BADGE OF HONOR

*W.E.B. Griffin's electrifying epic series
of a big-city police force . . .*

"DAMN EFFECTIVE . . . He captivates you with characters
the way few authors can."
                                    —*Tom Clancy*

"TOUGH, AUTHENTIC . . . POLICE DRAMA AT ITS
BEST . . . Readers will feel as if they're part of the investigation, and the true-to-life characters will soon feel like old
friends. Excellent reading."
                    —**Dale Brown, bestselling author of**
                    Day of the Cheetah* and *Hammerheads

"COLORFUL . . . GRITTY . . . TENSE."
                            —*The Philadelphia Inquirer*

"A REAL WINNER."
                            —*New York Daily News*

"NOT SINCE JOSEPH WAMBAUGH have we been treated
to a police story of the caliber that Griffin gives us. He cre-
ates a story about real people in a real world doing things
that are AS REAL AS TODAY'S HEADLINES."
                    —**Harold Coyle, bestselling author of**
                    Team Yankee* and *Sword Point

"FANS OF ED McBAIN'S 87TH PRECINCT NOVELS
BETTER MAKE ROOM ON THEIR SHELVES . . . *Badge
of Honor* is first and foremost the story of the people who
solve the crimes. The characters come alive."
                            —*Gainesville (GA) Times*

"GRITTY, FAST-PACED . . . AUTHENTIC."
                    —**Richard Herman, Jr., author of**
                    The Warbirds

Also by W.E.B. Griffin

HONOR BOUND
HONOR BOUND
BLOOD AND HONOR

BROTHERHOOD OF WAR
BOOK I: THE LIEUTENANTS
BOOK II: THE CAPTAINS
BOOK III: THE MAJORS
BOOK IV: THE COLONELS
BOOK V: THE BERETS
BOOK VI: THE GENERALS
BOOK VII: THE NEW BREED
BOOK VIII: THE AVIATORS

THE CORPS
BOOK I: SEMPER FI
BOOK II: CALL TO ARMS
BOOK III: COUNTERATTACK
BOOK IV: BATTLEGROUND
BOOK V: LINE OF FIRE
BOOK VI: CLOSE COMBAT
BOOK VII: BEHIND THE LINES
BOOK VIII: IN DANGER'S PATH

BADGE OF HONOR
BOOK I: MEN IN BLUE
BOOK II: SPECIAL OPERATIONS
BOOK III: THE VICTIM
BOOK IV: THE WITNESS
BOOK V: THE ASSASSIN
BOOK VI: THE MURDERERS
BOOK VII: THE INVESTIGATORS

MEN AT WAR
BOOK I: THE LAST HEROES
BOOK II: THE SECRET WARRIORS
BOOK III: THE SOLDIER SPIES

"Rousing." —*Kirkus Reviews* "Exciting." —*Publishers Weekly*

"The author once again proves himself a compelling storyteller."
—*Booklist*

continued . . .

BROTHERHOOD OF WAR

A sweeping military epic of the United States Army that became a New York Times *bestselling phenomenon.*

"A MAJOR WORK . . . MAGNIFICENT . . . POWERFUL . . . If books about warriors and the women who love them were given medals for authenticity, insight and honesty, *Brotherhood of War* would be covered with them."

—**William Bradford Huie,**
author of *The Klansman* and *The Execution of Private Slovik*

"*Brotherhood of War* gets into the hearts and minds of those who by choice or circumstances are called upon to fight our nation's wars." —**William R. Corson, Lt. Col. (Ret.) U.S.M.C.,**
author of *The Betrayal* and *The Armies of Ignorance*

"Captures the rhythms of army life and speech, its rewards and deprivations . . . A WELL-WRITTEN, ABSORBING ACCOUNT." —*Publishers Weekly*

"REFLECTS THE FLAVOR OF WHAT IT'S LIKE TO BE A PROFESSIONAL SOLDIER."

—**Frederick Downs, author of**
The Killing Zone

"LARGE, EXCITING, FAST-MOVING."

—**Shirley Ann Grau, author of**
The Keeper of the House

"A MASTER STORYTELLER who makes sure each book stands on its own." —*Newport News Press*

"GRIFFIN HAS BEEN CALLED THE LOUIS L'AMOUR OF MILITARY FICTION, AND WITH GOOD REASON."

—*Chattanooga Free Press*

SECRET HONOR

W.E.B. GRIFFIN

JOVE BOOKS, NEW YORK

This is a work of fiction. Names, characters, places, and incidents are either the product of the author's imagination or are used fictitiously, and any resemblance to actual persons, living or dead, business establishments, events, or locales is entirely coincidental.

SECRET HONOR

A Jove Book / published by arrangement with
the author

PRINTING HISTORY
G. P. Putnam's Sons edition / January 2000
Jove edition / December 2000

The Penguin Putnam World Wide Web site address is
http://www.penguinputnam.com

ISBN: 0-515-13009-5

A JOVE BOOK®
Jove Books are published by The Berkley Publishing Group,
a division of Penguin Putnam Inc.,
375 Hudson Street, New York, New York 10014.
JOVE and the "J" design
are trademarks belonging to Penguin Putnam Inc.

PRINTED IN THE UNITED STATES OF AMERICA

10 9 8 7 6 5 4 3 2 1

I would like to thank Mr. William W. Duffy II, formerly of the United States Embassy in Buenos Aires, and Colonel José Manucl Menéndez, Cavalry, Argentine Army, Retired, who both went well beyond the call of duty in helping me in many ways as I was writing this book.

W.E.B. Griffin
Buenos Aires/Fairhope
Sunday, February 28, 1999

Prologue

During the spring of 1943, 240 German submarines were operating in the North and South Atlantic Ocean. Their mission was the interdiction of Allied shipping carrying war supplies from the United States to England and North Africa, and of Allied shipping carrying wool, beef, and other foodstuffs from (primarily) Argentina to England. During that month German submarines sank fifty-six Allied ships, totaling 327,900 tons, at a cost of fifteen submarines sunk, most of them in the North Atlantic.

German submarines operating in the North Atlantic—often in groups called "Wolf Packs"—operated out of European ports and returned to them for replenishment.

German submarines assigned to the South Atlantic Ocean, however, were faced with the problems of the great distances between their European home ports and their operational areas. It took approximately a month for a submarine sailing from a French port to reach the mouth of the River Plate in Argentina. Once there, it had little fresh food or fuel—often barely enough to return to its home port. Once its torpedoes were expended, there was no resupply closer than France.

In the months before April 1943, the Germans tried to solve the problem in various ways. At first they dispatched replenishment ships—often flying the neutral flags of Spain or Portugal—to the South Atlantic. The Americans countered by furnishing specially modified (smaller bomb load, more fuel capacity) B-24 aircraft to Brazil, which had *declared war on the Axis in January 1942. These aircraft kept the South Atlantic coast off Argentina and Uruguay under surveillance. Any ship caught replenishing German submarines was considered a legitimate target under the Rules of Warfare, no matter what flag the ship was flying.*

The next German tactic was to anchor "neutral" merchant ships close to the Argentine shore in the River Plate. The Plate is 125 miles wide at its mouth, and is shared by Argentina and Uruguay. The government of Argentina, then led by pro-Axis president General Ramón Castillo, looked the other way.

It was politically impossible either to bomb ships flying the flags of nonbelligerent powers anchored in neutral waters, or to stop and search suspected vessels of neutral powers on the high seas.

April 1943 was a busy month in a world at war:

On 3 April, General George S. Patton launched an attack against the Germans near El Guettar, Tunisia; and two days later, British general Bernard Montgomery attacked the Italians on the Wadi Akarit line.

On 7 April, the Japanese sent 180 aircraft to attack the Americans on Guadalcanal and Tulagi in the Solomon Islands. A United States destroyer and two cargo vessels were sunk.

The same day, Adolf Hitler met with Benito Mussolini in Salzburg, Austria. They decided that Africa had to be held at all costs.

I

[ONE]
Near Sidi Mansour, Tunisia
1530 7 April 1943

A solitary Afrika Korps staff car—a small Mercedes convertible sedan—moved as quickly as it could across the desert. It had of course been painted in the Afrika Korps desert scheme: tan paint mimicked the color of the Tunisian desert, and crooked black lines on the hood and doors were intended to break up the form of the vehicle and make it harder to spot at a distance.

Nothing could be done, however, to keep the dust of the Tunisian desert road from boiling up beneath the wheels of the Mercedes and raising a cloud scores of feet into the air. If anyone was looking, the dust cloud formed an arrow pointing to the Mercedes.

And someone was looking—an American pilot in a P-51 Mustang.

The North American P51-C and -D aircraft used in the North African campaign were powered by a Packard version of the British Merlin engine. They had a top speed of 440 knots, and were armed with four .50-caliber Browning machine guns. Hardpoints in the wings permitted the use of droppable auxiliary fuel tanks and could also be used to carry 1,000-pound bombs.

Even at 500 feet and an indicated airspeed of 325 knots, it hadn't been hard for Captain Archer C. Dooley, Jr., U.S. Army Air Corps, to spot the boiling dust and then the Afrika Korps staff car that had caused it.

"Oh, shit!" Captain Archer Dooley, Jr., said sadly.

Finding a Kraut staff car running unprotected across the

desert did not please him. When young Archie Dooley first signed up to fly fighter aircraft, he expected to become a "Knight of the Sky"—flying *mano a mano* against other knights of the sky. He didn't expect to be killing people like cockroaches.

Fifteen months before, Archie Dooley had been the valedictorian of the 1942 class at St. Ignatius High School in Kansas City, Kansas. Six weeks before, he had been Second Lieutenant Dooley. He had come to Tunisia fresh from fighter school, looking forward to sweeping Nazi Messerschmitts from the skies with the four .50-caliber Brownings in the wings of his Mustang, much as Errol Flynn had swept the Dirty Hun from the skies over France in World War I in *Dawn Patrol.*

After which, with a little bit of luck, there would be a girl in the Officers' Club with an exciting French accent, long legs, long hair, and firm breasts, who would express her admiration for a Knight of the Sky in a carnal fashion.

It hadn't turned out that way.

For one thing, by the time Archie got to the squadron, the Allies had attained air superiority over the enemy. In other words, no German or Italian aircraft were left to be swept from the skies.

The day Archie reported in, the squadron commander had informed him that the 23rd Fighter Group had ordered the squadron to be engaged in ground support. That broke down into two missions: The first was to attack the enemy in front of American infantry and armor with either wing-mounted bombs or the .50-caliber Brownings. The second was reconnaissance and interdiction. This meant flying over enemy-held desert to see what you could see, and to interdict— which meant to shoot up—anything you found.

Second Lieutenant Archer Dooley, Jr.'s first mission had been to fly wingman to the squadron commander on a two-plane reconnaissance and interdiction mission. At first, that had been sort of exciting . . . even fun.

They had raced across the desert close to the ground at better than 300 knots, a maneuver flatly forbidden in flight school. Here it was perfectly acceptable.

Like drinking in the Officers' Club, even if you were a long way from being old enough to vote.

They had come across a railroad engine, puffing along tracks in the desert, dragging a line of boxcars. The squadron commander had signaled to Archie that they should engage the target. "Take the locomotive," he had ordered. "I'll get the boxcars."

Second Lieutenant Archer Dooley, Jr., had gotten the locomotive, enjoying the sight of his one-tracer-round-in-five stream of .50-caliber projectiles walking across the desert, and—as he raised the Mustang's nose just a hair—moving into the locomotive's boiler.

As he flashed over the locomotive, the locomotive had blown up. His first kill. Then there was a ball of fire, from which rose a dense black cloud of smoke.

As Archie pulled up to make a second run at the train, he realized that the ball of fire was several hundred yards from the railroad tracks. What else had they hit, he wondered, even by mistake, that had exploded like that?

Then, as he lowered the Mustang's nose for his second run, taking care not to collide with the squadron commander's Mustang, he realized that the squadron commander's Mustang was no longer in sight.

And then he realized what the ball of fire really was.

At the time, it seemed probable that the squadron commander had been hit by ground fire. The squadron commander had told him that some of the trains were armed with antiaircraft machine guns and light cannon, mounted on flatcars. Because his attention had been fixed on the locomotive, Archie hadn't noticed anything on the cars behind it.

That night, at the Officers' Club (empty, as always, of females—long-legged, firm-breasted, or otherwise), he learned about the Group's promotion policies: Everybody got to be a first lieutenant after eighteen months of commissioned service, which meant he had about ten days before that happened.

There were two ways to get to be a captain. If you lived to serve twelve months as a first lieutenant, then promotion was automatic. But promotion came a lot quicker in another circumstance. The senior first lieutenant was the squadron executive officer (senior, that is, in terms of length of service in the squadron, not date of rank). If the squadron commander got either killed or seriously injured (defined as having to spend thirty days or more in the hospital), then the Exec took the Old Man's job and got the captain's railroad tracks that went with it.

Four weeks and six days after Archie reported to the squadron, the squadron first sergeant handed him a sheet of paper to sign:

```
                    HEADQUARTERS
              4032ND FIGHTER SQUADRON
                23RD FIGHTER GROUP
                   IN THE FIELD
                                    2 MARCH 1943
         THE UNDERSIGNED HEREWITH
         ASSUMES COMMAND.
                                  Archer Dooley, Jr.
                            ARCHER DOOLEY, JR.
                            CAPT.          USAAC
         FILE
         201 DOOLEY, ARCHER, JR. 0378654
         COPY TO CO, 23RD FIGHTER GROUP
```

He hadn't gotten to work his way up to executive officer. The young man who had become the Old Man and the Exec had both gone in on the same day, the Old Man when his Mustang ran into a Kraut antiaircraft position that had gotten lucky, and the Exec when he banked too steep, too low to the ground and put a wing into the desert.

That left Archie as the senior first lieutenant in the squadron.

The colonel had driven over from Group in a jeep, told him to cut orders assuming command, and handed him two sets of railroad tracks, still in cellophane envelopes from the quartermaster officer's sales store.

Archie had pinned one set of captain's railroad tracks over the embroidered gold second lieutenant's bars still sewn to the epaulets of his A-2 horsehide flight jacket, and put the other set in the drawer of the squadron commander's—now his—desk. If he ever had to go someplace, like Group, he would pin the extras on his Class A uniform then.

Being a captain and a squadron commander was not at all like what he'd imagined. A lot of really unpleasant shit went with being the Old Man. Like writing letters to the next of kin.

He hadn't actually had to compose these, thank God. There were letters in the file that some other Old Man had written, full of bullshit about how your son/husband/brother/nephew died instantly and courageously doing his duty, and how much he would be missed by his fellow officers and the enlisted men because he had been such a fine officer and had been an inspiration to all who had been privileged to know him.

Not the truth, not about how he'd tried to bail out but had been too close to the ground and his 'chute hadn't opened; not that he'd been seen trying and failing to get out of the cockpit through a sheet of flame blowing back from the engine; not about how he'd tried to land his shot-up airplane and blew it, and rolled over and over down the runway in a ball of flame and crushed aluminum. Or that they really didn't know what the fuck had happened to him, he just hadn't come back; and later some tank crew had found the wreckage of his Mustang with him still in the cockpit, the body so badly burned they couldn't tell if he had been killed in the air or died when his plane hit.

He didn't have to type the letters, either. The first sergeant just took one from the file and retyped it, changing the name. But Archie had to sign it, because he was now the Old Man and that's what was expected of him.

And he was always getting bullshit pep talks from some major or light colonel at Group that he was supposed to pass down the line.

Like what he remembered now, staring down at the Kraut staff car:

"Dooley, what interdiction means is that you and your people are supposed to engage whatever you come across, like one fucking Kraut with a rifle, one motorcycle messenger, not pass him by to go looking for a railroad locomotive,

or something you think is important, or looks good when you blow it up. The motorcycle messenger is probably carrying an important message. Otherwise he wouldn't be out there. You take out a Kraut staff car, for example, you're liable to take out an important Kraut officer. Interdict means everything that's down there. You read me, Captain?"

"Yes, Sir."

"And pass the word to your people, and make sure they read you, and read you good."

"Yes, Sir."

And Archie had passed the word, and gotten dirty looks.

And now there was a Mercedes staff car down there, and it wasn't like being in a dogfight, it was like running over a dog with your car; but you had to do it because you had told your people they had to do it, and Archie believed that an officer should not order anybody to do what he wouldn't do himself.

Archie banked his Mustang steep to the right, lined up on the cloud of dust boiling out under the wheels of the Mercedes, and when he thought he had him, closed his finger on the trigger on the joystick. When he saw his tracer stream converge on the Mercedes and he didn't have to correct, he thought he was getting pretty good at this shit.

The Mercedes ran off the road, turned over, and burst into flames. Maybe a couple of bodies had flown out of the Mercedes, but Archie couldn't be sure, and he didn't go back for a second look, because if he did and saw somebody running, he wasn't going to try to get him.

He leveled off at about 500 feet and started looking for something else to interdict.

And at 2105 hours that night, at Afrika Korps General Hospital #3, near Carthage, Tunisia, the chief surgeon and hospital commander, Oberst-Arzt (Colonel-Doctor) Horst Friederich von und zu Mittlingen, pushed his way through the tent flap of the tent euphemistically called "Operating Theater Three" and reached beneath his bloodstained surgical apron for a package of cigarettes.

The hospital's name implied something far more substantial than the reality. General Hospital #3 (which served the Tenth Panzer Division) was a sprawling collection of tents and crude sheds, most of them marked with red crosses to protect against bombing or strafing. The tents served as operating theaters, the sheds as wards. Both were covered with the dust raised by the trucks and ambulances—and sometimes horse-drawn wagons—bringing in the wounded and dying.

Von und zu Mittlingen was a fifty-two-year-old Hessian trained at Marburg and Tübingen. Before the war, he had been professor of orthopedic surgery at St. Louise's Hospital in Munich.

The cigarettes were Chesterfields. One of the nurses, who didn't smoke but knew the Herr Oberst-Artz did, had taken them from the body of an American pilot who had survived the crash of his fighter plane but had died en route to Afrika Korps General Hospital #3. The lighter, too, was American, a Zippo, found on the floor of one of the surgical tents. There had been no telling how long it had been there, or to whom it had belonged, so he kept it.

He lit a Chesterfield, inhaled deeply, and felt with his hand behind him for one of the vertical poles holding up the corner of the tent. When he found it, he leaned against it, then exhaled, examining the glow of the cigarette as he did.

His hands were shaking. He willed them to be still.

It had been time to take a break, to leave the operating theater and step outside into the welcome cold of the night. And to light up a cigarette. And get a cup of coffee, if he could find one.

Though patients were still awaiting his attention, he had learned that he could push himself only so far. After so many hours at the table, his eyes did not see well, his fingers lost their skill, and his judgment was clouded by fatigue.

What he desperately wanted was a drink. But that would have to wait until later, much later, until there were no more wounded requiring his services. He would probably have to wait until the early morning for that. Then he would take several deep pulls from the neck of his bottle of brandy before falling into bed.

He took two more puffs on the Chesterfield, exhaled, and pushed himself away from the tent pole.

I will go to the mess and see if there is coffee. I will do nothing for the next ten minutes except smoke my cigarette and drink my coffee and take a piss.

His route took him past three tents on the perimeter of the hospital area. A medical team—a physician, a nurse, and stretcher bearers—stood outside the three tents as the ambulances and trucks brought the wounded to the hospital.

The physician categorized each incoming patient: Those who would most likely die if they did not go under the knife immediately, he ordered to be carried into the first tent, where a team of nurses would prepare them for surgery. As soon as a table was free, they underwent the knife. Those who had a reasonable chance of survival, but could wait a bit for surgery, were given morphine and moved into the second tent. As soon as the really critical patients had received attention, their turn in an operating theater would come. Those who stood little chance of survival were moved into the third tent and given morphine. When everyone in Tent A and Tent B had received treatment, an attempt would be made to save those in Tent C.

Oberst-Artz von und zu Mittlingen violated his own rule about never going into Tent C. The sight of dead men, and men in the last—too often agonized—moments of their lives, upset him. He knew it was better to be calm and emotionless when he was at the table.

There were six men on stretchers in Tent C.

The first two were dead. One looked asleep. The second's face was frozen with his last agony.

Von und zu Mittlingen covered their faces with blankets and went to the last man on that side of the tent.

He was surprised that he was still alive.

His entire head was wrapped in blood-soaked bandages. That implied, at the least, serious trauma to his eyes and probably to his brain. Both of his hands were similarly bandaged, suggesting to von und zu Mittlingen that he would probably lose the use of both hands, and might actually lose the hands themselves.

Another heavily blood-soaked bandage was on his upper right leg, and his torso was also bandaged; but the amount of blood on these last suggested to von und zu Mittlingen that the wounds on his torso were not as serious as the others, though internal bleeding of vital organs was of course possible.

It would probably be better if the poor bastard died; the alternative is living as a blind cripple.

He noticed that the patient was wearing U.S. Army trousers but an Afrika Korps tunic. That quickly identified him as an officer, someone in a position to ignore the rules forbidding the wearing of any part of the enemy's uniform.

Von und zu Mittlingen reached for the patient's ID tag.

"Who's that?" the patient asked, sensing the hand on the tag.

"I'm a doctor."

The tag identified the patient as Oberstleutnant (Lieutenant Colonel) von Stauffenberg.

Oh, my God! This mutilated body is Claus!

"You've got yourself in a mess, haven't you, Claus?" von und zu Mittlingen said.

"Who's that?"

"Horst Mittlingen, Claus," Horst Friederich von und zu Mittlingen said. "We're going to take care of you now."

"One of their Mustangs got me," Oberstleutnant Graf (Count) Claus von Stauffenberg said.

"Claus, what did they give you for the pain?"

"I decided I would rather be awake."

Oberst-Artz Horst Friederich von und zu Mittlingen stood up and walked to the flap of the tent and bellowed for stretcher bearers, then returned to the bloody body on the stretcher. "We'll take care of you now, Claus," he said. "You'll be all right."

"Really?" von Stauffenberg asked mockingly.

"Yes, really," von und zu Mittlingen said. "I am about to violate my own rule about never working on my friends."

Two stretcher bearers appeared.

"Put this officer on the next available table," von und zu Mittlingen ordered. "Tell Sister Wagner I will want her beside me."

"Jawohl, Herr Oberst."

"If I could see, I would say I'm glad to see you, Horst," von Stauffenberg said.

On 12 April, the Germans announced the discovery of mass graves in Poland's Katyn Forest. The graves contained the bodies of 4,100 Polish officers and officer cadets who had been captured by the Soviet army. They had been shot in the back of the head with small-caliber pistols. A week later, after refusing Polish Government in Exile demands for an investigation by the International Red Cross, the Soviet government said the whole thing was German propaganda.

On 17 April, in its largest operation to date, the 8th U.S. Air Force attacked aircraft factories in Bremen with 117 B-17 bombers, sixteen of which were shot down.

[TWO]
The Office of the Reichsführer-SS
Berlin
1545 17 April 1943

The interoffice communications device on the ornately carved desk of Reichsführer-SS Heinrich Himmler buzzed discreetly.

Though he was wearing his customary ornate black uniform, the forty-three-year-old Reichsführer's round spectacles and slight build gave him the look of a low-ranking clerk. It would have been a mistake to act on that assumption.

Without taking his eyes from the teletypewriter printout he was reading, Himmler reached for the box and depressed the lever that allowed his secretary, Frau Gertrud Hassler, to communicate. The Reichsführer-SS had had the device rigged in that manner. He was a busy man, and could not afford an interruption every time his secretary had something to say. If he was busy, he simply ignored the buzzing and she would try again later.

"Herr Reichsführer," Frau Gertrud Hassler announced. "Herr Korvettenkapitän Boltitz, from Minister von Ribbentrop's office, is here." Korvettenkapitän was the German Navy rank equivalent to major.

The Reichsführer-SS was not busy, but that did not mean he was prepared to be interrupted by the woman every time a messenger arrived in the outer office.

"And?" the Reichsführer-SS said impatiently.

"He insists that you personally sign for the message, Herr Reichsführer-SS."

"Mein Gott! Well, show him in, please, Frau Hassler."

Himmler rose from his desk and walked toward the double doors to his office. A moment later, one of them opened; and a tall, blond young man in civilian clothing stepped inside. In his hand was a briefcase. He raised his arm straight out from the shoulder. "Heil Hitler!" he barked.

Himmler raised his right arm at the elbow. "Korvettenkapitän Boltitz, how nice to see you," Himmler said.

"Herr Reichsführer," Boltitz said. "I regret the intrusion on your valuable time, Herr Reichsführer, but I was directed to give this to you personally."

Himmler knew that Boltitz's assignment to the office of Foreign Minister Joachim von Ribbentrop meant that he was really Admiral Wilhelm Canaris's man—read spy—in the Foreign Ministry. Canaris was Director of Abwehr Intelligence. Neither he nor von Ribbentrop was really a member of Adolf Hitler's inner circle, and Himmler wasn't entirely sure either of them could be completely trusted. "I understand," Himmler said, and put out his hand for the message.

Boltitz opened the briefcase and took from it a clipboard, whose clip held an envelope. He removed the envelope, and then handed Himmler the clipboard and a pen. Himmler scrawled his name, acknowledging receipt of the message, and the young man then handed him the envelope.

"Thank you, Herr Reichsführer."

"Are you to wait for a reply?" Himmler asked.

"No, sir, but I am at your disposal if you wish to reply."

"Just a moment, please," Himmler said, then tore open the envelope and read the message.

```
CLASSIFICATION: MOST URGENT

CONFIDENTIALITY: MOST SECRET

DATE: 15 APRIL 1943 1645 BUENOS
AIRES TIME

FROM: AMBASSADOR, BUENOS AIRES

TO: IMMEDIATE AND PERSONAL ATTENTION
OF THE FOREIGN MINISTER OF THE GER-
MAN REICH

HEIL HITLER!

STANDARTENFÜHRER-SS JOSEF GOLTZ RE-
QUESTS THAT APPENDIX ONE ATTACHED
HERETO BE IMMEDIATELY BROUGHT TO THE
ATTENTION OF REICHSFÜHRER-SS HEIN-
RICH HIMMLER.

MANFRED ALOIS GRAF VON LUTZENBERGER

AMBASSADOR OF THE GERMAN REICH TO
THE REPUBLIC OF ARGENTINA

BEGIN APPENDIX ONE

TO: REICHSFÜHRER-SS HEINRICH HIMMLER

FROM:    SS-STANDARTENFÜHRER   JOSEF
GOLTZ
```

SUBJECT: OPERATION PHOENIX, PROGRESS
REPORT

HEIL HITLER!

THE UNDERSIGNED HAS THE HONOR TO
REPORT TO THE HERR REICHSFÜHRER-SS
THE FOLLOWING:

(1) ALL ARRANGEMENTS HAVE BEEN MADE
TO OFF-LOAD THE SPECIAL CARGO ABOARD
THE MOTOR VESSEL COMERCIANTE DEL
OCÉANO PACÍFICO EARLY IN THE MORNING
OF 19 APRIL 1943.

(2) ALL ARRANGEMENTS HAVE BEEN MADE
TO TRANSPORT AND STORE THE SPECIAL
CARGO UNDER THE HIGHEST POSSIBLE
SECURITY ONCE IT IS ASHORE.

(3) ALL ARRANGEMENTS HAVE BEEN MADE
TO EFFECT THE TRANSPORT OF NAVAL
OFFICERS FROM THE GRAF SPEE FROM
THEIR PLACE OF INTERNMENT TO PUERTO
MAGDALENA ON SAMBOROMBÓN BAY ONCE
THE ACTIONS DESCRIBED IN (1) AND (2)
ABOVE HAVE BEEN ACCOMPLISHED.

(4) THE NAVAL OFFICERS WILL FIRST BE
TAKEN ABOARD THE OCÉANO PACÍFICO AND
THEN REPATRIATED TO THE FATHERLAND
AS SPACE BECOMES AVAILABLE ABOARD U-
BOATS RETURNING TO EUROPEAN PORTS.

(5) WHILE THE UNDERSIGNED HAS
ASSUMED PERSONAL COMMAND OF OPERA-
TION PHOENIX SINCE ARRIVING IN

ARGENTINA, HE WISHES TO ACKNOWLEDGE
THE CONTRIBUTIONS MADE BY AMBASSADOR
GRAF VON LUTZENBERGER AND MEMBERS OF
HIS STAFF, IN PARTICULAR FIRST SEC-
RETARY ANTON VON GRADNY-SAWZ, MILI-
TARY ATTACHÉ OBERST KARL-HEINZ GRÜNER
AND ASSISTANT MILITARY ATTACHÉ FOR
AIR MAJOR FREIHERR HANS-PETER VON
WACHTSTEIN. THEIR IMMEDIATE GRASP OF
THE IMPORTANCE OF OPERATION PHOENIX
AND THEIR DEDICATION TO THE PRINCI-
PLES OF NATIONAL SOCIALISM AND THE
FÜHRER HAS EARNED MY ADMIRATION.

RESPECTFULLY SUBMITTED:

JOSEF LUTHER GOLTZ

STANDARTENFÜHRER SS-SD

END APPENDIX ONE

END MESSAGE

The *Comerciante Océano Pacífico,* a Spanish-flagged
merchantman, had been sent to Samborombón Bay in the
Argentine section of the River Plate estuary ostensibly with
the clandestine mission of replenishing the increasingly des-
perate South Atlantic U-boats. Replenishment was not, however, its only secret mission. It was also charged with
smuggling into Argentina equipment and supplies intended
to aid the escape from internment of the crew of the German
pocket battleship *Graf Spee,* which had been scuttled in the
harbor of Montevideo, Uruguay, in December 1939, after a
running battle with the Royal Navy.

The repatriation of the *Graf Spee* crew was especially dear to the heart of Admiral Wilhelm Canaris, who had himself escaped internment in Argentina during the First World War.

There was a third, far more secret, mission for the *Océano Pacífico*. It had become clear to a number of Hitler's highest-ranking associates that the war might be lost—and probably would be—and that the life span of the Thousand-Year Reich was likely to be only a matter of years, perhaps less. With that in mind, it was deemed prudent to establish in South America a place of refuge. "Operation Phoenix" was set in motion. Money was obtained, largely from Jews, either from the dead—jewelry, gold fillings, and the like—or from the living, by way of extortion.

The equivalent of $100,000,000 (in various currencies, including American dollars) was aboard the *Océano Pacífico*. Once smuggled ashore, along with the material for the interned *Graf Spee* crew, the money would be covertly placed in Argentine banks and used to establish a South American refuge for Nazis who not only hoped to escape punishment for their crimes, but who also sought a place where the Nazi philosophy could be kept alive for an eventual return to Germany.

Himmler raised his eyes to Korvettenkapitän Boltitz.

"Please be so good as to thank Herr von Ribbentrop for me," he said.

"Jawohl, Herr Reichsführer."

"That will be all," Himmler said. "Thank you."

Korvettenkapitän Boltitz rendered another crisp Nazi salute, which Himmler again returned casually, then made a military about-face and marched out of Himmler's office.

Since the door to the outer office remained open, rather than returning to his desk and using the intercom, Himmler raised his voice and called, "Frau Hassler!"

Frau Hassler was tall, thin, and in her early fifties; and she wore her gray-flecked hair in a bun. When she appeared at his door moments later, she was clutching her stenographer's notebook and three pencils.

"Please ask Oberführer von Deitzberg to see me immediately." Oberführer was a rank peculiar to the SS that fell between colonel and brigadier general.

"Jawohl, Herr Reichsführer," Frau Hassler said, and pulled the door closed.

Manfred von Deitzberg, Himmler's adjutant, appeared in less than a minute. He was a tall, slim, blond, forty-two-year-old Westphalian; his black SS uniform was finely tailored, and there was an air of elegance about him.

He entered the room without knocking, closed the door after him, then leaned against it and looked quizzically at Himmler. He did not render the Nazi salute, formally or informally.

"We've heard from Goltz," Himmler said, and held the message out to him.

Von Deitzberg walked to the desk, took the message, and read it. When he'd finished, he looked at Himmler, returned the message to him, but said nothing.

"Comments?" Himmler asked.

"It looks like good news," von Deitzberg said.

"But?"

"The Operation has not been completed. Either part of it."

"He seems confident that it will succeed . . . that both parts of it will succeed. You aren't?"

"There is an English expression, 'a bird in the hand . . .' "

" '. . . is worth two in the bush,' " Himmler finished for him. "I agree. Anything else?"

"I hesitate to criticize Goltz. I recommended him for this mission."

"But?"

"When next I see him, I will have a private word with him and suggest that it is never a good idea to put so many details in a message."

"I saw that, but decided to give him the benefit of the doubt. He was obviously pleased with himself."

"And I think he wanted you and me to be pleased with him as well."

"Yes. Josef is not overburdened with modesty."

Von Deitzberg laughed dutifully. "I was a little curious about his fulsome praise for von Lutzenberger," he said. "And von Lutzenberger's people."

"Perhaps he really meant it."

"And he knew, of course, that von Lutzenberger would read the message."

"And that Grüner is one of us," Himmler said, smiling. "Do you think our Luther is becoming a politician, Manfred?"

"I think that's a terrible thing to say about an SS officer," von Deitzberg said.

It was Himmler's turn to laugh dutifully.

"What are you going to do about it?" von Deitzberg asked, nodding at the message. "Are you going to tell the Führer?"

"I thought I would solicit your wise counsel, Herr Oberführer."

"I have a tendency to err on the side of caution," von Deitzberg said. "I think I would wait until we have the bird in hand."

"If he hasn't already, von Ribbentrop is about to tell Bormann, knowing full well he will rush to the Führer, that there has been word from Himmler's man that Operation Phoenix will shortly be successful."

Party leader Martin Bormann was second only to Adolf Hitler in the hierarchy of the Nazi party and one of his closest advisers.

"You don't think he would wait until after we get the 'operation completed successfully' message, so he could say, 'Our man'?"

"I think von Ribbentrop would prefer to go to the Führer now, using 'Himmler's man.' Then, if something does go wrong, he could pretend to be shocked and saddened by that man's failure. On the other hand, if it does go well, it will naturally be 'our man.'"

Himmler looked at von Deitzberg for a moment, then continued: "I could, of course, get to the Führer first, either directly, or through Bormann—"

"The Führer's at Wolfsschanze," von Deitzberg interrupted. Wolfsschanze was Hitler's secret command post, near Rastenburg in East Prussia.

"—then through Bormann," Himmler went on. "And

take a chance our friend—actually he's your friend, isn't he, Manfred?—is everything he—and you—say he is. Claim him as our man now, taking the chance that he won't fail."

"Were you really soliciting my wise counsel?" von Deitzberg asked.

"Of course. And your wise counsel is that we should wait until we see what actually happens, right?"

"Yes, Sir."

"On second thought, what I think I really should do now is call Bormann and tell him that we have just heard from Oberführer von Deitzberg's man in Buenos Aires. That way, if Goltz is successful, I can claim the credit because he is one of my SS, right? And if he fails, it's obviously your fault, von Deitzberg. You recommended him for that job." Himmler smiled warmly at von Deitzberg.

"May I suggest, with all possible respect, Herr Reichsführer-SS," von Deitzberg said, "that is not a very funny joke."

"Joke? What joke?"

He pressed the lever on his intercom, and when Frau Hassler's voice came, told her to get Reichsleiter Bormann on the telephone immediately.

One of the telephones on Himmler's desk buzzed not more than ninety seconds later. Himmler picked it up and said "Heil Hitler" into it, then waited impatiently for whoever was on the line to respond.

"Martin," he said finally, and with oozing cordiality, "There has been good news from Buenos Aires. Our project there, under Standartenführer Goltz, of whom I am very proud, is proceeding splendidly. We expect momentarily to hear that the special cargo has been delivered, and that the first of the officers from the *Graf Spee* are on their way home."

There was a reply from Bormann that von Deitzberg could not hear, and then Himmler went on: "The SS exists solely to serve the Führer, Martin. You know that." This was followed by another pause, and then Himmler barked "Heil

Hitler!" into the mouthpiece and hung up. He looked at von Deitzberg and smiled. "That put our friend Bormann on the spot, you understand, Manfred?"

"Yes, indeed," von Deitzberg said.

"He doesn't want to go to the Führer with good words about the SS," Himmler added unnecessarily, though with visible pride in his tactics. "But he wants even less for the Führer to get his information from other people, such as our friend von Ribbentrop. So he will relay the good news about Argentina to the Führer, saying he got it from me, and the Führer will not only like the information but be impressed with my quiet modesty for not telling him myself."

"Very clever," von Deitzberg said.

"You have to be clever with these bastards, Manfred. They're all waiting for a chance to stab us in the back."

"I agree. Is there anything else?"

Himmler shook his head, "no," and von Deitzberg walked to the door.

"Manfred!" Himmler called as von Deitzberg put his hand on the knob.

Von Deitzberg turned to look at him.

"Are you, in your heart of hearts, a religious man, Manfred?"

"You know better than that," von Deitzberg replied.

"Pity," Himmler said. "I was about to say that now that the die has been cast, Manfred, it might be a good time to start to pray that Goltz is successful."

"Are you worried?"

"I'm not worried. But if I were you, I would be. You're the one who selected Goltz for this."

"I recommended him," von Deitzberg said. "You selected him."

"That's not the way I remember it, Oberführer von Deitzberg," Himmler said. "Thank you for coming to see me."

On 18 April, more than half of the 100 heavy German transport aircraft attempting to resupply the Afrika Korps in North Africa were shot down by American fighters.

And across the world, in the South Pacific, over Bougainville, P-38 Lightning fighters shot down a transport carrying Admiral Isoroku Yamamoto, chief of the Japanese Navy, and Japan's principal strategist. American cryptographers, in one of the most tightly guarded secrets of the war, had broken many high-level Japanese codes, and had intercepted messages giving Yamamoto's travel plans and routes. The decision to attack his plane, which carried with it the grave risk of the Japanese learning the Americans had broken their codes, was made personally by President Franklin D. Roosevelt.

On 19 April, the Argentine government of General Ramón Castillo was toppled by a junta of officers, led by General Arturo Rawson, who became President.

On 22 April, the U.S. II Corps, led by Lieutenant General Omar Bradley, began a major attack against the Germans in Tunisia. Another attempt by the Germans to supply the Afrika Korps by air resulted in the shooting down by American fighters of 30 of 50 transport aircraft.

[THREE]
Biscayne Bay
Miami, Florida
2215 23 April 1943

After a very long flight at 160 miles per hour from Caracas, Venezuela, the four-engined Sikorsky Flying Boat of Pan-American Grace Airways splashed down into the calm waters of Biscayne Bay in Miami, Florida. Among its thirty-four passengers was a tanned, balding man of forty-eight who wore a trim, pencil-line mustache. The name on his passport read Alejandro Federico Graham, and his occupation was given as "Business Executive." In the breast pocket of his splendidly tailored suit was another document:

THE JOINT CHIEFS OF STAFF

THE PENTAGON

WASHINGTON, D.C.

1 January 1943

Subject: Letter Orders

To: Colonel A.F. Graham, USMCR

Office of Strategic Services

Washington, D.C.

1. You will proceed to such destinations as your duties require by U.S. Government or civilian motor, rail, sea or air transportation as is most expedient. JCS Travel Priority AAAAAA-1 is assigned. The wearing of civilian attire is authorized.

2. United States Military or Naval commands are authorized and directed to provide you with whatever assistance of any kind you may require to accomplish your mission(s).

By Order of The Chairman, The Joint Chiefs of Staff:

```
Official:


                          Matthew J. Markham
                      Matthew J. Markham
                  Lieutenant General, USAAC
                                 J-3, JCS
```

[FOUR]
The Office of the Director
The Office of Strategic Services
National Institutes of Health Building
Washington, D.C.
1045 24 April 1943

Colonel William J. Donovan, the stocky, gray-haired, sixty-year-old Director of the Office of Strategic Services, rose from his desk and walked to the door when his secretary announced Colonel Graham's arrival. When Colonel Alejandro Federico Graham, USMCR, passed through the door, Colonel Donovan cordially offered his hand. "Welcome home, Alex," he said. "How was the flight?"

"From Buenos Aires to Miami, it was slow but very comfortable. Cold champagne, hot towels; Panagra does it right. From Miami to here it was very fast and very uncomfortable. That was my first ride in a B-26. What was that all about?"

"I'm going to have dinner tonight with the President. I really had to talk to you before I did."

Donovan had been a Columbia University School of Law classmate of Franklin Delano Roosevelt; he and the President remained close personal friends. In the First World War, he had won the Medal of Honor as a colonel, commanding the famous "Fighting Sixty-Ninth" Infantry in France. After the war, he had become a very successful Wall Street lawyer.

At the request of President Roosevelt, he had become the Director of the OSS at an annual salary of one dollar.

Graham grunted.

"Can I get you anything? Coffee?" Donovan asked.

"Coffee would be nice, thank you," Graham said.

Graham, who was now the Deputy Director of the OSS for Western Hemisphere Operations, had served as a second lieutenant in the Marine Corps in France in World War I. After the war he had been active in the Marine Corps Reserve, eventually rising to Colonel, USMCR.

An engineer by training, he had become president of the nation's second- or third-largest railroad (depending on whether the criterion was income or tonnage moved annually). He had made, additionally, a considerable fortune building railroads all over Central and South America.

A political conservative, he had made substantial financial contributions to the presidential campaign of his close friend, Wendell L. Willkie, who had been defeated in a landslide by Roosevelt in the 1940 election.

When called to active Marine Corps service, he had expected to be given command of a regiment; but Donovan—along with the Deputy Commandant of the Marine Corps, an old friend—had convinced him that his intimate knowledge of South America and its leaders made him more valuable to the OSS than he would be to the Marine Corps, and he had reluctantly given up his dream of commanding a Marine regiment.

"Sit down, Alex," Donovan said, and went to his office door and ordered coffee.

Graham lowered himself onto a green leather couch, took a long, thin black cigar case from the pocket of his well-tailored suit, extracted a cigar, and, after biting its end off, lit it with a gold Dunhill lighter.

"Nice-looking cigar," Donovan said. "Argentine?"

Graham started to take the cigar case from his jacket again. Donovan signaled he didn't want one. Graham shrugged. "Brazilian," he said.

"That's right," Donovan said. "There's a layover in Rio de Janeiro, isn't there?"

"And in Caracas," Graham said. "It took me four days to get here from Buenos Aires."

"Shall I get right to the point?" Donovan asked.

"That's often a good idea."

"I need to know the name of your intelligence source in Argentina," Donovan said, "the one who helped us with Operation Phoenix. I want to know who Galahad is."

"We've been over this, Bill," Graham said.

"That was an order, Colonel."

"Well, we are getting right to the point, aren't we? Sorry, I'm not in a position to tell you."

Donovan glared coldly at him.

"Bill," Graham said. "When I took this job, I had your word that you wouldn't try to second-guess my decisions."

"I can take you off this job, Alex."

"Yes, you can. Is that what you're doing?"

"What am I supposed to tell the President? 'Sorry, Mr. President, Graham won't tell me who Galahad is'?"

"When all else fails, tell the truth."

"What if the President asked you—*ordered* you—to tell him?"

"Same answer."

"What I should have done was order Frade up here."

"In the Marine Corps, Bill, they teach us to never give an order that you doubt will be obeyed."

"You don't mean he'd refuse to come?"

"That's a very real possibility."

"He's a major in the Marine Corps."

"And he's an ace. Who was just awarded the Navy Cross. And is smart enough to understand that court-martialing a hero might pose some public relations problems for you. And for the President. That's presuming, of course, that he would put himself in a position, coming here, where you could court-martial him."

"It wouldn't have to be a court-martial. . . ."

"Saint Elizabeth's? You're not thinking clearly, Bill."

In an opinion furnished privately to the President by the Attorney General, the provisions of the law of *habeas cor-*

pus were not applicable to a patient confined for psychiatric evaluation in a hospital, such as Saint Elizabeth's, the Federal mental hospital in the District of Colombia.

"I'm not?"

"Cletus Marcus Howell, who dearly loves his grandson, is a great admirer—and I think a personal friend—of Colonel McCormick."

Colonel Robert Rutherford McCormick, publisher of the Chicago *Tribune,* made no secret of his loathing for President Franklin Delano Roosevelt.

"And I suppose I could count on you to be with Howell when he went to see McCormick."

"That's a possibility I think you should keep in the back of your mind, Bill."

"You realize, Alex, that you're willfully disobeying a direct order? This is tantamount to mutiny."

"I'll split that hair with you, Bill. I thought about that on the way up here. You're not on active duty, Colonel; legally, you're a dollar-a-year civilian. I don't think that you have the authority to issue me a *military* order. But let's not get into that—unless you've already made up your mind to go down that road?"

"What road should we go down?"

"Be grateful for what we have."

"Which is?"

"Cletus Frade has done more for us than either of us dreamed he could. He *earned* that Navy Cross by putting his life on the line when he led the submarine *Devil Fish* into Samborombón Bay to sink the *Reine de la Mer.* Only a bona fide hero or a fool would have flown that little airplane into the aircraft weaponry on that ship, and whatever Cletus is, he's no fool."

"I wasn't accusing him of being either a fool or a coward," Donovan said.

"And because of what he did during the coup d'état, he's President Rawson's fair-haired boy," Graham went on. "Do I have to tell you the potential of that?"

"Point granted," Donovan said.

"Not to mention that his father—who was the likely next president of Argentina—was killed by the Germans during the process."

Donovan gave a snappish wave of his arm to acknowledge the truth of that.

"Not to mention that he was the one who located the *Comerciante del Océano Pacífico*," Graham went on. "Which really deserves mentioning—"

"She's in the middle of the South Atlantic," Donovan interrupted. "On a course for Portugal or Spain. There was a report from the *Alfred Thomas,* who is shadowing her, early this morning." The USS *Alfred Thomas,* DD-107, was a destroyer.

"Why don't we sink her?" Graham asked. "We know what she's carrying."

"The President made that decision," Donovan said. "There are . . . considerations."

"Getting back to the *Océano Pacífico,*" Graham went on. "If he hadn't flown Ashton and his team, and their radar, into Argentina, we never would have found her. And flew them, let me point out, in an airplane he'd never flown before. *We* sent him that airplane, Bill. *We* screwed up big time by sending him the *wrong* airplane. And he pulled our chestnuts out of the fire by flying it anyway."

"You sound like the president of the Cletus Frade fan club," Donovan said, tempering the sarcasm in his voice with a smile.

"Guilty," Graham said. "And while I run down the list, it was Frade's man, Frade's Sergeant Ettinger, who found out about the ransoming of the Jews. And got himself murdered."

"Can I stipulate to Major Frade's many virtues?"

"No, I want to remind you of them. Of *all* of them. And it was Frade who found out about Operation Phoenix."

"From Galahad. Which brings us back to him," Donovan said. "The President is very interested in Operation Phoenix. He wants to know—and I want to know, Alex—who Galahad is."

"In my opinion, and Frade's, Galahad is a Class I intelligence source whose identity must be kept secret, so that he won't be lost to us because somebody here does something stupid and the Germans find out about him. Or even have suspicions about him."

"That's not good enough, Alex. I want to know who he is. Who all of Frade's sources are."

"He's not going to tell you, and neither am I," Graham said. "I guess we're back where we started."

"And if Frade is taken out—which, after what they did to his father, seems a real possibility—that would leave only you knowing who Galahad is. That's not acceptable, Alex."

"There are others who know who Galahad is," Graham said. "But I won't tell you who they are, either."

Donovan looked at Graham, expressionless, for almost a minute before he spoke.

"I'm going to have to think about this, Alex," he said.

"Think quick, Bill. I want an answer right now, before I leave your office."

"That sounds like another threat."

"Either you fire me, which I think would be a mistake, or you tell me I can stay on under the original ground rules. You will not second-guess me. Your choice."

"That's not a choice. I can't do without you, and you know it."

"I have your word, Bill?"

"I can be overruled by the President," Donovan said. "He's not used to having anybody tell him something's none of his business."

"Roosevelt can't do without you, and both of you know it," Graham said. "What's it to be, Bill?"

Donovan exhaled audibly. "OK," he said. "You have my word."

"Thank you."

Graham pushed himself off the couch. "I need a long, hot shower and several stiff drinks," he said. He got as far as the door before Donovan called his name.

"Yes?" Graham asked, turning.

"This is a question, Alex, rather than second-guessing. Did you approve of Frade's killing those two Nazis—the military attaché and the SS guy—on the beach?"

"Frade didn't kill them," Graham said. "They were shot by two retired Argentine army sergeants."

"How did that happen?"

"*I* sent the lieutenant from Ashton's team to the beach to take pictures of the Germans landing the Operation Phoenix money from the *Océano Pacífico. I* sent the sergeants down to the beach to guard him. That's all they were supposed to do. But one of the sergeants not only had been el Coronel Frade's batman for thirty years, but the brother of the woman who was killed when they tried to assassinate young Frade. And they're Argentines, Latins, like me. Revenge is a part of our culture. The minute they saw who it was . . . bang! Ashton's lieutenant was very impressed. It was at least two hundred yards. Two shots only. Both in their heads."

"You sound as if you approve."

"I wouldn't have ordered it," Graham said. "And Frade didn't. But was I overwhelmed with remorse? No. You ever hear 'an eye for an eye'?"

"Yeah, I've heard that. I've also heard 'the devil you know is better than the one you don't.' They'll send somebody else."

"Yes, I'm afraid they will. Anything else, Bill?"

Donovan shook his head, "no," and Graham walked out of the office.

II

[ONE]
The Office of the Reichsführer-SS
Berlin
1430 26 April 1943

"Herr Reichsführer," Frau Gertrud Hassler's high-pitched voice announced, "Deputy Minister von Löwzer of the Foreign Ministry, Ribbentrop's office, asks to see you."

"Ask the gentleman to wait a minute or two, please,"

Himmler said courteously, and returned to reading the tele-typed report from Warsaw. It both baffled and infuriated him.

If the report was to be believed, and he had no reason not to believe it, the day before, "a group estimated to number approximately 2,000 Jews" in the Warsaw ghetto had risen up against their captors, protesting a pending "transport" to resettlement in the East. "The East" was a euphemism for the Treblinka concentration camp, but the damned Jews were not supposed to know that.

For one thing, a revolt of Jews against German authority is on its face unthinkable.

For another, these vermin, in their walled ghetto, have obviously somehow managed to obtain a few small arms. Someone will answer for this.

And even if it isn't "a few small arms," but many, and every slimy Hebrew in the ghetto has somehow managed to lay his hands on a pistol or a rifle, there is in Warsaw—in addition to the SS personnel—a division of German soldiers, a division of German soldiers!!!; the uprising should have been put down minutes after it became known.

According to the report, the uprising had been going on for twenty-four hours, and there was no estimate of when it would be contained.

The Reichsführer-SS grew aware that his knuckles on the hand pressing down the teletypewriter paper to keep it from curling were white with tension. When he lifted it from his desk, the hand was trembling.

Obviously, I am very angry, and—even though I have every right to be—therefore I should not make decisions that might be influenced by that anger.

One should never discipline children when angry, he continued, musing, his mind taking something of a leap. *One should discipline children very carefully, and with love in one's heart, not anger.* And then his focus returned to the matter at hand: *My God, that's incredible!—filthy Jewish swine confined to a ghetto having the effrontery to rise in arms against the German State! Whoever is responsible for this incredible breakdown of order will have to be disci-plined. Perhaps sent to a concentration camp, or shot.*

But I will make that decision calmly, when I am no longer angry.

The Reichsführer-SS pulled open a narrow drawer in the desk, rolled the teletypewriter print out into a narrow tube, then put it in the drawer and closed it.

Then he went to his private toilet, emptied his bladder, studied himself in the mirror, decided to have his hair cut within the next day or so, adjusted his necktie, and went back to his desk.

He pushed the SPEAK lever on his interoffice communication device. "Would you show the Herr Deputy Foreign Minister in, please?" he asked courteously.

The left of the double doors opened a moment later.

"Deputy Minister von Löwzer, Herr Reichsführer-SS," Frau Hassler announced.

Georg Friedrich von Löwzer, a plump forty-five-year-old in a too-small black suit, was carrying a leather briefcase. He took two steps inside the office and raised his arm and hand straight out from his shoulder in the Nazi salute.

"Heil Hitler!" he said.

Reichsführer-SS Heinrich Himmler stood up and returned a less formal salute: He bent his arm at the elbow and replied, "Heil Hitler!", then added, with a smile: "My dear von Löwzer, what an unexpected pleasure to see you."

"I regret, Herr Reichsführer-SS, that I am the bearer of unpleasant news."

Now what?

He smiled at von Löwzer. "Of such importance that someone of your stature in the Foreign Ministry has to bear it?"

"I believe when the Herr Reichsführer-SS reads the document, he will understand Herr Foreign Minister von Ribbentrop's concern that it be seen immediately and by no one but yourself," von Löwzer said. He unlocked the briefcase, took a sealed, yellowish envelope from it, and handed it to Himmler.

"Please, have a chair," Himmler said graciously. "Can I have Frau Hassler get you a coffee? Something a little stronger?"

"No, thank you, Herr Reichsführer-SS."

Himmler stood behind his desk and attempted to open the envelope flap with his fingernails. He failed in that attempt and had to reach for his letter opener—a miniature version of the dagger worn by SS officers. It had been a gift to him from one of the graduating classes of the SS Officer Candidate School at Bad Tolz.

When the envelope had been slit, he found that it contained another sheet of teletypewriter paper. He laid it on his desk, then placed a coffee cup at its top and his fingers at the bottom to prevent curling.

```
CLASSIFICATION: MOST URGENT

CONFIDENTIALITY: MOST SECRET

DATE: 23 APRIL 1943

FROM: AMBASSADOR, BUENOS AIRES

TO: IMMEDIATE AND PERSONAL ATTENTION
OF THE FOREIGN MINISTER OF THE GER-
MAN REICH

HEIL HITLER!

DEEPLY REGRET TO INFORM YOU THAT
STANDARTENFÜHRER JOSEF LUTHER GOLTZ
AND OBERST KARL-HEINZ GRÜNER WERE
KILLED BY GUNFIRE AT APPROXIMATELY
0945 19 APRIL 1943 NEAR PUERTO MAG-
DALENA, ARGENTINA. MAJOR FREIHERR
HANS-PETER VON WACHTSTEIN NARROWLY
ESCAPED DEATH IN THE SAME INCIDENT.

INASMUCH AS BRINGING THE MURDERS OF
THESE MEN TO THE ATTENTION OF THE
```

ARGENTINE GOVERNMENT WOULD HAVE MADE IT NECESSARY TO EXPLAIN THEIR PRESENCE AT PUERTO MAGDALENA, THE UNDERSIGNED HAS INFORMED THE ARGENTINE GOVERNMENT THAT BOTH OFFICERS, IN COMPLIANCE WITH ORDERS, HAVE RETURNED TO GERMANY, AND HAS ARRANGED FOR THE TRANSPORT OF THEIR REMAINS TO CADIZ, ABOARD THE SPANISH MOTOR VESSEL OCÉANO PACÍFICO, WHICH AS THE RESULT OF UNSUPPORTED CHARGES OF ATTEMPTED SMUGGLING HAS BEEN ORDERED TO LEAVE ARGENTINE WATERS IMMEDIATELY.

CAPTAIN JOSE FRANCISCO DE BANDERANO, MASTER OF THE OCÉANO PACÍFICO, WAS DENIED PERMISSION TO OFF-LOAD ANY OF HER CARGO, AND NONE OF HER CARGO OF ANY KIND WAS UNLOADED IN ARGENTINA.

ABSENT SPECIFIC ORDERS FROM YOUR EXCELLENCY TO THE CONTRARY, THE UNDERSIGNED IS RELUCTANT TO ENTRUST OTHER DETAILS OF THIS TRAGIC INCIDENT TO A RADIO TRANSMISSION. THE UNDERSIGNED SUGGESTS THAT A FULL REPORT OF THIS INCIDENT COULD BEST BE MADE TO YOUR EXCELLENCY AND OTHER OFFICIALS BY SOMEONE PERSONALLY FAMILIAR WITH THE INCIDENT.

IN ADDITION TO THE UNDERSIGNED, LISTED IN ORDER OF THEIR KNOWLEDGE OF THE INCIDENT, THESE ARE:

MAJOR FREIHERR HANS-PETER VON WACHTSTEIN

FIRST SECRETARY ANTON VON GRADNY-SAWZ

STURMBANNFÜHRER WERNER VON TRESMARCK OF THE EMBASSY OF THE GERMAN REICH IN MONTEVIDEO, URUGUAY.

THE UNDERSIGNED BEGS TO REMIND YOUR EXCELLENCY THAT A LUFTHANSA CONDOR FLIGHT IS EXPECTED TO REACH BUENOS AIRES IN THE NEXT FEW DAYS, AND RESPECTFULLY SUGGESTS THAT ANY, OR ALL, OF THE ABOVE-NAMED OFFICERS TRAVEL TO GERMANY ON THE RETURN FLIGHT SO THAT YOUR EXCELLENCY MAY BE MADE PRIVY TO THE DETAILS OF THIS UNFORTUNATE INCIDENT, AND OF OTHER RECENT DEVELOPMENTS HERE OF IMPORTANCE TO GERMANY.

THE UNDERSIGNED RESPECTFULLY AWAITS YOUR EXCELLENCY'S ORDERS.

HEIL HITLER!

MANFRED ALOIS GRAF VON LUTZENBERGER

AMBASSADOR OF THE GERMAN REICH TO THE REPUBLIC OF ARGENTINA

Reichsführer-SS Himmler looked up from the document and fixed his gaze on Deputy Minister von Löwzer, who was now sitting in the center of a small couch, his hands folded on his lap, his briefcase at his feet. "You are aware of the contents of this message?" he asked.

"I am privy to the details of Operation Phoenix, Herr Reichsführer-SS," von Löwzer replied solemnly.

So von Ribbentrop has told him of Phoenix? Is he smarter than he looks? Obviously, you don't get to be a deputy foreign minister unless you are bright.

I wonder how many others I don't know about are privy to Operation Phoenix?

"You may inform the Foreign Minister that I appreciate his entrusting the document only to someone like yourself, and that I will hold myself ready to meet with him at his earliest convenience."

"I will relay your message, Herr Reichsführer-SS."

Von Löwzer rose to his feet but made no move to leave the office.

"Something else, von Löwzer?"

"The message, Herr Reichsführer-SS. You still have it."

"I thought it was for me," Himmler blurted.

"The Foreign Minister thought that making copies of the document was unwise," von Löwzer said.

"Yes," Himmler said, signifying nothing.

"I am under the Foreign Minister's orders to show it as soon as possible to the others who have an interest," von Löwzer said.

"Bormann, for example?"

Von Löwzer nodded.

"Bormann hasn't seen this yet?" Himmler asked.

"You are the first to see it, Herr Reichsführer-SS," von Löwzer said. "Except, of course, for the Foreign Minister."

And yourself, of course. I'm going to have to find out about you.

But that's interesting. Von Ribbentrop sent the message to me first.

"And your next stop is where?" Himmler asked casually.

"Reichsleiter Bormann, Herr Reichsführer-SS, and then Admiral Canaris. Then I will go to Wolfsschanze, to see Generalfeldmarschall Keitel and Admiral Dönitz."

Generalfeldmarschall Keitel, chief of the German army, and Admiral Dönitz were with Hitler at his secret headquarters. As were Reichsmarschall Hermann Göring and Propaganda Minister Josef Goebbels.

Obviously, von Löwzer knows a good deal. The location of the Führer, and of those officials with him, is known to only a few wholly trustworthy people.

But does that mean von Löwzer knows everything *about Operation Phoenix?*

"Then I had best not keep you," Himmler said.

He picked up the message from Buenos Aires and read it through again carefully before handing it to von Löwzer.

"You will be good enough to tell the Herr Foreign Minister that I understand the gravity of the problem and am at his disposal to discuss it?"

"Of course, Herr Reichsführer-SS," von Löwzer said, rendered the Nazi salute, and walked out of Himmler's office.

Himmler waited three minutes—long enough for von Löwzer to have certainly left the outer office—and then pressed the lever on his interoffice communications device and ordered Frau Hassler to summon Oberführer von Deitzberg.

"The Reichsführer-SS requests your presence immediately, Herr Oberführer," Frau Hassler's voice announced metallically through the intercom device on von Deitzberg's desk.

Von Deitzberg had been sitting slumped in his high-backed chair with his feet resting on an open drawer. He put his feet on the floor, leaned across his desk, pressed the TALK lever, and very politely said, "Thank you very much, Frau Hassler."

He slumped back into his chair and smiled at his deputy, SS-Sturmbannführer Erich Raschner. "Raschner, I believe the Reichsführer has just seen the telex from Warsaw," he said.

The telex had been laid on his desk by a Signals Oberscharführer, the SS rank equivalent to technical sergeant, at 1120. As Adjutant to the Reichsführer-SS, von Deitzberg was charged with the administration of all correspondence—mail, teletype, or radio—that would come to Himmler's personal attention. That is to say, von Deitzburg was the gatekeeper for a good portion of the information flow to the Reichsführer-SS. He determined what was important enough for Himmler to see, what he himself could deal with, or what he could pass farther down the chain of command for action.

Next, he determined when the Reichsführer-SS actually saw the correspondence that in von Deitzberg's view merited his attention. Very rare pieces would be important enough for von Deitzberg to personally carry to Himmler himself. Immediately below that priority were messages that he would leave with Frau Hassler for delivery to Himmler the moment he was free. Below that priority were several categories: Some correspondence was stamped IMMEDIATE ATTENTION and placed in the box on his desk reserved for the Reichsführer-SS; some was stamped IMPORTANT and then placed in the box; and some, finally, was simply placed in the Himmler box without a stamp.

At least once an hour, a Signals messenger (always an SS noncommissioned officer) would make deliveries to von Deitzberg's In box and pick up the contents of the Out box. The Reichsführer-SS's correspondence would be immediately passed on to Frau Hassler, who would sort it (IMMEDIATE ATTENTION material on top, IMPORTANT below that, and unstamped on the bottom), and then place it on Himmler's desk at the first opportunity.

Reichsführer-SS Heinrich Himmler's time was, of course, very valuable. Oberführer von Deitzberg was a splendid manager—with the result that he was gatekeeper not only of Himmler's correspondence but of his appointments. He was the final arbiter of who got to see the Reichsführer-SS, when, and for how long.

Even senior government officials, like Deputy Foreign Minister von Löwzer, had to pass through von Deitzberg's "gates." When someone senior appeared unannounced to meet with Himmler, the SS officer on duty in the lobby of the building would pass the official into the elevator, then immediately telephone von Deitzberg. If von Deitzberg decided that the Reichsführer-SS had no time for the official, von Deitzberg would head him off in the corridor and explain that he was so very sorry, but the Reichsführer-SS had just left, and could he be of some help?

Today, von Deitzberg had decided that von Löwzer could be passed into the office of the Reichsführer. Whatever von Löwzer's business, asking him about it, and then checking with Himmler about that, would be more trouble than simply passing von Löwzer in. Thus von Deitzberg was not aware of the reason for von Löwzer's visit with the Reichsführer.

As for the teletype message from Warsaw announcing the Jewish insurrection, ordinarily, on receiving a message of that importance, von Deitzberg would have immediately carried it to Himmler and handed it to him personally. But today the Reichsführer had been lunching with his wife at the Hotel Adlon and hadn't been expected back until at least 2:30.

And besides, that message offered von Deitzberg a personal opportunity.

The only trouble with his job was that he was so good at it. That meant, in other words, that he had become indispensable to the Reichsführer-SS. And that meant Himmler always listened sympathetically to his requests for an assignment in the field, and more or less promised one at the earliest opportunity; but that never seemed to happen.

He didn't want to *stay* in the field, and wasn't asking for that. What he wanted was a brief assignment in the field—ten, fifteen days, no more than a month—so it would appear on his record when he was being considered for promotion. And besides, he had no doubt that he could clean up this Warsaw insurrection nonsense in ten days.

Moments after the teletype from Warsaw had reached his desk, von Deitzberg had ordered Raschner to call the Luftwaffe and order a Heinkel bomber flown to Templehof Airfield, where it was to be prepared to fly "senior officers of the office of the Reichsführer-SS" to Warsaw on twenty minutes' notice. Raschner had also reserved two compartments on each of the next three trains departing for Warsaw, in case the weather should preclude travel by air. Von Deitzberg's orderly had been instructed to pack luggage containing uniforms sufficient for a week in Warsaw.

Even before Himmler had ordered him to his office, as he had indeed just done, Von Deitzberg had the scenario clear in his mind: Himmler would summon him to ask him why he hadn't been immediately informed of the Warsaw affair, even if that meant interrupting his luncheon with his wife. Von Deitzberg would explain that the Reichsführer had left orders that he was not to be disturbed; and in any event, he had already done all that he felt the Reichsführer-SS would have ordered. An airplane was waiting at Templehof, et cetera, et cetera.

At that point, Himmler would wonder if the insurrection of some Jews was worth his personal attention.

"I think I had better tend the store, Manfred," he would say. "Who else could we send?"

At which point, von Deitzberg would say, "It would have to be someone who could act for you, Herr Reichsführer."

And then Himmler would say, "I hate to do this to you, Manfred, but I think it would be best if you went there. You will be acting with my authority, of course."

"Good afternoon, Herr Reichsführer. I trust you had a pleasant lunch?" von Deitzberg said as he entered Himmler's office.

"We have two problems on our hands, Manfred," Himmler said.

"*Two,* Herr Reichsführer?" von Deitzberg asked, surprised.

Obviously Löwzer brought the second one. Did I make a mistake in letting him in to see Himmler without knowing what he wanted?

"Deputy Foreign Minister von Löwzer was just here. To show me a message to von Ribbentrop from Buenos Aires," Himmler said. He paused and looked at von Deitzberg before going on, somewhat dramatically. "Goltz and Grüner are dead," he announced.

It took a moment for Oberführer von Deitzberg to absorb what he had just been told.

"*Dead,* Herr Reichsführer?" he finally asked.

"Murdered by person or persons unknown. Their bodies arc aboard the *Océano Pacífico . . .* which, by the way, the Argentine government has ordered from Argentine waters, on the grounds of attempted smuggling."

"And the cargo of the *Océano Pacífico?*" von Deitzberg asked carefully.

"The *Océano Pacífico* was not able to unload her cargo," Himmler said. "Von Lutzenberger was obviously reluctant to go into all the details in a cable, but he made that point quite clearly."

Von Deitzberg nodded.

"And said more details were available," Himmler went on. "Three people are familiar with them, in addition to the Ambassador himself. He suggested that von Ribbentrop arrange for at least one of them to come to Berlin on the next Lufthansa Condor flight."

"Did he provide their names?"

"Yes. Gradny-Sawz, von Wachtstein, and Sturmbann-führer von Tresmarck. I think your first order of business would be to have their dossiers sent up, so that you and I can have a fresh look at them."

"Jawohl, Herr Reichsführer."

"There will be a meeting of the others, and I would like to have that information before I go to that."

"I understand, Herr Reichsführer."

"And then I'd like your recommendations for someone to send to Warsaw to deal with *that* incredible problem."

"Before I knew of this, Herr Reichsführer, I made arrangements to take you there. There is a Heinkel at your disposal at Templehof."

"I thought perhaps you might suggest yourself. "

"If the Reichsführer-SS had decided going to Warsaw was not worth his time, yes, sir."

Himmler was aware that von Deitzberg was ambitious and that he stood a far better chance of promotion to

Brigadeführer (brigadier general) if he had some operational experience in the field.

"The problem, Manfred, is priority," Himmler said kindly. "The Argentine operation is of far greater importance to the Reich than the unfortunate business in Warsaw. I need you here, at least until some decisions are made about Argentina."

"I understand, Herr Reichsführer."

"Can you think of someone off the top of your head?"

"Three or four people, Herr Reichsführer. But I thought you might wish to go over their dossiers with me before you made your decision."

"Good idea. Get the dossiers as soon as you can."

"Jawohl, Herr Reichsführer."

[TWO]
The Chancellery of the German Reich
Wilhelmstrasse
Berlin
2230 27 April 1943

Though it was officially the Reich Chancellery Air Raid Shelter, everyone thought of it—and called it—"the Führerbunker."

Under the supervision of Hitler's personal architect, Albert Speer, a new Chancellery had been built in 1938–39 on the grounds of what was now known as "the old Reich Chancellery." The new structure was far more imposing than the old, in both size and style.

The Führer had studied the proposed plans for the new Reich Chancellery and the bunker carefully, made a few "suggestions" for improvement, and then had watched the actual construction with great interest.

After the bunker was finished, the courtyard of the old Chancellery looked very much like it had before the shelter was built. There were two exceptions.

The first was a round-roofed one-story building in a corner of the courtyard, which served as an above-ground observation post for the guards of the SS-Leibstandarte (Life Guards) Adolf Hitler Regiment, who had been assigned the duty of protecting the bunker. A three-story flight of stairs under this building led down into the bunker and provided an emergency exit from it.

The second was the main entrance to the bunker. Constructed of thick concrete, and equipped with theoretically bombproof doors, it clashed architecturally with the Chancellery Building, but aesthetics had to give way to practical military engineering when the lives of the Führer and his closest advisers were at stake.

Only two senior Nazi officials had their own quarters in the Führer bunker: the Führer's closest advisers, Martin Bormann and the clubfooted Dr. Josef Goebbels, Minister of Propaganda.

Not even Reichsmarschall Hermann Göring or Field Marshal Wilhelm Keitel had space in the Führer bunker. Nor did Admiral Karl Dönitz, head of the German Navy, nor Joachim von Ribbentrop, nor Rear Admiral Wilhelm Canaris, nor Reichsführer-SS Heinrich Himmler.

Space had been found, however, for Adolf Hitler's good friend, Fräulein Eva Braun, who had her own bedroom modestly apart from the Führer's.

Since it was useful to have an intelligent and trustworthy second pair of eyes and ears at important meetings, when Reichsführer-SS Heinrich Himmler went to the Reich Chancellery this afternoon, he took Oberführer Manfred von Deitzberg with him, but managed to get von Deitzberg only as far as the foot of the stairway leading downward from the courtyard of the Chancellery.

When Himmler and von Deitzberg passed through the two steel doors leading to the main bunker stairs, they were snappily saluted by the Schutzstaffel noncommissioned officers on duty and passed through without question. Himmler was, after all, the Reichsführer-SS, and the guards knew von Deitzberg was his adjutant.

But as Himmler reached the bottom of the last of the long

flights of stairs, he realized he wouldn't be able to take von Deitzberg any farther. Sitting in a row on steel chairs in the small area outside the bunker waiting room were Deputy Minister Georg Friedrich von Löwzer of the Foreign Ministry and the aides-de-camp to Admirals Dönitz and Canaris.

Someone has decided, Himmler thought, *that a deputy foreign minister, a Navy captain, and a Navy commander—not to mention an SS-Oberführer—are not important enough to wait in the actual waiting room.*

And there is no question in my mind that that someone is Martin Bormann.

"May I get the Herr Oberführer a coffee?" a Leibstandarte Hauptsturmführer politely inquired of von Deitzberg.

I wonder, Himmler thought as a Leibstandarte Obersturmführer opened the door to the waiting room for him, *if that bastard Bormann will have the effrontery to keep me waiting in here.*

There was no one in the long, narrow waiting room but another Leibstandarte Hauptsturmführer, who gave Himmler the Nazi salute.

"This way, if you please, Herr Reichsführer-SS," he said, and led him through a cloakroom lined with metal wall lockers into Martin Bormann's office. It was furnished simply with a metal desk and chair, a low filing cabinet, and a small table. The two admirals and the Foreign Minister were seated at the table.

Bormann, leaning against his desk, wore the brown uniform of the National Socialist Workers party. He was forty-three, a stocky man of a little less than medium height, and wore his hair close-cropped.

"Ah, there you are, Heinrich!" Bormann greeted Himmler with a smile, and offered his hand. "We've been waiting for you."

Himmler consulted his wristwatch. He forced himself to smile.

"You said half past seven," he said. "It is seven twenty-nine."

"No one comes in here," Bormann announced to the Leibstandarte Hauptsturmführer. "And no calls, except from the Führer. Or someone calling for the Führer."

"Jawohl, Herr Reichsleiter," the Hauptsturmführer said, and closed the door.

Himmler nodded in turn to Dönitz, von Ribbentrop, and Canaris. Each returned the nod.

"The Reichsmarschall, Generalfeldmarschall Keitel, and Dr. Goebbels are with the Führer at Wolfsschanze," Bormann announced. "Keitel is aware of the cable from Buenos Aires. I thought I would wait until we see what this meeting decides before seeking instructions from the Führer."

Himmler thought: *There is an implication in that which I don't like, that he alone decides what the Führer will or will not be told.*

In this case, since the Führer is likely to be furious when he hears about the mess in Argentina, I will allow him to indulge his vanity.

"Has there been anything more than the first cable?" Himmler asked.

Von Ribbentrop shook his head. He was wearing a business suit, the only one there not in uniform. He was fifty, a small, once-handsome man whose blond hair was turning gray.

"The cable said very little," Bormann said, addressing von Ribbentrop and making the observation an accusation. Ambassador von Lutzenberger was a diplomat, and diplomats were the responsibility of the Foreign Minister.

"It gave us the facts, Martin," Himmler argued reasonably. "And I rather admire von Lutzenberger's concern that our cables might not be as secure as we would like to believe."

"What did it tell you?" Bormann snapped.

"That we were lucky we didn't lose the *Océano Pacífico*'s special cargo—the Operation Phoenix special cargo—as well as Goltz and Grüner."

"It didn't say what happened, or who is responsible," Bormann said.

"I would hazard the guess that either the papal nuncio or

the American OSS is responsible," Himmler said sarcastically.

"There has to be someone in the embassy," Admiral Canaris said.

The others looked at him. Canaris, too, was a short fifty-five-year-old whose face was just starting to jowl. He had been a U-boat commander in World War I.

"I didn't know Goltz well, but Grüner was a good man," Canaris went on. "And from what little we know, I agree with Himmler that it was almost certainly the OSS—meaning that someone had to tell them not only what was going on but where and when."

"I will of course defer to the both of you in this area," von Ribbentrop said, nodding at Himmler and Canaris. "But I did have the thought that the Argentines themselves might be responsible. They are, after all, Latin. Latins practice revenge. The two killings might be in retribution for the unfortunate death of Oberst Frade."

"They're capable of it," Canaris said thoughtfully. "That's worth thinking about."

Canaris was the acknowledged expert in this group about things Argentine. Not only had he been interned by the Argentines during the First World War, but he had escaped from them.

"It was the OSS," Bormann pronounced.

"Von Lutzenberger's cable said other details were available," Himmler said. "Details he obviously did not wish to transmit in a radio message. And he provided us with the names of those people privy to those details."

"What do we know about those people?" Bormann asked.

"I took the trouble to review their dossiers," Himmler said, "this afternoon."

"And?" Canaris asked.

"Gradny-Sawz's family," Himmler began, "has served the Austro-Hungarian diplomatic service for generations, and Gradny-Sawz has followed in that tradition. Sometime before the *Anschluss,*" he went on, referring to the 1938 incorporation of Austria into the German Reich, which then became the German state of Östmark, "he was approached by one of my men, who solicited his cooperation. Gradny-Sawz not only readily offered it, but was of no small value to us during the Anschluss."

"From one perspective—the Austrian perspective—that could have been viewed as treason," Admiral Dönitz said.

Dönitz, the tallest of the group, was fifty-two, slim, and intelligent looking.

"Or enlightened self-interest," Bormann said, chuckling.

"The man who recruited Gradny-Sawz was Standarten-führer Goltz, who himself was recruited by Oberführer von Deitzberg," Himmler said. "Goltz had been close friends with Gradny-Sawz for years."

"And the others?" Bormann asked.

"Sturmbannführer Werner von Tresmarck," Himmler said, "was recruited for *this* assignment by Goltz. He worked for Goltz here. Goltz had absolute confidence in him."

"That leaves the aviator," Bormann said.

"Major Freiherr Hans-Peter von Wachtstein," Himmler said, "the son of Generalleutnant Graf Karl-Friedrich von Wachtstein . . ."

"Who is on the staff of the Oberkommando der Wehrmacht," Dönitz added. "The family has served Germany for hundreds of years." The Oberkommando was the High Command of the armed forces.

"The boy—I suppose I shouldn't call him 'the boy'—received the Knight's Cross of the Iron Cross from the Führer himself," Canaris chimed in.

"And whose two brothers have laid down their lives for the Fatherland in this war," Dönitz added.

"So these three are above suspicion, is that what you're saying?" Bormann challenged. "*Somebody* has talked to the Americans."

"Or to the Argentines," Canaris said. "Von Ribbentrop may well be onto something. The Argentines are quite capable of taking revenge. I was a little uncomfortable with the decision to remove Oberst Frade."

"You think that's possible, do you?" Himmler asked.

"Anything in Argentina is possible," Canaris replied. "We haven't mentioned von Lutzenberger himself. I have nothing to suggest that he is anything but wholly reliable. Do you?"

"No," Himmler said simply.

"So where are we?" Bormann asked. "Two very good men are dead. What we sent to Argentina is now somewhere in the South Atlantic Ocean en route to Cadiz. . . ."

"*Everything* we sent over there," Dönitz said. "We should not forget that in addition to the special shipment, the *Océano Pacífico* was carrying supplies for twenty-seven submarines operating in the South Atlantic."

"What about a rendezvous at sea?" Himmler asked.

"I began to work on that the moment I saw von Lutzenberger's cable," Dönitz said. "Possibly something can be worked out. But it is not easy. And so far as the *Océano Pacífico* is concerned, it's out of the question. She is being followed by an American destroyer. And, unless I am being unduly pessimistic, I don't think the new Argentine government will allow us to anchor a ship in their protected waters again."

"The more I think about it, the American involvement in this might be less than I thought at first," Canaris said.

"In any case," Bormann said, "our own priority, it seems to me, is to make certain that the special cargo of Operation Phoenix is safely landed in Argentina."

"*Safely* landed," Canaris agreed. "Not lost at sea, not falling into the hands of the Argentines. Or, God forbid, the Americans."

"Do you think the Argentines know—or suspect—anything about the special cargo?" Dönitz asked.

"You will recall, Admiral," Canaris said, "that one of the American OSS agents was reported to have asked questions on that subject."

"Reported by von Tresmarck," Himmler said, "who recommended his removal."

"That happened, didn't it?" Bormann asked.

"Von Tresmarck dealt with the problem," Himmler said. "We don't know how much he found out—or passed on—before he was removed," Canaris said. "And he was a Jew. Jews talk to Jews."

"It would seem to me, gentlemen, with all respect," Himmler said, "that we have only a few facts before us. Making decisions with so few facts is counterproductive. Thus we need to talk to someone who, as von Lutzenberger said, is 'personally familiar' with the incident."

Canaris grunted his agreement, then asked: "Which of them? All of them?"

Himmler did not respond to the question directly. "The first thing we have to do is learn what we're facing."

"I agree," Canaris said.

"And the way to do that," Himmler went on, "is to send people to Buenos Aires to find out, and bring some of the people on von Lutzenberger's list here, to get their stories. Once we have decided what the situation is, we can decide how to deal with it."

"Go on," Bormann said.

"What I suggest—what I intend to do immediately, unless there is serious objection—is to send my adjutant, Oberführer von Deitzberg, and his deputy, Standartenführer Raschner, to Buenos Aires. As you know, von Deitzberg is conversant with all the details of this program. Between the two of them they can determine how this disaster came about."

"You mean, conduct the investigation entirely in Argentina?" Canaris asked.

"Oh, no. The same plane that takes my men to Argentina will bring to Berlin some of the people on von Lutzenberger's list."

"Who, specifically?" Bormann asked.

"If I send von Deitzberg, that would permit me to bring von Tresmarck to Berlin," Himmler said.

"I would like to personally hear what von Tresmarck has to say," Canaris said.

"With that in mind," von Ribbentrop said. "What if I send von Löwzer? And bring back Gradny-Sawz?"

"Who is Löwzer?" Dönitz asked.

"Deputy Minister Georg Friedrich von Löwzer," von Ribbentrop said. "He is also privy to Phoenix. I don't want to leave him over there for long, however. I need him here."

"Our priority is the success of Operation Phoenix," Bormann said, somewhat unpleasantly. "Whether or not that is convenient for anyone."

"I was speaking of von Löwzer's value to Phoenix," von Ribbentrop said. "And once we have a talk with Gradny-Sawz, I think we'll probably be able to send him back to Buenos Aires. Then I can bring von Löwzer back here."

"Why not bring von Wachtstein to Berlin as well?" Dönitz asked. "If I read that cable correctly, he was physically present on the beach."

"I thought about that, " Himmler responded. "We don't know how much—or how little—he knows about Phoenix. But yes, I think it would be a good idea to have von Wachtstein come here."

"I agree," Dönitz said.

"If von Wachtstein was on the beach when the two men were killed, he has to know something about what was going on," Canaris said.

"And once we have a chance to talk to him," Himmler said, "we can decide whether to tell him more or eliminate him."

"You have some reason to suspect him of complicity?" Canaris asked.

"No," Himmler said. "That's my point, Admiral. We need information. And I have suggested a way to get it."

"I agree with the Reichsführer," Canaris said. "But I have a suggestion of my own. We need an immediate replacement for Oberst Grüner. In both his military and Sicherheitsdienst roles." The Sicherheitsdienst, SD, were the secret police within the SS.

"That's true," Himmler said. "Who do you have in mind?"

"One of my officers, Korvettenkapitän Boltitz—"

"Karl Boltitz?" Dönitz interrupted.

Canaris nodded.

"I know his father very well. And the son's a bright young man," Dönitz added.

"More to the point, he's a bright intelligence officer,"

Canaris said. "He's been my liaison officer to von Ribbentrop. I think he would be useful in Buenos Aires. But before we send to him to Argentina, I think we should have him talk, one sailor to another, so to speak, with Kapitän de Banderano. . . ."

"With who?" Bormann asked.

"The captain of the *Océano Pacífico,*" Himmler furnished. "He was also present at Puerto Magdalena." And then he had a second thought. "He wasn't on von Lutzenberger's list."

"An excellent reason to talk to him, wouldn't you say?" Canaris said.

Himmler chuckled.

"She should make Cadiz on the eighteenth or nineteenth of May," Canaris said, which told Himmler that Canaris had been thinking of Captain de Banderano before he came to the meeting. "That would mean Boltitz couldn't go to Buenos Aires immediately."

"I agree that talking to de Banderano is important," Himmler said. "I can send someone with Boltitz to Cadiz, to report to us here after Boltitz talks to de Banderano. Then Boltitz could leave for Argentina that much sooner."

"That's fine with me," Canaris said, then added: "And Herr Reichsführer, with all possible respect, I have another suggestion for you."

"Which is?" Himmler asked with a tight smile.

"An army officer would draw less attention in Buenos Aires than a senior SS officer. And the less attention in a situation like this, the better."

"You're suggesting we don't send von Deitzberg?"

"I was wondering how convincingly Oberführer von Deitzberg could wear the uniform of the Wehrmacht," Canaris said.

"I take your point, Admiral," Himmler said. "And I would say that Oberführer von Deitzberg would make a convincing Wehrmacht general officer. Do you think Keitel would object if I seconded him to the General Staff?"

"I think we can explain the situation to the Generalfeldmarschall," Canaris said, smiling.

"Is there anything else?" Himmler asked, looking at each of them in turn.

No one had anything to say.

"If there are no objections, I'll send the necessary cable, and arrange for their passage on the Condor," von Ribbentrop said.

"And what do we tell the Führer at this time?" Dönitz asked.

"I would suggest that the Führer has enough to occupy his attention without bringing this to his table until we know what we're talking about, and what we are going to do," Bormann said.

He looked at each man in turn, and each man, in turn, nodded his agreement.

[THREE]
The Chancellery of the German Reich
Wilhelmstrasse
Berlin
2325 27 April 1943

The first of the official Mercedeses lined up on Wilhelmstrasse to transport the senior officers who had attended the conference in the Führer bunker was that of Reichsprotektor SS Heinrich Himmler. The Leibstandarte Adolf Hitler Regiment knew on which side their bread was buttered.

As soon as the car had moved away from the curb, Himmler turned to Oberführer Manfred von Deitzberg.

"Manfred, how would you feel about going to Buenos Aires?" he asked.

"Whatever the Herr Reichsprotektor thinks is necessary," von Deitzberg replied.

"I asked how you would *feel* about going there."

"From what I've heard, it's a beautiful city," von Deitzberg said.

"It was decided in there that you should go to Buenos Aires to find out what happened there," Himmler said.

"Jawohl, Herr Reichsprotektor. May I take Raschner with me?"

Himmler nodded.

"And Canaris suggested that you go in a Wehrmacht uniform . . . that of a Generalmajor," Himmler said. "He said he thought you would attract less attention that way. How do you feel about that?"

"I think he has a point," von Deitzberg said. "But how could that be done? Wouldn't Keitel object?"

"There will be no objections from Keitel," Himmler said flatly.

"It will be a strange feeling putting on a Wehrmacht uniform again," von Deitzberg thought aloud.

Himmler smiled knowingly at him.

Actually, the thought of putting on a Generalmajor's uniform—and I won't just be putting it on, there will be some kind of official appointment, even if temporary; I will be a Generalmajor—is rather pleasant.

The von Deitzberg family had provided officers to Germany for centuries, and Manfred had been an Army officer—an Oberleutnant (first lieutenant) of Cavalry—before he transferred to the SS.

In 1911, when Manfred was ten years old, his father—then an Oberstleutnant (lieutenant colonel)—had been assigned to the German garrison in German East Africa. Manfred had clear memories of the good life in the African highlands, of their large houses, the verdant fields, the black servants.

His father had loved Africa and had invested heavily in German East African real estate, borrowing against the family's Westphalian estates to do so. When war came—Manfred was then fourteen—his father had been rapidly promoted to Generalmajor, and had served until the Armistice as deputy commander of German military forces in German East Africa.

The Armistice had brought with it an immediate reversal of the von Deitzberg family fortunes.

Under the Versailles Treaty of 28 June 1919, Germany lost 25,550 square miles of its land and seven million of its citizens to Poland, France, and Czechoslovakia. Its major Baltic port, Danzig, became a "free port" administered by Poland. Most of the Rhineland was occupied by Allied troops. The Saar was given "temporarily" to France; and the Rhine, Oder, Memel, Danube, and Moselle Rivers were internationalized. Austria was prohibited from any future union with Germany.

All German holdings abroad, including those of private German citizens, were confiscated. Almost the entire merchant fleet was expropriated. One hundred forty thousand dairy cows and other livestock were shipped out of Germany as reparations, as well as heavy machinery (including entire factories) and vast amounts of iron ore and coal.

Billions of marks were assessed annually as reparations, and German colonies in Africa and elsewhere were seized by the League of Nations and then mandated to the various Allies (though not to the United States).

Under the terms of the Versailles Treaty, all the von Deitzberg family property in what had become the *former* German East Africa had been lost.

And since the loans against the von Deitzberg estates in Westphalia had been still on the books of the Dresdener Bank, when payments could not be made, the estates were also lost.

Soon afterward, Generalmajor von Deitzberg had committed suicide. He had not only been shamed that his decisions had resulted in the loss of his family's estates, but he was unwilling to face spending the rest of his life in a small apartment somewhere, living only on his retirement pay.

Army friends of the family had arranged a place for Manfred in the cadet school, and in 1923, when he was twenty-two, he had been commissioned a lieutenant of cavalry like his father and his grandfather. The difference for Manfred was that the family could no longer afford to subsidize its sons' military pay—meaning that Manfred had to live on his army pay, and it wasn't much.

Furthermore, because the Army was now limited to 100,000 men by the Versailles Treaty, promotions had come very slowly. In 1932, when Manfred was finally promoted Oberleutnant, he was thirty-one and had been in the Army nine years.

A month before his promotion, he had joined the National Socialist German Workers party, recognizing in Adolf Hitler a man who could restore Germany—and the German army—to greatness.

The next year, he learned that Heinrich Himmler was expanding the "Protective Echelon" (Der Schutzstaffel, formed in 1925 to protect Hitler) of the Nazi party into a more heavily armed, army-like force to be called the Waffen-SS.

Manfred suspected that the Waffen-SS would become in time the most important armed force of Germany. And he knew that Hitler did not wholly trust the Army—an opinion shared by most of the senior National Socialist hierarchy. The majority of the army's officer corps came from the aristocracy, who looked down not only on Hitler himself (whom they referred to privately as "The Bavarian Corporal") but also on many in his inner circle. The Nazis were well aware of this.

Nevertheless, von Deitzberg had concluded that a professional officer who truly believed that National Socialism was the future would fare much better in the Waffen-SS than in the Wehrmacht, if for no other reason than that the Waffen-SS would in the beginning be short of professional soldiers, since its officer corps would come predominantly from one branch or another of the police (many police officers had joined the Nazi party very early on).

He was well aware that you can't make an Army officer out of a policeman—no matter how good a Nazi—by simply putting him in a uniform and calling him Sturmbannführer or Obersturmbannführer. It takes training and experience, and he had both.

His application for an SS commission was quickly approved, and within a year he had been promoted to Hauptsturmführer (captain). He was promoted to Sturmbannführer (major) two years after that—much sooner than he would have received the equivalent promotion in the Wehrmacht.

At the time of his promotion, von Deitzberg had been stationed in Munich, which exercised administrative authority over, among other things, the concentration camp at Dachau. His superior staff work in this position brought him to the attention of Brigadeführer Reinhard Heydrich, Himmler's adjutant.

Like von Deitzburg, Heydrich had been a professional officer (in the Navy, in his case). But for Heydrich it wasn't problems with making ends meet that sent him into the SS. Rather, he had been forced to resign his naval commission because of an unfortunate affair with a woman. His military experience still left him convinced—with von Deitzberg—that you can't make good officers just by pinning rank insignia on them.

Heydrich had von Deitzberg assigned to his office in Berlin, and there they became friends.

This turned out to be a mixed blessing. Heydrich liked fast cars, fast women, and good food. The SS provided his Mercedes, and the fast women were free, but usually only after they'd been wined and dined at Berlin's better restaurants, where Heydrich was seldom presented with a check. Since von Deitzberg did not enjoy Heydrich's celebrity, waiters and bartenders were not at all reluctant to hand the checks to him.

In August 1941, in the Reichschancellery, Hitler had personally promoted Heydrich to Gruppenführer (Major General) and von Deitzberg—newly appointed as First Deputy Adjutant to Reichsführer-SS Himmler—to Obersturmbannführer.

After a good deal of Champagne at the promotion party at the Hotel Adlon, von Deitzberg confided to Heydrich that, although the promotion was satisfying for a number of reasons, it was most satisfying because he needed the money.

Two days later, Heydrich handed him an envelope containing a great deal of cash.

"Consider this a confidential allowance," Heydrich said. "Spend it as you need to. It doesn't have to be accounted for. It comes from a confidential special fund."

With his new position as First Deputy Adjutant to Reichsführer-SS Himmler came other perquisites, including a deputy. Heydrich sent him—"for your approval; if you don't get along, I'll send you somebody else"—Obersturmführer Erich Raschner, whom Heydrich identified as intelligent and trustworthy. And, who "having never served in either the Waffen-SS," he went on, "or the Wehrmacht, has been taught to respect those of his superiors who have."

Raschner turned out to be a short, squat, phlegmatic Hessian, three years older than von Deitzberg. He had come into the SS as a policeman, but a policeman with an unusual background.

For one thing, he had originally been commissioned into the Allgemeine-SS, which dealt mainly with internal security and racial matters, rather than the Waffen-SS. Later, he had been transferred to the Sicherheitspolizei, the Security Police, called the Sipo, of the Reichssicherheitshauptamt or RSHA (Reich Security Central Office).

Early on in his time with von Deitzberg, Raschner made it clear that as von Deitzberg was judging him for a long-term relationship, Raschner was doing the same thing. Von Deitzberg understood that to mean that it was important to Heydrich for them to get along.

Two weeks later, Heydrich asked von Deitzberg for an opinion of Raschner, and von Deitzberg gave him the answer he thought he wanted: They got along personally, and Raschner would bring to the job knowledge of police and internal security matters that von Deitzberg admitted he did not have.

"Good," Heydrich said with a smile. "He likes you, too. We'll make it permanent. And tonight we'll celebrate. Come by the house at, say, half past seven."

At half past seven, they opened a very nice bottle of Courvoisier cognac, toasted the new relationship, and then Heydrich matter-of-factly explained its nature.

"One of the things I admire in you, Manfred," Heydrich said, "is that you can get things done administratively."

"Thank you."

"And Erich, on the other hand, can get done whatever needs to be done without any record being kept. Do you follow me?"

"I'm not sure."

"The confidential special fund is what I'm leading up to," Heydrich said. "I'm sure that aroused your curiosity, Manfred?"

"Yes, it did."

"What no longer appears on Erich's service record is that he served with the Totenkopfverbände," Heydrich said. The Death's-Head—Skull—Battalions were charged with the administration of concentration camps.

"I didn't know that."

"You told me a while ago you were having a little trouble keeping your financial head above water. A lot of us have that problem. We work hard, right? We should play hard, right? And to do that, you need the wherewithal, right?"

"Yes, Sir," von Deitzberg said, smiling.

"Has the real purpose of the concentration camps ever occurred to you, Manfred?"

"You're talking about the Final Solution?"

"In a sense. The Führer correctly believes that the Jews are a cancer on Germany, and that we have to remove that cancer. You understand that, of course?"

"Of course."

"The important thing is to take them out of the German society. In some instances, we can make them contribute to Germany with their labor. You remember what it says over the gate at Dachau?"

" 'Arbeit macht frei'?"

"Yes. But if the parasites can't work, can't be forced to make some repayment for all they have stolen from Germany over the years, then something else has to be done with them. Right?"

"I understand."

"Elimination is one option," Heydrich said. "But if you think about it, realize that the basic objective is to get these parasites out of Germany, elimination is not the only option."

"I don't think I quite understand," von Deitzberg confessed.

"Put very simply, there are Jews outside of Germany who are willing to pay generously to have their relatives and friends removed from the concentration camps," Heydrich said.

"Really?"

"When it first came to my attention, I was tempted to dismiss this possibility out of hand," Heydrich said. "But then I gave it some thought. For one thing, it accomplishes the Führer's primary purpose—removing these parasitic vermin from the Fatherland. It does National Socialism no harm if vermin that cost us good money to feed and house leave Germany and never return."

"I can see your point."

"And at the same time, it takes money from Jews outside Germany and transfers it to Germany. So there is also an element of justice. They are not getting away free after sucking our blood all these years."

"I understand."

"In other words, if we can further the Führer's intention to get Jews out of Germany, and at the same time bring Jewish money into Germany, and at the same time make a little money for ourselves, what's wrong with that?"

"Nothing that I can see."

"This has to be done in absolute secrecy, of course. A number of people would not understand, and an even larger number would feel they have a right to share in the confidential special fund. You can understand that."

"Yes, of course."

"Raschner will get into the details with you," Heydrich went on. "But essentially, you will do what I've been doing myself. Inmates are routinely transferred from one concentration camp to another. And, routinely, while the inmates are en route, members of the Totenkopfverbände remove two, three, or four of them from the transport. For purposes of further interrogation and the like. Having been told the inmates have been removed by the Totenkopfverbände, the receiving camp has no further interest in them. The inmates who have been removed from the transport are then provided with Spanish passports, and taken by Gestapo escorts to the Spanish border. Once in Spain, they make their way to Cadiz or some other port and board neutral ships. A month later, they're in Uruguay."

"Uruguay?" von Deitzberg blurted in surprise. It had taken him a moment to place Uruguay, and even then, all he could come up with was that it was close to Argentina, somewhere in the south of the South American continent.

"Some stay there," Heydrich said matter-of-factly, "but many go on to Argentina."

"I see," von Deitzberg said.

"Documents issued by my office are of course never questioned," Heydrich went on, "and Raschner will tell you what documents are necessary. You will also administer dispersals from the confidential special fund. Raschner will tell you how much, to whom, and when."

"I understand."

"We have one immediate problem," Heydrich said. "And then we'll have another little sip of this splendid brandy and go see what we can find for dinner."

"An immediate problem?"

"We need one more man here in Berlin," Heydrich said. "Someone who will understand the situation, and who can be trusted. I want you to recruit him yourself. Can you think of anyone?"

That had posed no problem for von Deitzberg.

"Josef Goltz," he said immediately. "Obersturmbannführer Goltz."

Heydrich made a "give me more" sign with his hands.

"He's the SS-SD liaison officer to the Office of the Party Chancellery."

Heydrich laughed. "Great minds run in similar channels," he said. "That's the answer I got when I asked Raschner for ideas. Why don't the two of you talk to him together?"

• • •

In addition to his other duties, Heydrich had been named "Protector of Czechoslovakia." On May 31, 1942, he was fatally wounded when Czech agents of the British threw a bomb into his car in Prague.

Before leaving Berlin to personally supervise the retribution to be visited upon the Czechs for Heydrich's murder, Himmler called von Deitzberg into his office to tell him how much he would have to rely on him until a suitable replacement for the martyred Heydrich could be found.

Meanwhile, von Deitzberg was faced with a serious problem. With Heydrich's death, he had become the senior officer involved with the confidential fund and the source of its money, and he had never learned from Heydrich how much Himmler knew about it.

He quickly and carefully checked the records of dispersal of money, but found no record that Himmler had ever received money from it.

It was, of course, possible that the enormous disbursements to Heydrich had included money that Heydrich had quietly slipped to Himmler; that way there would be no record of Himmler's involvement.

Three months later, however, after Himmler had asked neither for money nor information about the status of the confidential fund, von Deitzberg was forced to conclude not only that Himmler knew nothing about it but that Heydrich had gone to great lengths to conceal it from the Reichsprotektor.

It was entirely possible, therefore, that Himmler would be furious if he learned now about the confidential fund. The Reichsprotektor had a puritanical streak, and he might consider that Heydrich had actually been stealing from the Reich, and that von Deitzberg had been involved in the theft up to his neck.

When von Deitzberg brought the subject up to Raschner, Raschner advised that as far as he himself knew, Himmler either didn't know about the fund—or didn't want to know about it. Thus, an approach to him now might see everyone connected with it stood before a wall and shot.

They had no choice, Raschner concluded, but to go on as they had . . . but taking even greater care to make sure the ransoming operation remained secret.

No one was ever found to replace Heydrich as Himmler's adjutant.

In von Deitzberg's view, Himmler was unwilling to bring a stranger, so to speak, into the office of the Reichsführer-SS. And besides, he didn't have to, since von Deitzberg was obviously capable of taking over for Heydrich. It would have been additionally very difficult to keep Heydrich's replacement from learning about the confidential fund.

The thing to do now was make sure that no one was brought in. In what he thought was a fine example of thinking under pressure, von Deitzberg had never mentioned that he, a relatively lowly Obersturmbannführer, had been placed in the shoes of a Gruppenführer, which was of course a fitting rank for the Adjutant of the Reichsführer-SS.

Von Deitzberg recognized that when Himmler considered this disparity, he would conclude that anyone privileged to be of such high-level service to himself should be at least a Standartenführer (colonel)—a promotion for which von Deitzberg was eligible—and that he would in fact be promoted long before he would otherwise have a chance to be.

A week later, Himmler took him to the Reichschancellery, where a beaming, cordial Adolf Hitler personally promoted him not to Gruppenführer but to Oberführer, one grade higher, and warmly thanked him for his services to the SS and himself personally.

The risk of someone new coming into the Office of the Reichsprotektor and learning about the confidential fund seemed to be over.

Von Deitzberg immediately arranged for Goltz to be promoted to Sturmbannführer, Raschner to Hauptsturmführer and, six months after that, to Sturmbannführer. During that period, Goltz recruited a man—Sturmbannführer Werner von Tresmarck—to be sent to Montevideo, Uruguay, ostensibly as the Embassy security officer, but actually to handle the affairs of the ransoming operation.

Later, when Operation Phoenix was put in motion, von

Deitzberg had recommended Standartenführer Goltz as the man to set up and run the project in Argentina. This would also put him in a position to handle the South American end of the confidential fund. For several reasons, he was more capable, and more reliable, than von Tresmarck.

If Goltz did as well as von Deitzberg expected, his promotion to Oberführer could be arranged; and if that happened, he could subtly remind Himmler that his own promotion to Brigadeführer would be appropriate.

In that event, the risk of Himmler finding out about the confidential fund would have been even further reduced.

But that hadn't happened. Goltz was now dead, and there was a real possibility that when von Tresmarck was questioned, he would blurt out everything he knew about the confidential fund to save his own skin.

And who, von Deitzberg wondered, *is going to fill in for him while he is gone? One of his men? Or someone who will eagerly try to fill the vacuum? And might that man come across a clue that would lead him to the confidential fund?*

"I'm going to miss you in the office, Manfred," Himmler said as the Mercedes rolled down the Kurfürstendamm.

"I will do my best to see that you are properly served in my absence, Herr Reichsprotektor."

"But I think you and Raschner are the right team to send over to get to the bottom of this."

"I will do my best, Herr Reichsprotektor."

"My feeling, Manfred, is that there are three possibilities."

"Which are, Herr Reichsprotektor?"

"One, someone has betrayed us. Two, Canaris is right, and the Argentine army is responsible for the murders of Goltz and Grüner. And three, that the American OSS is involved."

"I agree, Sir."

"But the most important thing for you to find out is how much the Argentines and the Americans know about Operation Phoenix—and I hope they know nothing. Operation Phoenix is the priority, Manfred. That must go forward!"

"I understand, Herr Reichsprotektor."

"To that end—if I have to say this—you have my authority to do whatever you think is necessary."

"I understand, Herr Reichsprotektor. I am honored by your trust."

"*Whatever* is necessary, Manfred."

"Jawohl, Herr Reichsprotektor."

III

[ONE]
Office of the Director, Abwehr Intelligence
Berlin
0930 28 April 1943

"Korvettenkapitän Boltitz, Herr Admiral," Admiral Wilhelm Canaris's aide announced.

Canaris looked up from the work on his desk and saw the two young naval officers standing in his open door. He didn't reply, but made three gestures. First, with his index finger he beckoned Boltitz into the office; then he signaled him to close the door; and lastly he pointed to a chair placed squarely in front of his desk.

After that, he returned his attention to the report on his desk; he didn't look up again for five minutes.

When he had finished reading, he raised his eyes toward the ceiling. After a moment he nodded his head, as if in agreement with something, exhaled audibly, lowered his eyes to the desk, reached out for a pen, and wrote something quickly on the report before him.

A moment later, his aide-de-camp opened the door to his office.

There's probably a button on the floor, Boltitz thought.

Canaris again signaled three times with his hand without

speaking. He motioned the aide into the office, pointed to the report, which the aide came and took, and gestured a final time for the aide to close the door.

Then he looked at Boltitz, who started to raise himself from the chair.

Canaris held out his hand to signal him to remain seated. Boltitz sat back down.

Canaris almost visibly gathered his thoughts.

"There is always difficulty, Boltitz, when gathering intelligence that interests more than one agency; it becomes a question of priorities. Agency A, for its own reasons, is very interested to learn facts that are of little—sometimes no—interest whatever to Agency B, which, for its own reasons, is interested to learn a set of entirely different facts. I'm sure you're aware of this."

"I understand, Herr Admiral."

"The Führer has not found time in his busy schedule to share with me his thoughts about what happened in Argentina, or, for that matter, to convey to me the importance he places on Operation Phoenix. Possibly this is because the Führer—who not only believes, as we all do, in our ultimate victory, but is burdened with the leadership of the state—does not feel he should waste his time dealing with the contingency of being offered, or forced to seek, an armistice, and the ramifications thereof."

"I understand, Herr Admiral," Boltitz said.

This wasn't entirely true. Karl Boltitz was trying very hard to understand what Canaris was really saying.

Kapitänleutnant Boltitz recalled what his father, Vizeadmiral Kurt Ludwig Boltitz, had told him as he was about to report to the Oberkommando der Wehrmacht for duty with the Abwehr: "The best advice I can give you, Karl, is to listen to what Canaris is *not* saying."

Kapitänleutnant Boltitz had not been at all happy about his assignment to a desk in Berlin. After a brief service upon the *Graf Spee,* he had been reassigned to submarines. He had quickly risen to become the Number One (Executive Officer) of U-241, operating in the North Atlantic from the submarine pens at St. Nazaire, and there had been no question in his mind that he would shortly be given his own boat.

There had in fact been orders waiting for Leutnant zur See Boltitz when U-241 tied up at the underground pens of St. Nazaire after his seventh patrol. But rather than announcing that he was detached for the purpose of assuming command of another submarine, the orders told him to report for duty to Section VIII (H) of the Naval Element, Oberkommando der Wehrmacht.

He had been a bureaucrat in Navy uniform long enough to know what Section VIII (H) was. It was the purposely innocuous-sounding pigeonhole to which naval officers working for Admiral Wilhelm Canaris, the Chief of Abwehr Intelligence, were ostensibly assigned.

Earlier, he had had no doubt that his father had arranged his assignment to the *Graf Spee*; and now he had no doubt that Vizeadmiral Boltitz's influence was getting him off submarine duty . . . a situation that gave him a good deal to think about.

For one thing, he could not deny his first reaction to his orders . . . both the shame and the immense relief. Relief because he would no longer have to put to sea in U-241 and face the terrors of being depth-charged by British or American destroyers.

Shame because of the simple question of honor. His father had acted dishonorably in using his influence to remove his son from combat service. And consequently, as a man of honor, it was clearly his duty to protest the special treatment and to resist it in any way he could. If necessary, he decided, he would appeal upward in the chain of command all the way to Admiral Dönitz, even if that meant embarrassing his father. That couldn't be helped. His father should not have done what he did.

When he confronted his father in Berlin with the accusation, Vizeadmiral Boltitz's response was not at all what he expected.

"I had absolutely nothing to do with your transfer," his father said.

"I have your word?"

"If you feel that that's necessary, Karl."

"In that case, I offer my apologies."

"Don't. If I had the influence you think I have, you would never have gone to submarines in the first place. And I have tried and failed ever since you went to submarines to get you out."

"That's dishonorable!"

"Let me tell you something, Karl," his father said. "For reasons we can only guess at, God gives some men authority over others. How a man uses that authority, for good or evil, is between himself and God, as well as between himself and the State. We are engaged in an evil war, if I have to tell you that. If I can keep my son from being killed in an evil war, I will do that, and I think God will be on my side."

Karl didn't reply.

"Tell me, Karl," Vizeadmiral Boltitz said, "do you remember your first cruise out on the U-241?"

Karl did, vividly.

His first patrol aboard U-241—as the gunnery officer, in charge of the deck-mounted cannon and the conning tower–mounted machine guns—had not been quite what he had expected.

For one thing, firing his cannon at an old, battered, and rusty merchantman and watching her sink mortally wounded beneath the waves, and then leaving her crew afloat in lifeboats, three hundred miles from shore in the North Atlantic in winter, had not seemed to be much of a glorious victory at sea.

And what had happened in the captain's cabin immediately afterward was not in the honorable naval tradition of, say, Admiral Graf Spee.

The captain—Kapitänleutnant Siegfried von Stoup—had been two years ahead of Karl Boltitz at the Naval Academy. They had not been friends, but they knew each other. "Congratulations on your marksmanship, Boltitz," Kapitänleutnant von Stoup said.

"Thank you, Sir," Boltitz replied.

"You may examine the entry in the log," von Stoup said, and slid it across the tiny table to him.

1550 23 Feb On Patrol Zone A17

Sank by gunfire (Oblt Boltitz) SS Star of Bombay, Est. 12000 Gross
Tons. No survivors.

"No survivors, Sir?"

"I am sure, Boltitz, that if there were any survivors, you
would have seen them. In which case, in compliance with
orders from our Führer, you would, as an obedient officer,
have made sure there were no survivors. Nicht war?"

"You mean fire at the seamen?"

"I mean ensure there were no survivors, as our Führer has
ordered."

"That's the order?" Boltitz asked incredulously.

Kapitänleutnant von Stoup nodded. "So far, I have not
informed the enlisted men of the order," he said. "Except, of
course, the Chief of the Boat. Some of them might find
machine-gunning seamen in lifeboats distasteful."

"Good God!"

"The Führer is of course right, Boltitz. Survivors of a
sunk merchantmen are skilled seamen, who can serve
aboard other ships. This is total war—we can't permit that to
happen."

Karl had looked at him in disbelief.

"You will make sure, won't you, Oberleutnant Boltitz,
that no one on your gun crew saw any survivors either?"

"Jawohl, Herr Kapitän."

"That will be all, Karl, thank you."

It was the first time Kapitänleutnant von Stoup had ever
called him by his Christian name.

Later the same day, the Chief of the Boat told him that he
had served under his father when he was a young seaman
and would be grateful, when the Herr Oberleutnant had the
chance, if he would pass on his respects. The Chief added
that he had already spoken to the deck gun crew to make
sure no one had seen any survivors of the *Star of Bombay*.

• • •

"As an honorable officer," Karl's father was saying, "how did you feel about machine-gunning merchant seamen in their lifeboats?"

"That never happened on U-241," Karl said.

"You have sworn an oath of personal loyalty to the Führer. Was it honorable to disobey an order from the Führer? Or did you perhaps think that disobeying an order to commit murder was the more honorable thing to do?"

"I was never actually given the order," Karl said. "My captain—Kapitänleutnant von Stoup—was an honorable man, incapable of murder."

"It's always easier, of course, to let a superior decide questions of honor and morality for you. But sometimes you will have to make those decisions yourself. That, I suspect, is what you are going to have to do when you go to work for Wilhelm Canaris."

"Are you suggesting he's not an honorable man?" Karl asked, genuinely surprised.

"My experience with him, over the years, is that he is far more honorable than I am, and certainly more than the people he serves."

"What are you saying?"

"The best advice I can give you, Karl, is to listen to what Canaris is *not* saying."

The validity of his father's advice became immediately apparent on the second day of Oberleutnant Boltitz's duty with Section VIII (H).

His immediate superior—Fregattenkapitän Otto von und zu Waching, a small, trim, intense Swabian—took him to meet Admiral Wilhelm Canaris.

"I always like to personally greet officers newly assigned to me," Canaris began, looking intently into Karl's eyes. "To make a snap judgment, so to speak, about how well suited they may be for work in this area."

Karl could think of nothing to say in reply.

"You come highly recommended for this assignment, if I am to believe Kapitänleutnant von Stoup," Canaris went on. "He seems to feel that your belief in, your dedication to,

National Socialism and your unquestioned obedience to the orders of our Führer is to be expected from an officer of your heritage."

What the hell is that supposed to mean? I'm surprised that he even knows who Siegfried von Stoup is, much less that von Stoup recommended me for an assignment here.

God, what did the Old Man say? "Listen to what Canaris is not *saying."*

My God! Canaris is telling me that he knows von Stoup is disobeying the "no survivors" order; and that he also knows—the crack about "someone of your heritage"—that my father believes we are in an evil war.

"Where we're going to start you off, Boltitz, under Fregattenkapitän von und zu Waching, is as the liaison officer between this office and that of Foreign Minister von Ribbentrop. You will be expected to make yourself useful to both von Ribbentrop and von und zu Waching, and to keep your eyes and ears open over there for anything that might interest us. Additionally, to give you a feel for the conduct of a covert operation, I want you to come up with a plan to have the officers—and the men, if this is feasible—of the *Graf Spee* to be returned to service from their internment in Argentina."

"Jawohl, Herr Admiral."

"It would appear that you have some unusual qualifications for this assignment. You speak Spanish; you served aboard the *Graf Spee;* and it is self-evident that submarines will have to be involved. And it will serve as a learning experience for you. Both initial assignments will serve that purpose."

"Yes, Sir."

"I will be interested in your progress, Boltitz. I hope that you will not disappoint me. Or your father. Or Kapitänleutnant von Stoup."

"I will do my best, Herr Admiral."

"That will be all, gentlemen," Canaris said, dismissing them.

Though no one had told him anything specifically, Boltitz had quickly come to understand that making himself useful to both von Ribbentrop and von und zu Waching consisted primarily of carrying messages between von Ribbentrop and Canaris without anyone in the Foreign Ministry knowing about it. But he additionally made mental notes recording everyone in the Nazi hierarchy who called on von Ribbentrop, and passed this information in person to von und zu Waching in a daily report.

Most of his time, however, was occupied with planning the escape from Argentina of the two hundred–odd German officers interned there and bringing them back to Germany. Since he knew absolutely nothing about Argentina or about planning a covert operation, he at first imagined the assignment was intended (as Canaris had said) to be a learning experience and nothing more.

But in time he came to understand it was more than that. For reasons he couldn't imagine, Canaris and von und zu Waching wanted him to acquire extensive knowledge of Argentina. And in doing this, he found he had an unexpected ally in Foreign Minister von Ribbentrop himself, who ordered that he be given access to the files in the Argentine Section of the Foreign Ministry.

All of these loose strands came together in January 1943 at what had been announced as a small dinner party at von und zu Waching's home in Potsdam to celebrate Karl's promotion to Korvettenkapitän. He had expected neither the promotion nor the party.

The presence of some of the people at the von und zu Waching villa doubly surprised him—first because they were there at all, and second because they had come almost surreptitiously, in ordinary cars, rather than in the enormous and glistening Mercedeses and Horch limousines almost invariably used by the upper echelons of the Nazi hierarchy.

Martin Bormann was there, and Heinrich Himmler and Admiral Dönitz and Foreign Minister von Ribbentrop, and of course, Admiral Canaris. Only Canaris stayed for dinner, the others having wanted only to see for themselves the young Naval Intelligence officer whom Canaris wished to involve in Operation Phoenix.

Two SS officers, Oberführer Freiherr Manfred von

Deitzberg, Himmler's adjutant, and von Deitzberg's deputy, Sturmbannführer Erich Raschner, appeared ten minutes after Himmler left. Over dinner, Boltitz's role in Operation Phoenix—essentially liaison between the Navy, von Ribbentrop's office, Himmler's office, and the Abwehr—was discussed at some length.

"I think I should tell you, von Deitzberg," Canaris said, "with the exception, of course, that we will be using the *Océano Pacífico* and not a submarine, that the plan to repatriate the *Graf Spee* officers is Boltitz's. He has become our Argentine expert."

"Then perhaps we should send him over there. Or is that what you're suggesting?"

"I discussed that with both Himmler and Dönitz. We are agreed that he will be more valuable here. In case something goes wrong."

"Are you suggesting that something will go wrong?"

"Did you ever hear the phrase, my dear von Deitzberg, 'the best laid schemes of mice and men,' et cetera?"

"There is no room in Operation Phoenix for error," von Deitzberg said.

"Even the more reason to expect the unexpected, my friend," Canaris said.

And now it was 0930 on the twenty-eighth of April, and the unexpected had happened. The *Graf Spee* officers would not be repatriated aboard the *Océano Pacífico,* the special cargo had not been landed, the two officers in charge of the operation had been shot to death on the beach of Samborom-bón Bay, and Admiral Canaris had summoned Karl Boltitz to his office.

"The Reichsführer-SS," Canaris was saying, "has just about convinced himself that there is a traitor in Buenos Aires. He may well be right, and he may have information in that regard that he has not seen fit to share with me. The possibility exists, however, that the Argentines—knowing absolutely nothing about Operation Phoenix—are responsible for the deaths of Oberst Grüner and Standartenführer Goltz.

Ordering the elimination of Oberst Frade may well turn out to have been very ill-advised in this connection alone, not to mention the damage it did to our relations with the Argentine officer corps."

Karl Boltitz nodded but said nothing. He had long before learned that Admiral Canaris had no time to listen to verbal agreements. If there was no objection, he presumed full agreement with him.

"I have no doubt that a means will be found to land the special cargo in Argentina, and that Operation Phoenix, supported as it is at all echelons, will ultimately go forward. But I consider, and so does the Führer, that the repatriation of the *Graf Spee* officers is also very important to ultimate victory."

He glanced at Boltitz as if looking for an indication that Boltitz understood him.

"I have the feeling that the Führer will wish to see the reports from Spain and Buenos Aires. Read them himself, rather than trust a synopsis. The Führer does not like reports that offer ambiguities. So the report that you and whoever the Reichsführer-SS sends with you to Spain should contain no ambiguities. If there is any disagreement as to what the report to Himmler should contain, defer to the SS."

Now a reply was expected, and Boltitz gave it. "Jawohl, Herr Admiral."

"I would, of course, be interested in anything you develop there, or in Buenos Aires, that Himmler's man does not feel is worthy of the attention of either the Reichsführer-SS or of the Führer."

The translation of that is that I am to report to him, unofficially, anything in the report to Himmler I don't agree with, as well as anything I think—or suspect—he should know.

"I understand, Herr Admiral."

"If you can find the time, Boltitz, perhaps you could meet the Condor from Buenos Aires when it lands in Lisbon."

"Jawohl, Herr Admiral."

Admiral Canaris smiled at Boltitz, then signaled with his hand that their little chat was over.

[TWO]
Avenida Pueyrredón 1706
Piso 10
Buenos Aires
0405 29 April 1943

Alicia Carzino-Cormano was twenty years old, tall and slim; and when she came out of the bathroom, her intensely black hair hung down over her shoulders and almost below her bare breasts. The bedroom was flooded with moonlight, and she could see quite clearly.

What she saw made her smile tenderly. Twenty-four-year-old Major Freiherr Hans-Peter von Wachtstein was lying naked in his bed, on his back, arms and legs spread, breathing softly, sound asleep.

She walked to the bed and looked down at him.

He was *really* blond, she thought, blond all over, not just the hair on his head, but the hair on his chest, between his legs, and under his arms.

There were blondes in Argentina, of course. Dorotéa Mallín, Alicia's friend since childhood—and soon to marry Cletus Frade—was a natural blonde, an English blonde, but she had seen Dorotéa changing clothes, and she wasn't blond all over the way Peter was.

She sat down on the bed very carefully, so as not to wake him, and looked at him again. After a moment, she swung her legs into the bed.

She ran her fingers very softly over the hair on his chest, stopping when she encountered a line of scar tissue.

Peter had told her that he had gotten that falling off his bicycle as a child, but she didn't believe him. She was sure he'd gotten that scar in the war, just as he'd gotten the longer scars on his lower abdomen and on his right leg in the war.

He never talked to her about the war.

She wondered if Cletus Frade talked to Dorotéa about

what he'd done in the war. Or if Peter talked to Cletus about what they'd done in the war. Did they talk about war? Or about women?

When Alicia leaned forward to run her fingers farther down Peter's chest, her hair fell forward, blocking her view, and she pushed it back and over her shoulders.

Her fingers reached the blond hair at his groin. His thing looked like a long, wrinkled thumb, she thought. And ten minutes ago it had looked like . . . like a banana, a large banana!

She touched it, and that woke him up.

She quickly removed her hand.

"Sorry, baby," Peter said.

"For what?"

"I fell asleep."

"You don't have to be sorry for falling asleep," Alicia said.

He raised his hand to her breast, cupped it momentarily, and then put his index finger on her nipple, causing it to stiffen and rise.

"That's chocolate, right?" he said. "The *other* one's vanilla."

A moment later, he chuckled. "I love it when you blush," he said.

"I'm not blushing."

He snorted.

"Precious," she said. "I have to go."

"Damn!" he said, and sat up and reached for the wristwatch on the bedside table.

It was American, a Hamilton chronograph, an aviator's wristwatch. Cletus Frade had one exactly like it, and Dorotéa had noticed that, just as Alicia had noticed Peter's. Cletus had told Dorotéa that he'd stolen his from the U.S. Marine Corps, and Dorotéa wasn't sure if that was the truth or not. Peter had told Alicia that he had "found" his American watch, and obviously hadn't wanted to talk about it, so she hadn't pressed him.

"It's six and a half minutes after four," Peter announced indignantly.

That was the German in him, Alicia thought. She would have said "it's four" or "a little after four," not "six and a half minutes after four."

"I have to go to the house," she said. "We're going to Estancia Santo Catalina this morning."

"What time this morning?"

"Probably in time to have a late lunch at the estancia," she said, and computed the time. "Leave Buenos Aires at eleven." She paused. "You are coming out for the weekend?"

"Unless the Ambassador or Gradny-Sawz finds something for me to do," he replied, and then asked, "So why do you have to leave now? Is Mama sitting up in the foyer waiting for you?"

"She's sound asleep, but she will know five minutes after she wakes what time I came in. The maid will tell her when she brings her coffee."

"So if the maid tells her you came home at half past six? Half past seven? What's the difference?"

"The roof garden at the Alvear closes at half past four. She knows that. She will expect me to be home half an hour after that."

"That's," he consulted the watch again, "fifty-two minutes from now."

"Yes," Alicia said, and felt herself blushing again. "I didn't say I had to leave this instant. Just very soon."

"Oh, baby!"

"Can you?"

"Of course I can. I'm a fighter pilot."

Her smile vanished.

"I wonder how often you've said that in the past," she said.

"Once or twice, I admit—"

"Once or twice, hah!"

"Always before I met you," he said.

"Do you think you'll hear something today?" she asked.

"That was a quick change of subject," he said.

"Do you think?"

"I don't know. Maybe. Maybe today. Maybe not until next week."

"And if they tell you to go to Germany?"

"I'll cross that bridge when I get to it," he said.

She felt tears form, and she was not quite able to suppress a sob.

"Honey, don't do that," Peter said.

"God, Peter, I'm so frightened!"

He put his arms around her.

"It'll be all right, baby," he said.

She held him tightly. He kissed her hair.

"Sorry," she said.

"Oh, Christ!"

He ran his hand down her spine.

"Señorita, your question has been answered," he said.

"What?"

He took her hand and guided it to his groin. "Our friend has also waken up," he said.

She held him.

"If I could see your face, would you be blushing?" he asked.

"Shut up, Peter," she said, and lay back on the bed, pulling him down on top of her.

Major Freiherr Hans-Peter von Wachtstein, now wearing a shirt and trousers, knocked at the bathroom door.

"I'm brushing my hair," Alicia called softly, and he pushed open the door.

She was standing in front of the mirror in her underwear. She smiled at him. "You didn't have to get up," she said.

"I'm going to drive you home," he said.

"I'm going to take a taxi," she said. "We've been through this before."

"Christ, you're as hardheaded as you are beautiful."

She smiled at him. "I've explained the rules to you," she said. "I pretend to have been dancing with friends at the Alvear roof garden, and Mother pretends to believe me."

"You've had a lot of experience with this sort of thing, right?"

Her smile vanished, replaced by a look of hurt and anger. "You know better than that," she said.

He knew better than that. Alicia had been a virgin.

"Just a little joke," he said.

"I don't like your sense of humor," Alicia said, and began to furiously brush her hair.

After a moment she said, "I learned the rules from Isabela."
Isabela was the older of the Carzino-Cormano girls.

"And has el bitcho been dancing at the Alvear tonight, too?"

"Don't call her that, Peter, I've asked you."

It had been loathing at first sight when Isabela and Cletus
Frade had met. Clete had dubbed her "el bitcho." Though it
was neither Spanish nor English, the term had immediately
caught on. Alicia often caught herself thinking of Isabela
that way, and she had even overheard one of the maids calling her that to another maid.

"Has she?" he pursued.

"I don't know what she did last night. She's been . . ." Alicia
stopped herself just in time from saying "bitchy," ". . . difficult
about the wedding. She really doesn't want to participate."

Alicia finished brushing her hair and started to make up
her face.

"I like to watch you standing there in your underwear,
doing that," Peter said.

She smiled at him. "Go back to bed," she said.

"Not alone," he said.

"Sweetheart, I have to go."

"I'll put you in a cab," he said.

She nodded.

[THREE]
The Embassy of the German Reich
Avenue Córdoba
Buenos Aires
0915 29 April 1943

"And a very good morning to you, Fraülein Hassell," Peter
von Wachtstein said to the Ambassador's secretary as he
entered the Ambassador's outer office. He was wearing a
well-cut, nearly black pin-striped double-breasted suit, a
stiffly starched white shirt, and a striped silk necktie. She was
a middle-aged spinster in a black dress, and wore her graying
hair drawn tight and gathered in a bun at the nape of her neck.

"His Excellency wanted to see you the moment you arrived at the Embassy," Fräulein Ingebord Hassell said, sounding to Peter much like a scolding schoolteacher.

"And here I am," Peter said.

"It's sixteen past nine," she said. "He sent for you at eight twenty-five."

"I was caught in traffic," Peter said. "May I go in?"

"One moment, please, Herr Major," she said.

She pushed the TALK lever on her intercom box. "Excellency, Major Freiherr von Wachtstein is here."

"Send him in, please, Fräulein Hassell," the ambassador replied. "And would you bring us some coffee?"

"Jawohl, Excellency," she said, and glared at Peter. "One day, you're going to try his Excellency's patience too much."

"Oh, I hope not," Peter said.

He walked to the Ambassador's door, knocked, and then entered without waiting for a reply. "Heil Hitler!" he barked so that Fräulein Hassell would hear him, but he did not give the requisite salute.

"Heil Hitler," the Ambassador Extraordinary and Plenipotentiary of the Führer of the German Reich to the Republic of Argentina replied.

Manfred Alois Graf von Lutzenberger was a very slight man of fifty-three who wore his thinning hair plastered across his skull. He signaled for Peter to come in. "I sent for you forty-five minutes ago," he said.

"My apologies, Excellency, I was caught in traffic."

Fräulein Hassell scurried into the room with a tray holding coffee and sweets.

Von Lutzenberger waited until Fräulein Hassell had left and closed the door behind her, then pointed to the chair beside his desk, an order for Peter to sit down. "Traffic, eh? I thought perhaps you might have overslept." He pushed a sheet of paper across the desk to Peter.

"I wonder what Untersturmführer Schneider did from ten-fifteen to four A.M.," Peter said.

"His duty to his ambassador, von Wachtstein," von Lutzenberger said. "Making a report that will also be of great interest when the people arrive from Berlin."

Peter looked at von Lutzenberger with that question in his eyes.

"Not a word," von Lutzenberger said. "But it will come, Peter, as inevitably as the sun rises."

```
SECRET

ATTENTION OF AMBASSADOR AND FIRST
SECRETARY ONLY

SURVEILLANCE REPORT VON WACHTSTEIN,
MAJOR FREIHERR HANS-PETER

PERIOD 1735 28 APRIL 1943 TO 0630 29
APRIL 1943

28 APRIL

1700 SURVEILLANCE COMMENCED

1735 OFFICER LEFT THE EMBASSY IN
PERSONAL AUTO

1758 OFFICER ARRIVED AT HIS APART-
MENT

1805 OFFICER TELEPHONED 78342 AND
SPOKE WITH SEÑORITA ALICIA CARZINO-
CORMANO, ARRANGING RENDEZVOUS WITH
CARZINO-CORMANO AT RESTAURANT MÜN-
CHEN RECOLETA FOR 1930

1915 OFFICER TOOK TAXICAB TO RESTAU-
RANT MÜNCHEN

1932 OFFICER ARRIVED RESTAURANT MÜN-
CHEN, MET CARZINO-CORMANO
```

2115 OFFICER DEPARTED RESTAURANT
MÜNCHEN WITH CARZINO-CORMANO IN TAXI-
CAB

2148 OFFICER ARRIVED HIS APARTMENT
WITH CARZINO-CORMANO

2215 ALL VISIBLE LIGHTS IN APARTMENT
EXTINGUISHED.

29 APRIL

0353 LIGHT, MASTER BEDROOM ILLUMI-
NATED

0430 OTHER APARTMENT LIGHTS ILLUMI-
NATED

0442 OFFICER APPEARED WITH CARZINO-
CORMANO IN APARTMENT LOBBY AND
PLACED CARZINO-CORMANO IN TAXICAB

0600 SURVEILLANCE TERMINATED

SUMMARY:

DURING THE SURVEILLANCE PERIOD,
OFFICER MET WITH ONE (1) PERSON,
CARZINO-CORMANO AND MADE ONE (1)
TELEPHONE CALL, TO CARZINO-CORMANO.

HEIL HITLER!

SCHNEIDER, UNTERSTURMFÜHRER, SS-SD

Peter nodded.

"When do you next plan to see Señor Duarte?" von Lutzenberger asked. "I have something I want you to give him."

"I've been invited to the Carzino-Cormano estancia for the weekend. I'm sure he'll be there."

"Well, as we have had no word from Berlin, I think you should accept the invitation. Don't go out there before I give you what I have."

"No, Sir."

"That will be all, Peter, thank you."

"Yes, Sir."

Peter made it as far as opening the door when von Lutzenberger called out to him, loud enough for Fräulein Hassell to hear.

He turned.

"I expect you to be in the Embassy during normal duty hours, von Wachtstein. If traffic is a problem, then leave your apartment earlier."

"Jawohl, Excellency!"

[FOUR]
El Club De Belgrano
Barrancas Del Belgrano, Buenos Aires
1315 30 April 1943

The dark blue 1939 Dodge four-door sedan turned left off Avenida Libertador onto Calle José Fernandez and drove up its steep—for Buenos Aires—incline to the first corner. There the driver tried, and failed, to make a very sharp left turn into the drive of the Belgrano Club. He had to back up twice before he was lined up in the drive and the porter could open the gate.

If he had turned a block earlier and come down Arribeños, the passenger in the rear seat of the car thought, *he could have done this a lot easier.*

The Belgrano Club occupied most of a block in Barrancas del Belgrano, an upper-class district of Buenos Aires—a district that looked, its Deutsche-Argentinishe residents often commented, much like the Zehlendorf district of Berlin. Its tree-shaded streets were lined with large villas, and here and there a luxurious apartment building.

Once inside the compound, the driver (following the directions of his passenger) drove past the buildings housing the swimming pool and the restaurant, and finally stopped by the door to the men's dressing room, near the tennis courts.

The driver jumped from behind the wheel, came to attention by the rear door, and pulled it open.

A tall, fair-haired, light-skinned man in his middle thirties, wearing a well-cut gray business suit and a snap-brim felt hat, stepped out and looked at the driver, then at his watch.

There is time.

"Manuel," he said kindly. "A little less militarily, if you would. We're in civilian clothing."

"Sí, mi Coronel," Sargento Manuel Lascano said, still at attention.

Though Sargento Lascano was also wearing a business suit, he had spent five of his twenty-three years in the Army, and almost all of that in the infantry, and almost all of that in remote provinces. Two weeks earlier (after selection by the man in the well-cut suit as the most promising among ten candidates), he had been transferred to the Edificio Libertador Headquarters of the Ejército Argentino (Argentine Army) for "special duty."

The criteria for selection had been high intelligence, an absolutely clean service record, a stable marriage, a simple background, and, importantly, a reputation for keeping his mouth shut.

"And when we're in civilian clothes, Manuel," Coronel Bernardo Martín said, "please try to remember not to call me 'coronel.' "

"Sí, Señor," Sargento Lascano said.

"You'll get used to it all, Manuel," Martín said, meaning

it. He had already decided that he had made the right choice in Sargento Lascano. Lascano didn't know much about what was expected of him, but he wanted the promised—"if this works out, Sargento"—promotion to Warrant Officer, which meant he wanted to learn. So far, it hadn't been necessary to tell him anything twice.

Teaching him, Martín thought, *is like writing on a clean blackboard.*

"When you drop me off at a place like this," Martín said, "try to find a parking place that leaves the door I went in visible. Try to be inconspicuous, but failing that, park where you have to, and if anyone questions you, show them your identification and tell them you're on duty."

That morning, when he had reported to Coronel Martín for duty, Sargento Lascano had been issued a leather-bound photo identification card identifying him as an agent of the Bureau of Internal Security. He had also been issued a .45-caliber semiautomatic pistol manufactured in Argentina under license from Colt Firearms of Hartford, Connecticut, USA, and a shoulder holster.

"Sí, Señor."

"I'll probably be about fifteen minutes, Manuel," Martín said. "With a little luck, ten."

"Sí, Señor."

Martín entered the men's locker room, resisted the temptation to have a beer at the bar just inside, and went to his locker and stripped off his clothing.

The man he was looking for was not in the locker room.

I'm going to need a shower anyway. Why not?

Five minutes later, he came out of the tile-walled shower room, a towel around his waist. The man he was looking for, middle-aged, muscular, balding, was now in the locker room, sitting by his open locker, also wearing only a towel.

"Well, look who's here," Santiago Nervo said, almost sarcastically cordial. "Buenas tardes, mi Coronel."

Commissario Santiago Nervo was, more or less, Martín's

peer in the Policía Federal, in charge of their Special Investigations Division.

Martín did not particularly like him, and he was sure that Nervo felt much the same way about him. Policemen don't like soldiers, particularly soldiers in the intelligence business, which they believe should be their responsibility. And intelligence officers don't like policemen whose jurisdiction sometimes conflicts with their own.

"Putting on a little weight, aren't you, Santiago?" Martín said, offering his hand.

"Screw you," Nervo said without rancor, and turned to his locker and took an envelope from it.

"You can have that," he said. "You owe me."

Martín opened the envelope. It contained a single sheet of paper.

```
1623 ARENALES

APARTMENT 5B

45-707

MARIA TERESA ALSINA

2103 SANTA FE

APARTMENT 4H

DOB 16 MAY 1928
```

It was the address and telephone number of an apartment building. Martín searched his memory a moment and came up with a mental image. It was at the corner of Arenales and Coronel Díaz in Barrio Norte, a northern suburb of the city.

"You're sure about this, Santiago?" Martín asked.

"Yeah, I'm sure. I saw el Coronel Juan Domingo Perón go in there myself."

"Sixteen May 1928. That makes her fifteen," Martín said.

"Next month, she'll *be* fifteen," Nervo said. "Well, you know what they say, if they're big enough to bleed, they're big enough to butcher."

"Who else knows about this?"

"One of my lieutenants, two of my sergeants, and me."

"Can you keep it that way?"

"Of course."

"You're right, Santiago, I owe you."

"Yeah, you do," Nervo said.

Martín offered him his hand, then went to his locker and dressed quickly.

The moment he stepped into the street outside the men's locker room, he heard the starter of the Dodge grind, and a moment later the car started moving toward him. He signaled to Sargento Lascano to stay behind the wheel and climbed into the backseat. "The officer's sales store, please, Manuel," he ordered.

"Señor, I don't know where—"

"On the Avenida 9 de Julio, across the avenue from the French Embassy."

"Sí, Señor."

"You'll learn these places soon enough, Manuel," Martín said.

But I think it will be some time before I start telling you things like what I have just learned. That the new Assistant to the Minister of War, the distinguished el Coronel Juan Domingo Perón, has rented an apartment and installed in it his new mistress, who will be fifteen years old next month.

Lascano returned to Avenida Libertador by turning right onto Calle Arribeños, then making a right when the street dead-ended at one of the parks scattered throughout the Barrancas del Belgrano. As he did, Martín happened to glance up and saw the miniature Statue of Liberty that had been erected there about the same time the real one was going up in New York Harbor.

I wonder if Cletus Frade knows that's there? For that matter, I wonder if the American Ambassador does?

Lascano drove downtown at a shade under the speed limit.

By the time they had passed the Hipódrome, and the Frade family's guest house, a medium-size, turn-of-the-century mansion, which was across the street from it, Martín became aware of their pace.

The police are not going to stop this car, much less issue a summons to any car carrying me, or any other officer of the Bureau of Internal Security. So what do I do? Tell him to go faster? And give him the idea that he can ignore the speed limits?

"Manuel, pick it up a little, will you? I'm running late."

"Sí, Señor."

The speed increased another five miles an hour.

"A little more, please, Manuel."

Manuel added another five miles per hour to their velocity. Martín was pleased.

Lascano errs on the side of caution. That's a desirable characteristic in the intelligence business. The trick is knowing when to take a chance.

The officers' clothing store was in a turn-of-the-century mansion much like the Frade place on Libertador.

"Where should I park, Señor?" Lascano asked. "There are no-parking signs."

"Right in front," Martín said. "I won't be a moment. I have to pick up a uniform."

"Señor, I'd be happy to go in for you."

I wonder if he volunteered to go in for me because he would rather not sit at the wheel of an illegally parked car on the busiest street in Buenos Aires? Or because he is simply trying to please me?

"It will be quicker if I go," Martín said, giving him the benefit of the doubt. "But thank you, Manuel."

The uniform was waiting for him inside, with its new insignia in place.

This is the third time in three years I've been here. The last time was yesterday, when I came to see if they could take care of the insignia overnight. The time before that was three years ago, when I picked up this uniform, my present to myself, on my promotion to teniente coronel. I don't think I've worn it a dozen times in three years.

And if I am growing middle-aged flab, the way Santiago Nervo is, and can't get into this, then what?

Martín got back into the Dodge and ordered Lascano to take him to the Edificio Libertador.

When the car had stopped at a side entrance to the large, eleven-story building, Martín permitted Lascano to open the car's door for him.

"Manuel, have you ever heard of Estancia San Pedro y San Pablo?" Martín asked when he was standing by the side of the car.

"Sí, Señor."

"Do you know where it is?"

"Sí, Señor. Near Pila, in Buenos Aires Province."

"And how would you get there from here?"

"Señor, I would need a map."

"Where would you go for that?"

"To an ACA station, Señor," Lascano replied, referring to the Automobile Club of Argentina.

Martín was again pleased with his choice of driver/bodyguard.

"Go to an ACA station now. Buy every road map they have on sale. Get a receipt. Turn in an expense voucher. You have cash?"

"Sí, Señor."

"Personal or official?"

"Both, Señor."

"When you have the maps, bring the one for Buenos Aires Province to my office, and I'll mark Estancia San Pedro y San Pablo and the best way to get there. The estancia is not on the ACA map."

"Sí, Señor," Lascano said. "Señor, are we going to Estancia San Pedro y San Pablo? I will need fuel—"

"We may. In this business, one never knows where one might have to go, or when. So whenever there is the opportunity, make sure you have fuel, et cetera, et cetera."

"Sí, Señor."

Martín turned, and climbed a short flight of stairs to a metal door, carrying the bag with his uniform in it over his arm. A soldier in field gear, wearing a German-style steel helmet and with a Mauser rifle slung from his shoulder, pulled it open for him and came to attention, clicking his heels as Martín entered the building.

It made Martín a little uncomfortable, although he smiled at the soldier.

The soldier thinks he knows who I am, and that I am authorized to enter the building. The operative word is thinks. *One of his officers—or more likely one of the sergeants of the guard—has apparently told him that a "civilian" entering the building through this door, of such and such a height and description, is actually a coronel of the Bureau of Internal Security, and should not be subjected to close scrutiny.*

But how does he know, *without actually checking my credentials at least once—and if this soldier had done that, I would have remembered—that I am that BIS officer?*

The answer is he doesn't. It is one of the problems of the Army . . . and, for that matter, of Argentina. Even before he entered the Army, he was taught that it is not wise to question your superiors. That it is wise to give your superiors—and to this country boy in uniform, the fact that I am wearing a suit and have a car with a driver makes me a superior—the benefit of the doubt.

Martín walked down a long corridor almost to the center of the building, then rode an elevator to the ninth floor. There two BIS men in the elevator foyer did in fact examine him carefully before popping to attention in their civilian clothing.

"Buenas tardes, mi Coronel," the older of them, Warrant Officer Federico Attiria, said.

"Has Mayor [Major] Delgano come up recently?" Martín asked.

"Haven't seen him, mi Coronel."

"Do me a favor. Call El Palomar, and see if and when he's landed out there. If he hasn't, call Campo de Mayo, and see if he's taken off from there, and if not, why not."

El Palomar (literally, "The Dove") was Buenos Aires's

civilian airport. Campo de Mayo, on the outskirts of Buenos Aires, was the country's most important military base, and the Army Air Service kept a fleet of aircraft there.

"Sí, mi Coronel."

"If I ask Señora Mazza to do it, they give her the runaround," Martín said. "They'll tell you."

Señora Mazza was the private secretary to the Director of the Bureau of Internal Security. It was said, not entirely as a joke, that she knew more of Argentina's military secrets than any half-dozen generals.

Attiria chuckled.

"Anyone dumb enough to give her the runaround will suddenly find himself up to his ass in ice and penguin shit in Ushuaia," he said. "I'll let you know what I find out."

Because of its isolation and bitterly cold weather, Ushuaia, in Tierra del Fuego, at the southern—Cape Horn—tip of South America, was regarded as the worst possible place to be stationed.

Martín smiled at him, then walked down the wide, polished marble corridor. Near its end, hanging over a standard office door, was a sign reading, "Ethical Standards Office."

The corridor ended fifty feet farther down, at a pair of twelve-foot-high double doors, suspended in a molded bronze door frame. On them was lettered, in gold, "Office of the Director, Bureau of Internal Security."

At the moment, there was no Director.

In Martín's judgment, El Almirante Francisco Montoya, the former Director, had done a magnificent—and nearly successful—job of straddling the fence between supporting the government of President Ramón S. Castillo and the Grupo de Oficiales Unidos (GOU), which had, under El Coronel (Retired) Jorge Guillermo Frade, been planning its overthrow. When the revolution came, it had been far less bloody than it could have been, largely because of the careful planning of el Coronel Jorge Guillermo Frade. Frade had been determined that the Argentine revolution would not emulate the bloody Spanish Civil War.

Frade himself had been assassinated shortly before the revolution began, and his friend and ally, General de Division (Major General) Arturo Rawson, had stepped into the presidential shoes Frade had been expected to fill. Rawson was a good man, Martín thought. But he was neither as smart nor as tough as Coronel Frade.

He wasn't alone in this assessment. It was clear to Martín that the Germans had arranged for the assassination of Frade because he was smart enough and strong enough not only to control Argentina but to tilt his nation toward the Anglo-American alliance.

Montoya's careful neutrality had not sat well with the new Presidente Rawson, and he had ordered Montoya into retirement within an hour of the occupation by the revolutionaries of the Casa Rosada (the Pink House—the seat of government) and the Edificio Libertador.

He had at the same time offered the post to Martín, who had, with some difficulty, managed to turn it down.

As Chief of the Ethical Standards Office of the BIS (an office that made him directly subordinate to the Director), Teniente Coronel Martín had been responsible for keeping an eye on the GOU. Though he had regularly provided Admiral Montoya with intelligence that made the intentions of Frade and the GOU quite clear, Montoya had been unwilling—or unable; he was not a man of strong character—to bring himself to either suppress the revolutionaries or join them.

Shortly before the revolution began—after much thought, some of it prayerful, and for reasons he really hoped were for the good of Argentina—Martín had decided that his duty required him to support the revolutionaries. From that moment, he had worked hard—and at great personal risk—to conceal the plans of the GOU and the names of its members from Admiral Montoya and the Castillo government.

Martín felt little sympathy for Montoya, for he believed that he had failed in his duty as an officer to make a decision based on his oath to defend Argentina against all enemies. As far as Martín was concerned, el Almirante Montoya had made his decision to straddle the fence based on what he considered to be the best interests of Francisco Montoya. He deserved to be retired. Or worse.

But for reasons that were both practical and selfless,

Martín did not want to find himself sitting behind the ornately carved Director's desk as Montoya's successor.

For one thing, he had told el Presidente Rawson, the position called for a general or flag officer, and he was not even close to being eligible for promotion to General de Brigade (Brigadier General, the junior of the general officer ranks).

Rawson had replied that Martín's contribution to the revolution had not only been important but was recognized, and that he himself had been especially impressed with Martín's accurate assessments of the actions various officers in the Castillo government would take when the revolution began. As far as he was concerned, this proved that Martín could take over the Director's post with no difficulty. And with that in mind, he added, Martín's promotion to General de Brigade in several months was not out of the question.

Martín had countered by respectfully suggesting that if he were promoted out of turn, and named Director, the resentment from the senior officer corps of both the Army and the Armada would be nearly universal and crippling.

He also believed, but did not tell Rawson, that if he was named Director—with or without a second promotion—it would be only a matter of time before he was forced from the office. The generals—and senior colonels who expected promotion to general officer as a reward for their roles in the revolution—might swallow their disappointment and resentment toward a peer who was given the post, but they would unite against a Director who before the Revolution had been a lowly—and junior—teniente coronel.

That would leave (in what Martín liked to think was an honest evaluation of the situation) no one of his skill and experience to provide the government with the intelligence it needed. And when dealing with the North Americans and the Germans, gathering intelligence should not be left to an amateur.

Six general officers (in addition to two colonels, Perón and Sanchez, who were about to be promoted) considered themselves ideally qualified to be Director, and were vying for the post. No admirals were being considered. The only significant resistance to the revolution had come from the Armada.

Martín believed—but did not tell Presidente Rawson—that any of the eight would be delighted to have as their deputy a qualified intelligence officer who had already been given his prize—his promotion—for his role in the revolution, expected nothing more, and would not pose a threat.

He also did not tell Presidente Rawson that he could better serve Argentina from a position behind the throne of the Director of Internal Security than by sitting in the ornate gilded chair itself, and that he could train whomever was finally appointed to the post, much as he had taught Almirante Montoya, who had come from the School of Naval Engineering and had known nothing about intelligence.

Rawson attributed Martín's reasons for declining the directorship to commendable modesty, and decided that for the moment, until a Director could be chosen, Martín would serve as Interim Director. Rawson assured Martín he would seek his advice about which officer he should name Director.

Martín pushed open the door from the corridor to the foyer of his office. Three men rose to their feet. Two were in business suits, and by appearance could have been bankers or lawyers or successful shopkeepers. They were, in fact, agents of the BIS assigned to the Ethical Standards Office. The third man, who wore the uniform of a Suboficial Mayor, and was in fact a sergeant major, was also an agent of the BIS.

Martín motioned all three of them to follow him into his office. When they were all inside, he motioned to Suboficial Mayor Jose Cortina to lock the door.

"Who's with the President?" Martín asked.

Cortina provided two names.

Martín nodded his approval.

President Rawson was accompanied everywhere by his armed aide-de-camp. There was also a Policía Federal bodyguard detail. It consisted of two bodyguards and the drivers of all the cars in any presidential motor parade, which might be anywhere from two to six cars. All of these drivers were also armed.

The Policía Federal believed this was enough protection. Martín devoutly hoped it would be; but to err on the side of caution, he had ordered that two men from the Ethical Standards Office be with the President at all times.

The Policía Federal considered this an insult to their competence, but there wasn't anything they could do about it. Until a new Director of the BIS was named and took office, only the President himself could override Martín's decisions.

If the Germans were brazen enough to assassinate Coronel Frade, they just might be brazen enough to try to eliminate General Rawson. They might think he had been responsible for—or at least knew about and tacitly supported—the shooting of the two German officers on the beach near Puerto Magdalena, and be seeking revenge. Or they might decide to remove him because he shared Frade's pro-Anglo-American, anti-German beliefs. Or there might be an attempt on his life from officers or officials who had been deposed in the revolution. Because the threat was real, Martín saw it as his duty to do whatever he could to protect the President, whether or not the Policía Federal liked it.

"And if the President decides to go to the Frade wedding, how many people will we have at Estancia San Pedro y San Pablo to augment them?"

"Six, Señor," Cortina said.

"That should be enough," Martín said. "We do know, right, that he's going out there?"

"Sí, Señor," Cortina said.

There came a rapping at the closed doors.

Too sharp for knuckles, Martín thought, and signaled with his hand for someone to open the door.

Señora Mazza, a squarish, fiftyish woman in a simple black dress, marched into the office. She held a miniature cavalry sword—her letter opener, and obviously the source of the sharp rapping on the door.

"Excuse me, mi Coronel," she said, and went to his desk and picked up one of the telephones there.

"Here is el Coronel Martín, Señor Presidente," she said, and extended the phone to Martín.

"Coronel Martín," he said into it.

"General Rawson, Coronel," the President of Argentina said. "I'm glad I caught you in."

"How may I be of service, Señor Presidente?"

"Obregon," Rawson said. "How does he strike you?"

El General de Division Manuel Federico Obregon was one of the eight senior officers in the running to be Director of the Bureau of Internal Security.

"General Obregon, Señor Presidente?"

"How would you feel if he took over BIS, Martín?"

My honest answer is that Obregon is the one man I desperately hoped would not be given the appointment.

"I would be honored to serve under General Obregon, Señor Presidente."

"General Ramírez and Coronel Perón feel he would be the best choice."

He could tell from the pained looks of the faces of his three agents that they felt as he did.

The question now becomes: Is Rawson going along with Ramírez and Perón because of—or despite—Obregon's hatred for the English and the North Americans? Is it possible he doesn't know? Or is he afraid to defy Ramírez? Or Perón?

The question is moot. I am being told Obregon will be the Director of BIS, not really asked for my opinion.

"I would never question the judgment of either General Ramírez or Coronel Perón, Señor Presidente."

"How well do you know General Obregon?"

"Only slightly, Señor."

But well enough to know that he is intelligent and ruthless, and that nothing would give him greater pleasure than to become the Argentine version of Heinrich Himmler.

"I want to get the two of you together, privately, as soon as possible," Rawson said. "I want him to know how much I appreciate your services in the execution of Outline Blue"

The plan—in American military parlance, the operations order—for the coup d'état had been called "Outline Blue."

"The next few days will be out of the question, I'm afraid," Rawson went on, "but I am going to Estancia San Pedro y San Pablo for Señor Frade's wedding, and perhaps there will be the opportunity there."

"Señor, I am at your disposal."

"It would help if we knew when, precisely, the wedding will take place, wouldn't it?" the President said somewhat petulantly.

"I understand the Cardinal Archbishop has promised his decision by today, Mr. President," Martín said.

"Don't tell me you have someone in the Cardinal Archbishop's office?"

"An absolutely superb agent, Señor Presidente. My wife's sister. She considers Señor Frade's request outrageous."

Rawson chuckled, and then returned to the subject of General Obregon.

"Martín, while the appointment has not been made public, General Obregon has been told. I wouldn't be surprised if he came to Edificio Libertador to have an unofficial look around."

"I will hold myself at his disposal, Señor Presidente," Martín said.

"I really think, under the circumstances, Martín, that this was the best choice."

If he believed that, he wouldn't have said it. He has his doubts, which suggests that he gave in to some kind of pressure. Or was trying to solidify his position by appointing Obregon. Which is the same thing.

"I'm sure it was, Señor Presidente," Martín said.

IV

[ONE]
Estancia Santo Catalina
Near Pila, Buenos Aires Province
1005 1 May 1943

The wedding of Señor Cletus Howell Frade to Señorita
Dorotéa Mallín posed certain problems. The basic problem,
the blame for which had to be laid squarely at the feet of the
prospective couple, was that Dorotéa was three months pregnant.

Her condition precluded the events that would otherwise
surround a marriage between the offspring of two prominent
Argentine families. Ordinarily, there would have been a formal dinner party to announce the engagement. This would
have been followed by a six-month engagement period, during which there would be myriad lunches, dinners, bridal
showers, and the like.

Ordinarily, the wedding would have been held in the
Basilica of Our Lady of Pilar, in the Recoleta section of
Buenos Aires; and, considering the prominence of the
respective families, the nuptial mass would have been celebrated by the Cardinal Archbishop of Buenos Aires himself.

The bride's family would then hold a reception for the newlyweds at their home, or perhaps, considering the number of
people who would attend, at either the Plaza or Alvear Plaza
Hotel.

That was all now impossible, because of the careless carnal impetuosity of the couple.

An immediate marriage was the obvious solution, but that

itself posed problems, primarily because the groom was just beginning the year's mourning for his late father, during which, without a special dispensation from the Church, he could not marry.

Obedience to the canons of the Roman Catholic Church regarding marriage was required, even though the bride and groom were Anglican and Episcopalian, respectively. Roman Catholicism was the official religion of the nation, and therefore only Roman Catholic marriages were regarded as legally valid.

Father Kurt Welner, S.J., not without difficulty, had found solutions to the ecclesiastical problems. Welner was not only a close friend of the Frade family (and had been a trusted friend of Jorge Frade), he was an expert in canon law and an adviser to the Cardinal Archbishop.

First, he had obtained from the Right Reverend Manuel de Parto, bishop of the Diocese of Pila, in which Estancia San Pedro y San Pablo was located, a waiver of the year of mourning requirement for Cletus Frade. The waiver was not in fact difficult to obtain. He had had to mention to the Bishop only twice that more than half of the diocesan budget came from the pious generosity of *el Patron* of Estancia San Pedro y San Pablo.

Father Welner had not mentioned to Bishop de Parto that, in deference to the feelings of the bride and her mother, and the groom's almost belligerently Episcopalian family, he was also seeking from the Cardinal Archbishop of Buenos Aires a special dispensation permitting the bride's priest, the Very Reverend Matthew Cashley-Price, of the Anglican Cathedral of Buenos Aires, to take part in the wedding ceremony.

The Cardinal Archbishop had told Father Welner that he had to think long and hard about this, and it had taken him until last night to decide how to handle the granting of the dispensation needed to make the Anglican priest a part of the wedding ceremony. Once the decision was made, he himself had decided that he had to be the one to inform Bishop de Parto. Both Welner and the Cardinal were aware that the Bishop would be very uncomfortable with the notion of the Very Reverend Cashley-Price having anything to do with the wedding.

As would the two priests of El Capilla Nuestra Señora de los Milagros, who tended to the spiritual needs of the more than 1,400 people who lived and worked on Estancia San Pedro y San Pablo, and in whose chapel the wedding would be held.

And so would Monsignor Patrick Kelly, of the Archdiocese of Buenos Aires, who would celebrate the mass, representing the Cardinal Archbishop. The Cardinal would not be able to personally participate, as he would "unfortunately be tied up with pressing business," or so he had explained to the Jesuit.

Monsignor Kelly, the family priest of the bride's father and of the groom's aunt and uncle, had made it quite clear to Father Welner that he held him responsible for this outrageous business of having a bloody English Protestant involved in the wedding.

But there were other problems, of a more social nature.

Though Señora Carzino-Cormano—who had been "a very dear friend" of the groom-to-be's father and was a close friend of the bride's mother, and whose daughter Alicia and Dorotéa had been close since childhood—had felt that she had both the right and the obligation to provide any assistance she could, and would open Estancia Santo Catalina to the family of the bride to use as their home until the marriage was accomplished, her ministrations could not make straight what had long been crooked.

Enrico Mallín, for example, the father of the bride and Managing Director of the Sociedad Mercantil de Importación de Productos Petrolíferos (SMIPP), was having a very difficult—and only partially successful—time concealing his unhappiness with his daughter's intended.

Worse—or at least generating more problems—the groom's maternal aunt, Beatrice Frade de Duarte, had been under the constant care of a psychiatrist since the death of her son, the groom's cousin. The psychiatrist spent a large portion of his time feeding her just enough tranquilizing medicine to keep her behavior under control while not putting her into a trance. When not so controlled, she moved rapidly between euphoria and black depression. Usually, he was successful.

Señora Claudia de Carzino-Cormano, the mistress of Estancia Santo Catalina and its 80,599 (more or less) hectares, was a svelte woman in her mid-fifties, with a full head of luxuriant, gray-flecked black hair, drawn up from her neck to the top of her head.

When Sarita, her maid, entered to inform her that Padre Welner had just arrived and wished to see her, she was standing before a triple mirror in the dressing room of the master suite in the main house, wearing a simple black silk dress and holding a cross on a chain in each hand. "Where is he?"

"On the veranda, Señora."

"Offer him coffee, or something to drink, and tell him I will be with him in a moment."

"Sí, Señora."

Claudia dropped her eyes to the crosses she was holding. The simple gold cross on its delicate chain in her left hand was quietly elegant, and was entirely appropriate for luncheon. The cross in her right hand was maybe three times the size of the other. Its heavy gold chain looked sturdy enough to hold an anchor. There were four rubies on the horizontal bar of the cross and six on the vertical. At their junction was an emerald-cut 1.5-carat diamond.

It looks like costume jewelry, Claudia thought. *Of the type worn by a successful brothel madam.*

But it's real. The best that money could buy—if taste doesn't enter the equation.

I can't even remember any more what Jorge did, just that I had every right to be angry with him, and he knew it, and this was his peace offering.

She had imagined then, and imagined now, Jorge standing in the jewelry store off the lobby of the Alvear Plaza Hotel, being shown their entire collection of crosses and picking this one because it was the most expensive.

Anything to make peace. He couldn't stand it when I was angry with him. He really loved me.

Oh, Jorge!

Her eyes watered, and she closed them, and then she put the simple cross back in her jewelry box and fastened Jorge's cross around her neck.

Padre Welner will understand.

Señora Claudia de Carzino-Cormano and el Coronel Jorge Frade had been lovers—in fact, all but married—for many years. Though both of their spouses had died, for various reasons marriage had been out of the question.

She had just finished repairing the tear-caused damage to her mascara when Sarita returned.

"Father is on the left veranda, Señora."

"Thank you."

"You are going to wear *that* cross, Señora?"

"Obviously, wouldn't you say, Sarita?"

Claudia went into her bedroom, then passed through a French door to the walled private garden just outside, and then through a gate in the wall, and then walked to the veranda on the left side of the sprawling house.

The Reverend Kurt Welner, S.J., was a slim, bespectacled, fair-skinned, and elegantly tailored man of forty-four with thinning light brown hair. Claudia found him leaning against the wall. His legs were crossed, and he was holding a crystal Champagne glass by its stem.

As she approached, he raised it to his mouth and drained it. Then, stooping slightly, he set the glass on a small table beside him, took the bottle of Bodega San Felipe Extra Brut from its resting place in a silver cooler, refilled his glass, straightened up, and had another sip.

"A little early for that, isn't it, Father?" Claudia challenged.

"My dear Claudia," he said, smiling at her. "Certainly a good Christian like you is familiar with Saint Paul's words in his letter to Saint Timothy? 'Take a little wine for thy stomach's sake and thine other infirmities'? And besides, we have something to celebrate. The Cardinal Archbishop has come down, if not very firmly, on the side of indulging our Anglican brothers and sisters."

"Well, that's good news," she said. "When did you find out?"

"He called me to the chancellery about ten last night and told me. I decided it was too late to drive out then."

She smiled at him.

"There are two glasses," he said. "May I?"

"I shouldn't," she said.

"But you will?"

For answer she picked up the glass on the table and filled it herself. "To your amazing diplomatic skills," she said, raising the glass. "Thank you."

"No thanks required," he said. "I am but a simple priest doing what he can to ease the problems of the sheep of his flock."

She laughed.

"That's Jorge's cross, isn't it?" he asked.

"Jorge's *peace offering* cross," she said. "I don't even remember what he did, but to judge by this, it must have been something awful."

"They were doing *The Flying Dutchman* at the Colón," he said, smiling, referring to Buenos Aires' opera house. "You gave a dinner, at which he failed to appear. He showed up at the Colón during intermission, deep in the arms of Bacchus, and took improper liberties with your person."

"He was as drunk as an owl," she said, now remembering, without rancor. "He'd been playing vingt-et-un at the Jockey Club. And he'd won. A lot. Enough to buy this incredibly vulgar cross!"

"Which you have chosen to wear on the day we can schedule his son's wedding," Welner said. "How appropriate, Claudia! Good for you!"

"Oh, Father, I wish he was here."

"I was just thinking the same thing," Welner said. "I think he would be delighted with this union."

"That would make three of us," she said. "You, me, and Jorge."

"I think you must add the bride's mother, the groom's aunt, and even, believe it or not, Señor Howell to your short list. You may be right about the others, unfortunately."

"I thought the groom's grandfather hated all things Argentine," she said. "You really mean that?"

"Now that he is about to become the great-grandfather of another Argentine, I think he has been reevaluating his feelings vis-à-vis all of us."

She laughed. "When can we have the wedding?"

"Whenever we want," he said. "I was going to suggest that you schedule the date and present it as a *fait accompli*."

"That's really the bride's mother's business."

"Not, I would suggest, under these circumstances."

She chuckled.

"If I started right now," Claudia said, "and gave up the luxury of sleep, we could have it next Saturday. That would give me a week. There are so many people to invite. . . ."

"I gave the Cardinal the impression it would be a small ceremony, just the immediate families and the closest of friends."

"That's simply impossible, and you know it," she said.

"That's also the impression Cletus has," Welner pursued.

"Cletus better begin to understand who he is, and his obligations," she said. "He is not in a position to insult people who believe they are the closest of friends."

"Of his? Or of Jorge's?"

"You know what I mean," she said. "Stop being difficult."

"Cletus has inherited from his father a great capacity to make himself difficult."

"Why do I think you have something in mind?"

"Someone, actually. What are you going to do about Coronel Perón?"

"If you mean am I going to invite him, of course I am."

"When you showed Cletus your first rough draft of the guest list, he crossed the Coronel's name off with . . . what shall I say? A certain emphasis."

"Juan Perón is Cletus's godfather," Claudia said. "He was Jorge's best friend. I don't know what's happened between them, but Cletus is just going to have to work it out."

Welner didn't reply.

"You did call him and tell him the Cardinal granted the dispensation?" Claudia asked.

"I called Señor Mallín," he said. "I wanted to tell Cletus in person. After I told you."

"If you called Enrico, then I had better get onto the telephone with Pamela," she said, as much to herself as to him.
Pamela Mallín was the mother of the bride. "Can you find
something to occupy you until luncheon?"

"I thought I would go see Cletus—and his aunt and
grandfather—now."

She met his eyes.

"There will be others at luncheon," she said. "Humberto
and Beatrice Frade. And her doctor."

"Oh, really?" he said noncommittally.

"She called to tell me that they would be spending the
weekend at Estancia San Pedro y San Pablo. And I didn't
know how not to suggest they have lunch here on their way."

He smiled. "Be sure to give them my best regards."

"I suppose I can deal with Beatrice by not telling her about
the Cardinal's dispensation. All I need is her taking charge."

"I think that's a very good idea," he said. "She'll learn at
Estancia San Pedro y San Pablo, but Mrs. Howell can tell
her Pamela Mallín is handling everything. I'll have a word
with Mrs. Howell."

"I'd be grateful," Claudia said, then added, "For other
good news, Alicia's young diplomat friend will be here for
the weekend. I didn't know how to tell her no, either. My
cup runneth over."

"There's nothing you can do about that, Claudia, except
be grateful that he seems to be a fine young man. I like him."

"If he were an Argentine, I think I would, too," she said,
then asked, "You wouldn't be willing to talk to her?"

"It would do absolutely no good," he said. "Haven't you
seen the way she looks at him?"

"I don't want to have to arrange another hurried wedding," she said.

"You think it's gone that far?"

"Haven't you seen the way she looks at him?" she quoted
him, bitterly.

"If you like, Claudia, I will talk with her," Welner said.

"Now?"

"Let me deal with Cletus first. Am I invited to spend the
night?"

"Of course you are," she said.

"In that case, I will see you later this afternoon."

She nodded.

"And of course, Claudia, you could pray," he said.

"What makes you think I haven't been?"

"More often, then," he said.

She shook her head and walked away.

When Father Welner got behind the wheel of his black 1940 Packard 280 convertible coupe to drive to Estancia San Pedro y San Pablo, he remembered—as he often did—the not entirely good-willed ribbing he had taken from Jorge Guillermo Frade when he'd been given the car by another wealthy family in appreciation of his pastoral services.

Frade (the best friend he had ever had in his life) had asked him, smiling wickedly, "purely as a matter of curiosity, you understand, Kurt," how he reconciled the Packard, his custom-tailored suits, and his well-furnished apartment in the expensive Recoleta district of Buenos Aires with his Jesuit vows of poverty, chastity, and obedience.

With a straight face Welner had explained that since he readily admitted to being a weak man and a sinner, keeping two out of three of his vows wasn't bad. Frade had laughed heartily.

It took Welner forty-five minutes to drive the sixty kilometers of two-lane macadam roads between the main house (actually a complex of seven buildings) of Estancia Santo Catalina to the main house (a complex of nine buildings) of Estancia San Pedro y San Pablo. His route never took him off the property of the adjoining ranches. The terrain was the pampas, gently rolling hills extending to the horizon in all directions, broken here and there by clumps of trees and spotted all over by grazing cattle.

He saw the trees planted as a windbreak around the main house of Estancia San Pedro y San Pablo long before he reached the complex.

Protected by the trees was the big house itself, a rambling structure surrounded on three sides by wide porches; a small church, La Capilla Nuestra Señora de los Milagros; several houses for the servants and the senior managers of the estancia; a large stable; a polo field; the main garage; el Coronel's garage; and an aircraft hangar, around which were clustered three Piper Cub airplanes and a large twin-engine aircraft, a Lockheed Lodestar airliner, painted bright red.

In 1935, an enterprising Piper salesman had shipped two of the small, two-seater, high-wing monoplanes to Argentina and demonstrated their usefulness to cattle-raising operations on large ranches. He had almost lost the sale to Estancia San Pedro y San Pablo when he told the owner how useful they had proved to be on Texas's King Ranch; but Frade had been so impressed with the potential of the airplanes that he swallowed his dislike for anything Texan and ordered two Cubs on the spot, and later ordered two more.

Within six months of their arrival, he was flying one of them himself, first around Estancia San Pedro y San Pablo, and then to visit Señora Claudia de Carzino-Cormano at Estancia Santo Catalina. Within a year, there had been at least one Piper Cub at each of his four estancias, and landing strips had been built at both of his vineyards.

When Frade learned he was being appointed Deputy Commander of the 2nd Cavalry Regiment at Santo Tomé in Corrientes Province, he had ordered a larger six-place Beechcraft biplane, known as the "Staggerwing," its upper wing being placed to the rear of the lower.

As soon as he took command at Santo Tomé, Frade had put his cavalrymen to work turning one of its pastures into a landing field for the Staggerwing.

It was an overnight trip by rail from Santo Tomé to Buenos Aires, and there was only one train a day. In the Staggerwing, he could fly to Buenos Aires after the morning parade, spend several hours conducting the army's—and his own—business, and then fly back to Santo Tomé in time to take the salute of the regiment at evening parade.

El Coronel Frade had quickly become an advocate for the use of light aircraft in the army, and during the 1941 annual maneuvers (he had become by then Commanding Officer of the Húsares de Pueyrredón Cavalry Regiment, following in the steps of his father and his grandfather, who had founded the regiment), he had used Piper Cubs for reconnaissance and for message delivery.

This outrageously unorthodox behavior had shocked the cavalry purists, of course, but their criticism had been muted by their belief that Frade was almost certain to be become el General Frade, or El Presidente Frade, and most likely both.

Shortly afterward, Frade had with unconcealed pride shown Welner the story in the New Orleans *Times-Picayune* headlined, "Lt. Cletus H. Frade Earns Marine Corps Wings of Gold." At the same time, he had observed, "Of course, flying is in our blood."

The Staggerwing Beechcraft was now on the bottom of Samborombón Bay, having crashed in flames after Cletus H. Frade had flown it into the antiaircraft weaponry of the Portuguese-registered *Reine de la Mer.* But also on the bottom of the bay were the *Reine de la Mer* itself and the German U-boat tied up alongside her when she was torpedoed by the American submarine Cletus Frade had led to her.

The official Argentine story was that the *Reine de la Mer* had been destroyed by a mysterious explosion.

The Lockheed Lodestar had been sent by the OSS to replace the Staggerwing. The official US story was that it was a gift, a small token of the respect and friendship felt toward Colonel Frade by the President of the United States.

Father Welner finally pulled up in front of the big house.

A heavyset man in his forties, wearing a full mustache and carrying a 7mm Mauser cavalry carbine in one massive hand, came quickly off the porch and opened the Packard's door. "Padre," he said, not quite able to wholly restrain his Pavlovian urge to salute. It turned into an awkward wave.

Welner had known for years Sargento Rudolpho Gomez, Argentine Cavalry, Retired.

"Rudolpho," Welner said, offering his hand. "Señor Clete?"

"In el Coronel's garage," Rudolpho said. "With Enrico. Shall I put your bag in your room, Padre?"

For years, a small apartment in the sprawling structure had been set aside for Welner's exclusive use.

"No, thank you, I won't be able to stay."

Welner stepped onto the porch, then walked down it and around the corner of the house to the rear. The working buildings were behind the big house. In front of the house, in the direction of the airstrip, was a carefully tended, formal English garden.

When he reached what was still known as "El Coronel's Garage," he found Cletus Howell Frade nearly buried—both feet off the floor—in the engine compartment of an enormous black Horch convertible sedan. Only a soiled pair of khaki trousers and a battered pair of American cowboy boots were visible.

A heavyset man in his late forties, with a carefully cultivated, now graying cavalryman's mustache, was sound asleep and snoring on a leather couch near the door of the garage. He had a short-barreled Browning semiautomatic 12-gauge shotgun in his lap, and there was a leather cartridge belt beside him. He was Suboficial Mayor (sergeant major) Enrico Rodríguez, Retired. Sergeant Rodríguez had been born at Estancia San Pedro y San Pablo, and left it at sixteen to become batman to newly commissioned Subteniente Jorge Guillermo Frade. He had served his officer until his death, and had himself been left for dead in the bloody and bullet-riddled Horch.

Though still recovering from his wounds, he nevertheless now saw the protection of el Coronel's only son as his mission in life, and was determined not to fail him, as he thought he had shamefully failed to protect his father.

The last time Welner had seen the Horch, the hood, windows, and doors had all been pierced by bullet and buckshot holes, and the bright red leather upholstery and carpeting had been stained black with blood.

On the car there was no sign of any of that now. But against the wall of the garage were both bullet-holed sections of the split windshield, apparently replaced so recently there hadn't been chance to throw them out.

I wonder how Cletus is going to manage leaving Enrico home when he goes on his honeymoon?

Or, for that matter, whether he should? A number of people in Argentina, not only Germans, would like to see Cletus Frade dead.

Including Enrico Mallín.

That's not true. I should be ashamed of myself for even thinking that in jest.

No father likes to learn that his beloved nineteen-year-old unmarried daughter is about to become a mother, but Enrico would really not like to see the father of his forthcoming grandchild dead. Perhaps dragged across the pampas for a kilometer or two behind a galloping horse, but not dead.

Father Welner bowed his head without really thinking about it, and offered yet another prayer for the peaceful repose of his friend's soul. Then he walked up to the car.

As he approached the car, from beneath the hood came a profane, colorful string of expletives—an interesting combination of cultures, Father Welner observed with a smile: Texan, United States Marine Corps, with a soupçon of Spanish Argentine thrown in.

"I will pray to God, my son," Father Welner announced loudly, unctuously, in British-accented English, "that He may forgive, in His infinite mercy, your profane and obscene outburst."

Cletus Howell Frade, a lanky, dark-haired, 180-pound twenty-four-year-old, wiggled out of the engine compartment. His face was grease-stained, and he held several wrenches in his grease-stained hands.

"What brings you out into the country?" he challenged, smiling. "I thought you hated fresh air."

"I am the bearer of good news," Welner said. "The Cardinal Archbishop has agreed to permit Dorotéa's priest to participate in your wedding."

"That's great," Clete said. "So what happens now?"

"I think we can have the wedding next Saturday."

"Why not tomorrow?"

"Because things aren't done that way. Arrangements have to be made."

Clete snorted.

"I'm also here as your confessor, my son," Welner said. "To hear your confession."

"You know what you can do with your confession, Father," Frade said.

"Marriage is a sacrament," Welner said. "You are required to confess, and be granted absolution, before taking those holy vows."

"I'll give you 'marriage is a sacrament,' " Clete said. "But you can put your absolution in the same place you can put my confession."

"Nevertheless, having concluded that you do in fact heartily repent your sins, and intend to go and sin no more, I grant you absolution. In the name of the Father, the Son, and the Holy Ghost."

He made the sign of the cross.

"I wish you wouldn't do that," Clete said, no longer smiling. "It makes me uncomfortable."

"But on the other hand, I am now comfortable with assisting in celebrating the nuptial mass."

Clete shook his head in resignation.

"Let me have one more crack at this sonofabitch, and then I'll buy you a beer," he said.

"Unless it would strain your hospitality beyond the breaking point, I'd really rather have a glass of Champagne."

"My *vino* is your *vino,* Padre," Clete said.

Welner chuckled, and followed him down the cement stairs into the work area beneath the huge automobile.

El Coronel's Garage—Welner wondered how long it would take before it became known as "Señor Cletus's Garage"—was better equipped than most commercial garages. One wall was completely covered with tools, each in its own place, outlined in red paint.

Jorge Guillermo Frade had truly loved his Horch touring sedan, and had insisted on maintaining it himself, although there were more than a dozen mechanics on Estancia San Pedro y San Pablo.

From the moment it had arrived in Argentina until Cletus had suddenly appeared there five months before, only two people had ever been behind the wheel of the enormous German convertible touring car, el Coronel and Suboficial Mayor Enrico Rodríguez.

Father Welner looked up at the car's undercarriage, where Clete, standing on a wooden footstool, was illuminating the lower side of the engine with a work light.

"What exactly are you doing?" he asked.

"I'll be damned," Cletus Frade said.

"I was thinking in terms of mechanics, rather than your spiritual condition."

Clete chuckled, reached into his pocket for a wrench, and began to unbolt something.

He's obviously a skilled mechanic. Why should that surprise me?

In a moment Clete dropped off the footstool, clutching an eighteen-inch-long piece of metal tubing, bent into a contorted shape. He started to show it to the priest but was interrupted by the sudden appearance of a thin stream of lubricating oil. He quickly found a bucket, arranged it to catch the oil, then motioned for the priest to follow him out of the work pit. He headed for Enrico, then stopped and turned to the priest. "I had entirely too much oil pressure," he said. "The needle was almost off the dial. I couldn't figure out why."

"And now you can?"

He showed the priest the length of tubing. "Here," he said, pointing to a spot near one end, close to the connecting fastener. "See?"

"I don't know what I'm looking at."

"You see that dent?" Clete said. "Jesus, it damned near pinched the flow off completely."

"What did?"

"Whatever hit the pipe there," Clete said.

"What did hit the pipe there?"

Clete met his eyes. "I'll guess a buckshot," he said. "I

think a metal-jacketed .45 bullet would have just gone right on through."

The assassins of el Coronel Jorge Guillermo Frade had been armed with Thompson submachine guns firing copper-jacketed 230-grain bullets, and with shotguns firing 00-buckshot pellets.

What a stupid question for me to ask.

"Can it be repaired?"

"I don't know. I think it can be expanded from the inside; it's close to the end. If it can't, I'm fucked."

"Among the many gentling effects I devoutly hope Dorotéa will have on you is the cleaning up of your language."

Though they were not speaking loudly, their conversation was enough to wake Enrico. He opened his eyes and put his hand on the pistol grip of the shotgun, then recognized the priest and quickly rose to his feet. "Padre," he said.

"Enrico. How are you feeling?"

"I am fine, Padre."

"He's lying through his teeth, Father," Clete said in Spanish. "Isn't that a sin? Lying to a priest?"

"One of the worst," Welner said. "Unless, of course, it's in a good cause."

"Every morning, when I tell him to stay in bed," Clete went on, "he tells me that he can't sleep. So I let him come down here, and five minutes later he's sound asleep and snoring like a sea elephant."

"I just closed my eyes for a moment," Enrico said.

"Two hours ago," Clete said. He handed Enrico the piece of tubing. "See the dent?"

"Sí, Señor."

"That's why we had too much oil pressure," Clete said. "Can you get that out of there? Without ruining the tubing?"

"Of course, Señor Clete."

"If you rupture the tubing, I'm fu . . . in trouble, Enrico."

"I understand, Señor Clete."

"Father Welner and I are going up to the house."

"Sí, Señor."

[TWO]

There were perhaps twenty cases of wine and Champagne stacked against the side of the big house near the kitchen door. Clete reached into one of them and came out with two bottles. He looked at the priest and gestured at the stacked cases. "This goddamn thing is getting out of hand," he said. "This is all for the reception."

"The sacrament of marriage, Cletus, is not a 'goddamned thing.' "

"Sorry," Clete said. "You know what I mean."

"I'm not sure I do," Welner said.

"In Texas, in these circumstances, the guilty couple would make a quick trip to Reno, or maybe over the border into Mexico, and come back a married couple. This was supposed to be a small, private ceremony."

"This is not Texas," Welner said.

"How can it be—and that 'small, private ceremony' I got from you—how can it be small and private when there's going to be two hundred people here for the wedding?"

"This is not Texas," Welner repeated. "There are people who had to be invited."

Clete resumed walking toward his—formerly el Coronel's—apartment, a bottle of wine in each hand.

"Why?"

"Because they are family friends and would be deeply hurt if they weren't," Welner said. "For example, el Coronel Juan Domingo Perón, whose name you mistakenly crossed off of Claudia's guest list."

Clete opened a door into the house by standing on his left foot and then pushing on the lever handle with his cowboy-boot-shod right foot. He turned and looked at the priest. "That wasn't a mistake," he said. "I crossed the son-ofabitch's name off on purpose."

"And after discussing the matter with me, Señora de Carzino-Cormano put it back on."

"Christ!" Clete said disgustedly, and resumed walking down the wide corridor to his apartment. Welner walked quickly after him.

A tanned, stocky, short-haired, blond woman in her forties, who was wearing a simple black dress with a single strand of pearls, came out of the side door that led to one of the apartments and blocked Clete's path.

"I was about to come get you," she announced. "And where are you going with that wine?" And then she saw Welner. "How nice to see you, Father," she added and, smiling, offered him her hand.

"Mrs. Howell," Welner said.

That was a mother, a good strong mother, talking to a son. She may not have borne Cletus, but she raised him from infancy. They are mother and son.

"I was just about to tell him—I spoke with Claudia—that you were coming for lunch. And I wanted him to be cleaner than that." She gestured at his dirty clothing and grease-stained hands.

"I am en route to the shower," he said.

"With the wine?"

"With the wine," he said. "We're celebrating—you heard?—the Cardinal has agreed to have Dorotéa's priest in the wedding."

"I heard," she said. "And Claudia told me who was responsible. Thank you, Father."

"I did nothing," Welner said.

"Why don't you come with me? And we'll have a little Champagne to thank you."

"Father Welner and I are having a private little chat," Clete said, smiling at her. "You know, man to man? Things a bridegroom should know?"

She smiled and shook her head in resignation. "You don't have to go with him, Father," Martha Williamson Howell said. "He has a tendency to believe that what he wants is what everybody wants."

"In that, Mrs. Howell, he is very much like his father."

"We're having lunch in the gazebo," she said, "in," she looked at her watch, "twenty-five minutes."

"Yes, ma'am," Clete said.

"Go easy on the wine," she said, and stepped back through the door to her apartment.

Clete went the rest of the way down the corridor to his own apartment, which consisted of a sitting room, a bedroom, and what had been known as "el Coronel's study." As soon as he was inside he began to unbutton his shirt. "Open one of these, will you?" he said, handing the priest the wine. "I'll be out in a minute."

"With great pleasure," the priest said, and went to the bar in the sitting room to find glasses and a corkscrew as Clete disappeared into the bedroom.

Welner opened one of the bottles of wine, poured himself a glass, and then walked into el Coronel's private study.

A thought occurred to him that he'd had many times before: If some scholar ever decided to write *The Early Years of Cletus Howell Frade: A Biography,* he could do ninety percent of his research right in this room, which General Edelmiro Farrell, a close friend of el Coronel Jorge Guillermo Frade, had described as "Jorge's shrine to his son."

Years earlier, Cletus Marcus Howell, Clete's maternal grandfather, had blamed Jorge Guillermo Frade for the death during her second pregnancy of his daughter and the unborn child. She and her baby—Cletus—were in the United States when she died.

The Old Man had vowed that his grandson would never return to Argentina, where young Cletus had been born, and he had the influence to make good on his vow. When Jorge Guillermo Frade had appeared in Texas to claim his son, he had been arrested by Texas Rangers, thrown in jail for ninety days for trespassing, and then deported into Mexico. The Argentine Ambassador in Washington had reported that the U.S. government would never issue him a visa again.

Thus, Jorge Guillermo Frade had never seen his son from the time he was a year old until he had appeared in Argentina five months before. Nevertheless, with the help of a firm of lawyers in Midland, Texas, where Clete had been raised by his uncle and aunt, he had kept up with him.

There were more than a dozen thick scrapbooks in el Coronel's private study, filled with clippings from the Midland newspaper—and later, from other newspapers—tracing his son's life. There were guest lists from children's fourth-birthday parties; there were notices from the Future Farmers of America; there were reports about Clete's years at Texas A&M and Tulane in New Orleans, and then of his exploits when he became a Marine and a fighter pilot, whose seven victories over Guadalcanal made him an ace.

The walls of el Coronel's private study were covered with photographs of his son. And there was a large oil portrait of the late Elizabeth-Ann Howell de Frade holding their infant son Cletus Howell Frade in her arms.

It had been the war, and the war only, that had finally brought father and son together. It had come to the attention of the Office of Strategic Services that the man who would very likely be the next President of the Republic of Argentina had a son who was a Marine officer.

After being discharged from the Marine Corps, ostensibly for medical reasons, Clete had come to Argentina, ostensibly representing Howell Petroleum. Argentina (through the Sociedad Mercantil de Importación de Productos Petrolíferos) imported a substantial portion of its petroleum needs—refined and crude—from Howell Petroleum (Venezuela); thus the cover story was that Cletus was in Argentina to make sure that SMIPP was not diverting petroleum products to the German/Italian/Japanese Axis.

He was actually an OSS agent charged with two missions: First, to establish a relationship with the father he did not know, and if possible to tilt him in favor of the Americans in the war. Second, to somehow arrange for neutral Argentina (whose army was in fact pro-German) to stop offering shelter in Argentine waters to German vessels replenishing German submarines operating in the South Atlantic.

His first residence in Argentina was as a guest in the home of Enrico Mallín, SMIPP's Managing Director. Mallín had an English wife, a fourteen-year-old son, and a nineteen-

year-old blond-haired daughter named Dorotéa (whom
Clete thought of at the time as the Virgin Princess).

He had been in the Mallín home less than a week when he
met his father for the first time—a very emotional encounter
for both of them. That same day, el Coronel had taken him to
a mansion on Avenida Libertador overlooking the Buenos
Aires racetrack. The house had been built by Clete's grand-
uncle Guillermo, it was explained; since Guillermo's death,
it had been used by the Frade family as a guest house.

It was now Clete's, it was further explained.

Though el Coronel would brook no argument, the
arrangement in fact suited Clete. It would not only give him
a base of operations for his OSS activities he would not have
in the Mallín home, but also the Virgin Princess was making
it clear that she was not satisfied with the platonic little
sister role he had assigned to her.

Clete's OSS activities had exacted costs. For starters, the
Germans had sent a pair of assassins to the Avenida Libertador house. Warned that they were coming, he had been prepared, and had killed both of them, but not before they had
brutally murdered the housekeeper, Señora Marianna Maria
Dolores Rodríguez de Pellano, a lifelong Frade family ser-
vant who had cared for Clete as an infant and who was
Enrico Rodríguez's sister. But the highest price of all had
been the assassination of el Coronel Jorge Guillermo Frade,
also ordered by the Germans. Not only had El Coronel
assisted his American son in the sinking of the replenishment ship, but the Germans were well aware that el Coronel
Frade was the driving force behind the coup d'état the Grupo
de Oficiales Unidos was planning against the regime of President Ramón S. Castillo. If the revolution succeeded, el
Coronel Frade would become President of Argentina; and,
influenced by his son, he would certainly tilt Argentina
toward the Allies—or worse, engineer a declaration of war
on the Axis. In addition to preventing him from becoming
president, El Coronel Frade's assassination would send a
message to the GOU: that the Germans rewarded their
friends and punished their enemies.

When his father was assassinated, Clete was in the United

States (and newly promoted to major in the U.S. Marine Corps), where he was being trained to assume duties—as cover for his OSS activities—as the Assistant Naval Attaché of the U.S. Embassy in Buenos Aires.

His father's death changed the OSS's plans for him. As far as the Argentines were concerned, the Argentine-born Cletus Howell Frade was an Argentine citizen. And under Argentine law, on his father's death he had become sole heir to the Frade fortune, one of the largest in Argentina. Both of these things could be put to use by the OSS.

He had returned to Argentina under cover of a son come home to bury his father and claim his inheritance. On the day he placed his father's body in the Frade family tomb in the Recoleta cemetery, Dorotéa Mallín had coolly informed him that as a result of one of their (actually infrequent) liaisons, she was carrying his child.

Welner knew most of the details of Clete's involvement in the coup d'état—in no small part because el Coronel had written Outline Blue, its operations order. The success of Outline Blue had installed General Arturo Rawson in the Pink House as President, and General Pedro Ramírez as Minister of Defense.

During the coup, Clete had flown Rawson (in an Argentine Army Piper Cub) from the revolution's headquarters at Campo de Mayo, the military base on the outskirts of Buenos Aires, to observe the progress of the two columns of revolutionary troops advancing on the Pink House.

Meanwhile, the Lockheed transport had been kept ready at Campo de Mayo's airfield. If the coup d'état had failed, Clete would have flown the leaders of the revolution to safety in Uruguay.

The priest also knew that Clete had been involved in two more OSS operations since his return to Argentina. But— despite his normally excellent sources of information—he knew very little about these, except that the first had dealt with a second replenishment ship the Germans had sent into the River Plate, and that the second had something to do with the transfer of Nazi money into Argentina.

• • • •

Wondering idly what Dorotéa Mallín de Frade would do with the shrine to her husband once she was legally installed in El Patrón's apartment, Welner took a last look around the room and returned to the sitting room to replenish his glass.

A moment later, Cletus Frade emerged from the bedroom, wearing only a clean pair of khaki trousers, fresh from his shower. He helped himself to a glass of wine. "I don't like that sonofabitch, Padre," he said.

Welner had no doubt that the sonofabitch was el Coronel Juan Domingo Perón. "He was your father's best friend," he argued.

That's not entirely true, he thought. *Not only because I believe that I was Jorge Frade's best friend, but also because Perón and Jorge Frade had grown apart as they had grown older.* The two men, he knew, had been very close when they were cadets at the Military Academy, and Perón had been best man at Jorge's wedding, and was Cletus Frade's godfather.

It is really difficult for men of vastly different means— Perón has only his Army pay—to remain friends.

But not only that: Although publicly, Jorge loyally dismissed the rumors concerning Perón's personal life as outrageous, I think he knew they were true.

"Best friend?" Clete challenged sarcastically. "I find that very hard to believe."

"He's your godfather," Welner said.

"He's a goddamned Nazi, and you know it."

"I don't know that, and neither do you," Welner argued.

"He's toeing the Nazi party line," Clete said. " 'El Coronel was killed by bandits.' He knows goddamned well the Germans ordered him killed."

The priest shrugged. There was no point in arguing about that.

Clete chuckled bitterly. "And he's a dirty old man," he said. "Who likes little girls. And don't tell me I don't know that. I was in the house on Libertador when he brought one in. She was fourteen. Maybe younger."

"Judge not, lest ye be judged."

"I don't want that sonofabitch at my wedding," Clete said.

"I get back to my original irrefutable argument, Cletus:
This is not Texas. Things are different here. If you are wise,
you will learn to understand that, and make the necessary
adjustments."

Welner was very much afraid the argument was about to
get out of hand—Clete was his father's son, just as hardheaded—when Enrico came into the room.

"You're sorry, but the tubing split, right?" Clete challenged.

"The line is back on the car, Señor Clete, and the oil pressure is now correct," Enrico said.

"El Padre here has invited el Coronel Perón to my wedding," Clete responded. "I suppose you think that's a good
idea, too?"

"Of course, Señor Clete," Enrico said, making it clear the
question surprised him. "He was your father's friend. He is
your godfather."

"Jesus!" Clete said, and shook his head in resignation.

But from the tone of Clete's voice, Welner concluded that
the issue of Juan Domingo Perón had been defused. He was
relieved. Cletus Frade would have enough trouble in
Argentina without insulting Perón.

"I don't trust that oil line," Clete went on. "After lunch,
we'll take it for a ride."

"Sí, Señor," Enrico said, "I will bring it to the house." He
nodded his head respectfully to the priest and left the room.

[THREE]

Don Cletus Howell Frade, el patrón of Estancia San Pedro y
San Pablo and its 84,205 (more or less) hectares, sat at the
head of a table elegantly set for six in a gazebo in the formal
English gardens in front of the main house.

At the foot of the table sat his grandfather, Cletus Marcus
Howell, a tall, pale, slender, and sharp-featured septuagenar-
ian wearing a gray pin-striped suit. Howell was Chairman of
the Board of Howell Petroleum, and of Howell Petroleum

(Venezuela). Everyone thought of him, more or less fondly, as "the Old Man."

Father Welner was sitting to Cletus's right. Martha Williamson Howell sat across from him, while Martha's daughters, Marjorie, nineteen, and Elizabeth (Beth), twenty-one, dressed very much like their mother, sat opposite each other. The girls were Cletus's cousins, but their relationship was that of brother and sisters.

When one of the maids approached the head of the table with a bottle of wine, Cletus turned his wineglass over. The maid moved to Cletus Howell, poured a small amount of wine in his glass, and stepped back to await his judgment. He took a sip, smiled appreciatively, and made a thumbs-up gesture to the maid, who then walked around the table to fill Mrs. Howell's glass.

"No wine, Cletus?" the Old Man asked in Spanish, as if surprised.

"Don't encourage him, Dad," Martha Howell said, also in Spanish. "I don't know how much he had before lunch."

"I'm going to take the Horch for a ride after lunch," Clete said. "To change the subject. But don't let me stop you."

"Oh, I won't. This isn't bad," Howell said, unconsciously switching to English.

"You've got it fixed, Clete?" Marjorie asked.

"That's what I'm going to find out, Squirt," he said.

"Can I drive it?"

"Why not?"

"And me?" Beth asked.

"Females in love should not drive," Cletus said solemnly.

"What makes you think I'm in love?"

"You have been in love ever since you discovered there are two sexes," he said. "And I saw you making eyes at that gaucho at the stable last night."

"Oh, you go to hell, Clete," she said, blushing.

"What gaucho last night?" Cletus Marcus Howell demanded.

"I was just pulling her chain, Grandpa," Clete said quickly. "Yeah, Beth, you can come, if you want."

Is Jorge Guillermo Frade spinning in his casket, Father

Welner thought, *at the thought of two young norteamericano females driving his beloved Horch?*

Two maids began serving empanadas, half-moon-shaped dumplings filled either with chopped, seasoned meat, or blue cheese and ham.

"Is this lunch?" Cletus Marcus Howell asked, looking at the dumpling on his plate with suspicion.

"This is what we Argentines think of as an appetizer, Grandpa," Cletus said.

"They're delicious," Marjorie said. "I love them!"

"I hate to think what might be in them," the Old Man said.

The faint sound of an aircraft engine caught Cletus's attention and he tried to look up at the sky. The roof of the gazebo blocked his view. After a moment, he pushed his chair back and walked out of the gazebo and stood looking up at the sky.

Enrico, who had been sitting in a wicker chair in the shade of a tree twenty yards from the gazebo, got out of the chair and walked to where Frade was standing. He had his shotgun cradled in his arms.

"Binoculars, Enrico?" Clete asked.

Enrico went to the wicker chair and returned with a pair of leather-cased binoculars. Clete searched the sky and then put the binoculars to his eyes.

A moment later, Marjorie Howell, then the girls, and finally Mr. Howell and Father Welner joined the two men. They all looked skyward, where they saw a high-winged, single-engine monoplane flying in the general direction of Estancia Santo Catalina.

"May I please have those, Cletus?" Cletus Marcus Howell asked, and Clete handed him the binoculars. He started a moment. "What the hell is that, Cletus?" the Old Man asked.

"It's an airplane, Grandfather."

"With an iron cross on the body, and a Nazi—whatchamacallit?—*swastika* on the tail!" the old man announced.

"Really?" Clete asked innocently.

"Who was that, Clete?" Martha Howell asked.

"The Luftwaffe," Clete said. "They come over regularly. And once a week, tit for tat, I buzz the German embassy."

"What was that, Cletus?" the Old Man demanded.

Clete ignored him.

Martha Howell took the binoculars from her father-in-law and looked skyward. By the time she found the airplane, it was too far away to pick out what the Old Man had seen.

"I didn't see any swastika, Dad," she said.

The Old Man looked at his daughter-in-law. "You know what's going on, don't you?" he challenged.

"I don't know what you're talking about, Dad," she said.

"The hell you don't," the Old Man said. "God damn it, Martha!"

"Hey!" Martha Howell said warningly.

"And I'm expected to believe the old guy's carrying that shotgun to bag a few quail for dinner, right?"

"Dad, Enrico blames himself for what happened to Clete's father," Martha Howell said. "Clete doesn't have the heart to run him off."

His disbelief showed on his face. "And he had those binoculars handy in case Clete wanted to go bird-watching, right?"

"Let it go, Dad!" Martha Howell said, almost threateningly.

"I'm an old man, and in my lifetime I've made a lot of mistakes, but not one of them holds a candle to the one I made when I got suckered into getting my family involved in helping the goddamn OSS."

"Since we're telling all our family secrets, grandfather, why don't you tell Father Welner those are stolen binoculars?" Clete said.

Welner looked surprised.

"You think he's kidding, don't you?" the Old Man said. "They are. They were stolen from the U.S. Navy, and Clete bought them, knowing damned well they were stolen, from a hockshop in New Orleans."

"I have no idea what he's talking about," Clete said.

"The hell you don't! You boasted about it!"

By then they had walked back to the gazebo. The empanadas had been replaced with the main course, a *bife de chorizo* (the Argentine version of a New York strip steak) on a bed of spinach and mushrooms.

"Oh, isn't that attractive!" Martha Williamson Howell said.

The Old Man looked down suspiciously at his plate.

"What the hell is that? Spinach?" he asked.

"God, I hope so!" Clete said, which triggered giggles in the girls.

The Old Man looked at them indignantly.

He's old, Martha thought. *Very old. And when he's gone, Clete will be the only man in the family.*

"If you don't like it, don't eat it," she said.

"I didn't say I wasn't going to eat it. But that's a hell of a way to serve a steak. They're really strange, these people down here." He looked at Welner. "No offense, Father."

"None taken, Mr. Howell," Welner said.

V

[ONE]
Estancia Santo Catalina
Near Pila, Buenos Aires Province
1355 1 May 1943

Before landing, Major Freiherr Hans-Peter von Wachtstein made a low pass over the landing strip to make sure one or more five-hundred-kilo cows were not happily munching away on the runway. It was a necessary precaution in Argentina, where cattle roamed freely and landing strips were rarely protected by fences.

There were no cattle.

Three light aircraft were lined up beside the runway. Two were yellow Piper Cubs and the third was a Cessna C-34, a small four-seater. The Cessna, he knew, belonged to Estancia Santo Catalina, and probably the Pipers did, too, although Cletus Frade might have flown one over from his estancia.

He put the Fieseler Storch into a tight 180-degree turn, lined up with the runway, retarded the throttle, cranked down the flaps, and touched down smoothly at about forty knots.

While the Storch was not *much* of an airplane, compared to the Focke-Wulf 190 fighter he had flown in his last assignment (whose 1,600-horsepower engine propelled it to 418 mph), it was an *interesting* airplane. If the Piper Cub could be compared to an aerial bicycle, then the Storch was an aerial motorcycle, say a BMW four cylinder opposed, shaft-driven motorcycle.

By the time he had finished his landing roll and taxied the Storch to park beside the Cessna, three people had come out from the house to greet him. His heart jumped a little when he saw that one of them was Señorita Alicia Carzino-Cormano, although he had in fact expected her to come to the landing strip once she saw the Storch overhead. He had a quick mental image of Alicia two days before, naked in his bed, staring down at him with her large dark eyes, and he was as quickly ashamed of himself.

The others were the Duartes, Señor Humberto and Señora Beatrice Frade de Duarte, both of whom he had more or less also expected. Once Señora de Duarte had learned of his weekend visit to the estancia, he had known she'd be waiting for him anxiously.

He opened the side door of the Storch and climbed out.

"I am so happy to see you, dear Peter . . ." Beatrice Duarte said, grabbing his arms, pulling him to her, and planting a hard, wet kiss of greeting on his cheek—as opposed to a *pro forma* smack of lips in the general vicinity of his face, ". . . and you're just in time for lunch."

"It is always a pleasure to see you, Señora," he said in Spanish. His Spanish was perfect Castilian. He had learned Spanish in Spain when he was nineteen (a fact that he had passed on to Alicia). He had not told her that his instructress had been a twenty-five-year-old redheaded *Madrileña,* who had come to believe that a young blond German fighter pilot was the answer to her carnal frustration following the death of her husband, who had been killed in action in the Civil War.

He offered his hand to Humberto Duarte, a tall, slender, elegantly tailored man of forty-six years. "Good afternoon, sir," he said.

"It's always a pleasure to see you, Peter," Duarte said.

Peter turned to Alicia. "And an even greater pleasure to see you, Alicia."

She blushed, gave him a formal kiss on the cheek, and quickly backed away.

Peter inclined his head barely perceptibly toward the Piper Cubs. Alicia moved her head just perceptibly, telling him, no, Clete was not flying one of them.

"You flew?" Humberto said.

"Yes, sir," Peter said. "With the permission of the military attaché, I am making what they call a 'proficiency flight.' At the moment, I am the acting military attaché, so I gave myself permission."

"Can you really do that?" Alicia asked. "Does the Ambassador know?"

"Actually, no," Peter confessed said. "It's a case of what the ambassador doesn't know can't upset him."

"Oh, you naughty boy, you!" Beatrice cried happily. "He's just like Jorge, always doing something naughty, isn't he, Humberto? Isn't he *so* like Jorge?"

"Yes, dear," Humberto said, "he is."

She sounded as if Jorge, her son, was right around the corner and could be expected to appear at any minute. He was, in fact, dead.

El Captáin Jorge Alejandro Duarte, of the Húsares de Pueyrredón, had been serving with von Paulus's Army at Stalingrad as an observer when he'd been shot down while making an unauthorized flight in a Storch.

After his death (though it was in fact a consequence of

foolishness and not heroism), the Foreign Minister, von Ribbentrop had realized that, if properly handled, the sad occasion might accrue to the public-relations benefit of the Third Reich. Captain Duarte's corpse would be returned to Argentina accompanied by a suitable Luftwaffe officer. There Duarte would be posthumously decorated with the Knight's Cross of the Iron Cross. That could not fail to impress the Argentines: One of their own had laid down his life in their common battle against the anti-Christ Bolshevik Russians.

The commanding officer of Jagdstaffel (Fighter Squadron) 232, stationed on the outskirts of Berlin, met the requirements for a "suitable officer." Major Freiherr Hans-Peter von Wachtstein had not only received the Knight's Cross of the Iron Cross from the hands of Adolf Hitler himself, but, as a result of his service with the Condor Legion during the Spanish Civil War, he spoke Spanish fluently. Additionally, he was a Pomeranian aristocrat, whose father, Generalleutnant Graf Karl-Friedrich von Wachtstein, was assigned to the Oberkommando der Wehrmacht.

Major von Wachtstein was summoned to Berlin, and there introduced to an Argentine officer, Colonel of Mountain Troops Juan Domingo Perón. Perón had been in Europe for several years, both as an observer attached to the German and Italian armies, and to study the social programs of Germany and Italy, with an eye to their adaptation in Argentina. He was known to be quite sympathetic to the Axis cause, and more important, was a lifelong friend of Hauptmann Duarte's uncle, Oberst Jorge Guillermo Frade, who might very well be the next President of Argentina.

At this time, it was felt that Frade, too, was sympathetic to the Axis cause. Not only was he a graduate of the Kriegsschule, but his anti-American sentiments were well known (even if it was not generally known that his anti-Americanism was based on the Americans having forcibly denied him contact with his son).

Coronel Perón liked the young officer at first sight, and agreed that he was just the sort of man to escort the remains of Capitán Duarte to Argentina. This instant favor from such an important Argentine had long-lasting consequences for von Wachtstein. And in the office of Foreign Minister von Ribbentrop, he was told that after the funeral of Captain Duarte he would remain in Argentina as the Assistant Military Attaché for Air at the German Embassy. There his orders would of course be to do whatever the Military Attaché wanted him to do, but he was also expected to ingratiate himself as much as possible with the Duarte family, Oberst Jorge Guillermo Frade, and Oberst Juan Domingo Perón, whose return to Argentina was planned in the near future.

Before leaving for Buenos Aires, Peter met with his father on the family estate in Pomerania. There Generalleutnant von Wachtstein had words for his son that few Germans were speaking openly. There was a growing possibility, he told him, that Germany would lose the war. If that happened, he went on to explain, German currency would be worthless, and the von Wachtstein family could not meet its obligations to the people who lived on their estates and looked to them for protection, as they had for hundreds of years.

Neutral Argentina would be an ideal place to cache money (preferably exchanged for gold, Swiss francs, or American dollars). In fact, Peter's father had already transferred a great deal of money into secret, numbered Swiss bank accounts—a very risky act, Peter knew. If it came to the attention of the authorities, the penalty would be a court-martial and a possible death sentence, as well as the forfeiture of all the Wachtstein estates.

Before father and son parted, Generalleutnant von Wachtstein gave Peter all the cash he could lay his hands on—nearly a hundred thousand dollars in Swiss, English, and United States currency—together with the numbers of the secret bank accounts. He would have to somehow transfer to Argentina what was in the Swiss accounts.

If the worst happened for Germany—as Peter's father expected—this money could be the salvation of the von Wachtstein family and their estates.

Finally, and as a last resort, his father explained, there was a friend he might turn to, Manfred Alois Graf von Lutzenberger, the German Ambassador to Argentina.

On von Wachtstein's first night in Buenos Aires, Beatrice Frade de Duarte had arranged for him to be put up in the Frade family guest house on Avenida del Libertador, either blissfully unaware—or simply not caring—that her brother had already turned the house over to his onetime USMC fighter pilot son, Cletus.

The encounter between officers of warring powers could easily have been awkward, but it turned out quite the other way. In the library of the guest house, over a bottle and a half of el Coronel Frade's cognac, the two had quickly come to the conclusion that as fellow fighter pilots, intimately familiar with both the joys of flying and the horrors of war, they had far more in common with each other than they had with anyone else in Buenos Aires.

They knew, of course, that very few people indeed would understand this, and after Major von Wachtstein was provided with "more suitable" quarters, both officers discreetly kept their initial meeting—and their budding friendship—under wraps. And when they were formally introduced the next day at Capitán Duarte's funeral, both showed to each other the icy courtesy expected of officers of belligerent powers meeting in a neutral country.

Two weeks later, Oberst Karl-Heinz Grüner, the military attaché of the German Embassy, decided to have Cletus Frade assassinated—information that came to von Wachtstein. After a good deal of painful thought, he concluded that an honorable officer could not stand idly by while such a murder was committed, and he warned Frade.

Frade was therefore ready for the assassins when they appeared at the guest house, and killed them, though not before they had killed Enrico Rodríguez's sister, the housekeeper.

Cletus Frade, himself no stranger to honor (though the sense of formal chivalry that Major Freiherr Hans-Peter von Wachtstein had sucked in with his mother's milk was a little amusing to Frade), sought Peter out and announced that he was in his debt for his life. As far as he was concerned, von Wachtstein had a blank check on anything that was his to give.

Though Peter's initial reaction to Clete's offer was chilly (he had done what he had done, he explained, solely because his officer's code of chivalry demanded it), the respect of the two men for each other had grown, and their friendship had been cemented.

And then a letter came from von Wachtstein's father, carried, secretly and at great risk, to von Lutzenberger by the pilot of a Lufthansa Condor. The subject of the letter—in the very deepest sense—was chivalry and honor.

Schloss Wachtstein

Pomern

Hansel—

I have just learned that you have reached Argentina safely, and thus it is time for this letter.

The greatest violation of the code of chivalry by which I, and you, and your brothers and so many of the von Wachtsteins before us have tried to live is of course regicide. I want you to know that before I decided that honor demands that I contribute what I can to such a course of action, that I considered all of the rami cations, both spiritual and worldly, and that I am at peace with my decision.

A soldier's duty is rst to his God, and then to his honor, and then to his country. The Allies in recent weeks have accused the German state of the commission of atrocities on such a scale as to defy description. I must tell you that information has come to me that has convinced me that the accusations are not only based on fact, but are actually worse than alleged.

The of cer corps has failed its duty to Germany, not so much on the eld of battle but in pandering to the Austrian Corporal and his cohorts. In exchange for privilege and "honors" the of cer corps, myself included, has closed its eyes to obscene violations of the Rules of Land Warfare, the Code of Chivalry, and indeed most of God's Ten Commandments. I accept my share of the responsibility for this shameful behavior.

We both know the war is lost. When it is nally over, the Allies will, with right, demand a terrible retribution from Germany.

I see it as my duty as a soldier and a German to take whatever action is necessary to hasten the end of the war by the only possible means now available, eliminating the present head of the government. The soldiers who will die now, in battle or in Russian prisoner-of-war camps, will be as much victims of the of cer corps' failure to act as are the people the Nazis are slaughtering in concentration camps.

I put it to you, Hansel, that your allegiance should be no longer to the Luftwaffe, or the German State, but to Germany, and to the family, and to the people who have lived on our lands for so long.

In this connection, your rst duty is to survive the war. Under no circumstances are you to return to Germany for any purpose until the war is over. Find now someplace where you can hide safely if you are ordered to return.

Your second duty is to transfer the family funds from Switzerland to Argentina as quickly as possible. You have by now made contact with our friend in Argentina, and he will probably be able to be of help. In any event, make sure the funds are in some safe place. It would be better if they could be wisely invested, but the primary concern is to have them someplace where they will be safe from the Sicherheitsdienst until the war is over.

In the chaos that will ensue in Germany when the war is nally over, the only hope our people *will have, to keep them in their homes, indeed to keep them from starvation, and the only hope there will be for the future of the von Wachtstein family, and the estates, will be access to the money that I have placed in your care.*

I hope, one day, to be able to go with you again to the village for a beer and a sausage. If that is not to be, I have con dence that God in his mercy will allow us one day to be all together again, your mother and your brothers, and you and I in a better place.

I have taken great pride in you, Hansel.

Poppa

Peter was at first at a loss about how to accomplish his father's directives. He could not, he was all too aware, succeed on his own. Yet whom could he go to for help? Whom could he trust? Having nowhere else to go, and remembering Cletus's pledge, Peter brought the letter to Cletus Frade.

Since neither spoke the other's language, their conversation was in Spanish.

Cletus said, "I don't know what you want me to do. For one thing, I can't read German. So the letter won't mean a thing to me. For another, I don't know how I can do you any good. Secretly transferring money between countries is not one of my regular accomplishments."

"Forgive me for wasting your time, Señor Frade," Peter answered frostily.

"Don't get a corncob up your ass, Fritz," Cletus said. "My

father speaks German, and I think he would consider my debts his. And I owe you."

He saw the surprise and concern on von Wachtstein's face, and added, "I also suspect he's into this chivalry and honor shit, too."

When el Coronel Frade did in fact translate the letter for Clete (he was doing it aloud), the tears running down his cheeks and the tightness in his throat made it hard for him to make it through to the end.

Though he, too, had to admit that he was at a personal loss about handling Peter's problem, he knew who *could* handle it: "My sister's husband, Humberto Duarte, is Managing Director of the Anglo-Argentine Bank."

"You think he will help, mi Coronel?" von Wachtstein asked.

"Of course he will," el Coronel Frade said. "And not only because he is Cletus's uncle, and Cletus's debt to you is a family debt, but also because he has believed for years all the terrible things people have been saying about your Führer and the Nazi party."

Humberto Duarte not only proved to be willing to help, but more important, he knew all the tricks necessary to transfer funds in absolute secrecy from numbered Swiss bank accounts to accounts in Argentina.

Peter's relief was, however, short-lived. His father was not the only German who had been thinking about survival should Germany lose the war.

The very next Lufthansa Condor flight from Berlin to Buenos Aires had aboard—in addition to el Coronel Juan Domingo Perón, who had returned to take part in the coup d'état against President Castillo—Standartenführer-SS-SD Josef Luther Goltz.

Both Ambassador von Lutzenberger and Peter von Wachtstein thought the SS officer had been sent to find out what he could about the sinking of the *Reine de la Mer,* but that was not his purpose.

His orders had much more to do with the various missions associated with the soon-to-be-arriving "neutral" Spanish vessel *Comerciante del Océano Pacífico*—the repatriation of the interned officers from the *Graf Spee*; the replacement of the *Reine de la Mer* as a replenishment vessel for U-boats; and finally—and most secretly—the transfer of funds to be used for the implementing of Operation Phoenix.

Standartenführer Goltz presented this information to Ambassador von Lutzenberger and his old friend First Secretary Anton von Gradny-Sawz.

Ambassador von Lutzenberger, recognizing the threat Operation Phoenix posed to what he and Peter were doing with the von Wachtstein money—and other money entrusted to him by other friends—decided that Peter had to know, and told him everything.

The next day, Peter had flown Standartenführer Goltz to Montevideo in the Fieseler Storch, where Goltz met with Sturmbannführer Werner von Tresmarck, the SS-SD man at the German Embassy in Uruguay.

Von Tresmarck's wife, whom Peter had known in Berlin, presumed he knew what was going on and revealed to him the source of the Operation Phoenix funds available in Uruguay. It came from the families and friends of Jews in concentration camps in Germany. For a price, the SS would arrange for the release of Jews from the death camps and their travel to Uruguay and Argentina.

Peter had then been faced with another moral decision. On one hand, his stomach turned at yet another proof of the incredible moral bankruptcy of the Nazi hierarchy generally and the SS specifically.

On the other, to reveal this state secret, and what he knew about the *Océano Pacífico,* to a man he knew was an agent of the OSS was not only treason, pure and simple, but also personally painful.

The Kapitänleutnant of one of the submarines with empty fuel tanks in the South Atlantic was a close friend from college days, a wholly decent human being. Furthermore, if his treason ever became known, it would mean not only not being able to carry out the responsibility his father had given him to care for the people who depended on the von Wachtsteins, but would also be tantamount to signing an execution order for his father.

In the end, Cletus Frade gave him his word that he would never reveal the source of his information, and so Peter told him. Frade then told Peter that one of his agents, David Ettinger, a Jewish refugee from Nazi Germany, had heard the stories about the ransoming of Jews from concentration camps, and had been investigating them. Ettinger's obscenely mutilated corpse had been found a few days before, on the beach at Carrasco, outside Montevideo. The severed penis in Ettinger's mouth, Clete said, had been a message to the Jews who knew about the ransoming operation.

Standartenführer Goltz—who had not himself told Peter any more than he felt he absolutely had to know about Operation Phoenix—had been forced to press him into service when the *Océano Pacífico* arrived in Argentina.

Peter had managed to get word to Cletus Frade about where and when the "special cargo" would be unloaded, and Operation Phoenix and the other missions of the *Océano Pacífico* had been aborted on the beach at Puerto Magdalena.

Afterward, there was no *reason,* Peter knew, for anyone to suspect that he was in any way responsible for tipping the OSS off about the attempted landing operation, or that he was now a traitor to the oath he had taken, pledging loyalty unto death to the person of the Führer of the German people, Adolf Hitler.

But he knew that did not mean he was not under suspicion.

"Would you like to freshen up before coming to the table?" Señorita Alicia de Carzino-Cormano asked.

"Yes, thank you, I really would," Major von Wachtstein replied, exhibiting greasy hands as proof of the necessity.

"You take dear Peter to our room, Alicia," Señora Frade de Duarte ordered. "And I will see that there is a place set for him."

"Of course," Alicia said.

Señora Duarte laid her fingers on Peter's cheek. "Don't dally, dear," she said, and then, motioning her husband to follow her, she started to walk to the main house.

Humberto nodded, then walked after his wife.

"Give me a minute to take this off," Peter said as he pulled down the zipper of his gray flying suit and started to shrug out of it. Beneath it, he still wore the suit Gradny-Sawz had admired.

"I was afraid for a moment," Alicia said, "that she was going to take you to her room to wash your hands, and send me to make a place for you at lunch."

He smiled at her.

He freed his legs from the flying suit and hung it on the wing support. Then he followed Alicia into the house, where she led him not to the bedroom where the Duartes were staying, but to her own. The moment they were inside, she locked the door and threw herself into his arms.

"When you came by plane, I was afraid you'd been ordered to Germany," she said.

"No," he said. "So far, there's been no word from Berlin."

"I'm so frightened for you, Peter," she said.

That makes two of us.

"There's nothing to be frightened about, precious," he said, stroking her hair.

Do I believe that? Or am I pissing in the wind?

He gently extricated himself from her arms.

Another thirty seconds of feeling her against me like that, and I'll carry her to her bed.

And all we need is Clete's lunatic aunt coming to look for me, and finding us in Alicia's bedroom.

"Let me wash my hands," he said.

She nodded toward her bathroom.

He went into the bathroom and washed his hands with a clear bar of glycerin soap—concluding that while it might do wonders for the complexion of a young female, it was not ideal for removing oil from hands.

She was standing by her desk when he went back into the bedroom.

"If they do order you to go to Germany," Alicia asked, "then will you go to Brazil?"

"Baby, I don't think they're going to order me to Berlin."

"If they do!" she insisted angrily.

"If that happens, we will see what I have to do."

"Sometimes I hate you," she said.

"Baby, don't say that!"

"Why not? Right now, I mean it!"

He reached his hand to touch her face. She knocked it away, walked to the door, and unlocked it.

"They'll be wondering what's keeping you," she said.

He nodded, and started to walk past her. She stepped into his path, threw her arms around him, and kicked the door closed.

"Peter, I can't live without you!" she said against his chest.

"Ich liebe dich, meine hartz," he said, close to tears. I love you, my heart.

She pushed away far enough to look up at him.

"If I kiss you, we would never get out of my room," she said.

He kissed her forehead, gently took her hands from his arms, opened the door, and started walking down the corridor to the dining room.

[TWO]

"Over here, darling!" Señora Beatrice Frade de Duarte cried happily when she saw Peter and Alicia come into the dining.[*] She was sitting immediately beside Claudia Carzino-Cormano at the head of the table, and had made a place for Peter between herself and her husband. Seated across from her was a ruddy-faced, silver-haired Irishman, Monsignor Patrick Kelly, the Duarte family priest. Beside him was Isabela Carzino-Cormano, Alicia's older sister, a very beautiful, black-haired young woman of twenty-two. Beside her was a tall, handsome young Argentine Peter did not know. He was obviously another houseguest, Isabela's, to judge by

---

[*] Among the many ways the longtime presence of the British in Argentina was manifested was in the custom among upper-class Argentines of referring to rooms in homes by their English names. The living room, for example, was called "the living"; the dining room, "the dining"; and the foyer, or reception room, as "the reception," et cetera.

the fact that they were both dressed in riding clothing. Across from him sat Dr. Manuel Sporazzo, a middle-aged, well-dressed man whom Peter knew to be Beatrice Frade de Duarte's psychiatrist. The empty place beside him was obviously Alicia's.

Peter obeyed the summons, as Alicia made her way to the place set for her.

"How nice to see you, Peter," Claudia said.

"Señora Carzino-Cormano, I again thank you for your kind invitation," Peter said, clicking his heels and bowing his head to her.

"Don't be absurd," Claudia said. "You are always welcome here, Peter."

"Buenas tardes, Señorita Isabela," Peter said, repeating the heel clicking and bowing to her, and then repeating the gesture to Monsignor Kelly and Dr. Sporazzo. "Padre, Doctor."

"How nice to see you, Major von Wachtstein," Isabela said very formally, almost coldly.

"I don't believe you know Antonio—Tony—Pellechea, do you, Peter?" Claudia said.

"I have not had the honor," Peter said, and clicked his heels and bowed his head again.

The young Argentine rose halfway from his seat and offered Peter his hand.

"I don't believe I've ever seen an airplane like yours before," Pellechea said. "What is it?"

"It's a Fieseler Storch. What we call an 'Army Cooperation' airplane."

"My Jorge was riding in one just like it when God called him to heaven to be with Him and the Holy Angels," Beatrice announced brightly. "Isn't that so, Peter?"

Tony Pellechea looked at her in amazement. Isabela looked embarrassed.

"Yes, Ma'am," Peter said.

"Please sit down, Peter," Claudia said. "We're having a simple *lomo*"—filet mignon—"I hope that's all right."

"I am second to no man in my appreciation of Argentina beef," Peter said.

Claudia chuckled.

"Is that the diplomat speaking?" she asked.

"The man, Señora," Peter said.

Beatrice Frade de Duarte was not through: "Since Peter brought our Jorge home, Tony," she said, making it sound as if they had shared a taxi, "he's become almost a member of the family. Not *almost*—he *has become family*. Isn't that so, Humberto?"

"Yes, indeed," Humberto agreed.

"You are too kind, Señora," Peter said.

Tony Pellechea smiled uncomfortably.

"And not only of our family, Tony," Beatrice went on. "But of the Carzino-Cormano family as well. What would you say, Claudia, if I told you—judging from the way Alicia looks at him—that it looks very much to me as if Cupid has fired a second arrow from his quiver? And scored another bull's-eye?"

"I would say your imagination is running away with you again, Beatrice," Claudia said.

Unfortunately, you poor lunatic, Claudia thought, *I'm afraid you're right on the money.*

"But wouldn't it be nice if that were the case—and I think I'm right, no matter what you say? Alicia and Dorotéa have been friends since they were babies, and I'm sure that Peter and Cletus could be friends, if only they had the chance."

"Mi querida," Humberto Duarte said in a desperately transparent attempt to get his wife off the subject. "Weren't you telling Tony that you were at school with his mother?"

"*Yes,* I was," she said. "She was right down the corridor from me at St. Teresa's. I had a room with Elisa Frondizi—now Elisa Frondizi de Galeano, of course—and your mother shared one with Carmela Burmeister—now Carmela Burmeister de Manasaro, of course—and we were the dearest of friends, all of us."

She paused thoughtfully.

Tony Pellechea smiled uncomfortably.

Peter smiled gratefully at the maid who offered to fill his wineglass.

"Our favorite sister was Sister Maria Margareta," Beatrice resumed. "She was strict, but she was fair. You really couldn't say that about all the sisters. Sister Maria-Elena, for example . . ."

[THREE]
Estancia San Pedro y San Pablo
Near Pila, Buenos Aires Province
1425 1 May 1943

The Horch was parked on the red gravel on the curved drive in front of the main house. The roof was down, and the second windshield, which rose behind the front seat, had been raised.

"It looks good, Clete," Martha Howell said.

"Thank you," Clete said.

"God, it's big, isn't it?" Martha added wonderingly. "It's one and a half times the size of the Caddy."

"You want to drive it?" Clete asked.

"Give me a rain check. That was an enormous lunch. The Old Lady needs a nap."

"OK," he said.

He kissed her cheek. The gesture was somehow different, perhaps more intimate, than an Argentine cheek-kissing.

"Be careful," Martha said.

Clete walked off the veranda. Enrico, carrying his Browning shotgun, walked quickly ahead of him and opened both driver's-side doors.

"Let me drive it a little first, Marjorie," Clete said.

"OK," she said, and got in the front and slid across to the passenger side.

Clete got in beside her. Enrico waited until Beth had climbed into the rear seat, and then, after closing the driver's door, got in beside her.

"Hey, Adolf," the Old Man called, and when Clete looked

at him, Cletus Howell raised his arm in the Nazi salute. "Sieg Heil, Adolf!"

"Dad!" Martha protested, but when Clete and the girls laughed, she joined in too.

Enrico looked confused.

Clete started the engine, watched the oil-pressure gauge for a long moment, and then tapped the horn and drove off.

"That horn sounds like a bull in heat," Marjorie said.

Two minutes later, as Clete turned onto the macadam road, she said, "I thought so."

"You thought what so?"

"We're going to the radio station, aren't we?"

"Uh-huh."

"And Grandpa was right, wasn't he? That was a Nazi airplane, right?"

"Butt out, Squirt," he said.

Then he put his foot on the brake and stopped the car, pulled on the parking brake, and got out. Marjorie slid over behind the wheel.

"You think you can find it?" he asked.

"Sure," she said. "I was a Girl Scout, remember?"

He did in fact remember. Both Marjorie and Beth had been Girl Scouts. Beth had loved it; Marjorie had hated it from her first meeting. She had envisioned riding out on the prairie on horseback, pitching a tent, building a fire, and cooking supper under the stars. What the Girl Scouts wanted her to do, she had announced indignantly, was sell cookies that came from a factory.

She had absolutely no trouble driving the Horch, as enormous as it was. Since she had been driving tractors and trucks on Big Foot Ranch from the moment her feet could reach the pedals, this should not have been surprising.

But it was. Marjorie was slight, delicate, and feminine, and looked somehow out of place at the huge wheel of the gigantic car.

And Clete thought that now that her father was dead, the responsibility for protecting her—and Beth—was now his, and he was going to have a hard time doing that when he was here and she was back in Texas.

Ten minutes later, Marjorie gestured out the windshield toward a half-acre-size clump of pine and eucalyptus directly ahead of them.

"There it is," she announced.

The clump of trees looked no different from any of the countless other clumps of trees scattered all over the gently rolling pampas. The trees had been put there as windbreaks. And there were perhaps twenty-five similar clumps of trees scattered all over Estancia San Pedro y San Pablo. They contained cattle ramps, usually, and corrals, and houses for the gauchos and their families, and what would have been called toolsheds on Big Foot Ranch. They were in essence miniature ranches, self-sufficient enough that the gauchos usually didn't have to make more than a couple of trips a month to the main buildings.

In other words, a windbreak offered ideal concealment for a shortwave radio station and its antennae.

But she was right. That was what they were looking for.

She slowed the car, and three hundred yards farther down the road found a dirt road leading off to the right. She downshifted skillfully and turned off the macadam onto it.

As they got closer to the clump of trees, the outlines of four buildings could be seen inside it.

The first person they saw as they approached the larger of the four buildings was a large, florid-faced man in his middle forties wearing the billowing black trousers, broad sleeved white shirt, wide-brimmed hat, and leather boots of a gaucho. He was leaning on the fender of a Model A Ford coupe.

Two other automobiles were parked against the larger of the four buildings: a Model A Ford pickup truck and a 1940 Chevrolet coupe. The Chevrolet carried both the special license plates issued by the Argentine government to diplomatic personnel and an egg-shaped insignia with the letters CD.

As the gaucho walked up to them, two other men emerged from the building. Both were wearing business suits. The first was small, slim, mustachioed, and dark-skinned, with a long, thin cigar in his teeth. The other was young and muscular, his chest straining the buttons of his shirt.

"Buenas tardes, Señorita Marjorie," the man in gaucho costume said in fluent Spanish. "Señorita Beth. Mi Mayor."

"How are you, Chief?" Clete replied in English.

"Hi, Chief," Marjorie called cheerfully.

Chief Radioman Oscar J. Schultz was carried on the rolls of the United States Navy as being on "Temporary Duty (Indefinite Period) with OSS." He had been drafted—together with a large stock of radio room supplies, including the all-capital-letters radio room typewriter—into the OSS off the destroyer USS *Alfred Thomas,* DD-107, when she had called at Buenos Aires two months before. Schultz had been her chief radioman (and cryptographer). In addition to his communication skills, Schultz was fluent in Spanish (after two tours at the U.S. Navy base at Cavite, in the Philippines).

"Where did you get those wheels, honey?" the chief asked admiringly. "They're really something."

"Clete's giving it to me for my birthday present," Marjorie said.

"The hell I am," Clete said, and got out of the car.

"Welcome again to our happy little home away from home," the small man with the cigar in his mouth said.

His name was Maxwell Ashton III, and he was carried on the rolls of the War Department as "Ashton, Maxwell III, Captain, Signal Corps, AUS (Detail OSS)," and on the rolls of the OSS as "Commander, OSS Western Hemisphere Team 17."

"I was about to send somebody over to the main house," he said to Clete in Spanish. "You see the Fieseler fly over?"

Spanish was Ashton's mother tongue. He was the son of a Bostonian father and a Cuban mother, and had spent the first fourteen years of his life in Cuba, before going to the United States to attend Saint Andrew's School in Maryland, the preparatory school alma mater of his father.

"We did, and so did my grandfather," Marjorie said. "Swastikas and all. He gave Clete his 'I hate the OSS' speech."

"I keep forgetting you speak Spanish," Ashton said.

"Tex-Mex, anyway," Marjorie said. "But don't worry."

When he looked at her, she put both hands over her eyes, then over her mouth, and finally covered her ears.

Ashton chuckled.

"He flew pretty low over here," the muscular young man said, "But both the Chief and I were outside, and if he dropped anything, we didn't see it."

Pelosi, Anthony J., 1st Lt., Corps of Engineers, AUS, was carried on the rolls of the War Department as "Detail U.S. State Department"; on the personnel assignment charts of the State Department "as Assistant Military Attaché U.S. Embassy, Buenos Aires"; and on the rolls of the OSS as "Executive Officer, OSS Western Hemisphere Team 14."

Team 14 had originally consisted of Cletus Frade, Tony Pelosi, and Staff Sergeant David Ettinger. Chief Schultz had been drafted into it. Ettinger had been murdered in Uruguay. Ashton's Team 17 had been infiltrated into Argentina with a radar set.

"In that case, he's probably just going to Estancia Santo Catalina to see his girlfriend," Clete said. "In any event, my uncle is there for lunch; and if he has anything for us, he'll bring it when he comes for dinner tonight."

Pelosi grunted. Ashton shook his head in agreement.

"Anything for me? Clete asked.

"Uncle Milton said to say hello," Pelosi said.

Milton Leibermann (who in fact *looked* like a fond uncle: he was plump, balding, and forty-nine) was accredited to the Republic of Argentina as the Legal Attaché of the United States Embassy. It was technically a secret that he was also the special agent in charge of the Federal Bureau of Investigation's Argentine operations.

"Tell him to keep next Saturday free for my wedding," Clete said.

"The Archbishop came through, huh?" Tony Pelosi asked.

"I wish you two could be there," Clete said to Ashton and the chief, "but you don't exist, and there will be a lot of Argentine brass there. I even invited el Coronels Perón and Martín. Or I invited Martín and Father Welner, and Claudia invited Perón."

"I don't see how you could have not invited Perón," Ashton said.

"Et tu, Brutus?" Clete said.

"I won't be here anyhow," Ashton said.

"Oh?"

"There's one message," Ashton said, inclining his head toward the house.

"Tony, will you entertain the girls while the chief and Ashton and I have a look at it?" Clete said.

"Yes, sir," Pelosi said.

Clete walked into the larger building, and the chief and Ashton followed him.

In the center of the room were a sturdy table and simple chairs; two identical tables were against the walls. One of them held a communications receiver, a transmitter, and a battered Underwood typewriter. The other held an assortment of radio technician's tools and test equipment.

An ancient safe was under this table. Sitting neatly on top of it were two thermite grenades, to be activated in case of unwanted guests. The safe contained the radio codes.

The chief knelt by the safe, worked the combination, and handed Clete a single sheet of paper.

```
URGENT

TOP SECRET LINDBERGH

DUPLICATION FORBIDDEN

FROM AGGIE

MSG NO 133 1915 GREENWICH 30 APRIL
1943

TO TEX

BACARDI
```

BACARDI AT FIRST OPPORTUNITY WILL
EXFILTRATE BY ROUTE OF HIS CHOICE TO
CARIOCA REPORTING UPON ARRIVAL THERE-
AT TO MILITARY ATTACHÉ US EMBASSY
FOR FURTHER ORDERS.

POLO WILL ASSUME COMMAND DURING BAC-
ARDI ABSENCE.

INTEREST AT VERY HIGHEST LEVEL IN
IDENTITY OF GALAHAD AND IN ALL DE-
TAILS OF LINDBERGH CONTINUES.

NO ACTION REPEAT NO ACTION WILL BE
TAKEN WITH INTENT TO DISRUPT LIND-
BERGH WITHOUT SPECIFIC AUTHORITY
FROM AGGIE ONLY REPEAT AGGIE ONLY.

ACKNOWLEDGE

AGGIE

Aggie was Colonel A. F. Graham, USMCR, Deputy
Director of the Office of Strategic Services, who was a graduate of the Texas Agricultural and Technical Institute at College Station, Texas. Tex was Major Cletus H. Frade,
USMCR, whose home of record was Big Foot Ranch, Midland, Texas. Bacardi was Captain Maxwell Ashton III, AUS,
whose roots were in Cuba, known for its fine rum. Carioca
was Rio de Janeiro, Brazil. Polo was 1st Lieutenant Madison
R. Sawyer III, AUS, who had graduated from Yale University, where he had been captain of the polo team; he was
now Executive Officer of OSS Western Hemisphere Team
17. Galahad was Major Freiherr Hans-Peter von Wachtstein.
Lindbergh was the code name chosen to refer to the German
ransoming of concentration camp inmates.

"What do you think your orders from the attaché in Rio
will be?" Clete asked.

"If God is in his heaven, there will be a letter from the War Department telling me the war will be lost unless I return to Bell Labs, and I will proceed there immediately."

Before entering the service, Ashton had been an engineer at the Bell Telephone Laboratories.

Chief Schultz laughed. "What it says is 'during Bacardi absence,' " he said. "To a simple old sailor like me, Captain, sir, that means you're coming back."

"Taking a man's dreams is worse than taking his life, Schultz," Ashton pronounced solemnly. "And very, very cruel."

"What I think they're going to do is hand you a diplomatic passport and a ticket on the next Panagra flight to Buenos Aires," Clete said.

"After, probably, the Attaché works you over to find out who Galahad is," Clete.

"Who?" Ashton said.

"I'll bet that's on Donovan's agenda."

"In words of one syllable, fuck him. Don't worry, Clete."

"Max, how do you feel about Sawyer taking over your team?" Clete asked.

"Frankly, I was hoping it would annoy you more than it looks like."

"Chief, send Aggie a message saying that as senior officer present for duty, I will assume command of Team 17 while Ashton is gone."

"Aye, aye, Sir."

"It would be easier just to not tell Sawyer. That's liable to get you in trouble," Ashton said.

"What are they going to do? Send me back to the Marine Corps? Send the message, Chief."

"And if I refuse, will you send me back to the Navy?"

"Good try, Chief," Clete said. "Just send the message."

"Aye, aye, Sir."

"Now the question is, how do we get you to Brazil?" Clete asked.

"There's two ways," Ashton said. "The way I came in, black. Go back to Santo Tomé and somehow get across the river."

"I could fly you there, in a Cub," Clete said. "First refuel at my estancia in Corrientes, and then fly you across the river."

"Hey, you're getting married next Saturday. You don't want to be in a Brazilian jail."

"What's your second way?"

"If I could get into Uruguay, I have a Uruguayan passport. How risky would it be to rent a boat or something and get into Uruguay?"

"I could also fly you across, up by El Tigre, and put you out in a farmer's field someplace. Or, for that matter, I could fire up the Lockheed and fly to the airport in Carrasco—"

"Where, Mr. Frade?" Chief Schultz asked.

"The airport outside Montevideo," Clete said. "No one there would search that airplane."

"I'll come back to that wishful thought," Ashton said. "Who would you get to help fly the Lockheed?"

"I flew it to Santo Tomé by myself, you will recall."

"And safely only because God takes care of fools and drunks, and I qualify on both counts. Forget the Lockheed, thank you very much just the same."

"There's one other way that might work," Clete said. "Just get on the overnight steamer."

"How would I get through immigration? I'm in Argentina black, Clete."

"Black means secret. Nobody knows," Clete said.

"What?"

"Put yourself in Martín's shoes," Clete said. "He knows you're here. He knows your whole team is here. He's a good intelligence officer. Good intelligence officers don't make waves. If he arrests you, that would make big waves. If I were Martín, I would much prefer to watch you leave the country, bye, bye, gringo, with no waves."

"You really believe that?"

"I believe it, but it's your choice, Max."

Ashton thought it over for a full thirty seconds, which seemed longer.

"You really think you could fly the Lockheed to Montevideo all by your lonesome?"

"Yeah."

"When?"

"Whenever you want."

"Tomorrow? In the morning?"

"Come for breakfast, meet my family, and I'll have you in Montevideo in time for lunch."

"What's a nice young Cuban boy like me doing in this business?" Ashton said. "You really want me to come for breakfast?"

"Absolutely. I want you to meet the rest of the family."

"I'll be there," Ashton said.

VI

[ONE]
Zoological Gardens of Buenos Aires
Plaza di Italia, Buenos Aires
1530 1 May 1943

As the blue Dodge approached the Plaza di Italia, Coronel Bernardo Martín leaned forward and touched the shoulder of Sargento Manuel Lascano. Martín was wearing a brown tweed sports coat, gray flannel slacks, and a yellow polo shirt; Lascano was wearing a business suit. "Drop me at the main entrance, please, Manuel, and then wait for me at the entrance on Libertador."

"Can I stop there, mi Coronel?"

"I think, Manuel, if a policeman did come to the car, and you showed him your credentials, he would understand."

"Sí, Señor."

"And I can open the door myself when we stop, Manuel. The impression we are trying to give is that we are not in the Army."

"Sí, Señor."

Manuel pulled the Dodge to the curb and Martín stepped out. He walked toward the ticket booth, but stopped first at a kiosk and bought a copy of the tabloid newspaper *Clarin*. He opened it and stood for a moment looking over the paper to make sure that he was not being followed.

He was not about to do anything he wanted to hide. He wanted to know simply *if* he was under surveillance. General Obregon was entirely capable of wanting to know how he spent his weekends, and he had many friends in the Policía Federal who would be willing to do a favor for the new Director of the Bureau of Internal Security.

He saw no cars that could belong to the Policía Federal, but he waited until the traffic signal changed and the line of traffic moved off (no car had remained behind, or was moving unusually slowly). Then he folded the newspaper, tucked it under his arm, and went to the ticket window to purchase a ticket.

He walked slowly down the winding path until he came to the elephant enclosure, where several children and their parents were doling out peanuts to a pair of elephants. A somewhat ruffled middle-aged man was also there, doing the same.

"Buenas tardes, Milton," Martín said to him. "What a pleasant surprise."

"Ah, Bernardo," Milton Leibermann said, and offered both his hand and the bag of peanuts.

Martín took several peanuts and held them out to the elephant.

"So what's new, Bernardo?" Milton Leibermann asked.

"I have a new boss," Martín said.

"Oh, really?"

"General Obregon. You know the name?"

"I've heard it. When did that happen?"

"It hasn't been announced officially yet, but that should come in the next few days."

Leibermann grunted.

"Actually, a little bird told me that he might drop by his new office, unofficially, of course, this afternoon," Martín said.

"Where no doubt he will find you with your nose to the grindstone?"

"You know, Milton, first impressions?"

"Of course."

Leibermann's Spanish was fluent, but his accent marked him as neither a *Porteño* (a native of Buenos Aires) nor an Argentine. His Spanish was in fact Puerto Rican—more precisely, the modified Puerto Rican Spanish spoken in Spanish Harlem.

"And I have learned something else that has not yet been made public, and which I tell you in confidence," Martín said. "The Cardinal Archbishop has granted permission for the Anglican priest . . . what's his name?"

"Cashley-Price?"

". . . Cashley-Price to participate in the wedding of our friend Cletus Frade."

"Ah, young love!" Leibermann said. "I'm really impressed, Bernardo. I wish my budget were large enough to have someone in the Cardinal's office. I'll bet all sorts of interesting things go on there."

Martín laughed. "Actually, it's my wife's sister. And I learned that quite by accident."

"That happens to me a lot, too," Leibermann said.

"Recently, for example?"

"You do know that Mr. Graham has left Argentina?"

"I knew the day the Colonel left," Martín said.

"The Colonel?"

Martín smiled and shook his head.

"I was thinking, when I heard that our friend Cletus was going to be allowed to marry, that it would really be a shame if something happened to . . . what shall I say? Interrupt his newlywed bliss."

"Yes, it would."

"I don't know how much General Obregon knows about Cletus and his friends, but I'm going to have to tell him what I know. And I have no idea what he'll decide to do about it. Or them."

"I, of course, have no idea what you're talking about."

"Of course not. I was speaking hypothetically. And,

speaking hypothetically, I don't suppose you've heard anything about his plans? That he might, for example, wish to take his bride to the United States?"

"I don't think that's very likely to happen, Bernardo."

"I was afraid of that."

"Speaking hypothetically, what is it that you know about Cletus that you have to tell General Obregon?"

"There is a rumor that there is both a radio station and a radar station operating illegally on Estancia San Pedro y San Pablo."

"I wonder how a rumor like that got started?"

"Who knows? But it is the sort of thing that I'm going to have to tell General Obregon, and it's the sort of thing he'll probably want to look into."

"Oh, I don't know, Bernardo. A radar station? I can't think of any reason why there would be a radar station operating out there, except perhaps to look for German submarines being supplied in Samborombón Bay, and my government has your government's assurance that has never happened."

"From what General Rawson tells me, that sort of thing will never happen under his administration."

"Well, I'm certainly glad to hear that. Neutrality is so important, isn't it?"

Martín put out his hand. "So nice to run into you like this, Milton."

"And it's always a pleasure to see you, Bernardo," Leibermann said. "Are you sure you won't have another peanut?"

"No, but thank you."

They smiled at each other, and then Martín walked away, more quickly now, down the winding path to the other end of the zoo, and pushed through the turnstile onto Avenida Libertador.

Next Saturday, he thought, *we will meet in Recoleta Cemetery. And the week after that in the Café Colon.*

He spotted the Dodge. It was parked, illegally, twenty-five meters down Avenida Libertador. A sergeant of the Corps of Mounted Police had just parked his motorcycle and was advancing on it with a look of righteous indignation on his face.

Martín stopped and took the *Clarín* from under his arm.

The policemen bent down to look at the driver, and a moment later straightened up, saluted, and walked back to his motorcycle. Martín waited until he had kicked it into life and ridden off before folding the newspaper again and walking up to the car. He got in the backseat.

"Any problems, Manuel?"

"No, Sir," Manuel said.

"Let's go to the office," Martín said. "With a little bit of luck, we can both go home in about an hour."

"Yes, Sir."

[TWO]
Office of the Chief, Ethical Standards Office
Bureau of Internal Security, Ministry of Defense
Edificio Libertador, Avenida Paseo Colón
Buenos Aires
1620 1 May 1943

Coronel Bernardo Martín had just finished putting his uniform on and was examining himself in the full-length mirror on the back of his private rest-room door when there was a knock at his office door.

The uniform consisted of a brown tunic, a white shirt, a black necktie, light tan gabardine riding breeches, highly polished riding boots, a leather-brimmed high-crowned uniform cap, and a Sam Browne belt. The branch of service insignia was that of cavalry. He had once been a cavalry officer, and frequently wished he still was. The colonel's rank badges on the tunic's epaulets were brand new. He had been promoted to colonel only two weeks before, and had had the good luck to pick up the uniform with the proper insignia from the officer's sales store just in time to have it ready for General Obregon.

He hoped that good luck was an omen.

He went into his office, crossed to the door, and opened it to find Mayor Gonzalo Delgano, Argentine Army Air Service, standing there.

He motioned him into the office and closed the door. He didn't want anyone to hear their conversation.

Delgano was a short, muscular man in his early forties, and he too was in uniform. Martín saw that his insignia of rank was new, too.

"I just put this on," Martín said, indicating his uniform. "How does it feel to be back in uniform, Gonzo?"

"Good," Delgano said, meaning it.

Delgano was also an intelligence officer, who had been working undercover for Martín, charged with keeping an eye on el Coronel Jorge Guillermo Frade, the power behind the GOU. Frade had hired the ostensibly just-about-to-retire Capitán Delgano to pilot his Staggerwing Beechcraft.

The job had been personally difficult for Delgano. He liked el Coronel Frade—whom he had served under when Frade had been deputy commander of the 2nd Cavalry Regiment in Santo Tomé. Deceiving him, spying on him, had not come easy. Yet he had done his duty.

After el Coronel Frade's assassination, he had stayed on at Estancia San Pedro y San Pablo to surveille Frade's son—not only a Yankee gringo, but worse, an agent of the American OSS. However, Frade had learned during the revolution that Delgano was in fact a serving intelligence officer, and that of course ended his usefulness, insofar as keeping an eye on Cletus Frade was concerned.

Since the cover story about Delgano's retirement was now useless, Martín had arranged for the first postrevolution *Daily Army Journal* to announce that Captain Gonzalo Delgano had fully recovered from an unspecified illness and had been recalled to active duty in the grade of major.

Since that particular issue of the *Daily Army Journal* had consisted of sixteen pages of small type, most of it announcing the retirement of officers who had supported the deposed government, no one would pay much attention to an apparently routine personnel action for a lowly captain.

"The President telephoned me yesterday to say that, on the advice of General Ramírez and Coronel Perón, he has decided to name General Obregon as Director of BIS," Martín said. "He also suggested that the General might drop in for an unofficial visit. A friend told me when he planned to come. Hence, the uniform."

Martín knew that Delgano shared his opinion of General Obregon, but neither his large dark eyes nor his face suggested that he was surprised or disappointed.

Or anything, Martín thought with approval. *Intelligence officers should be like poker players. None of their feelings should show.*

"And I thought we should have a talk before you officially report for duty," Martín went on. "So I called you."

Delgano nodded and smiled. "May I say, mi Coronel, that the coronel's insignia looks very nice on your epaulets?"

"As does the mayor's insignia on yours, Mayor."

Their eyes met for a moment, and they smiled at each other.

"We are going to have to be very careful, Gonzo."

Delgano nodded. "I would like to know if some sort of deal was struck," he said. "Or whether Rawson was unwilling to resist a suggestion from Ramírez."

"Ramírez *and* Perón."

"I really thought Perón wanted the job," Delgano said.

"I think he has greater ambitions," Martín said.

Delgano nodded. "As does Ramírez," he said.

"And the ambitions of both require their man in here," Martín said. "They learned from Castillo's mistake in trusting Admiral Montoya."

"And how do they regard you? For that matter, us?"

"With a little bit of luck, they will regard us as technicians without ambition."

Delgano nodded his agreement.

"With your permission, Gonzo, I will suggest to General Obregon that you become his personal pilot."

"I would be honored with such an assignment, mi Coronel," Delgano said.

There was no sarcasm in Delgano's reply. Martín under-

stood why: Delgano was honored that he trusted him to surveille General Obregon, thus serving Argentina.

"Thank you, Gonzo," Martín said.

"It's nothing," Delgano said.

The red telephone—one of three—on Martín's desk
buzzed, and he picked it up.

"Coronel Martín," he said, listened, then said, "Muchas
gracias," and hung up.

He met Delgano's eyes. "El General Obregon has just
driven up downstairs," he said.

"And what do you want me to do?"

"I would rather he didn't know we're friends," Martín
thought aloud. "So stay here, in the outer office. I'll try to
avoid your meeting him right now, but that may not be possible."

Delgano nodded.

Martín walked quickly down the corridor to the bank of
elevators, and was standing there when the door opened and
General de Division Manuel Federico Obregon stepped off.

He was a large, heavily built man whose dark skin and
other features made it quite clear that Indian blood was in
his veins. That was unusual in the Argentine officer corps,
almost all of whom belonged to the upper class, if not the
aristocracy. Almost by definition, that meant they were of
European stock, unmixed with Indian.

Obregon was accompanied by his aide-de-camp, a major
whose features also suggested mixed blood. Martín had seen
him before but could not recall his name.

Martín came to attention and saluted. "Coronel Martín,"
he said. "A sus órdenes, mi general."

Obregon returned the salute. "You knew I was coming,
Coronel?" he asked, but it was a statement.

"I didn't know, Señor. But I am not surprised. President
Rawson telephoned to tell me of your appointment, and
mentioned he thought you would come by for a quick visit
to your new command."

*Will it hurt for him to know I have a connection with Raw-
son? It can't be helped. I do. And it would come out anyway.*

"You've been waiting for me on Saturday afternoon?"

"No, Sir. Actually, Sir, I came in to see if I could still fit in my uniform. I thought perhaps you might prefer that I work in uniform."

Obregon grunted noncommittally. "You know Hugo, of course?" he asked, nodding at his aide.

"Of course," Martín said. "It's good to see you, Mayor."

"And you, Señor," the aide said.

The name came: *Molina, Hugo. Class of 1934. Infantry.*

"May I show you your office, mi General?"

"You're very kind, Coronel."

Martín motioned the two of them down the corridor to the double doors of the Office of the Director, Bureau of Internal Security, where he stepped ahead of Obregon and pushed on the left door. Despite its enormity and weight, it opened effortlessly.

The Edificio Libertador had been designed and constructed under the supervision of a team of architects and engineers sent as a gesture of friendship to the Republic of Argentina by the German Reich.

And also, Martín believed, to demonstrate German engineering genius and efficiency. They had made their point with the Edificio Libertador. Everything was massive, impressive, and smooth-functioning, including the Seimens telephone system and the elevators. And the hinges on the massive doors.

Suboficial Mayor José Cortina, who had the duty, was sitting at the ornate desk ordinarily occupied by Señora Masa. He stood up quickly and popped to attention when he saw Obregon.

It was obvious that Cortina did not expect to see the General. His tunic was unbuttoned, his tie was pulled down, and a half-eaten piece of chocolate cake and a coffee thermos were on the desk beside his holstered pistol and the Thompson .45-caliber submachine gun that served almost as the insignia of whoever had the duty.

"This is Sergeant Major Cortina, General," Martín said. "He has the duty."

"Stand at ease, Sergeant," Obregon said, and offered his hand. "I'm pleased to meet you."

"I apologize for my appearance, Sir," Cortina said.

"I don't suppose you get many visitors here on Saturday afternoon, do you?" Obregon said.

"Almost never, Sir."

"Do you suppose, Cortina, that you could find some coffee for our new director?" Martín said.

"Immediately, Sir," he said as he hastily buttoned his jacket.

Martín walked to the doors leading to the Director's office, pushed it open, and waved Obregon inside.

The windows of the large, high-ceilinged office provided a splendid view of the River Plate.

With the exception of a leather desk pad, a double pen holder, and three telephones, the large, ornately carved desk was bare.

"Will you miss this splendid office, Coronel?" Obregon asked.

"Sir? Oh. General, I knew my interim appointment was just that. I never moved in here."

"President Rawson told me he had offered you the position," Obregon said.

"With all possible respect, sir, may I suggest that the offer was made in the excitement immediately following the success of Outline Blue? I respectfully suggest General Rawson was carried away momentarily in the euphoria of the moment."

"Well, his—what did you say, 'euphoria'?—wasn't all bad. It got you that coronel's badge, didn't it, Martín?"

"Yes, Sir, it did."

"Let me say, Coronel, that I feel your promotion was entirely deserved, both for your contributions to the success of Outline Blue, and also—perhaps primarily—because it was deserved. General Rawson is not the only one who has told me you're a fine intelligence officer."

"The General is very kind, even if he has been misinformed."

Obregon laughed. "I'm going to have to depend on you for a good deal until I get my feet on the ground around here," he said.

"I'm entirely at your service, mi General."

"Is there anything— Let me rephrase: What, in your judgment, Coronel, is the immediate pressing problem BIS faces?"

I should have anticipated that question, and I didn't.

"Señor, I can't speak for the entire BIS."

"The President said, as far as he's concerned, you're the only man here who really knows what he's doing," Obregon said.

"I'm sorry the President feels that way, mi General. There are a number of very competent officers here."

"Answer the question, please, Coronel."

"Yes, Sir. As far as Ethical Standards, which is my responsibility, is concerned, I would say our priority is to make sure that the officer corps poses no threat to President Rawson and the government. I know of no problem with the *serving* officer corps, and those officers who were retired when the new government took office will remain under surveillance."

"Including el Almirante Montoya?"

"Yes, Sir."

"Do you think he poses a problem?"

"No, Sir."

"What is the major problem facing BIS as a whole, in your judgment?"

"The violation of Argentine sovereignty by the belligerent powers, Sir."

"Could you be more specific?"

"The major problem is the Americans and the Germans, Sir, in my judgment."

"Do you believe the Germans were responsible for the assassination of el Coronel Frade?"

"Yes, Sir."

"El Coronel Perón does not agree with that conclusion."

"Then I think Coronel Perón is not adequately informed of the circumstances, Sir."

"One of the first things I want to do is have a look at your file about that."

"I can get it for you now, Señor, if you wish."

"Not right now, thank you. But it is available?"

"Yes, Sir, it is."

"And presumably there is a file about the alleged smuggling attempt by the Germans at Puerto Magdalena?"

"Yes, Sir. But there's not much concrete in it."

"I've heard a story that two of the three German officers on the beach were killed. Have you heard that?"

"Yes, Sir, and I believe it to be true."

"And who do you think killed them?"

"I have an opinion, Señor, but no proof."

"In your opinion, then, who killed them?"

"I believe they were killed at the direction of el Coronel Frade's son, Señor. Cletus Frade."

"Who is an agent of the American OSS?"

"Yes, Sir. I believe that to be true."

"The senior OSS man in Argentina?"

"I'm not sure about that, Sir. The senior OSS man may be the Military Attaché at the U.S. Embassy."

"The President is very taken with young Frade. He was apparently very useful to him during the execution of Outline Blue. Are you familiar with that?"

"Yes, Sir."

"And he is not only an Argentine citizen, but el Coronel Perón's godson, which poses certain problems in his regard, does it not?"

"Yes, Sir. Many problems."

"I'd like to hear what you think those problems are, Coronel."

Martín had mixed feelings about Cletus Frade.

In other circumstances, he knew they could have been friends. He liked him personally and admired him professionally. One of the very few errors he had made in judging opponents was to conclude that Frade was an amateur intelligence officer, who could easily be controlled by a professional such as himself. Frade had quickly shown him that he had a natural flair for the clandestine.

Unfortunately, friendship was obviously impossible under

the circumstances. Inevitably—and sooner rather than later—Frade was going to become embroiled with the Germans in something that might not be in Argentina's best interests.

"May I speak freely, mi General?" Martín asked.

"I expect you to, Coronel."

"There are two types of intelligence agents, Sir. The first kind is sent into a country by a foreign power. His activities are by definition espionage, and can be dealt with in that reference.

"The second is a citizen who is employed by a foreign power to conduct activities against his native country. That is considered treason and can be dealt with in that reference.

"Young Frade falls somewhere between the two. He is an Argentine citizen by birth. He is the great-grandson of General Pueyrredón. He is the son of a prominent Argentine who, had he not been assassinated, most likely would have become President of Argentina. And as you point out, he is the godson of el Coronel Perón, another prominent Argentine. And, finally, as you pointed out, Señor, he rendered considerable service to Argentina during the execution of Outline Blue.

"At the same time, he is a serving officer of the United States Corps of Marines. After distinguished service as a pilot in the Pacific, he was recruited by the OSS to come down here—I am sure because of his father.

"Under the Constitution, which the new government has promised to obey in every detail, a citizen may not be deported. That leaves the alternatives of arresting him and trying him for treason, or eliminating him. I respectfully suggest, Señor, that the government would need clear and convincing proof that Mayor Frade's actions seriously damaged Argentina before they brought him to trial for treason, and I confess, Sir, that I have nothing—"

"No proof that he was responsible for the assassinations of the Germans, you mean?"

"I have no proof of that, Sir. But even if I did, I respectfully suggest that no jury, much less a military court-martial, would convict Frade for avenging the assassination of his father."

"So how would you suggest we deal with the problem, Coronel?" Obregon asked.

"Señor, I have no suggestions to make. Frankly, I am glad that the responsibility for the decision is not mine."

General Obregon looked at Martín for a long time before he spoke. "Tell me about elimination, Martín," he said finally. "Presumably that's a last resort?"

"If Señor Frade were to be killed in an automobile accident, Señor, there would be demands for a full and impartial investigation from many quarters. Including, Señor, I would suggest, the office of the President."

"As well as from el Coronel Perón," Obregon said. "So elimination is not really an option, is it?"

"I would recommend against it, Sir."

"Presumably, you have him under surveillance?"

"Of course, Sir."

"Have you met him?"

"Yes, Sir."

"I saw him for no more than thirty seconds at Coronel Frade's funeral. But Coronel Perón has arranged to have me invited to his wedding. Maybe there will be an opportunity then."

"Yes, Sir."

General Obregon put his hands behind his back and paced back and forth to the window twice. Then he smiled at Martín.

"Thank you so much, Coronel, for the briefing. I won't officially be taking up the directorship for several days. But if anything happens, anything you feel should come to my attention, please get in touch immediately."

"Sí, Señor."

"And when I do come in, please have the files I asked for ready."

"Sí, Señor."

Obregon put out his hand. "I look forward to working

with you, Coronel," he said. Then he reclaimed his hand and came to attention.

Martín realized he was waiting to be saluted. He did so. Obregon returned it, gestured to Mayor Molina to open the door, and then marched out of the room.

[THREE]
Estancia San Pedro y San Pablo
Near Pila, Buenos Aires Province
1605 1 May 1943

The Lockheed Lodestar was a fourteen-passenger transport aircraft slightly smaller, but faster, than the twenty-one-passenger Douglas DC-3. It had a takeoff weight of 17,500 pounds and a 69-foot wingspan; and it was powered by two 1,200-horsepower Wright Cyclone engines, which gave it a top speed of 259 mph over a range of 1,800 miles.

Cletus Frade knelt by the left undercarriage of *his* Lockheed Lodestar (for it was his, having been his father's) and studied the wheel, the tire, the brakes, the piston, and even the cavity in the wing into which the landing gear would retract, for signs of damage and hydraulic leaks, and other indications of potential malfunction.

The trouble, he thought, *is that I don't have a clue what I'm looking for. Or, for that matter, at. The only thing I know for sure is that this is a great big sonofabitch, and the people who designed it were perfectly justified in deciding that it takes two people to fly it.*

On the other hand, you are a Marine aviator, complete with wings of gold, right? And you already have flown this big sonofabitch all by yourself three times—no, more than three times: From Pôrto Alegre to Santo Tomé. From Santo Tomé to the military field at Posadas. From Posadas here. From here to the field at Campo de Mayo. And from there back here. That's five times, right?

That's five successful takeoffs and five good landings—a

*good landing being defined as any landing you can walk
away from—right? So there is no reason you can't do it
again, right?*

Wrong.

*What you know you should do, pal, is tell Ashton you've
changed your mind, and what you're going to do is fly him to
Uruguay in one of the Piper Cubs and land him in some
farmer's pasture. That you know how to do.*

He ducked under the fuselage and examined the right
landing gear and its well.

He had his head in the wheel well when someone spoke
to him.

"May I be of some help, Señor Frade?"

There was a man standing by the engine. It took Clete a
moment to remember his name: Benito Leticri. He was an
aircraft mechanic, charged with maintaining the Cubs and,
before Clete had put it into Samborombón Bay, the Beech
Staggerwing.

Clete also had no doubt that even if Letieri wasn't actually
one of Coronel Martín's BIS agents, he reported to the BIS
whatever Clete did with the airplanes.

It was a moot point. There was no way he could fly to
Uruguay without Martín hearing about it. It didn't even matter if Martín learned after the fact that Ashton had been
aboard the Lodestar when he took off. He didn't think the
Argentine Army Air Corps would try to shoot him down.

For that matter, it was damned unlikely that the obsolete
fighters of the Argentine Army Air Corps—Seversky P-35s,
with a top speed of 275 mph—could be scrambled in time to
catch up with the Lodestar to shoot him down.

"Well, I want to run the engines up, Benito," Clete said.
"And I thought I'd give it a little test hop. Would you like to
go along?"

"Sí, Señor. Thank you."

"Get somebody to roll a fire extinguisher out here, and
then come on board."

"Sí, Señor."

Clete looked around until he found Enrico Rodríguez.

"You want to go for a little ride, Enrico?"

"Sí, Señor Clete," Enrico said with absolutely no enthusiasm.

The Dash One—*Pilot's Operating Manual for Lockheed Model L18-Series Aircraft*—was where he had left it, on the shelf under the windshield in the cockpit.

He sat down in the pilot's seat and read the STARTING PROCEDURE and TAKEOFF PROCEDURE and LANDING PROCEDURE sections very carefully.

Benito came into the cockpit. Clete looked out the side window and saw that a wheel-mounted fire extinguisher had been rolled into place, and two men were prepared to man it. He wondered if there was an auxiliary power unit around someplace to start the engines in case the batteries were dead, or whether they would have to recharge them.

He motioned to Benito to get into the copilot's seat, then fastened his harness, signaled to Benito to do the same, and then showed him the levers that controlled the landing gear and the flaps.

"When I tell you 'Gear up,' you pull that up. And when the green light comes on, you tell me, 'Gear up.' If the red light comes on, you tell me that. Got it?"

"Sí, Senõr."

"And when I tell you, 'Flaps up,' you set that lever to zero. When the needles match—see?—you tell me that, too. Got it?"

"Sí, Señor."

Clete reached up and threw the MASTER BUSS switch.

He looked out the window and signaled to the men with the extinguisher that he wanted the wheel chocks pulled, and when one of them went to remove them, signaled that he was about to wind it up.

He moved the carburetor control to FULL RICH, advanced the throttle of the right engine just a tad, and pressed the ENGINE ONE START switch.

For a moment, from the labored way it was grinding, it looked as if he was going to have to worry right now about how to get the batteries recharged, but then the engine spluttered, gave out a cloud of blue smoke, and caught. It quickly smoothed out, and he started the right engine.

As the needles began to move into the green, he released the brake and moved onto the runway. The windsock told him he was going to have to taxi all the way to the far end of the runway, but it was pointing parallel to the runway, which meant he wouldn't have to worry about crosswinds.

At the end of the runway he turned the plane around, checked the magnetos, set twenty degrees of flap, saw all the needles were in the green, and reached up and advanced the throttles. The plane began to move, very slowly at first. Then it began to pick up speed.

As he approached takeoff velocity, he eased the nose downward to raise the tail wheel. As the airspeed indicator showed takeoff velocity, the Lodestar began to take off by itself. The rumbling of the undercarriage suddenly stopped.

He was flying.

"Gear up," he ordered, and then, a moment later, "Zero flaps."

"Green light, zero flaps," Benito reported.

Clete smiled at him.

That wasn't too bad, pal, he thought as he put the airplane into a shallow climb. And then he remembered what his uncle Jim, who had taught him to fly long before he went through Pensacola, had told him over and over: "Just when everything seems to be going fine, everything will go wrong."

His later experiences as an aviator had given him many examples of how absolutely true that was.

He paid very close attention to what he was doing until he had reached 5,000 feet and trimmed it up and put it on autopilot, on a course that would take him over Estancia Santo Catalina. He wanted to see if the Feiseler Storch was still on the airstrip there.

It was, which meant that Peter was probably just visiting Alicia Carzino-Cormano for the weekend.

The Feiseler made Clete a little uncomfortable. It was a hell of an airplane just to direct artillery fire and cart people around. The Americans used Piper Cubs and other low-powered puddle jumpers for the same missions. The Storch obviously cost a lot more, in terms of money, time, and matériel, to build than it cost to build a Piper Cub.

It suggested to him that the Germans were a hell of lot better prepared to wage a war than the United States was. He had seen how ill-prepared the Americans had been on Guadalcanal, where the head stamps on some of the .30'.06 cartridges showed they had been manufactured for the First World War, as were many of the weapons they were fired from.

Was it possible the Germans could win the war? That didn't seem likely, but it was damned sure it was going to last a long time.

On the other hand, it seemed pretty clear that American industry was shifting into second gear as far as war production was concerned. The Lodestar seemed to be proof of that. The books showed that it was brand new when they shipped it to Brazil.

Does that mean we're making enough airplanes that the President can pass them out as presents to people he's trying to impress? Or was sending the Lodestar down here one more stupid thing the OSS set up, and did, even though it meant taking this airplane away from somebody who could really use it?

He changed course for the radar installation by using the autopilot, rather than by taking over manual control of the Lodestar. For one thing, it was self-educational, and for another he wanted to see how—or if—he could do so.

The Lodestar's autopilot system dutifully took him precisely where he wanted to go, to the high ground overlooking Samborombón Bay where he knew the radar installation was.

He could not, however, see it.

Polo obviously isn't the complete Yankee Yalie asshole he at first seemed. He's done a damned good job camouflaging the position, using fishing nets and grass from the pampas.

Clete noticed that Benito not only seemed to know where

the radar station was but seemed fascinated with what could be seen (or *not* seen) when they got close.

That wasn't important. Colonel Martín certainly knew where it was, and with that in mind, there were thermite grenades and cans of gasoline in place, ready to be set off the moment it was clear that the Argentines were coming to have a look at it.

If Martín decides to do something about the radar station, am I going to have time to burn the place down and get the team out of the country? Or are they going to find themselves in the military prison at Campo de Mayo charged with espionage? Or am I going to be in the pokey with them?

He flew out over the Bay for five minutes, and then, again using the autopilot, headed the Lodestar back to Estancia San Pedro y San Pablo.

When he got there, he devoted his full attention to getting what he now thought of, almost fondly, as "the great big sonofabitch" back on the ground in one piece. It was less trouble than he expected.

As he approached the hangar, he saw that Uncle Humberto was waiting for him.

Does that mean he's got a message from Peter?

He waved at him from the cockpit window, then went through the SHUT DOWN procedure, checking what he had done afterward with the Dash One.

"Benito," he asked, turning to look at him. "You know how to top off the tanks and check the oil, right?"

"Sí, Senõr. You're going to use the airplane again soon?"

Yeah, I'm going to exfiltrate an OSS agent into Uruguay right after breakfast in the morning. Make sure you tell el Coronel Martín.

"I was taught that if you keep the tanks topped off, it reduces the chances of condensation in the gasoline," Clete said.

"Yes, of course, Senõr," Benito said. "I'll see to it right away."

Clete unstrapped himself and made his way through the

passenger compartment. Enrico was still firmly strapped to his seat.

"You can unstrap yourself now, Enrico. This Marine has safely landed and the situation is well in hand."

Enrico looked at him without comprehension but began to unbuckle his belt.

Clete went to the door at the rear of the cabin, opened it, and climbed out of the Lodestar.

He offered his hand to Humberto, who ignored it, grasped his arms, and kissed Clete's cheek.

Did they get that from the French? Their men are always kissing each other. Christ, French generals kiss French PFCs when they hand out the "No Venereal Disease in Six Months" medals.

Or is that a standard European custom?

"I didn't expect you until a little later, Humberto," Clete said, claiming and firmly shaking his uncle's hand. "Did you see Peter?"

"He said to give you his regards," Humberto said. "He went riding with Alicia, Isabela, and Isabela's friend."

"Really?"

"His name is Antonio—they call him 'Tony'—Pellechea. Your aunt Beatrice invited him and his parents to your wedding," Humberto announced.

Clete's face showed his reaction.

"Beatrice and Tony's mother were at St. Teresa's together," Humberto said. "And Beatrice is, of course . . ."

As nutty as a fruitcake, you poor bastard.

". . . Beatrice."

"No problem," Clete said. "The more the merrier. But what happened to that 'small family and closest friends only' wedding I heard about? God, even Coronel Perón is coming."

"Claudia told me about that. He's your godfather; he thinks of himself as family. Be grateful for that."

Clete decided not to debate the point.

"What were you doing with the airplane?" Humberto asked as they started to walk toward the house.

"I wanted to make sure it worked," Clete said. "And I wanted to stay what we call 'current.' "

"What does that mean?"

"I'm drawing flight pay. Or at least I think I am; I haven't been paid in months. . . ."

"I don't think I understand."

"The Marine Corps pays pilots extra for flying. To qualify for it, you have to fly at least four hours a month."

"You don't need money," Humberto said.

"Uncle Humberto, I'm surprised at you. You, of all people, a banker, must certainly know there is no such thing as too much money!"

Uncle Humberto laughed dutifully. Then he put his hand on Cletus's arm and, when Cletus looked at him in surprise, met his eyes. "What were you really doing with the airplane, Cletus?" he asked. "Or what are you planning to do with it?"

"You don't really want to know, in case someone asks you about it."

"What, Cletus?"

"I'm going to fly to Montevideo in the morning."

"Why?"

"Captain Ashton has been ordered to Rio de Janeiro. Me taking him out of the country in the Lodestar seems to me to be the best way to do that. Once he's in Uruguay, no problem. He has a Uruguayan passport. Getting him out of Argentina is the problem."

"Am I allowed to ask why he's going to Rio?"

"I think when he gets there they're going to hand him a diplomatic passport and put him on the next plane back to Buenos Aires."

"So all you have to do is get him to Uruguay? You won't have to bring him back?"

"When he comes back, he'll be legal."

"And you are just going to illegally—that is, without going through customs and immigration—just going to fly to Montevideo?"

"Another option would be to fly him across the Río Plate in one of the Cubs and put him out in some farmer's field, but I think the Lodestar makes more sense. If I dumped the Cub landing it, that would be kind of hard to explain."

" 'Dumped the Cub'?"

"Crashed it."

"Yes, it would. You are planning to land at Carrasco?"

Clete nodded.

"And what about customs and immigration?"

"Don't I have an estancia over there someplace?"

"You have a small estancia and a large one, and you have a summer house near Puente del Este."

"And did my father ever fly the Beech to Uruguay?"

"The Staggerwing? Yes, he did. Often."

"And did he always cross all the *t*'s and dot all the *i*'s for immigration and customs, or did he just go?"

Humberto's shrug answered the question. "I see your thinking. You think that because your name . . ."

". . . is Frade, I can get away with a lot in Argentina, and presumably in Uruguay, too."

"And if that doesn't work?"

"I am hoping that my uncle Humberto will have enough influence to get me out of a Uruguayan jail."

Humberto smiled at him and shook his head. "There is another rule among bankers," he said. "And that is never to dip into capital unless you absolutely have to."

"Which means what?"

"When we get to the house, I will try to get through to Uruguay on the telephone," he said. "I will have at least one of your estancia managers, and the Managing Director of the Bank of the Río Plate, waiting to greet us at Carrasco when we land."

"When 'we' land?"

"When *we* land," Humberto said.

"Humberto, I don't want you involved in this."

"It would be best if the officials at El Palomar didn't know we were coming," Humberto went on, ignoring him. "So just before we take off from here, the telephone line will go out, and stay out—how long will it take us to fly to El Palomar, go through customs and immigration, and take off again?"

"You're not going anywhere with me," Cletus said flatly. "This is none of your business."

"We have had this discussion before, Cletus," Humberto said. "God in his wisdom has taken your father and my son, and given us each other. In my eyes, you are my son, and whatever you do is my business."

"Oh, Jesus, Humberto!"

"How long will it take us to fly to El Palomar?"

"Thirty minutes. Maybe a little less."

"And we'd best plan another thirty minutes to clear customs and immigration—they won't know we're coming, of course, which may cause a slight delay. So the telephone line should go down for at least an hour." Humberto looked at Enrico. "You can arrange for that, can't you, Enrico?"

"Sí, Señor Humberto."

"What time are we leaving?" Humberto asked.

"I invited Ashton for breakfast. Right after breakfast."

"If we have an early breakfast—say, at nine-thirty—we could leave at eleven."

Clete shrugged.

"Have the phone line go out the minute we leave the house, Enrico," Humberto ordered. "And have it stay out for an hour and a half."

"Sí, Señor Humberto."

"And now, Cletus, I suggest we go to the house and rescue your aunt Martha from your aunt Beatrice."

[FOUR]
Estancia San Pedro y San Pablo
Near Pila, Buenos Aires Province
2230 1 May 1943

Dinner, having been served early, was over. But, Clete thought unkindly, Señora Beatrice Frade de Duarte had a captive audience, and was obviously determined to make the most of that opportunity. The way she was going, they might still be here when the sun came up.

Only the Old Man had escaped, rescued by Father Welner, who announced as dessert was being served that he wanted to have a look at the Chapel of Our Lady of the Miracles, and perhaps Mr. Howell would like to accompany him?

The Old Man had jumped at the chance, and Clete was about to jump to his feet, too, when he saw the *don't you dare!* look on Martha's face.

Beatrice's memory had not been at all impaired by her psychological problems. She was now describing in excruciating detail his cousin Jorge's twelfth birthday party. She remembered who was there (children and parents), and the menu—including the brand of ice cream served, and that it had come from a sweets store that sadly was no longer in business, the wife of the proprietor having been called to heaven and the widower having turned to drink.

There was a sudden silence, and Clete looked around the dining room to see that Beatrice had interrupted herself to glower at Señora Lopez; the housekeeper had had the effrontery to enter the room while she was talking.

"Yes, Maria?" Beatrice asked.

"Excuse me, Señora, but there is a telephone call for Señor Duarte."

Humberto rose from the table.

Here's your chance, Martha. Yawn. Say you've had a long day and just can't seem to stay awake. Get us out of here!

"Don't be too long, dear," Beatrice called after him. "You know how I dislike having business intrude on family." She looked around the table. "Now, where was I?"

You were telling us about the ice-cream guy who hit the bottle when his wife died.

Beatrice remembered, and picked up where she had been when Humberto's business had had the effrontery to intrude on family.

Humberto was gone no longer than three minutes. "Carissima," he said. "Something has come up in Uruguay. I have to go there tomorrow."

"Can't you send someone else?"

"No, I have to deal with this myself, Carissima. Cletus, I

wondered is there any way you could fly me to Montevideo?"

"Absolutely," Clete said. "When would you like to go?"

"As soon as I can. Perhaps right after breakfast?"

"Sure."

"We may have to spend the night," Humberto added.

From the look on Martha's face, she smelled a rat, but Beatrice didn't. "Well, you'd only be in the way here," she announced. "Weddings are women's business, wouldn't you agree, dear Martha?"

"Absolutely," Martha said.

"What we'll do, as soon as the men leave, is drive over to Estancia Santo Catalina and discuss the whole thing with Claudia," Beatrice announced.

Martha smiled somewhat reluctantly.

Clete said, "Excuse me, please," stood up, and walked out of the dining room.

Martha gave him a look that was only partially questioning and mostly of disapproval, and she followed him with her eyes.

When he was in the corridor, out of sight of Beatrice, he turned and made a signal to Martha to come into the corridor. She shook her head, and he signaled again, this time with both hands.

Martha shrugged, excused herself, and came into the corridor. "What?"

"Martha, you don't have to put up with her lunacy. Have a headache. Or just don't go."

She looked at him. "I don't know whether you get it from the Old Man or your father," she said. "But there's a cruel streak in you, Clete, and I don't like it."

"What?"

"You planned this unexpected business trip, and don't tell me you didn't. You took that airplane up this afternoon, to make sure it would be ready, and you were oh-so-willing to fly Humberto to Uruguay when he asked."

"OK. You're right. But what's this 'cruel' business?"

"That poor woman loves you. She sees her son in you. I

could damned well be in her shoes. I almost was when your uncle Jim died. And if you hadn't come back from the Pacific . . ."

"I'm not going to Uruguay to get away from her, if that's what you're driving at. This is business."

Her eyes lit up. "What kind of business?"

"You don't want to know."

"Yes, I do. And Humberto is involved in that, too?"

"In the morning, I'm going to take one of the men with me—he's a Cuban named Max Ashton."

"That's a strange name for a Cuban."

"His father was American. You'll see him at breakfast. I have to get him out of the country without passing through immigration."

"You mean he's in Argentina illegally."

"Yeah."

"And you're involving Humberto in that?"

"He insists. And it's not really dangerous. Ashton has a Uruguayan passport. Humberto just wants to be very careful. He figures if he's with me, fewer questions—actually no questions—will be asked. There's two estancias over there that now belong to me, and he's going to have their managers meet us at the airport. And there will be somebody from a bank. All we have to do is land and put Max in a taxi."

"Your conscience is clear involving Humberto?"

"Yeah, it's clear. I'm an OSS agent, remember? And Humberto invited himself in, over my objections."

"Oh, Clete, I hate all of this OSS business!"

"It would be easier on me if you didn't know about it, but you asked."

"Thank you ever so much, you bah-stud," a British-accented voice called, "for calling me to tell me the good news."

Martha and Clete looked down the corridor.

Señorita Dorotéa Mallín was walking down the corridor toward them.

She was a tall, lithe young woman with shoulder-length

blond hair. Cletus Frade was not the only one who thought she was very beautiful.

Martha smiled, and shook her head. "You didn't call her?" He shook his head, "no."

"You're about as romantic as your uncle Jim."

"You I kiss," Dorotéa announced, kissing Martha. "Him, I may never kiss again."

"I'm on your side, Dorotéa, honey," Martha said. "I'd make him pay."

"Oh, he will," Dorotéa said. "Tomorrow, my beloved, no matter what you had planned to do, you will participate in the arrangements for the wedding. Mother's at Estancia Santo Catalina, and Claudia has asked everybody for lunch to discuss the details. You will sit, smiling bravely, through every bloody boring minute of it."

"Tomorrow morning, Humberto and I are going to Uruguay," Clete said.

"*Were* going to Uruguay," Dorotéa said.

"*Are* going to Uruguay," Clete said.

Dorotéa met his eyes. "You sound as if it's important," she said.

"It is."

"Then I'm going with you," she said. "I really didn't want to be at that luncheon anyway."

"You're not going with us."

"Hah!"

"Let's go into the dining room," Martha said. "You've had dinner, Dorotéa?"

"Yes, but I'll have some dessert. I'm getting fat anyway."

Without really being conscious of it, Clete looked at Dorotéa's stomach. *God, my baby is in there!* He saw on Martha's face that she had seen him looking.

Dorotéa turned and walked into the dining room. She kissed Beatrice first, then Beth and Marjorie, who seemed really glad to see her, said a polite hello to Dr. Sporazzo, Beatrice's psychiatrist, then went to Humberto and kissed him.

"What a pleasant surprise!" Humberto said.

"I'm going to Uruguay with you tomorrow," Dorotéa announced.

"No, you're not," Clete said.

"What a wonderful idea!" Beatrice proclaimed. "Beth and Marjorie have never been to Montevideo, and Dorotéa can show it to them while Humberto and Cletus are doing their business."

Clete looked at Humberto, who with a little luck would have some clever idea to stop Dorotéa's—and now Beatrice's—impossible idea right here and now.

"Why not, Cletus?" Humberto asked. "There's plenty of room in the airplane."

"Is it safe, Humberto?" Martha asked without thinking.

"Clete, please?" Beth asked. "I'd love to see Montevideo."

"It's settled," Dorotéa announced. "You're outvoted, darling."

"I think it's a very good idea," Humberto said.

Humberto's not a lunatic, Clete decided. *If he thought there was any chance of trouble, he would have squashed the idea right away. What he's probably thinking is that having three young women on the airplane will make us look even more innocent.*

Only an idiot would involve his sisters and his fiancée in exfiltrating an OSS agent, right?

Doesn't that make me an idiot?

Clete looked at Martha, who shrugged.

"OK, I give up," he said.

"You'd better get used to that, darling," Dorotéa said. "Your days of freedom are numbered."

He smiled at her.

Thirty minutes later, after Dorotéa had eaten a flan covered with dulce de leche, a sweet, chocolatelike substance made by boiling milk for hours, she kissed Clete chastely on the cheek, and marched off with Beth and Marjorie down a corridor in the right wing of the sprawling house to her guest room.

Twenty minutes after that, she came through the French doors of the master bedroom, wearing a dressing gown.

"I'm surprised you didn't go to sleep," she greeted him, "since I now know how little you care about me."

"Father Welner told me he'd told your father; I figured your father would tell you."

"*You* should have told me, in a voice bright with joy, excitement, and enthusiasm."

"I'm sorry."

She walked to the side of the bed. "As a good Christian girl, it is my duty to forgive," she said. "I forgive you!"

"Oh, thank you, thank you!"

She unfastened the dressing gown and let it slip off her shoulders onto the floor, revealing that the dressing gown had been all she had on.

"Jesus Christ, you're beautiful!" Clete said.

She smiled, and put her fingers onto her stomach. "I think it's getting bigger," she said. "What do you think?"

"I think you have a very attractive belly."

"Wait until later, when I'm swollen like a watermelon. You won't want to look at me."

"Yes, I will."

"You're saying that now," she said.

"I just wish this goddamn wedding was over," he said.

"Me, too."

"Are you going to get in bed, or just stand there in your birthday suit?"

"If I lie down, you know what's going to happen."

"I was hoping that's why you sneaked over here."

"I want to talk first."

"About what?"

"For example, are you going to tell me why you didn't want me to go to Uruguay?"

"Honey, I don't want you involved in this sort of thing."

"That's what I want to talk about."

"Huh?"

"I'm cold," she said, and got in bed with him. "Don't touch, me, Cletus. I'm not through."

"How long is this going to take?"

"Until you understand how I feel," she said. "And, of course, agree that I'm right."

"How you feel and are right about what?"

"For better or worse, in sickness and in health, until death do us part," she said. "This bloody war is worse, obviously. And we're going to have serious trouble unless you understand we have to share the worse, too."

"We're not married yet."

"Except for the little detail of the ceremony itself, we are," she paused, and then looked at him. "Damn you, don't you feel that way?"

"I really love you, Dorotéa. That's *why* I don't want you involved in . . ."

"You being an OSS agent?

"Yeah."

"But I want to be. I *insist* that I be."

"For Christ's sake, why?"

"For someone as smart as you are, you are sometimes really stupid," she said.

"Is that so?"

"I want to share your life, Cletus. That means what you do, what you're going to do. I want to help."

"How the hell could you help? For Christ's sake, you're carrying our baby! I don't want you in a cell someplace. Or worse."

"And I don't want to stand around not knowing what's going on, wondering what in the bloody hell you're up to, wondering if I couldn't help if only you'd let me. In that way, I realized, I'm lucky."

What the hell does she mean by that?

"I don't understand that."

"I know a dozen girls, women, here, whose husbands, whose boyfriends, got on ships and went wherever the Royal Navy or the RAF or whatever sent them. All they get is the odd letter saying 'sorry, I can't tell you where I am, or what I'm doing, but keep a stiff upper lip, old girl, and someday I'll be back.' At least you'll be fighting your war here, and—I admit I haven't a clue how, but I know that somehow I'll be able to—I can help, and at least we'll be together."

"Jesus, baby!"

"Unless you're too stupid to see this, to—"

"I'm sneaking Max Ashton out of the country."

"Just him? Not the others?"

"No, and I suspect that he'll be back here in a week or ten days, with a diplomatic passport."

"With the Lockheed?"

"If they don't know we're going beforehand—and the telephone line here will go out just before we take off from here, and stay out until I clear El Palomar—"

" 'Clear El Palomar'?"

"Go through customs and immigration."

"Oh."

"I don't think we'll have any trouble getting through El Palomar. And Humberto is arranging for people to meet us in Montevideo—my estancia managers and somebody from a bank."

"And with the girls along it will look even more innocent, right? Was that your idea?"

"Humberto's."

"Do your sisters know?"

"No. And they're not my sisters, they're my cousins. Martha knows."

"They're your sisters," she said. "I will take them to a place I know down by the port. Really marvelous leather goods. How long will your business take?"

"Aside from putting Max in touch with the OSS guy in our embassy in Montevideo, I don't have any business."

"But Humberto will arrange a lunch or something to make it look like you do," she said. "And we'll all be somebody's houseguests."

"Probably," Clete said.

"You can touch me now, Cletus," Dorotéa said. "I was going to let you anyway." She took his hand and guided it to her belly.

"Sometimes he moves," she said.

" 'He'?"

"God, I hope so," she said. "Don't you?"

VII

[ONE]
The Residence of the German Ambassador
1104 La Rambla
Carrasco, Uruguay
0845 2 May 1943

The Residence of the Ambassador Extraordinary and Plenipotentiary of the Führer of the German Reich to the Republica Oriental del Uruguay was a three-story red-tile-roofed villa of indeterminate architecture set against a small hill overlooking the beach of the River Plate.

There was a small balcony outside the master suite of the house, where Ambassador Joachim Schulker, a stocky Bavarian in his late fifties, was having his morning coffee in his bathrobe. From there he could see the small black embassy Mercedes moving down La Rambla, the road that ran from the Port of Montevideo to Carrasco along the River Plate.

At the wheel was his secretary, Fräulein Gertrud Lerner, a buxom woman in her late thirties who wore her straw-blond hair in a bun at her neck. She had a small apartment in the Embassy itself, which was in downtown Montevideo, but also on La Rambla.

Ambassador Schulker watched with his coffee cup in hand as Fräulein Lerner nosed the Mercedes against the gate of the driveway, stepped out of the car, and, marching purposefully in her sturdy shoes, approached the door. Then he set his coffee cup on the railing and went to meet her.

His wife was still asleep as he passed through their bedroom to the corridor outside.

When he reached the foot of the stairs, Fräulein Lerner was standing in the foyer, just inside the front door.

"Good morning, Trude," he said.

"There is an RCA radiogram, Excellency," she said, and handed him a yellow envelope.

When she was about the business of the Reich, Trude thought informality was inappropriate.

"Thank you very much, Fräulein Lerner," he said. "Will you wait just a moment, please?"

He tore open the envelope. It took him just a moment to confirm his suspicions about what the message would contain.

"That will be all, Fräulein Lerner, thank you very much."

"Jawohl, Excellency!" she barked, and rendered the Nazi salute.

The Ambassador returned it, somewhat casually.

Fräulein Lerner turned and left the building, and drove back to the Embassy.

She was very proud that the Ambassador had enough respect for her ability and trustworthiness to ask her to serve as duty officer on weekends and holidays, a responsibility ordinarily given only to officers and seldom to administrative personnel.

And she had no idea that the appointment had been Ambassador Schulker's solution to the interminable litanies of excuses about why the officers simply could not serve as duty officer this weekend, or over that holiday.

Ambassador Schulker closed the door, then went to the telephone on a small table in the foyer and dialed a number from memory.

It was answered by a female, speaking Spanish.

"Councilor Forster, please," he said. "This is Ambassador Schulker."

Councilor Konrad Forster was diplomatically accredited to the Republic of Uruguay as the Commercial Attaché of the Embassy. He was also—as only Ambassador Schulker knew—Hauptsturmführer Forster of the Geheime Staatspolizei—the German Secret State Police, known as the Gestapo.

Forster came on the line a minute later, sounding as if he had been asleep. "Heil Hitler, Excellency!"

"Heil Hitler, Forster. I need a few words with you. Would twenty minutes from now be convenient?"

"Jawohl, Excellency."

"Heil Hitler," Schulker said, and hung up.

He climbed the stairs and entered his bedroom.

His wife woke as he was pulling on his trousers. "Are you going somewhere?"

"I need to see Forster for a few minutes. I won't be long."

"Why don't you have him come here?"

Because whenever he's been in my home, I feel like a dog has shat on the carpet.

"I won't be long," he repeated.

"We're having the Paraguays for lunch," she said. She meant the Paraguayan Ambassador and his wife.

"I know. I'll be back in plenty of time."

"On your way out, would you ask Juanita to bring me my coffee?"

"Certainly."

He started for the garage, but changed his mind. It was a nice day, and Forster lived only five blocks away. It would be a nice walk, and good for him.

The message Fräulein Lerner had delivered to him was for Forster.

The German Embassy in Montevideo was not considered sufficiently important to the Thousand-Year Reich to have its own communications section. Thus routine messages to and from Berlin were transmitted over "commercial facilities," which in the case of this message meant they were routed, via the German Post Office, to Geneva, Switzerland, where they were retransmitted as ordinary radiograms over the facilities of RCA, which of course meant the Radio Corporation of America, which of course meant that copies were furnished to the American OSS detachment in Geneva.

Important messages—those it was hoped would not be read by the Americans en route—were routed through the German Embassy in Buenos Aires, 200 kilometers across the Rio Plate. They were usually sent to Montevideo by messengers, who three times a week rode the overnight steamer between the two capitals. In the case of something really important, the couriers were flown across the river in a light aircraft assigned to the Embassy in Buenos Aires.

The exception to this procedure was for messages between the SS in Berlin and Hauptsturmführer Forster. These were transmitted as routine messages—that is to say, via RCA to and from Switzerland—in a code known, at least in theory, only to Hauptsturmführer Forster.

Ambassador Schulker did not share the common belief that the Americans were intelligence amateurs and therefore incompetent. In his mind they had often proven this wrong, most recently when they had not only intercepted some sort of secret smuggling operation into Argentina, but in the process had not only eliminated the military attaché of the Buenos Aires Embassy and a senior SS officer but had accomplished that in such a manner that diplomatic protests could not be made.

He would not be at all surprised to learn that the message he was about to pass to Hauptsturmführer Forster had already been decoded and read by the Americans in Geneva.

But, of course, he said nothing. Forster had told him the transmission system was foolproof, and a wise man never argued with the Gestapo.

He reached Forster's quarters in five minutes. Forster lived in a neat little bungalow two blocks off La Rambla. His car, an Opel Kadet—appropriate to his rank—was parked inside the fence.

He rang the doorbell, and Forster opened it himself.

He was a slight man in his early thirties who wore his black hair slicked down, just long enough to part. There were also wire-framed glasses, with round lenses. In short, he looked very much like Heinrich Himmler. Schulker wondered whether this was intentional—brush mustaches like Hitler's had also become fashionable—or whether it was simply that Forster and Himmler were a type of German, as for example stout Bavarians were a type, and hawk-featured Prussians and Pomeranians were another.

Forster was wearing a silk dressing gown and a foulard, and held a silver cigarette holder in his hand.

He probably thinks he looks like a gentleman, Schulker thought. *God knows, he likes to play at being a diplomat. But he really looks like neither. He looks like what he is, a clerk, with an exaggerated opinion of his own importance, wearing clothing he associates with that of his betters.*

"Heil Hitler, Excellency! Good morning."

"It was such a pleasant day, I decided to walk," Schulker said, raising his arm to return the salute.

He stepped inside the house, and Forster closed the door.

"You have a message," Schulker said. "Fräulein Lerner just brought it to the residence."

He handed it to him, showing absolutely no interest in it.

He knew Forster well enough by now to know this was the best way to learn its contents. It was elementary psychology. Forster believed he was an important man. Indeed, he had almost certainly been told this by his Gestapo superiors.

But if you are an insecure little man—which was how Schulker thought of Forster . . . which did not challenge his belief that Forster was also a very dangerous man; the two characteristics were not mutually exclusive—*who continually needs the approval of peers and superiors. As Forster works alone and secretly in his Gestapo role, he has neither.*

The only person he can talk to about his important duties is me, and so long as I show no interest in his affairs, the only thing Forster can do to earn my admiration is to tell me more than he should.

"It may be important," Forster said self-importantly. "May I ask you to wait, Herr Ambassador?"

"Of course, if you think it is important."

"I'll have the girl bring you a coffee," Forster said, leading Schulker into the sitting room.

"Thank you."

Twenty minutes later, having decrypted the message, Forster was back, even fuller of self-importance.

"There has been a development, Excellency, vis-à-vis the incident in Argentina," he announced.

Schulker looked at him without expression.

"You will have certain responsibilities in this regard," Forster went on. "But for the moment, all I can tell you is that Sturm-bannführer von Tresmarck will shortly be ordered to Berlin."

Schulker nodded.

"Your instructions in this regard will come via Buenos Aires," Forster said.

Schulker nodded again.

"In the meantime, in other words, until you receive this information through your own channels, nothing must be said to the Sturmbannführer."

"I understand."

"At this moment, I can tell you only that these actions are being ordered at the highest level."

"I understand your position, Forster."

"I will be providing further details as it becomes necessary for you to learn of them."

"I'm at your disposal, Forster, if I have to say that."

"The Gestapo appreciates your cooperation as always, Excellency," Forster said.

"We are both serving the Reich and the Führer," Schulker said. "And now I must get back. We're having the Paraguayans for lunch."

"Let me know if you hear anything interesting," Forster said.

"Of course," Schulker said, and, raising his arm at the elbow, added, "Heil Hitler!"

[TWO]
Estancia de los Dos Caballos Blancos
Kilometer 87, Route National 1
Entre Rios Province, Uruguay
0945 2 May 1943

"You decent?" Beth Howell asked, putting her head in the door of the master bedroom.

"Yeah, come on in," Clete called. "I'm out here on the balcony, or patio, or whatever the hell it is."

She walked across the bedroom to where he was standing on a small area outside the room, which overlooked the rolling hills of the pampas. He was wearing a polo shirt, khaki trousers, and a battered pair of Western boots.

Clete smiled at her and pointed to a coffeepot. She helped herself.

"If breakfast is anything like dinner last night, it will be noon before it's ready."

She poured herself a cup of coffee.

"I knew you were alone, Clete," she said, smiling at him.

He looked at her. She was wearing a skirt, a pullover sweater, loafers, and white bobby socks. She looked very American.

"I just happened to open my door when I saw Dorotéa coming out of this one. In her bathrobe, looking as chipper as can be. What is that, Cletus, do as I say, not as I do?"

"Jesus, you didn't say anything to her, did you?"

"She said, 'Good morning, Beth,' and I said 'Good morning, Dorotéa.' "

He shook his head.

"Well, it will be legal on Saturday," Beth said. "What's the harm in jumping the gun a little, right?"

"So far as you're concerned, it *is* do as I say, not as I do."

"She really loves you, Clete, I can tell. I'm happy for you. For both of you."

"Thanks, Beth."

"And for a small consideration, I won't tell Mother."

"Well, I think Mom has figured out that we're already more than just good friends."

"I've been working on her—Mom asked me to—to get her to come to the States to have the baby."

"I wish she would, but I don't think that will work. She'll want to be around her mother."

"Mom's been working on her, too. Pamela, I mean."

"I hope she's successful," Clete said.

"You think everything's OK with Captain Ashton?" Beth asked.

"Once we got out of the airport at Carrasco, he was home free," Clete said. "By now he's probably already in Brazil."

"He's a nice guy. I like him."

"Yeah, he is."

"When he comes back to Argentina, what am I supposed to do, pretend I never met him before?"

"Since he was never in Argentina, how could you have met him?"

"OK. Marjorie told me to ask."

She sipped her coffee, then gestured around at the rolling hills.

"I like your spread, Clete," she said. "It's so green. . . ."

"As opposed to Big Foot Ranch, you mean? Yeah, this is great farmland. The topsoil is black and five, six feet deep. Too good, really, to graze cattle and sheep, which is about all they do with it."

"I like it down here," she said. "I almost hate to go back."

"Nobody special's waiting for you?"

She snorted. "Nobody who looks at me the way you look at Dorotéa."

"How do I look at Dorotéa?"

"Like she's everything you want in life."

"Guilty," he said.

"When the war is over, what are you going to do? Stay here? Or come home?"

"I don't know," he said. "Somehow I can't see Dorotéa in Midland."

"What about 'Whither thou goest,' et cetera, et cetera?"

"It's really strange, Beth, but I feel I belong here. Too, I mean. I will always be a simple roughneck-slash-cowboy from Midland, Texas, but—"

" 'Simple'? The one thing you have never been is simple. You're really a chip off the old blockhead."

"Which blockhead is that? My father? Or the Old Man?"

"I was thinking of the Old Man, but now that I think about it, probably both. I can see how you eat up this 'el patrón' business."

"Meaning what?"

"Just what it sounds like. You like it. That's an observation, not a criticism."

"There is something to be said for putting out your hand and somebody putting a cup of coffee in it."

"That's not what I mean. I mean, I thought about it. You're half Argentine. I knew that, but I never understood it until I saw you here. This is your country, too."

"You're speaking to Major Frade of the Marine Corps, the United States Marine Corps."

"You know what I mean, Clete. Face facts."

"What I'm doing right now is facing that fact. I am a Marine Corps officer. When the war is over, then I'll worry about what else I am."

"OK," she said. "Are you going to get married in that *gorgeous* Marine uniform, Major Frade?"

"I never thought about what I would wear," he confessed. "But, hell, yes, that's a great idea."

A maid came onto the patio and told El Patrón that breakfast was being served."

"El Patron and I will be there directly," Beth told her in Spanish, then smiled knowingly at Clete.

"It's easy to get used to," he said, and then waved her ahead of him out of the room.

He followed her down the corridor to the dining room, where everyone was seated at the table. Dorotéa was sitting at its foot—as she had at dinner—which meant, Clete thought, that as far as she was concerned she was already playing the role of La Patróna. It pleased him.

"Good morning, Cletus," Dorotéa said sweetly. "Did you sleep well?"

God, she's beautiful!

"Actually, no," he said seriously. "One thing and another kept me up most of the night."

"Perhaps your conscience was bothering you, darling," she replied without missing a beat.

"And how did you sleep, Dorotéa?" Beth asked innocently.

"Well, there was nothing on *my* conscience, so I slept like a baby," Dorotéa replied.

She picked up a small silver bell by her plate and rang it. Two maids immediately came out of the kitchen and started serving breakfast.

[THREE]
Control Tower
El Palomar Airfield
Buenos Aires
1435 2 May 1943

"Mi Coronel . . ." the senior control operator said, and when he had Coronel Bernardo Martín's attention, pointed his index finger toward the sky.

Martín picked up a set of earphones and put them on. He was in uniform because a colonel's uniform would be more useful than his Bureau of Internal Security credentials for what he wanted to do now.

"El Palomar Tower, this is Lockheed Zebra Eight Four Three."

Despite the slight static and clipped frequency of the control tower's radio, the voice was easily recognizable as Cletus Frade's.

Martín looked at the control tower operator, who was doing absolutely nothing. Martín gestured impatiently for him to get on with it.

The operator picked up his microphone. "Lockheed Zebra Eight Four Three, El Palomar, go ahead."

"Four Three is at 2,500 meters, indicating 250 knots—correction, 400 kilometers—per hour, approximately sixty kilometers due north of your station. Request approach and landing instructions. Over."

Four hundred kilometers per hour? My God, that's fast!

He did the arithmetic: *Four hundred kilometers an hour was six point six six six forever kilometers a minute. At that speed, it will take him nine minutes to fly sixty kilometers. I just got here in time.*

"Mi Coronel?" the control tower operator asked.

"Give him what he wants, por favor, Señor," Martín said politely, and added mentally, *You idiot!*

"Lockheed Zebra Eight Four Three, El Palomar. Permission to approach El Palomar on present course is granted. Descend to one thousand meters. Report when twenty kilometers from the field."

"El Palomar Four Three. Understand and will comply. Beginning descent at this time."

Four minutes later, Lockheed Zebra Eight Four Three called again.

"El Palomar, Four Three. At one thousand meters. Due north. Indicating four hundred kilometers. Estimate maybe 25 kilometers from your station."

This time Martín was waiting for the control-tower operator to ask for instructions.

"Do whatever you have to do to have him land," he ordered.

"Sí, mi Coronel," the control-tower operator said, and picked up his microphone. "Lockheed Zebra Eight Four Three, El Palomar."

"Four Three, go ahead."

"You are cleared to land on Runway One Eight. There is no other traffic. The winds are from the south at fifteen kilometers. Report when you have airfield in sight."

"Understand, One Eight. South at fifteen. I have the airfield in sight. I will require customs and immigration."

Again, Martín was waiting for the control-tower operator's request for orders.

"Inform the appropriate customs and immigration officials," he said, "and thank you for your courtesy, señor."

"It is nothing, mi Coronel."

Martín quickly went down the steep and narrow stairs from the control tower and walked toward the customs and immigration area. He was nearly there when, looking northward toward the Rio Plate, he saw the Lodestar making its approach to the field.

He stopped to watch it land.

The wheels came out of their wells. The airplane moved slightly to the right to precisely line up with the runway, and then it gracefully touched down, the tires giving off an audible squeal and puffs of smoke when they encountered the runway.

It's a beautiful machine. I'm glad I came to see this.

He resumed walking as the Lockheed rolled to the far end of the runway.

The day before, he had been informed that the Lodestar had taken off from Estancia San Pedro y San Pablo an hour and a half after the event. The report would have come immediately, Benito Letieri had assured him nervously, if the telephone line hadn't gone out.

Benito had also related that Señor Frade's two sisters were aboard, as were Señorita Mallín and Señor Duarte, but no one else, Benito seemed to think. His information was that they were bound for Uruguay.

Martín had immediately called El Palomar, not at all surprised to hear that the Lockheed had cleared customs and immigration and taken off ten minutes earlier with the announced destination of Carrasco airfield, outside Montevideo.

By the time Martín could get through to his man in Montevideo, it was of course too late for him to reach the airport when the Lockheed landed; but he had ordered him out there anyway, with orders to ask questions and immediately report the answers. And also to stay there, around the clock if necessary, to report the departure of the Lockheed.

Martín thought, more admiringly than angrily, that whatever the purpose of his flight, Cletus Frade had gotten away with it. It was of course entirely possible that the flight was wholly innocent, and that the telephone line going down so conveniently was Cletus Frade tweaking his tail.

But it was also highly possible—Cletus Frade not being the amateur intelligence officer he'd once assumed—that Frade had wanted to see if the people he knew were watching him at Estancia San Pedro y San Pablo could communicate with Buenos Aires by another means besides the telephone.

If I had had my people at El Palomar when he landed the first time, he would have known that I had another telephone line, or a radio, out there. And I suspect that if my men had gone over that airplane with a fine-toothed comb, they would have found nothing at all illegal.

His man in Uruguay had called several hours later to report that the plane had been met by the managers of Frade's Uruguayan estancias and by the Managing Director of the Bank of the Río Plate. Frade and Señor Duarte had gone off to an unknown destination with the banker and the managers, and the young ladies had gone off in another car.

And then today, when his man in Montevideo had called to report that Frade was in the process of clearing customs and immigration and about to take off for El Palomar, Martín had decided that the facts clearly indicated that the trip was as innocent as it appeared . . . or else Frade had succeeded in doing whatever he'd wanted to do.

Under ordinary circumstances, he would have simply sent one of his men to El Palomar to see what he could find out. If the clever fellow had succeeded in putting one over on him, he didn't want to give him the satisfaction of seeing him there. But under these circumstances—he would have to report the flight to General Obregon—he decided the best thing to do was go. He did not want General Obregon to think he was not doing all he could to keep an eye on Frade.

When he reached the airfield, he toyed briefly with having a word with the customs people to take a close look at the aircraft, but decided that it wouldn't be necessary. When they saw him in uniform, they would be inspired to show how dedicated they were to their duty.

The Lockheed was now taxiing up the taxiway parallel to the runway. Martín could not see Frade, but he could see the copilot, over whose long blond hair were cocked a set of earphones.

I wonder how much the beautiful Señorita Mallín knows about what he's doing? Or how much, if anything, she will learn as Señora Frade?

With a roar of its engines and a blast of air from its propellers (which blew Martín's uniform cap off his head), the Lodestar turned and stopped in the customs area.

When he had chased down his hat and turned back to the airplane, he saw Frade in the pilot's seat. Frade waved cheerfully, smiling in obvious amusement about the blown-off hat. Coronel Martín saluted.

A somewhat battered 1938 Ford station wagon drove up to the airplane, bearing customs and immigration officers. They did not seem at all surprised to see him, which meant that the man in the control tower had not only called them, but told them that a colonel of the Bureau of Internal Security was showing great interest in the aircraft.

The customs and immigration officials saluted him, wordlessly asking for instructions. He returned the salute but said nothing.

The engines died, and a moment later the door in the fuselage opened. Frade was the first person out. "Buenas tardes, mi Coronel," he said cheerfully. "How nice to see you. Just happened to be at the airfield, right?"

"A pleasant happenstance, Mayor Frade."

"Oh, really? When I saw you chasing your hat into the grass, I thought perhaps a little bird had told you we were coming."

"A 'little bird'?"

"A little bird in Uruguay. A man at Carrasco was fascinated with the airplane, and when I looked at him, I had the strangest feeling that you might know each other."

"Oh, I think your imagination is running away with you, my friend. Argentina would never station an intelligence officer on someone else's soil."

Clete chuckled, and Martín smiled at him. "Did you have a nice flight?"

"Lovely, thank you," Clete said.

"That's really a fine airplane. I've only seen it before at a distance."

"I'd be happy to show it you."

"I'd like that," Martín said.

Humberto Duarte was the next to step out of the airplane, followed by Dorotéa Mallín and Beth and Marjorie Howell, and finally by Enrico Rodríguez.

"How nice to see you, Señor Duarte," Martín said.

"What an unexpected pleasure, Colonel," Humberto said.

"Do you know my fiancée, Colonel? And my cousins?"

"I have not had the pleasure, but I know of Señorita Mallín by reputation."

"And what reputation would that be?"

"As one of Argentina's most lovely women."

"You are too kind, Coronel," Dorotéa said.

"And these are my cousins, Miss Marjorie and Miss Elizabeth Howell. Beth, Marj, this is Coronel Alejandro Martín."

"I am enchanted, ladies. Argentina is enriched by your beauty."

"I think I like you, Colonel," Beth said, giving him her hand.

"In that case, I am enchanted *and* delighted."

"Are you a friend of Clete's?" Beth asked.

"I like to think so," Martín said. "And while I have the opportunity, Señorita Mallín, may I offer my very best wishes for your upcoming marriage?"

"And what little bird told you about that?" Clete asked.

"My wife's sister, actually. She works in the office of the Cardinal Archbishop. It will take place next Saturday, correct?"

"And we look forward to seeing you there, don't we, darling?" Clete said. "You and Señora Martín."

"Absolutely," Dorotéa said without hesitation.

"I accept with great pleasure."

"The invitations will go out on Monday," Dorotéa said. "It will be at El Capilla Nuestra Señora de los Milagros on Estancia San Pedro y San Pablo."

"So I understand," Martín said.

"Your sister-in-law told you that too?" Clete asked. "Just out of personal curiosity, Bernardo, who does she work for, you or the Archbishop?"

"I think she is what people in the intelligence business refer to as an informal but usually reliable source of information," Martín said.

"I suppose people like that can be very useful," Clete said, "to someone in the intelligence business."

"Oh, yes, indeed."

"Mi Coronel," the customs officer interrupted hesitantly.

"With your permission, Señor, may we proceed with the inspection of the aircraft and the luggage?"

"Oh, I don't think that will be necessary," Martín said. "Señor Frade and Señor Duarte are prominent citizens of our country. I can't image that they would try to smuggle anything into Argentina. Or, for that matter, out of Argentina. You may have your records indicate that I waived the customs inspection. If you will have someone stamp their passports, they can be on their way."

"Sí, Señor."

"That's very good of you, Bernardo."

"It's nothing, Cletus. What are friends for?"

"But you would like a tour of the airplane?"

"I would very much like to see the inside."

Clete waved him onto the Lodestar.

Twenty minutes later, Martín watched the Lodestar lift off, genuinely impressed both with the technology it represented—*four hundred kilometers in one hour! And it isn't a fighter plane, which you expect to be very fast, but a transport, with leather-upholstered seats for fourteen people!*—and with the pilot—*Gonzalo Delgano says that two highly skilled pilots are needed to operate it, and here Frade is casually flying it by himself.*

He considered leaving instructions with the airport commander that the Lodestar was never again to be cleared for departure without his being notified beforehand, but decided against it.

It would be a waste of time and effort.

Cletus Frade would expect him to do something like that, and if he decided in the future to use the aircraft for anything illegal, he wouldn't bother to clear customs and immigration beforehand.

[FOUR]
Estancia Santo Catalina
Near Pila
Buenos Aires Province, Argentina
1645 2 May 1943

*I am not buzzing Estancia Santo Catalina with this great big
sonofabitch,* Cletus Frade told himself. *All I am doing is
making a very low, very slow approach to my airstrip.*

It wasn't very low, actually, about 500 feet over the roof of
the main house, but it wasn't very slow, either. The Dash
One said the Lodestar would stall at about 75 knots. Since
he hadn't had the opportunity to stall the Lodestar yet, the
safe thing to do was perform a maneuver like this at three
times stall speed, which translated to approximately 230
knots.

Only two people sitting in the gazebo near the main house
smiled when the Lodestar flashed overhead with a deafening
roar and even perhaps a little propeller wash.

Claudia Carzino-Cormano wasn't sure later whether the
tall flower vase had been knocked over by wind from the airplane, or whether Señor Enrico Mallín had jarred the heavy
table as he jumped to his feet and cried, "Holy Mother of
Christ!"

Major Freiherr Hans-Peter von Wachtstein, who was at
the gazebo to make his manners to his hostess for her weekend hospitality, smiled. Buzzing unsuspecting natives is
something that fighter pilots do, although rarely in a twin-
engine transport.

And Mrs. Martha Howell smiled, too, not sure later
whether she had forgotten her manners because of memories
of her husband and Clete buzzing Big Foot Ranch, or
because the look of absolute terror on the face of Enrico
Mallín was the funniest thing that had happened all day.

"He's out of his mind!" Enrico Mallín proclaimed, red-faced. "Dorotéa is on that airplane!"

"I would say he's exuberant, Enrico," Martha said, coming to Clete's defense. "He's actually a very good pilot."

"He shot down seven Japanese planes, you know," the Old Man said, looking at von Wachtstein.

"Did he really?" Peter replied politely. Countering that he had shot down thirty-two himself, including six Americans, would have been really bad form. And he liked the Old Man. In many ways he was like his father, with a definite opinion about everything.

"Yes, he did," the Old Man drove the point home.

"Well, at least we know they're back," Pamela Mallín said. "Which means we can go fetch her."

"I'll send someone over in a car. Or Cletus can bring her," Claudia said.

"Oh, no," Enrico said firmly. "Thank you very much, but we'd rather, wouldn't we, Pamela?"

The good-byes and expressions of mutual gratitude took almost twenty minutes, and Enrico Mallín's Rolls-Royce drop-head coupe had just reached the road paralleling the Estancia Santa Catalina landing strip when the Feiseler Storch flashed overhead.

Enrico Mallín looked at his wife across Little Enrico—a slender fifteen-year-old who had inherited his mother's blond hair and soft, pale complexion. "Peter's going to be at the wedding, is he?"

"You know how Beatrice feels about him," Pamela said.

You mean I know how crazy she is.

"That isn't going to cause problems with Cletus?" Enrico asked.

"Both of them are aware they are in a neutral country," Pamela said. "And will behave accordingly."

"The Germans killed Jorge Frade," Mallín said.

"I'm sure Major von Wachtstein had nothing to do with that," Pamela said. "And I know Cletus doesn't hold him responsible, either."

"Forgive me for saying this, darling, but has it ever occurred to you how much better off everyone would be if neither the Germans nor the Americans were here?"

"No," Pamela said, quietly angry. "I won't forgive you for saying that. That was a terrible thing to say. If I were in your shoes, Enrico, I would thank God that our daughter has found a man like Cletus."

Enrico Mallín looked at her for a long moment, but in the end decided not to argue the point. "If I offended you, darling," he said, "I offer my apologies."

"You had better get used to the idea that Cletus is about to become a member of the family," Pamela went on, warming to her subject, "and that we're about to become grandparents, and modify your attitude toward Cletus accordingly."

With a look of horror on his face that the shameful secret had been blurted out, Enrico Mallín smiled uncomfortably at his son.

"We are going to have to have a man-to-man talk very soon, Enrico," he said.

"I know Dotty's pregnant, if that's what you mean," Little Henry said. "I mean, everybody knows. I even heard the servants talking about it."

"We will still have a talk, man to man, my son," Enrico said.

Twenty minutes later, the Rolls topped a shallow rise in the rolling pampas, and Enrico Mallín could see the road now stretching before them in a nearly straight line for several miles. And a moment after that, a car appeared on the road, heading toward them.

"If I didn't know better," Enrico said, gesturing through the windshield at the car, "I'd say that looks like Jorge's Horch."

"That's it." Pamela said. "He had it repaired."

"My God, how fast is he going?" Enrico exclaimed, and added: "If I were him, I don't think I would ever want to see that car again."

"You're not him," Pamela said.

Mallín slowed, pulled to the side of the road, and stopped.

Less than a minute later, the Horch, braking heavily, stopped beside it. Dorotéa Mallín was driving. Clete was in the front seat with her. Enrico Rodríguez was in the backseat.

"Well, hello," Clete greeted them. "Something wrong?"

"I didn't want to be run off the road," Enrico Mallín said. "What's your hurry? Is something wrong?"

"No," Clete said, smiling. "We're just road-testing the car. How does it look, Enrico?"

Among the many things Enrico Mallín did not like about his son-in-law-to-be was that he addressed him by his Christian name.

"It looks splendid," Enrico said with a somewhat stiff smile.

Enrico got out of the Rolls Royce and walked up to the Horch, and Little Henry got out immediately and followed him.

"I thought they normally kept you locked in the attic," Clete said to him, smiling. "Got out on parole, did you?" Then he walked over and kissed Pamela. "No, I don't want to hear about the plans for the wedding," he said, "in case you were going to ask."

Among the many things Enrico Mallín did not like about his son-in-law-to-be was his sense of humor.

"Be careful," she said. "I still have not completely forgiven you. . . ."

"Forgiven me for what?" Clete asked innocently.

Little Enrico giggled.

You know damned well for what, Enrico Mallín thought. *For what you did to my Dorotéa. Taking her innocence and purity. Ruining her life! I will never forgive you!*

"How was Uruguay?" Pamela asked.

"The girls bought out a leather store down by the port," Clete said. "Each now has a lifetime supply of purses."

"We have to be getting back to Buenos Aires, Cletus," Pamela said, seeing that her husband was doing everything in his impatience but pawing the ground.

"We'd sort of expected you for supper," Clete said.

"Out of the question, I'm afraid," Enrico said. "Thank you just the same."

"Perhaps something light, if we had it early," Pamela said, adding, to her husband, "We have to eat."

He grunted.

"How about in an hour?" Clete said. "I've got a little errand to run."

"We'll take Dorotéa with us," Enrico said.

"We want to be alone, Daddy!" Dorotéa said.

"Can I go, Clete?" Little Enrico asked.

Among the many things Enrico Mallín did not like about his son-in-law-to-be was that Little Enrico idolized him.

"No," Clete said immediately, and somewhat abruptly, but then, when he saw the look of disappointment on the boy's face, added, "But I'll tell you what, Enrico Junior, when you get to the house, tell Beth I said to take you for a ride in a Model A. You can drive."

"Really?"

"Clete," Enrico Mallín said sternly, "I'm afraid Enrico is a little young for that. He doesn't know how to drive."

"He's fifteen and he can't drive?" Clete asked incredulously. "He doesn't *look* backward."

"He can't drive," Enrico Mallín repeated, somewhat coldly.

"Well, then, it's high time he learned. And Beth can teach him."

Among the many things Enrico Mallín did not like about his son-in-law-to-be was his presumption that he had the right to offer Little Enrico things—potentially dangerous things—without first seeking his approval.

"See you at the house in forty-five minutes," Clete said, and gestured for Dorotéa to get moving.

There was the sound of gunfire as they approached the radio station.

Clete knew what it was, and smiled.

Dorotéa looked at him in alarm and saw the smile. "What in the world is that?" she asked.

"An old Texas custom," he said. "Good ol' boys whiling away a dull Sunday afternoon, ventilating tin cans."

In a locked room in one of the outbuildings near the garage, Clete had come across small-arms ammunition—enough, in his professional judgment as a Marine officer, to supply a battalion about to land on a hostile beach.

He presumed his father had cached the ammunition there before the coup d'état. Whatever the reason, he had shown it to Chief Schultz, who had loaded a dozen cases of .45 ACP pistol ammunition—1,200 rounds per case—onto his Model A pickup and taken it to the radio station.

The marksmen turned out to be Chief Schultz and three of the men of Ashton's Western Hemisphere Team 17—Staff Sergeant Jerry O'Sullivan, a radar operator, a wiry little man with sharp features and intelligent eyes; Technical Sergeant Ferris, a trimly built man who ran the generator powering the radar and was the team's armorer; and the team's executive officer, First Lieutenant Madison R. Sawyer III, a large, good-looking, well-muscled young man.

O'Sullivan and Ferris were in casual civilian clothing, purchased for them by Ashton in Pila, the nearest town. Like the chief, Sawyer was wearing the billowing shirt, trousers, and boots of a gaucho.

If Sawyer was aware that he looked ridiculous popping to attention dressed that way and crisply saluting Clete, it didn't show on his face. "Good afternoon, Sir!"

Clete returned the salute, pretending not to see that Sergeants Ferris and O'Sullivan were shaking their heads in disbelief at Sawyer's parade-ground behavior.

"I was hoping to see you, Sawyer," he said. "Everybody's here?"

"Stein has the duty, Sir," Sawyer said.

Sergeant Siegfried Stein's family had fled Hitler's Germany in 1935; he now had a degree in electrical engineering from the University of Chicago. He was the radar expert.

By "has the duty," Sawyer meant that Stein was at the radar site, where the equipment was turned on once every two hours or so—never at a precise interval, but long enough to scan Samborombón Bay looking for a ship that might be a German submarine-replenishment vessel.

The crack he had made about good ol' boys whiling away a dull Sunday afternoon had been right on the money, Clete thought. Not only had they been ventilating tin cans—there was a pile of bullet-riddled cans twenty-five yards from the main building—but they had also been having a beer-and-beef barbecue.

"Gentlemen, I don't believe you know my fiancée. This is Dorotéa Mallín. Honey, the big gaucho is Lieutenant Madison Sawyer; the ugly Irishman is Sergeant Jerry O'Sullivan; and that's Sergeant Bill Ferris."

He waited until they had all gone through the polite motions with her, then added, "And in answer to the question that everybody's too polite to ask, yes, she knows what you're doing out here besides drinking beer."

"Speaking of which?" Sawyer asked.

"Yes, indeed. Thank you very much. I was afraid you were never going to ask."

"I'll go get a glass for the lady," Ferris said.

"Don't bother," Dorotéa said. "I like it from the bottle."

"How did things go yesterday, skipper?" the chief asked.

"Like you know what through a goose," Clete said. Dorotéa looked at him curiously. "I turned him over to Whatsisname—"

"Stevenson? Ralph Stevenson? Our guy in Montevideo?"

"Right. And Stevenson said he could get him to Pôrto Alegre with no trouble. From there, he should be able to travel to Rio de Janeiro in a matter of hours."

"Stevenson is a good man," Schultz said.

"We need to get a message out right away—" Clete said, and then interrupted himself. "If there had been anything for me, I guess you would have told me?"

"Nothing, skipper."

"OK. Message Graham that I took Ashton to Montevideo in the Lodestar and turned him over, without incident, to Stevenson, et cetera, et cetera."

"Aye, aye, Sir," the chief said. "You mean right now, or will it wait until the next scheduled call? That's in about an hour."

"It'll wait until then," Clete said.

"I'll do you a draft," the Chief said, and walked into the house.

"May I offer something to eat, Miss Mallín?" Sawyer asked politely.

"First of all, call me Dorotéa. And, no, thank you, we're going to eat just as soon as we get to the main house," Dorotéa said. "But do you suppose I could try that?"

"Try what?"

"One of those," she said, pointing to the .45 pistols on the table. "I've never fired a gun."

Sawyer looked at Clete, who nodded his permission.

"Baby, they make a lot of noise and they kick like a mule," Clete said.

"Forewarned is forearmed, right?" she said.

Sawyer picked up one of the pistols and began a lecture on the Pistol, Caliber .45 Model 1911A1, worthy of the Infantry School.

Her first shots went as wild as Clete thought they would, but within five minutes, she hit her first tin can, and turned to smile proudly and happily at Clete.

A moment later the Chief touched Clete's arm and handed him a sheet of typewriter paper.

"I included our routine crap, OK, skipper?"

```
PRIORITY

TOP SECRET LINDBERGH

DUPLICATION FORBIDDEN

FROM TEX

MSG NO 106 TIME TIME GREENWICH 2 MAY
1943

TO AGGIE
```

```
BACARDI  SUCCESSFULLY  EXFILTRATED  BY
TEX  IN  PARROT  TO  CARE  OF  COUTH  1  MAY

BACARDI  ETA  CARIOCA  VIA  BIRDCAGE  4
MAY

URGENTLY  REQUIRE  SIX  EACH  REPEAT  SIX
EACH  PART  NUMBER  23-34567

FOUR  EACH  REPEAT  FOUR  EACH  PART  NUM-
BER  23  8707

FOUR  EACH  REPEAT  FOUR  EACH  PART  NUM-
BER  23  8710

ABOVE  NOT  REPEAT  NOT  AVAILABLE  LOCAL
ECONOMY

NO  FISHING  LUCK  AT  ALL

ACKNOWLEDGE

TEX
```

"Parrot" was the code name of the Lodestar. "Couth" was
Mr. Ralph Stevenson, the Cultural Attaché of the American
Embassy in Montevideo. "Carioca" was Rio de Janeiro. And
"Birdcage" was the U.S. Army Air Corps base in Pôrto Alegre, Brazil. "No Fishing Luck" meant that no ship even suspected of being a German replenishment vessel had
appeared on the radar screen.

"'Urgently require,' Chief?" Clete asked.

"If I don't say 'urgently' they'll send it in time for Christmas 1945. There's no problem with the radar, skipper. Stein
is just being careful. Even Urgent, though, it takes two
weeks at least to fly parts down in the diplomatic pouch to
the Embassy, and a couple of more days before Lieutenant
Pelosi can get them out here."

Clete nodded his understanding.

"Looks fine, Chief," he said. "Send it."

"Aye, aye, Sir."

"Hey, honey, we have to get back," Clete called to Dorotéa. With obvious reluctance, she laid the .45 down.

VIII

[ONE]
**The Embassy of the German Reich
Avenue Córdoba
Buenos Aires, Argentina
0815 3 May 1943**

The moment Ambassador von Lutzenberger appeared for work, Fräulein Ingebord Hassell followed him into his office. He sat down at his desk and then looked up at her.

"Excellency," Fräulein Hassell said, "there is a Most Urgent, Most Secret from Berlin."

"Who did the decryption?"

"I did, Excellency."

He held his hand out for it. She gave it to him, took a step backward, and folded her hands over her stomach, awaiting her orders.

```
CLASSIFICATION: MOST URGENT

CONFIDENTIALITY: MOST SECRET

DATE: 24 APRIL 1943

FROM: FOREIGN MINISTER
```

TO: IMMEDIATE AND PERSONAL ATTENTION
OF THE REICH AMBASSADOR TO ARGENTINA
BUENOS AIRES

HEIL HITLER!

RECEIPT OF YOUR MOST SECRET OF 20
APRIL 1943 IN RE THE DEATHS OF
STANDARTENFÜHRER GOLTZ AND OBERST
GRÜNER IS ACKNOWLEDGED AND HAS BEEN
RECEIVED WITH THE GRAVEST CONCERN.
THE SITUATION IS BEING EVALUATED AT
THE HIGHEST LEVELS OF THE GOVERN-
MENT.

AT THE REQUEST OF GENERALFELDMAR-
SCHALL KEITEL, REICHSFÜHRER-SS HIM-
MLER HAS SECONDED SS-OBERFÜHRER
MANFRED VON DEITZBERG TO THE OBER-
KOMMANDO DER WEHRMACHT, WHERE HE
WILL SERVE AS GENERALMAJOR OF THE
GENERAL STAFF. FELDMARSCHALL KEITEL,
REICHSLEITER BORMANN, REICHSFÜHRER
HIMMLER AND I ARE AGREED THAT GEN-
ERALMAJOR VON DEITZBERG WILL SUPER-
VISE THE INVESTIGATION OF THIS
INCIDENT. VON DEITZBERG WILL PROCEED
TO BUENOS AIRES IN THIS CAPACITY ON
THE NEXT LUFTHANSA FLIGHT. DEPUTY
FOREIGN MINISTER GEORG VON LÖWZER
AND STANDARTENFÜHRER ERICH RASCHNER
WILL TRAVEL TO BUENOS AIRES AT THE
SAME TIME.

ADDITIONALLY, WITH THE CONCURRENCE
OF ADMIRAL CANARIS, I HAVE DESIG-
NATED KORVETTENKAPITÄN KARL BOLTITZ

AS NAVAL ATTACHÉ AND HE WILL PROCEED
TO BUENOS AIRES AS SOON AS CERTAIN
ADMINISTRATIVE MATTERS CAN BE CON-
CLUDED.

THE PRESENCE IN BERLIN OF FIRST SEC-
RETARY GRADNY-SAWZ, MAJOR FREIHERR
VON WACHTSTEIN AND STURMBANNFÜHRER
VON TRESMARCK OF THE EMBASSY OF THE
GERMAN REICH IN MONTEVIDEO WILL BE
REQUIRED IN THIS REGARD. YOU ARE
DIRECTED TO ADVISE THE GERMAN AMBAS-
SADOR IN MONTEVIDEO, AND TO ARRANGE
FOR THESE OFFICERS THE HIGHEST PRI-
ORITY FOR TRAVEL TO BERLIN ON THE
NEXT LUFTHANSA FLIGHT.

IT IS PRESENTLY INTENDED THAT THESE
OFFICERS WILL BE RETURNED TO THEIR
POSTS AS SOON AS POSSIBLE.

AT THE DIRECTION OF THE FÜHRER.

VON RIBBENTROP, FOREIGN MINISTER OF
THE GERMAN REICH.

If she were a man, von Lutzenberger thought for the five
hundredth time, *she would make an excellent Stabsfeldwebel*—Regimental Sergeant Major.

He read it carefully, without expression.

It was more or less what von Lutzenberger had expected.
The only good news was that he himself had not been
ordered to Berlin—an order that would have carried with it
the powerful suggestion that he was being held responsible
for the deaths of Goltz and Grüner, or, worse, the failed
attempt to smuggle the Operation Phoenix "special cargo"
into Argentina.

That good news could change, of course, when Gradny-Sawz, von Tresmarck, and von Wachtstein were questioned by the SS—probably by Himmler himself.

He thought a moment about the specific ways the good news could become bad.

Gradny-Sawz, for starters, now believed that von Wachtstein had nothing to do with how the Americans learned the details of the "special shipment" landing; but if it looked to him as if he were himself under deep suspicion, a man who had betrayed his country would have no compunctions about throwing someone to the wolves—anyone: von Tresmarck, von Deitzberg, von Wachtstein, or even Ambassador Graf Manfred Alois von Lutzenberger.

As for von Tresmarck, von Lutzenberger knew very little about him except that he was SS, and that meant that he would be perfectly willing to point his finger at anyone at all, to divert it from being pointed at him.

It was bad news pure and simple that von Ribbentrop was sending von Löwzer, a dangerous man and, even worse, a devout Nazi.

It was even worse news that they had chosen to send von Deitzberg, a far more dangerous Nazi, even though it had to be expected that the hierarchy would send someone from the SS to conduct an investigation.

The naval officer was obviously one of Canaris's agents, and was probably going to take over Grüner's Abwehr intelligence functions. And von Deitzberg's deputy, Raschner, was almost certainly going to take over Grüner's Sicherheitsdienst responsibilities.

Somebody—probably Canaris—had recognized that it had been a mistake for Grüner to serve as both the senior Sicherheitsdienst officer and the Abwehr's resident agent under cover of his military attaché function. Not only was it too much responsibility for one man, but the Abwehr liked to keep an eye on the Sicherheitsdienst, and vice versa, and that was impossible if both offices were held by the same man.

Of course, come to think of it, it is entirely possible that von Deitzberg's primary mission might be to make sure the

*next attempt to smuggle the "special cargo" into Argentina
is successful. Despite what the message said.*

*Speculation is useless. I will know what they are after only
after they arrive.*

He looked up at Fräulein Hassell. "Ingebord, is Herr
Gradny-Sawz in the Embassy?"

"Not yet, Sir. The First Secretary normally arrives at nine."

"And Major von Wachtstein?"

"The Herr Major will probably come at the same time,
Excellency."

"As soon as they find time to come to work, would you
ask them to see me immediately, Ingebord?"

"Jawohl, Excellency."

Fräulein Hässell left the Ambassador's office and immediately telephoned Peter von Wachtstein. He sounded sleepy
when he answered, as if he had just gotten up or was still in
bed.

She told him the Ambassador wanted to see him immediately.

She liked the young Pomeranian. She did not like First
Secretary Gradny-Sawz, and did not telephone his apartment.

[TWO]

Anton von Gradny-Sawz arrived at five minutes to nine. He
was forty-five, tall, almost handsome (with a full head of
luxuriant reddish-brown hair), and somewhat overweight
(von Lutzenberger privately thought of him as *Die grosse
Wienerwurst*—the Big Vienna Sausage).

As he stepped into von Lutzenberger's office, he raised his
right arm at the elbow. "Heil Hitler," he said. "Good morning, Excellency."

Von Lutzenberger returned the salute and the greeting.

Converts to National Socialism, von Lutzenberger

thought, *are something like converts to Catholicism: more Catholic than the Pope.*

"We have heard from Berlin, Anton," von Lutzenberger said, handing him the message. "Read this while we wait for von Wachtstein."

"They want us in Berlin," Gradny-Sawz said as he was reading the message.

Figured that out by yourself, did you?

"I suggested that either you or I might be helpful to explain what happened in Berlin," von Lutzenberger said. "They apparently feel that you could do that best. You and von Wachtstein. I have no idea what von Tresmarck—"

He interrupted himself. "Ah, there you are, von Wachtstein."

Major Freiherr Hans-Peter von Wachtstein (whom von Lutzenberger often thought could have been a model for an SS recruiting poster) gave a crisp Nazi salute, his right arm fully extended.

"Heil Hitler!" he barked.

Von Lutzenberger returned the salute.

"When you're through with that, Anton," he said, "let von Wachtstein see it." He turned to von Wachtstein. "Two questions, Peter. How soon can you fly to Montevideo? And how much luggage can you carry in that little airplane of yours?"

"There is room for one small suitcase behind the passenger's seat, Excellency."

"That's all?"

"The passenger might be able to hold a larger suitcase on his lap, Excellency, but it would not be comfortable."

"Here you are, Peter," Gradny-Sawz said, handing him the message. He then added, "That's a nice suit. New?"

"Thank you, Herr Baron," von Wachtstein said. "Yes, it is. Señor Duarte introduced me to his tailor."

"You'll have to give me his name," Gradny-Sawz said.

"Of course," von Wachtstein said, then read the message.

It was what he had expected, and he had steeled himself for the official notice.

Being prepared did no good. He felt a pain in his stomach.

I don't think Gradny-Sawz believes I have any responsi-

bility for what happened on the beach, and von Lutzenberger has done what he could to reinforce that belief. Or is that just wishful thinking?

Von Tresmarck doesn't have any reason to think I'm involved, either, but he is going to start shitting his pants when the SS questions him. He's lost Goltz as his protector. If they start suggesting that I had some responsibility, he'll go along with anything they say, just so long as it diverts attention from him.

And not only because of what happened on the beach: He doesn't want to wind up in Sachsenhausen with a pink triangle pinned to his shirt. (Homosexuals in concentration camps were required to wear a pink triangle.)

"I want you to go to Montevideo and bring von Tresmarck here," von Lutzenberger said, "as soon as possible. I don't know when the Condor will arrive, but I wouldn't be surprised if it is already en route."

"Jawohl, Excellency."

"How soon can you leave?"

Von Wachtstein looked at his wristwatch. "With a little luck, Excellency, I could probably make it over there and back today, Sir."

"Tomorrow morning will be soon enough for your return," von Lutzenberger said. "Von Tresmarck will need time to settle his affairs and pack. I'm going to give you a note to Ambassador Schulker, explaining all this."

"*All* this, Excellency?" Gradny-Sawz asked.

"So much of *all this,* Anton, as pertains to bringing von Tresmarck here for the flight to Berlin." He turned to von Wachtstein again. "Could you put him up, Peter? Or shall I arrange a hotel room for him?"

"There's plenty of room in my apartment, sir, and I would be happy to put him up. But it might be awkward vis-à-vis the Duartes."

"How so?"

"I am often invited to dine with the Duartes, and I'm not sure their invitations would include him."

"Anton?" von Lutzenberger asked.

Gradny-Sawz didn't reply for a moment. He was always

very careful when asked for an opinion. "My first reaction, Excellency," he finally said, "if you agree, is that von Wacht-stein's relationship with the Duartes is so important—"

"Vis-à-vis Operation Phoenix, you mean, Anton?"

"Yes, sir. I believe the Anglo-Argentine Bank can be very useful to us in carrying out Operation Phoenix. And Hum-berto Duarte is Managing Director of the Anglo-Argentine Bank." (In Argentine business, managing directors carried out the functions of presidents in American business.)

"Yes," von Lutzenberger said. "We wouldn't want them to think we were forcing anyone on them, would we—particu-larly an SS officer?"

"Not, I respectfully suggest, Excellency, if we can avoid that by putting up von Tresmarck in a hotel."

Von Lutzenberger appeared to be thinking that over. He wanted Gradny-Sawz to remember (in case he was asked by either von Löwzer, von Deitzberg, or Boltitz) that it was he who had recommended that von Tresmarck stay in a hotel rather than in von Wachtstein's apartment. "I think you are probably right, Anton," he said finally. "Put him in a good hotel—the Alvear, if you can. Or the Plaza."

"I'll see to it, Excellency," Gradny-Sawz said.

"And what, Herr Baron," von Wachtstein asked, "should I tell Sturmbannführer von Tresmarck?"

Gradny-Sawz again looked uncomfortable.

Von Wachtstein pressed the issue. "He's sure to ask, Herr Baron," he added reasonably.

"I would think, wouldn't you, Excellency," Gradny-Sawz finally replied, "that there would be little harm in telling von Tresmarck that the three of us are being summoned to Berlin to assist both the Foreign Ministry and the SS in their evalu-ation of the unfortunate events on the beach?"

"Tell him, von Wachtstein," von Lutzenberger said, "that all you know is that you're all being sent to Berlin, and that it self-evidently has something to do with 'the unfortunate events on the beach.' "

"Yes, Sir."

"How soon can you leave, Peter?" von Lutzenberger asked.

"It'll take me an hour, maybe a little longer, to drive to my apartment, pack a small bag, and get out to El Palomar," von Wachtstein said. "When I flew it over the weekend, the Storch had a little compass problem, but that should have been taken care of by now. . . ."

"Where did you go over the weekend?" Gradny-Sawz asked.

"I made a small training flight, to keep up my piloting skills, Herr Baron, and just coincidentally found myself over Estancia Santo Catalina, where, by another coincidence, Señor and Señora Duarte happened to be."

"Good for you!" Gradny-Sawz said. "And was there a chance to discuss investments?"

"I didn't want to be too obvious, Herr Baron. I share your opinion that it is a delicate relationship that must be carefully nurtured."

"Make sure you pay your respects before we go to Berlin."

"Of course, Herr Baron."

"You said something about a compass problem with the aircraft?" von Lutzenberger asked.

"A minor problem, Excellency. Probably a loose wire or corroded terminals. It should be repaired by now."

"Don't be too sure. This is Argentina," von Lutzenberger said.

Von Wachtstein chuckled, then went on: "At the very latest, I should clear Argentine customs and immigration, and get off the ground, by one-thirty or two o'clock. It's an hour, or a little more, to Montevideo, depending on the winds."

"Make sure the airplane is in perfect condition, von Wachtstein," von Lutzenberger said. "I really would rather not have to tell Berlin that you have disappeared into the Río Plate."

"I will make very sure it is as safe to fly as possible, Sir."

"If I can get through by telephone to Ambassador Schulker, I'll tell him to have someone waiting for you at the airport from two-thirty," von Lutzenberger said.

"Thank you, Sir."

"Give me a minute to dictate a note to Fräulein Hassell, and then you can be on your way."

"Yes, Sir."

"Have Loche follow you to your apartment and then take you out to the field," von Lutzenberger ordered. "Then you won't have to leave your car out there."

"That's very kind of you, Sir," Peter said, and left the office, hoping that no one—especially the Big Sausage (as he, too, thought of him)—had sensed his annoyance with the Ambassador's kindly gesture. The last thing he wanted right now was Günther Loche breathing down his neck.

Günther, a muscular, crew-cut-blond twenty-two-year-old, was an ethnic German—he had been born in Argentina to German immigrant parents and was an Argentine citizen—who was employed by the German Embassy as driver to the Military Attaché.

He—and his parents—saw Adolf Hitler as the greatest man of the twentieth century, and National Socialism as the hope of mankind. From the moment Günther had first seen von Wachtstein, he knew he had found his idol in life, a Luftwaffe fighter pilot who had received the Knight's Cross of the Iron Cross from the hands of the Führer himself.

Günther's worship had been bad enough when he had been Grüner's driver, but it was worse now that Grüner had nobly given his life for the Fatherland (which Günther had never seen) and the Herr Major Freiherr was acting as Military Attaché.

If I let him, Peter thought, *he would sleep on the rug outside my bedroom door, like an Alsatian.*

Peter had to tell Cletus Frade about the message from Germany, and having Günther around was going to complicate that.

Peter walked down the corridor from von Lutzenberger's office to his own, mentally repeating *von Deitzberg–Raschner–von Löwzer–Boltitz; von Deitzberg–Raschner–von Löwzer–Boltitz; von Deitzberg–Raschner–von Löwzer–Boltitz,* over and over.

Günther was sitting in a chair in the corridor outside Grüner's office—now temporarily Peter's. He stood up when he saw Peter, coming almost to attention. "Guten morgen, Herr Major Freiherr," he said.

Peter smiled and held up his hand to signal him to wait. He went into his office, sat down at Grüner's desk, and quickly scribbled "von Deitzberg–Raschner–von Löwzer–Boltitz" on a notepad.

He exhaled audibly in relief that his concentration had not been broken. Then he tore off the sheet of paper, as well as the eight sheets beneath it, folded them, and put them in his pocket.

"Günther!"

Günther appeared immediately. "Yes, Sir?"

"In five minutes, I will drive my car to my apartment and pack a small bag," Peter announced. "You will then drive me to El Palomar."

"Jawohl, Herr Major."

"Tomorrow, you will be at El Palomar at eleven o'clock to meet me when I return."

"Jawohl, Herr Major."

"I may be delayed by unforeseen circumstances. If I am, I will attempt to leave word at the embassy. If I am not at El Palomar by one o'clock, you will call the embassy and see if there is any word from me. If there is not, you will call the embassy every hour to see if I have called. If I have not, you may leave El Palomar at dark. You understand?"

"Jawohl, Herr Major Freiherr," Günther said, and waited for further orders.

"Now you may either drive to my apartment now, and wait for me, or follow me there when I'm finished here. Whichever you prefer."

Günther looked uncomfortable. "Whichever the Herr Major would prefer for me to do, Herr Major."

"Then go now. Then we won't have to worry about losing one another in traffic."

"Jawohl, Herr Major," Günther said. He clicked his heels, raised his hand in salute, and barked, "Heil Hitler!"

"Heil Hitler!" Peter repeated, and returned the salute crisply.

Is there something in the German character that makes us happy to receive orders—the more detailed, the better—and to comply with them precisely and without question? And, on the other hand, makes us uncomfortable when a decision is required?

When Günther had closed the door behind him, Peter took the sheets of notepaper from his jacket pocket, and then filled in the first names and ranks and titles and associations.

Then he composed his message to Cletus.

---

2 May 10 am

Bagman, Sausage and I ordered to Berlin on next Lufthansa flight, probably within 72 hours. Condor will bring here SS Oberführer Manfred von Deitzberg in uniform of Army General Staff Generalmajor, Standartenführer Erich Raschner, and Deputy Foreign Minister Georg von Löwzer. Korvettenkapitän Karl Boltitz, Abwehr, will follow later to be Naval Attaché. Hope to see you soon. Fritz.

He read it carefully to make sure it contained everything, then smiled, wondering what quaintly American code names Clete would assign to the newcomers.

"Bagman" was von Tresmarck, a reference to his function as the man taking money to ransom Jews from concentration camps; Clete had told him it was American slang for a gangster collecting bribes. Because he had told Cletus that von Lutzenberger called Gradny-Sawz "Die Grosse Wienerwurst," he was "Sausage." He had signed himself "Fritz," not only because that's what Cletus called him when he was angry, but also because his official code name, "Galahad," made him uncomfortable.

Sir Galahad, an honorable knight, had lived by the code of chivalry. His name seemed inappropriate for an officer who was consciously betraying his oath of allegiance and his country.

Günther was waiting outside his apartment, standing by the Embassy Mercedes, obviously relishing the right Corps

Diplomatique license plates gave him to ignore the No Parking signs on Avenida Pueyrredón.

Peter parked his own car in the basement garage, climbed the stairs to the lobby, and motioned through the plate-glass lobby window for Günther to wait for him, then rode the elevator to his apartment.

He quickly packed a uniform—he didn't think he would need it, but you never could tell—and a change of linen in a small bag. Then he went into the kitchen and took from a cabinet a small, cheap, patent-leather purse still in its original box. From another cabinet he took a three-inch-wide roll of bright red ribbon with waving rows of sequins glued on it.

He went back to his bedroom, opened the purse, and inserted the sheets of notepaper, then two large open ended wrenches. He closed the purse, then ripped off a fifteen-foot length from the roll of sequined ribbon, wrapped it firmly around the purse, and tied it. Next he took a flight suit from a hanger in his closet and, not without difficulty, managed to stuff the purse into the pocket on the lower right leg.

He picked up his small satchel, draped the flight suit over his arm, and started to leave the apartment; but then he remembered he had not left a note telling the maid he would be out of town overnight.

To hell with it. I'll have Günther come back here and tell her. It will give him something to do.

Günther saw him getting off the elevator and almost ran into the lobby to carry the Herr Major's luggage.

When he reached for the flight suit, Peter told him he would take it himself.

Then he got in the backseat. Günther closed the door, slid behind the wheel, and started for the airfield.

An hour later, Peter sat in the Feiseler Storch at the threshold of El Palomar's Runway Three Six, now wearing the flight suit over his shirt and trousers. The suit jacket was with the satchel, strapped to the backseat.

He was about to tell El Palomar he was rolling, when he remembered the purse. Getting it out of the pocket in the air would be a bitch.

After another struggle, he managed to tug it loose. He then rolled the red sequined tape into a neat tube and fastened everything to his lap with the seat belt. He picked up the microphone. "El Palomar, German Embassy One rolling," he called in Spanish. He shoved the throttle forward, and the Storch began to move. There was no need to worry about the flaps. He had all the runway he needed.

"Auf Wiedersehen, Herr Major von Wachtstein. Have a nice flight," the tower replied in German. In *good* German.

He picked up the microphone again. "Dankeschön."

Another ethnic German, obviously, is working in the control tower. The German was perfect. A little soft, so probably a Bavarian, or maybe a Swabian. And another Argentino-German who thinks Hitler is a splendid all-around fellow. An anti-Nazi Argentino-German would not have offered the cordial farewell to a Luftwaffe officer.

He felt life come into the controls, raised the tail wheel, and then let the plane take itself off. He flew to the Río Plate, then headed south.

Thirty minutes later, he was over Estancia San Pedro y San Pablo. He dropped to 500 meters, cranked in some flaps, and dropped to 250.

On his first pass over the radio station, he thought he saw someone in the open; but he wasn't sure, and he wanted to be sure. He stood the Storch on its left wing, turned, and made another pass. This time two men were in the open, looking up at him.

He flew level for a moment, while he pushed the upper half of the left-side window upward until it engaged the catches on the lower side of the wing. The slipstream caught the roll of tape in his lap and started to suck it out the window, but the seat belt held the purse in place.

He stood the airplane on its wing again and flew back toward the radio station. He pulled the throttle back so he was just above stall speed, and when he came very close to the men on the ground, he freed the purse from the seat belt and threw it out the window.

He applied throttle, dumped the flaps, and turned a final time to fly over the radio station to make sure they had the

purse. One of the men on the ground was waving at him to
show that they did.

He turned toward Estancia Santo Catalina. "Now comes
the tough part," he said aloud.

He remembered reading in a book about the American
Civil War what the Southern general Lee had said before
going out to surrender to the United States general, the one
who later became president, Grant: "I would rather die a
thousand deaths . . ."

"I know just how you felt, General Lee," he said aloud.

Alicia Carzino-Cormano was waiting for him—out of
breath, as if she had run to the airstrip when she heard the
sound of his engine.

Even before he climbed out of the airplane, she knew
there was bad news; and by the time he shut it down, she had
decided what it was. "When do they want you to go to Germany?" she asked.

"Very soon. In three or four days."

"If you loved me, you would go to Brazil."

"If I went to Brazil, my father would be shot."

"And they're not going to shoot you?"

He managed a smile and a light tone in his voice. "I don't
think anytime soon," he said. "I should be back in a month
or six weeks. Maybe even sooner."

She looked into his eyes. "You believe that?"

I wish I did. He nodded his head.

"If you believe that, I will believe that," she said. She
threw herself into his arms.

"We'll be OK, my precious," he said.

"Can you spend the night?" she asked against his chest.

"I have to leave right now for Montevideo."

"And when will you be back from Montevideo?"

"Tomorrow."

"I'll go to Buenos Aires tonight, or in the morning," she
said.

"Your mother may—"

She shrugged her shoulders impatiently, almost violently,
indicating that he should know that what her mother thought

or wanted was not important. "When you get back, call me at the house."

He nodded, and stroked her hair.

He very much wanted to cry.

And until I met her, I didn't think there was such a thing as love.

[THREE]
Estancia San Pedro y San Pablo
Near Pila, Buenos Aires Province
1220 3 May 1943

Cletus Frade, deep in thought, sat at the crest of a gentle rise astride Julius Caesar, a very large, magnificently formed black stallion. His mind jumped from one thought to another.

Next week this time, I'll be a married man.

Why did I give in to Claudia and that damned Jesuit and agree to have that goddamned Juan Domingo Perón at my wedding? A dirty old man who fucks little girls doesn't belong at a goddamn wedding.

By now Ashton's in Rio de Janeiro. I really hope I was right, and that he'll be on the next Panagra flight down clutching a diplomatic passport in his hand. I need him.

Jesus, this place isn't only enormous, they haven't touched the potential. All they do with it is raise enough food to feed themselves and let the cattle graze until they're ready to be slaughtered. That takes two years, maybe longer. This is farmland, not grazing land. What I should do is put in some feed crops. I can probably produce marketable beef in fourteen months.

God, I wish Uncle Jim was here. He'd really know what to do with this place.

There's an airport at Bariloche, and what's supposed to be the best resort hotel in Argentina. There's no reason I can't take Dorotéa there in the Lodestar.

It's too far to drive. It would take two days. It's twenty hours or something on the train. I can fly the Lodestar out there in four hours.

And if I go there in the Lodestar and something happens here, I can get back in a hurry.

Tragedy in Argentina. On the day after his marriage, Marine Aviator with Wings of Gold C. Frade flies himself and bride into a rock-filled cloud . . .

Enrico Rodríguez, astride a sorrel with brilliant eyes, his Browning shotgun cradled in his arm, was also deep in thought.

Julius Caesar, now docilely munching grass, had been el Coronel's favorite, and vice versa. Whenever anyone else tried to mount him, he was unruly, often successfully throwing the stranger. He had even tried to throw Señor Cletus the first time he mounted him.

He had not. Señor Cletus was almost as fine a horseman as his father. And Julius Caesar now seemed to understand he had a new master. At the stables, Enrico had stood stock-still while Señor Clete threw the sheepskin saddle and the hornless Recado saddle on the horse, and even when Señor Cletus had tugged hard at the tack, shortening the stirrups to the length norteamericanos preferred (for reasons Enrico did not understand), Julius Caesar had allowed it.

It usually took two men to get a saddle on Julius Caesar.

Enrico was not surprised that Señor Cletus had come out here to think. El Coronel also often rode slowly out onto the pampas under God's wide blue sky and stopped somewhere just to think. The longer he was around Señor Cletus, the more he saw how much he was like el Coronel.

In the important things.

There was not much of a physical resemblance. In these Señor Clete favored his mother.

Enrico took pleasure in the thought that el Coronel and Señor Clete's mother were together again in heaven with the blessed angels, and with Mariana Maria Dolores taking care of them there, as he was now taking care of Señor Clete in this life.

He believed that God always had a purpose, although that purpose had not been clear to him when God let those filthy bastards cut Mariana Maria Dolores's throat in Señor Guillermo's house by the Hipódromo.

And God's purpose had not been clear, either, when He let those filthy bastards kill el Coronel in the car. And he had had real trouble trying to understand why God had not let him die with el Coronel. Or even instead of him.

Now he knew. God in his infinite wisdom had put a baby in the belly of Señor Clete's blond woman. She wasn't a real Argentine, but she was half Argentine. As Señor Clete was half Argentine. Their baby would be entirely Argentine.

And that meant that Estancia San Pedro y San Pablo would go on as before, because it was now Señor Clete's home, where he would be married, where his baby would be born; and he would not return to the United States of America, and Estancia San Pedro y San Pablo would not be sold to strangers. Señor Clete would stay here and be el Patrón, as his father and grandfather and great-grandfather before him had been el Patrón, taking loving care of the people of Estancia San Pedro y San Pablo.

And God had sent Enrico a message. The all-knowing God knew that Enrico was shamed that he had failed to save the life of el Coronel, and that with Mariana Maria Dolores taken to heaven, too, he was all alone.

God had permitted him to take the vengeance that was His alone. He brought the German Nazi bastards who had ordered the murder of el Coronel and Mariana Maria Dolores to Samborombón Bay and put them in the glass sight on el Coronel's Mauser (which they had bought together in Berlin), so that he could kill them.

The message was *I know that you are unhappy and lonely, my son, and this is both to show you I understand and that you are part of my plan. Killing the German Nazi bastards is your reward on earth, and if you do your duty, when the time comes, there will be greater rewards in heaven.*

And Enrico understood what his duty was. He was to protect Señor Clete and the blond woman and the baby in her belly, and thus Estancia San Pedro y San Pablo and the good life it gave all the simple people who depended on it.

And he knew his reward when God finally took him to heaven. He would be with Mariana Maria Dolores and el Coronel again and could tell them that the Estancia San Pedro y San Pablo would go on as always.

That had been God's plan all along. He wondered why it had taken him so long to understand.

Enrico was brought back from his thoughts when he detected unusual movement on the pampas. "Señor Cletus," he said softly, and when he had Clete's attention, raised his arm and hand, the index finger extended, and pointed.

One of the Ford Model A pickups was bouncing across the pampas, headed for them.

"Who is that? Rodolfo?"

"I think so, Señor Cletus."

Sargento Rudolpho Gomez, Argentine Cavalry, Retired, pulled up to them three minutes later, got out of the Ford, and approached Clete, taking off his hat as a gesture of respect (all the while carefully staying away from Julius Caesar).

"Patrón, el Jefe asked me to find you," he said.

El Jefe was Chief Radioman Oscar J. Schultz, USN.

Most of the gauchos thought Schultz was very strange, even ludicrous—a man who wore the clothing of a gaucho but never mounted a horse and was visibly afraid of both horses and cattle. Enrico and Rudolpho, however, liked him and would not tolerate disrespect toward him—probably, Clete thought, because they recognized in him a fellow career serviceman.

Once he'd seen Rudolpho pointing a Cavalry sergeant's finger in the face of a gaucho and telling him the next time he laughed at el Jefe he would cut his balls off and feed them to the pigs.

"Did he say what he wanted?" Clete asked.

"No, Patrón. He is at the place."

"Señor Clete, we can take the Ford," Enrico said. "And Rudolpho can take the horses back."

"How far are we from the station? On horseback?"

"Twenty minutes, Señor Clete. And about as long by Ford," Enrico said, then added, "It has been some time since Julius Caesar has had a hard run. Then it would be a little less."

"Where is it from here?" Clete asked. Enrico pointed.

"Let's go for a run, Julius," Clete said, and touched the animal with his heels.

Enrico waited until Clete was out of earshot. "He is very much like el Coronel, may he rest in peace, is he not?"

"Sí," Rudolpho said thoughtfully.

"God has given us the duty of protecting him."

"Sí," Rudolpho repeated.

Enrico made a thumbs-up gesture to Rudolpho and then put his heels to the sorrel and raced after el Patrón.

Julius Caesar was breathing heavily and was spotted white with sweat when Clete rode up to the radio station.

"Beautiful animal, Sir," Lieutenant Madison R. Sawyer III said.

"Yes, he is. What's up, Sawyer? Is the chief here?"

Sawyer pointed to the Chief's Ford and waited for Clete to dismount.

Enrico rode up and slipped gracefully off the sorrel.

"Will you walk him for me, Enrico?" Clete asked.

"Sí, Señor."

"Galahad dropped a message to us about an hour ago," Sawyer said.

Chief Schultz appeared in the door of the house. "That's that vicious sonofabitch who tried to kick me, isn't it?" he asked.

"Nothing personal, Chief, he just doesn't like sailors."

"Thanks a lot. Just keep him away from me, thank you."

"What's the message?"

"He's been ordered to Germany."

"Oh, shit," Clete said. He walked to the building, and Sawyer followed him.

The chief handed him von Wachtstein's message. "Tough luck, huh?" he said when Clete had finished reading it.

"Yeah, that's what it is."

"You think he'll be coming back, skipper?"

"He seems to think there's some chance," Clete said. "We'll need to get this off right away."

The chief looked at his watch. "Skipper," he said, "if you can write it and I can encrypt it in nineteen minutes, we can get it off on the regular schedule."

"I won't be long," Clete said, and sat down at the table in front of the battered Underwood typewriter ("borrowed" by the chief from the radio room of the destroyer). He laid von Wachtstein's note down, then rolled a sheet of paper into the typewriter and started to type. After a few seconds he stopped and turned his head toward Sawyer, who was looking over his shoulder. "You're a man of imagination and culture, Madison," he said. "I need some names for the high-level Krauts who will be coming here."

"Sure."

"One is a deputy foreign minister," Clete said.

Sawyer grunted. "Metternich," he said immediately. "For the diplomat."

Clete chuckled and then typed quickly.

"Who else?" Sawyer asked.

"The SS Brigadier wearing a Wehrmacht uniform," Clete said.

"What's that all about, do you think, skipper?" the chief asked. "He'd rather not have people know he's SS?"

"I suppose," Clete replied.

"Did the wolf in sheep's clothes have a name?" Sawyer asked thoughtfully.

"If he did, I don't have a clue," Clete said. The chief shrugged.

"OK," Sawyer went on. "We have a máscarador—a guy in a mask—South America—What's that name? Got it. Zorro."

"As in 'the mark of'?" Clete replied. "I thought he was a good guy."

"I'm open to suggestion, Sir."

"Zorro it is," Clete said. "Now that I think about it, it has a nice ring to it."

He typed quickly.

"And for Zorro's aide? What was the name of Zorro's sidekick?"

That drew a blank.

"Little Zorro?" Chief Schultz suggested.

"How about Big Z and Little Z," Sawyer suggested.

"Better yet," Clete said, and typed again.

"That leaves the sailor," the chief said.

Clete and Sawyer spoke at the same time. "Popeye," they both said.

Clete typed for a few more seconds, then tore the paper from the typewriter and handed it to the chief.

```
URGENT

TOP SECRET LINDBERGH

DUPLICATION FORBIDDEN

FROM TEX

MSG NO #### TIME TIME GREENWICH 2
MAY 1943

TO ORACLE EYES ONLY AGGIE

1 GALAHAD REPORTS HE, SAUSAGE AND
BAGMAN ORDERED BERLIN PRESUMABLY
REGARDING INQUIRY INTO MARITIME
PROBLEMS. SUSPECT NEXT LUFTHANSA
FLIGHT DUE HERE WITHIN 72 HOURS WITH
DEPARTURE 24 HOURS LATER.

2 FLIGHT FROM BERLIN WILL CARRY GEN-
ERALMAJOR MANFRED VON DEITZBERG,
HEREAFTER BIGZ, STANDARTENFÜHRER
ERICH RASCHNER, HEREAFTER LITTLEZ,
AND DEPUTY FOREIGN MINISTER GEORG
FRIEDRICH VON LÖWZER, HEREAFTER MET-
```

```
TERNICH.    KORVETTENKAPITÄN    KARL
BOLTITZ, HEREAFTER POPEYE, WILL FOL-
LOW ETA UNKNOWN

3 BIGZ IS ACTUALLY OBERFÜHRER-SS AND
HAS BEEN HIMMLER'S ADJUTANT. LITTLEZ
IS  HIS  DEPUTY.  POPEYE  WORKS  FOR
CANARIS.

TEX
```

The chief read it.

"No problem, skipper," he said. "Give me the code book, and let me have the chair. You want to wait until it's acknowledged? There may be something coming in."

"Yeah," Clete said. "I don't suppose you'd have a cold beer?"

"Dorotéa!" the chief called loudly. "Cerveza, por favor."

A moment later, Dorotéa, the chief's "housekeeper," a widow of the estancia, came into the room with two bottles of beer in each hand.

Dorotéa doesn't know about Dorotéa, Clete thought. *I wonder how she's going to react when she finds out.*

He took two beers from her and went outside to give Enrico one.

There was no traffic from the States for them.

He got another couple of beers from Dorotéa, mounted Julius Caesar, and started in a walk back toward the Big House.

[FOUR]
1500 Meters Above the River Plate
Near Montevideo, Uruguay
1540 2 May 1943

The coastline of Uruguay was at first just a blur on the horizon, but then it began to take form as the small airplane neared the end of its flight over the 125-mile-wide mouth of the River Plate. Major Freiherr Hans-Peter von Wachtstein turned the nose of the Ficscler slightly, to point toward a rise in the coastline that he suspected was the old-fort-on-the-hill overlooking the harbor. A minute or two later, now positively identifying the fort, he reached above his head without looking and adjusted the trim tab to put the Storch into a gentle descent, then retarded the throttle a hair.

He looked at the Feiseler's fuel gauges and saw that he had more than an hour's fuel remaining. He glanced at the elapsed-time dials on his wristwatch, a Hamilton chronometer that had once belonged to a B-26 pilot who had gotten unlucky over France, and saw that he had been in the air two hours and fourteen minutes.

In the detailed records of the Luftwaffe, the downing of an American B-26 aircraft over Cherbourg was Peter's twenty-second victory. He had received the Knight's Cross of the Iron Cross from the Bavarian Corporal himself after his twenty-fifth victory, and his total was now up to thirty-two downed aircraft.

An asshole from the SS had come to the airfield three days after he'd shot down the B-26 and handed him the watch. He had taken it from the pilot of the B-26, he said, and thought Herr Freiherr Wachtstein would like to have it.

Stealing from prisoners of war was a clear violation of the Rules of Land Warfare; and in a better world, the American pilot would not only have gotten his Hamilton back, with the apologies of the Luftwaffe, but the SS asshole who had stolen it from him would have been brought before a Court of Honor and stripped of his commission.

But that wasn't going to happen, and Peter knew it. He could have told the SS asshole what he thought of him, and where he could stick the watch, but that would have meant that the SS asshole would have kept it to wear himself. So he had taken it, which at least kept it off the wrist of the SS Scheisskopf (shithead).

At the time, he had felt a little sorry for the B-26 pilot, who would have to spend the rest of the war in a POW camp. Now he was jealous. If you were a prisoner of war—and took your officer's honor seriously—all you had to do was try to escape.

Living in a POW camp in Montana or Wyoming or some other place in the United States, with no greater problem than trying to escape, seemed to be a splendid way to spend the rest of the war—especially compared to what he was doing now.

Among other things, POWs were released at the end of a war and could go home to the women waiting for them.

Argentina had interned the German officers from the *Graf Spee* in hotels in Villa General Belgrano in Córdoba Province; and they—on orders from Germany—had given their word as officers and gentlemen that they would not attempt to escape. That meant that they spent their days playing cards or tennis, or watching the grass grow. Some of them had actually taken up polo. Patriotic Argentino-Germans, doing their bit for the Fatherland, regularly visited them, bringing them *Apfel strudel, Knockwurst, Kassler ripchen,* and other little things to remind them of home.

Once a month, an officer from the Germany Embassy went to Villa General Belgrano to settle their hotel bills and give them their pay (Peter had flown Gradny-Sawz there in the Storch ten days before).

He had made the mistake of telling Alicia about the officers in Villa General Belgrano. And she had taken from that the obvious inference: All he had to do was go to Brazil and turn himself in, and he would be out of the war. She immediately saw herself visiting him on Sunday afternoons in a Brazilian version of the internment hotels, maybe with a picnic basket full of fruit and fried chicken.

Even putting aside the question of the trouble his desertion itself would cause for his father, there were serious problems connected with the OSS.

Specifically, there was no way it would not come to their attention. And the OSS maintained an Order of Battle, knew that he was his father's son, and would try to use that, even if they didn't know—or suspect—that his father was part of the small group of German officers who had decided that the only solution to Germany's problems was the assassination of Adolf Hitler.

Clete knew, of course. But Clete had given his word that he would not tell the OSS. And Peter believed him. So what did that make Clete? At least an officer willfully disobeying an order, and at worst, maybe some sort of traitor himself.

The war had once seemed so simple. When he'd been with the Condor Legion in Spain, it had been easy—and even pleasant—to think of himself as a latter-day Teutonic knight.

By day he brought death, in noble aerial combat, to godless Communists, and spent his nights half-drunk in the beds of women he now remembered only by the shape of their bodies, having long forgotten most of their names.

It had also been that way in Russia—except that there had been very few women—until he saw what the Einsatzgruppen were doing, and was shamed as an officer and as a German. (The Einsatzgruppen—literally "Task Forces"—were the SS mobile death squads that followed the German regular army into Poland and Russia and were charged with exterminating undesirables.)

Montevideo was now clearly in sight. On an impulse, he turned slightly away so that he could come in over the ship channel and maybe see the sunken hulk of the *Graf Spee*.

At first he thought he'd failed, but then he could make out parts of her masts rising from the murky waters where she had been scuttled.

As he turned his nose northward, he wondered why he had bothered. There was something sad about a sunken ship. And he had seen the hulk of the *Graf Spee* before.

He had also seen the grave of her captain. Langsdorff had put on a fresh uniform, carefully arranged the *Graf Spee*'s battle flag on the floor, and then stood in a position so that his corpse would fall on the flag after he had blown his brains out.

He wanted to leave the message that he had scuttled his ship to save the lives of his men, rather than because he was personally afraid of dying. The way to prove that was to kill himself.

That was something his father would understand, Peter knew . . . something Generalleutnant von Wachtstein would, in the same circumstances, do himself.

Major von Wachtstein wasn't sure if the act was heroic or cowardly. Or even worse, stupid. The more he thought about it, the more he realized that it would have taken more balls to stay alive and be accused of cowardice than to put a pistol in your mouth.

He flew over the old fort at the mouth of the harbor, close enough to see its battlements and ramparts and the old muzzle-loading cannon still pointing seaward, and then turned north. The altimeter showed 510 meters. He let it drop to a precise 500, then flew along the Rambla, just far enough out to sea so the black cross on the fuselage and the swastika on the vertical stabilizer couldn't be seen by the people sitting in the sidewalk cafés along the beach.

Both he and the Storch were diplomatically accredited to the governments of both Argentina and Uruguay, and flying between the two countries was perfectly legal, but he knew there was no sense in stirring up the natives.

In five minutes, he could see the hotel and gambling casino at Carrasco, and a minute after that, the runways and hangars of the airport. He turned the nose landward, flew over the villas and small business section of Carrasco, and then to the airport on its outskirts.

As he flew over the airport to have a look at the windsock, he saw a canary-yellow 1941 Chevrolet convertible parked at the terminal building. He knew the car. It belonged to Sturmbannführer Werner von Tresmarck, who had bought it to keep Frau Ingebord von Tresmarck happy. Peter knew that Ingebord von Tresmarck, for a number of reasons, was able to get from her husband just about anything she wanted.

He wasn't surprised to see the car. Ambassador von Lutzenberger had said he would try to let Ambassador Schulker know he was coming. As the Montevideo embassy's security officer, von Tresmarck would be the officer Schulker would send to meet an officer whose purpose in coming to Montevideo von Lutzenberger had been unwilling to discuss on the telephone.

As Peter taxied the Storch to the transient-aircraft ramp, two cars followed him—a 1937 Ford Fordor and the yellow convertible Chevrolet. The Ford carried uniformed Uruguayan customs and immigrations officers; in the convertible were von Tresmarck, in civilian clothing, and his wife. Peter had hoped that she wouldn't show up at the airport, but was not surprised that she had.

Peter shut the engine down, made the necessary entries in the flight log—turning his landing at Estancia Santo Catalina into "precautionary landing at Pinamar re: compass problem"—and then climbed out of the airplane.

He peeled off the flight suit, draped it over the cockpit window, then took his suit jacket and suitcase from the backseat. He had just finished pulling his necktie into place and was shrugging into the jacket when he saw that von Tresmarck and the others had walked up to the airplane.

"Heil Hitler!" von Tresmarck said. He was in his forties and sported a neatly clipped full—à la Adolf Hitler—mustache. "How good to see you, Peter!"

Peter raised his right hand from the elbow in a sloppy return of the Nazi salute.

"Herr Sturmbannführer," he said, and smiled at the Uruguayan officials. "Buenas tardes," he said, and handed them his diplomatic passport and his carnet, a small card issued by the Uruguayan government to diplomats. "Frau von Tresmarck," Peter said, smiling at her.

Ingebord von Tresmarck, a tall, slim blonde, perhaps fifteen years younger than her husband, gave him her hand. He bowed his head and clicked his heels.

"It's always a pleasure to see you, Peter," she said.

The taller of the two Uruguayans examined Peter's documents perfunctorily, handed them to the other official, and said: "Welcome to Uruguay. May I ask how long you will be staying, Sir?"

"I'll be leaving tomorrow," Peter said.

The second official returned the documents to him, and both saluted and got back in their Ford.

The three Germans walked to the Chevrolet. Peter held open the passenger door for Frau von Tresmarck. After she got in, he then tried to push the seat back forward so he could climb in the back.

"Don't be silly," she said. "There's plenty of room in front."

Von Tresmarck slipped behind the wheel and started the engine. "The Ambassador, Peter," he said, "said only that you were coming." It was a request for information.

"I have a message from Ambassador von Lutzenberger," Peter said.

"I thought perhaps it might have something to do with . . . that unfortunate business last week."

You bet your ass it does; we're being ordered to Berlin.

"I'm sure the Herr Sturmbannführer understands that I can't discuss the matter," Peter said.

"Of course," von Tresmarck said quickly. "I wasn't trying to pry, Peter."

"Where will I be staying, Herr Sturmbannführer?" Peter asked.

"With us, of course," Frau von Tresmarck said. "We have plenty of room."

Shit!

"That's very gracious of you," Peter said. "But I don't want to impose."

"Nonsense," von Tresmarck said. "You're our good friend, Peter. We wouldn't feel right if you were in a hotel."

"You're very kind," Peter said.

• • •

Ambassador Joachim Schulker raised his eyes from the envelope Peter had just handed him. "Are you familiar with the contents, von Wachtstein?"

"Yes, Sir."

"Did you say anything to Sturmbannführer von Tresmarck?"

"No, Sir, of course not."

"Well, then, I suppose I had better do so, wouldn't you think?"

How the hell am I supposed to reply to that?

"Yes, Sir."

Schulker picked up a silver bell from his desk and shook it. His secretary appeared a moment later at the door. "Will you ask Sturmbannführer von Tresmarck to see me, please?" Schulker asked. Then he looked at Peter. "I almost forgot, von Wachtstein, to congratulate you for your courageous behavior on the beach."

"I tried to do my duty, Excellency."

"There aren't many men who would have your icy courage under fire," Schulker said. "Who would have been so—what shall I say? . . . *visibly unaffected*—when two of their comrades died in such an awful fashion, right beside them."

"It was a very unpleasant incident, Excellency."

"Certainly, after both Standartenführer Goltz and Oberst Grüner were shot in the head, you must have thought you were next. And of course the next shot narrowly missed you, is that not so?" Peter gave an almost imperceptible nod. "Yet you saw to their bodies, carried them to the boat without assistance . . ."

He's been talking to somebody who knows exactly what happened at Puerto Magdalena, not just that Grüner and Goltz were killed. Who? I don't think von Lutzenberger, who would have told me if he had spoken to Schulker. That leaves Gradny-Sawz. Who else knew?

And did I detect a suspicion that it's odd I didn't have my brains blown out when Grüner and Goltz did? Or am I being paranoid?

There was a discreet knock at the door. Schulker looked

up and saw von Tresmarck standing there. "Come in, please, Werner," Schulker said.

Von Tresmarck walked in and gave a stiff-armed Nazi salute. "Heil Hitler," he said. "You wished to see me, Excellency?"

Schulker returned the salute casually.

"They want to see you in Berlin, Werner, in connection with the unfortunate recent incident," Schulker said. "Von Wachtstein will fly you to Buenos Aires in the morning."

Von Tresmarck tried very hard, and almost succeeded, to conceal his reaction to the announcement—terror. "Tomorrow, Excellency?" he asked.

"There is apparently a Lufthansa Condor flight en route to Buenos Aires. You will travel aboard it on its return flight."

"I understand, Excellency," von Tresmarck said.

"That doesn't give you much time," Schulker said.

"Excellency, did they say how long I am to be gone?"

"No, they didn't," Schulker said simply. "You will check in with me in the morning, though, before you leave, won't you?"

"Yes, of course, Excellency."

"There might be another message, or something," Schulker said, and then sat down, making it clear they had been dismissed.

"I'll have to clear my desk here, you understand," von Tresmarck said as they left the ambassador's office, "but there's no reason for you to wait for me. I'll have Inge run you out to the house."

"Wouldn't it be much simpler if I just went to the Casino and got a room?"

"Inge will be glad for your company," von Tresmarck said. "Especially if things don't go as quickly here as I hope they will."

Ingebord von Tresmarck was waiting for them in the foyer of the embassy.

"Take Peter to the house, please, Inge, and make him comfortable," von Tresmarck said. "I may be here awhile, so don't hold dinner for me."

She nodded. "What's going on, Werner?" she asked.

"I don't think it should be discussed in the lobby of the embassy," he said. "Peter will tell you what he can."

"I am not sure, Herr Sturmbannführer, if I am permitted—"

"She will have to be told something, Peter," von Tresmarck said. "Tell her what you think you can, on my authority."

"Jawohl, Herr Sturmbannführer."

Von Tresmarck turned on his heel and walked out of the lobby.

When they reached the Chevrolet, Inge asked Peter to drive. He got behind the wheel and drove toward Carrasco.

"What don't you think you are permitted to tell me?"

"I didn't want you telling him I told you everything," he said.

"You know there are some things I don't tell him," she said. "I don't want to get off the subject, but I am really glad to see you, darling." She leaned over and kissed him on the cheek. Her right hand moved to his upper leg and squeezed him playfully but almost painfully.

"Hey!" he said in surprise and protest.

"So tell me," she said, squeezing him one more time, then moving away from him.

"We've been ordered to Berlin," he said.

"Oh, my God!"

"I don't think there's anything to be worried about," he said.

"You don't think there's anything to be worried about," she parroted sarcastically.

"Considering what happened, it was to be expected that somebody in Berlin would want to talk to both of us, and since they wouldn't want to come here . . ."

"Are you going?" she asked.

"Of course I'm going. I think we'll be back within a month."

"You have the airplane. We could be in Brazil in three hours."

"Inge, calm down," he said.

"Calm down?" she snorted sarcastically. "What kind of a fool are you? What kind of a fool do you think I am?"

"Calm down, Inge," he repeated.

She snorted again but didn't say anything more in the car.

The von Tresmarck house was a medium-size, two-story, red-tile-roofed building two blocks from the casino. When they reached it, he stopped before the closed steel gate to the driveway.

"Leave it," Inge said. "I'll have someone park it and put your bag in your room. What I need is a drink."

He got from behind the wheel and followed her to the house. The large, ornate, varnished wood door opened as they reached it. A middle-aged maid stood there.

"Take the Major's things to the guest room," Inge ordered in heavily German-accented Spanish.

"Sí, Señora. Bienvenido, Señor."

"You're at the end of the corridor to the right," Inge said, gesturing up the stairs.

"Thank you," he said, and extended the Chevrolet keys to her.

She put them in her purse, then pointed to a door. "In there," she said.

It was the sitting. On a heavy wooden table against one wall was an array of bottles.

"What's your pleasure, Señor?" Inge said in her terrible Spanish. "We have English—scotch—and German, and native, and even some American. The local brandy's not at all bad."

"Sounds fine," Peter said.

"Then that's what we'll have," she said, and poured stiff drinks into short, squarish glasses. She handed him his drink and tapped her glass against it. "Prosit, Schatzie," she said.

"Prosit, Inge," he said, and took a swallow.

"Don't look so worried," she said, switching to German, when she had taken a healthy swallow. "I'm calm. OK?"

"Good," he said.

"Are you going to tell me what happened on that beach?

I've tried to get Werner to tell me, but he says he doesn't really know. I don't know whether he really doesn't know, or considers it a state secret."

"I have the feeling he knows," Peter said. "Ambassador Schulker knows, in some detail."

"So tell me. I want to know what he's facing."

"A little later," Peter said. "What I need right now is the toilet, and then a shower."

She looked into his eyes, then nodded. "I was in there this morning," she said. "So I know there's soap and towels."

"Thank you," he said, and drained his glass. She did the same thing, then turned to the table to pour herself another.

When he reached his room, the maid had just finished unpacking his satchel; she then informed him that, with his permission, she would touch up his uniform with an iron.

He thanked her, then waited for her to leave.

He locked the door after her, then undressed and took a shower. When he came out of the bathroom, naked, toweling his hair, to fetch his change of linens, Inge was in the bedroom, wearing a blue dressing gown.

"Oh," she said. "Is that what we're going to do? Play 'You show me yours, and I'll show you mine'? I *loved* playing that when I was a little girl."

She pulled her dressing gown open and then closed it, but not before he saw that she was naked under it.

"This is not smart, Inge," Peter said, quickly wrapping the towel around his waist. "What if he comes home?"

"First he's going to do whatever he has to do at the embassy, and then he's going to go weep on his lover's manly chest," she said. "He won't be home until very late. Not before ten or eleven, anyway. Maybe he won't come home at all. He knows how to find Brazil, too."

"I can't believe you're serious."

"Whatever Werner is, he's not stupid," she said. "One of his options is to obey his orders and go to Berlin. His problem there is that Goltz is dead, which means he doesn't know who now has his Kripo dossier"—Kriminalpolizei, the Criminal Police division of the Gestapo—"the one with all those pictures of him cavorting naked with handsome boys. If that's in the wrong hands, he's liable to be arrested the moment he steps off the plane. And that's even before they get around to asking what happened in Argentina. His other option is to empty the 'special' bank account—and the last time I looked, there was almost a quarter of a million American dollars in it—and put that money somewhere safe, go to Brazil, turn himself in to the Brazilians, or maybe even the Americans, and declare that he is now, after prayerful thought, really opposed to that terrible Adolf Hitler."

Christ, that possibility never entered my mind!

"You think that's possible, Inge?"

"Yes, of course it's possible. You are really terribly naïve, Peter."

"I suppose I am," he said.

"On the other hand, among his other vices, he's both a gambler and greedy."

"I don't understand."

"There's going to be a lot more money in that special account, and he knows it. The more there is, the larger his share. If he went to Brazil, he would have to worry for the rest of his life that the SS would come after him. He may decide to gamble on going to Germany and chancing that his dossier didn't fall into the wrong hands, and that he can credibly deny knowledge of what went wrong in Argentina. Do you think he had anything to do with what happened there?"

"I don't think so."

"The problem with that, of course, is that if he loses, I lose too. On the other hand, I have access to the special account, and can probably make it to Brazil—certainly, if you fly us there in your airplane—and be an even more convincing anti-Nazi than he would."

"I had nothing to do with what happened on the beach—" Peter said.

"Which brings us back to 'what did happen on the beach?' " she interrupted.

"—and if I took you to Brazil, my father would wind up in Sachsenhausen. I can't do that, Inge."

"No, of course not," she said sarcastically. "I keep forgetting you are a gentleman of honor."

"Your husband is too valuable to this ransom operation for anyone to decide he has to go, without damned good reason," Peter said. "And if he doesn't know anything about what happened on the beach, there is no good reason."

"Possibly," she said.

"I think your going to Brazil would be a mistake—at least until you know for certain he's in some sort of trouble."

"How would I know if he was in trouble, with him in Berlin and me here?"

"If someone tried to take control of the special account, or if you were told to come home."

"Home? I don't have a home, or a family, Peter, thanks to the Eighth United States Air Force," she said.

"You can always go to Brazil later," he said.

"This profound conversation is not what I had in mind when I climbed from my balcony to yours," she said.

"It's not? Well, what was on your mind, Inge?" he asked innocently.

She chuckled deep in her throat and walked to him. "You have no idea?" she asked.

"Not the foggiest."

She put her hand under the towel around his waist. "The hell you don't," she cried triumphantly. "Or are you going to try to tell me it's always in that condition?"

"Of course. I'm a Luftwaffe fighter pilot."

She jerked the towel loose and let it fall to the floor. Then, shrugging out of the blue dressing gown, she dropped to her knees and took him in her mouth.

Peter had a sudden mental image of Alicia, and with a massive effort forced it from his mind.

If Inge even suspected someone like Alicia was in my life, she would already be in Brazil. As far as she's concerned, I am the only friend she has in South America. And I probably am. If she went to Brazil, that would be the end of the only window we have onto this obscene ransoming operation. I have to keep her here.

What that means is that I am betraying two women at the same time.

Oh, you're really an officer and a gentleman, Major Frei-herr Hans-Peter von Wachtstein!

"Ouch!"

Inge looked up at him. "Sorry, darling," she said. "The last thing in the world I want to do is hurt him, at least before he's done his duty."

[ONE]
Restaurant Bernardo
La Rambla
Montevideo, Uruguay
2210 2 May 1943

During the course of their long and exhausting—though pleas-urable—afternoon together, Peter had many occasions to won-der, somewhat unkindly, if Inge was one of those insatiable females young men who don't know any better dream of find-ing. After actually finding one himself in Spain—or rather, after she had found him—he came to realize the error behind that fantasy. Two weeks into the relationship he actually began to dread her apartment (after two nights he had unwisely moved in, or she had moved him)—knowing that before he could even take a drink, or a cup of coffee, he was expected to prove yet again the legendary virility of Luftwaffe fighter pilots.

Inge was not quite in that league, he had to admit. It was in fact likely that she was simply taking advantage of the opportunity his presence presented. Her husband was totally uninterested in the gentle sex, and Inge had normal female hungers. And it was also possible that her enthusiasm was at

least partially feigned and intended to keep him in line. Inge
knew all about using sex to get what she wanted from men.

Peter and Inge had first met in Berlin during a five-day leave
after service in France and before assuming command of
Jagdstaffel 232, which was stationed outside Berlin. Inge
herself had been stationed in the lobby bar in the Hotel am
Zoo, one of those women who seemed to regard taking to
bed senior officers or dashing young Luftwaffe fighter pilots
as their contribution to the war effort. They were not technically prostitutes, but if there were presents, or "loans," so
much the better.

When he saw Inge back then looking at him over the edge
of her Champagne glass, he decided that the long-legged
blond beauty was going to be God's reward to a very tired
fighter pilot who had done his duty for the Fatherland.

Two hours later, they were in a suite overlooking the lake
in the Hotel am Wansee. And for two days they left the bed
only to eat room-service meals, meet calls of nature, and
shower.

Sometime during their licentious bacchanalia, she offered
her hard-luck story—her family home destroyed in an air
raid, the determination of the authorities to employ her in a
war industry—a ghastly plan, yet one she might be forced
into, unless she could find an apartment in Berlin, which was
a difficult proposition—by which she meant expensive—
because she didn't have permission to reside in Berlin, and
would have to find a place on the black market.

At the time, Peter was reasonably convinced that he was
running out of his allotted time in this world. The day before
arriving in Berlin, he'd encountered a P-51 Mustang over the
English Channel whose pilot was just as good as he was. At
the time, he was too busy to be afraid, and fortunately, the
dogfight ended in a draw: When Peter came out of the cloud
where he'd sought a few seconds' refuge, the Mustang was
nowhere in sight.

But afterward, in the air, and that night, and on the train to
Berlin, he had been forced to conclude that a number of Allied

pilots were just as good as he was, and flying aircraft just as good as his Messerschmitt or the Focke-Wulf he would be flying in his new squadron. It was only a matter of time before he ran into a better pilot, or made a mistake, or was just unlucky, and it would be *Sorry, your number came up. You lasted longer than most, but sooner or later, everybody's number comes up. Auf Wieder-sehen, Hans-Peter von Wachtstein!*

Inge's hard-luck story was in fact better than most—there was neither a sick mother nor a crippled little sister involved—and she had certainly been splendid in bed, so he wrote her a check. "A little loan," he said.

"I will repay you as soon as I can," she said.

And when their four days was over, he promptly forgot Inge, the loan, and even her name, although her incredible legs and the smell of her fresh from a shower remained for some time in his mind.

The next time he saw her was in Uruguay.

Peter had flown SS-Standartenführer Josef Luther Goltz there in the Storch to see his man von Tresmarck in Montevideo on behalf of his secret mission to provide an "insurance" refuge for high-ranking Nazis; and Inge, now Frau Sturmbannführer von Tresmarck, had been at the airport to meet them.

She was predictably glad to see him, and proved it that same night by coming to his room in the Casino Hotel in Carrasco. There she told him the story of her recent life since their four days together:

She had married a Waffen-SS Obersturmbannführer named Erich Kolbermann, and was widowed when he was killed at Stalingrad. She had then married von Tresmarck, of the Sicherheitsdienst.

"He needed a wife, and I would have married a gorilla to get out of Berlin," Inge reported matter-of-factly.

"He needed a wife?"

"Didn't Goltz tell you? You mean you couldn't tell the way he looked at you? It was either marry me or pink triangles and Sachsenhausen. That's how Goltz knows he can trust him."

"I knew there was someone like that here," Peter lied quickly. "But I didn't think he'd be married to you."

Five minutes later, Inge blurted out Goltz's other and far more secret mission in Argentina and Uruguay (under the presumption that Peter was as concerned with self-preservation as she herself was, that he had cleverly managed to get himself out of Germany, and that because he was now traveling around with Goltz, he was part of it). For a price, she explained, a stiff price, paid to von Tresmarck in Montevideo, a group of SS officers led by Goltz would arrange the release of Jews from certain concentration camps, and their safe passage though Spain to Argentina and Uruguay.

Peter reacted to Inge's revelation with shocked disbelief, for it was the first he'd heard about the ransom operation. And *this* terrified her. At which point she explained—and he believed—that if this came to the attention of the wrong people in Germany, Goltz, her husband, and everyone else in the know (e.g. Inge herself) would almost surely be shot or sent to a concentration camp.

Under these circumstances, Goltz and von Tresmarck were perfectly willing to kill anyone suspected of threatening the operation, or even of knowing too much about it. That, she pointed out, included him.

He promised her his silence.

Shortly afterward, Cletus Frade told Peter that one of his OSS agents had been brutally murdered in Montevideo. The man's name was Ettinger, a German Jew. While nosing around the Jewish community in Buenos Aires, he had picked up information about some kind of ransoming operation involving concentration-camp inmates. Though he himself did not give the story much credence, Frade had nevertheless reported it to Washington, where there was immediate, almost excited, interest. Ettinger had then gone to Montevideo to see what else he could find out, and had been murdered there.

When Clete then asked Peter if he knew anything about a ransom operation involving the German Embassy in Montevideo, Peter felt no compunction about telling him everything he'd learned from Inge, as well as everything else he had guessed about the operation. He also agreed to see what more he could find out. There was no question of treason here, no question of honor. Goltz and his ilk had no idea what honor was. And if the OSS had learned of the operation through their own sources, Inge could credibly deny leaking the secret.

He had not, of course, told Inge anything about his relationship with Cletus Frade. That made it entirely possible that her enthusiasm in bed was to insure his keeping his mouth shut.

For all of these reasons, but most of all because he needed a rest, Peter insisted—over Inge's objections—on dinner out. And so there they were at the Restaurant Bernardo.

"That's a lovely suit," Inge said, pausing while the tail-coated waiter refilled her wineglass. "New, isn't it? You got it here? In Buenos Aires?"

"Thank you," he said. "Yes, it's new. I found a very nice tailor."

"And nice wool. And no ration coupon, right? They have so much wool here, they practically give it away."

"And the same can be said for the beef," he said, putting his knife to a large, perfectly broiled *Bife lomo*. "I was thinking a moment ago how much a meal like this costs in Berlin."

"A fortune," she said matter-of-factly. "But that won't bother you, will it? You're rich."

"Whatever gave you that idea?"

"You remember Oscar, the bartender at the am Zoo?"

He shook his head, "no."

"Tiny little man, with a head as bald as a baby's bottom?"

He vaguely remembered a very small, bald bartender. "What about him?"

"I asked him about you," she said. "When I first saw you."

"And?"

"He told me who you are," she said. "A von Wachtstein. More important, the *only* son of Generalleutnant Graf von Wachtstein, who will one day be the Graf, and come into the von Wachtstein estates in Pomerania, including Schloss Wachtstein, one of the nicest castles in Pomerania."

"He knew me?"

"That's his business," she said. "He's a terrible snob."

"And until this moment," Peter said, "I thought it was love at first sight."

"That, too." She giggled. "But it's good for a girl to know who she's meeting before she meets him. You can understand that."

"And how did you meet your late husband—what was his name?"

"Erich," she said. "Obersturmbannführer der Waffen-SS Erich Kolbermann. You would have liked him, Peter."

"You met him in the am Zoo? The bartender told you who he was?"

"Actually, it was the Adlon," she said, either not catching the sarcasm or choosing to ignore it. "Heine, the bartender there, told me that poor Erich—whose family owns a shipyard in Bremen—had arrived from the Eastern front on home leave two days after his wife and children were killed in an air raid."

"The poor bastard!"

"And I thought the least I could do was offer him what solace I could," she said.

"Like marrying him?"

"That was, honestly, darling, his idea."

"And when he proposed, it took you all of ten seconds to make up your mind, right?"

"Closer to fifteen," she said, chuckling. "I didn't want to appear too eager."

"You're really something, Inge," Peter said, smiling at her. "I like you."

"After what we've been doing, I should certainly hope so."

He smiled at her. She ran her bare foot up his trouser leg.

"Have you thought about getting your money out of Germany?" Inge asked conversationally.

"They put people who get caught doing that in Sachsenhausen," he said. "And confiscate all their property."

"I got some of mine—Erich's—out," she said. "Werner helped me. Maybe he'd help you."

"Why would he want to do that?"

"Well, maybe you could be *very* nice to him," she said. "I saw the way he looks at you."

"Oh, for God's sake, Inge!"

"I'm just trying to figure a way to make you see that you, me, and lots of money in Brazil is a very interesting thought," she said. "I like you, Peter, but I don't have enough money for both of us."

"Going to Brazil is out of the question for me, Inge," he said seriously. "You'd better understand that."

"It is possible," she said, ignoring him, "that when you get to Berlin—" She interrupted herself. "You really didn't have anything to do with what happened to Standartenführer Goltz, did you?"

"I didn't even know where we were going, much less what he and Grüner were trying to do. I was just taken along because of my strong back to carry the crates."

"That's a little hard to believe, darling," she said. "You and Goltz seemed pretty chummy."

"I probably shouldn't tell you even this much," he said, thinking he better tell her *something*.

"But you will?" she asked, rubbing her foot against his calf again. "Because you know it will earn you a prize just as soon as we get back to the house?"

"Oh, God, Inge!"

"What were you about to say?" she asked, chuckling.

He proceeded with what he considered his own "official" version of the truth: "Goltz told me that since I was a pilot, I probably knew enough navigation to take a boat from El Tigre—"

"From where?"

"It's a port in Buenos Aires. Like Venice, lots of streams and boats, but without the old buildings."

"I've always wanted to see Venice," Inge said. "It's supposed to very romantic."

"Anyway," Peter went on, "Goltz had bought a boat in El Tigre, a little one. And with Grüner's driver and his father—they're Germano-Argentines—as my crew, I took the boat down the coast to Samborombón Bay. Goltz told me I didn't need to know what was going on. When I got to this little port, I spent the night in the house of another Germano-Argentine. Goltz showed up in the middle of the night, and the first thing in the morning, I took him out to a Spanish ship anchored in the bay. The idea was to use the boat I had to make the landing, but the captain of the ship took one look at it and decided it was useless to land on a beach.

"That was the first I had heard of a beach. They loaded some crates into one of the lifeboats from the ship, and we went ashore. I still don't know where we were. Grüner was waiting for us. The minute Goltz and I got out of the boat, people started shooting at us. I have no idea who. Grüner and Goltz were killed; I almost was. I put their bodies into the lifeboat and went back to the ship.

"They took the bodies aboard the ship, and I took the little boat I'd come down the coast in back to El Tigre. I still don't know what the hell was going on, except that they were trying to smuggle whatever was in the crates into Argentina, and got caught."

Inge looked at him thoughtfully, as if trying to make up her mind whether or not to believe him.

"Werner thinks the OSS has a spy in the German Embassy," she said finally.

"Here, or in Buenos Aires? If he means Buenos Aires, he's wrong. Grüner was in charge of security there. And if he didn't trust even me enough to tell me what was going on, how could anyone else know about it?"

"Well, somebody told whoever shot at you where you were going to be," she said.

"Well, it wasn't me," he said. "So I have nothing to worry about."

"In Berlin they may decide they need somebody to blame. And if they decide on you, it won't matter if you didn't know anything about it or not."

"Can we get off this subject?"

She looked into his eyes for a moment, then smiled. "For dessert, you can have a lime sherbet in what looks like an enormous cocktail glass. They pour champagne over the sherbet. It's supposed to be an aphrodisiac," she said.

"You think I need something like that?"

"Well, we'll see, won't we, darling? It can't do any harm to be sure, can it?"

Sturmbannführer Werner von Tresmarck was waiting for them, somewhat impatiently, in the sitting.

Will I now be spared servicing Inge?

"I was wondering where you were," he said.

Does that mean that you were thinking we had taken off for Brazil?

"Peter insisted on taking me to dinner," Inge said. "You said you would probably be late."

"That was unnecessary, von Wachtstein," he said. "We have a first-rate cook."

"It was my pleasure, Herr Sturmbannführer," Peter said.

"Inge, if you will excuse us, I have a little business to discuss with Peter."

"Of course. If you don't mind, either of you, I think I'll go to bed. It's been a busy day."

"I asked the maid to pack for me," he said. "Would you please check to make sure I have everything to last me two or three weeks?"

"Certainly," Inge said.

"Excuse me, Herr Sturmbannführer," Peter said. "We'll be in the Storch. It will have to be a small case that you can hold on your lap during the flight."

"Damn it," von Tresmarck said, looking at Peter with annoyance. Then he went on. "In that case, Inge, you will have to repack my things. Put what's absolutely necessary in the small black bag. And then pack everything else I might need for three weeks in a larger bag, or bags. It's possible we won't leave Buenos Aires immediately, and a messenger can bring them to me before we go."

"All right," Inge said agreeably.

"May I suggest, Herr Sturmbannführer," Peter said, aware that he was enjoying discomfiting von Tresmarck, "that there are liable to be very stringent weight requirements on the Condor?"

"I'm very much aware of that, von Wachtstein," von Tresmarck said, almost angrily. "We'll deal with that when the time comes."

"Yes, of course, Herr Sturmbannführer," Peter said.

"I'll see you, of course, in the morning, Peter," Inge said. "Good night."

"Sleep well, Frau von Tresmarck," Peter said, and bowed and clicked his heels.

Von Tresmarck waited until Inge had closed the door behind her, then touched Peter's shoulder. "I didn't mean to snap at you, Peter, but I don't want to arrive in Berlin looking like a refugee."

"I understand, Herr Sturmbannführer."

"Do you think you could bring yourself to call me Werner?"

"That's very good of you, Sir."

"We are, after all, so to speak, in this mess together, aren't we?" von Tresmarck said, and before Peter could form a reply, went on. "Let me get us a little brandy, and then you can tell me what you know about what happened on the beach in Argentina." Von Tresmarck went to the bar, where he poured generous drinks of French cognac into snifters, then handed one to Peter.

Peter raised his. "Unser Führer!" he barked, correctly.

"Adolf Hitler!" von Tresmarck said, and took a swallow.

"What, *exactly*, happened on the beach, Peter? In fact, tell me all you know about the whole tragic incident."

"With all possible respect, Herr Sturmbannführer, I don't believe I am at liberty to discuss this."

Von Tresmarck looked at him intently for a long moment. "I told you a moment ago you could address me informally," he said. "But perhaps you're right. You may consider, Herr Major Freiherr von Wachtstein, that we are now dealing with one another officially. That, in other words, I put that question to you as a Sturmbannführer of the Sicherheitsdienst."

"Yes, Sir," Peter said.

"Well?" von Tresmarck asked impatiently.

"Where would you like me to begin, Herr Sturmbannführer?"

"At the beginning," von Tresmarck snapped.

Peter began at the beginning. Though he told von Tresmarck essentially the same "official" version he had told Inge earlier, he fleshed it all out in great detail.

Thus he provided von Tresmarck with a detailed description of Günther Loche and his father, including their dedication to National Socialism and their loyalty to Oberst Grüner, to Ambassador von Lutzenberger, and to Peter himself. He followed this with a detailed description of El Tigre, the river launch *Coronel Gasparo,* and the difficulty of sailing such a vessel into the oceanlike River Plate estuary.

By the time Peter reached the end of the tale, Von Tresmarck was visibly relieved. There were a few questions, mostly in an attempt to get Peter to admit to more knowledge than he claimed to possess, and to having learned this somehow beforehand.

But those questions seemed perfunctory.

Which means either that he believes me—I think Inge does—or that he thinks I'm lying, and that since there's not much he can do about that here, he'll wait until we get to Berlin.

Von Tresmarck looked at his watch. "It's later than I thought, Peter," he said. "And we have an early day tomorrow. Why don't we have a nightcap, and then turn in?"

"May I pass on the nightcap, Herr Sturmbannführer? I don't like to drink very much if I'm flying the next day."

"I understand," von Tresmarck said, and then remembered something that now obviously bothered him. "What is the rule? Nothing to drink for twenty-four hours before you're scheduled to fly?"

"The body, Herr Sturmbannführer, will neutralize one drink each hour. My body will be alcohol-free when it is time for us to fly."

Von Tresmarck seemed relieved to hear that. "I think, Peter," he said, smiling at him, "we can go back to a first-name basis, at least when we're alone."

"Thank you."

"So, good night, Peter."

"Good night, Werner. Thank you for your hospitality."

Von Tresmarck gestured toward the door, and Peter followed him through it, then up the stairs to the second floor.

He undressed and went to bed. It had been freshly made. He wondered what the maid thought.

He could hear the sound of Inge's and von Tresmarck's voices, but could not make out what they were saying.

He closed his eyes and went immediately to sleep.

Sometime later—it couldn't have been more than thirty minutes—he became aware not only of Inge's presence but that she had decided to begin without his full attention.

"I didn't expect to see you again in here," he said, and then, involuntarily, "Jesus, be careful!"

"Sorry," she said, and moved up the bed so that her face was beside his.

"You could have stayed awake," she said coyly.

"I didn't think you were coming," he said.

Actually, I was delighted that I didn't think you would.

"I told you, he wants to weep on the manly chest of his lover."

"And he won't be back?"

"Not for a while," she said. "Did you like what I was doing?"

"If I could get you in my suitcase, I'd take you along as my alarm clock," he said.

"Not me, darling. I love you, but not enough to go to Berlin with you."

"I'm crushed."

"Maybe to Brazil," she said.

And then she straddled him, and he was no longer in the mood to rehash a conversation they'd already had.

[TWO]
Calle Martín 404
Carrasco, Uruguay
O805 3 May 1943

Inge was shaking his arm. He opened his eyes and looked at her. It took him a moment to realize that it was light, and that she was fully dressed.

He did not remember her leaving his bed.

"Good morning, sleepyhead," she said. "You didn't answer my knock."

"Sorry."

"Breakfast in fifteen minutes, all right?"

"Fine. Thank you very much."

She walked out of the room, wiggling her rear end for his benefit.

He got out of bed and took a long hot shower and shaved. The mirror told him he looked like a man who hadn't gotten much sleep.

When he went down to the dining, he saw that Sturmbannführer Werner von Tresmarck looked very much the same.

Frau von Tresmarck looked as if she had spent a long, restful, and entirely satisfying night in bed.

There was nothing in von Tresmarck's attitude that suggested he knew Peter had been anything but a houseguest.

Does that mean he doesn't know, or suspect? Or that if he knows, or suspects, he doesn't care?

After they reached the embassy, von Tresmarck announced that there was no reason for them to come inside and they could wait in the car; but soon after entering the building, he returned to announce that Ambassador Schulker wanted to see Peter.

Peter got out of the car and followed von Tresmarck to Schulker's office.

"Heil Hitler, Excellency!" Peter barked, giving a straight-armed salute and clicking his heels. "I was not aware that the Herr Ambassador wished to see me."

Schulker returned the salute and the greeting. "I have two envelopes for you to take to Buenos Aires, von Wachtstein," Schulker said.

"Jawohl, Excellency!"

"Forster, this is Major Freiherr von Wachtstein," Schulker said. "Herr Forster is our commercial attaché."

Peter clicked his heels and nodded his head. "Herr Councilor," he said.

Forster gave him his hand. "A pleasure to meet you, von Wachtstein," he said. "I've heard of your heroic behavior on the beach."

Peter smiled broadly at him. "I regret, Herr Forster, that I have no idea what you're talking about."

Schulker chuckled. "The world of diplomacy, von Wachtstein," he said, "may be compared to peasant women gathered around the village pump. A lot of things people would rather not have talked about are discussed in some detail."

"I am a soldier, Excellency. I try very hard to comply with my orders."

"And do so admirably, von Wachtstein," Schulker said. "Well, here's what needs to be taken to Buenos Aires." He handed Peter two envelopes, a large one apparently containing routine papers—it was addressed to Gradny-Sawz—and a smaller one, bearing Schulker's embossed family crest and addressed to Ambassador von Lutzenberger.

"I would like to make the point," von Tresmarck said, "that whatever my friend Forster has heard about some beach, he did not hear from me."

"Or from me," Schulker said. "But doesn't that prove that Forster has been doing what we diplomats are supposed to do, keep our eyes and ears open for something of interest?"

"Your discretion is admirable, von Wachtstein," Forster said.

"It is very nice to have made your acquaintance, Herr Councilor," Peter replied. "And may I say that I am grateful that you understand my position?"

"I have no doubt that we'll see each other again," Forster said. "And may I wish both of you a very pleasant home leave?"

"Now, *that* I told him, von Wachtstein," Schulker said.

"In that case, Herr Councilor, thank you very much."

"Have a drink for me at the Adlon," Forster said.

"I'll do that," Peter said.

In the car on the way to the airport, von Tresmarck said, "Peter, there is a story going around—I don't know if it's true or not, and I tell you this in confidence—that Forster is not entirely what he represents himself to be, that he has other duties, if you take my meaning."

"He's the Sicherheitsdienst's man in the embassy," Inge said, "and everybody knows it."

"No one *knows* that, Inge," von Tresmarck said. "And you should be very careful about who you say something like that to."

"I wondered how he heard about the beach," Peter said.

"What beach is that, Peter?" von Tresmarck asked.

While they were loading the Storch, Peter saw that von Tresmarck was more than a little nervous about flying the 160-odd kilometers across the River Plate in the small single-engine airplane.

It easily occurred to him that once they were out of sight of land, he would add to von Tresmarck's discomfiture by causing the engine to backfire, or by perhaps adding some sudden up-and-down movement to the aircraft.

The customs and immigration officers showed up at the terminal while Peter was checking the weather. After they asked about his destination they immediately left (without bothering to proceed out to the parking ramp to check what he might be taking out of Uruguay).

Inge kissed her husband's cheek, offered her hand to Peter, then changed her mind and kissed his cheek, too.

"Be careful," she said. "Both of you."

Ten minutes later, they were off the ground. Peter flew out over the River Plate in a shallow climb, put the fort-on-the-hill on his tail, and set the compass course for Buenos

Aires. When he had climbed to 2,500 meters, he trimmed the aircraft up, and then, without really being aware he was doing it, took his feet momentarily off the rudder pedals and raised both hands above his head to check the condition of the trim.

"Can you do that?" von Tresmarck's voice came metallically over the intercom. "Take your hands off the controls?"

"For a few seconds," Peter replied. By then he had both his hands and his feet back on the controls. In that moment, he decided he would not cause the engine to backfire, or initiate maneuvers that would put von Tresmarck's stomach into a tighter knot than it already was in.

He remembered a whipping his father had given him when he was nine or ten. He had been cruelly teasing a retarded boy from the village. His father had seen him, grabbed his arm, and marched him all the way up the hill to the Schloss. There he had taken him into the tack room of the stable, bent him over, and had at his bare bottom with a quirt. Half a dozen lashes, several of which broke the skin, all of which were painful.

And all he said was, "A gentleman, Hansel, does not take advantage of someone who cannot defend himself."

The poor bastard in the backseat is frightened. And with good reason. It might well be decided in Berlin that he was the source of the information that resulted in the deaths of Goltz and Grüner. And of the three of us, he is the most expendable, and he must know that. Gradny-Sawz has many highly placed Nazi friends, and no reason to betray Operation Phoenix. They might in the end decide that I'm expendable, but not before they think long and hard about the cost. It will be difficult—which does not mean impossible—to tell Hitler that the son of Generalleutnant von Wachtstein, an officer around whose neck he had himself hung the Knight's Cross of the Iron Cross, was suspected of treason. It would be much easier to lay the blame on an SS officer, who, it had recently been learned, was a deviate.

"Inge likes you." Von Tresmarck's voice came over the intercom. "I can tell."

"And I like Frau von Tresmarck," Peter said. "A charming lady."

"There is a great difference in our ages," von Tresmarck said. "And, frankly, we have our problems. She, of course, misses Berlin and the young people. There aren't very many young people around Montevideo . . . suitable young people. She was so pleased when you took her to dinner."

"It was my pleasure," Peter said.

"When we return, I wonder if you would have the time to do it again. Perhaps, if I sent her to Buenos Aires, you could show her around. It's a much more sophisticated city than Montevideo."

"It would be my pleasure, of course," Peter said.

Freely translated, that means, "Peter, my friend, it's perfectly all right with me if you want to fuck my wife."

The Storch suddenly encountered turbulence, and the aircraft rapidly lost altitude, and then as rapidly regained it. It had just about leveled out when the engine suddenly spluttered, gave off clouds of smoke, and almost died. Then there was more turbulence.

In the backseat, Sturmbannführer Werner von Tresmarck became airsick.

Günther Loche and the Mercedes of the Military Attaché were waiting for them at El Palomar. "Herr Sturmbann-führer, this is Günther Loche," Peter said, "who does very fine work for the Office of the Military Attaché."

Günther popped to attention. "A great honor, Herr Sturm-bannführer," he said.

"Oh, yes," von Tresmarck said. "Major von Wachtstein has been telling me about you."

Is Günther really pissing his pants, or does it just look that way?

"What we're going to do, Günther, is drop me by the Embassy, and then, for as long as Sturmbannführer von Tresmarck is with us, you will be his driver, and otherwise make yourself as useful to him as you can."

"Jawohl, Herr Major."

"But he's your driver, Peter," von Tresmarck protested.

"Rank hath its privileges, Herr Sturmbannführer," Peter said. "Where is the Herr Sturmbannführer going to stay, Günther?"

"At the Alvear Palace, Herr Major."

"When I'm in the embassy, I'll tell Gradny-Sawz. I know he wants to see you," Peter said.

"And will we see each other while I'm here, Peter?"

"That, of course, will depend on what Gradny-Sawz has planned for you, but I'm sure we will."

Peter's maid, Señora Dora, was a forty-five-year-old Paraguayan Amazon who outweighed him by at least thirty pounds. As he came through the door of his apartment, she greeted him with the announcement that Señorita Carzino-Cormano had called him many times, most recently twenty minutes before, and seemed very anxious that he call her back.

"Make some coffee, please," Peter said.

"Sí, Señor."

"And if the señorita calls again while I am in the shower, tell her that you expect me in thirty minutes."

"Sí, Señor."

He started for his bedroom, then changed his mind and headed for the laundry room, off the kitchen.

As far as she could remember, Señora Dora had never seen the Señor Mayor go into the laundry, so she followed him there.

"Is there something I can do for you, Señor?"

There it is. I knew it would be here. Every laundry room in the world has a stiff brush and a bar of mostly acid yellow soap for really dirty jobs.

When she saw what he had in his hands, Señora Dora asked, "Is there something I can wash for you, Señor?"

"No, this is something I have to wash myself, but thank you anyway, Señora Dora."

He went to his bedroom and then into the bath. There he turned on the hot water, stripped off his clothing, and, taking the yellow soap and the scrub brush with him, stepped into the shower.

When he came out five minutes later, his skin was bright red and actually felt sunburned.

But he still felt dirty.

Please, God, he prayed, *don't ever let Alicia find out.*

[THREE]
Bureau of Internal Security
Ministry of Defense
Edificio Libertador
Avenida Paseo Colón
Buenos Aires
1240 4 May 1943

There were three telephones on the desk of Coronel Bernardo Martín. There was also a fourth in the credenza against the wall behind his desk. The fourth phone's number was known to no more than two dozen people, and it was tested at least once a day to make sure it had not been tapped.

It rang, and he quickly turned around, pulled open the credenza door, and reached for it. "Hola?"

"Bernardo, this is Milton," his caller announced.

"And how are you, Milton?"

"Very well, thank you. Bernardo, I have just been informed about some really fascinating buys at very good prices at Sant Elmo. Are you at all interested?"

Sant Elmo was a neighborhood not far from El Bocha where a number of dealers in antiques, silver, old books, and things of that nature were located. It was usually crowded with bargain hunters, and was a good place to meet.

"It sounds very interesting, but I'm not sure I can get away from the office."

"Oh, I'm sorry to hear that. You could probably make a very good bargain, and I really think you'd be interested."

"Well, I'll see what I can do. In any event, thank you for thinking of me."

"Don't be silly. What are friends for?"

Forty-five minutes later, Martín spotted Milton Leibermann, sitting over a cup of coffee, in a café on the Plaza de Sant Elmo.

"What a pleasant surprise," Martín said. "May I join you?"

"Of course," Leibermann said.

Martín pulled up a small chair and, when the waiter appeared, ordered a *café cortado*.

Leibermann slid a three-by-five-inch filing card across the table.

```
GENERALMAJOR MANFRED VON DEITZBERG

(HIMMLER'S  ADJUTANT,  ACTUALLY  SS-
OBERFÜHRER)

DEPUTY  FOREIGN  MINISTER  GEORG  VON
LÖWZER.

STANDARTENFÜHRER ERICH RASCHNER

WILL  BE  ON  NEXT  LUFTHANSA  FLIGHT,
PROBABLY IN 72 HOURS OR LESS

KORVETTENKAPITÄN KARL BOLTITZ, WORKS
FOR CANARIS, WILL FOLLOW, TO BECOME
NAVAL ATTACHÉ. DON'T KNOW WHEN.
```

"What's this all about, Milton?" Martín asked, slipping the filing card into his pocket.

"Argentina's a beautiful country. They may be tourists. Or they may be here to eat. I understand there's a growing food shortage where they're coming from."

"How good is this information?"

Leibermann held out his balled fist, thumb extended

upward. "You can take it to the bank, Bernardo," he said.

"And if you had to make a guess, why would you say they're coming here?"

"I don't know if this is true or not, but I've heard that the German Military Attaché left for home under somewhat mysterious circumstances."

"I've heard that myself," Martín said, and smiled. "And what can I do for you, Milton?"

"Odd that you should ask, my friend. As you know, I'm very interested in photography. If, wandering around Sant Elmo, you should happen to come across some photographs of interesting faces . . ."

"I'll see what I can do, Milton."

"It's always a pleasure doing business with you, Bernardo."

Martín reached into his pocket for money to pay for the coffee.

Leibermann stopped him. "My pleasure, Bernardo."

"You're very kind. Are we still on for Saturday?"

"Oh, I'm glad you brought that up. No. I have been invited to a wedding."

"In the country?"

Leibermann nodded.

"Well, if it's the same wedding I'm thinking of, perhaps I'll see you there."

"That would be nice, Bernardo."

On the way back to his office, Bernardo had an unpleasant thought. The Military Attaché of the German Embassy, the late Coronel Karl-Heinz Grüner, had as a gesture of friendship given two Leica I-C cameras, together with a wide assortment of lenses and other accessories, to the Bureau of Internal Security. It was entirely possible that the former chief of the BIS, el Almirante Francisco de Montoya, had considered at least one of the camera sets as a personal gift and taken it with him when he had been retired.

When he reached the Edificio Libertador, he was greatly relieved to find both camera sets in a locked cabinet.

Within two hours, they had been set up at El Palomar.

[FOUR]
El Palomar Air Field
Buenos Aires, Argentina
1545 5 May 1943

"Mi Coronel," the senior control tower operator said to el Coronel Bernardo Martín, Chief of the Ethical Standards Office of the Bureau of Internal Security, "the Lufthansa flight reports they are fifteen minutes from the field."

"Muchas gracias," Martín replied. He was wearing a brown tweed sports jacket, gray flannel trousers, and the necktie of St. George's School, where he had received his secondary education (as had his father). He had been at the Monthly Old Boys Association Luncheon at Claridge's Hotel before coming out to El Palomar.

The food, as usual, had been very nice, but it had been otherwise a sad occasion. He had known two (and possibly three) of the four Anglo-Argentine Old Boys who had died for King and Country during the past month.

He looked around the control tower, then out its plate-glass window. Everything was in place and ready. In the control tower itself was a Leica I-C 35mm camera, equipped with a telephoto lens and mounted on a tripod. A 1939 Ford panel truck was parked on the grass beside the tarmac where Lufthansa Flight 102 would soon be parked. A crew of workmen were standing by a ditch working on the electrical line that ran to the lights along the runway. Inside the truck, another photographer with another Leica I-C would photograph everyone coming down the stairs after it rolled up to the aircraft.

Fifteen minutes later, a very long, very slender, very graceful four-engine aircraft dropped out of the sky and lined up with the runway. The Focke-Wulf 200B Condor, first flown in 1937, was a twenty-six-seat passenger airplane, powered by four 870-HP BMW engines, and had been built for Lufthansa, the German airline. A military modification, the 200C, turned the aircraft into an armed, long-range reconnaissance plane/bomber.

To Martín, the Lufthansa Condor looked something like the American Douglas DC-3, particularly in the nose. It was painted black on the top of the fuselage, and off-white on the bottom. On the vertical stabilizer and on the rear of the fuselage were red swastikas, outlined in white.

It touched smoothly down, rolled to the end of the runway, then turned and taxied back to the terminal, where a ground crew waved it into a space near the 1939 Ford panel truck.

As it approached the terminal, a group of people came out of the terminal building. Martín recognized only two of them, First Secretary Anton Gradny-Sawz, and the acting Military Attaché, Major von Wachtstein. "Get those people waiting for the airplane," Martín ordered.

"Sí, mi Coronel," the photographer replied.

He hoped the photographer in the truck would have enough sense to also take their pictures.

Movable stairs were rolled up to the airplane, and in a moment the door opened and people began to descend.

At this point, Martín thought, *both cameras will suffer mechanical problems. Meaning first that I won't have pictures of these Nazis to distribute to my men or give to Milton Leibermann, and then that Milton will be justifiably suspicious when I tell him, sorry, we didn't get any pictures.*

The first down the stairs was a plump little man in his forties wearing a mussed black suit. He was carrying a leather briefcase.

That has to be Löwzer, the Deputy Foreign Minister.

Next was a tall, slim, well-dressed blond man.

Manfred von Deitzberg, Martín decided. *Himmler's adjutant? I wonder how Milton knew that? I also wonder how Milton knew these people were coming, and even when. Has he got someone in the German Embassy? Or was their arrival announced over RCA, and intercepted by the OSS, and they told him?*

And am I going to tell General Obregon that this man is Himmler's adjutant? He thinks Himmler is a great man.

Not now. Until I can verify that fact, it's unsubstantiated. I can always say I either didn't know or wasn't sure, and therefore did not think I should include it in my report.

A middle-aged woman, followed by a man who was probably her husband, came down next.

Who the hell are they?

I'll have the manifest. I can find out.

The next person to appear was a short, stocky man in a tight dark-blue suit. He stopped in the doorway for a moment and looked around before coming down the stairs.

That man is a policeman. He had a careful look around. Policemen always look around a room as they enter it, and getting off an airplane is like entering a room. That has to be Sturmbannführer Erich Raschner.

Confirmation came immediately. Once Raschner had reached the foot of the stairway, Gradny-Sawz marched up to the three men and gave the Nazi salute. Von Wachtstein, three steps behind him, repeated the gesture. They all shook hands, and then Gradny-Sawz gestured for them to proceed to the terminal building.

One of the immigration officers, also one of Martín's men, was under instructions to take their passports into a room where a camera was waiting to photograph them, if he could do so without causing any suspicion. There was often useful information on passports besides place and date of birth, and even those were sometimes useful.

Martín walked across the control tower to look out the window that gave a view of the terminal parking lot. Three Mercedeses with CD plates, two small ones and a larger one—presumably Ambassador Von Lutzenberger's—were parked illegally right in front of the entrance.

It was five minutes before any of the Germans came out of the building and got in the cars. Löwzer and Gradny-Sawz stepped into the larger Mercedes, von Deitzberg and von Wachtstein got into one of the smaller cars, and Raschner and a chubby forty-year-old, with a mustache like Hitler's, got into the third.

*Who's he? He's obviously important enough to be out
here to meet Löwzer and von Deitzberg. But he's not with
the German Embassy here; I know all their faces, if not
their names. Maybe a Germano-Argentine? I thought I knew
all of them, at least the Nazis, at least the important Nazis.*

Maybe Milton can tell me.

*Does who got in which car establish the pecking order?
Löwzer is more important than von Deitzberg, and gets to
ride in the big car? But is a deputy foreign minister more
important than Himmler's adjutant? I don't think so. A
major general is less important than a deputy foreign minister, and for some reason Himmler's adjutant wants people to
think he's a major general. Why?*

Martín turned away from the window and faced the photographer, who was still taking pictures of people around the
Condor. "Stay here another thirty minutes to make sure no
one else gets off the airplane," Martín ordered. "Then—you
personally—develop that film, and make three sets of large
prints."

"Sí, mi Coronel."

"Bring them, and the negatives, to my office. I'll probably
be there. If I am not, give them to Suboficial Mayor José
Cortina."

"Sí, mi Coronel."

[FIVE]

"I have something for you, von Wachtstein," von Deitzberg
said as they drove down Avenida Libertador. He reached into
his jacket pocket and came out with an envelope. It bore the
embossed crest of the von Wachtstein family. "I was at Wolfsschanze just before we left," von Deitzberg went on, "and
stopped by to see your father. He asked me to give you that."

"The Herr General is very kind," Peter said. He put the
envelope in his pocket.

"Have you been to Rastenburg?" von Deitzberg asked.

"Yes, Sir, I have."

"Oh, of course. That's where the Führer gave you the Knight's Cross, right?"

"Yes, Sir."

"Your father is in excellent health, and a valued member of the OKW," von Deitzberg said. "And very proud of you."

"I am very proud my father, Herr General," Peter said. "And I'm also in excellent health. I'm not so sure how valuable a member of the German Embassy I am."

"You would rather be at home, on active service, so to speak?"

"May I speak honestly, Herr General?"

"Of course."

"I am a soldier, Sir. I can only presume that my superiors have decided I can make a greater contribution to Germany here than in a cockpit. Having said that, there is a good deal to be said for being in Argentina."

"Well put, von Wachtstein," von Deitzberg said. "I appreciate candor."

"The food is magnificent, and the women spectacular," Peter said. "The people remind me of Hungarians. They have a zest for life."

"From what little I've seen," von Deitzberg said, gesturing out the window as they passed the Hipódrome, "I can already see that my prejudgment of this country was in error. This is not how I envisioned South America. This is European."

"In many ways, Herr General, it is. When I was ordered here, I expected it would be like Spain. It's not. It's *Argentina*."

"That's right, you served in Spain, didn't you?"

"Yes, Sir. Three tours with the Condor Legion."

"Three?"

"I was given the choice twice, Sir, of returning to Spain, or doing a tour in Germany teaching people how to fly."

"And you preferred active service to teaching?"

"I decided that if it was my destiny to die for the Fatherland in an airplane, I would prefer to do so in a war, rather than teaching some farmer how to fly."

Von Deitzberg laughed. "And the women in Spain had nothing to do with it, of course?"

"Oberstleutnant Aschenburg, my commanding officer—"

"Dieter von und zu Aschenburg?" von Deitzberg interrupted.

"Yes, Sir."

"An old acquaintance. He's now flying Condors for Lufthansa, you know."

"Yes, I do," Peter said. "The Oberstleutnant used to say that in the land of the blind, the one-eyed man is king; and in Spain, the land of the black haired, dark-skinned, dark-eyed male, the blue-eyed, blond-haired, fair-skinned Aryan is king."

"He being a blue-eyed, blond-haired, fair-skinned Pomeranian like you, right, von Wachtstein?"

"I believe he's Prussian, Herr General."

"I believe you're right," von Deitzberg said.

"We're almost there, Herr General. The Alvear Palace is two blocks down, once we reach the crest of the hill."

"Then it's time we get down to business," von Deitzberg said. "I'm going to have to talk to you, you understand, about what happened to Oberst Grüner and Standartenführer Goltz, and about what you can expect when you get to Germany."

"Jawohl, Herr General."

"But that can wait until tomorrow. What I have to do today is talk to Oberst Perón. I understand you're friends?"

"Sir, I am acquainted with Coronel Perón, but I don't presume to think we're friends."

"Do you think you could find him for me, present my compliments, and tell him I would consider it a great personal favor if he would receive me as soon as possible? Today?"

"I will do my best, Herr General. Oberst Perón is now the principal assistant to the Minister of War, General Ramírez. I'll try his office."

"Find him, von Wachtstein," von Deitzberg said, firmly. "While I'm taking a shower."

"Jawohl, Herr General."

• • •

Getting el Coronel Juan Domingo Perón on the telephone
was less difficult than Peter thought it would be. The number
of the Ministry of War was in the telephone book, and when
Peter dialed the number, gave his name, and asked to speak
to Perón, the Minister was on the line thirty seconds later.

"What can I do for you, my young friend?" Perón asked in
his melodious voice.

"Mi Coronel, I am calling to pay the compliments of Generalmajor von Deitzberg."

There was a pause, and the warmth was gone from Perón's
voice when he asked, "*Generalmajor* von Deitzberg?"

"Yes, Sir."

"I know an Oberführer von Deitzberg."

"Sir, I believe that Oberführer von Deitzberg has been
seconded to the Wehrmacht."

"I see. Are you telling me he's here, in Buenos Aires?"

"Sí, mi Coronel. He just got off the airplane. He's at the
Alvear Plaza."

"Well, Mayor, please extend my compliments to Generalmajor von Deitzberg and my warmest wishes of welcome to
Argentina."

"Si, Señor. Señor, the general asked me to tell you that he
would consider it a personal service if you would receive
him at your earliest convenience, preferably today."

There was another long pause.

"There are questions of protocol, Mayor, as I'm sure you
will understand. I would be delighted to receive the General
socially, as an old friend, but I'm afraid coming here . . ."

"I believe the General wishes to pay his respects as a
friend, mi Coronel."

There was another pause.

"I have yet to find myself a suitable apartment, Mayor.
For the time being, I'm staying at the house of an old friend,
at 4730 Avenida Libertador—that's right across from the
Hipódromo."

"Yes, Sir."

That's Cletus Frade's guest house.

"Would you please tell the General I would be pleased to

receive him there, as an old friend, at, say, half past seven tonight?"

"It will be my privilege, mi Coronel," Peter said.

"Socially, you understand, Mayor?"

"Sí, mi Coronel." The line went dead. Peter hung up and looked at the door to the bath. He could hear the shower running.

He reached in his pocket and opened the letter from his father. It was typewritten.

```
THE FÜHRER'S HEADQUARTERS

30 APRIL 1943

MY DEAR SON,

GENERALMAJOR   VON   DEITZBERG   HAS
KINDLY AGREED TO CARRY THIS TO YOU
IN BUENOS AIRES. IT WILL THUS ARRIVE
SOMETIME  BEFORE  MY  LETTER  OF  27
APRIL,  WHICH  UNFORTUNATELY  DEALS
WITH THE SAME SUBJECT.

I MUST, WITH PROFOUND REGRET, INFORM
YOU  THAT  OUR  FRIEND  COLONEL  GRAF
CLAUS  VON  STAUFFENBERG  HAS  BEEN
SERIOUSLY WOUNDED WHILE SERVING WITH
THE AFRIKA KORPS. AS NEAR AS I CAN
PIECE  THE  FACTS  TOGETHER,  HE  WAS
TRAVELING  IN  A  CAR  WHICH  WAS
ATTACKED BY AMERICAN AIRCRAFT.

HE HAS LOST HIS RIGHT HAND, HIS LEFT
EYE,  AND  THE  THIRD  AND  FOURTH  FIN-
GERS OF HIS LEFT HAND. HE WAS FLOWN
FROM AFRICA TO MUNICH, AND WHEN GEN-
ERAL  STABBEN  AND  I  VISITED  HIM  IN
HOSPITAL   THERE,   HE   WAS   REFUSING
```

PAIN-REDUCING MEDICINE IN THE BELIEF
THAT DOING SO WOULD FACILITATE HIS
RETURN TO DUTY.

I GO INTO THESE UNPLEASANT DETAILS
BECAUSE I AM SURE THAT YOU WILL WISH
TO WRITE TO HIM—YOU ALWAYS THOUGHT OF
HIM AS AN OLDER BROTHER—TO EXPRESS
YOUR BEST WISHES, AND I WANTED TO
MAKE SURE YOU SAID NOTHING, IN AN
ATTEMPT TO CHEER HIM UP, THAT WOULD
MAKE HIM FEEL WORSE.

I AM IN GOOD HEALTH, BELIEVE I AM
DOING MY DUTY TO THE FATHERLAND, AND
THINK OF YOU OFTEN.

THE WARMEST WISHES OF YOUR FATHER,
OF COURSE.

KFvW

*One hand, one eye, and fingers gone from the other hand.
He's a fucking cripple!*

Christ, Claus, I'm sorry!

Sonofabitch!

"Shit," Peter said aloud.

"I confess," von Deitzberg said from the bathroom door,
"that I knew the sad news that letter contained. I decided it
would be best if you heard it from your father, if only by
letter."

"Thank you, Herr General."

"I think I should also tell you that I did not tell your father
that you will shortly have the opportunity to see him. I
decided that it would be a nice surprise for him if he didn't
know you were coming to Germany."

"I'm sure you're right, Sir."

"Now, about Oberst Perón?"

"The Colonel will receive you at half past seven tonight, Herr General. At his temporary residence."

"Good man, von Wachtstein!"

"Sir, Oberst Perón took pains to make it clear that he is receiving you as a friend, and not officially. He said there were questions of protocol. . . ."

"I understand completely," von Deitzberg said. "And my reason to see him is entirely personal. Do you know where this 'temporary residence' is?"

"Yes, Sir."

"Good, then you can come with me."

"Jawohl, Herr General."

"How is the beer in this beautiful country, von Wachtstein?"

"Excellent, Sir. All the brewmasters are German."

"Why don't you get us some while I'm dressing?"

"Jawohl, Herr General."

[ONE]
4730 Avenida Libertador
Buenos Aires
1735 5 May 1943

"Have you seen much of Colonel Perón since you've been here, von Wachtstein?" von Deitzberg asked as Günther Loche drove them from the hotel.

"No, Sir."

"It might be wise to cultivate him," von Deitzberg said. "He is a power in Argentina, and I wouldn't be surprised if he becomes more powerful."

"Oberst Grüner told me the same thing, Sir. But he didn't

tell me how to do it. Perón's an oberst, a senior oberst, and I am a very junior major."

"But Perón likes you," von Deitzberg said. "Make an effort."

"Jawohl, Herr General."

That sounds as if he expects me to come back from Germany. Is he doing that to put me at ease, to lower my guard?

"There's a very interesting dossier on him," von Deitzberg said. Peter didn't reply. "The last thing in the world one would expect of a man like that," von Deitzberg went on. "But there's no question about it: The photographer was very good."

Is he telling me Perón is homosexual? Is that what that "but Perón likes you" remark meant?

"You're not curious, von Wachtstein?" von Deitzberg asked, smiling at him.

"Herr General, I went to Spain as a corporal. I asked then Major von und zu Aschenburg a question. I didn't get an answer, but I received advice from him that I have never forgotten. It is probably the most valuable advice anyone has ever given me about being a soldier."

"Which is?"

"'If your superiors think you should know something, they'll tell you. Don't ask questions.'"

Von Deitzberg laughed. "Dieter stood you tall, did he?"

"Very tall, Herr General. And one never forgets a Deiter von und zu Aschenburg dressing-down."

"So you're curious, but too smart to ask me what's in Perón's dossier?"

"Yes, Sir."

"I think I shall, von Wachtstein, see how good a detective you would make," von Deitzberg said. "After our meeting with Oberst Perón, you tell me what character flaw you suspect."

"If the Herr General wishes."

"You don't like being tested?"

"Not if I strongly suspect the test will reveal my stupidity," Peter said, and then leaned forward on his seat. "Günther, it's in the next block. The mansion."

"Jawohl, Herr Major," Günther replied as he slowed the car.

"You've been here before, have you?" von Deitzberg asked.

"Yes, Herr General. I spent my first night in Argentina in that house. It is the Frade family guest house."

"And that's Perón's 'temporary residence'?"

"That's what he said, Herr General."

"God is smiling on our mission, von Wachtstein."

"Sir?"

"I thought you didn't ask questions."

"I beg the Herr General's pardon."

"Did Deiter ever give you the lesson, vis-à-vis the behavior of officers in the presence of their superiors, that I myself have found very valuable?"

"I'm not sure what the Herr General means."

"Mouth shut, eyes and ears open."

"Jawohl, Herr General."

Günther pulled the Mercedes to the curb, stopped, and then raced around the rear of the car to open the door for von Deitzberg.

They walked across the sidewalk to the fence—made of what looked like gold-tipped ten-foot spears—and pushed a doorbell mounted in the gate.

"That," von Deitzberg said, pointing to a finely detailed family crest set in the gate, "is presumably the Frade coat of arms?"

"I would suppose so, Herr General."

The lock buzzed and Peter pushed the gate open, allowing von Deitzberg to walk ahead of him for the thirty feet from the gate to the shallow flight of stairs leading to the front door. The Frade crest was also in stained glass on the door of the large, four-story, turn-of-the-century masonry mansion. The door was opened by a smiling, middle-aged woman in a black dress with crisply starched white collar and cuffs. "El General von Deitzberg to see el Coronel Perón," Peter said.

"El Coronel will receive you in the library, caballeros," she said, and motioned them across the foyer.

A middle-aged woman, similarly dressed, had greeted Peter with the same kind of warm smile the last time he had been in the Frade guest house. The killers-for-hire Grüner had sent to the house to assassinate Cletus Frade had slit her throat in the kitchen before going upstairs to deal with Cletus.

"If the Herr General prefers, I could wait here," Peter said, indicating one of the chairs lining the foyer wall.

"I want you with me," von Deitzberg said. "I don't speak much Spanish, and you can interpret."

"Jawohl, Herr General."

"As well as hone your skills of observation and intuition," von Deitzberg added with a smile.

The housekeeper pushed open the door to the library and stepped inside. Juan Domingo Perón, in a well-cut dark-blue suit, rose from a dark red leather armchair and smiled when they entered the room. "Guten Abend," he said in correct but heavily accented German. "It is a pleasure to see you again, Manfred."

"Thank you for receiving me, Juan Domingo," von Deitzberg said in German, bowed, clicked his heels, and then put out his hand.

Perón took it and then looked at Peter.

"A sus órdenes, mi Coronel," Peter said, clicking his heels and bowing his head.

"And it is always a pleasure to see you, my young friend," Perón said, stretching out his hand with a warm smile. "And tonight especially, when you are going to be very useful to an Argentine who speaks terrible German, and a German whose Spanish is a little less than perfect."

"It will be a pleasure to be of service, mi Coronel," Peter said. "But your German sounds fine to me."

"First things first," Perón said, smiling, in Spanish. "Would you please translate 'What may I offer you to drink?' "

Peter did so.

"First, Juan Domingo, let me say what a beautiful house this is," von Deitzberg said in German. "Then I will have a glass, if that would be possible, of your very good Argentine beer."

Peter translated.

Perón nodded and looked at the housekeeper. "Señora Lopez, would you bring us some beer, and perhaps some cheese and ham and crackers?"

"Sí, Señor."

"And after that, we can take care of ourselves," Perón said.

Except for von Deitzberg, who walked to a wall and complimented the "exquisite paneling," not another word was said until the housekeeper and a maid had delivered two silver Champagne coolers, each holding several bottles of beer, and two silver serving trays loaded with hors d'oeuvres. This happened so quickly that it was obvious it had all already been prepared. They then left the room.

"This beautiful building, Manfred—please translate for me, Mayor von Wachtstein—was owned, until his murder, by my lifelong friend el Coronel Jorge Guillermo Frade."

Peter translated. Von Deitzberg did not reply.

"It is now owned by his son, my godson, Mayor Cletus Frade. In the kitchen of this house, the housekeeper, whom I knew for many years, was brutally murdered by assassins sent to kill my godson."

Peter translated again, hoping his surprise at what amounted to an accusation was not evident.

"I was not aware of the history of the house, Juan Domingo," von Deitzberg said, waited for Peter to translate, and then went on: "But I cannot think of a better place for me to tell you what I have been sent from Germany to say."

"And what would that be, Manfred?" Perón said, smiling coldly.

"I will presume to speak as both a friend, Juan Domingo, and as a brother officer." He waited for Peter to translate, and for Perón to nod, and then went on: "I come to you as a

Generalmajor of the Oberkommando der Wehrmacht, and bring to you their apology for the outrageous and unpardonable actions of an officer of the Sicherheitsdienst who was permitted, for reasons I do not pretend to understand, to wear the uniform of an army colonel. I refer, of course, to the late so-called Oberst Grüner."

"The last time I saw you, Manfred," Perón said, "you were wearing the uniform of the SS."

"I was sent to the SS, against my personal wishes, by the OKW, because it was believed that an Army officer, the son of an Army officer, the grandson of an Army officer, might be able to instill in the SS some understanding of the code of honor," von Deitzberg said. "This instance particularly—and certainly others—show how I have failed."

My God, von Deitzberg said that with a straight face, Peter thought in amazement, *and Perón seems to be swallowing it whole.*

Maybe because he wants to believe it?

"Translate, if you will, Mayor," Perón said. "I found it difficult to believe that Germany would order the murder of el Coronel Frade. But the facts—"

"No one in the Wehrmacht would do such a thing," von Deitzberg said. "Grüner disgraced the uniform he should not have been wearing in the first place. Questions of honor aside, it was a stupid thing to do. I'm sure it enraged the Argentine officer corps. . . ."

"Yes, it did," Perón said.

"And it enraged the German officer corps," von Deitzberg continued. "And if I have to say this, Juan Domingo, it shamed and enraged me."

Perón made a wave of dismissal. "It never entered my mind that you, or any German officer I know, had anything to do with it," he said, and then gestured for Peter to make the translation.

"So far as the German officer corps is concerned, Juan Domingo," von Deitzberg replied, "the late Oberst Frade was a friend. He earned the respect—and the friendship—of all who knew him when he was at the Kriegsschule. And his nephew died an honorable officer's death while serving with us in our mutual fight against the godless Communists at Stalingrad."

The poor, stupid bastard, Peter thought unkindly, *got himself killed playing soldier. He was supposed to be an observer, a noncombatant, and an observer is not supposed to fly around in a Storch directing artillery fire.*

Perón did not reply.

"The assignment of Major von Wachtstein, the distinguished scion of a noble family of German soldiers, to accompany the remains of Captain Duarte to his Fatherland was not accidental, but rather a gesture of the respect in which the officer corps held the late Coronel Frade," von Deitzberg said, and gestured for Peter to make the translation.

"And that was appreciated by the family," Perón said. "And by myself."

"May I speak indelicately, between soldiers?" von Deitzberg said, then went on without waiting for Peter to translate. "The question of what to do with the so-called Colonel Grüner has been solved for us—"

"I don't understand," Perón interrupted without any translation from Peter.

Obviously, Peter thought, *Perón's German is better than he's willing to admit.*

"There is a certain justice in what el Coronel Frade's son did at the beach at Samborombón Bay," von Deitzberg said. "An eye for an eye, so to speak."

"What was going on at the beach?" Perón asked.

"Admiral Canaris wants the officers from the *Graf Spee* to escape, as he himself escaped from internment here in the First World War. To that end, Grüner and Goltz were trying to bring ashore a radio transmitter."

"Then that was an intolerable violation of Argentine sovereignty," Perón said.

"With all respect, Juan Domingo, if I were in their shoes, I would try to return to active service, and I think you would too."

"Nevertheless, that is unacceptable behavior."

"The question, I respectfully suggest, Juan Domingo, is moot. They did not get the radios ashore."

"You understand, Manfred, that now that you have told me this, I will have to take the appropriate action to ensure that the *Graf Spee* officers remain interned."

"I knew that when I told you," von Deitzberg said. "The more important question, however, is 'how can we close the door on this unfortunate incident?' "

"I don't think I know what you mean," Perón said.

"Can you express to the Argentine officer corps the profound apologies of the German officer corps for the actions—however unauthorized—of the so-called Colonel Grüner? Will you accept my word of honor as an officer that we have taken steps that will prevent anything like this from ever happening again?"

Perón neither looked at Peter for a translation nor immediately replied. Finally, he said: "The murder of the man who was poised to become President of Argentina cannot be—and should not be—forgotten easily."

"I am well aware of that, Juan Domingo," von Deitzberg said sadly.

"I will have a word with my friends," Perón said. "More important, with my godson. In very many ways, he is like his father, and his father was capable of staying very angry for a very long time."

"In his place, I would feel the same way," von Deitzberg said. "But he has had his revenge, has he not?"

Perón took a long moment to reply.

"I will have to think about this, Manfred," he said. "Would you be willing to offer the apology of the German officer corps to him personally? That might be necessary."

"Privately, you mean?"

"Yes, of course privately."

Von Deitzberg appeared to be thinking that over very carefully. "If you think that would be necessary, Juan Domingo, of course I would."

Perón grunted.

"I think enough has been said for now," he said. "Let me think about this."

"Of course."

"Personally, Manfred, I very much appreciate your coming to me like this."

"I very much appreciate your receiving me," von Deitzberg said.

"You'll be at the Alvear Plaza?"

"Yes."

"I'll telephone you there," Perón said, "and let you know. . . ."

"Thank you, Juan Domingo."

"In the old days," Perón said, "that is to say, before my friend was murdered, I would have asked you to stay here, in this house. My friends, so to speak, were his friends. And his friends, my friends. But this house is now the property of Mayor Frade, and that's quite out of the question."

"I completely understand, Juan Domingo."

"I'll call you at the Alvear," Perón repeated, then looked at Peter. "I understand, my young friend, that you have been seen at the Alvear yourself, in the roof garden, with a lovely young woman."

The discussion of an apology is now obviously over.

"I plead guilty, mi Coronel."

"You are aware, are you, that the young woman's sister was the next thing to engaged to the late Capitán Duarte?"

"Yes, Sir, I am."

"You could do a lot worse than Alicia Carzino-Cormano," Perón said. "And this war won't last forever."

"Mi Coronel," Peter said. "My relationship with Señorita Carzino-Cormano is not anywhere—"

"The person who saw the way she looked at you in the roof garden is in this room, Mayor von Wachtstein," Perón said, smiling warmly. "But I appreciate your discretion."

"We will not take any more of your time, Juan Domingo," von Deitzberg said.

Perón looked at his wristwatch.

"And I do have a dinner appointment," Perón said, and put out his hand.

• • •

"So tell me about your señorita, von Wachtstein," von Deitzberg said when they were en route to the Alvear Plaza.

"Her mother and Oberst Frade had a relationship," Peter replied. "They have adjacent estancias—enormous estancias, Herr General, each more than eighty thousand hectares—"

"*Eighty thousand* hectares?" von Deitzberg interrupted incredulously.

"Yes, Sir. They're unbelievable."

"And you met this young woman in connection with the funeral of Hauptmann Duarte?"

"Yes, Sir."

"Perón was right. You could do a lot worse than a young woman whose family owns eighty thousand hectares. And the war won't last forever."

"Herr General, there is nothing serious between us," Peter said.

"A connection like that could be very valuable to the Reich," von Deitzberg said, as if thinking aloud. "This is not the time to get into that subject, but let me say that, for a number of reasons, I wish you every romantic success with the young lady with the eighty thousand hectares."

"Thank you, Sir, but I really don't think—"

"So tell me, von Wachtstein, what do you think is Oberst Perón's little secret? What dark side of his character do you think there is?"

"Herr General, I have no idea."

"What's the first thing that came to your mind when I mentioned his interesting dossier?"

"The Herr General is embarrassing me."

"I don't mean to," von Deitzberg said. "What did you think?"

"I thought you were suggesting that he might be homosexual, Herr General."

"And do you think that's what his dark side is?"

"I find it hard to accept, Herr General. He is such a . . ."

"Masculine man?"

"Yes, Sir."

"Röhm* was a masculine man," von Deitzberg said, obviously enjoying himself. "A picture of the rough, tough-as-steel warrior. And he spent his last night on this earth, indeed, his last moments, in bed with a delicate young man. I've seen those photographs, too."

"I still don't see Perón as a homosexual, Herr General," Peter said.

"Then guess again."

"Herr General, I have no idea."

"He likes young women, von Wachtstein."

"Sir?"

"Very young women. At the first blush of womanhood, so to speak. Nothing, I gather, over fifteen."

Peter looked at him in disbelief.

"There were several incidents while he was in Italy and Germany. He had diplomatic immunity, of course, and they were all kept quiet. But photographs are available, if they should ever be needed."

"I'm shocked," Peter confessed. "Does he know you know?"

"He knows he was arrested; he's not stupid. He knows there is a record somewhere. I don't think he knows *I* know. And I certainly don't intend to play that card unless it's necessary."

He smiled at Peter. "As I say, von Wachtstein, you should make an effort to cultivate Oberst Perón."

Peter nodded.

"Grüner mentioned nothing of this to you?" von Deitzberg asked.

"No, Sir. This is the first I've heard of it."

---

* Ernst Röhm was a member of the Nazi party before Hitler. He formed strong-arm squads of thugs, who wore brown shirts as a uniform and had the mission of protecting Hitler, other senior Nazis, and Nazi party meetings, and of disrupting, usually violently, meetings of Socialists and Communists. In 1921 the Brown Shirts officially became the SA (Sturmabteilung), in effect the private army of the Nazi party. As their commander, Röhm became one of the most powerful and feared men in Germany. Hitler considered him, and the Brown Shirts, a threat to his own power, and in June 1934, on "The Night of the Long Knives," he had Röhm and several hundred other people assassinated by the SS.

"What about Operation Phoenix?" von Deitzberg asked.

"Standartenführer Goltz told me something about that, Herr General, but not Oberst Grüner."

"And what did Goltz tell you?" von Deitzberg asked.

Peter did not reply. Instead he pointed at Günther Loche in the front seat.

"Quite right, quite right," von Deitzberg said. "We can get into that later."

"Jawohl, Herr General."

On 6 May 1943, in three separate thrusts, American infantry and armored divisions in Tunisia broke through the German defensive line and attacked toward Bizerta, Ferryville, and Protville.

Elsewhere in Tunisia, following a massive artillery and air bombardment, the British destroyed what was left of the German 15th Panzer Division and broke through the German defensive positions to strike toward Tunis.

[TWO]
The Embassy of the German Reich
Avenue Córdoba
Buenos Aires
0915 6 May 1943

Fräulein Ingebord Hässell pushed open the door to the private office of Manfred Alois Graf von Lutzenberger, Ambassador Extraordinary and Plenipotentiary of the German Reich to the Republic of Argentina, and very loudly and importantly barked: "Your Excellency! Baron Gradny-Sawz is here with Deputy Foreign Minister von Löwzer and General Major von Deitzberg!"

You really should have been a man, Inge. You would have been a splendid Stabsfeldwebel. I can just see you on a parade ground, screaming orders at conscripts.

"Ask the gentlemen to come in please, Inge," von Lutzenberger said, and got up from behind his desk.

Deputy Foreign Minister Georg Friedrich von Löwzer came into the office first and rendered the Nazi salute. "Heil Hitler!" he barked.

Was that preposterous gesture rendered in deference to Himmler's adjutant? Or has von Löwzer become yet another zealous convert to the New Order?

Von Löwzer was followed into the office by von Deitzberg, then Gradny-Sawz, Standartenführer Erich Raschner, and finally, von Wachtstcin. They all wore civilian clothing.

"Heil Hitler," von Lutzenberger replied. "How are you, Friedrich?" Without waiting for a reply, he walked to von Deitzberg and offered his hand.

"Welcome to Argentina, Herr Generalmajor," he said. "I presume Gradny-Sawz and von Wachtstein have been taking good care of you?"

"Splendid, thank you. Last night von Wachtstein fed me the best steak I have ever had."

"There are some compensations attached to being in this barbarous outpost," von Lutzenberger said. "The food, the women, and the pastry, not necessarily in that order."

Gradny-Sawz chuckled; von Wachtstein smiled. Von Deitzberg did neither.

Is that an indication I was supposed to cringe at your appearance, von Deitzberg?

"Standartenführer Raschner is my deputy," von Deitzberg said, and von Lutzenberger offered his hand—but said nothing—to Raschner.

"You understand, Herr Generalmajor, why I was unable to meet you at the airport, or entertain you myself last night?

"Gradny-Sawz said something about a diplomatic reception?"

"At the Swedish Embassy," von Lutzenberger said. "My absence would have been conspicuous."

"Why is that?" von Deitzberg asked.

"It was the first reception—the first by a neutral

power—since the unfortunate demise of Oberst Frade, the coup d'état, and the incident at Samborombón Bay. The entire diplomatic corps was waiting—rather shamelessly—to see the interaction between myself and the officials of General Rawson's—El Presidente Rawson's—new government."

Von Löwzer chuckled. "And that was?" he asked.

"Following a *pro forma* handshake between el Presidente and myself, I became invisible to the Argentines."

"Which you think signifies . . . ?" Von Löwzer pursued.

"The Argentines obviously wished to make it clear to me, and everyone in the diplomatic community, that they—el Presidente Rawson in particular; he and Frade were good friends—don't consider the deaths of Oberst Grüner and Standartenführer Goltz as payment in full for the assassination of Oberst Frade."

" 'Everyone'? " von Löwzer asked. "Are you suggesting that everyone in the diplomatic community is conversant with the details of both incidents?"

Von Lutzenberger nodded. "No one believes that Oberst Frade was murdered in the course of a robbery, and everyone knows what happed to Grüner and Goltz."

"What does 'everyone' think happened to Grüner and Goltz at Samborombón Bay?" Von Deitzberg asked.

"That when they attempted to land equipment—shortwave radios, and other items, intended to facilitate the repatriation of the *Graf Spee* officers—from the *Océano Pacífico,* Frade's son was waiting for them, and revenged the murder of his father."

"How did our intention to repatriate the *Graf Spee* officers become known?" von Deitzberg asked, surprised.

"I told, in the strictest confidence, my friend the Spanish ambassador—"

"You did what?" von Deitzberg interrupted, incredulously.

"—in absolute confidence that within hours Oberst Martín of the Bureau of Internal Security would hear what we were doing at Samborombón Bay," von Lutzenberger finished, somewhat coldly.

"And who gave you the authority to do this?" von Deitzberg demanded.

Von Lutzenberger waved his hand at Gradny-Sawz, von Wachtstein, and Raschner. "If you gentlemen will excuse us," he ordered. "Herr Minister von Löwzer and the Generalmajor and I would like a word in private."

Gradny-Sawz—whose face showed his surprise and concern—and von Wachtstein and Raschner left the office.

Von Lutzenberger looked at von Deitzberg.

"You were about to tell me who gave you the authority to reveal—" von Deitzberg said.

"Pardon me, Herr Generalmajor," von Lutzenberger said, holding up his hand to interrupt him.

Von Deitzberg glowered at him.

"Perhaps I can save us all some time," von Lutzenberger said. He turned to von Löwzer. "Friedrich, are you here to tell me that I am being recalled to Berlin for consultation? Or, perhaps, that you are replacing me 'temporarily' until this matter is resolved?"

"No," von Löwzer said, obviously surprised at the question. "Where did you get an idea like that?"

"Perhaps you are bearing orders of that nature for me, Herr Generalmajor?" von Lutzenberger asked.

"No," von Deitzberg said. "I don't quite understand the question."

"The question is one of authority, Herr Generalmajor," von Lutzenberger said. "May I presume, then, Friedrich, in the absence of orders to the contrary, that I remain the Ambassador Extraordinary and Plenipotentiary of the Führer of the German Reich to the Republic of Argentina?"

"Of course," von Löwzer said. "There never has been any question of that."

"Then perhaps you would be good enough, Friedrich, to tell the Herr Generalmajor that as the ambassador here, I exercise, in the name of the Führer, German authority in all things."

"I'm sure von Deitzberg understands that," von Löwzer said.

"I come here with the authority of the Foreign Minister, Herr Ambassador," von Deitzberg challenged.

"What you have, Herr Generalmajor, is the Foreign Minister's authority to conduct an investigation under my authority as the Führer's representative in Argentina. You have no more right to question my authority than you do to question that of the Führer. If there is any question in your mind about that, I suggest we can get clarification from Berlin in twenty-four hours or so."

Von Deitzberg backed down. "I had no intention of questioning your authority, Herr Ambassador," he said.

"I did not have that feeling a few moments ago."

"The plan to repatriate the *Graf Spee* officers is—was—a state secret of the highest order, Manfred," von Löwzer said, obviously pouring oil on the troubled waters. "Certainly, you can understand von Deitzberg's surprise that you felt you had to compromise it."

"I thought perhaps the Herr Generalmajor," Von Lutzenberger said, looking directly at von Deitzberg, "would consider that until the Argentine Bureau of Internal Security found an answer satisfactory to them for our presence at Samborombón Bay, they would keep looking. Of 'the three state secrets of the highest order' involved here, the *Graf Spee* officer repatriation was, in my judgment, the least important. If compromising that secret satisfied the curiosity of the BIS, then that price simply had to be paid."

"Well, I can certainly agree with your reasoning," von Löwzer said.

"You didn't inform Berlin of your action," von Deitzberg said.

That's still a challenge, von Lutzenberger thought. *But the arrogance factor has been reduced by—what? Say three-quarters?*

"I decided that it could wait until you and von Löwzer got here."

"I hope the Herr Ambassador will understand how much of a fish out of water someone like me is in the world of diplomacy," von Deitzberg said.

That's even getting close to an apology.

"As a soldier, you mean?" von Lutzenberger asked.

"Precisely."

You're not a soldier. You're Himmler's adjutant.

"Let me try an analogy," von Lutzenberger said. "I've often thought that an ambassador is something like a just-graduated lieutenant taking command of his first platoon in combat. He doesn't know where he is, or what his captain wants him to do with all the authority he's suddenly been given. Yet he has to do something, and can only hope that what he does is the right thing."

"Very well put, I would say," von Deitzberg said.

"And about the first thing he learns is that if he compromises his authority, he never gets it back," von Lutzenberger added.

"Well, from my own experience, I can certainly agree with that," von Deitzberg said.

"Now, there are some advantages to having authority, either as a young lieutenant, or an ambassador," von Lutzenberger said seriously. "And high among them is being able to meet nature's call without asking for permission. If you gentlemen will excuse me for a few minutes?"

It took both von Deitzberg and von Löwzer a few seconds to take his meaning. By then, von Lutzenberger was almost out of his office. Then both laughed at von Lutzenberger's sense of humor. Von Deitzberg's laugh sounded a little forced, and von Löwzer's a little relieved.

Von Lutzenberger entered the men's room, made sure it was empty, then locked the door. He went into a stall, carefully raised the seat, bent over it, and vomited. When he stood up he held his hands out in front of him. They were trembling, and it took him some time to will them to be still.

It is always a mistake to underestimate your enemy, but I think I have put that Nazi bastard in his place.

Von Lutzenberger washed his hands, then wiped his face with a cold water-soaked towel. He looked at himself in the mirror for a moment, then walked back to his office.

"Now, where were we?" he asked.

"While you were gone, Manfred," von Löwzer said, "I

wondered about the reaction of the diplomatic community to the murders."

"Generally speaking, of course, and vis-à-vis Oberst Frade, they thought that was a mistake," von Lutzenberger said. "As did I, you will recall, Friedrich. I advised against that action. And vis-à-vis Grüner and Goltz, they feel we should not have been surprised that the Argentine military did not turn the other cheek."

"I was opposed to the elimination of Frade myself," von Deitzberg said. "And said so. That decision was made at the highest levels."

You really are a stranger to the truth, aren't you, my dear Generalmajor?

"Then time has proven you and me right, hasn't it?" von Lutzenberger said.

"I confess to being a little surprised—if I understand you correctly—that the diplomatic community believes Germany was involved."

"They take their lead from the Argentine military, and the military never had any doubt who was responsible."

"Late yesterday afternoon, I went to see Oberst Perón," von Deitzberg said. "I conveyed to him the regrets of his many friends in Germany, especially within the officer corps, that an out-of-control SS officer, acting without authority, caused the death of Oberst Frade."

Von Lutzenberger looked at him with interest.

"Before you do anything like that again, Herr Generalmajor, please consult with me," von Lutzenberger said.

"I made it quite plain to Perón, Mr. Ambassador, that my visit was unofficial."

"And you said Goltz was the loose cannon on our deck?"

"No. Grüner," von Deitzberg said.

"Grüner? Do you think he believed you?"

"Yes. I think so. Von Wachtstein was with me. He said he thought Perón believed me."

"Von Wachtstein has become close to the Duarte family. The mother of Hauptmann Duarte, Frau Duarte, who is mentally unbalanced, is especially fond of him. When von Wachtstein came to me for guidance in the matter, I encouraged him—on the advice of both Goltz and Gradny-Sawz—to cultivate the relationship. Frau Duarte is the late Oberst Frade's sister, and her husband is the managing director of the Anglo-Argentine Bank. That could very well be quite valuable in connection with Operation Phoenix."

"How much does von Wachtstein know about Operation Phoenix?"

"Goltz was going to tell him what he thought he should know."

"And how much do you think he did tell him?"

"I'm sure he told him about the *Graf Spee* officers' repatriation. He was going to be involved in that."

"And nothing else?"

"I don't know what else he told him, but I wouldn't be surprised if he at least alluded to Operation Phoenix. And I would be very surprised if von Wachtstein—he's a very bright young man—hasn't wondered why we went to all that trouble to smuggle shortwave radios and civilian clothing from a Spanish vessel into Argentina, when one can buy radios and civilian clothing in Buenos Aires."

"He's asked questions, has he?"

"Oh, no. He's a soldier, General. He obeys orders and doesn't ask questions."

"Then you would say he's not the source of the information that permitted Oberst Frade's son to be waiting on the beach at Samborombón Bay?"

"For several reasons, I think that's highly unlikely."

"Would you tell me why?"

"First of all, I don't think he knew. Secondly, if he knew, I don't think he had a motive to tell anyone—or the opportunity. But even if he had both, I don't think he would have betrayed his country."

"Because you think he's a reliable young soldier?"

"Because he is a bright young man who would understand the consequences to his father."

"Well, if you had to guess, how would you say that Frade knew when and where the special shipment was going to be landed?"

Von Lutzenberger then spelled out the story of the river

launch in El Tigre: It had been purchased by Argentine-born ethnic Germans, he explained, who had no idea about the schedule for the landing of the special shipment. Nor did von Wachtstein, who was brought into the picture because he knew how to navigate.

"Given that," he continued, "I strongly suspect that our involvement with the boat came to the attention of the BIS. As I've said before, Oberst Martín is very good. Why would a German immigrant sausage maker be buying a riverboat? More important, where would he get the money? Perhaps from the German Embassy? The word goes out, watch the boat. The boat sets out with the German Assistant Military Attaché for Air as her captain. Not up the river, but down the river, into the River Plate estuary. What's in the River Plate estuary? The *Océano Pacífico,* which is suspected of being a German replenishment vessel. It goes to Puerto Magdalena, where, as the Argentine police watch, her crew goes to the home of Herr Steuben, another ethnic German. The BIS agents watching Goltz report that Goltz gets up in the middle of the night and drives to Puerto Magdalena to the home of Herr Steuben, and then gets on the river launch and heads out to the *Océano Pacífico.* The BIS agents watching Grüner report that he, too, gets up very early in the morning and drives in the same direction.

"Now Oberst Martín has a problem. If Goltz and Grüner are really smuggling, he can't arrest either of them because of their diplomatic status. He can make a report through channels, and at worst I will be chastised by the Foreign Minister, and he will get in trouble with some of our friends in the Argentine military who will think he should have looked the other way.

"I don't think it strains credulity to suspect that Oberst Martín told young Frade that Oberst Grüner and Standartenführer Goltz were going to land on the shores of Samborombón Bay in the next couple of hours—"

"My God!" von Löwzer said.

"—in circumstances that would preclude any diplomatic indignation on my part if something happened to them there."

"And, after the fact, the reaction of the Argentine military was 'Good for young Frade, he revenged his father'?" von Deitzberg asked.

Von Lutzenberger nodded. "That is all speculation, of course," he said. "I don't know."

"It's the best theory I have heard so far," von Deitzberg said. "But I wondered . . . Why did von Wachtstein come through unscathed? Why wasn't he shot along with Grüner and Goltz?"

"He was shot at, and they missed. Or so Kapitän de Banderano with whom I managed to speak for an hour—told me. Von Wachtstein came under fire while he courageously pulled Grüner and Goltz into the boat from the *Océano Pacífico*. Banderano seemed to feel he acted with great courage."

"Well, he does have the Knight's Cross, doesn't he?" von Deitzberg said agreeably.

I don't think he accepted that explanation nearly as much as he wants me to think he has. And if he doesn't believe that, he questions the rest of the story as well.

"In the belief that both you and von Löwzer would like to go through our records, I instructed Untersturmführer Schneider, who is in charge of surveilling the Embassy's officers, to have his records available for you this morning."

"All the Embassy's officers?"

"Everyone but myself and Gradny-Sawz," von Lutzenberger said.

"I would very much like to see them," von Deitzberg said, "and to talk to Untersturmführer Schneider."

"He is at your disposal, Herr Generalmajor."

"And there is another thing, of a somewhat indelicate nature," von Deitzberg said with a smile. "How do you feel about giving a diplomatic reception, to afford the diplomatic community, and the more important Argentines, an opportunity to meet von Löwzer? And, of course, myself."

"I think that's a splendid idea. I'll have Fräulein Hässell get started right away."

"You're very kind. This Saturday, perhaps?"

"That could be arranged, but I don't think the important Argentines will be available this Saturday."

"Why not?"

"Young Frade is getting married on Saturday. Presidente Rawson will be there, and so will most of the important Argentines."

"You and I are going to have to have a long talk about young Frade," von Deitzberg said, smiling. "But not now. I know you're busy, and I want to talk to Schneider. And we're having dinner tonight, I understand?"

Von Lutzenberger nodded. "At the Alvear. I think you'll like it."

"I'm sure I will," von Deitzberg said, and stood up and gave the Nazi salute.

"Heil Hitler!" he barked.

[THREE]
Estancia San Pedro y San Pablo
Near Pila, Buenos Aires Province
0925 6 May 1943

Martha Howell had heard thunder during the night, and when she looked out of her window when she woke, she saw dark clouds hovering over the pampas. When she went into Marjorie's room, she wasn't there; and when she went into Beth's room, Beth said that her sister was flying with Clete.

In this weather?

She said nothing to Beth. Clete was no fool and a good pilot; he wouldn't fly if it was dangerous. But she was a mother, and after she'd had her breakfast, she walked down to the airstrip with a cup of coffee in her hand.

Enrico Rodríguez was sitting in a chair under the wing of the Lockheed Lodestar. When he saw her coming, he rose to his feet. "Buenos dias, señora," he said politely.

She was not surprised to find him there. "Keep your seat, Enrico," she said in Spanish, with a smile.

I would have been surprised if he wasn't here. His devotion to Clete is doglike.

That thought triggered a memory. Of Jim's dog. Oscar. A black Labrador. Although Jim had been dead a year now, Oscar still spent most of his days lying on the porch of the house at Big Foot Ranch with his head between his paws, waiting for Jim to come home.

James Fitzhugh Howell, her husband, the only man she had ever loved, and whom she missed desperately, had stepped away from the bar at the Petroleum Club in Midland and dropped dead before he got to the men's room.

She saw a lot of Jim in Cletus, some of it genetic, but most of it in his character—although she had to admit, after seeing so many pictures of Clete's father, that in his physical features he favored the Frades more than the Howells. They had been like father and son, and Clete had copied Jim in many ways. He even walked like him.

She forced the memories of her husband and Oscar from her mind and looked at the Lodestar. It was painted a brilliant red—Clete said the color was called "Staggerwing Red" because many Beechcraft Staggerwing aircraft were painted that color.

Clete had been very vague about why this plane was painted that color, or even why President Roosevelt had sent it as a gift, "an expression of friendship and admiration," to the late Colonel Frade to replace the Staggerwing Beechcraft that had been lost in an "accident."

She looked down the runway and thought that the pampas were much like the plains around Midland, except that here there was rich topsoil, five and six feet deep. Around Midland the land was arid and the topsoil shallow. It took ten times as much acreage to sustain a beef on Big Foot Ranch as it did here.

Two minutes later, her ears picked up the peculiar sound of a Piper Cub's engine. A minute later, the plane came into view.

As it made its approach, Martha saw her daughter in the front seat. It touched down, immediately took off again, and repeated this process three times before finally completing its landing roll and taxiing up to the hangar.

She was annoyed but not surprised.

Clete said he was going to give Marjorie some instruction, and that's what he's doing. He's like Jim in that, too. If he says he's going to do something, he does it.

Jim had taught all of them to fly, Martha included. Clete had been flying all over the ranch by himself long before he was old enough to get a license. And he had regularly flown to and from College Station on weekends when he was at Texas A&M. Jim had waited until the girls were sixteen before teaching them how to fly.

"How'd it go?" Martha asked when they had climbed out of the Cub.

"Another two hundred hours of dual," Clete said, "and she'll be ready to taxi it by herself."

"You can go to hell, Clete," Marjorie said.

"Actually, she's not bad," Clete said. "She was trying to find Buenos Aires, and she was actually pointed in the right direction—"

"Go to hell twice," Marjorie said.

"—but I didn't like the weather, so we came back."

They walked back to the big house, with Enrico trailing behind them with his shotgun. As they approached the steps to the wide veranda, one of the maids came out. "Patrón, you have a telephone call," she said. "A Captain Ashton."

"He's on the phone?" Clete asked, doubtfully.

"Sí, Patrón. I heard the airplane coming, and . . ."

Clete trotted up the stairs, went to the desk in his apartment, and picked up the telephone. "If this is who I think it is, what a pleasant surprise," he said.

"Captain Ashton, Sir."

"Where are you, Max?"

"At the embassy."

"And you've called to tell me you've found work?"

"Sir, I have been appointed as an assistant military attaché."

"When did that happen?"

"We arrived last evening, Sir," Ashton said. "Sir, I need to see you, at your earliest convenience."

What's with this "Sir" business?

"Will it wait until Saturday? Consider yourself invited to my wedding."

"Thank you, Sir. Would it be possible to see you today, Sir?"

"Sure, come on out."

"Sir, perhaps there's someplace we could meet in Buenos Aires?"

Whatever this is all about, he's serious.

"The weather's closing in—I can't fly. It'll take me two hours, a little longer, to drive in. How about lunch?"

"Yes, Sir. That would be fine. Where, Sir?"

"You know where the guest house is, on Libertador?"

"Yes, Sir."

"No. That's out. I just remembered somebody's staying there. It'll have to be the museum. Noon OK?"

"The museum, Sir?"

"Seventeen twenty-eight Avenida Coronel Díaz, in Palermo," Clete said. "I'll call ahead and tell them you're coming, in case you get there before I do."

"Seventeen twenty-eight Avenida Coronel Díaz at twelve hundred," Ashton said. "Yes, Sir. We'll be there, Sir."

The line went dead.

"We'll be there"? He said "we" twice. Who's "we"? What's this all about?

He put the telephone in its cradle and turned and was not at all surprised to find Enrico standing in the door. "Get the Horch, Enrico, we're going into Buenos Aires."

"Señor Cletus, they are working on the polish of the Horch."

"OK, then get the Buick."

"We will be coming back today?"

"I think so."

[FOUR]
1728 Avenida Coronel Díaz
Palermo, Buenos Aires
1150 6 May 1943

Unnecessarily, for Clete had already noticed it, Enrico touched his arm and then jerked his thumb toward a gray 1939 Dodge sedan parked across the street from the massive mansion. Two men were sitting in it.

"The clowns are here," Enrico said. He held the agents of both the Bureau of Internal Security and of the Policía Federal in equal contempt; he called both "the clowns."

"They're probably following Ashton," Clete said. "He's here." He pointed to a 1941 Chevrolet sedan with Corps Diplomatique license tags parked directly in front of the mansion.

Hell, that's almost certainly Milton Leibermann's car. As the "legal attaché," he gets CD plates. That's what this is all about. Leibermann wants to see me. He's the "we" Ashton meant.

As he drove the Buick across the sidewalk to the left of the mansion's two twelve-foot-high wrought-iron gates, one of the double doors to the mansion opened and a short, squat maid—who obviously had been watching from behind the curtains for Señor Frade to arrive—trotted to the gates and pulled them open. Clete pulled into the curved cobblestone drive, stopped in front of the mansion, and got out and started up the stairs.

A dignified, silver-haired man in his sixties, dressed in a gray frock coat, opened the door as Clete reached it. Antonio had been the butler in the Frade family's Coronel Díaz mansion for longer than Clete's lifetime. "Señor Frade," Antonio said. "Your guests are here. I put them in the downstairs sitting."

The downstairs sitting in this place is about as warm and comfortable as the room in a funeral home where they put the casket on display. Maybe less warm and comfortable.

"Thank you, Antonio," Clete said. "How are you?"

"Very well, thank you, Sir."

"Can we feed these people?"

"If I had had more time, Señor . . ."

"But we can feed them, right?"

"Of course, Señor."

As Clete walked across the marble-floored foyer past the curving double stairways leading to the second floor (the steps were marble; the railings were cast bronze), he remembered his father telling him that his mother had refused to live there (she was the one who'd given it its name, "The Museum"). His father himself had described it as "my money sewer on Avenida Coronel Díaz."

It *was* like a museum, both in its dimensions and in the plethora of artwork, huge oil paintings and statuary that covered the walls and open spaces. He always had the somewhat irreverent thought that two subjects seemed to fascinate Argentine artists and sculptors: La Pampa, at dusk, during a rainstorm; and buxom women dressed in what looked like wet sheets that generally left exposed at least one large and well-formed breast.

He was far more comfortable in the guest house on Libertador; but, as he had told Max on the phone, there was a guest there. He had an unkind thought as he pushed open the door to the downstairs sitting: *If I hadn't let that damned Jesuit con artist sweet-talk me into having Perón at my wedding, Perón would have been insulted. Maybe then the sonofabitch would move out of my guest house. I am really pissed at the thought of that bastard doing whatever the hell he does with young girls in my house.*

The first person he saw was Milton Leibermann, sitting on one of the half-dozen unbelievably uncomfortable straightbacked, brocade-upholstered, two-seater couches. They were set so close to the floor that Leibermann's knees were higher than his waist.

Milton looks ridiculous.

There was a tiny porcelain coffee set on a silver tray on a small table in front of the couch, and an identical set on a small table before the matching chair where Captain Maxwell Ashton sat. He had two more unkind thoughts: *Max is so short, he fits in that chair. And where did he get that awful suit? He looks like a Mexican sharpie in Matamores. "You want pesos, señor? I give you best deal. Or how about a sixteen-year-old virgin?"*

And then he saw a third man in the room.

Well, that explains the "we arrived last night" remark, doesn't it?

Colonel A. J. Graham, USMCR, was standing by the heavily draped windows overlooking Avenida Coronel Díaz. He was in uniform, complete to ribbons and a thick gold cord hanging from his epaulet that Clete recognized, from his aborted assignment as Naval Attaché, as the insignia of an attaché.

He really looks like a Marine colonel. Starchy, and mean as a junkyard dog.

"Well, look who's here!" Clete said. "How long are you going to be here? Can you stay for the wedding?"

Graham was not smiling, and he did not reply for a long moment. "Tell me, Frade," he said finally, "you do understand, don't you, that you are a serving officer of the United States Marine Corps?"

"Well, this is hardly Quantico, is it?" Clete replied without thinking. "But sure."

"Come to attention, Major, and stay at attention until I give you further orders," Graham said coldly.

Clete looked at him for a minute before he saw that he was absolutely serious. There was proof of that in the embarrassed looks on the faces of Milton Leibermann and Maxwell Ashton III. He felt his face flush, as, feeling foolish, he came to attention.

In my own house? What the hell is going on?

"One of the first things I learned as a young lieutenant, Major, was that in ordinary circumstances, when one is reprimanding a subordinate, one does so in private, so the offi-

cer being reprimanded won't be embarrassed or humiliated,"
Graham said matter-of-factly, almost conversationally.

"These are not ordinary circumstances," he went on. "I
asked Mr. Leibermann—and ordered Captain Ashton—to be
here because I wanted witnesses. If the by-product is that
you are embarrassed and humiliated, that's unfortunate."

"Sir, may I ask what's going on?"

"You do not have permission to speak, Major," Graham
said. "Don't open your mouth again until I give you permission to do so, not even to say 'Yes, Sir.' "

Clete managed, at the last split second, to overcome his
Pavlovian urge to say "Yes, Sir."

"The reason I wanted witnesses is that, given your
demonstrated willingness to disobey orders, I was forced to
consider the real possibility that you are entirely capable of
deciding—perhaps have already decided—that you no
longer have to obey orders.

"So I will begin by explaining to you what will happen the
very next time you elect to either disobey orders or take any
action on your own which in my judgment violates the spirit
of the orders I have given you.

"You will be ordered to return to the United States. You
will become a patient at St. Elizabeth's Mental Hospital in
Washington, and you will stay there, your records marked
'National Security Patient,' until this war is over. If you
behave while in St. Elizabeth's, you may be allowed, once
the war is over, to resign your commission for the good of
the service. The other option is a court-martial, on a wide
variety of charges, not all of them, frankly, justified.

"Your wife will not be granted a visa to enter the United
States, which is probably a moot question, because you will
not be allowed visitors while you are in St. Elizabeth's. Any
children born of your marriage will not be considered to
have been born to an officer serving outside the United
States, and will not, therefore, be American citizens.

"As you have already almost certainly begun to think,
'Fuck Graham, I'll just stay here,' let me touch on that. If
you choose to ignore an order to return to the United States,
charges will be brought against you for desertion in time of

war. Steps will be taken to have you expelled from Argentina. I think they will probably be successful, despite your connections here, because we will give the Argentine government reason to believe you are acting against the best interests of this country.

"Even if that fails, you will remain on the rolls as a deserter-at-large. If you should ever return to the United States, you will be arrested at the port of entry. Law-enforcement officials in Texas and Louisiana will be regularly contacted by the FBI to make sure that you haven't managed to enter the country without being arrested. I will personally make sure that your photograph—Deserter Wanted By FBI—hangs on the bulletin board of every post office and police station in Texas and Louisiana."

He paused and looked at Clete with loathing. "Are you getting the picture, Major Frade? You may speak."

"What orders am I accused of disobeying, Colonel?"

"Oddly enough, I can remember them almost word for word. My last orders to you, Major, when I agreed to keep von Wachtstein's identity secret, were 'If something happens to you, Clete, the deal is off. So don't do anything dangerous—like falling out of your wedding bed—or anything else risky down here. Go on the canapé and small-talk circuit. Keep your ears open. Say a kind word for our side when you get the chance.' That may not be verbatim, but it's pretty damned close."

Graham looked at Leibermann. "You were there, Milton. Did I leave anything out?" Leibermann shook his head "no," but didn't speak. "For the record, I just repeated those orders to you, Major Frade. You are advised they are direct orders."

"Yes, Sir," Clete said.

"What the hell were you thinking when you flew Ashton to Uruguay in the Lockheed? Who do you think you are, goddamn it, Jack Armstrong, All-American Boy? Commander Don Winslow of the goddamned U.S. Navy?"

"In my judgment, Sir, it was the best way to exfiltrate Ashton," Clete said.

"Then your judgment is fatally flawed! Goddamn you! Didn't you consider the risk you were taking?"

Clete didn't reply.

"Let me explain, since your stupidity is of such monumental proportions that you may not even know: First of all, you arrogant pup, you're not qualified to fly that airplane. You're a fighter pilot, not a multiengine transport aircraft pilot."

"Sir, I flew the Lodestar from Braz—"

"Close your mouth!" Graham interrupted furiously. He paused a moment, as if considering what he wanted to say. "OK. My fault. I should have pulled you up short when that happened. That was a stupid thing for you to do. Really stupid. A combination, I suppose, of Marine Corps fighter pilot arrogance and this Jack Armstrong complex you have. What you should have done was get word to me you had never been inside a Lodestar. I could have had a qualified pilot there in forty-eight hours. Or you could have asked the Marine Corps pilot you got to give you—what, four hours instruction?—to fly it. But you got away with it, you got Ashton and the radar into Argentina, and because I didn't think you would be so stupid as to go on flying the Lockheed without getting fully checked out in it, and certainly not by yourself, without a copilot, I said nothing. Major error in my judgment."

He stopped, and collected his thoughts again.

"Did it even occur to you what would happen if you crashed that airplane? And I'm not speaking of killing Ashton, your fiancée, your uncle, and your sisters—"

"Colonel, if I had thought there was any danger—"

"Goddamn you, shut your mouth until I give you permission to open it!"

He paused, visibly getting his temper under control, before going on.

"For one thing, that would have given the Bureau of Security all they needed to come on your estancia and grab the radar and Ashton's team. Two weeks after that, another German freighter would be anchored in Samborombón Bay refueling German submarines.

"For another, it would have meant that I would have had to tell Colonel Donovan who Galahad is. And von Wachtstein is the only window we have on this obscene concentration camp inmate ransoming business. There are thousands of lives at stake there, for God's sake.

"And von Wachtstein—and you're right: If Donovan gets his name, it will be only a matter of time before we do something stupid, and the Germans will learn we've turned him—is the only window we have on Operation Phoenix." He paused and took a breath. "And you were willing to risk all this so that you could play Jack Fucking Armstrong. Now do you know why I'm furious?"

"Sir, I didn't think—"

"You bet your stupid ass you didn't think!"

"I'll find somebody to fly the Lockheed," Clete said.

"And here's another instance of where I find it difficult to believe that you're so incredibly stupid: Ashton tells me that you crossed Juan Domingo Perón's name off the guest list for your wedding. Is that true?"

"He will be at the wedding," Clete said.

"Don't tell me you actually reconsidered one of your stupid acts?"

"Somebody told me I couldn't afford to insult him," Clete said.

"Who somebody?"

"A Jesuit priest. Named Welner. He and my father were friends."

"I'll tell you what you're going to do with Perón. You're going to get so close to him you'll think you're a fucking Band-Aid. You're going to be the son that sonofabitch never had." He paused and looked at Clete. "I sent you down here in the first place because I thought you could get close to the powers that be. When the Germans killed your father, you should have known, for Christ's sake, that the next-best thing to your father is your goddamned godfather. I think that sonofabitch is going to end up running this country. You want to tell me why you didn't want him at your wedding?"

"He's a pervert, for one thing," Clete said, and the moment he heard the words come out of his mouth, he realized how inane his answer sounded.

"Pervert?" Graham asked with obvious interest. "Perón's queer?"

"He likes little girls. Fourteen-year-olds."

"You're sure about that?"

"He brought one to the house on Libertador. I saw him with her."

"It could have been a niece or something."

"I asked Enrico about it, and he told me."

"I'll be damned," Graham said. "That's interesting. And that's what I meant when I ordered you to keep your eyes and ears open. You didn't think we would be interested in hearing about that?"

"It never occurred to me, Sir," Clete said.

"Start thinking, for God's sake!" Graham snapped. He turned to Leibermann. "You hear anything about Perón, Milton?"

Leibermann shook his head. "You're sure about that, Tex?" he asked.

"I told you what I know," Clete said.

"I agree, that's interesting," Leibermann said.

"You said, 'for one thing,' " Graham said.

"Sir?"

"You said you didn't want him at your wedding for one thing because he's a pervert. What else?"

"Well, in the face of the facts, he refuses to admit the Germans killed my father."

"Milton, are you thinking what I'm thinking?" Graham said.

"Clete, it could be because the Germans know about his sexual appetites," Leibermann said. "In a society like this, Perón would do or say whatever they want him to to keep that from coming out."

"That may be very useful information, for use somewhere down the pike," Graham said.

"I would hold that card a long time before playing it," Leibermann said.

"Of course," Graham said. "As far as you're concerned, Frade, aside from keeping your eyes and ears open to confirm this little-girl business, you say and do nothing. You got that?"

"Yes, Sir."

"I think that concludes our conversation," Graham said. "We understand each other, right, Frade?"

"Yes, Sir. Sir, I'm sorry—"

"Save your breath. In our business, sorry doesn't count."

Leibermann grunted as he raised himself out of the too-low couch.

"One more thing," Graham said. "Mr. Leibermann and I accept your kind invitation to your wedding."

"Yes, Sir," Clete said, and then thought of something else, decided to hell with it, it was his business, but in the end decided it probably was Graham's business—or Graham would think it was. "Sir, I plan to get married in my uniform," he blurted.

Graham looked at him and took fifteen seconds to think it over. "Fine," he said finally, then started to walk out of the room.

[ONE]
1728 Avenida Coronel Díaz
Palermo, Buenos Aires
2245 6 May 1943

Clete had wasted the evening at a not entirely pleasant dinner at the home of his fiancée. Rather than spending time with Dorotéa, he had had to "get to know" Dorotéa's paternal grandmother and some of her father's brothers and sisters, none of whom he had previously met.

The grandmother in particular, as well as most of the uncles and aunts, had—through a haze of icy courtesy—managed to make it clear what they thought of norteamericanos and Protestants in general, and of a Protestant norteamericano who had despoiled the family virgin in particular.

At the time, he had resisted the temptation to drink, but as he walked through the door to the Museum, he told Antonio to bring American whiskey to his sitting.

He was halfway through his third Jack Daniel's, and listening to the news from the British Broadcasting Corporation's Foreign Service, when Antonio reappeared.

"Are you at home, Señor?" Antonio asked. "There is a Señor Freets on the telephone."

"I'll take it," Clete said, and quickly got out of the chair, where—in addition to listening to the news—he had also been wincing mentally at the (richly deserved, he was forced to admit, hook, line, and sinker) tongue-lashing he'd gotten from Colonel Graham, and wondering how many Mallín family genes the baby would inherit.

He crossed the room to the telephone, then had to wait until Antonio said, "One moment, please, Señor Freets," before he handed it to him.

"Fritz? What's up?" Clete asked.

"I'm going to Germany tomorrow. I'm about to go to dinner in the Alvear with von Deitzberg, the Ambassador, and Gradny-Sawz. I'd like to see you for a few minutes. I can't get away from here for more than twenty minutes. Any ideas?"

Clete had no ideas at all. It would take more than twenty minutes for Peter to travel back and forth from the Alvear Palace Hotel to the Museum; and if he himself went to the hotel, they would be seen together.

"Call me back when you get to the Alvear," Clete said. "I'll think of something."

"Right," Peter said, and the line went dead.

Clete looked around for Enrico and found him asleep in an armchair in the small foyer of the master suite. He touched his shoulder.

"Señor Clete?" Enrico asked, suddenly wide awake.

"Mayor von Wachtstein is going to be at the Alvear in maybe fifteen minutes. He can't get free long enough—twenty minutes, no more—to come here. He wants to see me. Obviously, it's important. Any ideas? Is there some-place near the Alvear where we could meet without being seen?"

"You have an apartment in the Alvear," Enrico said.

"I do?" Clete asked. It was the first he'd heard about that.

Enrico reached into his pocket, came out with an enor-mous bunch of keys, found the one he was looking for, and held it up triumphantly.

"Why do I have an apartment in the Alvear?" Clete asked.

"El Coronel used it for entertaining," Enrico said. "When discretion was necessary."

"What does that mean? And I thought that's what the house on Libertador is for? A guest house."

"The house on Libertador *is* used to house guests," Enrico said, smiling. "Normally, men who come to Buenos Aires from the country with their families."

"That's what I thought."

"Some men, Señor Clete, if their wives do not accompany them to Buenos Aires, and sometimes even if they do, grow very lonely at night. And even sometimes in the afternoon."

"What are you saying, Enrico? That my father kept an apartment in the Alvear so that his friends could—"

"El Coronel, Señor Clete, was famous for his hospitality."

"I'll be damned," Clete said. "But I still don't see why an apartment. Why not in the house on Libertador?"

"Señora Pellano, my beloved sister, Mariana Maria Delores Rodríguez de Pellano, Señor Clete, may she be rest-ing in peace now for all eternity with all the saints in heaven, was a good Christian woman. El Coronel would never insult her by asking her to house inappropriate women in a house she thought of as her own."

"Inappropriate women meaning whores, right?"

"No, Señor Clete. Your father would not insult his friends, his guests, by asking them to associate with whores."

"Then with what?"

"A whore, Señor Clete—is this not true in the Estados Unidos as well?—will go to bed with any man who pays her—"

"That's a *prostitute,* Enrico," Clete interrupted. "A whore just likes men, all men."

"She will sleep, a whore, with just about any man?"

"That sums it up neatly, Enrico. I guess you could say that Señora Pellano would regard both whores and prostitutes as inappropriate women. As would Señora Howell. And, of course, Señora Carzino-Cormano."

"You understand, Señor Clete," Enrico said approvingly.

"And did Señora Carzino-Cormano know about the apartment in the Alvear?"

"She did not want to know about the apartment, and therefore she did not know. You understand, Señor Clete?"

"Maybe," Clete said. "What I *don't* understand is who *did* my father get to entertain his friends who got lonely at night and sometimes in the afternoon, who we now understand were inappropriate women but neither whores nor prostitutes?"

"You are making fun of me, Señor Clete?"

"Absolutely not, Enrico," Clete said. "I am asking you, as a friend, to explain these matters to me, so I will not do or say anything inappropriate. In case I should happen to bump into one of these inappropriate women, or if I should have to entertain some lonely friends of my father."

"You are making fun of me, and I will say no more," Enrico said, at once sad and indignant.

"Goddamn it, Enrico, I am not making fun of you. You're my best friend in Argentina."

Enrico met his eyes. "Except perhaps for the good Father Welner, I am," he said.

"You're my best friend, Enrico," Clete said flatly.

Enrico considered that for a moment. "You have decided, Señor Clete, to use the Alvear apartment to meet el Mayor von Wachtstein?"

"If that makes sense to you," Clete said.

"Then I will have to explain the inappropriate women to you," Enrico said. "If you don't understand, you are likely to say something inappropriate. I say that with all respect, as your friend."

"Please do."

"There are young women in Buenos Aires, whose families are poor, or who have no family, or whose family is in the country, and who in any event do not make enough money to support themselves as well as they would like to live. You understand?"

Yeah, I understand. Like Tony Pelosi's Maria-Teresa. Who provided my father-in-law-to-be with a little afternoon bedroom gymnastics because he slipped her money and held the mortgage on her father's restaurant.

And then when she met Tony, and told him no more, was going to call the goddamn mortgage.

And that hypocritical sonofabitch sat there tonight, wallowing in the sympathy he was getting from his family because I made Dorotéa pregnant.

My God, did my father have a Maria-Teresa stashed away someplace? In this apartment in the Alvear?

"Go on, Enrico."

"They *meet* people," Enrico went on. "There is an understanding that there will be a gift—"

"Money, you mean?"

"Money, or jewelry—that can easily be sold back to the jeweler—something like that. If they meet the same man regularly, sometimes there is an apartment. Or an account at Harrod's. You understand?"

"But they do go to bed with the man, right?"

"Sometimes yes, and sometimes no, it depends on whether they like the man."

"Or the size of the present?"

"It is not like that, Señor Clete. You will make a gift to the Minas tonight—"

"Whoa! What tonight?"

"These girls are called Minas. You will give them a gift—"

"I don't want any women tonight, for Christ's sake. Jesus, I'm getting married on Saturday! What the hell is the matter with you?"

"You will be so kind as to permit me to finish, Señor?"

Enrico asked, his tone eloquently indicating how deeply his feelings had been hurt.

"Go ahead," Clete said, managing to restrain a smile.

"The Mina is an accepted custom in Argentina for people of your position, Señor. If you and el Mayor von Wachtstein spend fifteen or twenty minutes in the apartment with two Minas, the staff of the hotel will see nothing unusual. If, however, you and el Mayor spend time in the apartment alone . . ."

He put one hand on his hip, and with the other pretended to moisten his eyebrow.

"You're kidding," Clete said.

"You cannot afford to draw attention to el Mayor and yourself, Señor Clete. And the staff of the Alvear is worse than women when they think they have seen something scandalous. It would be all over Buenos Aires within hours."

"OK," Clete said.

"You understand, Señor?"

"I understand, Enrico. There will be Minas in the apartment."

"And you will give them a gift, even though nothing will pass between you."

"How much?"

"A man in your position, Señor Clete, is expected to be generous. El Coronel was. I think there are probably some emerald earrings in the safe. I will see. If not . . ."

"My father kept a stock of earrings on hand?"

"Of course. A gift of earrings is more delicate than money."

"Of course," Clete said.

Enrico opened the wall safe. There were no earrings. There was a .32-caliber Colt automatic pistol, two gold watches, and a stack of currency. Enrico held the currency in his hand for a moment and, after some thought, peeled off six bills. He folded three of them very carefully twice, handed them to Clete, then folded the other three and handed them to Clete.

"What you will say, Señor Clete, is, 'Since you were so kind as to accept my invitation, please permit me to take care of the taxi for you.' "

"That's enough money to take a taxi from here to Estancia San Pedro y San Pablo," Clete said. "And back."

"It is an appropriate gift for someone of your station, Señor," Enrico said.

"What do I do now, wait for von Wachtstein to call and give him the room number?"

"I suggest, Señor, that we go to the Alvear now—"

"Wachtstein's going to call here," Clete interrupted.

"—and then when Mayor von Wachtstein calls here, Antonio will tell him that you will contact him at the Alvear."

"How am I going to do that?"

"Jorge, the concierge, will send a bellman to el Mayor and tell him that he has a telephone call. When he goes to the telephone, the bellman will give him a key to the room, or take him there."

Clete thought a moment, and then said, "That'll work. Have the bellman tell him Señorita Carzino-Cormano is calling."

"Yes," Enrico agreed. "Are we agreed, Señor Clete?"

"We are agreed, Enrico. Thank you, my friend."

Enrico nodded and picked up the telephone and dialed a number from memory. "I need to speak to Jorge," he said. There was a pause and then Jorge-the-concierge came on the line. Enrico inquired into the state of his health, that of his family, assured him that he himself was in fine health, and then said that Señor Frade wished to have a little cocktail party in his apartment, starting immediately, and would be grateful if two suitable young women could be enticed to accept his invitation. Apparently they could, because Enrico told Jorge he would see him in a few minutes.

Enrico hung up the telephone. "It is arranged, Señor Clete," he said. "I will have a word with Antonio, and then we will go."

"But you said 'suitable young women,' " Clete said. "I thought we had agreed on not suitable young women?"

"Suitable for the Alvear apartment, not for the house . . . You are making fun of me again, Señor Clete!"

"I wouldn't do that to you, Enrico," Clete said.

"You would and you are, Señor Clete," Enrico said very sadly.

"I don't know if I should tell you this or not. I'm afraid it will hurt your feelings," Clete said to Enrico as they turned onto Avenida Alvear in the Buick convertible.

"Tell me what, Señor?"

"You forgot your shotgun."

"Reach under the seat and see for yourself, Señor Clete."

Clete put his hand under the seat and encountered the barrel of a shotgun.

"There is more than one shotgun," Enrico said. "I leave one there, and another in the Horch. And I always have a pistol."

"I apologize profusely, Enrico."

"You are very much like your father, Señor Clete. He was always making fun of me too."

Clete didn't reply.

"When I was a very young soldier, and away from Estancia San Pedro y San Pablo for the first time—we were stationed in Entre Rios province with the 2nd Cavalry—it was very painful for me. When I told Mariana Maria Delores—may she be resting in peace with all the angels—who was then your grandmother's—may she be resting in peace—personal maid, she told me that if your father didn't love me, he would not tease me."

"I'm sure that was true."

"And is that why you make fun of me?"

"Yes, it is," Clete said.

"I have come to love you as I loved your father, Señor Clete. It is good that you love me too."

"I am honored to have your love, Enrico."

"We will say no more," Enrico said.

●   ●   ●

Clete pulled the Buick off Avenida Alvear into the small, curving driveway under the first floor of the hotel and stopped. He left the engine running, because he knew that a bellman would come quickly to take the car to the garage; there was space for only three cars in the drive.

Enrico reached over and snatched the keys from the ignition.

"How are they going to park the car if you have the keys?" Clete asked.

"We do not allow them to park our cars, Señor Clete," Enrico said. "I will park it myself shortly." He gestured toward the revolving door, where a silk-hatted doorman was prepared to turn it for them.

Jorge-the-concierge, who was fiftyish and bald, came from behind his desk as they entered the lobby. The symbol of his office, a large gold key on a gold chain, hung from around his neck and rested on his ample stomach. He offered his hand to Clete. "How nice to see you again, Señor Frade," he said.

Clete, who could not remember ever seeing the man before, said: "And it's nice to see you, Jorge."

"We will go to the apartment, Jorge," Enrico announced.

"Of course," Jorge said. He snapped his fingers—it sounded like a pistol shot—and when he had the instant attention of one of the bellmen standing against the wall, motioned for him to take his position at the concierge's desk. Then he bowed Clete ahead of him toward the bank of elevators.

They rode to the fifth floor.

"To the right, Señor Clete," Enrico said softly, and then, a moment after Clete had started walking down the corridor, added: "There, Señor Clete."

A waiter was rolling a cart out of an open door. "Buenas noches, Señor Frade," the waiter said as Clete waited for him to clear the door.

"Buenas noches," Clete said, and went through the door.

Inside was a comfortably furnished sitting overlooking Avenida Alvear. Two enormous silver wine coolers had been set up, each holding two bottles of Champagne. A coffee table held an array of dishes covered with silver domes, and a table against one wall held an array of whiskey bottles.

"The German Ambassador is having dinner—" Enrico began.

"In the main dining room," Jorge interrupted.

"With him is a young German caballero, el Mayor von Wachtstein," Enrico went on.

"A tall blond gentleman," Jorge said.

"Would it be possible to have a bellman tell him—loudly enough for the others to hear—that Señorita Carzino-Cormano wishes to speak to him on the telephone, and bring him here?"

"It will be done," Jorge said.

"Do it, Jorge, please," Enrico said, and shook his hand. This last was done in such a manner that Clete had no doubt that Jorge was suddenly much better off financially than when he entered the room.

"Your guests, Señor Frade," Jorge said, "will be here momentarily. And if there is anything else you require . . ." He pointed at the telephone.

"Thank you very much, Jorge," Clete said.

"I will now park our car," Enrico announced. "And then I will be in the room off that room until you need me." He pointed to one of the three doors opening off the sitting.

"Thank you, Enrico."

Enrico followed Jorge out of the room.

Clete looked around the room, and then went to the door Enrico had pointed out. It was a bedroom with a double bed. It, too, had two doors opening off it. Behind the first door was a bathroom, and behind the second was a smaller room equipped with a small, single bed, an armchair, and a small table. An ashtray and a copy of *La Prensa* were on the table.

I wonder how often Enrico has waited there before? And who was with my father when he did?

Clete explored the other rooms—another bedroom and a small kitchen, complete with refrigerator. It held at least a case of wine and Champagne.

Then he went back into the sitting and looked out the window onto Avenida Alvear. The off-the-street drive to the hotel was concealed from his view, and thus he couldn't tell if Enrico had moved the Buick, but on Avenida Alvear a backed-up line of six cars was waiting to enter the hotel drive.

There was a gentle knock at the door. Clete walked to it and pulled it open.

Two young women were standing in the corridor, a red-head and a blonde. They were well-dressed and good-looking.

They don't look like whores or prostitutes. But, then, what does a whore or a prostitute, by any name, look like?

"Won't you please come in?" Clete said, pulling the door all the way open.

The women walked to the center of the sitting and turned to look at him.

"My name is Frade," Clete said.

"It is a pleasure to meet you, Señor," the redhead said, and offered her hand. "My name is Estela Medina, and this is Eva Duarte."

Duarte, like Humberto? A distant cousin from the country, maybe?

"I'm very pleased to meet you both," Clete said.

"May I express my most sincere condolences on your loss of your distinguished father, Señor Frade?" the blonde asked. "And be permitted to offer my best felicitations on your upcoming marriage?"

Well, at least she gets the message I won't be playing around.

Unless she thinks—everybody thinks, starting with Jorge-the-concierge—that this is my farewell-to-bachelorhood party. Cigarettes, and whiskey, and wild, wild women.

"You are very kind, Señorita . . . Duarte, you said?"

"Yes. I believe I am distantly related to the family of your uncle."

"Is that so?" Clete replied politely. "May I offer you a glass of Champagne, ladies? And there are some hors d' ouveres. . . ."

"That would be delightful," the blonde said. "I so love Champagne."

"Then let me get you some," Clete said.

She talks funny, he thought, and then, as he unwound the wire on a bottle of Champagne, understanding came: *She is trying to sound like an Argentine aristocrat by using big words. She's trying to sound like Dorotéa or my Aunt Beatrice. Or as she thinks they talk.*

It doesn't work. She sounds like someone from the country, who had to look up condolences *and* felicitations *in the dictionary. There's something sad about that.*

He poured Champagne into crystal glasses, wondering idly if they belonged to the hotel or whether, like the apartment, they were his.

He handed glasses to the women. "Thank you for accepting my invitation on such short notice," he said.

Neither replied, but the redhead, Estela, asked if he wasn't having any Champagne.

"Of course I am," he said, and poured himself a glass.

"This is such an exquisite apartment," the blonde, Eva, said. "It has such élan."

Does she think people swallow that phony elegance? Christ, I speak Tex-Mex Spanish, and even I can tell the difference.

"Thank you very much, Señorita Duarte," Clete said, and raised his glass. "To your very good health, ladies," he said.

They tapped glasses.

"You are both from Buenos Aires, I take it?" Clete asked.

I'm not good at this trying-to-be-charming business. I feel like a character in a bad high-school play.

"I'm from Cordoba, the city of Alta Gracia. Do you know it?"

They call a city "High Grace"?

"I'm afraid not," he said.

"It was founded by the Jesuits in 1588," she said proudly.

"I didn't know that," he said. "May I inquire as to your profession, Señorita—"

What the hell is your last name?

"—Medina?"

"I am in the administration division of the Banco Roberts," she said.

In other words, you're a clerk.

"How interesting," Clete said. "And you, Señorita Eva?"

"I am an actress," she said.

You're an actress like I'm a bullfighter. Neither one of us has the talent.

"On the stage? In the movies?"

"Right now I'm a radio actress. On Radio Belgrano," Eva said.

Radio Belgrano? That rings a bell. My father had money in a radio station. Was it Radio Belgrano? Maybe I own Radio Belgrano; every time I turn around, I bump into something else that belonged to el Coronel, Incorporated. That would sure explain how she knew who I am and that I'm getting married.

There was a knock at the door. When Clete opened it, Major Freiherr Hans-Peter von Wachtstein was standing there. "Oh, Señor Gonzales," Clete said. "Please come in."

Peter walked in, took a quick look at the redhead and the blonde, and then looked at Clete.

"Ladies, may I present Señor Pedro Gonzales, of Madrid?" Clete said. "Pedro, the ladies are Señorita Medina and Señorita Duarte."

Peter went to each of them and told them he was enchanted. And both of them seemed delighted that Señor Gonzales was not forty-five, bald, and overweight.

"Can I offer you a glass of Champagne, Pedro?" Clete asked.

"I'd like nothing better, but I'm a little pressed for time."

"We can talk in there," Clete said, nodding to one of the bedrooms. "But take a glass of Champagne with you." Clete poured a glass of Champagne, handed it to Peter, and then motioned him ahead of him into the bedroom. "Will you please excuse us, ladies?" he said. "We won't be long."

He didn't close the door. Peter looked at him as if he thought Clete was either drunk or had lost his mind, and went to the door and started to close it.

"Leave it open," Clete said.

"You want to tell me what's going on here?" Peter asked.

"If we close the door, the girls will think we're faggots, and it will be all over Buenos Aires by morning."

"You're kidding."

"Trust me. Enrico set it up. Leave the door open."

"Jesus Christ!" Peter said, but then the humor got to him. "What the hell, close the door. Give them something to talk about."

"Fuck you, Fritz!"

"How did you set this up so quickly?"

"I didn't know about it, but the apartment is mine. Enrico got the concierge to get the girls—"

"Prostitutes?"

"No. Not quite. But with them here, no one will talk about us. Got the picture?"

"OK," Peter said.

He took Clete's arm and led him into the bathroom, leaving that door open.

"You told me one time you felt in my debt," he said.

"What I said was you have a blank check," Clete said.

"Excuse me? Blank check?"

"If I've got it, it's yours," Clete said. "Except, of course, for Dorotéa and my toothbrush."

Judging by his face, Clete sensed that Major Freiherr Hans-Peter von Wachtstein did not understand the humor. "What do you need, my friend?" Clete asked seriously.

"I'm going to Germany in the morning," Peter said. "I think I will be coming back. I don't think I'm really under suspicion of telling you about the *Océano Pacífico*. They don't think I knew beforehand, in other words."

"That's good news."

"It may be whistling in the dark. I may not come back."

"You'll be back," Clete said. "They also need you for Phoenix."

"I may not come back," Peter insisted. "That possibility is real and has to be considered."

"Peter," Clete said thoughtfully, "why do *you think* they *don't think* you knew beforehand where that boat was going to come ashore?"

"When Goltz was showing de Banderano—"

"Who?"

"The captain of the *Océano Pacífico*."

"OK."

"—where he was to land the boat, he made a point of giving me that information, saying something like 'it's time for you to know.' De Banderano picked up on that. He told the Ambassador and Gradny-Sawz."

"And the guy who gave you the information? What about him?"

"I got it from the father of an embassy driver, a man named Loche. And he didn't know what he was giving me."

"I don't understand. Why did Loche have it? And he didn't know what it was?"

"He didn't know about the landing. All he knew was that he had been ordered to have a truck at a certain spot. I knew why the truck was supposed to be there; he didn't."

Peter looked at him thoughtfully for a moment, then shrugged. "OK," he said. "That makes sense. So what do you need from me?"

"Alicia thinks she is in love with me."

"I've noticed," Clete said.

"If I don't come back, she will want to wait for me."

"OK."

"If I don't come back in two months, I will not be coming back," Peter said.

"You don't know that."

"I don't want her to wait for something that's not going to happen."

"How am I supposed to stop her?"

"I don't know. Maybe Dorotéa could help."

"This is all noble as hell of you, Fritz, but I think you'll be back."

"I am now asking you, Cletus, for repayment of the debt you say you feel you owe me," Peter said, very seriously.

"You have my word, my word of honor," Clete said, just as seriously.

"Thank you," Peter said, and put out his hand.

"You're welcome," Clete said. "What else?"

"What else?"

"What else do you want?"

"You gave me what I wanted when you gave me your word of honor," Peter said.

We went through this whole absurd routine just so you could tell me to tell your girlfriend to forget you?

And it isn't only absurd, it's dangerous.

And you're no fool, you knew that it was dangerous when you called me.

Which means (a) you're really in love with Alicia; (b) you think there's a very good chance you're not coming back; and (c) you really think I'm your friend and can be trusted.

Which means I am a prick for mocking you.

Particularly since you are about to go In Harm's Way and, as of about 1300 hours this date, Major Cletus H. Frade of the Marine Corps has been under a direct order to get and stay out of the fucking line of fire.

"I will take care of Alicia for you, my friend," Clete said, and meant it.

Peter grasped Clete's arms at the shoulders.

"Watch it," Clete said. "You don't want the ladies to see us like that!"

"Fuck you, Cletus!" Peter said, and smiled.

"Now what?" Clete asked.

"Now I go back to the dinner," Peter said. "And in the morning, to Germany."

"Without seeing Alicia again?"

"How can I see her again?"

"Would she come here if you called her?" Clete said.

"You mean here?"

Clete nodded. "You could get another telephone call, and this time when you came here, she'd be here."

"Von Deitzberg would be suspicious," Peter said.

"So he follows you up here, and what does he find? A fighter pilot doing what fighter pilots do."

"It is not like that between us," Peter said indignantly. "Alicia is pure."

"Is or was? This is me you're talking to, Fritz."

"Oh, God, I want to see her before I go."

"You got her number? There's the phone."

After Peter had given the hotel operator the number, Clete took the phone from his hand. "This is Cletus Frade. Put Señorita Alicia on the line," he said. "And don't go through that 'I'll see if she's at home' routine." There was a minute's wait. "Alicia, Clete. A friend of yours wants to see you. Be standing on the curb in front of your house in fifteen minutes. I'll pick you up in the Buick. Just do it." He hung up.

"She'll do it? Just like that?"

"Actually no, she told me to go fuck myself. Of course she'll do it. She trusts me. Now say good-bye to the girls and go back to your dinner. I'll have Alicia here in thirty minutes."

"And now I owe you, my friend," Peter said.

"Pay me when you get back."

Peter touched Clete's shoulder and then left the bedroom. He nodded at the blonde and the redhead, said it had been a pleasure to meet them, and quickly left the apartment.

The blonde and the redhead looked at Clete.

Fuck it. When all else fails, tell the truth.

"Ladies," he began, somewhat awkwardly, "the truth of the matter is, something has come up, and the party's just about over."

"Did I in some manner offend?" Eva Duarte asked.

"Absolutely not, my dear lady," Clete said. "It is I who owe you both an apology." He reached into his pocket and found two small wads of money Enrico had given him. "Please allow me to take care of your taxis," he said, and gave them the money.

The redhead took it, tucked it into her brassiere, and left.

The blonde seemed reluctant to leave.

"If you will excuse me, Señorita?" Clete said, and passed through the other bedroom into the room where Enrico waited. "How long will it take you to get the car? I told Alicia Carzino-Cormano I'd pick her up in fifteen minutes."

"Señorita Alicia?" Enrico asked, obviously confused.

"Von Wachtstein is going to meet her here. I just paid off the girls."

"You made a little gift to your guests," Enrico corrected him.

"Have it your way. The car?"

"Wait here ten minutes. I will have a word with Jorge, and then I will be in the drive." .

"OK."

He left the small room by a door to the corridor. Now he had a short-barreled Browning auto-loading shotgun in his hand.

I wonder what people in the corridor are going to think about that?

Clete looked at his watch so that he would know when to go down to the drive, then went into the sitting room and helped himself to a straight shot of Jack Daniel's.

And then he saw the blonde, Eva, standing in the door to the bedroom. He smiled at her uneasily.

"I thought you would not mind if I finished this exquisite Champagne," she said.

"Absolutely not," he said. "But I have to leave, myself, in just a minute."

"Oh, what a pity," she said. "I would really hate to think that you do not find me attractive."

"I think you are very attractive, Señorita."

She walked up to him. "And I find you very attractive, Señor," she said, and after brushing her fingers over his lapel, let them drop below his belt.

He felt them lightly, but unmistakably, travel the length of his organ. Then she stepped away.

"Do you really have to leave in the next few minutes?" she asked.

"I really do," he said, and walked to the door to the corridor and opened it.

"And if you said 'another time, Señorita,' could I believe you?"

"Yes, you could."

"But you're not going to say it?"

"Another time, Señorita," Clete said.

She smiled at him, then drained her Champagne glass.

She walked to the door, paused just long enough to touch him again, said, "Another time, Señor," and left.

He closed the door, walked back to the display of whiskey bottles, and had another straight shot of Jack Daniel's.

[TWO]
1728 Avenida Coronel Díaz
Palermo, Buenos Aires
0820 7 May 1943

Cletus Frade was eating breakfast at a small table at the window overlooking the formal gardens in the sitting of the master suite when Antonio entered to inquire if he was at home to Padre Welner, who was on the telephone.

What the hell does he want this time of morning?

"I am as much at home as you can get in a museum, Antonio," Clete said. "Put him on."

His breakfast—a small *bife de chorizo,* two fried eggs, a large glass of grapefruit juice, a glass of milk, and coffee made half as strong as the Argentine variety—had struck both the cook (when he had gone to the kitchen to order it) and the maid (who had delivered it) as another manifestation of the oddity of norteamericanos. An Argentine breakfast usually consisted of a cup of coffee and a couple of very sweet croissants.

The look in the maid's eyes when she laid the breakfast before him made him wonder what the boys at Fighter One on Guadalcanal were having for breakfast—if they were lucky, some rehydrated dried eggs—and how they had dressed for the occasion.

He was wearing a red silk dressing gown that had more or less been his father's. He had found it, still in it's Sulka's Rue de Castiglione Paris box, apparently forgotten since his father had returned from his last European trip in 1940.

Antonio headed for the telephone, which was on a table against a wall.

Clete stood up and waited for Antonio to announce that Señor Frade was at home, then took the telephone from him.

"And how is my favorite devious Jesuit this fine morning?"

"I am involved in my pastoral duties, Cletus, and the odd thought just struck me that you might he able to help."

"Exactly what did you have in mind?"

"You wouldn't happen to know where Alicia Carzino-Cormano is, would you, Cletus?"

"Why do you ask?"

"Why do I think I have just struck the bull's-eye? Where is she, Cletus? Claudia is nearly out of her mind."

"Why?"

"Is she there with you?"

"Why is Claudia nearly out of her mind?"

"Alicia went out of the house last night a little before eleven. Without telling anyone. And she hasn't come home."

"Oh, shit."

"You do know where she is?" Welner asked, but it was a statement rather than a question.

"I've got an idea," Clete said.

"Where?"

"Where are you?"

"I'm in Recoleta, in my apartment. Where is she, Cletus?"

"There's nothing really to worry about," Clete said. "I think I know where she is. Let me see if I can find out for sure. Why don't you come over here?"

"Why should I do that?"

"By the time you get here, I should be able to tell you where she is," Clete said, and added, "And she's probably going to need your pastoral services."

Father Welner hung up without saying another word.

Clete went into the bedroom off the master suite and woke Enrico up. "Get on the phone and discreetly inquire if Alicia Carzino-Cormano is still in the apartment," he ordered.

"She didn't go home?"

Clete shook his head, "no."

"The Germans would do nothing bad to her, Señor Clete."

"I hadn't even thought about that," Clete thought aloud,

then added, "I'm more worried about Señora Carzino-Cormano. Get on the phone, Enrico."

It took ten minutes to learn that while one of the beds in the apartment in the Alvear Plaza showed signs of use, no one was in the apartment now, and—the shifts having changed—none of the staff was available to be questioned about when the persons in the apartment had left. Bellmen would be sent to the homes of the night-floor waiter and elevator operator to ask what they knew.

"She's either at von Wachtstein's apartment," Clete said, "or maybe she went to the airport to see him off. Or maybe she jumped in the River Plate."

"You really think she would do that, Señor Clete? That is a mortal sin."

"Christ, I'm just kidding," Clete said. "Bad joke, sorry."

On the other hand, who knows? Her world has just flown off. Women in love have been known to do stupid things. See Anna Karina, or whatever the hell her name was, the Russian who jumped under the train.

Jesus Christ, what did I do?

Antonio appeared to inquire if Señor Frade was at home to Padre Welner, who was in the foyer.

"Of course," Clete said.

The Reverend Kurt Welner, S. J., who had decided that under the circumstances he did not wish to wait in the foyer, came into the room.

"Where is she?" he demanded.

"Right now, I don't know," Clete said. "Enrico, is there anyway we can call El Palomar and find out if the Lufthansa flight has left?"

Enrico thought the question over. "I can send Rudolpho out in a car to see, Señor Clete."

"It's a big, four-engine airplane with a swastika on the tail," Clete said. "If it's still there, he can't miss it. Send him."

"Alicia is with her German?" Welner asked.

"She was. His plane was scheduled to leave very early this morning. She may have gone out there to see him leave, or she may still be in his apartment. I've got the number in my wallet. You can call."

*Well, if he didn't know that Peter and I are more than ene-
mies being polite to each other in a neutral country, he does
now. Damn!*

Welner followed Clete into his bedroom, waited until
Clete found Peter's apartment telephone number, and then
called it.

The maid answered, and said that el Mayor von Wachtstein was out of town and she didn't know when he would
return.

"Now I have absolutely no idea where she could be,"
Clete confessed.

Unless, of course, she did take a jump into the river.

"I think you had better tell me what has been happening,"
Welner said.

Clete had just started when another visitor arrived who
had decided that under the circumstances it was not necessary to wait in the foyer while Antonio determined if the
master of the house was at home.

Claudia stood just inside the door, her hands on her hips,
her eyes flashing.

What we have here is an outraged mother.

"Good morning, Claudia. What a pleasant surprise! Can I
offer you a little breakfast?"

"You sonofabitch," she repeated, and marched toward him.

"Have you heard from Alicia?" Father Welner asked.

"She came in just after you called," Claudia said. "She's in
her room, crying her heart out, and she won't unlock the
door."

Clete had a sudden, very clear memory of Marjorie pulling hysterical young female *I hate you I locked the door
crap* on Martha, whose response had been a well-placed
kick to open the door, followed by a rush into the room, a
slapped Marjorie, and the announcement that the slap was
nothing like what she was going to get the next time she
locked the door.

*That wouldn't work in the Carzino-Cormano house, a
slightly smaller version of the Museum, whose doors are like
bank vaults. Claudia would have needed four men on a bat-
tering ram to do what Martha did with her boot.*

"But she's all right?" Welner asked.

"That depends on how you define 'all right,' " Claudia said. She stood beside Clete and glowered down at him. Then she pulled up a chair and sat down.

Clete had another mental image, an unpleasant one, of Claudia, genuinely concerned, rather than angry, in the corridor outside Alicia's closed door, being refused entrance.

He picked up the silver coffeepot and filled a cup.

"One lump or two?" he asked as he picked up the sugar tongs.

"Black, thank you," she said, adding, "Goddamn you, you're just like your father."

"Why doesn't that sound like a compliment?"

"It wasn't intended as one. What in the world were you thinking of last night, Cletus? When you got her out of the house?"

"You heard about that, huh?"

"When the butler came in about the same time she did. If I had known that last night, I would have come here and—"

"Actually, she wasn't here," Clete said.

"Then where was she?"

"Peter's going to Germany this morning," Clete said. "He wanted to see her again before he left. He was having dinner at the Alvear with the ambassador and the SS guy, and couldn't get away for more than a few minutes. So I picked her up and took her to the apartment in the Alvear."

"What SS guy?" Welner asked.

Clete looked at him. "His name is von Deitzberg. They sent him from Germany to find out who was responsible for what happened on the beach on Samborombón Bay."

"And what happened on the beach?"

"Enrico and Rudolpho shot the German military attaché and another SS guy who ordered the murder of my father. They were trying to smuggle something into Argentina."

"You ordered this?" Welner asked.

"No. But I'm not sorry they shot those bastards, and don't give me any of that 'Vengeance is mine, saith the Lord' crap."

"Watch your mouth, Cletus, you're talking to a priest," Claudia said.

He didn't reply.

"He wanted to see her for a few minutes?" Claudia went on. "She spent the night with him! And in the apartment in the Alvear!"

Well, that answers whether or not she knew about the apartment, doesn't it?

"They're in love, Claudia. He really loves her."

She met his eyes. Hers were really sad. "And what if he put her in the family way? Did you think about that?"

"What I thought was they deserved some time together. He thinks he may not come back. I had no idea they were going to spend the night together. I would have tried to talk them out of that."

"And what does that mean?" Welner asked. "'He thinks he may not come back'?"

"The Germans need somebody to blame for what happened on the beach. Peter thinks they may blame him."

"Oh, God!" Claudia said, and then had a second thought: "Then why did he go?"

"If he didn't go, it would be all the proof they needed that he was involved with what happened. They would have killed his father."

"Oh, my God," she said. "Oh, poor Peter."

"As a general rule of thumb, Claudia, the Nazis are not very nice people."

"How was Peter involved?" Welner asked.

"You don't really expect me to answer that, do you?" Clete snapped.

"You should be ashamed of yourself, Cletus, speaking to Father Welner in that way. He's a friend. My friend, your friend, and he was your father's best friend."

"It's all right, Claudia," Welner said. "I understand Cletus's concerns."

She looked between them for a moment, then asked, "Would they really have killed Peter's father if he hadn't gone?"

"Innocence doesn't count as far as the Nazis are concerned, Claudia. They kill anybody who gets in their way. They killed my father, they killed one of my men, they killed Enrico's sister, and they would have killed Peter's father."

"I'm afraid Cletus is right, Claudia," Welner said.

Clete's mouth ran away with him. "Why don't you tell that to my godfather? El Coronel Perón thinks the Nazis are the salvation of the Christian world."

"I don't understand that," Welner confessed.

"I've got a couple of theories I may tell you sometime," Clete said. "But not in mixed company."

"That's enough about Juan Domingo, Cletus," Claudia said.

"OK. Subject closed."

"He'll be at Estancia San Pedro y San Pablo for the wedding," she said. "You are going to behave, right?"

"I will be so good, Claudia, as to be unbelievable."

"I don't like the sound of that," she said. "My God, you're like your father! I even know when you mean something else than what you say."

"That sounded like a compliment, in which case, thank you. You're no longer mad at me, I take it?"

"If she's pregnant, I'll kill you."

"Changing the subject, do I own a radio station?"

"Three of them. Specifically, your father and I—*you and I*—own one in Córdoba, and another in Santa Fe together, and you own another here."

"Radio Belgrano?"

"Yes, Radio Belgrano. Why do you ask?"

"Just taking inventory."

"You mean you're not going to tell why you asked?"

"You don't want to know why I asked."

"What am I going to do about Alicia?" she asked.

"I will speak with her, of course, Claudia," Welner said.

"She'll come out of her room when she feels like it, and she will tell you whatever she feels like telling you," Clete said. "Moral indignation will get you nowhere. She did nothing she's ashamed of, nothing she should be ashamed of."

"What makes you think you're an expert on women? Or on questions of morality?"

"I'm my father's son, of course," he said, and before she could protest, added, "I have two sisters, Claudia. Well, two cousins, who act like sisters."

"And if one of your sisters was involved with someone like Peter, would you have done the same for her? Arrange for her to go to spend the night with him in the Alvear apartment?" she challenged.

He met her eyes. "Yeah, I would," he said. "Under these circumstances, I would. You ever hear 'it's better to have loved and lost, et cetera'?"

"Oh, come on, Cletus," Welner protested. "That's poetry, bad poetry, not life."

"And did you ever hear, Father, that those that can, do, and those that can't, teach?"

"And what is that supposed to mean?" Welner asked.

"I find it hard to pay a lot of attention to advice about love—sex—from someone who's not supposed to know anything about it firsthand," Clete said.

"Cletus!" Claudia protested, but she could not restrain a smile.

"Touché, Cletus," the priest said. "Your father often said much the same thing to me."

"Father!" Claudia said, shocked, and then laughed. Then she went on: "Since this indelicate subject has come up, can I ask a personal question, to satisfy my feminine curiosity?"

"You can ask," Clete said, smiling.

"What did your aunt Martha and your sisters say to you when they found out about Dorotéa?"

"Don't you really mean, 'when they found out Dorotéa's pregnant'?"

"As a matter of fact, yes," she said, and smiled.

"Beth was delighted, according to Mom, and Marge and Mom—before they met Dorotéa—were afraid I'd been seduced by some hot-blooded Argentine tango dancer."

"They weren't!"

"Yes, they were. Their sighs of relief when they saw her

for the first time sounded like someone let the air out of a truck tire."

Claudia laughed. "I'd like a little cognac for my coffee," she said. "And don't tell me it's too early. After last night—thanks to you—I deserve it."

"There's a button around here someplace to call a maid," Clete said.

"No need," she said. "Or at least I don't think so."

She got up, walked into the bedroom, and returned a moment later clutching a bottle of Rémy Martin in one hand and three brandy snifters in the other.

"Your father always kept a bottle in the bedside table," she said. "Against the chill."

"You mean, when you were mad at him?" Clete asked innocently.

Claudia's not at all embarrassed to display her intimate knowledge of my father's bedroom before Welner. Good for her!

She didn't answer. She poured brandy in the glasses, then emptied hers into her coffee cup.

"I think your father would like it that you and Dorotéa will be in there," she said, indicating the bedroom. "Damn, I miss him."

"Me, too," Clete said.

"And I," Welner said. "A little more every day."

She raised her coffee cup. Clete picked up the snifter, raised it to her, and took a sip.

"You know, this is why we can't lose the war," Clete said.

"The cognac?" Welner asked, confused.

"It's the first thing they hand Winston Churchill when he wakes up," Clete said. "Before his coffee."

"How do you know that?" Claudia challenged,

"I don't know. I must have read it someplace."

She shook her head and had another sip of coffee.

Antonio came through the door from the corridor. "Señor, are you at home to el Coronel Perón?"

"Hell, no . . . ," Clete responded immediately, and then changed his mind. "Of course I am," he said, oozing synthetic enthusiasm. "What a wonderful way to begin the day."

He looked at Claudia. "What is this, Claudia? Speak of the devil?" he asked, and then got up.

"I don't know what's going on, but you behave!" she ordered.

"Señor Frade, mi Coronel," Antonio said, and handed Clete the telephone.

"Good morning, mi Coronel," Clete said.

The others could hear only his side of the conversation:

"No, Señor. It's always a pleasure to hear from you."

"Well, actually, Señor, I am sitting here over coffee discussing current events with Señora Carzino-Cormano and the good Father Welner."

"Damn you, Cletus," Claudia hissed.

"Yes, Señor. He is standing right beside me."

"Of course, Señor. One moment, please."

Clete extended the telephone to Welner. "Father," he said, loud enough for his voice to carry over the telephone, "el Coronel Perón asks to speak to you."

Welner took the telephone.

Now Clete and Claudia could hear only the priest's side of the conversation:

"How are you, Juan Domingo?"

"I'm very well, thank you."

"Is that so?"

"I am sure that I can convince the good lady to do that, Juan Domingo. But you are a busy man. Couldn't it be done on the telephone?"

"I understand."

"We will expect you shortly, then, Juan Domingo," Welner finished, and hung up the telephone.

"Don't tell me the bast . . . good Coronel's coming here?" Clete asked.

"You can convince me to do what?" Claudia asked suspiciously.

"Juan Domingo says he has something quite important to say to Cletus, and he wants us to be here when he tells him."

"What the hell is that all about?" Cletus asked.

Welner shrugged. "Whatever it is, he thinks it's important," Welner said.

"And he's coming here now?" Claudia asked.

"He said he will leave the Edificio Libertador immediately," Welner said.

El Coronel Juan Domingo Perón, Special Assistant to General Pedro Ramírez, Minister of Defense of the Republic of Argentina, arrived twenty minutes later.

Antonio, Clete noticed, had not asked Perón to wait in the foyer while he inquired if Señor Frade was at home.

He was my father's best friend. Family, so to speak. Like Claudia; she wasn't told to wait either. Then why did Antonio at least try to make Father Welner wait? Were there occasions when my father didn't want to see Welner?

Perón was in uniform, with glistening boots and a Sam Browne belt, the brown tunic festooned with an array of decorations.

The Marine in Clete was forced to recognize that—with the exception of the leather-brimmed, gold-braid-decorated cap, with its ridiculous huge, high crown—he looked like a soldier, a senior officer.

Perón saluted, crisply touching the brim of the outsized hat. "Buenos días," he said. "Thank you for receiving me on such short notice."

"My house is your house, mi Coronel," Clete said, hoping he sounded far more sincere than he felt.

Perón went to Claudia and kissed her cheek. "Claudia, thank you for being here," he said. He turned to Welner. "It is always a pleasure to see you, Padre."

"And for me to see you, Juan Domingo," Welner said.

Perón did not try to kiss Welner, although kisses of greeting between men were standard procedure.

You don't kiss priests? Or aren't they close enough for that?

Perón nodded at Enrico, who came to attention and said, "Mi Coronel."

Then Perón walked to Clete and grasped him by both shoulders. "Cletus," he said emotionally.

"Mi Coronel," Clete said.

"We're having coffee, Juan Domingo. Mine with brandy," Claudia said. "Would you like either?"

"A coffee, please," he said.

Claudia poured a cup and handed it to him.

He took it, sat it down, took off his cap, and then picked up the coffee again. "What I have to say to you must never leave this room," he said solemnly. "Agreed?"

That depends on what you have to say, Colonel.

He looked at them one at a time.

"Sí, Señor," Enrico said.

"Certainly, Juan Domingo," Claudia said.

Welner nodded.

Perón looked at Clete, who nodded.

"First, let me say, Cletus that I owe you an apology." He turned to Claudia and Welner. "When Cletus told me he held the Germans responsible for the murder of our beloved Jorge—may he now be resting in peace for all eternity united again with his beloved Elizabeth-Ann . . ."

And where's that going to leave Claudia, you pious fraud? She loved my father too, and spent a hell of a lot more time with him, taking care of him, than my mother did.

What is Claudia supposed to do, for all eternity, ride around on a cloud by herself, strumming on a harp?

". . . I found the suggestion so monstrous that I was unable to believe it, and told him so . . ."

Who else could have done it, had any reason to do it, you stupid bastard?

". . . which caused bad feelings between us, which, as his godfather, caused me much pain."

Not as much pain as a load of double-ought buckshot in my father's face caused. What the fuck are you up to?"

Perón turned back to Clete. "I now tell you, Cletus, that I was wrong, and can only hope you can find it in your heart to forgive your godfather, who looks upon you as the son God never saw fit to give him."

Maybe you can knock up one of your little girls and have one of your own.

"I'm not sure what you're saying, mi Coronel," Clete said.

"A distinguished German officer recently arrived from Berlin, Cletus," Perón began, then turned and looked at Claudia and Father Welner. "This is, of course, what must go no further than this room." He turned back to Cletus. "This distinguished German officer, like yourself, Cletus, an honorable officer, the son and grandson of general officers—"

Clete was horrified to hear himself ask, not very politely, "Has this distinguished German officer got a name?"

Watch it, stupid! Keep your goddamned mouth shut! Hear the bastard out!

Perón obviously didn't like the question. "Given your word of honor as an officer and a gentleman that it will go no further than this room?"

"You have my word," Clete said. *Why am I uncomfortable giving him my word when I don't mean it?* "But if giving me the name is awkward for you, don't—"

"Generalmajor Freiherr Manfred von Deitzberg," Perón said. "Of the General Staff of the Oberkommando der Wehrmacht. You have a right to know. Do you know what this is, the Oberkommando der Wehrmacht?"

"Yes, Sir."

And I also know, mi Coronel, that von Deitzberg is no more a Wehrmacht officer than I am. The sonofabitch is not only SS, he's Heinrich Himmler's adjutant.

"General von Deitzberg was sent to Argentina to offer the assurances of the Wehrmacht that the German officer corps had absolutely nothing to do with murder of our beloved Jorge."

"If the Germans didn't kill him, Juan Domingo," Father Welner asked in an innocence Clete suspected was as phony as a three-dollar bill, "who did? I don't understand."

"There was an officer—a man at least wearing the uniform of a German officer; actually he was in the SS. Do you know what the SS is, Father?"

Welner shook his head.

"It is the German secret police."

"I see," Welner said. "And?"

"Acting without any authority at all, he ordered Jorge's assassination."

"Do you think this man also ordered the attempt on my life?" Clete asked, and was immediately sorry.

There goes your goddamned runaway mouth again!

Perón considered the question. "I don't know, but it certainly seems likely, doesn't it?"

Jesus! Either he's the greatest actor since John Barrymore, or he actually believes this bullshit!

"And where is this officer now?" Welner asked.

"I hope he is burning in hell," Enrico said. "I shot him, and Rudolpho shot the other SS bastard."

"Oh, my God!" Claudia exclaimed.

"None of us heard that," Perón announced. "And you, Suboficial Mayor Rodriguez, will never say that again to anyone. You understand that is an order?"

"Sí, mi Coronel."

"And you will go to Sargento Gomez, Suboficial Mayor, as soon as you can, and tell him that is my order to him as well. You understand?"

"Sí, mi Coronel."

"We must now do what I know our Jorge would have wanted us to do," Perón announced. "We must put aside our personal feelings and think of the good of our beloved homeland. What has happened has happened, and nothing will bring our Jorge back to us."

"I don't think I know what you mean, mi Coronel," Clete said.

"Discreetly, of course, under the circumstances, I am carrying to the Argentine officer corps the profound apologies of the German officer corps, as well as their assurance that nothing of this sort will ever happen again."

At least until somebody else gets in their way.

"It is their hope, and mine, that this unfortunate business can be put behind us."

Maybe you and the Argentine officer corps are going to kiss and make up with the Germans, but if it's all the same to you, I think I'll pass. Grüner didn't order my father's murder. The order came from Germany, and I wouldn't be a damned bit surprised if it came personally from your honorable officer pal, von Deitzberg.

Perón looked at Clete. "Can you find it in your heart to forgive your godfather, Cletus?"

"Of course, mi Coronel" Clete said after a moment.

"Can you find it in your heart to think of me, rather than as el Coronel, as Tío Juan?"

Oh, shit!

"That is very kind, Tío Juan," Clete said.

"I am your father in God, and while I never could take your father's place, with God's help I can be a good uncle to you."

"Thank you very much."

"And now I must return to my duties," Perón announced. "And I feel duty-bound to repeat that what has just been said in this room must go no further."

"We understand, Juan Domingo," Father Welner said. "Thank you for telling us what you have."

Perón and Welner shook hands.

Perón put on his uniform cap, then kissed Claudia.

"You have my orders, Suboficial Mayor."

"Sí, mi Coronel."

He turned to Clete and grasped his shoulders. "Be strong, my son," he said, and kissed him on the cheek.

The feel of Perón's beard against his made him uncomfortable. "I will try, Tío Juan," Clete said.

Perón saluted him, did an about-face, and marched out of the room.

Clete watched him, and as soon as he had left the room, picked up the cognac bottle. "Jesus!" he said, and poured an inch and a half into the snifter.

"I would love to know what you're thinking," Welner said.

"The one thing I never expected from that sonofabitch was stupidity. He actually believes that line of horseshit he just laid on us."

"Clete!" Claudia protested.

"If el Coronel had not had his geography examination taken for him, he never would have been promoted teniente coronel," Enrico said.

"Really?" Welner asked, amused.

"I am glad I told him I killed his Germans," Enrico said.

"I'm not sure that was smart," Clete said.

"I'll tell you something else I think he believes," Welner

said. "I think he does look on you as 'the son God never saw fit to give him.' "

"Jesus!" Clete said.

"What would really not be smart," Welner said, "would be to underestimate your tío Juan, much less get on the wrong side of him."

Jesus, judging from that sarcastic tone, Welner doesn't like him any more than I do.

"Meaning what?" Clete challenged.

"Meaning—also not to go any further than these walls—a reliable story is going around—encouraged by Tío Juan—that General Ramírez is going to try to take General Rawson's place as president."

"Really?" Clete asked, surprised.

"And who knows what your Tío Juan wants after that for himself?" Welner said. "Tío Juan may be very valuable to you, Cletus."

"I can't believe that," Claudia said.

"That he would be valuable?" Welner asked.

"You're not suggesting he wants to be president?" Claudia asked.

"Of course he would like to be president," Welner said. "He saw himself as vice president under Jorge. That's why he came home from Europe. Now Jorge is gone."

"I'll be damned," Clete said, and took a thoughtful sip of the cognac.

[THREE]
El Capilla Nuestra Señora de los Milagros
Estancia San Pedro y San Pablo
Near Pila, Buenos Aires Province
1134 8 May 1943

"You may kiss your bride, Cletus," the Very Reverend Matthew Cashley-Price said softly in English, earning him a dirty look from the Right Reverend Manuel de Parto, bishop of the Diocese of Pila, who didn't speak English, and who was already more than a little annoyed that he had been ordered to allow the Anglican clergyman to participate in the wedding.

"Huh?" the groom asked, startled, and then added, "Right. Sorry."

He was in dress blues, complete to medals—not just the ribbons—and Marine officer's sword.

He had been looking at the bride, who was wearing a bridal gown that had been her grandmother's and, for the last minute or so, a wedding ring. It had just struck the groom, like a baseball bat in the back of the head, that he was now a married man, that the incredibly beautiful woman looking up at him had just sworn, until death did them part, to share his life, and as undeniable proof of that was carrying their baby under all that lace and silk.

With great tenderness—as though if he did it wrong, she would break, like an eggshell—he pushed her veil up over her head and bent and kissed her.

A murmur of approval came from the spectators in the chapel.

"Now we take communion," Dorotéa whispered. "Kneel down."

"Right," he said, looking down at two prie-dieux placed in front of them. He somewhat awkwardly got on his knees, knocking his uniform cap off his prie-dieu as he did so.

As they hurried to put the cap back where it belonged, First Lieutenant Anthony J. Pelosi, Corps of Engineers, Army of the United States, who was in his Class A uniform, complete to medals, glistening Corcoran jump boots, and the thick golden rope that identified him as a military attaché, bumped into Suboficial Mayor Enrico Rodríguez, Retired, who was in the incredibly ornate dress uniform of the Húsares de Pueyrredón—the design of which had obviously been strongly influenced by the uniforms of King and Emperor Franz Josef's Hungarian cavalry. Suboficial Mayor Rodríguez won the race and put the cap where it belonged with a gesture of triumph.

"Now get up," Mrs. Cletus H. Frade ordered when they

had received the wafer representing the body of Christ. "And don't forget your hat."

The groom rose to his feet, tucked his uniform cap under his arm, performed an about-face, and, when his bride had taken his arm, marched with her down the aisle of the chapel.

On the groom's side of the church, sitting in one of the rows of upholstered chairs, Mrs. Martha Howell was blowing her nose. Mr. Cletus Marcus Howell nodded his head, apparently in approval. Sitting beside him was Señora Claudia Carzino-Cormano, who was also wiping her nose. Beside her was Señora Beatrice Frade de Duarte, who was wearing a dazzling smile and waving at the bridal couple, while her husband dabbed at his eyes with a handkerchief.

In the first wooden pew on the groom's side of the aisle were the Misses Howell, who each gave a thumbs-up to the newlyweds; Señorita Isabela Carzino-Cormano (her sister Alicia had been the bride's only attendant, and, with her arm in Lieutenant Pelosi's, was now following the couple down the aisle); Coronel Juan Domingo Perón, who was wearing his dress uniform; and Señorita Maria-Teresa Alberghoni, who had been introduced as Lieutenant Pelosi's fiancée, and whom Coronel Perón obviously found charming.

The second pew held General Arturo Rawson, President of the Republic of Argentina; Señora Rawson; Capitán Roberto Lauffer, General Rawson's aide-de-camp; and Coronel Bernardo Martín. Capitán Lauffer and Coronel Martín were in uniform; General Rawson wore a business suit.

In the third pew were Colonel A. F. Graham, USMC, and Captain Maxwell Ashton III, AUS, both in uniform and wearing the silver aguillettes of military attachés; Sargento Rudolpho Gomez, Argentine Cavalry, Retired, who had sold his uniforms on retirement and was in a blue serge suit that looked to be two sizes too small; and Mr. Milton Leibermann, Legal Attaché of the American Embassy. The four pews behind held members of the upper hierarchy of Estancia San Pedro y San Pablo and their wives.

On the bride's side, the row of upholstered chairs held Señora Pamela Mallín, who was wiping her eyes; her hus-

band Enrico; his mother; and Little Enrico Mallín. Señor
Mallín, the father of the bride, looked very unhappy, and had
looked unhappy since he had entered the church and noticed
Señorita Alberghoni sitting across the aisle with el Coronel
Juan Domingo Perón.

The pews behind them held Mrs. Cashley-Price, various
members of the Mallín family, and more members of the senior staff of Estancia San Pedro y San Pablo and their wives.

Immediately outside the chapel, the newlyweds passed
between and under the raised sabers of eight officers of the
Húsares de Pueyrredón in full dress uniform. This was el
Coronel Perón's surprise contribution to the wedding. The
Special Assistant to the Minister of Defense had called the
regiment's colonel commanding and suggested this might be
an appropriate honor to render to the son of the former
colonel commanding, who happened to be a distinguished
soldier himself.

The path from the chapel to the main house was lined by
the workers of Estancia San Pedro y San Pablo. The men
removed their hats and bobbed their heads as the couple
passed by, and the women curtseyed. Some of both sexes
crossed themselves. Halfway to the house, when he caught
the groom's eye, one of the gauchos popped to attention,
saluted crisply, mouthed the words "Beautiful bride, skipper, good luck!" and then resumed the arrogant posture of a
gaucho.

The staff of the main house was lined up on the steps and
on the veranda.

The bride and groom entered the house and passed down
the corridor to the master suite.

The groom closed and locked the door, turned to his bride,
and tried to kiss her.

"Wait a moment," she said, startling him.

Then she startled him even more by reaching behind her,
unbuttoning something, shrugging out of the top of the
dress, and then stepping out of the skirt and its petticoats.
She then stood before him wearing nothing but a very frag-
ile brassiere and matching pants.

"Now," she said. "God, that dress is uncomfortable!"

The groom kissed the bride.

When the kiss became passionate, she freed herself from his arms.

"Take that off," she ordered. "The medals and the buttons hurt."

"Sorry," he said, and complied with the order.

"You may now kiss your bride, Cletus," Dorotéa said, mimicking the Reverend Cashley-Price. "Where in the world were you when he said that?"

"I had just realized we were married," he said.

"That hit me outside the church," she said. "I thought, 'My God, I now live here. This is where I'm going to raise my baby.' "

"I love you, Dorotéa," Clete said.

"I saw that in your eyes while the Bishop was going through that Latin rigmarole," she said.

"I said you could kiss me," she repeated.

He hesitated.

"Is something wrong?" Dorotéa asked.

"Sweetheart, by now the house is getting full of people. They'll expect us to come out. If I start now, I may not be able to stop."

"To hell with them," she said. "They can wait. The whole world can wait. I want my husband to make love to me. Now."

XII

It had been a very long and dangerous flight. They had to travel 2,700 miles from Buenos Aires to Cayenne in French Guiana in the northeast of the South American continent, and then 2,500 miles across the Atlantic Ocean from Cayenne to Dakar, on the west coast of Africa, and then 1,800 miles from Dakar to Lisbon. These great distances posed enormous problems of a purely aeronautical nature.

For starters, communication between the points of departure and the en route destinations was unreliable, if it worked at all. And even if there was communication, the weather reported at Cayenne might change completely by the time the Condor—which cruised at 215 knots—arrived there after a thirteen-hour flight from Buenos Aires, and the weather in Dakar might have changed drastically also after another twelve-hour flight.

And then they had to take off on each leg with the expectation that the aircraft would not encounter unusually strong headwinds (which would exhaust the fuel supply) or a storm that could not be flown around with the available fuel.

The weight of the fuel severely limited the Condor's passenger and cargo weight allowances. Thus, on this flight the twenty-six-passenger aircraft carried only eight passengers in addition to First Secretary Anton Gradny-Sawz, Sturmbannführer Werner von Tresmarck, and Major Freiherr Hans-Peter von Wachtstein. Five of them were diplomats—two from Argentina, two from Chile, and one from Paraguay. The other three were Germano-Argentine businessmen.

Peter suspected the Germano-Argentines had been more or less ordered to take the Condor, and he thought the diplomats were fools. Either they didn't comprehend the risk or they were flying despite it, for reasons of prestige or Latin machismo.

Brazil was at war with Germany, and under the rules of warfare the Condor was fair game. Because it could not fly over Brazil, it had to fly at least a hundred miles off the coast, in hopes that it would not be spotted by the American-supplied B-24 aircraft that patrolled the South Atlantic Ocean off Brazil and Uruguay looking for German submarines.

Cletus Frade had told Peter about the B-24s in Brazil. While they weren't as heavily armed as the B-24s bombing Germany—since there were no German fighters operating in the area, they could dispense with the weight of the machine guns and ammunition they would normally have carried—they still carried enough Browning .50-caliber machine guns to shoot down a Condor.

Clete did not, in fact, think there was a great chance that the Condor would run into a patrolling B-24, and even if a B-24 pilot saw the Condor, he probably wouldn't attack. Shooting down an unarmed transport, almost certainly carrying civilians, wasn't the sort of thing a pilot would want to do.

"You might find yourself offered the choice between landing in Brazil, though, or getting shot down," Clete said, "but what you really have to worry about is the Dakar–Lisbon leg."

There was an active war in North Africa, with German bombers patrolling to interdict Allied shipping, and American fighters based in Morocco patrolling to interdict German bombers. Any aircraft with a swastika on its tail would be fair game.

With the exception of the steward, the Condor crew had just about ignored the passengers until they reached Dakar. Peter thought that was understandable. Von Tresmarck was in his SS uniform, and no one with the brains to find his ass with both hands wanted to get any closer to anyone in the SS than necessary. Peter himself had boarded the plane in civilian clothing, and on his diplomatic passport, and the crew naturally assumed he was a diplomat—like Gradny-Sawz, who had lost no time informing the pilot he was First Secretary of the German Embassy.

When they had refueled in Dakar, however, Peter had changed into his uniform, partly because his civilian clothes showed the signs of all that time in the air, and partly because he decided that he'd rather be in uniform if he was going to get shot down by some American P-51 Mustang pilot operating out of Morocco—*which, come to think of it, would probably be a better way to check out than what's liable to happen to me in Germany; my father wouldn't be involved, and Alicia could get on with the sort of life she deserves.*

That changed things, as far as the Condor pilot was concerned. The blond young man he had mistaken for a diplomat was not only a fellow pilot but the recipient of the Knight's Cross of the Iron Cross. They were still climbing out of Dakar when the steward came to him and told him the pilot wanted to see him in the cockpit.

He had the chart laid out on his lap, with their intended course marked on the celluloid with a grease pencil.

Out to sea, then a turn right, and up the North Atlantic 250 miles off the Moroccan coast, then another right turn straight into Lisbon. An *X* about halfway on the grease-pencil line indicated the Point of No Return, beyond which they would be closer to Lisbon than to Dakar.

"The Americans sometimes come this far offshore—but not often," the pilot explained, "but they're looking for surface shipping and submarines, which means they seldom fly higher than twenty-five hundred or three thousand meters, and usually lower. And they're usually in something we can outrun—B-24s, B-17s, sometimes B-26s, and sometimes a twin-engine Navy amphibian.

"But they have radios, and if they spot us, they just get on the radio and give our position. There's Amis, and even some English, all over the area around the mouth of the Mediterranean. So the trick is not to get spotted. The way to do that is to fly high—not so high as to make contrails, but higher than they usually fly. They're generally looking down, for subs and shipping, and for our boys, who're doing the same thing.

"The nightmare is that we get spotted by a Mustang patrol. They've got droppable auxiliary tanks and can range pretty far. And we can't outrun a Mustang."

"There's not much that can," Peter agreed.

"I'll keep you posted," the pilot said, and Peter knew his invitation to visit the cockpit had expired.

The steward came down the aisle to Peter, who was dozing, spread out over two seats. He had made a bed, or sorts, from the cushions of the empty seats.

"The Captain has sent for you, Herr Major."

We changed course ninety degrees thirty minutes ago. Which either means we are within Portuguese airspace, and have made it, or there are a couple of Mustangs chasing us.

"Thank you," Peter said, got up, and walked with difficulty—his right leg was painfully asleep—to the cockpit.

The pilot handed him the celluloid-covered chart and pointed to a spot, their location, off a town called Faro, on the coast of Portugal, right above the Spanish border. It was not on the grease-pencil course marked on the chart.

"I don't like to fly the same course every time. Or, for that matter, twice in a row. So I took a chance the Amis would be working off the Morocco coast. I guessed right. No Amis. We should be on the ground in forty-five minutes. It'll be a short stop, just for fuel, and then on to Madrid, where we'll spend the night."

Portuguese immigration officials and a representative of Lufthansa came aboard the Condor as soon as it had parked in front of the terminal.

The man from Lufthansa, a tall, muscular blond who looked healthy enough to be wearing a uniform (which made Peter wonder if he might also be the local Gestapo representative), informed them that after their passports had been examined, they would be taken to the transient lounge while the Condor was being serviced. This would probably take no more than an hour.

As they descended the portable stairway, Peter saw Portuguese policemen lining their path to the terminal building.

An In Transit lounge had been set up in the terminal to take care of international passengers who were only passing through Portugal and thus would have no reason to require customs and immigration.

Inside, just after he had spotted and started toward the men's room, Peter saw two well-dressed men in the lounge. Neither of them—they were both blond and fair-skinned—looked Portuguese.

[TWO]
1610 8 May 1943

When Korvettenkapitän Karl Boltitz had been introduced to SS-Obersturmbannführer Karl Cranz in Berlin, Boltitz had not been at all surprised that he was outranked by the SS officer who would accompany him to Spain, but he had been surprised by Cranz the man.

For one thing, he was affable, even charming. Boltitz's experience with the Gestapo—at all levels—had taught him that they were usually surly and suspicious; and as their rank rose, so did their arrogance.

Cranz, a tall, slender blond-haired man of maybe thirty-five, had taken him from Himmler's office to the Hotel Adlon, then had suggested that since they were about to spend so much time together, they might as well be on an informal, first-name basis.

As they talked, though Cranz had looked with obvious approval at the young women at the bar, he identified himself as the last faithful husband in Berlin, and showed Boltitz, with obvious pride, photographs of his wife and three children.

Their dinner together was quite pleasant—and Cranz grabbed the check. During the meal, he expressed apparently genuine admiration for those who'd served in U-boats, and he confessed relief that at least one of them spoke Spanish fluently enough to talk easily to Kapitän de Banderano in Cadiz.

Boltitz was of course aware that the charm and affability were almost surely part of Cranz's professional technique (to put the enemy, so to speak, at ease), and reminded himself to be careful. But he was nevertheless relieved that he would not have to spend the next two or three weeks with a typical Gestapo asshole.

During most of their train trip across Germany, France, and Spain, Cranz kept himself occupied by burying his nose in a book; then, in Madrid, he quickly got rid of the resident Gestapo agent and took Boltitz on a two-hour shopping trip for clothing and toys for his family.

They traveled from Madrid to Cadiz, accompanied by a consular officer from the embassy, to make the arrangements to transfer the bodies of Oberst Grüner and Standartenführer Goltz from the *Océano Pacífico* to the hands of a local undertaker. After the bodies had been placed in sealed caskets, arrangements would be made to transport the caskets out of Spain, through France, and finally to Berlin.

Once that was accomplished, Cranz took Boltitz on another shopping expedition, and then they returned to Madrid. That night, over dinner in a first-class restaurant, and well into their second bottle of wine, Cranz asked for the first time, conversationally, what Boltitz thought "went wrong" in Argentina.

Boltitz replied, quite honestly, that he really had no idea . . . only questions.

"One of the theories, you know," Cranz said, "is that it had absolutely nothing to do with Operation Phoenix; that it was simply the Argentine officer corps' expression of disapproval over the elimination of Oberst Frade."

"How would the Argentines have known when and where the landing from the *Océano Pacífico* would be made?"

"You think, then, do you, that treason is involved?"

"It's not unlikely that the Argentines have someone in the embassy. That makes it espionage, or, if you like, counterespionage, on the part of the Argentines, rather than treason on the part of a German."

"Interesting," Cranz said.

"The problem with that theory—and it's only a theory—is that if the Argentines do have somebody in the embassy who had access to the when-and-where information, they might also have access to the what information."

"If they had known the *what*—the nature of the special shipment—wouldn't they have tried to seize it?"

"That would have made it pretty obvious that they have someone in the embassy, wouldn't you think?"

"There's a man in their Bureau of Internal Security, an Oberstleutnant named Martín—"

"Who is supposed to be very clever," Boltitz interrupted, "and who, incidentally, has been promoted Oberst."

Cranz had looked at him thoughtfully. "I hadn't heard about the promotion," he said, and then: "In other words, you're suggesting that if he had to give up something—the special shipment or his man in the embassy—Oberst Martín decided to give up the special shipment?"

"It's a possibility," Boltitz said. "But I repeat, I really have no idea what I'm talking about."

"Neither of us does, I'm afraid," Cranz said, and then, making it sound as if the thought had just occurred to him, asked, "What do you think about going to Lisbon to meet the Condor from Buenos Aires?"

"That's a very good idea," Boltitz replied honestly.

Cranz smiled and nodded. "And since Portugal is not involved in this war," he said, "I wouldn't be a bit surprised if I found some really nice things in Lisbon for the wife and kids."

In Lisbon, Boltitz was once again taken on shopping expeditions, during the course of which Cranz found it necessary to buy a huge suitcase to carry all the nice things he'd found for the wife and kids.

That night at dinner, Cranz threw another idea on the table, again making it sound as if it had just occurred to him. "What if we take our people off the airplane?" he asked. "They're certain to be tired after their flight. We could take them out to dinner. . . ."

"In vino veritas?" Boltitz asked.

Cranz nodded. "We could put them on the Swiss Airways flight to Zurich tomorrow," he said. "I really would like more than an hour or two with them."

And you didn't think about that until just now, right?

"And if we did that, and went with them, there would be another advantage," Cranz went on with a conspiratorial smile. "We wouldn't have to spend hours typing up a report."

"And then we'd fly back to Cadiz?"

"Why not?"

"What about tickets and visas for them to enter Portugal?" Boltitz asked.

Cranz tapped the breast of his suit jacket and winked, making it clear that he had considered that some time before.

Boltitz and Cranz rode to the airport in a Mercedes sedan assigned to the Naval Attaché of the German Embassy, with a second car, an embassy Opel Kapitän, following them. Boltitz had known the attaché from their cadet days at the Naval Academy.

At the airport, they found that the people they wanted to see were effectively sealed off in the Transit Lounge since, *de jure,* the In Transit passengers had not been admitted into Portugal. That meant that Boltitz and Cranz had more than a little difficulty getting in

However, a combination of diplomatic indignation (they were carrying diplomatic passports and carnets issued by the Portuguese Foreign Ministry identifying them as diplomats attached to the German Embassy), Cranz's charm, and a small gift of cash got them through the locked doors fifteen minutes before the Condor landed.

Though the lounge was small and sparsely furnished, there were comfortable leather armchairs. There was also a counter that offered sandwiches and coffee, and, of course, there were rest rooms. On a small table between the doors to the rest rooms someone had erected a neat triangle of rolls of toilet tissue.

"I suppose," Cranz said with a smile, "that the first thing

most arriving passengers will want to do is answer the call of nature."

When a waitress came into the room, she offered them coffee and very sweet biscuits.

"When the plane lands, I'll have a word with the crew about unloading their luggage," Cranz said. "And you explain to them that their travel plans have been changed."

Boltitz nodded, at the last second restraining his impulse to acknowledge the order by saying, "Jawohl, Herr Obersturmbannführer."

If Cranz wants to think that he has convinced me we're pals, fine.

As soon as the ground handlers had rolled the stairway up to the Condor, Cranz left the terminal and walked toward the airplane without speaking to any of the arriving passengers as they came off the airplane.

And he knows who they are as well as I do. There are photographs in all their dossiers.

The first man off the plane was First Secretary Gradny-Sawz. Boltitz followed Cranz's example and let him pass into the transient room without giving him any sign of recognition. Sturmbannführer Werner von Tresmarck, in uniform, followed him. As he passed, he looked at Boltitz carefully, obviously suspecting he was German and wondering why he was there.

Major Freiherr Hans-Peter von Wachtstein came in next.

Although Boltitz knew from his dossier that von Wachtstein had won the Knight's Cross—indeed, had gotten it from the hands of Adolf Hitler himself—it was a little strange to see the man in person. The Knight's Cross was one of the few decorations that still meant something. It was awarded only in cases of really unusual valor in the face of the enemy, not as a reward for long and faithful service to the Nazi party.

"Major von Wachtstein?"

Von Wachtstein looked at him carefully. One eyebrow rose just perceptibly before he nodded.

"I'm Karl Boltitz of the embassy," Boltitz said.

Von Wachtstein waited expressionless for him to go on.

"Actually, Major, I'm Korvettenkapitän Boltitz."

"Oh, the new naval attaché," von Wachtstein said, and offered his hand. "How do you do?"

Von Wachtstein's grip, not surprising Boltitz, was firm.

"What are you doing here?" von Wachtstein asked.

"The opportunity came up, and I thought it might be valuable to have a word with you before I went to Buenos Aires."

Von Wachtstein's eyes showed his disbelief.

If he's involved, he's doomed. You can read his face like a newspaper.

"Actually, I'm here—"

"Will this wait, Boltitz, until I take a piss?"

Well, he's obviously not afraid of me. Is that an indication of innocence? Or ignorance?

"Absolutely," Boltitz said with a smile.

The first of the three to come out of the men's room was Sturmbannführer von Tresmarck. He marched purposefully to Boltitz. "I understand you're from the embassy?"

"That's right," Boltitz said. "And you're . . . ?"

"Sturmbannführer von Tresmarck," he replied, and then went on: "I . . . uh . . . had rather expected someone from the SS would meet us."

"Obersturmbannführer Cranz is here," Boltitz said with a nod toward the window and the Condor outside, "arranging to have your luggage removed from the airplane."

"What did you say?" von Tresmarck asked quickly.

This one's afraid.

"We're going to spend the night here," Boltitz said, "and then fly on to Berlin via Zurich on Swiss Airways."

"What's that all about?"

"I'm sure Cranz will explain everything," Boltitz said.

That scared him even more. What's he got to hide? Was he turned by the Argentines? By what's-his-name? Colonel Martín? Or is it something else?

Gradny-Sawz came out of the men's room and walked up to them. "Baron von Wachtstein tells me you're from the embassy," he said. "I'm Gradny-Sawz, the First Secretary of our embassy in Buenos Aires."

"Yes, I know, Herr Baron," Boltitz said.

"What is your exact function at the embassy? What did you say your name is?"

"I'm Korvettenkapitän Boltitz, Herr Baron. Actually, I'm with the Abwehr."

Boltitz looked quickly between the two men.

Von Tresmarck looks even more uncomfortable. Possibly because I said "Abwehr"? The Austrian doesn't look worried at all.

"They're taking our luggage off, Anton," von Tresmarck said. "We're going from here to Berlin via Zurich tomorrow on Swiss Airways."

"Thank God! I need a night in a good bed."

Von Tresmarck laughed dutifully.

Cranz came through the door a moment later, and was the picture of charm and affability as he introduced himself and explained the change in plans. "Boltitz thought it would be a good idea if we had a word with you before we both go to Cadiz to chat with Kapitän de Banderano. And before he goes on to Buenos Aires. And we didn't think we'd have the time to do that while the airplane was being refueled, so we arranged for us all to travel on Swiss Airways tomorrow."

"But Foreign Minister von Ribbentrop expects me in Berlin as soon as possible," Gradny-Sawz said.

Did he say that because he doesn't want to talk to us? Because he wants to get to Berlin for some other reason as quickly as he can? Or to impress Cranz and me with his importance?

"Herr von Ribbentrop was kind enough to tell me the Sicherheitsdienst had wide discretion in this matter," Cranz said, just coldly enough to put Gradny-Sawz in his place. Then he turned on the charm again. "And really, Herr Baron, after that long flight—which must have been grueling—I rather thought a good dinner and a night in a comfortable bed would be appealing."

"Obersturmbannführer Cranz," Boltitz said as von Wachtstein walked up to them. "This is Major Freiherr von Wachtstein."

"It's always an honor to meet a holder of the Knight's Cross, Herr Baron," Cranz said.

Von Wachtstein clicked his heels and bowed.

"We're apparently going to spend the night here, Hans," Gradny-Sawz said. "Before flying on to Berlin tomorrow on Swiss Airways."

"You don't seem very pleased, Herr Baron," Cranz said.

"To the contrary, Herr Obersturmbannführer," von Wachtstein said, smiling. "I'm always delighted to fly in an airplane I know the Amis are not going to try to shoot down."

[THREE]
1810 8 May 1943

Five minutes after Boltitz left Cranz in the bar of the Grand Palace Hotel to go to his room for a shave and shower before dinner—just long enough to be standing naked next to the bathtub, waiting for the water to heat up—there was an imperious knock at his door.

It was Cranz, as always smiling and affable, but also all business. "Sorry to burst in on you like this, Karl."

"What's up?"

"Before dinner, I want your first reaction to our three friends."

"I don't know if I have one," Boltitz said.

"We all have first reactions," Cranz said. "My first reaction to you in Himmler's office was that you looked like a submarine officer, not an Abwehr officer."

Boltitz smiled.

"And you certainly had one of me," Cranz said.

"I thought you didn't look very menacing for someone in your line of work."

Cranz laughed. "That's what I want now, about these three, the first thoughts that came to your mind."

"Von Tresmarck is nervous, as if he has something to hide. The Austrian is a typical aristocratic bureaucrat. Von Wachtstein is a soldier."

"And which of the three is the guilty party?"

"None of them may be."

"But if you had to guess, which one would it be?"

"I don't like to guess about something like that."

"Which one, Boltitz?"

"Especially when the man who comes to mind wears the same uniform as the man asking the question."

"Because von Tresmarck's nervous?"

Boltitz nodded.

Cranz met his eyes for a long moment. "I agree that von Tresmarck's hiding something. A man may have many reasons for looking nervous, many skeletons in his closet. But none of them may be treason."

"That's why I don't like to guess about this sort of thing."

"The traitors most difficult to detect, Karl, are those who believe their treason is holy. If I had to guess, it would be the pilot."

"Why not the Austrian? He's already demonstrated his willingness to betray an oath."

"Interesting point," Cranz said. "That, for the moment, slipped my mind."

Why do I think that very little ever slips your mind—especially something like Gradny-Sawz's change of sides?

"And he's a diplomat; diplomats are taught to lie," Boltitz said, tempering it with a smile.

Cranz returned the smile. "After we've had our dinner, why don't you take von Wachtstein out and get him laid?"

"You're serious?"

"Absolutely. It would establish a camaraderie. People tell their friends things they ordinarily wouldn't talk about."

"Says the friendly Obersturmbannführer."

Cranz laughed.

"But I really like you, and I'm not sure about von Wachtstein. I have a feeling. . . ."

And if you have a feeling about von Wachtstein, you probably have one about me.

"I would have no idea where to look for women in Lisbon."

"But you're resourceful, Karl. I know that."

[FOUR]
2305 8 May 1943

Over dinner the wine and Champagne flowed freely. When they'd finished, Cranz announced he knew about a nightclub famous for its floor show they all might want to see.

"I'm not much for floor shows," Boltitz announced. "I thought I'd take Hans on a tour of Lisbon's other cultural attractions."

Obviously, Peter decided, *our separation has been pre-arranged. Cranz is going to find out what he can from Die Grosse Wienerwurst and von Tresmarck, and Boltitz will do the same with me.*

"I'm going to have a nightcap in the bar and go to bed," Peter announced.

"We'll *start* in the bar and see where that leads us."

"I think the señorita likes you, Hans," Boltitz said after the bartender had delivered a second cognac. He nodded toward two young women sitting in a banquette.

"Do me a favor, Karl," Peter said. "Don't call me 'Hans.' "

"OK. Why not?"

"When I was a kid, they called me 'Hansel,' as in 'Hansel and Gretel.' "

Boltitz laughed. "I think the señorita likes you, *Peter.* OK?"

"Why shouldn't she like me? Not only am I handsome beyond her wildest dreams, but I look as if I can probably afford her."

"You think they're whores?"

"I would say there is a very strong probability that two young women sitting in a hotel bar smiling at two obvious foreigners are business girls."

"But such attractive business girls—"

"If you want to get your ashes hauled, Karl, go ahead."

"I could put both of them on my expense voucher as 'research expenses.' "

" 'In connection with investigating what happened on the beach of Samborombón Bay'?"

"Well, that's why I'm here."

"Why don't you just ask me, and save the Reich some money?"

"Is there anything wrong with mixing business with pleasure?"

"Look . . . you don't have to. Just ask me what you want to know."

"You have a girl," Boltitz challenged. "You're being *faithful*! Will wonders never cease? A Luftwaffe *fighter pilot* turning down some hanky-panky!"

"With all possible respect, Herr Korvettenkapitän Boltitz, whether I have a girl or not is none of your goddamn business. But I will tell you this: Despite the damage it might do to the reputation of Luftwaffe fighter pilots as the world's greatest swordsmen, I am uncomfortable with the notion of this one hopping into bed with the first available prostitute who spreads her legs, even at the expense of the SS."

"I'm not SS, I'm Abwehr," Boltitz blurted.

"Is there a difference?"

"Yes, Herr Major von Wachtstein, there is."

Peter didn't reply, but his face clearly showed that he didn't believe this at all.

And, of course, neither do I, Boltitz had to admit to himself. *So what does this mean?*

He does have a lady friend. Where? Is she German, and he doesn't want to go to her bed in Berlin fresh from a whore's bed here? Or is she Argentinian? Why do I suspect that? And if she's Argentinian, it's entirely possible that she works for our friend Oberst Martín of their Bureau of Internal Security. Von Wachtstein is a fighter pilot, not an intelligence officer. He would probably find it difficult to believe that the love of his life is an agent.

And if she is, there's the leak from the embassy.

If, of course, von Wachtstein knew where they were going to land the special cargo from the Océano Pacífico.

"I've been told the women in Argentina are beautiful," Boltitz said.

"And they are, and can we change the subject?"

"One more question: Am I going to meet this lady when I'm in Buenos Aires?"

Von Wachtstein met his eyes. "I was just thinking about that," he said. "I don't see how I can keep that from happening. Yeah, you'll meet her. But let me tell you beforehand that she's nineteen years old, doesn't work for the BIS, and doesn't even know anything happened at Samborombón Bay."

"I had to ask, Peter," Boltitz said.

"Yeah, I guess you did," Peter said.

"What if we take the bottle with us, go to your room, and you tell me what happened at Samborombón Bay?"

"Why do I feel that I don't have any choice?"

"Probably because you know you don't," Boltitz said.

The bartender came to them.

"We'll take the bottle," Peter said. "My friend from the Abwehr will pay."

"Señor?"

Boltitz put down some money, grabbed the bottle, and followed Peter out of the bar.

[FIVE]
The Office of Strategic Services
National Institutes of Health Building
Washington, D.C.
0825 9 May 1943

Colonel A. (Alejandro) F. (Federico) Graham, USMCR, the Deputy Director for Western Hemisphere Operations of the Office of Strategic Services, was already in a bad mood when the door to his office opened and OSS Director William J. Donovan walked in and almost immediately made things worse.

Almost exactly twenty-four hours before, Graham had been eating breakfast in his hotel room in Mexico City when the Mexico City Station Chief unexpectedly appeared and wordlessly handed him a message.

```
URGENT

TOP SECRET

DUPLICATION FORBIDDEN

FROM DIRECTOR

MSG NO 2072 1310 GREENWICH 8 MAY 1943

TO STATION CHIEF MEXICO CITY

FOR DIRECTOR WHO

YOUR   PRESENCE   REQUIRED   HERE   NOT
LATER THAN 0800 TOMORROW.

STACHIEF   MEXICO   CITY   DIRECTED   TO
PROVIDE    FASTEST    AVAILABLE    TRANS-
PORTATION  TO  SAN  ANTONIO  WHERE  AIR
CORPS   WILL   PROVIDE   FURTHER   TRANS-
PORTATION TO WASHINGTON.

ACKNOWLEDGE   RECEIPT   AND   ETA   SAN
ANTONIO.

DONOVAN
```

Graham had tried to telephone Donovan to ask if whatever was so important couldn't wait twenty-four hours while he finished his business in Mexico City, but all he could get was "the Director is not available and won't be until sometime after six tonight." By six, he thought, he could be in San

Antonio, so he really had no choice but to break his dinner date with a Mexican attorney with close ties to the Mexican president and head for San Antonio.

He could not, of course, explain to the Mexican lawyer that he had been suddenly ordered to Washington, which rubbed the lawyer the wrong way. And then he didn't get to San Antonio until after seven. And then the B-26 that was flying him to Washington had been forced to make a "precautionary landing" in northern Alabama.

He had arrived in Washington with barely time to stop at his apartment for a quick shave, shower, and change of clothes, before reporting at the proper place and the proper time.

At two minutes before eight, he had arrived at OSS Headquarters, in what had once been the National Institutes of Health Building. There Donovan's secretary told him she had no idea when the Director would be coming in, "but probably a little after nine."

"Well, you made it," Donovan greeted him. "Good."

"I thought the hour was 0800," Graham said.

Donovan ignored him.

"I was supposed to have dinner last night with a guy who probably could have been paid to let our people into the telephone company," Graham said.

" 'Could have been paid'?" Donovan parroted.

"Right. Past tense. He was miffed when I had to break our dinner date. Latins tend to be miffed when people are late for important meetings."

"And you're Latin, right?" Donovan said, and immediately regretted it.

"Yes, I am."

"Raise the ante," Donovan said. "That's important."

"I thought it was important," Graham said. "I'd rather that we intercept German communications than have the Brits do it for us and then send us a 'You Owe Us' bill every month for the next fifty years."

"I want to talk to you about Galahad," Donovan said, sailing on.

"Jesus Christ, Bill!" Graham said incredulously, contemptuously, "You brought me back to talk about Galahad?"

Donovan nodded.

"We've been over that before," Graham said, coldly furious, and added: "You're as bad as the goddamn Mexicans! You never know when to quit!"

"'The goddamn Mexicans'?" Donovan quoted mockingly. "Why, *Alejandro Federico,* I didn't expect to hear something like that from someone like you."

That pushed Graham over the edge. "Goddamn you!" he exploded. "I'm an American, not a goddamn Mexican! When your ancestors were rooting for potatoes in some Irish bog, my ancestors were fighting this country's wars, starting at the Alamo! When my great-grandfather was marching on Mexico City with General Winfield Scott, your goddamn ancestors, the goddamn San Patricio Brigade, deserted to the Mexicans!" The San Patricio Brigade had been made up of Catholic Irish-Americans who'd deserted to the Catholic Mexicans. After the war, they were caught and executed.

Donovan smiled but said nothing for almost a full minute.

"Got it out of your system enough to listen to me, A. F.?" he said finally.

Graham glowered at him for a moment, then smiled. "If you're waiting for an apology, gringo, don't hold your breath."

"I wasn't asking for an apology," Donovan said.

"Then let me save you some time. No, I won't tell you who Galahad is. Do you want my resignation?"

Donovan ignored the question. "The Navy and the Brits know about him," he said. "Or at least that we have someone in the German Embassy in Buenos Aires."

"The Navy *and* the English?" Graham asked.

"I don't know who told the other," Donovan said. "But from what you tell me, the Argentine Navy brass is close to the Brits, so that seems likely."

"Our naval attaché down there is ONI," Graham said, thoughtfully, referring to the Office of Naval Intelligence.

"It's possible he has some kind of arrangement with the English."

Donovan nodded but said nothing.

"Or the reverse," Graham said. "The English found out first, and told the ONI. How do we know the English know?"

"Because Churchill wants Roosevelt—Hands Across the Sea, of course—to give him Galahad's name."

"Do they have 'Galahad'?" Graham asked quickly. "The code name, I mean?"

"No. Or at least it didn't come up."

"What happened on the beach at Samborombón Bay has to be common knowledge to the Argentine brass," Graham said. "Army and Navy. And they are not stupid. They know there's no way Cletus Frade could have known when and where the *Océano Pacífico* was going to try to put that stuff ashore unless he had someone in the German Embassy. And they would like to know who he is. And use him. El Coronel Martín of the BIS is as good as they come—"

"What do you think the Argentines know, or suspect, about Operation Phoenix?" Donovan interrupted.

"If they know, or suspect, anything, they didn't get it from Frade."

"Do you think they have somebody in the German Embassy?"

"I'd be very surprised if they didn't. I told you, Bill, this guy Martín is good. But—presuming they do have somebody there—I don't think that he, or she, knew anything about the *Océano Pacífico*. Frade said Galahad himself didn't know the details until shortly before they made the landing. If he didn't know—"

"The question was what do you think the Argentines know, or suspect, about Operation Phoenix?"

"I have no idea," Graham said.

"And Lindbergh?"

"I don't think they know about that," Graham said firmly.

"The President told me he wants Galahad's name," Donovan said.

"And what did you tell the President?"

"I told him you wouldn't give it to me."

"And?"

"He asked me how I thought you would react if he personally ordered you to identify Galahad."

"Is that what this is about, goddamn it?" Graham replied, his temper visibly on the rise. "I'm to face Roosevelt?"

"I told the President I believed you would tell him the same thing you told me," Donovan said.

"And?"

"He said, 'Well, if Colonel Graham feels that strongly about it . . .' Or words to that effect."

Their eyes met.

"Why don't I like that?" Graham asked finally.

"Actually, there was a little more to it. Before we got to the 'What if I order Graham myself?' part, I told him that I thought you would resign before you told me. And I told him I didn't want to lose you. That I couldn't—the country couldn't—afford to do without your services."

"And he caved in?" Graham said, quietly sarcastic.

"You have to understand, A. F., that FDR really does not want to tell Winston Churchill that his intelligence people are reluctant to share their knowledge with their brothers in London. It might suggest we don't trust them. And that's what he'd have to do, unless he wanted to tell Churchill Galahad's identity is none of his business."

"In other words, he didn't really cave in?"

"I think Roosevelt, the consummate politician, decided there was no sense in having a confrontation with either of us to get something he can get by other means."

"Huh," Graham grunted.

"If, for example, he gave the task of identifying Galahad to our friend J. Edgar Hoover, Edgar would turn to it with a relish beyond his thrill in being personally handed an intelligence mission by FDR. He would know that if he succeeded, it would humiliate me and the OSS. Or if Roosevelt ordered ONI to come up with the name, they would turn to the task with a zeal based on their opportunity to show up both the FBI *and* the OSS. And Franklin Roosevelt likes to bet on a sure thing—I know, I still play poker with him. It's highly likely that by now—my meeting with him was two nights ago—both the FBI and the ONI have identifying Galahad at the head of their lists of Things To Do."

Graham grunted again.

Donovan smiled, then asked: "The FBI's guy in Buenos Aires—what's his name? Leibermann? He knows who Galahad is, right?"

Graham met Donovan's eyes again but said nothing.

"Let me rephrase, A. F. Is Leibermann one of your good guys? Or is he associated with those you think of as the forces of evil?"

Graham chuckled. "I'm very fond of Milton Leibermann, Bill."

"Then I don't suppose you would be willing to listen to my argument that since the FBI is sure to find out who Galahad is anyway, you could get your gringo friend Bill Donovan back in the good graces of FDR by telling him now?"

"That is correct, Mr. Director," Graham said, smiling.

"Then I won't offer that argument."

Graham grunted again. "Bill, you didn't have to tell me this," he said.

"Yeah, I know."

"Thank you."

"I'm trying to be one of your good guys, A. F.," Donovan said. "I guess I didn't really realize how much I need you until I had to start defending you."

"Is that what they call 'blarney'?"

"No, A. F.," Donovan said. "It isn't. Let me know how you make out with the goddamn Mexican telephone company."

"I'll do that," Graham said. "Thank you again, Bill."

Donovan smiled broadly. "Vaya con Dios, mi amigo," he said, and walked out of Graham's office.

[SIX]
The Office of the Reichsführer-SS
Berlin
1545 10 May 1943

SS-Obersturmbannführer Karl Cranz took one step inside the office of Reichsprotektor Heinrich Himmler, came to attention, and with a click of his heels rendered a stiff-armed Nazi salute. "Heil Hitler!" he barked.

Himmler returned the salute with a casual wave of his hand, but said nothing for a moment. "I didn't expect to see you so soon, Cranz," Himmler said finally. It was both a statement and a question.

"I'm afraid I might be wasting the Herr Reichsprotektor's valuable time—"

Himmler interrupted him by raising his hand from the wrist. "What do you have, Cranz?"

"I met the Condor from Buenos Aires—"

"*You* met?" Himmler interrupted again.

"Boltitz and I, Herr Reichsprotektor."

"To properly set the stage, don't you think you should tell me about Korvettenkapitän Boltitz?"

"My initial reaction, Herr Reichsprotektor, is that he is highly intelligent and quite competent."

"I didn't think Canaris would send a man who wasn't," Himmler said.

"I saw nothing that suggests, Herr Reichsprotektor, that he is anything but a reliable professional officer."

"Fully qualified to take Grüner's place in Buenos Aires?"

"Yes, Herr Reichsprotektor."

"Perhaps I should have said '*reliable enough* to take Grüner's place'?"

"Based on what little I have seen of him, yes, Herr Reichsprotektor."

"I don't like qualified answers, Cranz."

"I beg the Herr Reichsprotektor's pardon. My judgment is that he will unquestioningly obey his orders."

Himmler thought that over a second, and then said, "You went to Lisbon?"

"Yes, Herr Reichsprotektor. We took the three of them from the Condor, took them to dinner that night, and then brought them to Berlin via Swiss Air today. I came here directly from Templehof."

"And which of the three do you suspect?"

"Permit me to say, Herr Reichsprotektor, that I have nothing that removes any of them from suspicion."

"I was rather hoping that it was the Austrian," Himmler said. "He has already proved capable of treason."

"He is, I think, the sort of man whose nervousness would betray something like that."

"He's a diplomat," Himmler argued. "He has been trained to conceal what he's thinking, and to lie."

"With respect, Herr Reichsprotektor, I considered that."

"And our man?"

"Von Tresmarck is nervous—Boltitz quickly picked up on that—but that may very well be because of what is in his dossier."

"Refresh my memory about that."

"There are Sicherheitspolizei files——"

"Homosexuals cannot be trusted," Himmler protested, suddenly remembering. "When Goltz came to me with that argument—that von Tresmarck could be trusted *because* that was hanging over him—I was struck by how charmingly Machiavellian it was, and I indulged him. His error in judgment may have cost him his life. That might be poetic justice, except that I don't want to face the Führer after knowingly giving someone like that so much responsibility."

"Herr Reichsprotektor, may I respectfully suggest that if the traitor does turn out to be von Tresmarck, the situation can be dealt with without von Tresmarck's sexual predilections coming to the Führer's attention?"

Himmler looked at him thoughtfully for a long moment.

"And apparently neither you nor Boltitz thinks von Wachtstein is the traitor?"

"Herr Reichsprotektor, a shot—or shots—were fired at von Wachtstein, yet I think it odd that he wasn't killed when Grüner and Goltz were shot in the head."

"So do I," Himmler agreed.

"And I hope to get the true story of that when I speak to the master of the *Océano Pacífico,* Kapitän de Banderano."

"When will the ship be in Spain?"

"On the sixteenth or seventeenth, Herr Reichsprotektor."

"And what do we do with our three friends until then? Or until we hear something from von Deitzberg in Buenos Aires that will clear this up?"

"I was going to suggest, Herr Reichsprotektor, that after they give us their statements—"

"You haven't taken their statements yet?"

"Herr Reichsprotektor, so far the interrogation has been informal. In my experience, when suspects are required to give a formal statement after they've been interrogated informally, the guilty tend to act nervous. My suggestion is for someone they haven't met before to take their official statements—say, as a surprise, tomorrow morning. And then give them a few days' leave. Meanwhile, we'll let them stew while we wait for all the rest of the information to come in—the result of my interrogation of de Banderano, and what we get from von Deitzberg in Buenos Aires. And then you and the other senior officers must examine everything. We'll explain this to the three, and then that you will almost certainly want to talk to them personally after all that has taken place."

"Give them something to think about while they're on leave?"

"That is my suggestion, Herr Reichsprotektor. If you approve, I will see that the commanding officer of the Leibstandarte Adolf Hitler—I sent von Tresmarck to their barracks—authorizes him leave within Berlin. If the Herr Reichsprotektor could suggest to the Foreign Minister that Gradny-Sawz be given a few days to visit his beloved Vienna . . ."

"Keep them separated, right? And under surveillance?"

"That is my suggestion, Herr Reichsprotektor."

"And the pilot?"

"I'm sure von Wachtstein would like to visit his father."

"At Wolfsschanze?"

"Unless Generalleutnant von Wachtstein could be spared for a few days from his duties."

"I'll have a word with Keitel," Himmler said. "I'm sure he'll understand the situation."

He looked at Cranz for a moment, as if making up his mind, then went on: "Putting down the insurrection in the Warsaw ghetto has proved to be a greater problem than anyone imagined."

"Oh, really?" Cranz asked, genuinely surprised.

"When the SS troops in Warsaw saw they would be unable to put it down immediately, they sought assistance from the Wehrmacht. The Wehrmacht also underestimated the situation, and have found it necessary to bring in tanks and artillery —"

"Excuse me, Herr Reichsprotektor. Do I understand you to say the Jews are still giving us trouble?"

"As incredible as it sounds, Cranz, yes. It's only a matter of time, of course, until the situation is under control, but at the moment Generalfeldmarschall Keitel finds himself in the unenviable position of having to report to the Führer twice a day on the situation in Warsaw."

"I see."

"And as you yourself know, Cranz, our Führer—"

"Is sometimes an impatient man, Herr Reichsprotektor?"

Himmler's lips curved in a very tight smile, and he nodded. "Keitel and I, and Canaris and Bormann, have decided that it is not necessary to burden the Führer with Operation Phoenix problems until we have that situation under control."

"I understand, Herr Reichsprotektor."

"It occurs to me, Cranz, that if young von Wachtstein were to go to Wolfsschanze, his father would probably arrange for him to pay his respects to the Führer. And the Führer would very likely wonder why he was back in Germany."

"I understand, Herr Reichsprotektor."

"Where is young von Wachtstein now?"

"At the Hotel am Zoo, Herr Reichsprotektor."

"Why don't you keep him there until I have a word with the Generalfeldmarschall about giving Generalleutnant von Wachtstein a few days off?"

"Jawohl, Herr Reichsprotektor."

[SEVEN]
Office of the Director, Abwehr Intelligence
Berlin
1605 10 May 1943

When he looked up at Fregattenkapitän Otto von und zu Waching standing in his open door, Admiral Wilhelm Canaris's face darkened with annoyance, but he said nothing and waited.

Von und zu Waching did not offer an apology for disturbing the Admiral. He knew the Admiral was aware that he regretted wasting his valuable time, and that an apology would do nothing but waste more time. "Boltitz just called, Herr Admiral," von und zu Waching said. "He's at the Hotel am Zoo with Major von Wachtstein."

A flicker of surprise crossed Canaris's face. "Did you know he was coming to Berlin?"

Von und zu Waching shook his head.

Canaris looked at the ceiling for a moment. "Otto, present my compliments to Korvettenkapitän Boltitz, and tell him that you and I would be pleased to accept his kind invitation to have a drink with him and Major Freiherr von Wachtstein."

"At what hour, Herr Admiral?"

"There is no time like the present, is there, Otto? Have the car in front in five minutes."

"Jawohl, Herr Admiral."

Having just concluded that the glass of Berliner Kindl beer he was drinking in the bar of the Hotel am Zoo, while vastly superior to the beer in Portugal, really had nothing to recommend it over the Quilmes cerveza of Buenos Aires, Major Freiherr Hans-Peter von Wachtstein turned on his stool as Korvettenkapitän Karl Boltitz slid onto the stool beside him.

"From the look on your face—" Peter said, smiling at him.

"What look?" Karl interrupted.

"Utter disbelief. What's wrong? Has your beloved been swept off her feet by a dashing Luftwaffe pilot?"

"Admiral Canaris has accepted my offer to share a drink with you and me," he said.

"Mein Gott! What's that all about?"

"I think a good guess would be that the Admiral wants a personal look at the dashing Luftwaffe pilot. Fregattenkapitän von und zu Waching will be with him. And Peter . . ."

"What?"

"They should be here directly."

Mein Gott! Karl thought. *I stopped myself just in time from warning him not to judge von und zu Waching by his friendly face and simplicity.*

"Who is Whatsisname?"

"I think of him as the Minister Without Portfolio," Karl said. "He and Canaris are very close."

And I shouldn't have even said that.

Karl reached out and touched the shoulder of a passing waiter. "We will be joined by a senior officer," he said. "We will require a table."

The waiter looked at him dubiously. "That may be difficult, Mein Herr."

"Arrange for it," Karl ordered coldly.

"I will see what I can do, of course," the waiter said, and walked away.

Von Wachtstein laughed.

"What's funny?"

"He wanted you to give him money."

"To hell with him."

"If you had given him money, he would have scorned you. Now he respects you. He understands that you are speaking for the senior officer, not sucking up to him."

"Is that what happened?"

"Your father is a senior officer, you should know the drill."

"I suppose you're right."

Is that what it is? Is that why I like von Wachtstein? Because we are both children of senior officers?

The waiter unsmilingly provided a banquette in the rear of the bar. Three minutes later, Canaris and von und zu Waching entered the room, standing for a moment just inside so their eyes could adjust to the darkness. As soon as the waiter saw them, he approached them and, now smiling broadly, led them to the table.

Canaris impatiently waved the two young officers back into their seats after they'd popped to attention. "My name is Canaris, Major von Wachtstein," he said, offering his hand.

"I am honored to make your acquaintance, Herr Admiral," Peter said.

"Fregattenkapitän von und zu Waching," Canaris said, pointing to him.

Von und zu Waching offered Peter his hand but said nothing, then offered his hand to Boltitz and said nothing to him either.

"Good evening, Sir," Boltitz said.

"We'll have whatever these gentlemen were drinking," Canaris said to the waiter.

"Immediately, Herr Admiral," the waiter said.

"I understand you had a difficult time at Samborombón Bay, Major," Canaris said, "the details of which I am sure will be in Boltitz's report. I wanted to talk to you about the *Graf Spee* internees."

Gott! Boltitz thought, chagrined. *I didn't ask von Wachtstein one question about the internees!*

"I'm afraid I don't know much about them, Herr Admiral," Peter said.

Canaris ignored him. "For one thing, despite repeated requests, the late Oberst Grüner was until very recently unable to provide aerial photographs of the place of their internment. And they weren't very good photographs."

"Villa General Belgrano was overcast, and it was raining

the day they were taken, Sir," Peter said, adding, "and with a Leica, not an aerial camera."

Canaris looked closely at him. "You were about to add, Major?"

"That it's a bit difficult, Herr Admiral, to shoot pictures with a Leica while taking off in a small aircraft from a dirt strip."

"You couldn't just . . . ?" Canaris asked, describing a circle with his hands.

I'll be damned, Boltitz thought. *Peter took the aerial photographs I used. Why didn't that occur to me before?*

"Not under the circumstances, Herr Admiral."

"Which were?"

Peter looked uncomfortable. "Herr Admiral, the Argentines forbid aerial photography. My orders were to do the best I could without giving the Argentines cause to revoke our privilege to fly to Villa General Belgrano."

"Your orders from whom?"

"Ambassador von Lutzenberger, Herr Admiral."

"Don't you—didn't you—normally get your orders from Oberst Grüner?"

Peter's answer had to wait until the waiter, with a flourish, served four glasses of Berliner Kindl. When he had gone, Canaris looked at Peter, waiting for him to go on.

"Herr Admiral, in this case," Peter said, "there was some question whether the photographs should have been taken at all. First Secretary Gradny-Sawz was concerned that the Argentines would revoke our privilege to fly to Villa General Belgrano and brought the matter to the Ambassador for a decision."

"And why do you think Gradny-Sawz was so concerned about losing the privilege?"

Peter hesitated.

"The first thing that came to your mind, Major!" Canaris said sharply.

"Herr Admiral, Villa General Belgrano is a two-day trip by rail and car from Buenos Aires. Four days round-trip—"

"I know the Luftwaffe doesn't think much of the Navy,

Major," Canaris interrupted almost rudely. "But most of us really can multiply by two."

"I beg the Herr Admiral's pardon."

"Go on."

"In the Storch, you can fly there and back in one day."

"So you're suggesting that Gradny-Sawz believed his convenience was more important than my request for aerial photographs?"

"Herr Admiral—" Peter began uncomfortably.

Canaris chuckled, and stilled Peter with a raised hand. "Those of us in the services tend to have difficulty finding diplomatic ways to say something awkward, don't we, Major von Wachtstein?"

"Yes, Sir," Peter said.

Why is Admiral Canaris so interested in these aerial photographs? Boltitz wondered. And then he remembered what his father had said about listening to what Canaris was *not* saying. *Canaris doesn't really give a damn about those aerial photographs. So what is he doing? Seeing how von Wachtstein behaves under pressure?*

Canaris looked at Boltitz, then back at von Wachtstein. "Did you ever wonder, when you got to Buenos Aires, von Wachtstein, why they had an airplane there and—until you got there—no one to fly it?"

"Yes, Sir."

"The airplane was Foreign Minister von Ribbentrop's idea," Canaris explained. "It was his idea that when the opportunity presented itself, Ambassador von Lutzenberger would make a gift of it to the Argentine Army as a gesture of friendship."

He looked between Peter and Karl again. "So the airplane was sent to Buenos Aires and parked in a hangar at El Palomar to await the propitious moment to manifest our great respect for the Ejercito Argentine," Canaris went on. "And then I had a thought, which I shared with Oberst Grüner. Did he think, and more importantly, would Ambassador von Lutzenberger think, that perhaps the aircraft might be more useful to Germany than as a public relations gesture?"

The translation of that, Karl decided, *what Canaris was*

not *saying, was that he had somehow talked von Ribbentrop into making a gift of an airplane to Argentina and all along intended that it be used by Grüner.*

And is he saying, by not saying that, he has Ambassador von Lutzenberger in his pocket?

"Apparently, von Lutzenberger has not yet found the propitious moment to make the gift," Canaris said. "And in the meantime, the airplane has proven useful, has it not?"

"Yes, Sir," Peter said. "It's been very useful."

"And if you accommodate Gradny-Sawz again, sparing him a two-times-two-day—how much is that, four?—trip by train and auto, perhaps the next time the weather will be such that we'll have some better photographs."

"I'll try, Herr Admiral," Peter said. "And I now know the buildings where the officers are being housed."

"What is your assessment of their morale? Are they to a man anxious to return to active service?"

Peter opened his mouth to reply. But before he could speak, Canaris held up his hand to silence him.

"When I ask you a question, von Wachtstein," Canaris said, "I want to hear the first thing that comes to your mind, rather than what you think you should say."

"Jawohl, Herr Admiral," Peter said. "I would suggest that most of them are like me. While we recognize our duty as serving officers, living in Argentina doesn't offer much to complain about."

"That's what I want," Canaris said. "The truth."

He looked at Karl and then back at Peter. "The investigation of the Samborombón Bay incident can't be concluded until Boltitz and Cranz speak with Kapitän de Banderano," Canaris went on. "And, of course, until we hear from von Deitzberg in Buenos Aires. Which means you will have a few days on your hands here. What are your plans?"

"I'd hoped to see my father, Sir."

"Well, perhaps that can be worked out," Canaris said. He turned to Boltitz. "I'd like a few minutes with you, Boltitz."

"Of course," Karl said.

Canaris stood up.

Peter and Karl immediately rose.

Canaris put out his hand to Peter. "It is always a privilege to meet a holder of the Knight's Cross," he said.

"It has been my privilege, Herr Admiral," Peter said, and clicked his heels as he curtly bowed his head.

"If you do see your father, please give him my compliments; I get to see very little of him these days."

"Of course, Herr Admiral," Peter said.

Canaris nodded at Peter, then marched out of the bar, followed by Boltitz and von und zu Waching—who neither spoke nor offered his hand.

The Admiral's Horch was parked in front of the hotel. There was the sound of solemn organ music—*funeral music*, Karl thought—from the Kaiser Wilhelm Memorial Church a few yards away. Canaris motioned for Boltitz to get in front beside the driver. Von und zu Waching sat in the back, followed by Canaris.

"I don't want him going to Wolfsschanze," Canaris said.

"Jawohl, Admiral," von und zu Waching said.

"Interesting young man, Boltitz," Canaris said. "An honest one, I think. Possibly because of his heritage. I would be very distressed to learn that he has been lining his pockets by taking thirty gold coins from the enemy."

He means more than he said. What didn't he say?

"Herr Admiral, I have the feeling that he is honest."

"I'm disappointed to hear you say that, Boltitz," Canaris said. "In our business, we can afford to trust no one. Or practically no one."

Then he made an impatient gesture with his hand, a signal that he had said all he was going to say.

"Until further notice," von und zu Waching said, "stay as close to him as you can, and call every few hours."

"Jawohl, Herr Fregattenkapitän," Karl said, and left the car.

XIII

[ONE]
The Lobby Bar
The Hotel am Zoo
Kurfürstendamm, Berlin
1720 10 May 1943

Major Freiherr Hans-Peter von Wachtstein watched Admiral
Canaris, von und zu Waching, and Boltitz walk out of the
bar and then sat down at the banquette.

What the hell was that all about?

Canaris didn't touch his beer; the other guy drained his.

Obviously, Canaris wanted to see me personally.

But why here?

Did I let anything slip?

A short, muscular, blond Luftwaffe officer in his early
twenties slid onto the banquette seat beside him. "If the Herr
Major doesn't mind, I will have the Admiral's beer," he said,
and reached for Canaris's untouched beer.

"Willi! Jesus Christ!" Peter said.

"He's not coming back, is he? I mean, when I was coming
back from the pisser, I saw him head for the door."

"He's not coming back," Peter said. "Help yourself."

"Waste not, want not, I always say," Hauptmann Wilhelm
Johannes Grüner said, and took a deep swallow from the
glass.

Peter and Willi Grüner had flown in France together. His
father was—had been—Oberst Karl-Heinz Grüner, late Military Attaché of the German Embassy in Buenos Aires.

Maybe he's drunk. He doesn't act like a man whose father

was murdered less than a month ago. Or even particularly surprised to see me in Berlin.

"How's it going, Willi?" Peter asked.

"Can't complain," Willi said. "And how are things in far-off Argentina? My old man been riding your ass?"

My God, he doesn't know!

"What have they got you doing these days?" Peter asked.

"I have—had—your old squadron."

"Had?"

"New assignment."

"Doing what?"

"I can't tell you, as much as I would like to. State secret."

Korvettenkapitän Karl Boltitz walked up to the banquette and looked down at them.

"Willi, say hello to Karl Boltitz. Karl, this is my old friend Willi Grüner. *Wilhelm Johannes* Grüner, known throughout the Luftwaffe as 'Grüner the Great.' "

"And justifiably so," Willi said. "Aside from Peter, here, of course, I am both the greatest fighter pilot and the greatest swordsman in the Luftwaffe."

Boltitz chuckled and put out his hand. "Hello, Willi," he said.

I said "Grüner" three goddamned times, and he didn't pick up on it!

Maybe he doesn't want to?

"U-boat man, are you?" Willi asked.

Karl nodded.

"You guys have more balls than I do," Willi said. "More than Peter and I do combined. Can I buy you a beer?"

"I haven't finished this one yet," Karl said, and picked his up.

"Grüner's been telling me he now has, or had, my old squadron," Peter said.

" 'Had'?" Karl parroted.

"And Hansel here was about to tell me how badly my father has been riding his ass," Willi said, almost visibly wanting to change the subject.

Karl looked at Peter and met his eyes. "And your father is?" Karl asked.

"He's the Military Attaché in Buenos Aires," Willi said. "Where Hansel here has been sitting out the war." He turned to Peter. "Not that I blame you, Hansel."

When Peter didn't reply, Willi grew serious. "You used to erupt when I called you Hansel, Hansel. So what's wrong? What's going on here that when I sat down made me think I was the last guy in the world you wanted to see?"

"Jesus!" Peter said, and looked at Karl.

"Obviously, Hauptmann Grüner," Karl said, "there has been some sort of administrative slipup, some breakdown in communications—"

"Whatever you're trying to say, say it," Willi interrupted rather unpleasantly.

"Not here," Karl said. "I think we should step outside."

"What's wrong with here?" Willi asked. "What the hell is going on?"

"Please come with me, Hauptmann Grüner," Boltitz said formally, making it unmistakably an order. "And you, too, von Wachtstein."

He stood up, and Peter followed his example. Willi Grüner looked up at them for a moment, then shrugged and got to his feet and followed them out of the bar, through the lobby, and onto the Kurfürstendamm.

[TWO]
Führerbunker #3
Wolfsschanze
Near Rastenburg, East Prussia
1720 10 May 1943

Generalleutnant Graf Karl-Friedrich von Wachtstein—slight, nearly bald, and fifty-four years old—had been in his small, windowless, two-room suite only ten minutes, just long enough for a quick shower and shave, when he heard a barely audible knock on the steel door.

He was reasonably sure that his caller was either his aide-de-camp or, more likely, his batman; he had left his boots in the corridor outside his room so his batman could have them polished by the dinner hour.

Von Wachtstein was barefoot and bare-chested, and he was wearing only his riding breeches, with the broad red stripe of a general down the seams, which were held up by normally out-of-sight—and almost shabby—dark blue braces. His tunic was on the bed, where he had tossed it when he entered his quarters.

A good deal had been done, of course, to make the quarters of the senior officers assigned to the Führer's Wolfsschanze headquarters as comfortable as possible. But Führerbunker #3 *was* a reinforced-concrete bunker, designed to withstand direct hits from heavy artillery and even the largest aircraft bombs. Despite the genius of German engineering, its construction gave it two temperatures—too hot and too cold.

Today was a too-hot day, and von Wachtstein had been reluctant, after his shower, to climb into his uniform again. He had instead made a pot of coffee on a small electric burner. He didn't like coffee, and this was bad coffee, but he was drinking it for the caffeine. He knew that he would have trouble staying awake at dinner—the Führer liked to speak, often at length, after dinner. Since coffee was not served at the Führer's table, staying awake was sometimes difficult.

"Come!" von Wachtstein called loudly, so his voice could he heard through the door.

Field Marshal Wilhelm Keitel, head of the Oberkommando der Wehrmacht, entered the room. More than a little embarrassed, Generalleutnant von Wachtstein jumped to his feet. "I hope the Generalfeldmarschall will excuse my appearance—"

Von Wachtstein was really surprised to see Keitel. When Keitel had something to say to him, one of his aides would be dispatched to summon him either to the Führer's personal bunker or to the bunker he shared with Admiral Wilhelm Canaris and Generaloberst Alfred Jodl, the chief of the Armed Forces Operations Staff.

Wolfsschanze was about four hundred miles from Berlin and about four miles from Rastenburg. It was a large compound—an oblong approximately 1.5 by .9 miles—which was entirely surrounded by two rings of barbed wire, machine-gun towers, machine-gun positions on the ground, and an extensive minefield.

Just inside the outer wire perimeter—separated as far as possible from each other to reduce interference—were some of the radio shacks and antennas over which instant communication with the most remote outposts of the Thousand-Year Reich was maintained.

Inside the compound itself were two compounds, both ringed with barbed wire and machine-gun positions.

One of them was the Führer's compound, which contained thirteen bunkers, including the largest of all, the Führer's bunker, which stood apart from the others.

Across a narrow street were two bunkers that housed Hitler's personal aides and doctors, Wehrmacht aides, the Army personnel office, the signal officer, and Hitler's secretaries.

To the east, Reichsmarschall Hermann Göring had both an office building and his own personal bunker. Between these and the Führerbunker was a VIP mess called the "Tea House."

Next closest in distance from the Führer's bunker were the offices and bunker assigned to Keitel, Jodl, and Canaris. It was a five- or six-minute walk from that bunker to the Führerbunker, and when the Führer wished to speak to someone, he was usually annoyed if it took that long for that individual to make an appearance.

Keitel never wanted to be far away when the Führer summoned him.

The bunker where Generalleutnant von Wachtstein and a dozen other general officers had their quarters was an additional four- or five-minute walk.

Von Wachtstein could not remember Keitel ever coming to his quarters.

Keitel held up his hand to silence von Wachtstein's apology, and what could have been a small smile crossed his aristocratic face. He closed the door behind him, then turned back to von Wachtstein. "Karl," he said. "How would you like a few days off?"

"I don't think I understand, Herr Generalfeldmarschall."

"A day, perhaps two, in Berlin, and then perhaps another few days in Pomerania?"

"I have not requested leave, Herr Generalfeldmarschall."

"That wasn't the question, Karl," Keitel said, smiling. "The question was if you would like a few days'—say a week's—leave?"

"It's been quite a while since I had some time off, Herr Generalfeldmarschall," von Wachtstein said.

"Yes, I know," Keitel said. "And what is it the English say, 'all work and no play makes Jack a dull boy'?"

"I've heard that, Herr Generalfeldmarschall."

"When you're in Berlin, you might want to stop at the Hotel am Zoo."

"I'm afraid I don't understand, Herr Generalfeld-marschall."

"Just a suggestion, Karl. I thought that since you were on leave, perhaps you might want to spend a little time with your son. He's staying at the am Zoo. Canaris just telephoned. Apparently, the admiral brought him back from Argentina for some sort of conference."

"That was very kind of the Admiral," von Wachtstein said. "And the leave is very kind of you, Sir."

"You and Canaris are close friends, are you not?" Keitel asked.

"I cannot claim that privilege," von Wachtstein said. "I have the privilege of the Admiral's acquaintance, of course."

"Odd. I somehow had the feeling you were close."

"No, Sir."

"I wouldn't mention this at dinner, Karl," Keitel said. "Just go out to the airfield in the morning and catch the Dornier courier. With a little bit of luck, perhaps no one will even notice you're gone."

"Jawohl, Herr Generalfeldmarschall."

"Give my best regards to your son, Karl."

"Thank you, Herr Generalfeldmarschall."

[THREE]
The Hotel am Zoo
The Kurfürstendamm, Berlin
1720 10 May 1943

Boltitz walked across the narrow lane to the tree-lined island
that separated the main traffic on the Kurfürstendamm from
the rows of hotels, restaurants, and expensive shops.

"Where are we going?"

Boltitz pointed to the Kaiser Wilhelm Memorial Church
and started walking in that direction.

"You don't think the SS has gotten around to putting
microphones in there? Don't be too sure," Willi said.

"Watch your mouth, Herr Hauptmann," Karl snapped.

"Yes, Sir, Herr Korvettenkapitän, Sir," Willi said, and
saluted Boltitz contemptuously.

"Willi!" Peter protested.

They entered the foyer of the church. There was no longer
the sound of organ funeral music, but a dozen or more people—obviously mourners—filed past them.

Boltitz waited for the last of them to leave before speaking. "Hauptmann Grüner," he began finally. "I'm afraid
there's very bad news."

"About my father, obviously," Willi replied. "What?"

"You should have been notified, Herr Hauptmann—"
Karl said.

"Let's have it, for God's sake!" Willi interrupted.

"Von Wachtstein," Boltitz said.

"Willi, your dad is dead," Peter said. "I'm really sorry I
had to be the one to tell you."

Willi looked at Peter, then, after a moment, nodded and
asked, his voice low but under control: "How did it happen?"

"I'm afraid I don't have the authority to provide details,"
Boltitz said.

"Obviously, I'm an English spy, right?"

"For God's sake, Karl!" Peter protested.

Boltitz met his eyes but said nothing.

"We were on an intelligence operation that went wrong," Peter said.

" 'We were on'?" Willi asked. "You were there?"

Peter nodded. "I was there."

"What happened?" Willi asked. "What kind of an intelligence operation?"

"That, I'm sorry to have to say, is a state secret," Karl said.

"Fuck you and your state secrets, U-boat," Willi said.

"We were trying to get the officers from the *Graf Spee* out of Argentina—" Peter said.

"That's quite enough, Major von Wachtstein," Boltitz snapped.

"—and when we landed, they were waiting for us," Peter said. "Your father was shot. He died instantly, Willi."

"And they missed you, right?"

Peter nodded.

"You always were a lucky bastard, Hansel," Willi said.

He shrugged and then looked at Peter again. "Who is they, as in 'they were waiting' for you?"

"Maybe the Argentines, maybe the Americans," Peter said. "I don't really know."

"I strongly advise you, Major von Wachtstein, to heed my order that you have already said more than you should have," Boltitz said.

"Or you'll turn me in, Herr Korvettenkapitän? Do what your duty requires you to do."

"Don't get your ass in a crack, Hansel," Willi said, and turned to Boltitz. "One more question, Herr Korvettenkapitän. If it's not another of your fucking state secrets, that is. Where is my father buried?"

"Goddamn it, Karl, he's entitled to know that," Peter said. "If you won't tell him, I will."

"The remains of your father, Herr Hauptmann," Boltitz said, "are being returned to Germany for interment. With full military honors, of course."

"When? Now? Or after the Gottverdamnte war?"

"They are en route to Germany now," Boltitz said. "I'm sure you will be given further details when they are available."

Willi considered that for a moment, then looked at Peter. "Stick around a minute, Hansel," he said. "I won't be long."

Peter nodded.

Willi went into the nave of the church and walked up the aisle to the third row of chairs. He stopped there, with his hands behind his back, and looked toward the altar.

"You didn't expect to see him, did you?" Boltitz asked.

Peter looked at him but didn't answer.

Willi stood motionless for a full minute, then suddenly came to attention and saluted the cross crisply—a military, stiff-fingers-to-the-brim-of-his-uniform-cap salute, rather than the Nazi salute—then did a crisp about-face movement and walked back to Peter and Karl.

"I'm going back to the am Zoo," he announced. "If U-boat will let you come with me, Hansel, I'll buy you a drink." He turned to Karl. "Come with us or not, U-boat, I don't really give a shit."

"Karl's all right, Willi," Peter said. "He's just doing his duty."

"I don't want to intrude," Boltitz said.

Willi walked out of the church foyer.

"I have the feeling I should come with you, von Wachtstein," Karl said. "To make sure you don't run off at the mouth."

"Do what you think you have to do," Peter said, and walked quickly to catch up with Willi.

After a moment, Boltitz trotted after them.

The table where they had been sitting was, surprisingly, still available. As soon as they had taken seats, the waiter reappeared.

"A bottle of your finest schnapps, Herr Ober," Willi ordered. "Actually, a bottle of your best cognac would be better."

"Jawohl, Herr Hauptmann."

"The old man hated schnapps," Willi said. "But he did like his cognac."

Peter and Karl didn't reply.

"Did you know him, U-boat?" Willi asked.

"I did not have that privilege, Herr Hauptmann," Karl said.

"I thought maybe you did," Willi said. "Since you both work for Canaris. And if you're going to keep calling me 'Herr Hauptmann,' take a walk."

"Are you going to stop calling me 'U-boat'?" Karl asked.

Willi considered the question for a moment. "Probably not," he said with a smile. "I have a tendency to name people, don't I, Hansel? And U-boat seems to fit you, U-boat."

Willi reached in his trousers pocket and came out with a stuffed and well-worn wallet. He searched through it, came out with a photograph, and handed it to Boltitz.

"The late Oberst Karl-Heinz Grüner," Willi said.

Karl looked at it for a long moment, then handed it back.

"When did it happen?" Willi asked.

"Nineteen April," Peter said, "about quarter to ten in the morning."

He looked at Karl defiantly, but Karl said nothing.

The waiter delivered a bottle of Martel cognac and three brandy snifters, and began to pour as Willi returned his father's photograph to his wallet.

"I'll be damned," Willi said. "Here's another moment in time captured on film."

He took another photograph from his wallet and laid it on the table.

It showed Leutnant Freiherr Hans-Peter von Wachtstein and Leutnant Wilhelm Johannes Grüner, both wearing black leather flight jackets, onto which were pinned second lieutenant's insignia and Iron Crosses. They were standing under the engine nacelle of a Messerschmitt ME-109, holding between them the bull's-eye fuselage insignia torn from a shot-down Spitfire.

"A momentous occasion, Hansel," he said. "The day before we were enlisted swine, and here we are as commissioned officers."

"I remember," Peter said. "France. Calais, I think. Or maybe Cherbourg. Nineteen-forty."

Did I shoot that Spit down? Peter wondered. Or did Willi? Or was that piece of fuselage fabric just one of the half dozen around the officers' mess and we picked it up to have the photo taken?

"The Old Man was more pleased to see that goddamn officer's pin on my epaulet than he was with the Iron Cross."

"Mine, too," Peter said. "It really bothered him when he had to say, 'my son, the sergeant.' "

Willi chuckled. "You're an academy man, right, U-boat?" Willi challenged. "You never served as an enlisted swine?"

"I was never an enlisted man," Karl said, and picked up his glass. "Gentlemen, the late Oberst Grüner."

Willi looked at him for a moment before touching his glass to his. "Papa," he said.

"Oberst Grüner," Peter said.

They drained their glasses. Willi immediately picked up the bottle and refilled them. "That was taken just before I was shot down," he said. "During which process Hansel here saved my ass."

"Excuse me?" Karl said.

"A Spitfire got me," Willi said. "Sonofabitch came right out of the sun and did a real job on me. Took off the whole left stabilizer. And my engine, of course, was gloriously on fire. I didn't think I was going to get out of the airplane."

"And you said Peter—"

"*Hansel* got the Englishman, and then circled around me until he saw me safe on the ground."

"I don't understand," Karl said.

Willi looked at him for a moment before speaking. "Some asshole who never flew anything but a desk got the idea that it would be a good idea—to keep parachuting Englanders from getting back into another airplane, you see—to make targets of them after they bailed out. And some of our guys were stupid enough to listen to him. The natural result of that—which apparently never occurred to our asshole—was that the English started shooting at us when we had to bail out."

Karl looked as if he was about to say something but then changed his mind.

"You were a POW?"

"Oh, yeah. For four happy months."

"You escaped?"

"The Old Man somehow arranged for me to be the escort officer when we exchanged seriously wounded," Willi said.

"And what are you doing now?" Karl asked.

"I was hoping you'd ask, U-boat. Sorry, I can't tell you. State secret."

"You're not flying anymore?"

"I didn't say that," Willi said, then turned to Peter.

"So tell me, Hansel, are you back for good, or are you going back to Argentina?"

"I'm going back to Argentina," Peter said.

"And how is Argentina? And don't tell me about the beef; the Old Man already did. You getting any?"

"Beef, you mean?"

Willi laughed. "You know what I mean, Hansel."

"There are some very good-looking women in Argentina," Peter said.

"The question was 'Are you getting any?' "

"A gentleman never discusses his sex life," Peter said.

"You're not a gentleman, you're a fighter pilot," Willi said. "Or were." He turned to Karl. "You ever been to Argentina, U-boat?"

"I'm going to Argentina very soon," Karl said.

"To do what?"

"Where I will fly him around in my Feiseler Storch," Peter said.

"Is that what they have you doing, flying a *Storch*?"

Peter nodded.

"And you can look yourself in the mirror in the morning?"

"Absolutely," Peter said.

Willi shook his head.

"Speaking of sex," he said.

"Who was speaking of sex?" Peter asked.

"I'm going to have to get a room, since I think I am going to be too shitfaced to take one of the girls home." He inclined his head toward the bar, where half a dozen young women were sipping cocktails and looking their way.

"I've got a room here," Peter said.

"My apartment isn't far," Karl said. "You're welcome to stay with me."

"U-boat, don't tell me you're a faggot," Willi said.

Boltitz's face whitened. "You have a dangerous mouth, Grüner," he said.

"Jesus Christ, Willi!" Peter protested.

Boltitz stood up.

"Oh, for God's sake, U-boat! Can't you take a joke?"

"I'm going to the pisser," Boltitz said. He walked toward the men's room in the lobby.

"So what's with you and U-boat, Hansel?" Willi asked.

"He's investigating . . . what happened in Argentina."

"What's that got to do with you?"

"Somebody had to tell the Americans, or the Argentines, that we were coming."

"And you're one of the suspects?" Willi asked incredulously.

"They brought three of us back to make reports," Peter said.

"Four eight six six one," the man who answered the telephone said.

"Korvettenkapitän Boltitz for Fregattenkapitän von und zu Waching."

"What's up, Boltitz?" Von und zu Waching asked.

"Sorry, Sir, I didn't recognize your voice."

Von und zu Waching said nothing, and it took Karl a moment to recall Canaris's habit—now obviously adopted by von und zu Waching—not to waste time with unnecessary words, such as accepting an apology.

"Oberst Grüner's son—he's a Luftwaffe Hauptmann—was in the bar when you and the Admiral were here. He's now with von Wachtstein."

There was another long silence.

"It was necessary to tell him that Oberst Grüner is dead."

"And in what detail?"

"Von Wachtstein told him that it was in connection with the *Graf Spee* officers."

"Hold on," von und zu Waching said.

A long moment later, Admiral Canaris's voice came over the telephone: "Before I see you tomorrow," he began without any introduction, "I want you to think about von Wachtstein's reaction to Grüner."

"Jawohl, Herr Admiral."

"What are they doing now?"

"Drinking. They're old friends. Von Wachtstein saved Grüner's life—"

"Stay with them," Canaris interrupted. *"In vino veritas."*

"Jawohl, Herr—"

"I have just been informed von Wachtstein's father will be on the first flight tomorrow," Canaris interrupted again. "Von und zu Waching will telephone von Wachtstein there in a few minutes to tell him."

"Yes, Sir."

The telephone went dead.

"I will require two rooms," Karl said to the desk clerk.

"I'm very, very sorry, Herr Korvettenkapitän, but there are simply no rooms."

Karl took his credentials from his coat and showed them to the clerk.

"This is official Abwehr business," he said. "If you can't provide the rooms, get the manager."

The desk clerk turned from Karl and made some sort of signal with his hand, which confused Karl until a man in his middle thirties, wearing a well-cut suit, got out of an armchair and walked to the reception desk.

"Papers, please," he said to Karl.

"Who are you?"

The man said nothing, but produced a Gestapo identity disk. This was a serially numbered, elliptical piece of cast aluminum embossed with the Seal of State. It gave the bearer immunity from arrest, authority to arrest anyone without specifying the charge, and superior police powers over all other law-enforcement agencies. Illegal possession of a Gestapo identity disk was punishable by death, and loss of his disk by a member of the Gestapo was punishable by immediate dismissal.

Karl showed him his Abwehr credentials.

"The gentleman," the desk clerk said helpfully, "has requested two rooms for official business."

"It had better be official business," the Gestapo agent said.

"I beg your pardon?" Karl said.

"I saw you with those two Luftwaffe officers in the bar. This *is* official business?"

"As I understand the arrangement, Abwehr officers don't question the Gestapo, and the Gestapo doesn't question us," Karl said coldly. "I presume the rooms are equipped for surveillance?"

"Of course," the Gestapo agent said.

"Good," Karl said. "Please have the still photography film processed immediately, two copies. One should be sent to Obersturmbannführer Karl Cranz—"

"Obersturmbannführer Cranz? I don't seem to know the name."

"That's surprising," Karl said. "He's on the personal staff of the Reichsprotektor."

The Gestapo agent stared intently into Boltitz's eyes for a moment, then took out his notebook. "That's C-R-A—"

"A second set of prints should be sent to Fregattenkapitän von und zu Waching at the Abwehr," Boltitz interrupted. "Is there any reason why this can't be done by eight in the morning?"

"No, I can't think of any."

The desk clerk now had two room keys in his hand.

Boltitz put his hand out for them. The desk clerk looked to the Gestapo agent for directions. The Gestapo agent nodded, and the desk clerk dropped the keys into Boltitz's hand.

"Good," Boltitz said. He looked at the Gestapo agent. "Fregattenkapitän von und zu Waching and Obersturmbann-führer Cranz will be expecting those photographs at eight in the morning."

"I understand," the Gestapo agent said.

"Thank you for your cooperation," Boltitz said.

The Gestapo agent nodded but didn't speak.

Boltitz walked back to the lobby bar with irreverent thoughts running through his head: *What Cranz and von und zu Waching—for that matter, Himmler and Canaris—are liable to see in the photographs are two heroic Luftwaffe pilots sleeping off a drunk. Alone.*

Well, at least they'll have proof that I've been doing my job.

What a despicable way to earn your living, hanging around a hotel lobby, waiting for the opportunity to photograph officers in bed with some slut!

Where do they recruit Gestapo agents? In a sewer?

Major Freiherr Hans-Peter von Wachtstein and Hauptmann Wilhelm Johannes Grüner were no longer at the table where Boltitz had left them.

They were now at the bar, with the young women who had been smiling at them before and a Wehrmacht General Staff Oberstleutnant and an SS-Hauptsturmführer.

To the visible annoyance of the Army and the SS men, the young women seemed far more fascinated with the two fighter pilots (one of whom had the Knight's Cross of the Iron Cross hanging around his neck) than with them.

If one is a nice German girl, one does not go to bed with a young man one has met thirty minutes before in a bar. Unless, of course, he is a hero, in which case one is not a slut but a patriotic German woman making her contribution to the Final Victory.

Grüner saw him. "U-boat!" he cried. "You're back! We thought you'd submerged!"

Boltitz dangled the hotel keys in front of him.

"How the hell did you get those?" Willi asked. "They told me there wasn't a room in the house."

"Never underestimate the submarine service, Willi," Boltitz said.

"Ladies, may I present Korvettenkapitän Boltitz?" Willi said.

The young women all offered their hands. One of them, a tall, buxom woman with dark red hair who looked Hungarian, held on to Boltitz's hand far longer than the circumstances demanded. "And does the Korvettenkapitän of the Submarine Service have a first name?" she asked.

"He does," Boltitz said. "It's Karl, and Karl suggests that it might be very pleasant to go upstairs and sip Champagne while we watch the people walk up and down the Kurfürstendamm."

"That would be very nice," the red-haired woman said. "My name is Charlotte."

She gave him her hand again.

The waiter appeared. "Major Freiherr von Wachtstein?"

Peter nodded.

"You're a baron?" one of the women, a brunette with a short haircut and a low bodice, asked.

"Only on odd Thursdays," Peter said.

"There is a telephone call for you, Herr Baron," the waiter said. "The house phone is in the lobby, to the right."

"Who the hell can that be?" Peter asked.

"It's probably the loving mother of your four precious children," Willi said.

"You're married?" the brunette asked, disappointed.

"Only his wife is married," Boltitz said.

The joke won more laughter than it deserved.

Peter turned and walked toward the lobby door.

"And while he's lying to his wife about how he plans to spend the evening," Willi said, "I think I'll jettison some fuel. Can I trust you, U-boat, not to lose the girls while I'm gone?"

"I'll do my best," Karl said.

Charlotte swung on her stool so that her calf pressed against Boltitz's leg.

Von Wachtstein returned to the bar first.

"Was that your wife, Herr Baron?" the brunette asked.

"He doesn't have a wife," Boltitz said.

Peter flashed him a quick, dirty look.

"Actually, it was a sailor," he said. "A friend of the Herr Korvettenkapitän."

"Von und zu Waching?" Boltitz asked. "Or the other sailor?"

"Von und zu Waching," Peter said. "My father's going to be here in the morning."

"Your father's coming?" the brunette asked.

"Generalleutnant Graf von Wachtstein," Boltitz offered helpfully.

The brunette's face showed how pleased she was to have snared a Luftwaffe fighter pilot with the Knight's Cross, whose father was a both a nobleman and a senior officer.

The question, then, is whether Peter will nail her or remain faithful to the nineteen-year-old Argentine he told me about.

And if he does nail the brunette, does that mean he's not really in love with the Argentine, or simply that he's a healthy young male who is not about to kick something like the brunette out of bed?

[FOUR]
The Hotel Provincial
Mar del Plata, Argentina
0830 11 May 1943

"What are you doing out of bed?" Señora Dorotéa Mallín de Frade inquired of her husband as she entered the sitting of the hotel suite where they had spent the second and third nights of their marriage.

The question was in the nature of an indignant challenge.

The General Belgrano Suite was in the center of the top—fifth—floor of the hotel. It consisted of a bedroom, a sitting, a dining, and a maid's room (where Enrico Rodríguez had insisted on sleeping). It was furnished with what Clete considered typical Argentine furniture: large, heavy, dark, and uncomfortable—particularly the bed.

Its windows overlooked the promenade, a wide concrete walk that separated the curved-front hotel from the beach and the South Atlantic Ocean.

Cletus Frade, who was wearing the red silk bathrobe he had found in his father's closet still in its Sulka Rue de Castiglione Paris wrappings, turned from the window to look at his wife. She was wearing a white lace negligee that did virtually nothing to conceal the details of her anatomy.

"I tried very hard not to wake you, baby," he said, genuinely contrite. "I couldn't sleep."

"And what have you been doing?"

"I've been looking out the window," he said, indicating the window.

"And what did you see?"

"The waves are still going up and down," he said. "Aside from that, not much is happening out there."

That wasn't exactly true.

Leaning against the wall of the promenade was a man in a snap-brim hat and a business suit, looking up from his newspaper from time to time toward the General Belgrano Suite. Clete was sure he was in the service of the Bureau of Internal Security.

Enrico Rodríguez was leaning on the same wall, ten feet from the BIS agent, keeping *him* under surveillance. His broad smile indicated that he found the very idea of keeping a man on his honeymoon under surveillance ludicrous.

Dorotéa walked to the window, pushed the curtain aside, and looked for herself.

"Who's the man in the suit? One of Coronel Martín's men?"

"Probably," Clete said.

"That's ridiculous," Dorotéa said. "Is that going to happen all the time?"

"I don't know," Clete said. "Probably."

"They obviously think you're up to something," she said.

"I'm not," Clete said.

"I know," she said. "You promised to tell me if you were, and I trust you."

"My orders, baby, are not to fall out of the marriage bed," he said. "And to keep my eyes and ears open. That's all."

"So you told me," she said. "And I trust you."

"Just so I understand, you trust me, right?"

"Are you getting a little bored, my precious?"

"I may not be very bright," Clete said, "but I am smart

enough to know that the wise bridegroom on his honeymoon does not tell his bride he's bored."

"That, of course, means you are, my precious," Dorotéa said. "I rather hoped you would be."

"Excuse me?"

"Why don't we get out of here? We could be in Buenos Aires in time for a late lunch. I could do what I have to do this afternoon. We could have a nice dinner—maybe at the Yacht Club—and then we could drive home in the morning."

Clete was surprised at the emotion he felt when Dorotéa referred to Estancia San Pedro y San Pablo as "home." He put his arms around and hugged her. "Why go to Buenos Aires? Why don't we just go home, baby?"

"There are some things at Mother's I want to take home," she said. "And then I have to see my obstetrician."

She did it again. Not "things at my house," but "things at Mother's." And whatever it is, she wants to take it "home."

Clete hugged her a little more tightly.

Obstetrician? What the hell is that all about?

"You want to see your obstetrician? Honey, is everything all right?"

"As far as I know."

"Then why do you have to see your obstetrician?"

"I've never seen him."

"You told me you'd been to the doctor."

"I went to Dr. Schimmer, our *family* doctor," Dorotéa explained. "And he said I should go to see Dr. Sarrario—he's the *obstetrician*; he delivered me and Little Henry—as soon as I could."

"Why haven't you been to see him before now?"

"Before now, I didn't have this," she said, holding up her left hand, now adorned with a wedding band. "I couldn't go to Dr. Sarrario in the family way without being married."

"And you don't think he'll be able to guess that you got pregnant a couple of months ago?"

"Of course he will, but now that I'm married, he won't say anything."

He laughed. "And with a little bit of luck, he will spread

the word that for a premature child, our baby was born remarkably large and healthy?"

"Of course he will. That's understood," Dorotéa said. "I like it when you say 'our baby.' "

"Yeah, me too."

She gave him what she intended to be—and Clete initially accepted as—a very tender kiss and nothing more. But somehow things got out of control, and it was twenty minutes later when Clete opened the window, put his fingers in his mouth, and summoned Enrico with a shrill and piercing whistle.

He smiled when he saw the whistle had startled the people walking along the promenade, including Coronel Martín's BIS agent, who immediately looked up at the hotel in something close to alarm, saw Clete, and then pushed himself off the railing and turned around and began to study the waves lapping at the beach.

[FIVE]
The Hotel am Zoo
The Kurfürstendamm, Berlin
1230 11 May 1943

When Generalleutnant Graf Karl-Friedrich von Wachtstein caught sight of his youngest son coming down the stairway into the lobby of the hotel, his first thought was that—to judge from his pallor and bloodshot eyes—Hansel had spent the previous evening in the arms of Bacchus, and probably in those of one of the young women who frequented the hotel's bar.

His second thought was that he was a fine-looking young officer. And his third thought was that Major Freiherr Hans-Peter von Wachtstein was his only remaining son and thus the last of the von Wachtstein line.

Peter spotted his father and walked quickly up to him. He gave the Nazi salute, muttered "Heil Hitler!", and then gave his father the military salute.

The Graf raised his right arm from the elbow in a sloppy Nazi salute.

"Poppa!" Peter said.

"It's good to see you, Hansel," the Graf said, putting out his hand.

They shook hands.

The Graf turned to the officer standing beside him, an erect, tall, dark-haired Hauptmann. "I don't believe you know my aide, do you?" the Graf asked. "Hauptmann Sigmund von und zu Happner."

"A very great honor, Herr Baron," von und zu Happner said, popping to attention, clicking his heels, and nodding his head in a bow.

Peter gave him his hand. "Hello," he said.

"The ever-efficient Ziggie has found a compartment for us on the three-oh-five to Wachtstein . . . from here, right, Ziggie?" The Graf made a vague wave in the general direction of the am Zoo railroad station.

"Yes, Herr Generalleutnant."

"And once you go to the station and get the tickets, Ziggie, you are also on leave," the Graf said.

"The Herr Generalleutnant is very kind, but I am perfectly willing to stay with you, Sir."

"Hansel and I are going home, where we are going to drink beer and eat sausages and do nothing that will require your services. Go see your family, Ziggie. I'll meet you here a week from today, or get other word to you."

"If the Herr Generalleutnant—"

"Go get our tickets, Ziggie," the Graf interrupted.

"Jawohl, Herr Generalleutnant."

Von und zu Happner came to attention again, clicked his heels, and walked away from them.

"Very efficient young man," the Graf said. "And a devout National Socialist. He was recommended to be my aide by Generaloberst Jodl. His mother is Jodl's cousin."

Their eyes met.

Peter wondered if Jodl had simply been seeking a posting for his cousin's son far from the sound of guns, or whether

Jodl wanted someone he could trust watching Generalleutnant von Wachtstein. Or perhaps both.

This is not the time or the place to ask.

"I thought perhaps we would spend a couple of days at Wachtstein, and then perhaps go to Munich. Claus von Stauffenberg is in a hospital there."

"How is he?" Peter asked.

"His recovery has been slow, I'm afraid," the Graf said. "The question before us now is how do we pass the time until our train leaves? Would you like a glass of beer?"

"There are two people I would like you to meet," Peter said.

"Here?"

"One of them is Korvettenkapitän Boltitz. He works for Admiral Canaris. The other is an old comrade, Hauptmann Willi Grüner. I had the unfortunate duty yesterday of having to inform Willi that his father has given his life for the Fatherland. There was some communications problem."

The Graf asked only, "Where are these officers?"

"I thought we could have lunch together. They should be here any minute."

The Graf nodded. "Would you like a glass of beer?" he asked. "Whenever I fly, I seem to dehydrate."

Peter waved his father ahead of him toward the lobby bar. They found an empty banquette, and a waiter quickly appeared.

"Two Berliner Kindl, please, Herr Ober," the Graf ordered.

"Jawohl, Herr Generalleutnant."

Willi Grüner came into the bar first, moments before Karl Boltitz.

"I have your photograph in my office, Hauptmann," the Graf said. "It was taken, I believe, the day after you and Hansel were commissioned."

"Yes, Sir," Willi said.

The Graf waved him into the banquette.

"Please accept my condolences on the loss of your father," the Graf said. "Hansel just informed me."

"That's very kind of you, Sir. Thank you."

"Korvettenkapitän Boltitz, Herr Generalleutnant," Karl said, rendering a bent-elbow Nazi salute.

"I believe I have the privilege of your father's acquaintance," the Graf said, returning the salute. "Vizeadmiral Boltitz?"

"Yes, Sir."

"I'm always happy to meet a friend of my son who is the son of one of my friends," the Graf said.

"Thank you, Sir."

Unfortunately, Karl thought, *I am not his friend. I am an intelligence officer who has been forced to conclude that your son may well be a traitor.*

"Hansel tells me that you work for Admiral Canaris," the Graf said. "I knew him years ago, but unfortunately, even at Wolfsschanze, I hardly ever get to see him."

"The Admiral is a very busy man, Herr Generalleutnant."

The waiter appeared with two large glasses of beer.

"What will you gentleman have?" the Graf asked.

"The same," Willi and Karl said on top of each other.

"Are you stationed in Berlin, Hauptmann Grüner?"

"I am—or was—outside Berlin. I had Hansel's old squadron, Sir, but I've been transferred."

"Oh? And where are you going now?"

"With all respect, Sir, I'm not allowed to say."

So he does have something to do with a state secret, Karl thought. *Last night, I thought he was just being clever about that. I'll have to find out what that is.*

Hauptmann von und zu Happner came into the bar and found them. Introductions were made.

"Will you have a beer, Ziggie, before you go home?" the Graf asked.

"If the Generalleutnant is sure that—"

"We've been over that, Ziggie," the Graf interrupted.

"Then I will decline with thanks, Herr Generalleutnant. There's a train to Dresden in about twenty minutes."

"Have a nice time, Ziggie. Please present my regards to Frau von und zu Happner."

"Thank you, Sir," von und zu Happner said, clicked his heels, gave the Nazi salute, and walked out of the bar.

"Hauptmann," the Graf said. "Hansel and I are on the three-oh-five to Wachtstein. There's not much to do there but drink beer and eat sausages, but if you don't have better plans, wc both would be pleased to have you join us."

"That's very kind of you, Sir," Willi said, "but I'm on the five-fifteen to Augsburg."

"Pity," the Graf said.

I wonder, Boltitz thought, *what the state secret in Augsburg is?*

"And I have to leave you, too, Peter," Boltitz said. "Fregattcnkapitän von und zu Waching telephoned me a few moments ago to tell me I have been charged with organizing Oberst Grüner's funeral. He wants to talk to me about it now."

Willi looked at him but said nothing.

"Willi, I'll want to talk to you about that, obviously," Boltitz said. "Where can I get in touch with you?"

"That may pose a problem," Willi said. "I am under very specific orders to tell no one where I'm going."

"I'm sure the Luftwaffe will know," Boltitz said. "And be able to tell me."

"Good luck," Willi said wryly. "They couldn't find me to tell me my father had . . . died, could they?"

"I'm sure that can be straightened out," Boltitz said.

He stood up. "It was a very great pleasure to meet you, Herr Generalleutnant Graf," he said, clicking his hcels and bobbing his head in a curt bow.

"It was my pleasure," the Graf said.

"Have a pleasant leave, Peter," Boltitz said, putting out his hand to him.

"I'll try," Peter said.

Boltitz came to attention again, gave a stiff-armcd Nazi salute, then walked out of the bar.

The Graf, Peter, and Willi watched him walk out, but none of them said anything.

[SIX]
The Admiral's Mess
Office of the Director, Abwehr Intelligence
Berlin
1305 11 May 1943

Korvettenkapitän Karl Boltitz stepped into the small, darkly paneled private dining room of the Director of Abwehr Intelligence, came to attention, rendered the Nazi salute, and barked, "Heil Hitler!"

Canaris's reply was to point to a chair.

"Good afternoon, Herr Admiral, Herr Fregattenkapitän," Boltitz said, and sat down.

A steward in a stiffly starched short white jacket immediately began to ladle soup onto their plates.

"If we are to judge from the excellent photography so kindly provided to us by the SS," Canaris said, his fingers grazing over a large brown envelope, "von Wachtstein was not at all interested in the recreation available to him at the am Zoo—"

"Certainly less interested than Hauptmann Grüner," von und zu Waching said, "and yourself."

My God, that Gestapo swine photographed me and the Hungarian redhead!

Canaris looked at Boltitz.

What the hell am I supposed to say?

"It has been my experience, Boltitz," Canaris said after a long moment, "that when one has nothing to say, one should say nothing."

"You might consider it a learning experience," von und zu Waching said. "The SS is second to no one in their zeal."

What could have been a smile crossed Canaris's face. Then he picked up the brown envelope and held it out to the steward.

"Have this burned," he said.

"Jawohl, Herr Admiral."

"Do you see some significance in von Wachtstein's chastity?" Canaris asked.

"Herr Admiral, he is involved with a woman in Argentina. I believe he thinks he's in love."

"You would say, then," Canaris said, "that he is not a candidate for a pink triangle?"

"No, Sir. I saw nothing that would suggest that at all."

"And his reaction to his unexpected encounter with Hauptmann Grüner?" Canaris asked.

It was the question Canaris had told Boltitz to expect, and he had given a good deal of thought to it. Providing an answer posed ethical problems for him.

There was no question in his mind that there was an element of guilt, perhaps even shame, in von Wachtstein's reaction to Willi Grüner. The question was, however, what the guilt or shame meant.

Von Wachtstein's version of what had happened at Samborombón Bay—related in his hotel room in Lisbon, when he had been drinking but not drunk—was straightforward. He and Goltz had just stepped ashore from the *Océano Pacífico*'s ship's boat, and were greeting Grüner, when they were suddenly fired upon, before they had even begun to unload the special shipment from the boat.

Von Wachtstein claimed there were at least three shots. The first two killed Grüner and Goltz. The third—but perhaps there'd been more—had been aimed at him as he was bending over Grüner's body.

According to von Wachtstein, the sailors from the *Océano Pacífico* had been "terrified and useless," and he had had to drag both bodies from where they had fallen to the ship's boat. They had then returned to the *Océano Pacífico*.

The only people who could verify—or disprove—von Wachtstein's story were the sailors from the *Océano Pacífico*, including Kapitän de Banderano, and Boltitz couldn't interrogate them until the ship tied up in Cadiz. In a week or more.

In the meantime, he had to consider that it was entirely possible that von Wachtstein had not been harmed because the riflemen did not want to kill him. If they were good enough snipers to kill two men with two shots to the head, why had they missed a third?

The most logical reason for their "miss" was that they regarded von Wachtstein as a friend, or if not a friend, as someone who had been useful to them.

That line of reasoning presumed von Wachtstein was a traitor. Boltitz was not willing to make that accusation. Not yet, not without further proof.

It was possible, of course, that the shame and guilt that showed on his face when he saw Willi Grüner could simply be the reaction of an officer who felt doubly guilty, doubly shamed, because he had not been able to carry out his orders, and was still alive when Oberst Grüner—who was both his commanding officer and the father of his comrade-in-arms—was dead.

Boltitz was aware that he would like to believe that von Wachtstein had simply been lucky. That the Argentine—or American—sharpshooters had shot at him and missed. He had to admit it was significant that none of the six *Océano Pacífico* crewmen had been shot, either.

That could suggest that the snipers had fired three—or more—carefully aimed shots as quickly as they could, then immediately left the area to avoid detection.

Boltitz was aware that he liked von Wachtstein and that Generalleutnant von Wachtstein reminded him of his father, and that this might tend to color his reasoning. Yet he knew his duty was to find the truth, whether or not he liked it.

And his duty was to report to Canaris the truth, not his suspicions. An officer like Major Freiherr Hans-Peter von Wachtstein, who practiced, as Boltitz himself did, adherence to the officer's code of honor was entitled to the benefit of the doubt.

"Herr Admiral," Karl Boltitz said carefully, "von Wachtstein and Hauptmann Grüner served together. Grüner believes that when he was forced to parachute from his aircraft over

England, von Wachtstein saved his life—at considerable risk to his own—by protecting him until he landed."

"I didn't know that," Canaris said,

"And, Sir, I learned that before France, they served together in Spain, and were commissioned from the ranks on the same day. They are good friends."

"And what was von Wachtstein's reaction to seeing his old friend?"

"He was very uncomfortable, Sir."

"And you have an opinion about that?"

"Hauptmann Grüner had not been informed that his father had been killed, Sir. Von Wachtstein had to tell him. I would have been uncomfortable in that circumstance. And, in my opinion, I felt that von Wachtstein was made more uncomfortable because he wasn't injured or killed at Samborombón and Oberst Grüner was."

Canaris nodded but said nothing.

"Herr Admiral, Hauptmann Grüner told us both—and Generalleutnant von Wachtstein—that he is under orders not to reveal his present assignment to anyone. He let slip that he's going to Augsburg."

Canaris looked at von und zu Waching and nodded his head.

"Messerschmitt has developed a new fighter for the Luftwaffe," von und zu Waching said. "They call it the ME-262. It is propellerless, and supposedly capable of speeds approaching nine hundred kilometers per hour. When it is operational, the Führer expects it will remove the Allied bomber fleet from our skies. Adolf Galland has been charged with its final testing and making it operational. Hauptmann Grüner has been selected by Galland as one of his pilots."*

---

* The Messerschmitt ME-262, developed in great secrecy, was first flown on 18 July 1942. It was powered by two Junkers Jumo turbojet engines, each producing about 2,000 pounds of thrust, which gave it a maximum level speed of approximately 540 mph. It was armed with four 30mm MK108 cannon and had a range of approximately 650 miles. Adolf Galland, one of the Luftwaffe's most successful fighter pilots, and a national hero, became Germany's youngest general officer when he was promoted in 1942 at age thirty. Shot down flying an ME-262 in the last days of the war, he was captured by the English.

"In Augsburg?" Boltitz asked, then asked the question that had sprung to his mind, "Nine hundred kilometers per hour?"

"Sounds incredible, doesn't it?" Canaris said. "One should never underestimate German engineering genius. Or the genius of Reichsmarschall Göring."

He looked at Boltitz for a moment, then went on:

"Galland is a friend of mine," he said. "Despite the press of his duties, I am sure that he will feel Grüner can be spared long enough to participate in the funeral of his father. And I'm sure that von Wachtstein would like to be there, to pay his last respects to Oberst Grüner. Perhaps it might be wise for you to plan to leave for Argentina immediately afterward. It might be possible for you and von Wachtstein to travel together."

"Jawohl, Herr Admiral."

"What are the von Wachtsteins' plans?"

"They are going to Pomerania, Herr Admiral. Generalleutnant von Wachtstein mentioned something about going to see a friend of theirs, an Oberstleutnant von Stauffenberg, who is in a hospital in Munich."

"The families are old friends," Canaris said. "Von Stauffenberg was severely wounded in Africa."

"What would the Herr Admiral have me do?" Boltitz asked.

"Just what you are doing now, Boltitz," Canaris said.

"Jawohl, Herr Admiral."

What I'm really going to have to do, Karl Boltitz thought, *is remember this conversation as carefully as I can, and then hope I can guess what he really means by what he has not said.*

XIV

El Coronel Juan Domingo Perón, fresh from a shower and wearing a blue silk robe, was sitting on the bed in the top-floor master bedroom of the mansion across from the Hipódrome Argentino. There he consulted a small leather-bound address book and found the number he was looking for.

He dialed all the digits but one, laid the address book on the bedside table, adjusted the pillows of the bed against the headboard, and, swinging his legs up onto the bed, arranged himself comfortably against the pillows.

He dialed the last number. It was answered on the second ring.

"Coronel Martín."

"Juan Domingo Perón. Buenas tardes, Alejandro."

"Buenas tardes, mi Coronel. How may I help you?"

Perón chuckled. "You're going to have to remember, Alejandro, that you are now a coronel yourself, and that protocol permits coronels to address one another by their Christian names."

"That's very gracious of you, Juan Domingo," Martín replied. "But may I suggest, with all possible respect, that there is a vast difference between a coronel so junior that the shellac is still on his insignia, and a very senior coronel who is also the Special Assistant to the Minister for War?"

"That of course, would have to be taken into account, Alejandro, by a wise officer—such as yourself—who understands the value of discretion," Perón said charmingly. "But I really wish you would call me Juan Domingo."

"I will be honored, Juan Domingo. Thank you."

"Juan Domingo is calling, Alejandro, not the Special Assistant to the Minister for War."

"And how may I help you, Juan Domingo?"

"I have a small problem that you might possibly help me with."

"Whatever I can do, Juan Domingo."

"I can't imagine that the BIS would have Señor Cletus Frade under surveillance, Alejandro, but I really have to get in touch with him, and I thought perhaps that—perhaps you heard something over a cup of coffee—you might have an idea where he is."

"Oddly enough, Juan Domingo, just a few minutes ago, while I was having a cup of coffee, I did hear something about Señor Frade. He and Señora Frade were seen on the highway from Mar del Plata not more than an hour ago."

"If you had to guess, Alejandro, were they headed for Estancia San Pedro y San Pablo?"

"No, Sir, it was this side of Estancia San Pedro y San Pablo. If I had to guess, I would guess that Señor and Señora Frade are coming to the city."

"I tried both the estancia and Llao Llao," Perón said—referring to a luxury hotel in San Carlos de Bariloche.

"I believe the story that the Frades were going to Llao Llao on their wedding trip was a diversionary maneuver, Juan Domingo."

"I can understand that. A man is entitled to be left alone on his honeymoon."

"My mother-in-law couldn't seem to understand that, Juan Domingo."

Perón laughed appreciatively.

"I would say, Juan Domingo—just a guess, you understand—that you could probably reach Señor Frade in about an hour at his home on Coronel Díaz, or at the home of Señor Mallín."

"Not at the Frade guest house?" Perón asked.

"I think they would go to either Señora Mallín de Frade's family home, or to the house on Coronel Díaz."

"I have the Coronel Díaz number. You wouldn't happen to have the Mallín number?"

"I think I've got it here somewhere, Juan Domingo," Martín said, and a moment later furnished it. Perón carefully added it to the correct page in his address book.

"You have been very obliging, Alejandro," Perón said.

"It has been my pleasure to be of some small service."

"I'll call one day next week, and if you can find the time, we'll have lunch."

"That would be delightful."

"Thank you again, Alejandro," Perón said, and hung up.

He swung his legs out of bed and telephoned both numbers, leaving the same message at each: He would be grateful if Señor and Señora Frade would take dinner with him tonight, that he would call back in an hour to confirm the details.

He hung up, and sat thoughtfully for a moment. He was pleased that he had finally thought of calling Martín. He should have thought of that before wasting time calling the estancia and Llao Llao.

He consulted his address book again and dialed a number. "Generalmajor von Deitzberg, por favor. Coronel Perón of the Ministry for War is calling."

Von Deitzberg came on the line a moment later. "Buenas tardes, Juan Domingo. It's always a pleasure to hear from you."

"Likewise, Manfred," Perón said. "About tonight . . ."

"Unfortunately, he's more interested in his bride than in sipping Champagne with a group of diplomats?"

"Actually, the problem was finding him. I have finally done so."

"Then he'll be at the hotel . . . the Plaza . . . tonight?"

"I think under the circumstances that it would be nice if an invitation was waiting for him at the door."

"He's coming alone?" von Deitzberg asked.

"An invitation for both Frade and his wife," Perón said. "And unless something happens, we will arrive together."

"There will be invitations at the door, Juan Domingo,"

von Deitzberg said. "And I look forward to seeing you. Incidentally, Señor and Señora Duarte have accepted."

"Splendid. I think this personal meeting is important, Manfred."

"And I quite agree, Juan Domingo."

"The . . . unfortunate . . . business has to be put behind us."

"I agree."

"I'll see you tonight, then, Manfred," Perón said, and hung up.

It isn't enough, Perón thought, *that I arrange for Cletus to attend the reception for von Deitzberg and von Löwzer. He is so like his father, unpredictable, unwilling to forgive. I have to make sure that he accepts the apology of the German officer corps for the death of Jorge. And that he understands the importance of doing so.*

Which means I will have to have a word with him—in private; not with his bride listening—before we go to the Plaza tonight.

"Tío Juan," Maria-Teresa said, "are you about finished? I'm hungry."

Perón turned to look at her, and then smiled. She was in the bed beside him in a pink bathrobe. "You are hungry, my precious?" he asked, and crawled onto the bed on his knees and looked down at her.

She was tall and thin, with long, rich dark-brown hair, which she wore parted in the middle.

"Yes, I am," she said, pouting.

"Would you like to go somewhere for a pastry? Some ice cream? Or are you *really* hungry?" He reached down and gently tugged at the bow of the cord holding the bathrobe together.

"Where?" she asked.

"Well, we could drive downtown," he said. The belt came loose and he unfastened it completely, then very slowly opened the bathrobe. Her breasts were small and firm, and the light brown tuft of hair between her legs was adorable.

I don't care how beautiful a woman is otherwise, disgusting pendulous breasts overwhelm any other physical charms. And if her pubic hair looks like a pampas swamp that could conceal a herd of feral pigs, she has absolutely no appeal to me.

"Are we going to be naughty?" Maria-Teresa asked.

"Well, I don't know. Would you like to be naughty?"

"Oh, I don't know. Sometimes I like it and sometimes I don't."

He leaned down and kissed one of her nipples.

"That's *naughty,* Tío Juan!" Maria-Teresa said. It was more a comment than a protest.

"Not as naughty as I would like to be," he said.

"I think I would rather walk across the street and have a strawberry cake in the Jockey Club."

"You would, would you?"

"Can we do that?"

"If I do that for you, what are you going to do for me?"

"You mean 'what am I going to do *naughty to you*?'" she said.

He bent over her and kissed her other nipple. "Well?"

Maria-Teresa slipped her hand inside his dressing gown. "Is this naughty enough for you?"

"It's a beginning," he said.

"If I'm *really* naughty, will you take me to Harrod's and buy me a dress?"

"Yes, but not today. Today Tío Juan has things to do. Perhaps tomorrow."

"Oh," she said. "You really want to be naughty, don't you? You're ready right now."

"You are so beautiful!" he said.

[TWO]
1728 Avenida Coronel Díaz
Palermo, Buenos Aires
1305 11 May 1943

The mansion's twelve-foot-high cast-iron gates were already open when Clete turned off Avenida Coronel Díaz, and he drove to the front door without stopping.

He was still in the process of leaving the car when the

door opened and a parade of servants, led by Antonio the butler, marched out of the house. Antonio and the house-keeper walked to the car's passenger side. The maids and cooks—the females—formed a line to the left on the stairs, and the gardeners, the handyman, and the other males formed a line on the right.

At the last moment, Sargento Rudolpho Gomez, Argentine Cavalry, Retired, stepped out of the house, took a quick glance around, and took up a position next to the men.

Clete smiled.

This is not the first parade you've been a little late for, is it, Rudolpho? I know the feeling.

That's a new suit. The one you had on at the wedding looked like something you borrowed.

You thought you were the picture of civilian sartorial splendor, but obviously Antonio did not.

Antonio opened Dorotéa's door. "Welcome to your home, Señora," he said. "It is a great pleasure for all of us to have you here."

"Thank you very much, Antonio," Dorotéa said. She shook the housekeeper's hand, then followed Antonio to the stairs. There she was introduced to the men. After shaking hands and saying a word or two to each, she crossed the stairs to the women, who curtsied as Antonio gave their names.

She knows the drill, Clete thought admiringly. *She handled that like a pro. Did her mother include how to do things like that in their little "what every bride should know" chats?*

Antonio bowed Dorotéa into the foyer, and Clete trotted up the stairs after them.

"Nice suit, Rudolpho," he said as he passed him, and was not at all surprised to hear Rudolpho call after him,

"Antonio got it for me, Señor Clete. Three of them. He said it was your wish."

Just inside the massive doors, a Winchester Model 12 riot gun was leaning against the wall, and a leather bandolier filled with brass 12-gauge 00-buckshot shells for it hung from the back of a chair.

And somewhere under his new suit there's a .45.

He caught up with Antonio and Dorotéa, who were standing in the center of the foyer.

"And when would Señora like luncheon?" Antonio asked.

"As soon as it's convenient," Dorotéa said.

"Would broiled chicken be satisfactory, Señora?"

"Broiled chicken would be fine," Dorotéa said. "I'll need a few minutes to freshen up. Anytime after that."

"Sí, Señora. Señora, Padre Welner is in the downstairs sitting. Is it your desire that he join you for lunch?"

What the hell does he want? Clete wondered. Then: *How did he know we were going to be here?*

Dorotéa paused just perceptibly before replying. "Please tell Father Welner that Señor Frade and I would be delighted if he was free to join us for luncheon."

"Sí, Señora," Antonio said, and added: "Señor Clete, el Coronel Perón telephoned. He said that he hopes you and the Señora are free this evening, and that he would telephone again at one-twenty to explain."

Sonofabitch! The last thing I want to do tonight is have dinner with that sonofabitch! What the hell's going on? Is that damned Jesuit involved?

"How interesting," Dorotéa said. She looked at Clete, and he shrugged to indicate he had no idea what Perón wanted. She turned to Antonio. "We'll be down directly," she said.

"I'm all right, baby," Clete said. "Maybe Welner knows what's going on. I'll ask him."

"Don't you think you'd better freshen up?" she asked.

The translation of that is I either go upstairs with you or I will be sorry.

Oh, Jesus! Is that what she's thinking? A little quickie before lunch? It must be at least five hours since we have shared the now-sanctioned joys of connubial bliss.

"Your wish, my dear, is my command," Clete said, à la Clark Gable.

She started walking up the wide staircase. He followed, which gave him reason—again—to think that her rear end was one of the wonders of the modern world. But when they were inside the master suite with the door closed behind them, he quickly learned that she did not have anything carnal in mind.

"Not now!" she said, holding him at arm's length.

"Sorry."

"What are we doing here?" she asked.

"Huh?"

"I thought we were going to the house on Libertador."

"Tío Juan is in the house on Libertador," he said.

"I'd forgotten," she said. "How long is that going to go on?"

"You want me to tell him to move out?"

"I don't suppose you could really do that, could you?" she asked, and then, without giving him a chance to reply, asked: "And Rudolpho?"

"Rudolpho comes with your wedding present," Clete said a little awkwardly. "He was here making sure it glistens."

"Whatever are you talking about?"

"You've always liked the Buick," he said. "So, happy marriage, Dorotéa, the Buick is yours."

She didn't reply.

"I thought you'd like it," he said. "If you'd rather, you can have the Horch."

"Don't be absurd," she said. "If I started to drive your beloved Horch, you would have a fit."

"Then what's wrong?"

"I'm trying to get used to the idea that Rudolpho is going to follow me around with a shotgun, the way Enrico follows you."

He didn't say anything.

"You really think it's necessary?" she asked.

"My uncle Jim used to say that you never need a gun unless you need one badly. I suppose the same thing could be said about a—"

"A bodyguard?" she interrupted.

He shrugged, then nodded.

"Do you think he would mind if I got him one of those little caps, so he would look like a chauffeur?"

Clete thought about that briefly, then replied, "Yes, I do. I think he would mind."

"Well, then, I'll guess I will have to get used to Rudolpho the bodyguard, won't I?"

"Baby, I wouldn't want to live if anything happened to you," Clete blurted.

"Odd," she said. "That was precisely what I told myself when I realized that Enrico was going with us on our wedding trip." She looked at him a minute, then touched his cheek with her hand and changed the subject. "Why don't you ask Father Welner how we can get Perón out of the guest house? I really hate the prospect of calling this museum home."

"OK," he said.

"I'll be down in about fifteen minutes," she said. "I want to take a good bath before I go—*Rudolpho and I go*—to see Dr. Sarrario."

"OK," he said.

"Cletus, thank you very much for the Buick," she said. "I really like that auto."

"With all my worldly goods, baby, you are now endowed. Weren't you listening?"

"I must have missed that part," she said. "Anyway, if you have convinced me that you have been a good boy while I was off to the baby doctor, I may have a little present for you myself."

"What kind of a present?"

"What kind of a present can a wife give a man who has everything?" she asked.

Then, looking into his eyes and smiling sweetly, she placed her hand firmly on the symbol of his gender.

"Think about it, husband of mine," Dorotéa said, and walked into the bedroom.

The telephone in the downstairs sitting began to ring as Cletus walked through the door.

"Well, if it isn't my favorite Jesuit," he said.

Father Welner, a Champagne glass in his hand, rose gracefully to his feet from a red leather couch and, smiling, walked to Clete with his hand extended. "The value of the compliment would depend, of course, on how many members of the Society of Jesus you know."

"Counting you?" Clete chuckled, and began to count by folding down the fingers of his left hand. When he stopped, two fingers remained extended.

"That many?" Welner chuckled. They shook hands. "And how do you find married life?" he asked.

The door opened, and Antonio announced, "Señor Clete, el Coronel Perón is on the line."

Clete could see no reaction on the priest's face. He walked to a telephone and picked it up. Just in time, he stopped himself from saying "mi Coronel." "Tío Juan," Clete said. "What a pleasant surprise."

If I sound as insincere as I feel, he's going to know just how pleased I really am.

"So you two didn't go to Bariloche, to Llao Llao, as you announced you would," Perón said. "That was very naughty of you, Cletus, but under the circumstances probably a very wise thing to do."

"How did you find out about that?" Clete asked.

"I called out there," Perón said. "I really had to talk to you."

"How'd you know I was here?"

"I took a chance, and Antonio told me you were expected within the hour."

That'll be the last time you'll tell this bastard anything about me, Antonio.

"Well, I'm glad you tried here. What's up?"

"Ambassador von Lutzenberger is giving a reception tonight—eight o'clock at the Plaza Hotel—in honor of Deputy Foreign Minister von Löwzer and Generalmajor von Deitzberg."

"Oh, really?"

Something touched his arm, and he looked. Welner was offering him a glass of Champagne.

"And I really think you—and, of course, Dorotéa—should attend."

"If I may speak frankly, Tío Juan," Clete said. "I have two problems with that. . . ."

Welner jabbed him painfully in the ribs with his index finger. Clete glowered at him.

"Which are, Cletus?" Perón asked.

"First, I'm on my honeymoon; and second, we haven't been invited, so far as I know."

"There will be invitations at the door," Perón said. "I thought the three of us could go together."

Welner jabbed Clete again, not quite so hard as the first time, and when Clete looked at him, nodded his head "yes."

"That would be very nice, if it's convenient for you," Clete said.

Welner nodded approvingly.

"And I would like to have a few words with you privately," Perón said. "Before we go to the Plaza."

"You mean this afternoon?"

"What are your plans for this afternoon?"

"Dorotéa's going to the doctor. . . ."

"Nothing wrong, I hope?" Perón asked.

There was something in his voice that caused Clete to think, *I'll be damned. The bastard sounds genuinely concerned.*

"Just checking in with her obstetrician," Clete said.

"Good," Perón said. "A young woman, a delicate young woman like Dorotéa, cannot be too careful during her first pregnancy."

And that sounded sincere, too. Damn!

"You're right, of course."

"Then Dorotéa will not be at Coronel Díaz this afternoon?"

"She's going right after lunch," Clete said.

"Do you suppose I could come there then?" Perón asked.

"Better yet, Tío Juan," Clete heard himself saying. "Why don't you come over here right now, if that would be convenient, and have lunch with us? Father Welner is already here."

As I suspect you damned well know. Welner's presence here is not a coincidence.

"You sure I wouldn't be intruding? It is important that we have a word—"

"Don't be silly, Tío Juan," Clete said.

"Then I shall leave directly," Perón said. "I'm at the Libertador house."

"Fine, then we'll see you in just a few minutes."

Clete put the telephone it its cradle, looked at the Champagne glass in his hand, raised it to his mouth, and drained it.

"You're supposed to sip Champagne," Welner said.

Clete extended his right hand, the fist balled, except for the center finger, which pointed upward.

"You don't have an invitation to where?" Welner asked, smiling.

"To a reception at the Plaza. A German Embassy reception. You didn't know?"

Welner shook his head.

"You being here is just one of those coincidences, right?"

"Claudia was sure you wouldn't be here."

"Excuse me?"

"She wants to remove some personal things," Welner said. "She wanted to do that when she was sure you wouldn't be here, and she asked me to be here when she did it."

"Where is she?" Clete asked.

"She should be here any minute," Welner said.

Clete pulled a bell cord hanging next to the door. Antonio appeared a moment later. "Señora Carzino-Cormano and probably one or both of her daughters will be here shortly. And so will el Coronel Perón. Is feeding them going to be a problem?"

"None whatever, Señor Clete."

"In the future, Antonio, I don't want you telling anyone—in particular el Coronel Perón—where I am, or where my wife is."

"I never have, Señor Clete, and I never would."

"Then how did he know we were going to be here?"

"I have no idea, Señor Clete."

"Then I owe you an apology," Clete said. "I should have known better. Sorry, Antonio."

Antonio inclined his head, accepting the apology. "Will there be anything else, Señor?"

"No, thank you."

When Antonio had left the sitting, Clete looked at the priest. "In English, we call that 'el footo in el moutho,' " he said. "I'm very good at it, as you just saw."

Welner chuckled. "So was your father," he said. "Why do you think Perón wants you to go to the German's reception?"

The door opened before Clete could reply, and Señora Claudia Carzino-Cormano walked into the sitting. She was alone. She went to Welner and gave him her cheek. Then she turned to Clete. "You weren't supposed to be here," she said as she gave him her cheek.

"I didn't know I was going to be," he said. "Dorotéa has to go to the obstetrician."

"Everything's all right?"

"So far as I know. We got a little bored in Mar del Plata," Clete said. "And she hasn't been to the obstetrician yet. Name of Sarrario. You know him? Is he any good?"

"The best," Welner said.

"He delivered both Isabela and Alicia," Claudia said. "Why hasn't she seen him before?"

"Because she didn't have a wedding ring before," Clete said.

"He is something of a prude," Claudia chuckled. "Did Father Kurt tell you what we're doing here?"

"He said you were going to burgle the place, and wanted him here for an alibi. Claudia, you don't ever have to sneak in here. And take whatever you want."

"There are some personal things . . ."

"You wouldn't be interested in buying the place, would you?" Clete said.

"No, I wouldn't."

"You can't be thinking of selling the place, Cletus," Welner said.

"Why can't I be?"

"Because it's the Frade mansion."

"The Frade museum is more like it. I don't like it, Dorotéa

hates it, and, for that matter, my father referred to it as 'my money sewer on Coronel Díaz.' "

"Yes, he did." Claudia laughed.

"But it never entered his mind to sell it," Welner argued.

"Why not? Do you know how many people are working here? In this almost-always-empty marble barn? The only reason we're here today is because Perón is in the guest house, and I can't think of a way to get him out."

"It is the Frade mansion," Welner repeated. "If you sold it, people would talk."

"Not that I give a damn, but what would they say? 'Gee, it took him a long time to figure out he was pouring money into that museum of his for no good reason, and to decide to get rid of it'?"

"It would suggest you are having financial difficulty . . . ," Welner said.

"Yes, it would, Cletus," Claudia agreed. "Try to think of it as an advertising expense."

". . . and had to move into the guest house. That would almost certainly cause you business problems, Cletus."

"He's right, Cletus," Claudia said.

And you really don't want Juan Domingo Perón out of there, either."

"The hell I don't."

"And I was right on the verge of saying, 'You're learning, Cletus' when I heard you talking so nicely to Tío Juan on the phone just now."

"What did Juan Domingo want?" Claudia asked.

"He wants Clete to go to the German reception tonight," Welner said. "Are you going?"

"I don't think I'm up to that," Claudia said.

"And he's coming here for lunch," Welner said.

"Are you going, Cletus?" Claudia asked.

He nodded.

Their eyes met for a moment, and she looked as if she was going to say something but decided against it.

"There is something of yours I would be willing to buy," Claudia said. It was an obvious change of subject.

"Really?"

"Your radio station. Radio Belgrano."

"Why would you want to buy that?"

"Because I think there is a lot of money to be made in broadcasting."

"If that's so, why should I sell it? I mean, I have all these advertising expenses, you know."

"I'm serious about this, Cletus," she said. "If you want to sell it, I'd like to buy it."

"If you want it, it's yours," he said.

"I don't want it that way," she said. "Don't toss me a bone, Cletus!"

"Excuse me?"

"Have it appraised. Find out what it's worth, then make an offer," she said. "Your father and I did a lot of business together, but that's what it was, business. I don't want you doing me any favors."

"Claudia . . ." Welner came to his defense. "There's no reason to take offense."

"OK, Claudia," Clete said. "To hell with you. It's not for sale. I've never even seen it. Or, for that matter, heard it."

"God," she said. "He's as hard to deal with as his father."

"I accept that as a compliment," Clete said.

"Poor Dorotéa's going to have her hands full with you!"

Clete had an immediate mental recall of Dorotéa's hand, full, which had nothing to do with what Claudia was saying. This caused him to smile.

"You think it's funny, do you?" Claudia snapped. "You're just going to have to get along with people."

Antonio came into the sitting. "Señora," he said. "Your things have been packaged and put in your car."

"Thank you, Antonio," she said.

"Perhaps Señora would care to take a look around, to make sure I found everything."

"That won't be necessary, Antonio. Thank you."

"Have another look yourself, Antonio," Clete ordered. "If you have any question about anything, decide in favor of Señora Carzino-Cormano."

"Sí, Señor."

"Damn you, Cletus, now I'll have to go with him," Claudia said.

Clete waited until she had followed Antonio out of the room, then went to the Champagne cooler and refilled his glass. He held the bottle up to Father Welner.

"Of course," Welner said.

"What the hell did I say that made her so mad?"

"She has a lot of memories of this house," Welner said. "And of your father. Taking her things is painful for her. And then you were condescending to her . . . just as your father often was."

"I didn't mean to be."

Welner shrugged.

The door began to open.

"That didn't take long," Clete said softly.

"Señora de Mallín and I arrived at exactly the same moment!" el Coronel Juan Domingo Perón announced.

He walked to Welner and shook his hand, and then walked to Cletus. "My boy!" he said, clasping Clete's shoulder.

"Tío Juan," Clete said. "It's always a pleasure to see you."

Like watching a dog get run over.

Pamela Holworth-Talley de Mallín, grandmother-to-be, walked to Clete and offered her cheek.

Good-looking woman, Clete thought, remembering what his uncle Jim had once told him: "When you really get serious about some female, Clete, take a good look at her mother. That's what your beloved will look like in twenty, thirty years."

Looking at Pamela, the prospect is not at all frightening.

"Is this the day you start calling me 'Mother Mallín'?" Pamela asked.

"I don't think so," Clete said firmly. "But I must admit the prospect of watching my father-in-law squirm when I call him 'Father Mallín' has a certain appeal."

"You're terrible, Cletus," Pamela said, laughing.

"Would you like a little Champagne?" Clete asked.

"It's early, and I shouldn't, but of course I will."

Clete went to the cooler and poured her a glass of Champagne. "Ol' Whatsername's upstairs having a shower," he said as he handed it to her.

"I know," Pamela replied, giggling. "She called me, and asked me to go to Dr. Sarrario's consulting with her. She said you didn't want to go."

"If there was a subtle tone of accusation in that, the question never came up. I wasn't invited."

"But you didn't want to go, did you?" Pamela challenged. "Wives have a way of knowing what their husbands want and do not want."

"Listen to Mother, darling," Dorotéa said, coming into the room.

When Clete saw her, his heart jumped.

Goddamn it, she's beautiful!

She came to him and kissed him on the cheek. He could smell her shampoo.

Clete tugged the bell cord again, and the housekeeper appeared.

"We need a little more Champagne in here, please," Clete ordered. "And we can have lunch as soon as Antonio and Señora Carzino-Cormano finish their tour of the museum."

Luncheon was served in the upstairs dining, whose bay windows overlooked the formal gardens in the rear of the mansion, and whose table could comfortably accommodate fourteen people. As master and mistress of the household, Clete and Dorotéa were seated at the head and foot of the table. El Coronel Juan Domingo Perón sat next to Clete, with Señora de Mallín across from him, and Father Welner was next to Dorotéa, with Señora Carzino-Cormano across from him.

At least four feet of highly polished wood separated the lace place mats of the diners. Antonio circled the table, filling wine and Champagne glasses as the housekeeper and one of the maids offered a choice of beef or Roquefort-and-ham empanadas as the appetizer.

I wonder, the master of the house thought, *what the boys are having for an appetizer on the wooden-plank tables of the Fighter One officers' mess on the 'Canal?*

Maybe, if the mess sergeant is in a good mood, Spam chunks on toothpicks. Most likely, the Spam will be the entrée.

And I wonder what Claudia thinks, seeing Dorotéa sitting there, Mistress of the Mansion, on the day she's removing the last of her personal possessions from a house that by all rights should be hers?

Father Welner rose to his feet and invoked, in the name of the Father, the Son, and the Holy Spirit, the blessings of the Deity upon those about to partake of His bounty. After he sat down, both he and Clete reached for their glasses of Merlot. El Coronel Juan Domingo Perón rose to his feet.

Now what? Clete wondered as he took his hand away from the glass.

"If I may," Perón began. "As I looked around this table, I could not help but think that our beloved Jorge may well be looking down on us from Heaven at this moment. And if he is, I like to think he's smiling." He paused to let that sink in, then went on. "The time came to Jorge to leave this world for a better one . . ."

With a load of buckshot in his head, Clete thought.

". . . as it will come to all of us," Perón went on.

Clete saw that Claudia was looking at Perón incredulously.

"And all of us, myself included, thought his going on to a better place was the end," Perón said.

Clete glanced down the long table at Dorotéa. She was looking at him with a look he recognized as a wifely imperative signal: NO!!!!!

She thought I was going to say something I shouldn't.
I wasn't.
Or was I? My mouth sometimes shifts into high gear all on its own.

He flashed Dorotéa a small, reassuring smile.

"But it was not the end, I submit, my dear friends, my dear family," Perón continued solemnly.

Family? What the hell do you mean, family? That "Tío

Juan" crap again? What the hell is that all really about, anyway? Are you playing with a full deck, "Tío Juan"?

"It was instead a change of the guard," Perón intoned. "A beginning. God sent our beloved Jorge's beloved son Cletus back to the land of his birth . . ."

If that's so, then God is an OSS Tex-Mex full-bull Marine colonel named Alejandro Federico Graham.

". . . so that Cletus could step, so to speak, into his father's boots and assume the responsibility for the land and the people of the land, as Jorge had assumed it from his father.

"And, at the risk of indelicacy, my dear Dorotéa, God in his wisdom and generosity has seen fit to put a new life in your womb . . ."

That wasn't God, Tío Juan, it was a Good Ol' Midland, Texas Boy named Clete who done that.

". . . to carry on the family, someone who, when the time comes, will take the burden of responsibility from your and Cletus's shoulders and take it on his own."

Does he believe this shit? He sounds like a West Texas Baptist preacher at the end of a four-day Come-to-Jesus-in-a-Tent revival.

Clete looked at Claudia. Her face was expressionless. He looked at Pamela. She looked as if she was about to cry. He looked at Dorotéa. Tears were running down both cheeks, and Clete saw her chest jump as she sobbed.

"So I think . . ." Perón went on, raising his eyes to the fourteen-foot ceiling of the upstairs dining, ". . . I *believe* with all my heart . . . that our beloved Jorge is looking down at this table and smiling. The guard has changed. What is past is past. This is the beginning!" He raised his glass. "Salud, mi amigo!" Perón said.

I'll be damned, Clete thought as he realized he was on his feet with his glass raised toward the fourteen-foot ceiling.

And I'll be twice damned—so is Father Welner.

Perón sat down.

Dorotéa came running down the side of the table, knelt beside Perón, threw her arms around him, and kissed his cheek.

I guess that makes me a cynical prick.

He glanced around the table again. Pamela de Mallín was dabbing at her eyes with a napkin. Claudia Carzino-Cormano, her face expressionless, met his eyes. And a moment later, so did the intelligent blue eyes of Father Kurt Welner.

What is that? Two cynical pricks and a cynical lady?

Dororéa got to her feet and walked back to the foot of the table.

Claudia waited until Dororéa was sitting down. "While Dororéa and Pamela are at the doctor's, Juan Domingo," she said. "I'm going to take Cletus to Radio Belgrano."

Is that what they call changing the subject, Claudia?

"Oh, really?"

To judge by the look on his face and the tone of his voice, that's what Tío Juan thinks it is.

"I know how busy you are these days, but I thought you might like to come with us."

"As a matter fact, Claudia . . ."

Thank you very much, but no thanks?

". . . I've never seen it, and I'd like to. And I need a few minutes alone with Cletus. We could have our little chat as we drove over."

Claudia couldn't quite manage to conceal her surprise. "I'm trying to get Cletus to sell it me," she said.

"Is that so?"

[THREE]
Radio Belgrano
1606 Arribeños
Belgrano, Buenos Aires
1535 11 May 1943

They had driven from the museum in Palermo to Radio Belgrano in three cars. Claudia's 1940 Buick Roadmaster, carrying her and Father Welner, led the way. Clete followed in the Horch, with Juan Domingo Perón beside him and Enrico in the backseat. Perón's official Ministry of War car, a 1941 Chevrolet driven by a sergeant, brought up the rear.

The owner of Radio Belgrano was not very impressed with his property the first time he saw it, although he was enormously relieved to get there. From the moment Perón had slid onto the seat beside Clete, he'd delivered a nonstop sales pitch about how happy he was that Clete was going to hear for himself how deeply Generalmajor Manfred von Deitzberg—speaking, of course, for the entire German officer corps—regretted losing control of an SS officer in Wehrmacht uniform, which had resulted in the death of Clete's beloved father and his own beloved friend.

And how important it was that Clete—for his own personal peace, for the good of Argentina, indeed for the good of the new generation of the Frade family—be willing to put the tragic incident behind him.

Clete had managed to keep his mouth shut, but it had not been easy.

Radio Belgrano occupied a small, old, and run-down two-story masonry house. The house's trim needed a paint job, and a not-very-impressive antenna rose from the faded tile roof. To Clete it looked as if it had been welded together of thin iron rods on the spot—far less substantial than the windmill water pumps that dotted the fields of Estancia San Pedro y San Pablo. What had been the lawn of the house was now a muddy gravel parking lot. Two somewhat battered automobiles, a Ford and a Citroen, were parked facing the house, leaving room for only two more.

Claudia's driver pulled into one of the slots, and Clete drove in beside it. That left no room for the Army Chevrolet, and the sergeant simply stopped in the street, holding up traffic, until Perón ordered him to circle the block and find a place to park.

Claudia was by then at the door of the building, which was at the same moment pulled open by a mustachioed man in a business suit whose thinning hair was plastered against his skull. He kissed Claudia's cheek, then smiled broadly at Clete as he and Perón walked up to the door.

"How nice to see you again, Señor Frade," he said, enthusiastically pumping Clete's hand, and confusing Clete—"*see me again"?*—until Clete realized that the man had probably been one of the long line of managers and other executives of El Coronel, Incorporated, who had shown up at Estancia San Pedro y San Pablo for his father's memorial service.

"It's good to see you, too, Señor," Clete said. "Do you know Coronel Perón?"

"Only by reputation," the man said, and began to pump Perón's hand. "It is a great privilege to have the Special Assistant to the Minister of War visit our little radio station, mi Coronel."

Perón smiled at him.

The man bowed them into the building, where there was a variation of the King Comes Home ceremony they had gone through when Clete and Dorotéa had arrived at the museum.

The employees of Radio Belgrano were lined up in the inside foyer, waiting to be introduced to El Patrón. Among these was Eva Duarte, the blonde from the Alvear Palace Hotel.

They worked their way down the line, with Claudia in the lead, shaking everyone's hand.

"And this, Señor Frade," the plump little man said, "is Señorita Evita Duarte, one of our dramatic artists."

"I have the privilege of Don Frade's acquaintance," the blonde said. "How nice to see you again, Señor."

"You know each other?" Perón asked, obviously surprised.

"We met at a social event at the Alvear. . . . It was the Alvear, wasn't it, Don Frade?"

"I think so, yes," Clete said.

"I am Juan Domingo Perón," Perón said, taking her hand.

"Oh, I know who you are, mi Coronel," the blonde gushed. "Everyone in Argentina knows who you are. I consider it a great privilege to make your acquaintance."

"The privilege is mine, my dear young woman," Perón said, beaming at her.

She's a little old for you, isn't she, Tío Juan? I'll bet she's the far side of twenty.

The procession moved into the manager's office—it had obviously previously been the house's dining—where a brass sign on his desk identified him as Manuel de la Paz, General Manager.

Clete was surprised that the blonde was one of the privileged few permitted to share a tiny cup of coffee with the visiting brass, and about as surprised to see that Tío Juan was charming the hell out of her.

That was followed by a tour of the station's facilities: Administrative offices were on the first floor, and three studios, a record library, and a control room—once obviously bedrooms—were on the second. These were covered with squares of sound-deadening material, some of which were in the process of falling off the wall.

And then the procession moved downstairs and out into the parking lot.

If Claudia wants to buy this, she can have it.

Hands were shaken, Manuel de la Paz announced that he hoped to see more of Don Frade, and he informed Perón that his visit had been a great honor.

Perón and the blonde beamed at each other.

"Where are you headed, Claudia?" Clete asked.

"To Estancia Santo Catalina," she said.

"I can't convince you to come to the Ambassador's reception for Generalmajor von Deitzberg?" Perón asked her.

"I really have to go to the estancia," Claudia said firmly.

Perón looked at his watch. "And I really must return to my duties," he said. "I'll come by Coronel Díaz for you and Dorotéa about seven, Cletus?"

"I'll see you there, Tío Juan," Clete said.

Perón set off to find his car.

"Come by the museum a minute," Clete said to Claudia when Perón was out of earshot.

"All right," she said.

"Curiosity is a female prerogative," Claudia said, helping herself to a snifter of cognac in the downstairs sitting. "Was that 'social event' where you met the blonde in your apartment at the Alvear?"

Clete nodded. "Juan Domingo seemed fascinated with her," he replied.

"I noticed. I thought she was a little old for him." Claudia laughed.

"If you want to buy that place, come up with a price," Clete said.

"Don't do me any favors, Cletus."

"I've got too much on my plate as it is," Clete said. "I don't know anything about radio stations, and I don't have either the time or the inclination to learn. I have some Texas ranch-hand's ideas about improving production on the estancias."

"Such as?"

"There's a better use for more than four feet of good, thick topsoil than to raise grass for cows to chew."

"Such as?"

"Putting in corn, for example. If I feed them corn, I can get a beef to market months before I can by feeding it grass."

"You mean that, don't you?"

"Yeah, I mean it. My uncle Jim used to say, 'When you have a chance to make some money, take it. Next year, there'll damned sure be a drought.' "

Claudia chuckled. "Your father used to talk about feed-lots," she said. "He apparently saw them in the United States. Which may be why he never got around to doing any-thing about it."

"I'm one of the good gringos, Claudia."

"Your father would be pleased to know that you're taking an interest in the estancias."

"That—and flying airplanes—is about all I know, and I have some ideas about making money with airplanes, too, that I want to play with."

She met his eyes. "I'll get some estimates," she said. "Top peso and bottom peso, and we'll split it down the middle. Fair enough?"

"Fair enough."

"You behave yourself tonight with those Nazis."

"I will."

She drained her brandy, then walked to him and kissed him tenderly—rather than *pro forma*—on the cheek and walked out of the downstairs sitting.

[FOUR]
Wachtstein Bahnhof
Kreis Wachtstein, Pomerania
2105 11 May 1943

The train was an hour late, having been sidetracked three times by military trains headed for Russia, which of course had higher priority. One had been a troop train—two second-class coaches for the officers and a long line of third-class coaches for the enlisted men. The other two had been freight trains, loaded with military equipment and vehicles. Each of the three had two special flatcars, one immediately behind the locomotive, the other about halfway down the line of cars.

These held machine-gun positions, steel plates further protected by sandbags. Generalleutnant Graf von Wachtstein identified them as *Waffenwagen,* armed cars. They were unfortunately necessary because the army and the SS, despite valiant effort, had not been able to completely suppress partisan activity in Russia.

Their own train had one first-class car, no second-class, and a line of third-class cars. The first-class car was nearly empty, and its few passengers were either army or SS officers.

Though there was opportunity for talk in their compartment, Peter's father showed no inclination to do so, and Peter knew his father well enough not to press him. There would be ample opportunity for that once they reached Wachtstein and the Schloss.

They were the only passengers to leave the train at Wachtstein, and at first glance the station seemed deserted. But just as they were about to enter the small station building, a man in a leather overcoat stepped out of the shadows, showed them his Gestapo identity disk, and demanded their papers.

"When I see Reichsprotektor Himmler next week, I will report your zeal," the Graf said.

The Gestapo man handed the Graf his identity documents, looked him in the face, raised his hand in the Nazi salute, and then turned away without speaking.

The Graf motioned for Peter to precede him through the station. The street outside was empty and dark, with the only light coming faintly through the shuttered windows of the gasthaus a block away.

"How do we get from here to the Schloss?" Peter asked.

"If we're lucky, the battery in the Horch will not have run down," the Graf said. "It's in the stable behind the gasthaus."

"Why?"

"I didn't know what to do with it," the Graf said, "after you went to Argentina."

"I meant, why at the gasthaus?"

"The Schloss has been pressed into service as a hospital," the Graf said. "I didn't want the Horch being used by the officer in charge. And of course, I couldn't have it at Wolfsschanze."

They walked down the cobblestone street to the gasthaus and pushed open the door. Though it smelled of beer, just as Peter remembered it, it was now also somehow more drab, less happy, than before.

The proprietor, Herr Kurt Stollner, was leaning on the bar, a white apron tied around his ample middle. Stollner's father and grandfather had been the proprietors before him, but his son would not be. His son, ten years older than Peter, had died for the Fatherland in Poland.

Eight men and an old woman were sitting at three of the tables. Once they recognized the Graf, the men rose respectfully to their feet.

The Graf nodded to Herr Stollner, then went to the old lady and called her by name to tell her that he had Hansel with him. She smiled toothlessly at Peter. Then Peter followed his father around the room and they shook hands with all the men. Two of the older men called him "Hansel." The others called him Herr Baron.

Herr Stollner handed Peter and the Graf gray clay mugs of beer. The Graf raised his and called "Prosit!", then signaled for Stollner to give everyone a beer.

It was a ritual. As a small child, Peter remembered coming to the gasthaus with his grandfather. Everyone had stood up and waited for the Graf to shake their hands. Then the Graf was handed a beer, took a sip, and ordered beer all around. Afterward, the village elders had come, one at a time, for a private word.

Herr Stollner came close to the Graf.

"Do you think we will be able to start the Horch?" the Graf asked.

"I have charged the battery once a week, Herr Graf."

"I knew I could rely on you."

"It will take us a moment to get it for you," the proprietor said. "To move the hay."

Peter had a mental image of the car buried under bales of hay in the stable behind the gasthaus to keep it out of sight.

"I'm sorry to put you to so much trouble, Kurt."

"I am happy to be of service," the proprietor said. He made a motion with his hand to several of the men in the room, then led them through the kitchen and out to the stable.

Five minutes later, they filed back in. "I left the engine running, Herr Graf," the proprietor said.

The Graf, with Peter following, moved again to each of the men and shook their hands, and then they went outside.

The Horch was covered with dust from the hay it had been buried under, and the Graf read Peter's mind: "It will blow off long before we reach the Schloss." The Graf signaled for Peter to get behind the wheel, then climbed in beside him.

Peter got the car moving.

"We can talk now," the Graf said. "About the only place I am reasonably sure the Gestapo doesn't have a microphone is in this car."

"In the Schloss?"

"We will have to be discreet in the Schloss," the Graf said. "We're going to drive to Munich to see von Stauffenberg in hospital. That should give us the time we need."

"He is going to live?"

"Yes. But he was really badly hurt. At first, he was even blinded . . ."

"Damn," Peter said.

". . . but he has the sight of one eye, and the use of one hand and arm."

Peter didn't reply. His mind was full of images of Claus von Stauffenberg as a handsome, athletic young man, and of what he must look like now, as a scarred, horribly wounded, one-eyed cripple.

"What are you thinking, Hansel?" the Graf asked.

Peter didn't want to tell his father what he was thinking. "A friend of mine in Argentina has a car like this. Almost identical, I think."

"What friend is that?" the Graf asked. There was a tone of impatience, perhaps of annoyance, in his voice.

"My friend is an enemy officer," Peter said. "A major of the U.S. Marine Corps. He was once a fighter pilot, and now he is an agent of the American OSS."

"And?"

"On orders from Berlin, my friend's father was murdered while riding in his Horch."

"His father was?"

"Oberst Jorge Guillermo Frade, who was probably going to be president of Argentina. A fine man."

"And the son and you are friends?"

"Yes," Peter said. "We are friends."

"He's not just using you?"

"I suppose you could say we are using each other," Peter said. "You want the whole story?"

"Please."

Peter told his father the whole story of his relationship with Cletus, up to Operation Phoenix and a plan for a refuge in South America if the war was lost.

"Apparently, starting with the Führer," Peter concluded,

"there is less absolute confidence in the Final Victory than they would have us believe."

"Just before I left Wolfsschanze this morning, Hansel, there was a final message from General von Arnim in Tunisia."

"A final message?"

The Graf stilled him with a quick wave. "According to von Arnim, his troops have done all they could. But he is out of ammunition, has many casualties, the situation is hopeless, and to preserve the lives of his men, he has sent emissaries to the Americans. He believes there will be a cease-fire as of 0700 tomorrow."

"So we have lost Africa," Peter said.

The Graf waved his hand again. "Von Arnim concluded his message 'God Save Germany!' " He went on. "It fell to me to take the message to the Führer."

"Why you?"

"Probably because Generaloberst Jodl decided that if a head was to roll, mine was the most expendable. When something goes wrong, the Austrian corporal often banishes the messenger."

"And what happened?"

"Whatever he is, Hitler is no fool," the Graf said. "His face whitened, but he took the news quite calmly. He touched my shoulder. He knew it wasn't my fault, he said, and that I was one of a very few of his generals in whom he had complete trust. He then very courteously asked me to ask Generalfeldmarschall Keitel and Generaloberst Jodl if they could tear themselves from their duties to confer with him."

The Graf sighed, then went on: "When they went in, we could hear him screaming at them, despite the thick walls. His tantrum lasted ten minutes. He actually picked up chairs and smashed them against the floor. And then Keitel came out, ashen-faced, and ordered me to message Von Arnim that surrender was out of the question; that the officers who had recommended such action to him were to be shot; and that he was to fight to the last cartridge and the last man."

"Mein Gott!"

"When I went to the communications bunker, there was a

final message from Africa. They were destroying their cryptographic equipment and radios so it would not fall into the hands of the Americans."

The Graf paused, looked at his son, and almost visibly changed his mind about what he was going to say.

"And now tell me why you are here."

Peter then explained what happened on the beach, and how Boltitz and Cranz were trying to establish who was responsible.

"Do they suspect Ambassador von Lutzenberger?" the Graf asked when Peter had finished, and then answered his own question. "Of course they do. My God, what a mess!"

"The possibility exists, of course, that they will, in the absence of some proof to the contrary—"

"These people don't need proof, Hansel," the Graf interrupted. "There is no presumption of innocence."

"—conclude that the Argentines were responsible. They have a very efficient counterintelligence service, the Bureau of Internal Security, run by an Oberst Martín. The Argentine officer corps was furious when Oberst Frade was murdered."

"That sounds like wishful thinking," the Graf said.

Peter slowed the car. His headlights had picked up a striped pole barring the road, and a guard shack. Two soldiers wearing steel helmets, with rifles slung over their shoulders, came out of the guard shack.

"We'll talk no more tonight," the Graf said. "There's a lot for me to think about."

When Peter had stopped the Horch and the soldiers came to the car, Peter saw they were both Stabsgefreiters (lance corporals), and both well into their forties. And both were surprised and nervous to see a Generalleutnant of the General Staff appearing at their guard post.

Peter cranked down the window.

"Generalleutnant Graf von Wachtstein," he said rather arrogantly.

One of the Stabsgefreiters rushed to raise the barrier pole.

A few minutes later, the headlights illuminated the gate in

the wall of Schloss Wachtstein. A sign had been erected next to the gate:

Recuperation Hospital No. 15

[ONE]
Schloss Wachtstein
Kreis Wachtstein, Pomerania
2150 11 May 1943

An elderly Oberstleutnant Arzt was commandant of Recuperation Hospital No. 15. He appeared in the main hall of the castle as the Graf and Peter were climbing the stairs to the second floor, where the family apartments were located. "Heil Hitler!" he said, giving the Nazi salute. "Oberstleutnant Reiner at your service, Herr Generalleutnant Graf."

The Graf returned the salute casually.

"Your aide, Herr Generalleutnant Graf, telephoned to say you would be coming. I have been waiting for your call to send a car to the Bahnhof. These days, there is no telling when a train will arrive—"

"Hauptmann von und zu Happner was apparently unaware that we would be driving," the Graf interrupted him.

"Your staff was informed of your coming, Herr Generalleutnant Graf, and I believe they have prepared a dinner for you."

"This is my son, Major von Wachtstein," the Graf said.

Peter saluted the old man and shook his hand.

"If there is any way I may be of service while you're here, Herr Generalleutnant Graf . . ."

"That's very kind of you, but I can't think of a thing we'll need," the Graf said. "Good evening, Herr Oberstleutnant."

He started up the stairs, and Peter followed him.

A pedestal-mounted sign—ENTRANCE STRICTLY FORBID-DEN—stood in the corridor leading to the family apartments on the second floor. The door was unlocked, and there were lights in the corridor inside, and the smell of sauerkraut.

The Graf went directly to the kitchen. All that remained of the staff—an old woman and her even older husband, too old to do anything but care for the empty apartments—were sitting at a table drinking coffee. They stood up quickly, but not without visible effort, when they saw the Graf and Peter.

"Good evening," the Graf said.

"Herr Graf," they both said, and bobbed their heads.

The old lady said, "Hansel," and Peter went to her and let her embrace him.

The old man called him "Herr Major."

"It won't be much, Herr Graf," the old woman said, pointing to a large pot simmering on the stove. "If I had more time . . ."

"It smells marvelous," the Graf said. "We have missed your cooking, Frau Brüner, haven't we, Hansel?"

"Absolutely," Peter said. It was true. The smell of the pork and sauerkraut was actually making him salivate.

Frau Brüner smiled.

"When will it be ready?" the Graf asked.

"Whenever Herr Graf is ready."

"I'm ready now," the Graf said. "Is there any beer?"

"Of course, Herr Graf."

Peter followed his father into the dining room. Two places had been set at one end of the large table. Herr Brüner came in with gray pottery mugs of beer as soon as they sat down.

The Graf raised his mug. "To being home," he said.

Peter touched his mug to his father's and took a deep swallow.

The beer, brewed locally, was good—the brewery, like much of the farmland, was the property of the family.

A little sharper, Peter thought, *than the beer in Argentina.*

That triggered a memory of Alicia. He wondered how she would look sitting at this table; what she would think of the Schloss, of the estate. For Pomerania, the von Wachtstein estate was very large. But compared to Estancia Santo Catalina, it was tiny.

"What's in your mind, Hansel?" the Graf asked. "You seem far away."

"I was thinking . . . a friend in Argentina has an eighty-odd-thousand-hectare estate."

"I was thinking of your mother," the Graf said. "And your brothers."

Peter didn't reply. *Is he implying that I should have been thinking of them too?*

"Eighty *thousand* hectares?" the Graf asked incredulously, and went on before Peter could reply. "Your American friend, you mean?"

"No," Peter said. "His is even larger, and he has three or four of them. I was thinking of the estancia of a young lady I know."

"How well?"

"Sir?"

"How well do you know the young lady?"

"Very well, Poppa. I want to marry her."

The Graf raised an eyebrow in surprise but said nothing.

Frau Brüner came in with a large china tureen and ladled onto their plates thick pea soup with chunks of ham floating in it.

"My favorite, Frau Brüner," the Graf said. He put a spoon to his plate, tasted the soup, and nodded his approval.

Frau Brüner beamed.

"Eat your soup, Hansel," the Graf ordered.

Frau Brüner waited for Peter's reaction, then left the room.

"Have you actually proposed marriage to this young woman?" the Graf asked.

"Not formally. But it is understood between us."

"Was that the honorable thing to do?"

"This is the girl for me, Poppa."

"That's not what I asked. Does she understand your prospects? Have you considered that?"

"She knows everything," Peter said.

"You told her?"

His tone made it very clear the Graf was surprised and disappointed.

"It's like . . . I don't quite know how to explain this, Poppa . . . it's like one enormous family down there. Alicia's mother—"

"Alicia? That's a very pretty name."

"Alicia's mother, Señora Carzino-Cormano—"

"The family is Italian?" The Graf's tone suggested he didn't like that either.

"Not the way you suggest. They're like Americans down there. They immigrated from all over Europe, they intermarried. They don't think of themselves as Germans, or Italians, or English, or whatever, but as Argentinians."

"But they speak Spanish?"

"Yes, but they're not like the Spaniards. They're Argentine."

"Interesting. What about her mother?"

"Señora Carzino-Cormano had a very close relationship with Oberst Frade. . . ."

"Indeed? With the approval of their respective mates? That sounds Italian."

"Both mates, Poppa, were dead."

"But they didn't marry?"

"They had their reasons, one of which has to do with Argentine inheritance laws."

"She was, in other words, his mistress?"

"Are you determined to disapprove of these people, Poppa?"

"I would like to know about the family of a girl my son wishes to marry."

"There are two Carzino-Cormano daughters. One of them had an understanding with Hauptmann Duarte, who was killed at Stalingrad. That's how I came to meet Alicia."

"I see."

"When I went to Oberst Frade for help, I presume he confided in Señora Carzino-Cormano."

"Everything?"

"I suppose everything. They were like husband and wife."

"Except they weren't married."

"It would have been impossible for Oberst Frade to help me—help us—Poppa, without her knowing. They're helping me because they know that I could not honorably permit Cletus Frade to be murdered."

"The more people who know a secret, Hansel, the less chance there is to keep it a secret."

"I trust these people with my life, Poppa."

"You don't have much choice, do you?"

Peter met his father's eyes for a long moment. "You would like Alicia, Poppa. You would like all of them."

"If you say so," the Graf said. "What was—what is—the reaction of your Alicia to what you're doing?"

"She's frightened."

"She should be."

"She wants me to go to Brazil and turn myself in as a prisoner of war."

"That may be the wise thing to do. That's possible?"

"And what would happen to you?"

"What will probably happen to me anyway."

"Alicia understands why I can't go to Brazil," Peter said.

"My feeling, Hansel, presuming you find yourself back in Argentina, is to tell you to go to Brazil. That way, you will survive. The von Wachtstein family would survive. And so would our money. After the war, you could deal with the problems of our people here."

"I can't do that, Poppa."

"If things go wrong, unless you go to Brazil, it will be the end of the von Wachtsteins. It is a question of obligation, Hansel."

"I can't do that, Poppa."

"Our assets would be safe with your friends?"

"Of course."

"And if neither of us is around when this is over, then what?"

"Alicia knows how I feel about the estate, and our people. And so does Cletus. They would—"

"It would be better if you went to Brazil," the Graf interrupted.

"If I went to Brazil, you would go to Sachsenhausen or

Dachau," Peter said. "How could you help deal with the problem of our Führer from a concentration camp?"

The Graf met his eyes for a moment. "That, of course, is a consideration," he said, finally.

Frau Brüner came into the dining room with another china tureen, this one full of pork and sauerkraut.

"We will talk more on the way to Munich," the Graf announced. "This is the time for us to think and pray over our possible courses of action."

"I am not going to Brazil, Poppa," Peter said.

The Graf looked at his son, and after a moment nodded. "There are a number of problems here that I will have to deal with tomorrow," he said. "And there will be time to think."

After spending most of the next day dealing with the problems of the estate, the Graf, in the late afternoon, announced that he was "going to visit with the men in the hospital."

"You don't have to join me, Hansel," the Graf said. "You weren't responsible for sending them to war."

"Neither were you, Poppa," Peter protested. "You were simply doing your duty."

"The whole point of this, Hansel, is that I forgot my duty is to God first, and then to Germany. Like the others, I put my duty to the state—to Hitler—first, ignoring that it contradicted the laws of God and was bad for Germany." He met Peter's eyes. "The men in here, Peter, did their duty to Germany as they saw it. I didn't. I can't tell these men I'm sorry, obviously, but perhaps if I visit them, they will at least think that a German officer appreciates what they have done and that they are not forgotten."

"I'll go with you, Poppa."

"Where is your Knight's Cross?"

"In my luggage."

"Wear it, please."

Peter nodded.

The wards were as depressing as Peter thought they would be.

The three, enormous, high-ceilinged rooms on the lower floor of the Schloss had at other times been party rooms. Not something out of a Franz Lehar operetta, with elegantly uniformed Hussars and elegantly gowned and bejeweled women waltzing to *The Blue Danube,* but parties for the people in the village.

There they had celebrated "the-harvest-is-in," the birthdays of his father and mother, the weddings of villagers, birthday parties for octogenarians, and sometimes, in the case of village elders who had been close to the von Wachtsteins, there had been a little bite to eat and a glass of beer after their funerals.

The people of the village had come to the Schloss in their Sunday best to dance to a five-piece band—piano, accordion, tuba, trumpet, and drum—gorge themselves on food laid out on ancient plank tables, and drink beer from a row of beer kegs on another table.

Somebody always got drunk and caused trouble. Fathers went looking for their nubile daughters who'd sought privacy with their young men in dark and distant parts of the Schloss. There was usually at least one fistfight. And always there was a good deal of singing.

The three stone-floored rooms branching off the entrance lobby were now lined with white metal hospital beds, one row against each wall, another row in the middle. Each bed was separated from its neighbor by a wall locker and a small table.

Peter quickly saw that most of the men in the long lines of beds had been injured beyond any hope of recuperation. They had lost limbs, or their sight, or been badly burned, sometimes in a horrible combination of mutilations.

They should call this place War Cripples Warehouse No. 15, Peter thought, not Recuperation Hospital No. 15.

The Graf stopped at each and every bed and said a variation of the same words to each man: "I hope you're feeling better." . . . "Are they treating you all right?" . . . "Is there anything you need?"

Peter walked two steps behind his father and—with an effort—smiled and gave to each what he hoped was a crisp nod.

Peter thought: *Some of them wouldn't know if their visitor was the Führer himself.*

But some actually tried to come to attention in their beds, as a soldier is supposed to do when spoken to by an officer.

The tour went on and on, but finally it was over and they went back up the stairs to the family apartments. Peter went directly to the liquor cabinet and poured himself a stiff drink of cognac.

"I'll have one of those, too, I think, please," the Graf said.

Peter poured a drink for his father, and then another for himself. They touched glasses without comment.

"Oberstleutnant Reiner and some members of his staff will be dining with us," the Graf announced.

Peter nodded.

What the hell is that all about? Because he feels it's expected of him? Or because he doesn't want to be alone with me again at dinner, as we were last night, with the ghosts of the family looking over our shoulders?

Dinner was very good, roast wild boar with roasted potatoes and an assortment of preserved vegetables, everything from the estate. Peter wondered what the patients of Recuperation Hospital No. 15 were having, then wondered who was asking. Flight Corporal Peter Wachtstein (for he had not used the aristocratic 'von' until he was commissioned)? It had been Pilot Cadet Wachtstein and Flight Corporal Wachtstein and even Flight Sergeant Wachtstein, winner of the Iron Cross First Class. As far as he knew, he had been the first von Wachtstein ever to serve in the ranks (much to his father's embarrassment).

Or was it Major von Wachtstein asking? He had learned as an enlisted man that a good way to judge an officer was by how deeply he was concerned with the men in the ranks, and had tried to remember that, and practice it, when he had become an officer.

Or was it Baron Hans-Peter von Wachtstein, the Graf-to-be?

Their guests at dinner were four doctors in addition to Oberstleutnant Reiner, as well as the two senior nurses and two administrative officers, all of whom seemed very impressed with the privilege of dining with the Herr Generalleutnant Graf von Wachtstein and the heir apparent.

The Graf made polite small talk, and took nothing to drink but a sip of wine. A glare from him when Peter reached yet again for a wine bottle was enough to make it Peter's last glass of wine.

That night, Peter had a little trouble getting to sleep. His mind was full of Alicia, and memories of his mother and brother, and the uncomfortable feeling that this might be the last night that anyone named von Wachtstein would ever sleep in Schloss Wachtstein.

They left early the next morning. Frau Brüner packed a large wicker basket with ham and cheese sandwiches, cold chicken, and a bottle of wine and two of beer. They drove as far as Frankfurt an der Oder the first day. There were virtually no private automobiles on the highway, and they passed through Feldgendarmerie checkpoints every twenty-five kilometers or so.

They spent the night with an old friend of his father's, Generalleutnant Kurt von und zu Bratsteiner, who was in the process of reconstituting an infantry division that had suffered heavy losses in the East. They had dinner in the officer's mess, and Peter noticed that his father and his old friend carefully avoided talking about what was happening in Russia, what had happened to von Arnim in Tunisia, or what was likely going to happen in the future.

In the morning, very early, they set out again, the gas tank of the Horch full, and with four gasoline cans in the trunk.

To Peter's surprise, his father had very little to say between Wachtstein and Frankfurt an der Oder.

And about all he said between Frankfurt an der Oder and Munich was that General von und zu Bratsteiner had learned unofficially that the Wehrmacht had not yet contained the rebellion of the Jews in the Warsaw ghetto. "Putting the rebellion down will apparently take more troops than was originally anticipated," the Graf said without emphasis. "It is apparently also going to be necessary to bring in tanks and more artillery. The issue is not in doubt, of course. It's just going to be more expensive than anyone would have believed."

"What's going to happen to the Jews when it is over?"

"Well, inasmuch as they are not entitled to treatment as prisoners of war, I would suppose that Reichsprotektor Himmler will order the survivors transported to the concentration camps in the area. There are six, if memory serves: Auschwitz, Birkenau, Belzec, Chemlno, Maidanek, and Sobibor."

"And what will happen to them there?"

"They will be exterminated," the Graf said. "Men, women, and children."

"My God!"

"On arrival at the camps," the Graf went on unemotionally, "a medical doctor—sometimes an SS medical officer, but as often as not an Army doctor—will make a cursory examination to determine which prisoners are fit for labor. They are segregated from the others. Since there is no point in feeding anyone who cannot contribute his or her labor to the State, the unfit prisoners and the children are immediately exterminated."

"The children too?" Peter asked softly.

The Graf ignored him and went on: "At one time—and today in the East—extermination was accomplished by having the prisoners dig a mass grave. Then they were—are—forced to kneel at its edge. When they received a pistol shot to the back of the head, their bodies fell into the grave.

"But German science has been applied to the problem. German efficiency. In the Dachau and Auschwitz camps, extermination has been modernized. Those to be exterminated are stripped of their clothing and herded into rooms marked 'Shower Baths.' The doors are then locked and a poison gas—it's called Zyklon-B—is introduced by way of the showerheads. As many as a hundred and fifty people can be exterminated in fifteen minutes.

"The gas is then evacuated, and other prisoners are sent in to remove gold teeth fillings from the mouths of the corpses, and to shear the women's hair. This is used primarily to stuff mattresses, but sometimes to make wigs."

"Oh, my God!" Peter said.

"And then the corpses are taken to furnaces specially designed for the purpose and incinerated."

"Poppa, you're sure of this?"

"Of course I'm sure. And it cannot be argued that the blood is only on the hands of the Nazis, Hansel. It is on the hands of the army. We put the Austrian Corporal in power."

"But how could you have known?"

"We didn't want to know, Hansel. That's our guilt." He looked at his son. "Whenever I waver in what I now know is my duty, Hansel, I think of children being led to the slaughter."

[TWO]
Recuperation Hospital No. 3
Munich, Germany
1015 16 May 1943

Starting at breakfast in the Hotel Vier Jahrseitzen, where they had spent the night, and continuing in the Horch as they drove to the Munich suburb of Grünwald, Generalleutnant Karl Friedrich Graf von Wachtstein delivered to Major Freiherr Hans-Peter von Wachtstein a detailed briefing concerning what he could expect to find at Recuperation Hospital No. 3.

The briefing contained as many details as an operations order for a regimental assault on an enemy fortress, and was very much in character for Peter's father, a reflection of his many years as a planning and operations officer of the General Staff Corps. Minute details are the stock-in-trade of a planning and operations officer; nothing that can possibly be included in an operations order is ever omitted.

Peter had a hard time restraining a smile.

The Graf began with a description of the terrain, informing Peter—quite unnecessarily; he had been to Grünwald before—that Grünwald was an upper-class suburb of Munich, much as Zehlendorf was of Berlin. "It contains a large number of substantial villas," the Graf pronounced, "most of them built before the First World War by successful businessmen and merchants of Munich, and a number built in the late 1930s for actors, writers, producers, and the like—people connected with the motion picture studios, which were built at the same time."

Peter knew that, too. There was a small hotel on Oberhachingerstrasse in Grünwald, called "The Owl," where young women connected with the movie business could be found. Many of them were as fascinated with Luftwaffe fighter pilots as were the girls in the bars of the Hotels Adlon and am Zoo in Berlin, and as willing to hop into their beds.

Peter had not infrequently arranged to be "forced to land for necessary repairs" at Munich late enough in the day that the "repairs" to his aircraft would require a night in Munich.

"When recuperation hospitals became necessary to care for officers whose condition did not require all the facilities of a general hospital," the Graf went on, "private homes with adequate space were requisitioned—those that were not needed to house other military facilities, and were located where the patients would not be visible to the public. . . ."

Nobody wants to look at mutilated cripples, right? There's nothing very glamorous about those kinds of heroes, right?

". . . Schloss Wachtstein and similar large houses on estates met those criteria, and so did the some of the larger villas of Grünwald."

There were at least three hundred "recuperating" patients at Schloss Wachtstein—all of them enlisted men, and most of them horribly mutilated and disfigured.

What does that mean? Is that another manifestation of "rank hath its privileges"? Crippled enlisted men are sent to spartan accommodations in an old castle in the country, and officers to requisitioned villas in Grünwald?

Or is it just that there are so many more torn-up enlisted men than officers?

"How many officers are in . . . where Claus is?" Peter asked.

"There are facilities for approximately one hundred," the Graf replied. "The hospital consists of three villas. Claus has been given a pleasant private room on the second floor of the largest of them. It was the home of a Munich businessman who accumulated a large fortune making candy for children."

"A private room? Because he's senior? Or because he's so badly shot up?"

"I don't know," the Graf replied, his tone making it clear he did not like either the question or the interruption. "Obviously, both factors were considered." He paused and went on, more gently. "You are going to have to be ready to face Claus's injuries, Hansel," he said. "And when I saw him last, he had lost a good deal of weight."

"I have seen wounded men before, Poppa."

"The last thing Claus wants is your pity," the Graf said, paused, and then went on: "There are, as I said, three villas, each on what I suppose is about a hectare of land. They were originally walled off from the street and each other—three-meter-high steel-mesh fences, concealed by shrubbery. A portion of the interior fencing has been removed, so now there is what amounts to a single compound."

"I understand," Peter said.

"The building where Claus is quartered holds officers who have been blinded, or who have lost a leg," the Graf went on, "probably because the stairways are wider and shallower than those in the other villas—thus more easily negotiable by someone on crutches, or learning to navigate with the aid of a cane."

"And the others?" Peter asked softly.

"The building next to his—it belongs to Max Stammt, the motion picture producer—houses officers who have lost both legs, or both arms, or who suffer from mental distress, and consequently require greater attention. And the third building was once owned by Peter Ohr."

Peter nodded his understanding. Peter Ohr, a well-known actor, was a Jew who had had the good sense—and/or the good luck—to abandon the movie studios of Grünwald for those of Hollywood while there was still time.

"That is utilized to care for officers considered unlikely to recover."

In other words, those waiting to die.

"Slow down a little, Hansel," the Graf said. "It's the second turn to the right after the Strassenbahn stop ahead."

Peter made the turn.

"On the right, in the second block," the Graf said.

As he approached the entrance to the compound, Peter could see little of the villas behind the fence but their roofs. At the entrance itself, there was a helmeted soldier with a rifle slung over his shoulder.

He turned off the cobblestone street and stopped.

The soldier approached the car, saw that Peter was a major, and saluted. Then he saw the Graf, and popped to rigid attention. Like the guards at Schloss Wachtstein, the soldier was in his forties and didn't look fit for active service.

Peter rolled the window down. "Generalleutnant Graf von Wachtstein," he said. That announcement had quickly gotten him past the guards at Schloss Wachtstein. It didn't work here.

"Heil Hitler!" the guard said, adding, "May I have your authorization, please, Herr Major?"

"What authorization? We are here to visit a patient."

"I regret, Herr Major, that you must have an authorization to visit the hospital."

"Summon your officer," Peter said. He looked at his father, who shrugged.

Three minutes later, the gate opened and a Wehrmacht doctor—a major in his late fifties—emerged. He gave the Nazi salute the moment he saw the Graf's collar tabs, then gave it again as he walked to the passenger side of the car. "Heil Hitler! How may I be of service to the Herr Generalleutnant?"

"We're here to see one of your patients, Oberstleutnant von Stauffenberg," the Graf said.

"I regret, Herr Generalleutnant, that we were unaware of your coming."

"Is there some sort of a problem?" the Graf asked.

"The hospital has been closed to visitors, Herr Generalleutnant."

"Certainly not to a general officer of the OKW," the Graf said impatiently.

"I'm sure an exception can be made in your case, Herr Generalleutnant, but I will have to ask you to come with me while I speak with the Munich Area Medical Commandant's office for permission."

"Let's get on with it, then," the Graf said.

The doctor signaled the soldier to open the gate, and then got onto the running board of the Horch.

Peter drove through the gate, which belonged to the middle of the three villas. The doctor signaled him to drive to the right, toward the villa where Claus had his room. The Major stepped off the running board when Peter stopped the car.

"If you will come with me, gentlemen," he said, then turned to the Graf. "I regret the inconvenience, Herr Generalleutnant."

The Graf didn't reply, but the moment they were inside the foyer of the villa, he looked at the Major. "Is Graf von Stauffenberg still in the room at the left corner of the second floor?" he asked, gesturing toward the wide staircase.

"Yes, Herr Generalleutnant, he is. Has the Herr Generalleutnant been here before?"

"You go up, Peter, while I deal with the Munich Area Medical Commandant. I'll see you in a moment."

The Major was visibly uncomfortable with that announcement, but in the German Army, as in any other, majors do not challenge general officers.

Peter went up the stairs and started down the wide corridor to the left. A doctor in a white smock and a nurse were in the corridor, about to enter one of the rooms. The doctor looked at him curiously but said nothing.

Peter continued down the corridor to the door that was almost certainly the one he wanted and knocked. When there was no answer, he knocked again, and harder. The door was obviously thick, and would mute the rap of his knuckles.

When again there was no answer, he tried the handle, then pushed the door open.

When Oberstleutnant Graf Claus von Stauffenberg heard the first faint knock, he was sitting in an upholstered chair, facing the door opening to his balcony. He ignored the knock. He was occupied, and preferred not to be disturbed. He was buttoning his shirt. This simple task was now possible, but very time-consuming.

His equipment for accomplishing that task was a three-pronged claw—the thumb and the first and second fingers of his left hand.

The stump where his right hand had been was for all practical purposes useless. Moreover, it was taking an unusually long time to heal. The suppuration had only started to diminish in the last few days, but the bandage still had to be changed at least twice a day. Thus, even trying to use it was painful.

It was difficult to force the button through the buttonhole with the claw, but he was getting much better at it, probably because he had been able to bring the three remaining fingers back to some measure of flexibility by faithfully exercising them.

The surgeons had done a splendid job with his now-empty left eye socket. One of the doctors believed an artificial eye might be fitted after another operation or two. But the eye—or, properly, the lost eye—didn't bother him at all except when he washed his face and the empty socket stared at him from the mirror. There was no pain, and he didn't have as much trouble with lost depth perception as he had feared. The ugliness could of course be concealed beneath his eye patch, which was in any case necessary to keep the still-raw socket from becoming infected.

There was a second, louder knock, and a moment later Claus von Stauffenberg heard the door quietly creak open. He did not turn to see who it was, primarily because he didn't care.

Nina, his wife, the Grafin von Stauffenberg, would not be able to visit until the following Friday. A personal appeal to the Munich Area Medical Commandant—he was a friend of a friend—had gotten her a waiver to the No Visitors Rule, but for only four hours every other Friday.

The silver lining to the black cloud of No Visitors was that he was no longer subjected to almost daily visits from adolescent girls of the Bund Deutscher Mädel, the League of German Girls, who felt it was their patriotic duty to come to Recuperation Hospital No. 15 to stare with pity at the mutilated heroes of the Third Reich.

That meant that whoever was entering the room was staff, which term included everyone from the surgeon-in-charge to a cleaning woman.

"Don't tell me," a somehow familiar voice said, "he said 'shut up' and you thought he said 'stand up.' "

He turned in curiosity.

"How are you, Claus?" Peter asked.

Von Stauffenberg held up his claw and stump and pointed at his eye patch. "How do I look, Hansel?"

"Goddamn you, don't call me that!"

"If you promise to try not to blaspheme, I'll try not to call you Hansel, Hansel."

Von Stauffenberg lifted himself out of his chair. After a moment's hesitation, they embraced. It seemed to embarrass them both. After a moment they stepped apart. "How did you get in?" von Stauffenberg asked.

"My father's downstairs," Peter said.

"You're supposed to be in Argentina," von Stauffenberg said.

"They brought me back," Peter said. "I think temporarily."

Von Stauffenberg pointed at the corners of the room, then at the light fixture.

My God, he's warning me they have surveillance microphones in here!

Peter nodded his understanding.

"You look well fed," von Stauffenberg said.

"The food is magnificent!"

"And the ladies?"

"Even tastier," Peter said.

"Anyone in particular?"

"As a matter of fact, yes."

"Tell me."

"How's Nina?"

"Tell me, Peter."

"Her name is Alicia," Peter said. "A really nice girl, Claus."

"That's a change."

"How's Nina?"

"Fine. Every other Friday, she is permitted to visit."

"And the kids?"

"Growing amazingly."

"You get to see them?"

"Before they instituted the No Visitors Rule, I did," von Stauffenberg said. "I hope to be given a leave." He held up the stump. "As soon as this thing stops leaking."

"What happened?"

"I was driving across the desert when an American P-51 strafed me. I woke up in a field hospital, and then I woke up again here in Munich, at the General Hospital." He paused, and added: "At first—my eyes were covered with bandages—I was afraid I was blind."

"You look like a pirate," Peter said. "One-Eyed Claus, the scourge of the Spanish Main. All you need is a hook for your right arm."

"I knew I could count on a comforting word from you, old friend."

"Well, at least you're not in an American POW camp. You—"

Von Stauffenberg pointed at the ceiling again.

Peter stopped himself, just in time, from saying, "You heard about von Arnim?" and instead finished, ". . . and you're obviously well on the road to recovery."

"I'm anxious to get back to active duty," von Stauffenberg said.

"I'm sure it won't be long."

"You were telling me about Argentina," von Stauffenberg said.

Somewhat uncomfortably (imagining a listener hoping to

hear disloyal or defeatist remarks), Peter delivered what was becoming a stock speech about the good food in Argentina, the incredible size of the farms, and the beauty of the women.

The door opened, and the Graf appeared.

"Heil Hitler!" von Stauffenberg said. "How good to see you again, Herr Generalleutnant."

"Heil Hitler," the Graf said. "It's good to see you looking so well, Claus."

Neither saluted. An eavesdropping microphone was possible, but it was unlikely that anyone was watching them.

"I've spoken both to the Munich Area Medical Commandant and to Generaloberst Jodl," the Graf announced. "The bad news is that our leave is over. My presence is required at Wolfsschanze immediately."

Peter looked at his father curiously, but said nothing.

"I will fly to Berlin at 1530," the Graf went on. "And you, Peter, have been designated to represent the OKW at the interment of Oberst Grüner. Korvettenkapitän Boltitz is on his way to Augsburg to arrange things with Hauptmann Grüner. You are to meet him there today."

"And the good news?" Peter asked.

"The medical commandant has given us his permission to take Claus to luncheon."

Curiosity got the best of von Stauffenberg. "Oberst Grüner?" he asked. "Who's he?"

"A very fine officer who made the supreme sacrifice for the Fatherland, Claus," Peter said. "In circumstances I'm not at liberty to divulge."

"The prospect of a good lunch is pleasing," von Stauffenberg said. "I have always loved the venison sauerbraten at the Vier Jahreseitzen."

In the car on the way back into Munich, Peter turned to von Stauffenberg in the backseat and asked: "Is there really a microphone in your room, Claus?"

"I don't know. I do know I have to be careful. And so should you, Peter."

"I have been trying to impress that on him, Claus," the Graf said, and then asked: "Claus, have you ever heard of Operation Phoenix?"

"No," von Stauffenberg said simply. "Should I have?"

"It's apparently a closely guarded state secret," the Graf said. "One I think you should know about."

"With all possible respect, Uncle Friedrich, should Peter hear this?"

"I heard it from Hansel, Claus. It is a state secret to which I have not been made privy. Tell him about it, Hansel, while we show our Claus the tourist sights of Munich."

As they made a sedate motor tour of Munich, Peter related all he knew about Operation Phoenix, including the deaths of Oberst Grüner and Standartenführer Goltz while they were attempting to smuggle the Operation Phoenix funds ashore, but he did not discuss his role in informing Cletus Frade of the landing.

"And that's not all, that's not even the worst, Claus," the Graf said. "Tell Claus about the ransoming operation, Hansel."

"I'm surprised, but not really surprised," von Stauffenberg said when Peter had finished. "There are some really criminal types around our Führer, especially in the SS. Their uniforms have not changed their basic character." Then he had another thought. "Do the Allies know about the ransoming operation?"

Peter looked at his father for permission to answer. After a moment, the Graf nodded. "The Americans do," Peter said. "I told them."

"Was that wise, Peter?" von Stauffenberg asked.

"They were about to find out themselves."

"So you decided to tell them? Why?"

"Peter has ... an arrangement ... with an agent of the American OSS," the Graf said. "It has proven useful. It may prove even more useful in the future."

"The risks of that are enormous," von Stauffenberg said, obviously thinking out loud. "That's treason on its face."

"And what are we doing, Claus?" the Graf asked.

"How much have you told Peter about that, Uncle Friedrich?" von Stauffenberg asked.

"As little as possible," the Graf said. "But it should be self-evident that our Little Hansel isn't so little anymore. I'm sure he's concluded that you're with us. I don't think he should know any more than that, and that may be too much. He is one of those suspected of being implicated in the deaths of Oberst Grüner and the SS man."

"Were you, Peter?" von Stauffenberg said. But before Peter could reply, he had a second thought: "I don't want to know the answer to that question."

"But you already know, Claus, don't you?" the Graf said. "What is that English cliché about, 'Oh, what a tangled web we weave'?"

" 'When first we practice to deceive,' " von Stauffenberg finished.

"I think that's everything," the Graf announced, and looked at his watch. "Take us to the Vier Jahrseitzen, please, Hansel. We can have a nice leisurely luncheon, and then you can take me to the airport, and Claus back to the hospital."

"What do I do with the car?" Peter asked.

"I'd say leave it with Claus, but I don't think they'd let him use it. But what about leaving it with your friend Hauptmann Grüner at Augsburg? Perhaps Nina —"

"Hauptmann Grüner?" von Stauffenberg asked.

"The son of Oberst Grüner," the Graf explained. "He and Hansel are comrades in arms."

Von Stauffenberg shook his head but said nothing.

"I was about to suggest, Claus, that if Hansel left the car with his friend, Nina could pick it up."

"If she drove, there would be questions," von Stauffenberg said.

"Would there be a place for it at your home?" the Graf asked. "I don't see how we could get it back to Wachtstein, and I am determined to keep it out of the hands of some Nazi swine."

"She could say that she was taking it to our place for you."

"I will prepare a note to that effect," the Graf interrupted.

"And once it was there, that would be the end of the problem," von Stauffenberg said. "Done, Uncle Friedrich."

The venison sauerbraten at the Vier Jahrseitzen was as delicious as von Stauffenberg had predicted.

As they were having their coffee, the Graf called for a sheet of paper, wrote a few words, and handed it to von Stauffenberg.

Der Hotel Vier Jahrseitzen

München

16th May 1943

To whom it may concern:

Frau Oberstleutnant Nina Grafin von Stauffenberg is, as a personal service to me, taking my Horch automobile to her home, where I will pick it up in the near future.

Any questions concerning this matter should be referred to the undersigned.

Karl Friedrich, Graf von Wachtstein

Generalleutnant,

Oberkommando der Wehrmacht

"That should do it," von Stauffenberg said after he'd read it. Then, with some difficulty, he unbuttoned a breast pocket on his tunic, inserted the note, and, with as much difficulty, buttoned the pocket again. He smiled with satisfaction. "Nina should be here this coming Friday," he said. "Consider it done, Uncle Friedrich."

"I'm grateful," the Graf said.

At the airport, a Heinkel bomber was parked in front of the terminal. The pilot—a Luftwaffe Hauptmann—and a crewman were waiting for them. The crewman took the Graf's luggage from the car and put it aboard the airplane.

The Graf gave his hand to his son. "Perhaps we will have another chance to be together before you return to Argentina, Hansel," the Graf said. "It was very good to see you."

"It was very good to see you, Poppa," Peter replied.

The Graf put out his hand to von Stauffenberg, who shook it as well as he could with his claw. "And it's always a pleasure to see you, Claus. I'm delighted that you are well on the way to recovery."

"The pleasure is, as always, mine, Herr Generalleutnant Graf," von Stauffenberg said.

The Graf nodded at both of them, then raised his hand in the Nazi salute. "Heil Hitler!" he barked.

Peter and von Stauffenberg returned the salute. "Heil Hitler!" they said, almost in unison.

The Graf turned and marched out to the airplane, where the pilot and the crewman gave the Graf the Nazi salute.

He climbed aboard, and the pilot and crewman climbed in after him. Peter could not see his father inside the airplane as it taxied to the runway. In his mind he saw his father rendering the Nazi salute he hated. He wondered if that would be his last memory of his father.

Claus von Stauffenberg was silent most of the way back to Grünwald, but as they turned off the main road, he said, "Peter, keep in mind that we are doing the right thing in the eyes of God, and that, in the final analysis, is all that matters."

Peter nodded but didn't reply.

Their farewell inside the Recuperation Hospital No. 15 compound was brief. "I'll give your regards to Nina," von Stauffenberg said. "And you give ours to . . . what did you say her name was, Alicia?"

"I will."

"And I thank you for a delightful lunch, Hansel, even if your father paid for it." He raised his left hand, gave the Nazi salute, and marched inside the villa built by the man who had made a lot of money making candy for children.

Peter, his eyes watering, wondered if his last memory of Claus von Stauffenberg would be of him giving the Nazi salute with his horribly maimed left hand.

He got the car moving, and wondered if he remembered where to find the road to Augsburg.

[THREE]
Pier 3
The Port of Montevideo, Uruguay
0830 16 May 1943

When the motor vessel MV *Colonia* tied up, without assistance, at the pier after an overnight voyage from Buenos Aires, three automobiles from the German Embassy were lined up on the pier. One of the three was Ambassador Joachim Schulker's Mercedes.

Two days before, the diplomatic courier from Buenos Aires had carried a letter from Ambassador von Lutzenberger announcing that Generalmajor Manfred von Deitzberg wished to make an unofficial personal visit to Uruguay, accompanied by Herr Erich Raschner of his staff. During his visit, the Herr Generalmajor would require suitable separate accommodations, preferably at the Casino de Carrasco, for himself and Herr Raschner, and the use of two automobiles, with trustworthy drivers. Since Herr Raschner had important matters to discuss with Herr Konrad Forster, the Commercial Attaché, every effort should be made to make Councilor

Forster available from the time Herr Raschner and General-major von Deitzberg arrived in Montevideo at 0830 16 May 1943.

Forster's Opel Kadet was the third car in line, behind the small, black embassy Mercedes assigned to Fraülein Gertrud Lerner. Ambassador Schulker had intended for one of the Embassy's junior officers to drive the Mercedes, but when he spoke to Fräulein Lerner, her normally blank face had mirrored her heartbreak at being denied what she considered her right to render service to the distinguished visitors, so she was at the wheel of the car.

His own car was driven by Manuel Ortiz, a Uruguayan who had worked for the German Embassy for nearly twenty years. Schulker had decided that if Manuel did not meet von Deitzberg's criteria for a reliable driver, he would call the embassy and have Ludwig Dolmer, the administrative officer, meet them at the Casino de Carrasco to chauffeur von Deitzberg around.

On the deck of the MV *Colonia,* Generalmajor Manfred von Deitzberg stood with his hands on the rail, watching the docking process. Erich Raschner stood beside him. Von Deitzberg had risen early, shaved, and dressed very carefully in a new double-breasted faintly striped dark-blue woolen suit. It was cut in the English manner—the tailor had tactfully said "Spanish," but von Deitzberg knew an English-cut suit when he saw one. It was one of three suits the tailor had run up for him in a remarkable nine days as a service to Ambassador Manfred Alois Graf von Lutzenberger.

The suits were remarkably inexpensive considering the quality of the cloth and the workmanship—about the equivalent of one hundred American dollars each. Not that cash was a problem. Before leaving Berlin, von Deitzberg had drawn for his personal expenses the equivalent of five thousand American dollars from the SS's confidential special fund. He had already ordered three more suits on a rush basis, and had strongly suggested to Raschner that he have some suits made for himself. Someone in his position really should not look like a policeman. With fine clothing available inexpensively and without the clothing coupons necessary in Berlin, there was no reason he had to.

Von Deitzberg had also bought three pairs of high-quality shoes at amazingly low prices. As he put on a pair of new black wing tips this morning, it occurred to him that custom-made shoes would almost certainly be available in Buenos Aires; he would look into that when he returned to the city.

"It would seem, Erich, that we are expected," von Deitzberg said, taking his hand from the rail to point vaguely at the cars lined up on the wharf.

Raschner grunted.

"And I did make the point, I hope, that I don't want . . . What's his name? Forster? The Gestapo man?"

"Hauptsturmführer Forster, Konrad," Raschner furnished.

". . . to get the idea that we are any more interested in Frau von Tresmarck than we are in anyone else."

"I understand," Raschner said. "It won't be a problem. I'll ask him for a roster of embassy personnel, and get that to you immediately. Her address and telephone number should be on that."

"My primary interest in Forster, really, is to see how much he knows about Operation Phoenix. And, even more important, if he knows anything, or even suspects anything—has even heard rumors—about our arrangement with von Tresmarck."

"I understand," Raschner repeated, just a trifle impatiently. He had heard all this the night before, standing on the stern of the *Colonia* after dinner.

"The trouble with the Gestapo, Erich, is that they are accustomed to looking into whatever they want to look into, and I don't want Forster looking into von Tresmarck's operation."

Raschner had heard this the night before too. "My feeling is that the man with the most to gain and the least to lose by 'cooperating' with the Argentines is Gradny-Sawz," he said. "And we already know that his loyalty is to whichever side he thinks will win."

"So you said," von Deitzberg said. "And you may well be right; you usually are."

"I'll find out what Forster knows," Raschner said.

"Ah, they are about to put the gangplank in place," von Deitzberg said. "Shall we go?"

[FOUR]
The San Martín Suite
The Casino de Carrasco
Montevideo, Uruguay
1015 16 May 1943

Manfred von Deitzberg was sitting on the balcony of the suite when he heard the somewhat tinny doorbell sound. The suite, on the top floor of the right wing of the five-story building, looked out over the Rambla and the beach.

The Rambla was a wide, attractive, four-lane avenue. A graceful promenade of colored blocks separated it from the beach. The beach was nice, not spectacular, but at least as wide and clean as a North Sea beach, and far superior to the touted—for reasons von Deitzberg could not understand—beaches of the French Riviera. The water was disappointing. Rather than blue, it looked muddy, even dirty. Von Deitzberg, curious, had asked the room-service waiter about it when he brought his coffee and sweet rolls.

The water out there, the waiter explained, was not, as von Deitzberg thought, the South Atlantic Ocean, but rather the River Plate. It was, in fact, still the river's mouth—an incredible 230 kilometers wide. The blue waters of the South Atlantic, the waiter told him, finally overwhelmed the silted waters of the river at Puente del Este, some 100-odd kilometers north of Montevideo.

When the bell sounded, von Deitzberg was in his shirt-sleeves, with his feet up on a small table. He was smoking a cigarette and had almost finished the really nice sweet rolls.

He went into the sitting room of the four-room suite—according to Schulker, it was the best in the Casino—and retrieved the jacket to his new suit and put it on.

"Just a moment," he called toward the door, and went quickly into the bedroom to check his appearance in a full-length mirror on the door.

Very pleased with his appearance, he went to the door and pulled it open.

Raschner stood there with a slight man in his thirties wearing a too-tight suit and wire-framed glasses. He bore more than a slight resemblance to Heinrich Himmler. "Councilor Forster," Raschner said.

Von Deitzberg motioned the two of them into the sitting room and closed the door.

Forster came to attention, and his right arm shot out in the Nazi salute. "Heil Hitler!" he nearly shouted. "Hauptsturmführer Forster at your orders, Herr Oberführer!"

Von Deitzberg did not return the salute. "Do not use my SS rank again," he said coldly, and added, "Wait here." He took Raschner's arm and led him out onto the balcony.

"I now understand why he's in the dark about von Tresmarck," Raschner said. "If we are to believe him, he is the only loyal man in the embassy."

Von Deitzberg chuckled. "Maybe he is," he said.

"He's an idiot," Raschner said. "They must have sent him here to get rid of him. Or does he have highly placed friends we don't know about?"

"Not as far as I know, and I think I would," von Deitzberg said.

"He told me he has strong suspicions that von Tresmarck is queer."

"Only suspicions?" von Deitzberg said, unable to restrain a smile.

"His investigation is continuing," Raschner said sarcastically.

"Does he have names?"

"He has a dossier," Raschner said, holding his hands three inches apart to indicate the thickness of the dossier. "He can't wait to show it to me."

"You better have a look at it, Erich," von Deitzberg said. "You have the embassy roster for me?" Raschner took an envelope from his suit pocket and handed it to him. "What do you think he knows about Operation Phoenix?" von Deitzberg asked.

"He further suspects that von Tresmarck has been investing in the local economy; in fact, that the local real estate man is one of his good friends. He even has a price on a farm that he thinks von Tresmarck has bought."

"So he's not entirely stupid, eh?"

"And he suspects von Tresmarck has bank accounts he hasn't listed with the embassy."

"They say there is nothing more dangerous than a zealous stupid man," von Deitzberg said, as much to himself as to Raschner. And then he added, "Does he have any idea where von Tresmarck is getting the money?"

"I've only been with him an hour," Raschner said. "But if you're really asking, does he know about the concentration-camp connection, I don't think so."

"Or he can have decided he knows something he doesn't think you should."

"That's possible."

"Spend as much time with him as you think necessary," von Deitzberg ordered. "The priorities—in this order—are who knows about the special business; Operation Phoenix; and—in connection with number two—who here in Uruguay knew about the details—for that matter, the operation itself—of landing the stuff from the *Océano Pacífico*."

Raschner nodded.

Von Deitzberg went on: "Going further on that, find out what he knows about what happened on the beach at Samborombón Bay, and, as important, where he got that information." Raschner nodded again. Von Deitzberg waved him back into the suite.

Hauptsturmführer Konrad Forster was standing where they had left him, in the center of the sitting room. When he saw them, he came to attention.

"We have a somewhat delicate situation here, Hauptsturmführer," von Deitzberg said. "Herr Raschner and myself have been sent by Reichsprotektor Himmler himself to look into certain matters here and in Buenos Aires. These matters concern a state secret of great importance. That state secret is none of your concern. Or that of Ambassador Schulker."

"Jawohl, Herr Oberfu . . . Generalmajor."

"The very next time you use either my or Herr Raschner's SS rank, Hauptsturmführer Forster, I will see that you are relieved of your duties here and assigned to the East," von Deitzberg said matter-of-factly.

"It will not happen again, Herr Generalmajor," Forster said.

"Herr Raschner and I believe that you, quite innocently, may possess certain information of value to our inquiry, acquired during the course of your normal duties. As Ambassador Schulker may also. Consequently, Raschner will interview you at length, and I will interview the Ambassador and some others. The questions we put to you may not seem to make much sense, but you will not only answer them as fully as possible, but volunteer any other information you have that may have a bearing. Do you understand me?"

"I understand you, Herr Generalmajor."

"To avoid drawing attention to these interviews, I would rather not conduct them in the embassy. Have you a secure room in your quarters?"

"I have a small office in my home, Herr Generalmajor."

"And it is secure?"

"Yes, Herr Generalmajor."

"And where is your home?"

"Not far from here, Herr Generalmajor."

"Very well," von Deitzberg said. "Go with the Hauptsturmführer now, Herr Raschner. Take as much time as required. Telephone me here when you have something to say."

"Jawohl, Herr Generalmajor," Raschner said.

He made a gesture with his hand toward the door.

"Heil Hitler!" Forster said, giving the Nazi salute.

Von Deitzberg returned the salute with a casual movement of his right arm, but said nothing.

He waited until the door had closed, and then took the envelope Raschner had given him, found the number he wanted, and walked to the telephone. He dialed the number but got nothing more than a series of clicks and a dial tone. He dialed "O" and the hotel operator came on. She explained that it was not possible to dial directly from a telephone in the suite. Von Deitzberg wondered why they bothered to install telephones with dialing mechanisms if they didn't work, but politely gave her the number he wanted.

A soft-speaking woman answered.

"Señora von Tresmarck, por favor."

She came on the line a moment later.

"This is Generalmajor von Deitzberg, Frau von Tresmarck. How nice to hear your voice again."

"What a pleasant surprise, Herr Generalmajor. Ambassador Schulker told me you would be visiting. Will I see you while you're here?"

"That's actually why I'm calling, Frau von Tresmarck," he said. "I have a little time to spare. I was rather hoping you could give me a little tour of Montevideo, and afterward we could have luncheon."

"It would be my pleasure," Inge said. "You're at the Casino?"

"In the General San Martín suite," he said.

"How appropriate, Herr Generalmajor," Inge said. "I can be there in half an hour. Would that be convenient?"

"That would be perfect," he said. "How kind of you! I'll be waiting for you outside."

He broke the connection with his finger, held the button down for a moment, and then released it. He waited for the hotel operator to come back on the line, but she didn't. After a moment, he dialed "O," and she came on.

If you can dial "O," why can't you dial an entire number?

"Would you be good enough to send the waiter to my room, Señorita?" he asked politely.

When the waiter appeared, von Deitzberg told him, man to man, that he intended to entertain a lady at luncheon, and that while he wished to make it a very nice luncheon—"I think it would be best to chill at least two bottles of Champagne"—he didn't want it interrupted by anyone after it had begun.

Under those circumstances, the waiter suggested a cold luncheon would perhaps be best. A selection of cheeses and meats and sausages, with a side of smoked salmon for the entrée, and for the *postre,* a selection of petits fours and other sweets.

"That's what we're after," von Deitzberg said, and took a wad of money from his pocket and peeled off a very generous tip.

[FIVE]

When von Deitzberg went down to the entrance of the Casino twenty minutes later, Ingebord von Tresmarck was already waiting for him at the wheel of a yellow Chevrolet convertible. The top was down.

She really is an attractive female.

She waved cheerfully at him, and he smiled and walked down to the car, bent over, and kissed her on the cheek.

"You are quite as lovely as I remembered, my dear Frau von Tresmarck," he said, then walked around to the passenger side of the car and stepped in.

Inge turned on the seat and smiled at him. "Herr Generalmajor, is there anything in particular you'd like to see?" she asked.

Was there a double entendre in her question? And why do I suspect that her skirt is not accidentally hiked so far up?

"Why don't we start by you showing me your house?" von Deitzberg said.

"If you like," she said. "It's just two squares away."

He smiled at her, and she put the car in gear and drove off.

When she raised her hand and pointed to the house, von Deitzberg smiled at her and said, "As long as we're here, Frau von Tresmarck, why don't you run in and get Sturmbannführer von Tresmarck's bank records? The special ones."

"Excuse me, Herr Generalmajor?"

"Stop the car, please," von Deitzberg ordered.

Inge pulled the car to the curb in front of the house and looked at him.

"The special bank records?" she asked, confused.

"And the rest of the records, as well."

"I'm not sure I understand," Inge said.

"By the rest of the records," von Deitzberg explained patiently, "I mean the books, Frau von Tresmarck, and the deed to the estancia, unless there is more than one deed by now, and the records of the Sturmbannführer's expenses. I want to take a look at everything."

"I don't know what you mean," Inge said.

He didn't reply for a moment. "Go get the records, Frau von Tresmarck," he said, still patiently. "I know they are here, and I know there is no one else in whose care your husband would have dared to place them when he went to Berlin."

"I think I may know what you want," Inge said.

"Frau von Tresmarck, your husband would not have left his records with you without explaining their importance," he said, as if admonishing a stubborn child. "You know what records I want. Now please go get them."

"Herr von Deitzberg, my husband said I was to give the records to no one."

"As well he should have. But obviously, I'm not 'no one,' am I, Frau von Tresmarck?"

"No. Of course not. I meant no disrespect, Herr von Deitzberg."

"Go get the records," he said. "All of them. And then we can have our tour of Montevideo and our lunch."

She smiled somewhat uneasily at him and opened the car's door. "I won't be a moment," she said.

He smiled at her.

Three minutes later, she came quickly out of the house carrying a soft black leather briefcase.

• • •

"Oh, what a lovely suite," Frau von Tresmarck exclaimed as she walked into the sitting room. She turned and looked at von Deitzberg, smiled, and walked around, inspecting both the bedroom and the dining room, and then the balcony.

She walked close to him and smiled. "It really is very nice," she said. "And lunch is ready, I see."

He nodded. "A cold lunch," he said. "I thought you wouldn't mind."

"Not at all," she replied, and then added, a little naughtily, "And I saw that someone has turned the bed down."

"Take off your clothing, please," von Deitzberg said.

She looked at him in surprise, then smiled naughtily. "I'm to be the hors d'oeuvres? Why, Herr von Deitzberg!"

Von Deitzberg struck her in the face with his fist. The blow came without warning, and was forceful enough to knock her backward onto the floor.

She looked at him with terror in her eyes, put her hand to her face, and then looked at her fingers, which now had blood on them.

"I'm not going to tell you again, Frau von Tresmarck," von Deitzberg said.

She looked into his eyes and saw something that quickly made her avert her eyes. She put her fingers to the buttons of her blouse, saw the blood on them, and licked them clean. Then she began to unbutton the blouse.

Von Deitzberg walked to the desk, placed the black briefcase on it, and sat down.

Inge shrugged out of the blouse and laid it on the carpet beside her. She looked at him. He was carefully removing large envelopes from the briefcase. She lifted herself to her feet, unbuttoned the skirt, and stepped out of it. She glanced quickly at him again, then pulled her slip over her head. She was afraid to look at him, but somehow she sensed that he wasn't even watching her. She unfastened her stockings from the garter belt and removed them. As she did so, she tasted blood on her lip, proved this by putting her fingers to her mouth, and then bent over, took a handkerchief from her purse, and wiped her nose, mouth, and fingers with it.

She looked at him once again. Now he had one of the files open on the desk and was flipping through it. She put the bloody handkerchief in her purse. "May I go to the rest room and clean my face?" she asked after a moment.

He raised his eyes from the file. "No," he said, and dropped his eyes back to the file.

She stepped out of the garter belt, looked at him again, exhaled audibly, and reached behind to the clasp of the brassiere. She took that off and dropped it onto the skirt. Then she slid her underpants off and stepped out of them. She put her left arm across her breasts and covered her pubic area with her right hand.

Von Deitzberg looked at her. "Put your hands to the side," he ordered matter-of-factly, and then demonstrated by extending both his arms from his body so that they were midway between vertical and horizontal.

She complied. Tears ran down her cheeks.

He returned his attention to the documents on the desk.

"Why are you doing this to me?" she asked, plaintively, a long moment later.

He raised his eyes, looked at her from forehead to toes, and then returned his attention to the documents without speaking.

Five minutes later, he closed one of the file folders and looked at her again from head to feet. "Feel a little humiliated, do you, Inge?" he asked.

"What is it you want?" she asked.

"That's the whole idea," von Deitzberg said conversationally. "To humiliate the person being interrogated, to deprive him—or her—of his—or her—dignity."

He let that sink in.

"You're a more than ordinarily attractive female, Inge. One might even say beautiful. That was my reaction to you when I saw you in your car, when you gave me a look at your legs. You were then in charge, so to speak. Or at least thought you were."

She didn't reply.

"Right now you are a naked female, and frankly, your

body isn't nearly as attractive as I expected. Your breasts are starting to sag, and there is too much flesh between your legs."

Her lips quivered.

"More important, I think you're getting the idea just how vulnerable you are, how completely you are at my mercy."

"What is it you want from me?"

"That standard line from any film about a court trial, 'the truth, the whole truth, and nothing but the truth.' "

"I would have answered anything you asked me," she said. "You didn't have to do this."

"I think I did. Otherwise I wouldn't have done it," he said matter-of-factly. "Please turn around, Inge. Turn completely around."

She looked at him for a moment, then complied.

When she had completed the turn, he let her stand there for a long moment. Then he said, "Your buttocks are beginning to sag, Inge. You are losing the charms of youth."

Inge could not entirely restrain a sob.

"You might actually have trouble picking up officers in the Adlon Hotel Bar if I sent you back to Berlin, Inge. Moot question. If I send you back to Germany, you won't get anywhere near the Adlon Bar."

"I'll tell you anything you want to know," Inge said. "You don't have to do this."

"First question. How much do you know about the special operation your husband has been conducting?"

"He's been conducting two special operations," Inge said.

"Very good, Inge. That suggests you are willing to tell me the whole truth. What are the two operations?"

"One is Operation Phoenix."

"Which is?"

"He has opened bank accounts and bought an estancia—a farm."

"I know what an estancia is. To what end?"

"To provide a refuge for our leaders if the war doesn't go as well as they think it will."

"And the second operation Werner is involved in?"

"Jews give him money to get people out of concentration camps in Germany."

"And how is that done?"

"I don't know. I really don't know. I just know that it happens, and that the money goes into accounts at the Banco de Río Plate and the Banco Ramírez. Different accounts than the money used for Operation Phoenix. I know which ones—"

"So do I," von Deitzberg cut her off. "Who besides Werner has access to those accounts, the *special* accounts?"

"Just me."

"You're sure of that?"

"I'm sure."

"Tell me about Werner's friends," von Deitzberg said. "Is there anyone in particular?"

"I don't know," she said.

"Stimulate your memory," he ordered. "Jog your brain. Jump up and down."

"What?"

"Jump up and down," he said. "Until I tell you to stop."

"He is closer to the imobilerio, the real estate—"

"I really hoped that I would not have to strike you again," von Deitzberg said, and rose from behind the desk.

Inge began to jump, awkwardly, up and down.

He kept her at it until her face was flushed with the exertion, then waved his hand to signal her to stop. "When you do that, your breasts flop up and down," he observed. "It's not attractive."

She looked at him and shook her head, but said nothing.

"You were telling me about the imobilerio," he said. "Whose name is?"

"Nunzio. Alfredo Nunzio."

"And would you say, Inge, that Señor Alfredo Nunzio and your husband are lovers?"

"I think so," she said.

"Do you think that, as lovers are wont to do, Werner may have shared secrets with his beloved Alfredo?"

"I don't think so," Inge said.

"Why not?"

"Werner is too smart for that," Inge said.

"Because he is aware of the consequences?"

"Yes."

"Inge, what I'm wondering now is what you thought when Werner was ordered to Berlin."

"I was frightened," she said.

"For yourself? For your husband?"

"For myself," Inge said.

"Good girl, Inge! I'm actually starting to think that you understand the importance of telling me the truth, not what you think I want to hear."

"I am."

"Now tell me about your friends," von Deitzberg said. "Anyone special?"

"No."

"You said that so quickly, I'm tempted not to believe you."

"There is no one special," she said. "I understand the necessity for discretion."

"This is not Berlin, Inge. There is no Hotel Adlon, no Hotel am Zoo. So where do you find your lovers?"

"I . . . sometimes meet people at social events, diplomatic receptions, that sort of thing."

"And where do you go with these people you meet?"

"Usually here," she said. "They take a room here in the Casino."

"These people include diplomats?"

"Two or three times."

"Is that discreet? For the wife of a senior German official?"

"I'm very careful."

"Have you become friendly with any German officer?"

There was a just-perceptible hesitation. "Just once."

"And who was he?"

"He wasn't from here. He's assigned to the embassy in Buenos Aires."

"And his name?"

"Major von Wachtstein."

"Major Freiherr Hans-Peter von Wachtstein," von Deitzberg said.

"I knew him in Berlin," she said.

"One of the handsome dashing aviators at the Hotel am Zoo?"

She nodded.

"And the circumstances of your touching reunion with an old lover from Berlin?"

"He came here with Standartenführer Goltz."

"You know that Standartenführer Goltz is dead?"

She nodded.

"Von Wachtstein came here with Goltz?"

She nodded again.

"And the two of you jumped into bed? Was that discreet on either your part or his?"

"He knew what Werner is, of course."

"How did he know that?"

"I presume Standartenführer Goltz told him."

"Why should he do that?"

"They were close."

"Would you say that von Wachtstein knew about Operation Phoenix?"

"I'm sure he does."

"And the special operation?"

"I don't know about that. I don't know how much Standartenführer Goltz told him."

"Did you discuss anything about it with him?"

"Of course not. Or about Operation Phoenix. I just had the feeling von Wachtstein knows about Operation Phoenix. I don't know if he knows about the other thing."

"Would you be surprised if he did?"

"I wouldn't be surprised one way or the other."

"How often were you together with von Wachtstein?"

"Twice. The first time he came to Montevideo with Standartenführer Goltz, and then when he came here to take Werner to Buenos Aires—after whatever happened to Goltz."

"What do you know about what happened to Goltz?"

"The gossip is he was murdered."

"Under what circumstances?"

"I don't know."

"Your husband didn't talk to you about this?"

She shook her head.

"Did he tell you that what happened to Standartenführer Goltz was one of the reasons he was recalled to Berlin?"

"No. But I knew that's what it had to be."

"You're a very bright girl, Inge. You are also skilled in the art of self-preservation. You see things as they are."

"I try to," she said.

"Your nipples are standing up," von Deitzberg said. "Does that mean you are sexually aroused? Or that you're feeling a little chill?"

Inge sucked in a breath but didn't answer.

Von Deitzberg rose from behind the desk, walked around it, and leaned back against it. "That raises a question, Inge," von Deitzberg said. "Given these facts. You understood that your husband was under suspicion—of what doesn't matter—and was being called to Berlin. You surely had to consider the possibility that he had done something wrong and would not be coming back here. You also understood that you possess information that is dangerous for you to possess. And that you would be suspected of complicity in whatever your husband had done wrong—"

"I have done nothing wrong!" Inge said.

"And you had access to all the money in the special accounts in the Banco de Río Plate and the Banco Ramírez," von Deitzberg went on. "Frankly, Inge, were I in your shoes, I would have at least considered taking the money from those accounts and disappearing."

"I did," Inge said.

"Thank you for your honesty," von Deitzberg said. "But you didn't, when there was time to do so. Why not?"

"Because I knew there was nowhere I could go that the SS couldn't find me," Inge said.

"That was a wise decision, Inge," von Deitzberg said. "There is no place in the world where you could hide from us."

"I know."

"It almost certainly saved your life," von Deitzberg said. "I hope you appreciate that."

"I do."

"No matter what the investigation of your husband's role in the Goltz matter reveals, perhaps you could still be useful to me here."

"I'm sure I could," Inge said.

"In that circumstance, it would be important for me to believe that you would do whatever I told you to do without question."

"Of course."

"Get on your knees, Inge, please."

She dropped to her knees.

"Now walk to me on your knees," von Deitzberg ordered softly. "The truth is, despite the unkind things I said before, I really do find you sexually attractive."

By the time she reached him, he had freed his erect organ from the fly of his new suit.

XVI

[ONE]
Luftwaffe Flughafen No. 103B
Augsburg, Germany
1755 16 May 1943

When Peter von Wachtstein returned Claus von Stauffenberg to the hospital, it was half past four. At that time, he had thought the trip to Augsburg would take him less than an hour; Augsburg was only eighty kilometers or so from Munich.

He had not counted on having to pass through three road

checkpoints. They were apparently intended to keep rationed foodstuffs from being moved illegally. He had no difficulty passing through them—no rural Bavarian policeman was about to subject a Horch driven by a Luftwaffe major to an intense search for a couple of chickens or three kilos of sausage—but at each one, he had to wait his turn in line until he reached the inspection point.

When he finally reached the gate to the Augsburg airfield, a Luftwaffe enlisted man, who was wearing a too-large uniform and looked as if he should be in high school, waved him to a stop. "Your identification please, Herr Major."

Peter produced it.

"Herr Gefrieter," the young man called, and a Luftwaffe corporal, who looked old enough to be the kid's grandfather, stuck his head out of the guard shack. "We have Major von Wachtstein, Herr Gefrieter," the kid said.

The ancient corporal came out of the guard shack slinging his Mauser rifle over his shoulder. He gave the Nazi salute. "Guten Abend, Herr Major," he said with a smile. "With the Herr Major's permission, I will stand on the running board and direct the Herr Major to Hangar IV-A."

"Thank you," Peter said.

Hangar IV-A was across the field from the main section of the airfield. They had to drive slowly around the end of the north-south runway to reach it; Peter was afraid the old corporal might fall off the running board. When they got close to the hangar, Peter saw that it was of heavy concrete construction and built for some depth into the ground.

You can't just push aircraft in and out of that hangar, he thought. *At least not easily. I wonder if anyone ever thought of that when they designed this thing.*

He tried to get a better look, but the hangar's windowless steel doors were closed.

The corporal showed him where to park the car.

"How will you get back to the gate, Gefrieter?" Peter asked. "Or are you going to wait for me?"

"I will walk, Herr Major," the old man said, as if the question surprised him. "There is the entrance, Herr Major. They expect you."

"Let me see if I can get you a ride," Peter said.

The corporal looked as if he didn't believe what he was hearing.

"Wait here," Peter said.

"Jawohl, Herr Major."

Peter pushed open the door to the hangar.

Inside, behind a desk, was an Oberfeldwebel (staff sergeant), a lithe man in his mid-twenties. On the desk lay a Schmeisser submachine gun. He rose to his feet when he saw Peter.

"Major von Wachtstein?"

"Right. Sergeant, I don't want the corporal who brought me here to die of old age or exhaustion hiking back to the gate. Can you get him a ride?"

"Yes, Sir," the sergeant said with a smile.

"Thank you," Peter said. "I guess you expected me?"

"Yes, Sir."

"Well? What's this all about? Who am I supposed to see?"

"Through the door, Sir. There's an officer inside who wants to see you."

Peter pushed open the door, went down a flight of stairs, and then pushed open another door.

The hangar was larger than he had imagined. And it held four aircraft of a type he had never seen before. Peter walked toward the closest one, oblivious to everything else in the hangar.

It looks like something from the future!

It has to be a fighter! It's larger than a Focke-Wulf or a Messerschmitt, but it's too small to be a bomber!

And it's sleek! My God, is it sleek!

There were four heavy barrels protruding from the nose of the machine.

Those aren't machine guns, they're machine cannons!

Twenty-millimeter machine cannons.

No! Thirty-millimeter cannons!

Where the hell is the engine, the propeller?

He looked around the hangar at the other three aircraft. He could see one of them more clearly than the others. It was bathed in the glare of work lights, as mechanics crawled over it. A man wearing a sheepskin high-altitude flight jacket and trousers—obviously a pilot—was standing with his hands on hips talking to a mechanic standing on a wing.

There's no engine or propeller on that, either!

What is this, a pusher? He knew that experimental aircraft, called "pushers," because their propellers were mounted at the rear, had been tested without much success by all the belligerent powers. The idea was to lessen aerodynamic drag at the nose.

He walked to the side of the aircraft and looked toward the rear. And for the first time took a closer look at what he had assumed were droppable fuel tanks suspended beneath the wing.

Those aren't fuel tanks!

What the hell are they?

Peter bent and looked into the forward opening of whatever the hell this thing that looked like a fuel tank was. He had no idea what he was looking at. He walked around the wing tip and looked in the rear opening of whatever the hell this tubular-shaped object was. There was a pointed, round object projecting three inches or so out of the opening. It disappeared inside the body of the object.

"Major von Wachtstein," a pleasant voice inquired courteously. "Do you suppose you could spare me a moment or two of your valuable time?"

Peter stood up and looked over the wing at the pilot he had seen a moment before. He knew the neatly mustachioed, smiling face beneath the pilot's cap perched irreverently—fighter pilot's style—atop his head.

A Pavlovian reflex took over. He popped to attention. His heels clicked as he snapped his hand crisply to the brim of his uniform cap.

"I beg the Herr General's pardon," he said. "I did not see the Herr General."

"Hansel," Generalmajor Adolf Galland, the youngest general officer in the military service of Germany, said, returning the salute with a casual gesture in the general direction of his brimmed cap, "you were always a lousy soldier. Not too bad a pilot, but a lousy officer."

And then Galland held his arms wide. This exposed at Galland's neck the Knight's Cross of the Iron Cross with Swords and Diamonds, Germany's highest award for valor.

Peter understood that he was now expected to approach the General, who had every obvious intention of embracing him.

He did so.

"It's good to see you, Hansel," Galland said, and then put his arms around him.

"It's very good to see you, Sir," Peter said.

"Normally, when I send for someone, they come on the run," Galland said. "Not stopping to take in the sights."

"I beg the Herr General's pardon," Peter said. "I had no idea—"

Galland punched him in the arm. "Ach, Hansel!" he said fondly, smiling. "Aren't you going to ask me what it is?"

"What is it, Sir?"

"It just may be the airplane that wins this war for us. Officially, it's the Messerschmitt ME-262A1."

"Those are the engines?" Peter asked, pointing.

"Those are the engines," Galland confirmed. "Turbojet engines. Junkers Jumo 004B-4s."

"There're no propellers?" It was both a statement and a question.

"No. Not conventional propellers. There's a kind of a propeller inside the engine. It—they—force air out the rear with tremendous force."

"It's amazing! How many of them do we have?"

"Not nearly enough yet."

"How fast will it go?"

"Almost nine hundred K."

"Nine hundred kilometers?" Peter asked incredulously. "In level flight?"

"Almost," Galland said, and then abruptly changed the subject: "What brings you here, Hansel? I tried to find you. The word was that you were in Argentina."

"Yes, Sir, I was."

"And then, today, I get word from Berlin that you will be

meeting someone from Canaris's bureau here. A Korvettenkapitän Boltitz?"

"Yes, Sir."

"You're involved in that slimy business, Hansel? How did
that happen?"

"I didn't volunteer, Sir."

"No, I didn't think you would volunteer for something
like that," Galland said. "I'll get you out of it, Hansel. I need
you here."

Peter didn't reply.

"You haven't forgotten how to fly?"

"I've been flying a Feiseler Storch," Peter said.

"Karlsberg!" Galland called, raising his voice.

A Luftwaffe captain, also wearing high-altitude sheepskins, appeared. He was wearing both pilot's wings and the
insignia of an aide-de-camp to a general officer, and he held
another set of bulky high-altitude sheepskins under his left
arm.

"You remember Hansel, Johann?"

"Yes, Sir, but I never thought *I* would be saluting *Hansel*,"
Hauptmann Karlsberg said, touching the brim of his uniform
cap.

"The Herr General can call me 'Hansel,' Herr Hauptmann," Peter said. "You can't." He smiled, returned the
salute, and put out his hand. "Hello, Johann, how are you?"

"Sometimes I wish we were back in Spain," Karlsberg
said. "You know who else is here, Peter? Willi Grüner."

"He knows," Galland said. "Put on the gear, Hansel. The
bird over there is a two-seater. We'll take a hop."

"Jawohl, Herr General," Peter said happily.

Peter stuffed his legs through the heavy sheepskin
trousers, and then Galland held the jacket for him.

"The higher these things fly, the more efficient they are,"
Galland said. "Fuel consumption is lousy near the ground.
So the cold-weather gear—and oxygen—are necessary most
of the time."

Peter nodded his understanding.

"Have them roll out Two One Seven, Johann," Galland
ordered.

"Jawohl, Herr General. Just Two One Seven, Herr General?"

"You'd like to come along, would you?"

"Whatever the Herr General desires."

"OK, Johann," Galland said with a smile, and turned to Peter and winked. "Come on, Hansel, I'll show you around the cockpit."

When they reached the two-seater, Galland waved Peter up the ladder against its side. It was immediately apparent that the two-seater arrangement was a jury rig. Only the front of the two in-line seats had a full instrument panel. The rear seat had a stick and rudder pedals, a second oxygen mask, a microphone/earphones facemask, and little else.

Galland motioned Peter into the front seat. There was barely room to get in.

Galland seemed to read Peter's mind. "We put the backseat in here," he said. "The factory said it would take three months to do it 'properly.' "

The instrument panel looked familiar, not very different from the ME-109F's. The airspeed indicator was larger, and was red-lined at 1,200 kilometers per hour; the red line on the ME-109 had been at 850. And there were controls and indicators completely new to Peter.

He heard large electric motors, and the hangar doors began to slide open. A tow truck appeared, and a moment later there was a slight jolt as it connected to the plane's single front wheel.

Galland's explanation of the controls and their functions was not nearly as detailed as Peter would have liked, but he told himself it didn't matter; once they were in the air, their purpose would quickly become apparent.

The plane began to move. The hangar floor was below the surface of the tarmac, and it was an effort for the small tow truck to pull the plane up the ramp. They were towed to the end of the runway, where two trucks awaited them.

"It's not supposed to," Galland's voice came metallically over the earphones, "but more often than not, it takes auxiliary power to get the engines going. You can't jump in one of these, throw the Master Buss, crack the throttle, and hit ENGINE START."

Ground crewmen from the trucks plugged a thick cable into the fuselage. Peter saw that Karlsberg, in a second ME-262, was on the threshold ten meters to the left behind him.

"Wind it up, Peter," Galland said. "Brakes locked. Check for control freedom after you've got it running." He pointed out the applicable controls in the order they would be used.

On orders, Peter depressed the LEFT ENGINE START lever. There was a whining noise, slow at first, then increasing in intensity to a roar.

"Throttle back," Galland ordered. "Let it warm slowly. Start the right."

"Two One Seven and Two Two Three ready for takeoff," Galland's voice came over the earphones.

"You are cleared for takeoff from Two Eight at your discretion. The winds are negligible. There is no traffic in the area. Air Warning Status, Blue."

"To your right, Hansel, under a protective cover, is the rocket firing switch. Get your engines to takeoff power—it's marked on the gauges—release the brakes, then fire the rockets. It steers surprisingly well, but watch it when you break ground. Sometimes it veers to one side or the other."

"Jawohl, Herr General."

"Don't lift off until I tell you," Galland said. "If you don't have sufficient velocity, it'll mush."

"Jawohl, Herr General."

"Controls all right?" Galland asked.

Peter felt the stick move through its range, and the rudder pedals moving, as Galland checked the rear seat controls, then tested his own. "Controls free," he reported.

"Ready, Johann?" Galland called over the radio.

"Ready, Herr General," Karlsberg replied.

"Two One Seven rolling," Galland said. "OK, Hansel, let's see if you can still fly."

The runway lights came on.

Oh, that's nice. That means it will be totally dark in an hour, and I will have to make my first landing in this thing in the dark.

What the hell, you're a Luftwaffe fighter pilot, aren't you? You can fly anything with wings, anywhere, anytime.

Peter advanced both throttles until their indicator needles touched the green line on the dials. He released the brakes, felt the plane just barely start to move, then pushed the protective cover over the rocket fire button out of the way and pushed the red button.

There was a cloud of billowing white smoke as both of the rockets ignited. Peter expected the plane would immediately accelerate rapidly. It did not. But a moment later, as he lined up the nose of the accelerating aircraft on the centerline of the runway, he became aware that he was being pushed slowly, but with great force, back against his seat.

He saw the airspeed indicator jump to life at about 70 kilometers, and then the needle continued to move upward very quickly. He felt life come into the controls.

A moment later, Galland ordered: "Lift it off."

Peter dropped his eyes to the airspeed indicator. It was indicating more than 120 kilometers. He edged back on the stick. The rumble of the landing gear ceased almost immediately, and he felt that he was flying.

"Gear up," Galland ordered.

The gear came up very quickly.

There *was* a tendency for the aircraft to turn to the right. Peter made the necessary corrections without thinking about it.

"Drop the rockets," Galland ordered.

Peter pressed that button. He glanced out the window. The ground was dropping away quickly, and as he watched, the runway lights died.

Runway lights were turned on only when aircraft were taking off or landing. Otherwise, they served as lovely target markers for B-17 bombardiers.

This sometimes caused problems for fighter pilots trying to find their fields after radios or antennae had taken one or more .50-caliber Browning bullets, or were not functioning for some other reason.

He saw Karlsberg's ME-262 slightly behind and just a little above him. And then there was backward pressure on the stick. He fought it at first, then realized it was coming from Galland, pulling backward on the backseat's stick. He gave in to it.

The nose rose at an impossible angle.

Christ! What's he trying to do, put it in a stall?

There was no stall. With the nose approaching straight-up, the ME-262 continued not only to climb, but at an ever-increasing velocity.

Peter looked over his shoulder. Galland was smiling at him. "Put on the mask, Hansel," he said. "We'll be going through three thousand meters very soon."

Peter pulled the clammy rubber mask over his mouth, twisted the valve, and felt the oxygen on his face. He looked at the altimeter. The needle seemed to be almost spinning around the dial, and as he watched, it indicated 3,000 meters. "This is fantastic!" he said.

"It's not a bad little airplane, Peter," Galland said, and with an exaggerated gesture—holding up both hands at the level of his shoulders—signaled that he had let go of the stick.

The airspeed settled down at about 600 knots, but the altimeter continued to wind rapidly.

"Level off at six thousand," Galland said. "And then you can play with it a little."

"Are we going to find any Amis or Brits up here tonight?" Peter asked.

"I don't think so," Galland said. "You heard the tower. The aircraft warning status is blue. The Amis are usually long gone by this time of day—they like to land in the daylight. And the Brits usually time their night raids so they arrive home just after first light. Which is why we're flying at this hour. The longer we can keep them from learning about the ME-262, until we get enough of them to really do some damage, the better."

"Understand," Peter said.

"If we do see a Lancaster, Peter, or anything, we will not engage. Not engage. Understand?"

"Jawohl, Herr General."

"If you see something, do a one-eighty and get the hell out of there."

"Jawohl, Herr General."

The airplane was as agile in the sky as anything Peter had ever flown. He engaged in a brief mock dogfight with Karlsberg and lost sight of him in a turn. And then Karlsberg flashed past him.

"All things considered, I'd say you're dead," Galland said. "But that's not too bad for your first fifteen minutes."

Peter went looking for Karlsberg, spotted him, and put the ME-262 into a sharp diving turn to the left.

What seemed like two or three minutes later, Galland spoke again: "If you don't plan to make a dead stick landing—and these birds drop like a stone, I think I should tell you—I think you should try to find the field."

Peter found the fuel gauges. The needles were close to empty. He looked down at the ground. Darkness was already concealing the details of the terrain.

Where the hell is Augsburg?

He looked at the Radio Direction Finder, then banked the ME-262 toward the Augsburg transmitter.

"With a little reserve, you have about fifty minutes at altitude," Galland said. "You aren't going to be able to strafe the King in Buckingham Palace in one of these. We just don't have the range. But once we get these airplanes operational, I think my friend Spaatz is going to get far fewer B-17s back to England than he sends here." General Carl Spaatz, USAAC, directed the bombing of Germany by the Eighth U.S. Air Force.

"With those thirty-millimeters," Peter thought out loud, "you don't have to come in range of the guns on a B-17."

"And if you're quick," Galland said, "you can come out of the sun at them at a thousand K, and get two, maybe even three of them, and still be out of the range of their guns."

"Jesus!" Peter said.

"I think I should warn you, Hansel, that the standard punishment for my pilots who bend one of these on landing is castration with a very dull knife."

"Yes, Sir."

"Two other things: One, you have to land hot. They don't handle well at low speeds, which means you should put the wheels down as close to the threshold of the runway as you can."

"Yes, Sir."

"Two, you don't get instant throttle response from a turbojet engine. It's five to seven seconds before you get any usable power."

"Yes, Sir."

"You want me to shoot a touch-and-go so you can see how it's done?"

"Why don't you let me try it, and take it away from me if I start to lose it?"

"If I start to take it away from you, don't fight me."

"Yes, Sir."

"Jaegerhaven," Galland called over the radio. "Two One Seven and Two Two Three for approach and landing."

The control tower responded with landing instructions, and all of a sudden, two parallel lines of lights showed him the runway.

"Sometimes, if a dull knife isn't immediately available, I use a dull saw," Galland said.

Peter lined up with the field, turned on final, and touched down hot but smoothly on the yellow and black stripes that marked the end of the runway. The runway lights went off before he had finished the landing roll. Tow trucks were waiting for both fighters on the taxiway, and had hooked up before the whine of the turboprops had stopped. When they reached the hangar, the doors were opening, and the moment the airplanes were inside, they began to close again. The hangar lights did not come on until the doors were fully closed.

Ground crew appeared and put a ladder up to the cockpit. Galland got out first, and then Peter climbed down after him. Karlsberg appeared. He had removed his sheepskin trousers but was still wearing his now unbuttoned high-altitude jacket. Galland unbuttoned his jacket and somewhat awkwardly pulled off the trousers. He waited until Peter had done the same thing.

"Karlsberg, you may say something appropriate to Major von Wachtstein for having successfully passed the appropriate flight tests qualifying him in ME-262 Series aircraft."

Karlsberg smiled and gave Peter a thumbs-up. Peter suspected that Galland was serious about his passing a check ride.

And again Galland seemed to be reading his mind. "Don't let it go to your head, Hansel," he said. "You'll get a good deal of further instruction before I let you go on your own. But when I go to Unser Hermann to get you transferred here, I want to tell him that you're already qualified in these birds." Reichsmarschall Hermann Göring—Unser Hermann, Our Hermann—was the head of the Luftwaffe.

"Yes, Sir."

There was something in Galland's tone of voice when he referred to "Unser Hermann" that gave Peter pause.

In a moment, he knew what it was. In the early days, when Peter had flown with the Condor Legion in Spain, and in Poland, and in the defeat of France, "Unser Hermann" had been spoken of with affection and respect. Unser Hermann was one of them; he was everybody's fond uncle; he worried about them; by taking care of the Luftwaffe, he took care of them.

But as British and American bombers began to strike at German cities, which Göring had sworn would never happen, and as stories of his drug addiction, his erratic behavior, his homosexual advances to decorated fighter pilots invited to his Karin Hall estate, and more important, his unwillingness to stand up for the Luftwaffe, were whispered about in Luftwaffe ready rooms and officers' clubs, "Unser Hermann" had become a more derisive appellation.

But by captains and majors, not general officers.

Did I really hear a sarcastic tone in Galland's voice? Or was it just my imagination?

A Luftwaffe Oberstleutnant marched across the hangar, the heels of his glistening boots ringing on the concrete. He came to attention in front of Galland and rendered a crisp Nazi salute. "Heil Hitler!"

Galland and Karlsberg returned the salute, and a moment later, Peter did too.

That's the first time I've seen Galland do that.

"Herr General, there has been an urgent teletype from Berlin about Major Wachtstein."

"Saying what?"

"Herr General, the message states that Korvettenkapitän Boltitz has been delayed approximately twelve hours. He will arrive at approximately 1000 hours tomorrow morning. We are directed to ensure that Wachtstein is available to him at that time."

"It's *von* Wachtstein, Colonel," Galland corrected him. "Colonel Deitzer, may I present Major Freiherr Hans-Peter von Wachtstein?"

Peter came to attention and clicked his heels.

Colonel Deitzer offered his hand and a weak smile. "Major," he said.

"Major von Wachtstein has just taken, and passed, his flight examination for ME-262 aircraft," Galland said. "Make sure that Luftwaffe Central Records is promptly made aware of that."

"Jawohl, Herr General."

"I don't want any administrative problems with that," Galland said. "Make sure you have a record of their acknowledgment."

"Jawohl, Herr General. Herr General, Berlin requests an acknowledgment of their order regarding the major."

"Then telex them that I personally guarantee Major von Wachtstein will be available to the Korvettenkapitän when he arrives."

"Jawohl, Herr General," he said, and turned to Peter.

"If there's nothing else, Colonel, I'll be in my quarters," Galland said.

"Jawohl, Herr General," Deitzer said, then raised his arm in the Nazi salute and barked, "Heil Hitler!"

The three pilots returned the Nazi salute, and Oberstleutnant Deitzer turned on his heel and marched away.

Galland waved his hand toward the stairway of the hangar, and the three started walking to it. "Napoleon said, 'An army marches on its stomach,' " he said. "I have learned he was wrong. An army marches—in our case, flies—on the backs of people like Deitzer. We may not like them, and God knows they're not warriors, but we need them. I have to keep reminding myself of that."

Neither Karlsberg nor Peter could think of a reply.

When they had climbed the stairway and left the hangar, Galland pointed to the Horch. "Hello! What's that?"

"It's my father's car, sir," Peter said.

"I was afraid for a moment we were having another important visitor," Galland said. "And I'm not in the mood to entertain important visitors."

"Grafin von Stauffenberg . . . Herr General—do you know Oberstleutnant von Stauffenberg?"

Galland nodded. "I heard he really caught it bad in Africa. Blinded, wasn't he?"

"He has the sight of one eye, Herr General. I just saw him in hospital in Munich. His wife is going to come here and take the car to their place. I hope that's all right."

"Of course it is," Galland said. "Just give Deitzer the details. That's my point. Those paper pushers *are* really useful."

A young sergeant was standing at attention beside a gray military Volkswagen.

"Otto," Galland called to him. "We're going to ride in style with Major von Wachtstein. Follow us to my quarters."

"Jawohl, Herr General."

[TWO]
Quarters of the General Officer Commanding
Luftwaffe Flughafen No. 103B
Augsburg, Germany
2035 16 May 1943

Hauptmann Willi Grüner was leaning against a pillar of the fence in front of the two-story masonry house provided as quarters to General Galland. He pushed himself off the wall when he saw the Horch and the Volkswagen approach. He saluted—the military, stiff-hand-to-the-brim-of-his-cap salute, not the Nazi—when he saw General Galland.

"Why are you standing on the street, Willi?" Galland called as he got out of the car. "You should have gone in."

He punched Grüner affectionately on the arm, then led him through the gate in the fence and toward the house with his arm around his shoulder. Karlsberg and Peter followed. The door was opened by a young Luftwaffe soldier in a short, crisply starched white jacket. Galland led them all into a sitting room, and to a bar set against one wall. "Anybody hungry?" Galland asked.

No one was.

Galland went behind the bar, came up with beer and glasses, and handed them around. When they had all poured beer, he raised his. "Prosit!" he called.

They repeated the toast and sipped at their beer.

"I didn't expect to see you here," Willi Grüner said.

"I'm the Luftwaffe representative for your father's funeral," Peter said. "I was ordered to meet Boltitz here."

"Boltitz? U-boat?" Willi asked.

Peter remembered that was what Willi had christened Boltitz in the bar in Berlin. He nodded.

"I don't know what to think about U-boat," Willi said, then went on before giving Peter a chance to reply: "Have you seen what they're flying here?"

"I just flew one," Peter said. "As a matter of fact, Galland made it a check ride."

"And you passed it?" Willi asked in mock surprise.

"Go fuck yourself, Willi," Peter said.

The room was decorated with photographs and paintings, all with a Luftwaffe connection. Peter wandered around the room, looking at them. He found one of special interest. It was a photograph of then Oberst Galland standing in front of the wing of an ME-109 with three young pilots, one of whom was Flight Sergeant Peter Wachtstein. It had been taken, he recalled, on a Polish military airfield outside Warsaw.

Peter remembered the tall, thin Swabian standing beside him. He couldn't remember his name, but he remembered that he had gone down into the English Channel, and that they had never been notified that he had been taken prisoner.

The other guy, too—what the hell *was his name?—had also caught it, later, in France.*

Peter examined a rather good oil painting of a Focke-Wulf Fw-190 taking off, accurate to the point that the left gear was nearly in its well, and the right still dangling down, making the sleek fighter look like a one-legged bird.

One of the first things a new Fw-190 pilot was told was that when you went to GEAR UP, you should be prepared for the bird to veer to the right, because the gear went up unevenly.

That triggered memories of the Fw-109 squadron he had commanded before being sent to Argentina, and he went from that to wonder somewhat bitterly how many of his men had caught it since he'd left them.

He turned from the painting and looked around the room. There was something about it that made it seem more like an officer's mess than a living room in a home. There was no evidence of a feminine touch, although he knew there was a Frau Generalmajor Galland and a family; he had met them—a nice lady, and nice kids—once in Paris, right after Paris had fallen, and another time in Berlin.

I wonder where she is?

Galland again seemed to read his mind. "For some reason, Hansel—never try to understand female reasoning—Liesel doesn't like it here. She says she never sees me but an hour or two a day. Why she thinks that's not better than seeing me for a day only once every other week at home, I don't pretend to understand."

"And the kids?" Peter asked.

"Whenever it can be arranged, the oldest boy spends a couple of days with me here."

That relationship doesn't seem to upset him very much. Maybe he has trouble with his wife?

It's none of your business.

Three other officers joined them, one at a time, during the next fifteen minutes. Two were young captains (Peter remembered one vaguely from Poland), and an old—relatively speaking; he was probably not yet thirty—Oberstleutnant who had been one of his instructors at flight school.

Peter saw that Oberstleutnant Henderver also wore the Knight's Cross of the Iron Cross around his neck. At roughly the same moment, Henderver saw Peter's and headed for him.

"Your face is familiar, Major."

"Von Wachtstein, Sir," Peter said. "You taught me to fly the Stosser, Herr Oberstleutnant."

The Focke-Wulf Fw-56 "Stosser," first flown in 1933, was a single-engine 240-hp, low-wing monoplane designed as a fighter, which after 1937 was used as an advanced flying and gunnery trainer.

"And you're still alive? Amazing!" Henderver said.

"Lucky, Sir, I'd say."

"You'd better hope it holds," Henderver said. "The 262 is a dangerous little bitch."

"I flew it this afternoon, Sir."

"Under the circumstances, you and the Herr General may address me by my Christian name," Henderver said. "Of course, the Herr General may anyway. But somebody that I long ago taught to fly the Stosser and is still alive is obviously a special person."

He's drunk, Peter realized.

"Thank you, Sir," Peter said. "I think it was probably the quality of your instruction."

"And you're an ass-kisser, too. . . . What was your Christian name?"

"Peter."

"I like to have my ass kissed, Peter," Henderver said, "but only by members of the other sex." He raised his voice: "Herr General, were you aware that I taught this splendid officer to fly the Stosser?"

"And he's still alive? Amazing!" Galland replied.

"My point exactly, Herr General," Henderver said. He turned to Peter and smiled. "Let's have a drink."

Peter held up his beer glass.

"That's a *beer*," Henderver said. "I said a *drink*." He

dragged Peter to the bar and reached under it and came up with a bottle of Dewar's scotch whiskey.

Scotch? Here in Germany? I wonder where that came from?

Henderver poured stiff drinks in glasses and then raised his to Peter.

"To those of us who have survived," Henderver said. "For as long as it lasts."

Peter touched his glass to Henderver's.

He hadn't finished the drink when he heard female voices in the foyer, and six young women came into the sitting room a minute later. They were neither quite as good-looking nor as elegant as the young women who could be found in the bars of the Adlon and am Zoo Hotels in Berlin, but they obviously were a Bavarian version of the same breed.

There were several ways to look at them, Peter decided. The most kind was to see them simply as young women looking for eligible young men, with the three *K*'s as their basic ambition: Kinder, Kirche and Küchen—Children, Church, and Kitchen. According to the Nazi philosophy, these described the female function in life.

Or else they could be considered to be young women looking for attractive young men; and, by and large, Luftwaffe pilots met that description.

Less kindly, they had come to understand that while the chances of getting a Luftwaffe fighter pilot into a wedding ceremony ranged from poor to none, Luftwaffe fighter pilots almost always could be counted on to provide access to food and luxuries not available elsewhere.

Including, of course, to French wine, cognac and Champagne, and even scotch whiskey.

With a couple of drinks of Rémy Martin or Martell to warm your heart, it seemed less important that the young man who had just given you a kilo box of Belgian chocolate, or two pairs of French silk stockings, was interested in getting you in bed, not to the marriage registry office.

Or to convince yourself that it was obviously your patriotic duty to bring joy, or solace, to a young hero of the Third

Reich who daily risked his life to protect the Fatherland from the Bolshevik hordes.

"And this, my dear Trudi," Generalmajor Galland said, "is another old comrade-in-arms, Major Freiherr Hans-Peter von Wachtstein."

"I'm very pleased to meet you, Herr Baron," Trudi said.

Trudi looked enough like Alicia to bring her picture clearly into Peter's mind.

And she looks like a nice girl, like Alicia; there is nothing of the whore, or the slut, in her face.

So what is she doing here?

If the Brazilians were bombing Buenos Aires and I was an Argentine, flying one of their antique American Seversky fighters out of El Palomar, would Alicia be in a place like this smiling at me because I looked like a source of silk stockings or chocolate?

Maybe. If the Gendarmerie Nacional was setting up roadblocks on the highway to Estancia Santo Catalina, to keep people from moving food around, maybe she would.

No, she wouldn't, not Alicia.

"The pleasure is mine, Fräulein," Peter said, and bowed his head at the neck and clicked his heels.

The white-jacketed steward rolled in a tray of hors d'oeuvres.

"Oh, I think I'm going to have some of that!" Trudi declared. "It all looks delicious."

"I think, Hansel," General Galland said thirty minutes later, "that you could take Trudi home."

"Herr General?"

Trudi was smiling at them from across the room. She was warming a brandy snifter in her hands.

"I think she likes you," Galland said. "But I am not sure, under the circumstances, that that would be such a good idea."

"It was not my—"

"I was about to suggest if you told her you had to fly first thing in the morning, she might be amenable to spending the night here."

"Am I flying first thing in the morning?"

"The Navy's coming first thing in the morning," Galland said. "How much of the scotch have you had?"

"Korvettenkapitän Boltitz," Peter said. "He slipped my mind for a minute."

"That's understandable, Hansel. I've never seen a sailor nearly as attractive as Trudi," Galland said, smiling. "But under the circumstances, I will, Major von Wachtstein, change that suggestion to an order."

"Sir?"

"If you feel, Major von Wachtstein, that it's your duty to maintain the reputation of Luftwaffe fighter pilots by providing what the lady so obviously wants, you will do so on the premises."

Peter didn't reply.

"I gave my word, you will recall," Galland went on, "that I would have you here for the Korvettenkapitän in the morning. I don't want to tell him you're off God only knows where attempting to increase the Bavarian birth rate."

"Jawohl, Herr General."

"I had my orderly put your bag in the second bedroom to the left, at the top of the stairs," Galland said. "And he will take Trudi home in the morning."

"I wish I shared your high opinion of my irresistibility, Herr General," Peter said. "I don't think she's all that interested in me."

"Oh, I'm sure she is."

"With all possible respect, Herr General, I disagree."

Galland winked at Peter, smiled knowingly, punched him affectionately on the arm, and walked away.

Across the room, Trudi saw that Galland had left Peter, and she walked to him, offering the glass.

"I've got scotch, thank you."

"Scotch tastes like medicine to me."

"And the cognac?"

"Like . . . cognac," Trudi said.

There was the sound of music, a phonograph playing in an adjacent room.

"That's Glenn Miller," Peter said.

"Well, I won't tell if you won't tell," Trudi said.

It took him a moment to take her meaning. "Is Glenn Miller proscribed?" he asked.

"He's decadent," Trudi said. "Are you decadent, Herr Baron?"

"I really wish you wouldn't call me that," Peter said without thinking.

"Herr Major?" she asked with a smile.

"Peter will do nicely," he said, and thought aloud: "He's in the American Air Corps, you know. Glenn Miller, I mean."

"Really?" She seemed surprised. "How do you know?"

"I read it in the English newspaper, the Buenos Aires *Herald,* when I was in Argentina. He and his whole band."

"I thought reading enemy newspapers was proscribed," Trudi said. "They're decadent."

"Actually, it was my duty to read them."

"Really?"

"There's a German newspaper in Buenos Aires—actually two of them, and some magazines. And I'm sure my counterparts—the military attachés in the British and American embassies—read them. The military principle involved is 'know your enemy.' "

Cletus Frade, for example.

"Do you think you could get to know the enemy better if we went in there"—she inclined her head toward the door of the room where the sound of the music was coming from—"and danced to the decadent music of Glenn Miller?"

I don't want to dance with Trudi, and I don't want to take her to bed.

Because of Alicia?

Or because I know Trudi knows getting in my bed is expected of her, and I feel bad about taking advantage of her?

That never bothered me before.

Why now?

Alicia, of course. I wonder where she is now?

It's early. There's five hours' time difference between here and Buenos Aires.

Maybe she's having tea with Dorotéa Frade in Claridge's Hotel.

Or shopping with her for baby clothes in Harrod's.

Why did I ever get involved with Alicia?

All I am going to do is bring her grief.

"Why not?" Peter said. He drained his scotch, set the glass down, smiled at Trudi, and motioned for her to precede him into the adjacent room.

One of Galland's white-jacketed orderlies stood almost at attention beside the table that held the phonograph. When one record was finished, he replaced it with another, all the time pretending not to see that Oberstleutnant Henderver's hands were pressing the girl he was dancing with against him by holding her buttocks, and that Hauptmann Grüner had his hand under the sweater of the girl dancing with him.

"General Galland really likes you," Trudi said, her mouth close to his ear.

"How do you know that?"

She smells good. That's French perfume. I wonder where she got it?

You know damned well where she got it, from someone like Henderver, or Willi, maybe from Galland himself.

"He told me," Trudi said. "He said that I shouldn't be misled by your looks. . . ."

"My looks?"

"How young you look. He said that you were one of the old-timers, starting in Spain."

"We were in Spain," Peter said.

"And then in Poland and France, and England . . ."

"Guilty."

"And that you got the Knight's Cross from the Führer himself."

"Absolutely," Peter said. "I was the only man in my squadron with a perfect record for six months of never missing Sunday mass."

Trudi laughed delightedly, and far more enthusiastically than the bad joke merited. And when she leaned back to look up at his face, she pressed her midsection against his. That she left it there proved it was not accidental.

It produced an immediate reaction, and Peter withdrew his midsection. Trudi's groin followed his.

"Meine Damen und Herren," an orderly announced, "dinner is served."

"I'm hungry," Trudi said, stopping the dancing movements but not withdrawing her groin from his. "But I hate to stop dancing."

"We'd better go in," Peter said.

She moved her hand from his back to the base of his neck and pulled his face to hers and kissed him.

Not really lewdly, Peter decided. *Not wide-open-mouthed with a tongue hungrily seeking mine, accompanied by a grinding of her pelvis against my hard-on.*

A slightly opened mouth, with the tip of her tongue daintily touching my lips, and a just barely perceptible increase of pelvic pressure.

A promise of more to come.

And you like it, you sonofabitch!

You get near any reasonably good-looking female and you're instantly ready to play the bull.

Jesus Christ! You really should be ashamed of yourself!

You don't deserve Alicia.

General Galland, standing at the head of the table, smiled knowingly at Peter and Trudi as they took their seats.

Two white-jacketed orderlies served the meal. It was roast loin of wild boar, oven-roasted potatoes, creamed onions, and a salad. There was Champagne and wine.

Trudi tapped her Champagne glass against his and smiled. Peter smiled back.

You are probably a very nice girl, Trudi.

And you are probably very good in the sack.

But thank you, no thank you.

After dinner, I am simply going to disappear.

I am not, so help me God, going to take you to bed.

[THREE]
Guest Room #1
Quarters of the General Officer Commanding
Luftwaffe Flughafen No. 103B
Augsburg, Germany
0715 17 May 1943

Major Freiherr Hans-Peter von Wachtstein was naked and spread-eagled on his back. Trudi pushed him in the ribs. She had been trying to wake him for at least ninety seconds. He grunted.

"Liebchen," Trudi whispered fiercely, "there's someone at the door."

Peter opened his eyes and looked around the room, as if wondering where he was.

"Liebchen," Trudi whispered again, "there's someone at the door."

He looked at Trudi. She was supporting herself on an elbow, which served to put her left nipple about six inches from his eye.

Oh, God!

"There's someone at the door," Trudi hissed a third time.

With a tremendous effort, Peter pushed his torso off the bed. "What is it?" he called as loudly as he could, which was not very loud, as the inside of his mouth was absolutely dry.

"Ruttman, Herr Major," a male voice responded, "the Herr General's orderly."

"What is it?" Peter demanded.

"I am to drive the young lady into Augsburg, Herr Major."

"Wait downstairs," Peter ordered.

"Jawohl, Herr Major."

"You were really sleeping, Liebchen," Trudi said.

"Liebchen"? *Oh, my God!*

"How much did I have to drink last night?"

"Not very much," Trudi said. "Do you feel bad?" She ran her fingers across his forehead.

Not very much? The way I feel? That's absurd.

But enough obviously to bring Trudi up here.

"Poor Liebchen," Trudi said.

Oh, my God, and Boltitz is coming this morning!

Was I out of my mind, to get drunk?

He let himself fall back against the bed.

Trudi looked down at him, smiled, and ran the tips of her fingers over his chest. And then lower. "And how is he this morning?" she asked naughtily.

"I suspect he's out of service," Peter said.

I don't even remember bringing her up here, much less anything about what obviously happened last night.

The last thing I remember is standing at the bar, arguing with Oberstleutnant Henderver about the best way to fight a Mustang.

What happened after that?

"He doesn't act as if he's out of service," Trudi said as she manipulated him.

"Trudi, I've got to get up and have a shower and get dressed."

"Oh, really?"

She sounds genuinely disappointed. Is that because I am the greatest lover since Casanova? Or because she's a nymphomaniac?

Oh, Jesus Christ, I'm really hard!

"I would really hate to waste that," Trudi said.

"Trudi, I'm beat," Peter said. "I don't have the energy . . ."

"Ssssh," Trudi said, putting her finger on his lips. Then she straddled him and guided him into her.

Oh, my God!

Peter opened his eyes. Someone was knocking at door.

Christ, I told him to wait downstairs!

He looked around for Trudi. She wasn't in the bed with him, and there was no sign of her in the room—no purse, no clothing. He remembered that she had collapsed on him, and he hadn't particularly liked that, and he remembered that he was just going to have to close his eyes and get a couple of minutes sleep.

"What is it?" Peter called.

"Herr Major, the Herr General and the other gentlemen are downstairs."

"I'll be there directly," Peter said.

He found his watch. The U.S. Army Air Corps chronometer said that it was 12:09.

Christ, I remember telling Henderver—and, my God, Galland too—about that slime of an SS officer who stole it from the American pilot.

What else did I run off at the mouth about last night?

And the orderly said "gentlemen." More than one. Who's with Boltitz? That charming slime, Obersturmbannführer Karl Cranz, who met us in Lisbon?

Galland had been disgusted with the story. Disgusted enough to tell Obersturmbannführer Karl Cranz about it?

You goddamn irresponsible fool!

Getting drunk out of your mind!

He swung his feet out of the bed and walked unsteadily to the bathroom. He turned on the cold water of the shower and stood under it until he was shivering nearly out of control. He hoped the cold water would clear his head.

All it did was make me shiver.

Keep your goddamn mouth shut when you go downstairs.

Peter cut himself in three places while shaving.

Generalmajor Adolf Galland, Obersturmbannführer Karl Cranz, Korvettenkapitän Karl Boltitz, Oberstleutnant Henderver, Oberstleutnant Deitzer, and Hauptmann Willi Grüner were in the sitting room when Peter walked in. "Heil Hitler!" Peter said, giving the Nazi salute. "My apologies, Herr General, for my tardiness."

The Nazi salute was returned with varying degrees of enthusiasm.

"You may notice, Cranz," Galland said, "that Major von Wachtstein looks a bit pale."

"So he does."

"Yesterday," Galland went on. "Major von Wachtstein flew a new aircraft—"

"You're not referring the ME-262?" Cranz asked.

"Indeed I am. Are you familiar with the aircraft, Cranz?"

"I've seen photographs," Cranz said, "and read its characteristics."

"And von Wachtstein flew it, Herr General?" Boltitz asked, obviously surprised.

"I personally qualified Major von Wachtstein in the ME-262," Galland said.

"Isn't that a little unusual?" Cranz asked.

"Major von Wachtstein is a very unusual pilot," Galland said. "And if you're familiar with ME-262 characteristics, you're aware of the great increase in speed it offers?"

"I heard nine hundred kilometers," Boltitz said.

"In level flight. The figure is considerably higher in a dive."

"Amazing," Cranz said.

"Naturally, flying an aircraft at those speeds subjects the human body to great stress."

"I'm sure it does," Cranz said.

"But nothing like the stresses placed upon the human body—in this case Hansel's body—by the party that always follows a pilot becoming rated in the ME-262. What you see before you, gentlemen, bleeding from his shave and looking like death warmed over, is a brand-new ME-262 pilot."

Cranz laughed dutifully. Boltitz chuckled.

"And he went beyond that, gentlemen," Galland said. "Delicacy forbids me to get into specifics, but let me assure you that Major von Wachtstein gave his all—to judge by his bloodshot eyes, all night—to maintain, even polish, the reputation Luftwaffe fighter pilots enjoy among the gentle sex."

"Hansel," Willi Grüner said. "You look awful."

Peter gave him the finger.

"Ruttman!" Galland called. The orderly appeared. "The emergency equipment for Major von Wachtstein, if you please."

"Jawohl, Herr General!"

Ruttman left the room and returned in a minute with a face mask and a portable oxygen bottle. He handed them to Peter.

"What is that?" Boltitz asked. "Oxygen?"

"The best—so far as I know personally, the only—cure for a hangover," Galland said.

The cool oxygen felt marvelous.

"With a little luck, Major von Wachtstein may live through lunch," Galland said. "He may wish he were dead, but I think he may live."

Obersturmbannführer Cranz kept Galland's orderly from refilling his wineglass by covering it with his palm. "To get to the sad business before us," he said. "Specifically, Hauptmann Grüner, the details of the interment of your father."

Willi Grüner looked at him and just perceptibly nodded his head.

"It has been proposed by Reichsprotektor Himmler, in consideration of your late father's distinguished service to the SS, that his interment and the accompanying ceremonies be joined with those of the late Standartenführer Goltz. Have you any objection to that, Herr Hauptmann?"

Willi shook his head.

"The Reichsprotektor also suggests that an appropriate place for the interment of both of these fallen heroes would be in the SS section of the Munich military cemetery. He has ordered that two grave places immediately adjacent to the Horst Wessel monument be made available. Does this also meet your approval, Hauptmann Grüner?"

Willi knew that was meant to be an honor. Horst Wessel, a student, who had been in trouble with the police "for rowdyism," had joined the Nazi party in 1926, and become a storm trooper. In 1930, political enemies, possibly Communists, had killed him in a brawl in his room in the Berlin slums. Nazi propagandists had blamed three Jews for his murder, executed them, and elevated Wessel to martyrdom. "The Horst Wessel Lied" was now the anthem of the Nazi party.

"Yes, Sir."

"The arrangements haven't been finalized, of course, but

it is anticipated that company-size units from each of the armed forces will participate. Would providing such a unit, to represent the Luftwaffe, pose any problems for you, General Galland?"

"No," Galland said simply.

"I know the SS unit at Dachau can be counted upon," Cranz said. "And that leaves the Wehrmacht and the Navy. Boltitz?"

"There's a Navy Signals school at the air base at Fürstenfeldbruck," Boltitz said. "I'm not sure how large . . ."

"Why don't you call them after lunch and find out?" Cranz said.

Boltitz nodded.

"The Munich military garrison has the troops, obviously," Cranz said thoughtfully. "And now that I think about it, a quite good band. I'll get on the telephone to them."

"When is this going to happen?" Willi Grüner asked.

"Reichsmarschall Göring has made an aircraft available—a Junkers Ju-52. It should be here sometime today. It will take Korvettenkapitän Boltitz, Major von Wachtstein, me, and, if General Galland permits . . ." Cranz paused and looked at Galland, ". . . you to Cadiz to meet the *Océano Pacífico*."

Galland nodded. "Of course," he said.

"The remains of your father and Standartenführer Goltz will be flown here," Cranz went on. "The actual date and time of the interment ceremonies will depend on whether Reichsprotektor Himmler or Admiral Canaris, either or both, feel they can take the time from their duties to participate. Both, Hauptmann Grüner, really wish to do so."

Grüner nodded.

Major Freiherr Hans-Peter von Wachtstein thought: *This is insane.*

These people are insane.

Hundreds of thousands of German soldiers are in unmarked graves in Russia, hundreds of thousands more are in Russian POW enclosures because Unser Hermann failed on his promise to supply von Paulus by air.

On 19 November 1943, the Soviets had launched pincer

movements north and south of Stalingrad. By 23 January they had encircled General Friedrich von Paulus's 6th Army. German attempts to relieve and resupply von Paulus failed. Under orders from Adolf Hitler, von Paulus continued to fight on, but on 31 January 1943, von Paulus disobeyed Hitler and surrendered the last of his remaining (91,000) troops. The Soviets recovered 250,000 German and Romanian corpses in and around Stalingrad, and total Axis losses (Germans, Romanians, Italians, and Hungarians) were estimated at 800,000 dead.

And here we sit, at a table loaded with food and wine, served by orderlies in white jackets, talking about a funeral parade for two people, whose bodies we are going to fly here in an airplane desperately needed in Russia, so they can be buried in the shadow of a monument of a storm trooper who never heard a shot fired in anger.

These people are insane.

And they are taking Germany down with them.

XVII

[ONE]
Estancia San Pedro y San Pablo
Near Pila, Buenos Aires Province
0805 May 18, 1943

El Patrón of Estancia San Pedro y San Pablo, Don Cletus Frade, had left instructions with the butler, Antonio La Valle, that, following his morning ride, he wished to take breakfast at eight A.M. with Señora Frade in the gazebo in the formal garden. He had also specified, in some detail, what he wished to eat.

Señora Frade had left instructions with her maid that she

wished to be awakened at half past seven (which she frankly thought was an obscene hour to rise), in the belief that thirty minutes would give her time to perform her toilette and arrive at the gazebo in time to make sure her husband's wishes vis-à-vis his breakfast had been met.

At five minutes to eight, Señora Frade arrived at the gazebo, wearing a light blue dressing gown over a pink peignoir, her blond hair perfectly coiffured in a modest bun appropriate to her status as an expectant young matron. At the gazebo, she found everything to her satisfaction.

Two places had been set with silver and crystal on the central round table. There were two large silver pitchers, one containing coffee and the other tea. A smaller silver pitcher held cream. Crystal pitchers contained orange juice, grapefruit juice, and water. Just outside the gazebo, two portable grills had been set up, fueled by coals from the wood fire of the *parilla* in the kitchen. A cook was prepared to fry eggs, make toast, and broil a *bife de chorizo* for the master of the house. A housemaid stood by to serve.

It was, she thought, actually rather elegant.

When her husband rode into the formal garden on Julius Caesar, he was not at all elegant. He was wearing a red polo shirt, khaki trousers, a Stetson hat, and battered Western boots he had owned since he was sixteen and his feet had stopped growing, at which point a good pair of boots made by a Mexican boot maker was justified.

He was followed by Enrico Rodríguez, on a magnificent roan. Enrico was wearing the billowing shirt, trousers, wide-brimmed black hat, and wide leather belt of a gaucho. The stock of a Mauser 7mm cavalry-model carbine rested on his thigh, and a .45 ACP pistol was in his wide belt.

When Señora Frade examined her husband more closely, she saw that he, too, was armed. An old Colt six-shooter was stuck in his waistband (he had shown her the weapon with great pride; it had belonged to his grandfather, el Coronel Guillermo Alejandro, and it had been his "working gun"—whatever that meant), and he had what Señora thought of as another "cowboy gun" in a scabbard attached to Julius Caesar's saddle. This weapon, she had learned when her husband had found it in the estancia armory—with all the joy of a ten-year-old finding an electric train under his Christmas tree—was a Winchester Model 94 30.30 lever action.

One just like it—"my first high-power"—had been presented to Clete by his uncle Jim on his thirteenth birthday. This occasion had also been marked by "my first whitetail six-point buck." He had explained to her this meant a deer with an unusually large rack of horns.

Dorotéa Frade could not imagine a responsible adult making a present of a dangerous weapon to a thirteen-year-old, much less taking him out to slaughter a helpless animal with it the same day—and this provided her with yet another opportunity to remind herself that she had married a Texan, not an Argentine, and that a Texan could not be expected to behave like an Argentine.

Don Cletus Frade dismounted from Julius Caesar with what Dorotéa Frade thought was effortless grace, tied his reins to one of the supporting poles of the gazebo, and walked to his wife. "Goddamn, you're beautiful," he said, then kissed her.

Julius Caesar began to munch on the flowers that grew up on the supporting pole of the gazebo.

"We're going to need a place set for Enrico," Clete said.

"Oh, no, Señor Clete," Enrico said.

"I thought we had been over this," Clete said. "You're my best friend, right?"

"Sí, Señor."

"When I eat, my best friend eats," Clete said. "Get off that ugly nag and sit down."

Enrico looked at Dorotéa.

"Please, Enrico," Dorotéa said.

"Sí, Señora. Gracias."

"I'll have a small glass of grapefruit juice, please," Dorotéa ordered, "and a piece of toast. And tea with milk and two lumps of sugar, please."

Enrico ordered a *café cortado* and helped himself to a croissant.

"I don't understand how you people manage without a real breakfast," Clete announced as the maid served him orange juice, milk, the steak, two eggs fried sunny-side up, home-fried potatoes, and toast. "A good breakfast is the most important meal of the day."

Dorotéa glanced at Enrico, who rolled his eyes.

"What I'm going to do, baby," Clete announced, "is run some tests."

"What kind of tests?"

"I'm going to put in about twenty acres—eight hectares—"

"I know what an acre is, darling."

"—of corn. That's where I was this morning, looking at the soil. Enrico and I found a place. I don't know where I'm going to get the seed—good seed—but I'll deal with that somehow. And then, when the corn has come in, I'm going to segregate maybe two hundred, maybe three, of calves when they're weaned. There will be two groups of calves. One will eat nothing but grass. The other I'll start on corn and grass. We'll weigh them once a week."

"You're going to weigh three hundred calves once a week?" Dorotéa asked incredulously.

"And keep accurate records, to see if I'm right or not."

In his mind, Dorotéa thought, *the chances of his being wrong about this are about the same as those of the sun not setting this afternoon.*

Antonio appeared, carrying a telephone on a silver tray. "Pardon the interruption, Señor Clete. Are you at home to Señor Leibermann?"

Clete gave the question some thought before replying. "Sure," he said finally. "Why not? Plug it in."

Antonio plugged the telephone into a jack mounted on one of the supporting poles.

Clete, smiling smugly at Dorotéa, picked it up.

With the assistance of Chief Schultz, Clete had "fixed" the telephone service at the estancia. One "fix" was to install jacks all over the main house and the outbuildings, including the gazebo, and another was to replace the short cords that connected the instruments to the wall with cords at least four meters long.

It was no longer necessary to return to the house from the gazebo, for example, to take a telephone call. The telephone went to the gazebo.

Clete was proud of the improvements—just a little childishly proud, Dorotéa thought.

Dorotéa could hear both sides of the conversation.

"Hello, Milton," Clete said cheerfully into the mouthpiece. "Why do I suspect I'm not going to like this call?"

"I had hoped marriage would reduce your cynicism," Leibermann chuckled. "How was the wedding trip?"

"Compared to what?"

"What did I do, wake you up?"

"Actually no. I got up at first light and had a little ride on the pampas. I am now just finishing my breakfast. Until you called, I didn't think I had a care in the world."

"You fell off the horse?"

"I'm an Aggie, Milton. We don't fall off horses."

"Never?"

"Never," Clete said firmly. "So what's new, Milton?"

"There's a story making the rounds in Buenos Aires that Señor and Señora Frade, following their return from their wedding trip to Bariloche, are going to have a little "we're back" soiree tonight for their many friends."

"Why do I suspect that you suspect that my good señora and I, despite the stories making the rounds in Buenos Aires, could not find time to fit Bariloche into our busy social schedule?"

"Because by nature you are a suspicious cynic who fell off his horse before breakfast?"

Clete laughed heartily. "Then may I cynically suspect that you've mentioned the intimate little soiree my señora is having tonight—there won't be more than five thousand or so people here—because you would like to come?"

"I thought perhaps you didn't like me anymore," Leibermann said.

"My house is your house, Milton. I thought you understood that."

"I'd like to bring someone with me," Leibermann said.

"Male or female?"

"Male. The new assistant military attaché for air. I thought you would like to meet him. He tells me that he's a multi-engine instructor pilot."

"That's fascinating!" Clete said. "By all means, bring him. While he and I are exchanging lies about flying, you can share social notes with el Coronel Martín."

"You invited Bernardo, and you didn't invite me?"

"My Tío Juan suggested I should."

"Your Tío Juan will be there?"

"Of course."

"Thank you so much for thinking of me, Don Cletus."

"Don't mention it, Milton."

Clete was still smiling when he put the telephone back in its cradle.

"What was that all about?" Dorotéa asked. "And there will be no more than fifty people, not five thousand."

"I think Milton is bringing someone who can give me the time I need in the Lockheed," Clete said. "There's a new attaché for air at the American Embassy."

"You like him, don't you?" Dorotéa said, and went on without giving him a chance to reply. "It doesn't sound like it."

"Yeah, I like him," Clete said. "Don't you?"

"If you like him, I do," Dorotéa said, then changed the subject: "I really hope you can find time in your 'busy social schedule' to be here for lunch. At one sharp. Mother and Claudia—and most likely Alicia and Isabela—will be here."

"OK, baby," Clete said. "I'll be here, and I will even try to smile at Isabela."

[TWO]
The Airstrip
Estancia San Pedro y San Pablo
Near Pila, Buenos Aires Province
1240 18 May 1943

Clete didn't see Dorotéa and Alicia Carzino-Cormano standing by the hangar until he had almost reached the spot beside
the hangar where he was going to park the Lockheed
Lodestar.

And from the looks on both their faces, he knew something was wrong.

He very carefully turned the Lodestar around and went
through the procedure for shutting it down, and then got out
of the pilot's seat and started to walk through the cabin.

Dorotéa and Alicia were standing outside when he opened
the door. They were both dressed in sweaters and skirts, and
each wore a single strand of pearls. He had the idle thought
that both of them would look quite at home on the porch of a
Tulane sorority house.

"I was afraid for a moment you were going flying,"
Dorotéa said. It was an accusation. He had made the mistake
of telling her he wasn't really well qualified to fly the transport. To which her wifely response had been "then don't fly
it again until you are."

"With something this big," he explained patiently, "the
tires get flat on the bottom if it sits for a while. Since it's too
big to push, I had to start the engines. Since I had the
engines started—which is something else you have to do,
every couple of days, to keep a little oil circulating—I figured I might as well get some taxi practice. OK?"

She nodded her acceptance of the explanation, then asked:
"Can we talk in there?"

"I'll have to put the steps down," he thought aloud. He

was reluctant to use the electrically powered steps more than he had to. They were making a funny noise. He had no idea what it was, but he suspected that something in the mechanism was about to fail, and he didn't think there were replacement parts available in Argentina.

"Yes, darling, I guess you will," Dorotéa said, a little impatiently.

He found the switch, and the stairs began to unfold. He heard the funny noise again.

Dorotéa waved Alicia up the stairs, and she gave Clete's cheek the ritual kiss as she walked past him. Dorotéa passed him. He patted her buttocks.

"What's up?" he asked softly.

She didn't reply.

He followed her up the aisle.

Alicia had taken one of the seats on the left. Dorotéa slipped into the seat across the aisle.

He faced them, then squatted in the aisle. "What's up?"

Alicia sobbed and looked out the window.

"Alicia thinks she's in the family way," Dorotéa announced.

"Oh, shit!" Clete blurted, and then asked, "Are you sure?"

Alicia bobbed her head and put her hand to her mouth.

"She thinks it happened that night at the Alvear," Dorotéa said.

Clete had been married long enough to Dorotéa to understand what she was not saying: "If you hadn't put them together in your apartment in the Alvear, you stupid man, this wouldn't have happened." And he had a selfish thought: *My God, Claudia will kill me!*

"Does your mother know?" Clete asked, realizing it was a stupid question even as the words left his mouth.

If Claudia knew about this, Alicia wouldn't be here.

Alicia turned to look at him and shook her head. "Cletus, what am I going to do?" she asked plaintively.

"The first thing you're *not* going to do is tell your mother," he said, "until we work this out. Can you handle that?"

"Work this out"? What the hell am I talking about? This is a goddamn problem without a solution if I ever heard one.

Alicia nodded her head. "Will Peter be coming back, Cletus?" she then asked.

"For all we know, he may be on his way back right now," Clete said.

On the other hand, they may have already stood him in front of a firing squad, or whatever those bastards do to a traitor, or someone they suspect might be.

"I wanted him to go to Brazil," Alicia said, softly. "If he was in Brazil, I could have gone to him there."

And if he had gone to Brazil, the Nazis would by now have shot his father.

"That wasn't an option, honey," Clete said gently.

"Can we find out when he's coming back? If he's coming back?"

"I'll try," he said.

German Embassy? Good afternoon. This is Major Cletus Frade of the OSS. I wonder if you'd be good enough to tell me if Major Hans-Peter von Wachtstein is coming back to Argentina? And if so, when can I expect to see him?

Welner! Can Welner help?

"Honey, is Father Welner coming today?"

"You think he could help?" Dorotéa replied. "I didn't think of him."

"I don't want him to know," Alicia said.

"He's going to have to know eventually," Clete said. "He can be trusted." He turned to Dorotéa. "Is he coming, baby?"

"Of course," Dorotéa said.

Alicia sobbed.

"If your mother sees you crying," Clete said, "she's going to wonder why."

"Cletus is right, Alicia," Dorotéa said. "You're going to have to act as if nothing—"

"How can I do that?" Alicia challenged.

"We'll work this out," Clete said. "You're just going to have to hang tight until we do."

She looked into his eyes, then nodded her head.

She trusts me. Goddamn it!

"We'll go back to the house," Dorotéa said. "So you can wash your face. Cletus will come up with something."

Is she saying that to make Alicia feel good? Or is she, too, placing faith in me that's absolutely misplaced?

He stood up.

Alicia raised herself out of the seat. "Thank you, Cletus," she said, and then turned and walked down the aisle.

Dorotéa stood up and met his eyes for a moment but said nothing, then followed Alicia down the aisle.

Clete followed them to the door, watched them walk away from the Lockheed, and then flipped the switch that activated the electrical motor for the stairs. They began to retract, with the funny noise again, but finally came in place. He exhaled audibly and jumped to the ground.

"Shit!" he said.

[THREE]
Gendarmeria Nacional Post 1088
Route Nacionale No. 2
Near Pila, Buenos Aires Province
1530 18 May 1943

Sargento Manuel Lascano abruptly braked the blue 1939 Dodge sedan. This act awakened el Coronel Bernardo Martín, who had been dozing in the front seat beside him. Martín looked out the window.

Fifty meters down Route 2 was a Gendarmeria Nacional Post. The two-lane highway divided around an island on which sat a guard shack. On the right of the road was a two-story administrative building. Martín knew the plan; he'd been inside many such buildings. Offices and a detention cell occupied the first floor, and the second was a barracks for the dozen or so men who manned the post.

There were three gendarmeros on the island. A sargento

was signaling the Dodge to stop with a somewhat imperiously raised palm. This could mean any number of things. It could mean, for example, that the Gendarmeria Nacional sargento was bored and was stopping them for something to do. Or else he had had a fight with his wife and was looking for someone on whom to vent his unhappiness.

But probably it meant that Lascano had been caught speeding. The Gendarmeria Nacional sometimes hid men in roadside ditches a kilometer apart, who timed how long it took a car or truck to cover the kilometer. Speeders were reported to the next post, where offenders were pulled over and issued citations.

There were two kinds of speeding. Manuel could have been going like hell, say 120–130 kph (75–80 mph), which was really a bit much for Route 2 in this area, or he could have been going just a few kilometers over the absurd posted speed limit of 75 kph (45 mph).

Gendarmeria Nacional road checkpoints were all over the country; this was the third they'd passed since leaving Buenos Aires. El Coronel Martín regarded not only the checkpoints but indeed the Gendarmeria Nacional itself as a monumental waste of effort and money.

Though organized on military lines, the Gendarmeria was a law-enforcement agency. They were policemen, in other words, who dressed like soldiers. But they were not very good policemen. On one hand, they didn't have the requisite training. On the other, they felt they were far too good to stop a man who was beating his wife, for example, or who was selling farmers tickets in a nonexistent raffle.

Manuel stopped the Dodge and rolled the window down.

The Gendarmeria Nacional sargento saluted. "Buenas tardes," he said. "Documents, please."

The saluting also annoyed Coronel Martín—as it did many other Army and Navy officers—who felt the salute was a greeting of mutual recognition between warriors, and should not be rendered by a policeman to a civilian who was about to be cited for a traffic violation.

Perhaps for that reason, though he usually displayed his

BIS credentials reluctantly, Martín found himself reaching into the breast pocket of his well-tailored, faintly plaided suit for his papers. Agents of the Bureau of Internal Security were immune to arrest by any law-enforcement or military agency.

He leaned across Sargento Lascano.

This earned him another salute from the Gendarmeria Nacional sargento—a much crisper salute than the first. "If you will be so good as to wait a moment, Señor," the sargento said, and trotted across the road to the Administration Building.

Lascano looked at Martín, who held his hands up helplessly.

Martín was tempted to tell Lascano to just drive off, but there might be a reason why they'd been stopped.

That appeared a moment later.

Commisario Santiago Nervo, Chief of the Special Investigations Division of the Policía Federal, emerged from the building, leaned down, put his hands on the window frame, and smiled. "Shame on you, mi Coronel. *One hundred thirty-five* in a seventy-five-kilometer zone."

"Been promoted, have you, Santiago? Out here catching speeders! Before you know it, they'll let you wear a uniform."

Nervo laughed. "Before I throw you in a cell, Bernardo, I'll buy you a cup of coffee."

"You are so kind," Martín said.

Nervo pointed to the parking area beside the Administration Building and got out of the car.

Martín followed him into the building, where Nervo was considerably less jovial to the Gendarmeria Nacional lieutenant in charge. "El Coronel and I will require coffee," he announced, "and we do not wish to be disturbed."

"Sí, Señor."

"Would you be good enough to get my driver a cup of coffee, too, Lieutenant?" Martín asked courteously.

"Sí, mi Coronel."

Nervo waved Martín into an office with OFFICER COM-

MANDING lettered on the door, and then onto a couch. He sat at the other end of the couch and offered Martín a cigarette. Martín held up his hand to decline.

The sargento who had stopped Martín's Dodge carried in a tray with coffee cups and a thermos of coffee.

Nervo nodded at him

"You're very kind, Sargento," Martín said.

"Close the door as you leave," Nervo ordered. He poured coffee for Martín, who declined milk and sugar.

"What a pleasant coincidence meeting you here, of all places," Martín said.

"Well, *I* don't get invited to the estancias of the high and mighty," Nervo said. "I have to park by the side of the road and watch them drive by."

My God, is he really jealous?

"What can I do for you, Santiago?" Martín asked.

"I would like your honest opinion about a political matter. Make that opinions, political matters."

"Certainly. Ask away."

"Ramírez has appointed Perón Minister of Labor."

"Yes, he has."

"Why?"

"Why not? Juan Domingo Perón is a very capable man."

"Why isn't he Minister of Defense?"

"General Farrell is Minister of Defense," Martín said. "Nobody told you?"

"Don't fence with me, please, this is serious," Nervo said.

"Perón doesn't have to be at the Ministry of Defense so long as Farrell is there. Farrell does exactly—no more and no less—what Perón tells him to do."

"Why does Perón want to be Minister of Labor?"

"Because he wants to be president of the Republic. The Minister of Labor can do nice things for the laboring class, who vote. What can the Army and the Navy do for the voters?"

"You think Perón will make it? Become the president?"

"Yes, I do."

"And if he does, will we get into the war?"

"I don't think so. I can't believe he could be that stupid."

"Meaning?"

"Meaning the English and the Americans are going to win the war, and I think that Perón knows that—no matter how much he would wish otherwise."

Nervo nodded. "We have finally found something we agree upon, Bernardo," he said.

"We agree upon many things, Santiago, and you know it."

"Perón will be at Estancia San Pedro y San Pablo today?" Martín nodded.

"Is that why you're going out there?"

"I was *invited* out there," Martín said.

"What's that all about?"

"I don't really know," Martín said. "But it will give me a chance to see who's there, won't it? And maybe even see who's talking to whom, and with a little bit of luck, hear what is said."

"And will Perón like that?"

"Perón has Don Cletus Frade calling him 'Tío Juan.' "

"You're kidding!"

"I am not. I have the feeling that Juan Domingo will be delighted to see me. The more Argentine friends Frade makes, the better his Tío Juan likes it."

"Isn't that letting the fox into the chicken coop?"

"By now, everyone knows that Frade is in the OSS. I don't think he will be told anything he should not be told."

"Even by his Tío Juan?"

"That's really in my half of the football field, Santiago, but I'll answer you anyway: No. Whatever else he might be, Juan Domingo Perón is both intelligent and a patriot."

Nervo paused, considered the reply, then nodded. "Speaking of whatever else an unnamed gentleman might be, are you aware of the new lady friend?"

"He sent the other one home to Mommy?"

"No. Señorita Maria-Teresa Alsina will probably celebrate her fifteenth birthday in the Arenales apartment."

The two exchanged glances of wonderment and contempt.

"How old is the new one?" Martín asked.

"A little older, twenty-two or thereabouts. I have it reliably that he is looking for another apartment for her. When I have the address, I'll give it to you."

"The new one has a name?"

"Her name is Eva Duarte. Blonde. She works at Radio Belgrano."

"You're sure about them?"

"Of course, it could be my cynical mind, but the lady has spent the last two nights in the Frade place on Libertador."

"What do we know about her?"

"Not much. She's from the country. I'm working on it. All I know now is that she is a very friendly lady if she thinks you can do her any good. You don't know the name?"

"I'll check. We'll exchange notes?"

Nervo nodded.

"Anything else?" Martín asked.

"If you learn anything interesting today?"

"You'll be the first to know."

Martín got up and extended his hand to Nervo. Nervo held on to it.

"What would happen if it got out that Perón likes little girls?" he asked.

"Why should it get out? As far as I'm concerned, if it doesn't endanger the nation's security . . ."

"If it got out, who do you think Perón would blame?"

"Well, *I* would blame you, Santiago, because *I'm* not going to tell anybody. And I trust the very few of my people who know to keep their mouths shut."

"It's something to think about, isn't it?"

"With a little bit of luck, maybe he'll marry the blonde."

"I think if the blonde got out, he'd be in trouble. She is not some virgin of good family."

"But she's twenty-something, you said. Maybe that would make the difference between a caballero with an eye for the ladies, and a dirty old man?"

"Interesting question," Nervo said, and finally let go of Martín's hand. "Drive slow, mi Coronel. Respect the nation's laws."

"How could I do otherwise, with police officers like you on the job?" Martín asked, then walked out of the room.

[FOUR]
El Estudio Privado del Patrón
La Casa Grande
Estancia San Pedro y San Pablo
Near Pila, Buenos Aires Province
1605 18 May 1943

As the Reverend Kurt Welner, S.J., walked through the door with a smile, Cletus Frade began to push himself out of his overstuffed, dark-red leather armchair. The Jesuit motioned for Cletus to stay where he was. The two shook hands, then Welner sat on the edge of another overstuffed, but not matching, leather armchair. This one was smaller, green, and sat closer to the floor.

"Yes, thank you, I will," he said, reaching for the bottle of Merlot sitting on the low table between the chairs.

"Mi vino es su vino, Padre," Clete said. "And yes, I think I will have another drop." He leaned forward and shoved his glass toward the priest, who topped it off.

"This is new," Welner said, indicating the green chair.

"Dorotéa put it in here."

"How does Dorotéa feel about this?" Welner asked, waving his hand around the room that had been described as Coronel Jorge Guillermo Frade's Shrine To His Son.

"I don't know," Clete said. "So far she hasn't suggested we turn it into a nursery."

"And you?"

Clete met his eyes. "I don't know. Sometimes I'm . . . what? Embarrassed . . . and sometimes it makes me a little sad, thinking of all the hours my father spent in here because my grandfather was such a sonofabitch."

"Maybe it would be more useful as a nursery," Welner said.

"On the other hand, it's the only room on the estancia where I know nobody's going to come through the door."

"Your father made it rather plain this was his, period."

"Did he let you in?"

"Not often. Usually when you had done something that made him proud of you. He'd show it to me before he had it framed, or put it into one of the scrapbooks."

They looked at each other.

"I suppose it's too much to hope that I am being allowed into the sanctum sanctorum to hear your confession—"

"Don't hold your breath." Clete chuckled.

"—but something is on your mind."

"Oh, yeah," Clete said. "Tell me about this business of what I tell you as a priest—"

"As your priest, Cletus."

"—going no further. Does it apply if I tell you something about somebody else?"

"That would depend," Welner said.

"I was afraid you would say something like that. Yes or no, Padre?"

"I can give you my word as a man, as your friend. You have it."

"Alicia is with child," Clete said.

Welner shook his head sadly. "The German?" he asked.

Clete nodded.

"How far is she along?"

"She thinks it happened that night in my apartment in the Alvear."

"When you played Cupid?"

"You really know how to go for the nuts, don't you?"

"I take your meaning, even if I never heard it phrased so graphically before. 'Go for the nuts.' I'll have to remember that one."

"We Episcopals don't believe we automatically go to hell because we tell a priest to go to hell."

Welner smiled. "That would depend, of course, on the circumstances. Whether you really wish for me to spend eternity in the fires and agony of hell, or whether that is simply

a paraphrase of 'fuck you,' in which case it would be a cru-
dity, not a curse."

Clete laughed.

Welner took a sip of his wine. "Very nice," he said, then
added, "You do bear a certain degree of responsibility,
wouldn't you say?"

"That occurred to me. And, of course, to Dorotéa. As it
will to Claudia when she finds out. Alicia's not blaming me."

"Claudia doesn't know?"

"Alicia, Dorotéa, and me, that's all."

"Claudia will have to know sooner or later."

"Dorotéa told me sometimes women miss a period, particularly if they're upset. This may be a false alarm."

"Is that what Alicia is hoping?"

"It's what Dorotéa and I are hoping. Alicia is convinced
she's pregnant."

"You want me to go to Claudia, is that it?"

"Maybe later. Not yet. What I was hoping you could do is
find out what's happened to Peter."

"I don't think I understand."

"Peter is suspected of being involved in what happened at
the beach of Samborombón Bay."

"In still other words, he is suspected of being a traitor. Is
he?"

"Another shot to the nuts, Padre," Clete said. "I can't
answer that."

"You don't have to; the answer is in your eyes. But I
don't understand what you want me to do, what you think I
could do."

"Don't you have some back-channel communication with
Germany? With other Jesuits in Germany? People who
could ask questions and get straight answers?"

"What questions?"

" 'Is Peter von Wachtstein dead?' is the most important
one."

"You think that's likely?"

"I think the possibility has to be considered," Clete said.

"There is a much easier way to get what you want done

than using my channels," Welner said. "I'm surprised you haven't thought of it."

"I don't understand," Clete said.

"Tío Juan," Welner said.

"Perón? How the hell could he help?" Clete asked, and the answer came to him even before Welner replied.

"The Germans think he's important to them," Welner said. "Von Deitzberg's apology to him about your father seems proof of that."

"They think he's going to be el Presidente," Clete agreed thoughtfully. "You think they'd tell him about von Wacht stein?"

"His interest in von Wachtstein might even . . . be helpful."

"Christ, I hate to go to him," Clete said, and then thought of something else: "And if I do, he'll know Peter and I—"

"Not necessarily," Welner replied. "You heard of Alicia's . . . problem . . . from your wife, her dear friend. And, as your father's son, despite the natural animosity you feel toward an enemy officer, you feel obliged to help a young woman who is like a sister to you."

"Jesus! You are devious, aren't you?" He chuckled and added: "Thank God!"

"Ignoring the blasphemy, my son, I will accept that as a compliment. Or—what is it you say—'a left-handed compliment'?"

"You think my Tío Juan will help?"

"I think he will if you can force yourself to say 'Tío Juan' with a shade less sarcasm."

"When necessary, Father, I can—here's another Americanism for you—charm the balls off a brass monkey."

Welner laughed.

"And if Tío Juan can't—or won't—help, then what?" Clete asked.

"I'll do what I can, of course."

"And what do we do if . . . things have gone wrong with von Wachtstein and he won't be coming back?"

"There are a number of young men of good family . . . a suitable marriage can be arranged. Not only is she an attractive young woman, but she will ultimately own half of Estancia Santo Catalina."

"Jesus, that's awful!"

"Yes, it is," Welner agreed. "The best thing that can be said about a marriage like that is that it's in the best interests of the child."

Clete shook his head and reached for the bottle of Merlot.

[FIVE]
La Casa Grande
Estancia San Pedro y San Pablo
Near Pila, Buenos Aires Province
1905 18 May 1943

With a glass of Merlot in his hand, Don Cletus Frade stood at the window of the cloakroom looking through the slats of the blind at the drive where the cars of his guests would arrive for the reception. The drill, as he thought of it, was that when a car pulled up before the house, one of the servants would approach it, open the door, and lead the guests into the house and into the small sitting, which was across the foyer hall from the cloakroom.

There they would be greeted by a reception line of women. At the head of the line would be Señora Dorotéa Mallín de Frade. Beside her would be Señora Claudia Carzino-Cormano; then Señora Pamela Holworth-Talley de Mallín; and then the Señoritas Carzino-Cormano, Alicia and Isabela.

Though Señora Beatrice Frade de Duarte naturally felt entitled to a prominent place in the reception line—she had been born and raised in the Casa Grande—it was the unspoken hope of everyone concerned that her arrival would be delayed (either inadvertently, or intentionally by her husband) until the guests had passed through the reception line and gathered in the large sitting for cocktails and Champagne.

That was not to happen. The very first car to arrive was

the black Rolls-Royce of Señor Humberto Duarte, and Beatrice was out of the backseat before the chauffeur could open his door.

"Shit," Clete muttered, and put his glass on the windowsill. Then he had a second thought. Beatrice's early arrival might disturb the women—God alone knew what she would do or say in the reception line—but he needed to talk to Humberto.

He walked onto the veranda and allowed himself to be emotionally greeted by his aunt.

"You look so elegant, Cletus!" she cried happily. "So much like your father, may he be resting in peace with your sainted mother and all the angels."

Clete was wearing a tweed sports coat, a checkered shirt, a blue silk foulard, gabardine breeches, and glistening British-style riding boots. Their reception was informal, Dorotéa had announced, and the riding costume would set the proper tone.

After examining himself in a full-length mirror in his dressing, Clete had come to two conclusions. First, he looked *like the Duke of Whateverthehell about to have tea and crumpets—whatever the hell a crumpet is—with the Duchess of Windsor.* The second, *truth to tell, Cletus Frade, you do look pretty spiffy.*

"And you are as beautiful as ever, Beatrice," he said. "Dorotéa's still dressing."

"Then I will go to her," Beatrice announced, and marched into the house.

Clete and Humberto embraced with genuine affection.

"You do, you know, look elegant," Humberto said.

"In Texas, we have a name for people who wear these things," Clete said, pointing at the foulard.

"Please don't tell me what it is." Humberto chuckled. "And, as you may have noticed, Cletus, you are not in Texas."

"Have I ever," Clete said, and adding, "We have to talk." He led Humberto into the cloakroom and closed the door after them.

"Something's wrong?" Humberto asked.

Clete walked to a table on which sat an array of bottles and glasses. "You want wine, or something stronger?" he asked.

"A little wine, tinto, please," Humberto said. "I think it may be a long day."

Clete poured Merlot in two glasses and handed one to Humberto, then stationed himself where he could look through the slats in the blind. He glanced out, and then faced Humberto. "Alicia's in the family way," he said.

"Oh, my God!" Humberto said softly. "Peter's the father?"

Clete nodded. "I found out a couple of hours ago."

"Does Claudia know?"

"Just Dorotéa, me, now you, and in a few minutes, Juan Domingo Perón."

"Why him?"

"Add Welner to the list," Clete said. "He thinks my Tío Juan's influence with the Germans may be helpful."

"Alicia went to Father Kurt?"

"I did," Clete said then. "Oh, shit, I forgot about them."

Humberto walked to the window. Four men were getting out of a 1942 Buick Super with diplomatic tags. Three of them were in the pink-and-green uniform of U.S. Army officers, all with the golden rope of military attachés hanging from the epaulets. The third man was in a somewhat rumpled suit. Humberto recognized two of the officers and the civilian. They were Milton Leibermann, "Legal Attaché of the American Embassy"; Captain Maxwell Ashton III; and Lieutenant Anthony J. Pelosi. The third officer he had never seen before. "Who's the officer?" Humberto asked.

"I don't know his name. He's the new military attaché. Milton thinks I should meet him."

"And meet him in public," Humberto said.

Clete shrugged to indicate he had no idea of Leibermann's motives.

"You were telling me what Father Kurt had to say," Humberto said.

"I asked him if he could find out what's going on with Peter von Wachtstein," Clete said. "He suggested Perón would be useful. I told you about this von Deitzberg character bringing the apologies of the German officer corps for murdering my father. . . ."

"What do you think has happened to Peter?"

"I don't like to think about that," Clete said. "They obviously suspect he was involved with what happened at Samborombón Bay. That's enough to put him in front of a firing squad, without even getting into the rest of it."

The door opened without a knock. Clete glowered at it and then smiled. Señora Dorotéa Mallín de Frade, wearing a simple black dress and a double strand of pearls that had belonged to Clete's grandmother, entered the room. "Tío Juan is five minutes out," she announced.

Enrico had stationed gauchos near the road from Pila to the estancia with orders to notify him the moment el Coronel Perón's car appeared on the road. By galloping across the pampas, a gaucho could reach the Casa Grande at least five minutes before an automobile could do so by road.

She walked to Humberto and kissed him. "He told you?"

Humberto nodded.

"You think Tío Juan will be able to help?"

"I tend to think Father Kurt is usually right," Humberto said.

Dorotéa went to Clete and adjusted the foulard. "Now you look fine," she said. "Go easy on the wine, darling."

Clete exhaled audibly. "I hope I can charm the sonofabitch," he said, then added: "You haven't said anything to Alicia?"

"Of course not," she said.

She leaned upward, kissed him rather chastely on the lips, and left the room.

Almost exactly five minutes later, the 1939 Packard 280 touring car provided by the Republic of Argentina for the use of its Minister of War rolled majestically up before the Casa Grande and stopped. The chauffeur jumped out and ran around the front, almost succeeding in reaching the rear passenger door before Sargento Rudolpho Gomez, Argentine Cavalry, Retired, who had been waiting on the veranda.

The passengers in the rear seat got out. Everyone—the chauffeur, Rudolpho, Minister of War General de Division

Edelmiro Farrell, Minister of Labor Coronel Juan Domingo
Perón—was in civilian clothing, and the canvas roof of the
enormous Packard was up; but Clete had no trouble envi-
sioning the roof down, everybody in uniform, and Farrell
and Perón standing up in the backseat, hanging on to the
chrome of the rear-seat windshield and trooping the line of
the Húsares de Pueyrredón.

Rodolfo led them into the house, and a moment later, the
door to the cloakroom opened. "Patrón," Rudolpho barked,
"el General Farrell and el Coronel Perón."

Clete walked across the cloakroom. "A sus órdenes, mi
General," he said. "Thank you for coming."

Farrell spread his arms wide. "Ah, Cletus," he said, "thank
you for including me."

They shook hands.

Clete turned to Perón. "Tío Juan," he said. They embraced
and went through the kissing ritual of intimate males. The
touch of Perón's mouth on Clete's cheeks made him uncomfortable, but he forced himself to return the intimacy.

"My boy," Perón said, patting Cletus's back.

Farrell kissed Humberto's cheeks—*pro forma,* Clete
decided; there was no lip contact—and they each spoke the
other's Christian name.

"What are we doing in here?" Perón asked.

"Tío Juan," Clete said. "With your permission, I want to
introduce you and General Farrell to an old Texas custom."

"Which is?" Perón asked, smiling.

"We call it 'cutting the dust of the trail,' " Clete said.

He led them to the table with the array of bottles. He
picked up two glasses half full of whiskey, handed them to
Farrell and Perón, and then picked up two more, handing
one to Humberto and raising the other one. "Welcome to
Estancia San Pedro y San Pablo," he said.

"I think I like your custom," Farrell said, and drained his
glass.

"I am pleased, mi General," Clete said.

Perón chuckled. "And the Champagne, Cletus?" he asked,
pointing at the open bottle in a cooler.

"The dust of the trail having been cut," Clete said, "you

now can pick up the Champagne glasses and carry them into the small sitting to join the ladies. And if the ladies presume you have cut the dust of the trail with nothing stronger than Champagne . . ." Farrell and Perón both laughed. "On the other hand, if the dust is still thick in your throats . . . it is a long ride from Buenos Aires." Clete picked up a bottle of scotch.

"Now that you mention it, Cletus," Perón said, holding his glass out.

Cletus refilled his glass.

"Does everyone get this treatment?" Farrell asked.

"Sargento Gomez has a very short list," Clete said, "of those he suspects have dusty throats."

Humberto took Farrell's arm and led him to the window so he could see Gomez at work.

Clete went to Perón and touched the sleeve of his dark blue double-breasted suit. "Tío Juan," he said softly. "I have a problem. Can I talk to you about it?"

"Of course," Perón said. "Of course you can, Cletus. We will make the time."

"Thank you," Clete said. "Perhaps now?"

Peron looked at him and then nodded. "Edelmiro," he said, and when Farrell turned to look at him, went on: "Why don't you and Humberto go in to the ladies? I need a moment alone with Cletus."

That was an order, and he called Farrell by his first name. Colonels don't normally call generals by their first names. I guess that establishes the pecking order, doesn't it?

"Of course," Farrell said.

When they had gone, Perón looked at Cletus.

"I don't know where else to go with this, Tío Juan," Cletus said.

"I am touched that you are coming to me, Cletus. How may I help?"

"I learned today that Alicia Carzino-Cormano is with child," Clete said.

"My God! Yours?"

You filthy-minded bastard!

"Tío Juan, I have come to look on Alicia as a sister."

"Then whose?"

"I can tell you in absolute confidence," Clete said.

"Of course."

"The father is the German officer von Wachtstein."

Perón took a long moment to think that over. "I was not aware they had . . . become so close," he said finally.

"The dirty sonofabitch!" Clete said. "Taking advantage of a decent girl like that."

Perón smiled tolerantly. "There are those, Cletus, who would say the same thing of you," he said, and chuckled. "Your wife's father, for example."

"That was different," Clete said with what he hoped was just the proper amount of indignation and embarrassment.

"I happen to know Major von Wachtstein better than you do, Cletus. And I can see why Alicia was attracted to him. He's very much the same kind of young man as you. In different circumstances, I'm sure that you would become friends."

"With that Nazi sonofabitch?" Clete said. "Never!"

"Major von Wachtstein is an honorable man," Perón said. "A highly decorated officer from an ancient German family of officers. Did you know that his father is a teniente general?"

"No, and I really don't care."

"I happen to know that Teniente General von Wachtstein is an honorable man, Cletus. Just as honorable, just as decent, as your father. Blood tells, Cletus. There is absolutely no doubt in my mind that when Major von Wachtstein learns of this situation—I presume he *doesn't* know?"

"According to what Alicia told Dorotéa, he doesn't know."

"When he *does* know, I am sure that he will behave as honorably as you did when you learned the consequences—forgive me for saying this, Cletus—of allowing your lust to overcome your good sense."

"I wish, Tío Juan, that I shared your confidence in that bastard's sense of honor."

"He is not a bastard, Cletus," Perón said. "And I am sure

that he will be as anxious as you were to ensure that the product of his indiscretion will not be a bastard either."

"He's in Germany, as I guess you know. Alicia doesn't even have an address to write to him."

Perón thought that over. "Does Claudia know?"

"Not yet," Clete said.

"I think the thing to do about that is to say nothing to her until I have a chance to talk to Generalmajor von Deitzberg. Perhaps to Ambassador von Lutzenberger as well, but certainly to von Deitzberg. He's a soldier, and will understand. And he is very highly placed in Germany. I'm sure he will be willing to help."

"That would be wonderful," Clete said.

And if von Deitzberg tells you to go fuck yourself, then what?

"Do you think you could find out when the bastard's coming back to Argentina?" Clete asked.

"You have your father's weaknesses as well as his strengths. He had great difficulty controlling his anger. I would be grateful if you would stop calling Major von Wachtstein a bastard."

"Sorry," Clete said.

"It's too late to do anything about it tonight," Perón said. "But I will call von Deitzberg tomorrow and ask him to lunch."

"And you really think he will be willing to help?"

"I'm sure he will," Perón said. "As soon as I have talked to him, I'll call and tell you what he said."

"I don't know how to thank you," Clete said.

"No thanks are necessary. We're family. Not only you and I, but by extension, Claudia and Alicia as well. Your father loved them as his own."

"I know."

"And now, Cletus," Perón said, affectionately putting his arm around Cletus's shoulder. "I think we should join your guests. Your Tío Juan will do whatever he can."

[SIX]
La Casa Grande
Estancia San Pedro y San Pablo
Near Pila, Buenos Aires Province
1930 18 May 1943

Clete found Milton Leibermann, Maxwell Ashton, Tony Pelosi, and the new assistant military attaché for air standing together against the wall of the large sitting. Coronel Bernardo Martín was with them. They all held glasses of Champagne.

"Ah, our host," Leibermann said. "I was beginning to wonder where you were, Don Cletus."

"I was having a private word, actually, with Coronel Perón," Clete said. "I'm so glad you could make it, Milton." He switched to Spanish, and smiled at Martín. "And you, too, mi Coronel."

"So good of you and Señora de Frade to have me, Major Frade," Martín said.

"I thought we'd already had a little chat about your use of my former military title," Clete said.

"And so we have. My apologies, Don Frade. I seem to have trouble remembering that."

"Cletus, may I introduce Colonel Dick Almond, our new assistant military attaché for air?" Leibermann said in English.

Clete by then had had time to run his eyes over Almond—a tall, sharp-featured man he guessed was in his early thirties—and over the ribbons and insignia pinned to his tunic. There were a Distinguished Flying Cross, a Purple Heart, and ribbons indicating he had served in both the Pacific and European Theaters of Operation. There were other ribbons Clete didn't recognize, but the star above the shield of his pilot's wings he did.

It was the badge of an Air Corps senior pilot, awarded for flying so many years and/or for so many hours in the air. There were no comparable wings in the Marine Corps. A second lieutenant fresh from Pensacola wore the same golden wings as the two-star chief of Marine Aviation, who had been flying longer than the lieutenant was old.

Nevertheless, Clete liked what he saw.

This guy has been around.

"Welcome to Argentina and Estancia San Pedro y San Pablo, Colonel," Clete said as they shook hands.

"It's very kind of you to have me, Señor Frade," Almond said in very good Spanish. "And actually, it's *lieutenant* colonel."

"I haven't been out of the Marine Corps that long, Colonel," Clete replied in Spanish. "And—my memory being better than my friend Coronel Martín's—I still remember the difference between an eagle and a silver oak leaf."

Martín laughed good-naturedly.

Clete put his arm around Ashton's shoulders and shook Tony's hand.

"And is one permitted to ask 'how was the honeymoon'?" Leibermann asked.

"One is permitted to ask, Milton, but only a goddamn fool would answer."

Leibermann laughed.

"I'm sure you have much to talk about," Martín said. "So I will—what is it they say?—circulate?"

"Don't let me run you off, Coronel," Clete said.

Martín ignored the comment, shook Almond's hand, told him he was sure they would see one another again, and walked away.

"I was telling Dick that Martín is very good at what he does," Leibermann said.

"Oh, yes," Clete said. "Whatever you do, Colonel, don't underestimate Coronel Martín."

"I try not to underestimate anyone, Señor Frade," Almond said. "May I ask you a question?"

"As long as it's not about my honeymoon."

"The last place I expected to see a Lockheed Lodestar is on a dirt strip in Argentina."

"I think you'll be surprised by many things down here, Colonel," Clete said. "You're familiar with the Lodestar?"

"As a matter of fact, last month, I flew one from the States to Brazil—our air base at Pôrto Alegre. You know it?"

"I know it's there."

"They're nice airplanes," Almond said.

"Is that what you've been doing? Ferry pilot?"

"No, actually, I was going through the attaché course in Washington before coming here, when a brigadier general I never heard of before or since called me up, asked if I was current in the Lodestar, and when I told him I was—I'd been flying brass around the Pacific in one—told me I was going to ferry one to Brazil the next morning. So I flew one to Pôrto Alegre, parked it, and they put me on the next C-54 headed for the States. I never got an explanation."

He either suspects that's the Lodestar he flew to Brazil, or knows it is. But I don't think he's going to ask.

"You didn't get a DFC flying brass around," Clete challenged.

"I've got some P-38 time, too," Almond said. "I like to think of myself as a fighter pilot."

"We were getting an Air Corps P-38 squadron on Guadalcanal just when I left."

"Then we apparently just missed each other," Almond said. "I made three missions off Fighter One, took a chunk of shrapnel strafing a freighter, and got sent home."

"And that's where you got the Purple Heart?"

"And the DFC. The freighter blew up."

Clete snatched a glass of Champagne from a tray in the hand of a passing maid. "I wonder what the boys on Fighter One are drinking?" he asked.

"Warm Kool-Aid," Almond said. "War is hell, isn't it?"

"I've got a few hours in that Lodestar," Clete said. "But I need about twenty hours with a good IP."

"You're serious?"

"Absolutely," Clete said.

"Hell, I'm available, Señor Frade."

"I owe you, Milton," Clete said.

"It's nothing, Don Cletus," Leibermann said with a smile.

XVIII

[ONE]
Office of the Director, Abwehr Intelligence
Berlin
1425 22 May 1943

"Korvettenkapitän Boltitz, Herr Admiral," Admiral Wilhelm Canaris's aide announced.

Canaris signaled Boltitz to enter. Boltitz took six steps inside the office, came to attention, clicked his heels, and said, "Good afternoon, Herr Admiral."

"I expected you earlier," Canaris replied, and pointed to the upholstered chair in front of his desk. "We are expected by Himmler at four-thirty."

"The aircraft was delayed, Herr Admiral."

"I didn't ask for an explanation," Canaris said, then: "You came here directly from Templehof? Then you missed your lunch, Boltitz?"

"It's not important, Sir."

"I didn't ask if you thought it was important," Canaris said.

"I have not had lunch, Sir."

Canaris nodded. "Neither have I," Canaris said. "The brain requires sustenance, a fact I frequently forget."

Boltitz didn't reply.

The door opened.

"Herr Admiral?" Canaris's aide asked.

"One, I thought I asked you to remind me to eat at twelve o'clock."

"I did, Herr Admiral. The Herr Admiral's response was 'Later. Not now.'"

"Two, get Boltitz and me something to eat. Sandwiches and milk and coffee will do, as long as we can have it in five minutes."

"Jawohl, Herr Admiral."

"Three, ask Fregattenkapitän von und zu Waching to come in."

"Jawohl, Herr Admiral."

Fregattenkapitän Otto von und zu Waching appeared in Canaris's office less than two minutes later. When Karl Boltitz started to get out of his chair, von und zu Waching waved him back into it.

"Have you had your lunch, Otto?" Canaris asked.

"Yes, Sir."

"Boltitz and I have not," Canaris said. As if on cue, a white-jacketed steward appeared with a tray of sandwiches.

The aide had them waiting outside; there's no way they could have been prepared this quickly.

Canaris signaled for the tray to be laid on his desk in front of Boltitz, and then for Boltitz to help himself.

"Thank you, Herr Admiral."

The first bite of the *leberwurst mit sempf* was in his mouth, but he had not had time to chew when Canaris ordered, "Begin with the master of the *Océano Pacífico,* Boltitz."

He saw that I was chewing. Is this a reproof for thanking him?

Nearly choking with the effort, he managed to quickly swallow the liverwurst. "Kapitän de Banderano," he reported, "stated very clearly that von Wachtstein was in his presence when von Wachtstein learned where the *Océano Pacífico*'s boat was to land on Samborombón Bay. And that that information came from Standartenführer Goltz, who used the phrase 'it's time for you to see where we're going,' or words to that effect, before telling him—or actually showing him on a chart."

"Is there an implication that Goltz did not trust von Wachtstein?"

"I asked that question, Herr Admiral. Kapitän de Banderano felt that Goltz had confidence in von Wachtstein. Goltz introduced von Wachtstein to de Banderano as 'my assistant in this undertaking,' or words to that effect. Kapitän de Banderano felt that Standartenführer Goltz was simply being careful. He also said that it would have been impossible for von Wachtstein to communicate with the shore from the time that Goltz showed him the landing spot to the time of the landing."

"Somebody told the Americans or the Argentines—one or the other, or both—where the landing was to be made," Canaris said.

"Kapitän de Banderano also stated with great firmness that von Wachtstein's behavior on the beach after the shootings was heroic. According to de Banderano, many shots were fired—this differs from von Wachtstein's account that there were not more than four or five—and that despite this fire, von Wachtstein carried both bodies to the *Océano Pacífico*'s boat, and then returned for the two crates which had been put ashore."

"How could de Banderano know this?" Korvettenkapitän von und zu Waching asked. "Could he see it? How far offshore was the *Océano Pacífico*?"

"Kapitän de Banderano commanded his ship's boat himself," Boltitz said. "He apologized profusely for the cowardly behavior of his crew for not helping von Wachtstein."

"Then you are satisfied that von Wachtstein is not the man who informed the Argentines—or the Americans?"

"I believe, Herr Admiral, that he is less likely than Gradny-Sawz and von Tresmarck."

"Let's hear what you have on them," von und zu Waching said.

"Let's finish with von Wachtstein," Canaris said. "He went to see von Stauffenberg?"

"Yes, Sir, he and Generalleutnant von Wachtstein."

"A purely personal question, Boltitz. How is von Stauffenberg?"

"He's badly injured, Sir."

"He will live, would you say?"

"Yes, Herr Admiral. I don't think there's any chance of his dying now."

"Good. Germany needs officers like him," Canaris said. "And you would say they—he and young von Wachtstein, I mean—are close?"

"Yes, Sir. When von Wachtstein was drunk at Augsburg—"

"Tell us about that," Canaris interrupted.

"Well, he's apparently sort of a protégé of General Galland, Sir—the general put him up in his quarters, and told both Cranz and myself that he intends to have von Wachtstein assigned to the ME-262 project—"

"Von Wachtstein getting drunk, Boltitz, if you please," Canaris interrupted again, somewhat impatiently.

"Yes, Sir. There was a good deal to drink, apparently, in the General's quarters, and von Wachtstein got very drunk."

"You were there?"

"No, Sir, but General Galland told me not to judge him harshly. He had come from Oberstleutnant von Stauffenberg, and was terribly upset by his condition. General Galland believed that was the reason he got drunk."

"Galland is another good man," Canaris said. "We might be a good deal better off with more very young general officers who've earned their rank in battle. Was there anything unusual in von Wachtstein's behavior when he was with Hauptmann Grüner? Did he look guilty, in other words?"

"I thought his behavior was what one could expect," Boltitz said.

"Now tell us what you have learned about Gradny-Sawz and von Tresmarck."

"Very little, I'm afraid, Sir. Obersturmbannführer Cranz put it to me that the SS had assets in place to observe them; that I didn't; and that to attempt to set up some sort of surveillance would not only be unnecessary but might tend to alert them."

"And you agreed with that?" Canaris said.

"I didn't think I was in a position to argue with Obersturmbannführer Cranz, Sir. And in this case, I think he had a point."

"Do you think Galland will be able to have von Wacht-stein transferred to him, Sir?" von und zu Waching asked.

"If he goes to the Führer, and the Führer is in the right frame of mind, he might. And actually, that might be the best solution to the situation. I'm sure von Wachtstein would rather be flying than doing what he's doing. I wonder . . . do you know, Boltitz . . . if having him assigned to the ME-262 project was von Wachtstein's idea, or Galland's?"

"I don't know, Sir. I know he flew the ME-262, what they call a check ride, with General Galland."

"And did he pass the check ride?"

"Yes, Sir."

"Then I would tend to think that Galland really must have a high opinion of von Wachtstein's skill as a pilot," Canaris said. "The Führer has ordered that he be informed—by Gal-land—of the loss of each ME-262 in training. What is that phrase aviators use? 'Pilot error'? I don't think our Führer believes there is any excuse for it."

He looked at Boltitz. "Eat your sandwich. We have to leave shortly."

"Jawohl, Herr Admiral," Boltitz said, and reached for the liverwurst sandwich.

[TWO]
The Office of the Reichsführer-SS
Berlin
1455 22 May 1943

SS-Obersturmbannführer Karl Cranz marched into the office, came to attention, gave a stiff-armed Nazi salute, and barked, "Heil Hitler!"

Without rising from his desk, or even straightening up, Himmler returned the salute with a casually raised palm. "I understand there was aircraft trouble," he said.

"We had to make an unexpected landing at Leipzig, Herr Reichsprotektor," Cranz said. "But the reason I am this late is that I have been at the Propaganda Ministry's film laboratory."

"What's that all about?"

"The funeral service was filmed by Propaganda Ministry photographers. I arranged with General Galland to have it flown here in a fighter so that it could be processed immediately. It was ready—a rough cut, they called it—by the time I got here." He exhibited a small black can of film.

"And the purpose of this?"

"You told me, Herr Reichsprotektor, that you always felt you could judge far more about an individual from studying his face than by what came out of his mouth."

Himmler looked at him and smiled. "It's true, Karl."

"I believe it is, Sir."

"So you had a movie made? And what did you tell von Tresmarck and the others was the purpose? That I wanted to study their faces?"

"They don't think I had anything to do with it," Cranz said. "And neither did the photographers. It's not very long, Sir. May I suggest you have a look at it?"

"Canaris and the others will be here at four. We have to talk before then. One of the other things I believe, Karl, is that one should go to a meeting as well prepared as possible."

"And I have found that to be true, too, Herr Reichsprotektor."

"As you have learned that imitation—the most sincere form of flattery—goes a long way with Heinrich Himmler?"

"I wouldn't quite put it that way, Herr Reichsprotektor."

Himmler reached for his telephone. "I will require a projectionist immediately," he announced, and hung up.

The projectionist, a handsome young blond Stabsscharführer, came into Himmler's private projection room from the corridor as Himmler and Cranz entered from Himmler's office. He gave a stiff-armed salute with his right hand and held out his left hand for the can of film.

"As soon as you can find time, Karl, there is film of that

disgusting business in the Warsaw ghetto you will probably find interesting," Himmler said.

The private projection room was a small theater. There were two rows of chairs. In the front row were three comfortable leather armchairs, each with a table beside it holding a lamp, a telephone, a pad of paper, and a glass containing six freshly sharpened pencils.

Himmler waved Cranz into one of the chairs and raised his voice slightly. "Whenever you are ready, Stabsscharführer."

A moment later, the room went dark and the film began to play.

The first shot showed two tracked vehicles, normally used to tow heavy artillery, but now towing trailers, moving between two lines of uniformed men, black-uniformed Waffen-SS on one side of the road and gray-uniformed soldiers on the other. They stood with their rifle butts between their feet, their helmeted heads bowed in respect. Officers with drawn swords stood in front of the ranks of soldiers.

A casket covered with a Nazi flag was on each trailer.

The officers raised their swords in salute as each casket passed.

The next shot showed the mourners and dignitaries following the caskets, headed by General Galland.

"Major von Wachtstein is the fellow walking with Hauptmann Grüner, the two young Luftwaffe officers," Cranz said. "Behind them, the chubby fellow is Gradny-Sawz, and the SS officer is Sturmbannführer Werner von Tresmarck, our man in Uruguay."

"I know the Austrian and von Tresmarck," Himmler said.

The next shot showed the procession moving through the gates of the cemetery. There were close-ups of von Wachtstein, Grüner, von Tresmarck, and Gradny-Sawz. Next came a shot of the Horst Wessel Monument, with the camera moving down it to reveal the caskets, now poised above the empty graves. The mourners and dignitaries were lined up at the head of the grave.

Two clergymen appeared, one in Army uniform, the other in the vestments of a Catholic priest. Though there was no sound track, it was obvious that both were performing funeral rites.

They were followed by two officers, first an Army generalmajor and then a Waffen-SS SS-Brigadeführer. They each delivered a brief eulogy, followed by the rendering of the Nazi salute.

There were more close-ups of the faces of von Wachtstein, Grüner, von Tresmarck, and Gradny-Sawz.

The next shot was of a small battery of 57-mm antitank cannon, which fired a salute. Then came a shot of the troops and the mourners—with the camera lingering a moment on each of their faces—and the dignitaries rendering the Nazi salute as the flags were removed from the caskets, and the caskets being lowered into the ground.

This dissolved into a shot of Adolf Hitler, wearing his Iron Cross First Class, rendering the Nazi salute, and then the screen went white.

"Interesting," Himmler said, and then raised his voice slightly. "I'd like to see it again, Stabsscharführer. I am particularly interested in the faces of the mourners. Can you stop the film, or run it slowly, when those appear?"

"May I suggest, Herr Reichsprotektor, that I put the film in a still projector? There is a risk that the film might be damaged if I 'hold' too long in the motion picture projector."

"Then do that," Himmler said. "And tell the supply officer I want a motion picture projector in here that I can have stopped when I want it stopped without ruining the film."

"Jawohl, Herr Reichsprotektor. It will take me just a second, Sir."

Himmler picked up the pad of paper and scrawled on it. "I am making a note to myself, Karl, about the Horst Wessel Monument. I don't think it's quite what it should be. Maybe Speer will have some ideas."

"I thought it was very impressive, Herr Reichsprotektor."

"Not impressive enough," Himmler said flatly.

There was a blur of images on the screen, and then the screen was full of a close-up of Hauptmann Grüner.

The Stabsscharführer appeared with a small box connected to a cable. "With your permission, Herr Reichsprotektor," he said, handing it to Himmler. "The top button moves the film rapidly backward; the button below, backward, one frame at a time. The next button moves the film forward, one frame at a time, and the lower button forward rapidly."

"Thank you, Stabsscharführer," Himmler said, and began to experiment with the switch. He spent ten minutes looking at the close-ups, and then raised his voice: "How do I turn the projector off?"

The screen went blank and the lights came on.

"All right, Karl, tell me what you saw in the faces."

"Of the three, von Tresmarck, in my judgment, Herr Reichsprotektor, looked most nervous. Gradny-Sawz slightly less nervous, and von Wachtstein least nervous of all."

"Nervousness, or guilt?"

"There was, I thought, some guilt on the face of von Wachtstein."

"And to what do you attribute the guilt?"

"In my judgment, Herr Reichsprotektor, I felt that he holds himself responsible for the death of Oberst Grüner."

"You think he's our traitor, then?" Himmler asked evenly.

"No, Sir. What I meant to say is that he and Hauptmann Grüner are close friends, and he was—for lack of a better word—feeling guilty that his friend's father had died in his company; that he had not been able to prevent it from happening, that he had somehow failed his friend."

"Not because he was responsible for telling the Americans where the landing was to be made?"

"After speaking with Kapitän de Banderano—"

"Who? Oh, the captain of the Spanish ship?"

"Yes, Sir. Kapitän de Banderano said that he was present on the ship when von Wachtstein learned from Goltz where the landing would be made, and that at the time, Goltz made reference to its being time for von Wachtstein to learn. He said that it would have been absolutely impossible for von Wachtstein to communicate with anyone on shore after he had the information. And he painted quite a picture of von Wachtstein's courage under fire on the beach itself."

"I have to tell you, Karl, that I was surprised a moment ago when you said you thought von Wachtstein held himself responsible. I watched his face very carefully. That was not the face of a man who had anything shameful to hide. I could tell by the eyes, the lip movement . . . even the way he held his shoulders."

"Everything I have been able to learn about him makes the idea of treason sound unreasonable. General Galland thinks so highly of him that he will go to the Führer if necessary to have him assigned to the ME-262 project. And he is a close friend of Oberstleutnant von Stauffenberg."

"Who?"

"Oberstleutnant Graf Claus von Stauffenberg, Herr Reichsprotektor. Who was severely wounded in Africa, nearly blinded, and who refused painkilling drugs in the belief they would slow his recovery."

"I heard about von Stauffenberg," Himmler said. "Anything else on von Wachtstein?"

"Well, we have a lady, using the word loosely, in Galland's circle. She got him drunk—"

"A man who has secrets would think long and hard before abusing alcohol, wouldn't you say, Karl?"

"With that in mind, Herr Reichsprotektor, the lady—her name is Trudi—made sure he got drunk."

"How? Prurient curiosity overwhelms me."

"One pours cognac in a wide-mouthed jar, or a measuring cup, something on that order. Then it is placed in a freezer for however long it takes to bring the temperature of the cognac below zero. The cognac does not freeze because of the alcohol, you see. Then you drop a chip of ice into the jar. The water in the alcohol/water mixture is attracted to the chip of ice and adheres to it. The ice chip is then removed. This is done several times. Eventually, the remaining liquid has a much higher percentage of alcohol. One drink equals two or three."

"And you can't taste the difference?" Himmler asked.

"If one's first drink is ordinary cognac, one might notice a slight change. . . ."

"You obviously have put this to a personal test, have you, Karl?"

"In the line of duty, of course, Herr Reichsprotektor. After the first drink of the special cognac, one cannot tell the difference."

"And what did Trudi learn from von Wachtstein?"

"That he was very upset by the injuries suffered by Graf von Stauffenberg, and that he had been present when Oberst Grüner was killed."

"Huh," Himmler said.

"And also that even great amounts of alcohol in his system did not adversely affect his . . . romantic capabilities. I got the impression Trudi rather liked him."

"And what did we learn about Gradny-Sawz?"

"That he had a lockbox in the Credit Anstalt bank in Vienna we had not previously known about, in which he apparently kept what was left of the family jewels. He apparently plans to take them with him to Buenos Aires. If he returns to Buenos Aires."

"Nothing else?"

"The same sort of thing he does in Buenos Aires, ladies of the evening. Nothing extraordinary."

"And von Tresmarck?"

"Although temptation was placed in his path, he went to bed with neither male nor female. Neither did he drink to excess at any time—hardly at all, as a matter of fact."

"From which you infer?"

"I don't know what to infer, Herr Reichsprotektor. Von Tresmarck is SS, so he would assume that he's being watched. That doesn't necessarily mean he sold out to the Americans. And doing so, I think, would be illogical. He is not in a concentration camp with a pink triangle on his jacket; he is making money. And from what we have heard from Montevideo, he has his friends there."

"Keep on," Himmler said.

"I think we can assume that von Wachtstein didn't know the details of the landing. Goltz said so. And he is a junior officer, so I think Goltz would not have told him. Gradny-

Sawz, on the other hand, is the number two in the Buenos Aires Embassy. Though he says he didn't, he could have known the details of the landing. Even more likely, I think, is that Goltz did confide the details to von Tresmarck, perhaps accidentally. Von Tresmarck's position is that he knew nothing about the special shipment except that it was coming. And I get back to why would selling out be in his best interests?"

"To guarantee him refuge should we lose the war," Himmler said. "Men like that are dangerous." He chuckled. "They think like women."

"The same thing would apply to Gradny-Sawz, and we know he is willing to turn traitor," Cranz said. "He's done it once, why not again?"

Himmler grunted, thinking that over, and then asked, "Presumably you have compared notes with Canaris's man?"

"I think he agrees just about completely with me."

"Unless he has other theories to be shared only with Canaris?"

"That's possible, Herr Reichsprotektor, but I think unlikely," Cranz said, and then: "Would it be valuable for me to know what Oberführer von Deitzberg has learned in Buenos Aires and Montevideo?"

"Ambassador von Lutzenberger confirms that Goltz did not tell von Wachtstein the details of the landing, and that he himself didn't know the position, only the time and general area. It is also his opinion that the Argentines, who have a patrol and surveillance capability, were keeping an eye on the *Océano Pacífico*. Von Lutzenberger offers as a possible scenario that there would be a relatively senior officer—an oberst, for example—in charge of the surveillance. That such an officer would certainly have known Oberst Frade, and might well have been a close friend, and that when he saw Oberst Grüner and Standartenführer Goltz—whom the Argentine officer corps blames for the death of Oberst Frade—landing from the ship, he simply behaved like a Latin and ordered them shot. Knowing, of course, that we could not protest whatever happened to them without getting into what they were doing."

"Interesting. If that's true, there would be no traitor."

"I don't think we can take that as any more than a possibility. Although when I think of Oberst Juan Domingo Perón, I am tempted to believe an Argentine officer might behave that way."

"You're suggesting Perón might have been involved?"

"No. No. What I'm suggesting is that an officer like Perón would be capable of doing what von Lutzenberger suggests."

"I understand."

"Von Deitzberg also reports that Frau von Tresmarck doesn't believe Goltz told von Wachtstein anything more than he absolutely had to know, and that she doesn't think her husband would be involved, because he would be—as she is—afraid of the consequences."

"We seem to getting back to Gradny-Sawz, would you agree?"

"I just don't know," Himmler said. "I have been thinking that if we do something about young von Wachtstein—without anything to go on—there is the problem of Generalleutnant von Wachtstein. He would demand a Court of Honor for his son, and I think Keitel and others would go along with him. And if we do something about von Tresmarck—without anything to go on—we will lose his valuable services in Montevideo. That makes it tempting to go after Gradny-Sawz, but without anything to go on . . ."

"I understand, Herr Reichsprotektor."

Himmler looked at his watch. "We have enough time, I think, to watch the film of the Warsaw ghetto," he said thoughtfully, and then raised his voice: "Stabsscharführer! How long is the Warsaw film?"

"Twenty-three minutes, Herr Reichsprotektor," the Stabsscharführer called from the projection room."

"Would you show it, please?"

"Jawohl, Herr Reichsprotektor."

"I find the whole Warsaw ghetto business simply inexplicable," Himmler said. "Inexplicable and inexcusable!"

A moment later, the lights dimmed and an image of a battery of field howitzers lined up on a Warsaw street came onto the screen. They were firing at a block of apartment buildings, most of which were in flames.

The film ended with a line of Jews, men, women, and children, their hands in the air, walking between rows of German soldiers toward a line of trucks.

[THREE]
The Private Projection Room
The Office of the Reichsführer-SS
Berlin
1605 22 May 1943

"What are we doing in here?" Admiral Wilhelm Canaris asked as he—the last man to arrive—walked into the small, well-furnished miniature theater, trailed by Fregattenkapitän Otto von und zu Waching and Korvettenkapitän Karl Boltitz.

Already present were the Reichsführer-SS, Heinrich Himmler; Foreign Minister Joachim von Ribbentrop; Parteileiter Martin Bormann; Feldmarschall Wilhelm Keitel; and SS-Obersturmbannführer Karl Cranz.

"We are going to see a short film the Propaganda Minister intends to have in every theater in Germany by the end of the week," Himmler said with a smile.

"Do we have time for this?" Canaris asked, not bothering to conceal the disgust in his voice. "What kind of a film?"

"It has a dual purpose," Himmler said. "Goebbels is quite excited about it. He feels that those whose family members have made the supreme sacrifice for Germany can vicariously experience the honor they would have been paid had circumstances permitted."

"I have no idea what you're talking about, I'm afraid," Canaris said.

"Actually, this was Cranz's idea," Himmler said. "A picture is worth a thousand words, so to speak, right, Karl?"

"As I told you, Sir, inasmuch as some of the gentlemen

have never seen the people we brought back from Buenos Aires, I thought seeing what they looked like—how they behaved in this particular circumstance—would have merit."

"The film was shot by Propaganda Ministry cameramen," Himmler went on, obviously pleased with himself, "after Cranz telephoned to Goebbels and suggested that the interment ceremonies of Standartenführer Goltz and Oberst Grüner might well have a certain propaganda value. Goebbels immediately saw the possibilities, and ordered the interment filmed."

"I still don't understand," Canaris said. "But let's get it over with."

"Herr Admiral," Cranz said, "the idea is that many German families who have lost people naturally wonder where they are buried and how. The unknown is often unpleasant. What I suggested to the Herr Propaganda Minister was that this film would leave in the minds of such people images of a dignified ceremony in which the deceased were honored by the Fatherland."

"Let's see the film," Bormann said.

Himmler snapped his fingers. The room went dark, and after a moment the projector came to life.

"There will be, of course, a narrative, and appropriate music, and some final editing," Himmler said. "Goebbels's people are working on that as we speak."

The film of the funerals played.

The screen went blank, then white, and the lights in the room came on.

"I can see why this excited Goebbels," Martin Bormann said, "but I cannot see what the film has to do with the purpose of this meeting."

"The Reichsprotektor believes that one can often learn a great deal by looking at people's faces," Cranz said. "And I am convinced he's right."

"To get to the point," Bormann said, "has the investigation turned anything up?"

"Nothing concrete. I think Korvettenkapitän Boltitz will agree with me."

"I'm afraid that's true, Herr Parteileiter," Cranz said.

"In other words, you cannot tell me—so that I can report to the Führer—whether or not Operation Phoenix has been compromised?" Bormann replied, just a little nastily.

"We have learned nothing, Martin," Himmler said, "either here, or from von Deitzberg in South America, that suggests Operation Phoenix has been compromised."

"You don't think that the murders of the military attaché and your man Goltz has anything to do with Operation Phoenix?" Bormann pursued, sarcastically.

"It is entirely possible that both were killed in revenge for the death of Oberst Frade," Himmler said. "And that those who perpetrated that barbarous act did not know, or even suspect, anything about Operation Phoenix."

"And that's what I'm supposed to report to the Führer?"

"Inasmuch as I was given responsibility—together with Admiral Canaris—for conducting the investigation, that's what *I* will report to the Führer," Himmler said. "And I am extremely reluctant to go to the Führer without something concrete."

"Canaris?" Feldmarschall Keitel asked.

"The incident on the beach at Samborombón Bay, Herr Feldmarschall, is consistent with the character of the Argentine officer corps. They deeply resented the murder of Oberst Frade."

"I wondered if that was necessary," Keitel said. "So what are you recommending, Canaris?"

"I will defer to the Reichsprotektor," Canaris said.

"Unless there are objections, I think we should send von Tresmarck and Gradny-Sawz back to South America," Himmler said.

"And young von Wachtstein?" Keitel asked. "Why not him?"

"General Galland wants him assigned to the ME-262 project," Himmler said. "And knowing Galland, he's prepared to go to the Führer to get him."

"He's not needed over there for Operation Phoenix?" Bormann asked.

"He knows very little of Operation Phoenix, Herr Parteileiter," Cranz said. "From everything Korvettenkapitän Boltitz and I have been able to determine—and from what the Herr Reichsprotektor tells me we have learned in South America—von Wachtstein believes the material they attempted to take ashore was in connection with Admiral Canaris's plan to repatriate the officers from the *Graf Spee*."

"I think it would be easier to go along with Galland," Himmler said, "to let him have von Wachtstein, than to open that can of worms with the Führer."

"You're suggesting, Herr Reichsprotektor," Canaris said, "that if he was needed later, von Wachtstein could be sent back over there?"

"Yes, that was my thinking."

"I have no objection to that," Canaris said.

"Nor I," Feldmarschall Keitel said.

"And that's what I'm supposed to report to the Führer?" Bormann asked.

"*I* am going to tell the Führer, Martin," Himmler said, "that in my judgment, and that of Admiral Canaris, Operation Phoenix has not been compromised, and that he no longer has to spend his valuable time thinking about it."

"Obersturmbannführer Cranz and Korvettenkapitän Boltitz are also going to South America, presumably?"

"Only Korvettenkapitän Boltitz, Martin," Himmler said. "And I'm going to bring Oberführer von Deitzberg back. I need both von Deitzberg and Cranz here, and I have great faith in Boltitz to continue the investigation and institute appropriate security measures in South America. Furthermore, Boltitz will have the services of Sturmbannführer Raschner, who will remain in Argentina."

"Then that winds up our business?" Von Ribbentrop asked. It was the first time he'd spoken.

"I think so," Himmler said, and looked around the room.

Keitel got to his feet. "I am pleased, I must say, that we are not going to have to trouble the Führer further with this."

He picked up his field marshal's baton, touched it to his forehead, and walked out of the room.

"I have film of the Warsaw ghetto," Himmler said. "If anyone has time to see it—it's about twenty minutes."

No one had the time.

[FOUR]
Café Tortoni
Avenida de Mayo
Buenos Aires
1505 25 May 1943

"I don't think this will take long," Coronel Bernardo Martín said to Sargento Manuel Lascano as Lascano stopped the blue 1939 Dodge on Avenida de Mayo in front of the Café Tortoni. "Why don't you go around the block and park across the street?"

Lascano nodded his head vigorously to indicate he understood his orders. He was still having trouble following el Coronel's orders not to say "Sí, Señor"—much less "mi Coronel"—when they were in civilian clothing. He had tried "Sí, Señor Martín," but Martín hadn't liked that, either, ordering him not to use his name unless absolutely necessary.

Martín sensed Lascano's discomfort and smiled. "Try 'OK,' Manuel," he said. "It's an Americanism, but it'll work for us."

"Sí, Señor," Manuel replied, adding, somewhat uncomfortably, "OK."

Martín laughed, then stepped out of the car and walked across the wide sidewalk to the café. It was a historical landmark, the gathering place of Argentina's literati, thespians, and musicians for nearly a century. Photographs—or sometimes oil paintings—of the more famous of these decorated the paneled walls of the large main room, and even hung on the walls of the stairway leading down to the rest rooms.

Though the place was crowded with patrons of all ages, there was, Martín thought somewhat unkindly, a high percentage of dramatically dressed and coiffured ladies well past their prime, but still with a coterie of admirers.

He walked slowly through the room until he saw Milton Leibermann, sitting alone at a small table, reading *La Nación*. "Well, what a pleasant surprise," Martín said. "May I join you, Milton?"

"It would be my great pleasure," Leibermann said, laying the newspaper down.

Their rendezvous was scheduled; they had decided upon it at the Frade reception at Estancia San Pedro y San Pablo. That was fortunate, because something had come up that Martín considered—a gut feeling; he could offer no explanation—he should pass on to Leibermann.

An elderly waiter appeared and took their order for coffee.

"Anything interesting in the paper?" Martín asked.

"Actually, there's a pretty good piece in here—from Reuters, which I suppose will make you think it's British propaganda—saying that fourteen thousand Jews were killed in the suppression of the uprising in the Warsaw ghetto."

"That seems an incredible number," Martín said.

"And forty thousand were arrested," Leibermann went on. "The number of dead and prisoners doesn't really surprise me, actually, but how long it took the German army to do it does. We hear all these stories about the invincible German army, and here they are, forced out of Africa, and taking six weeks to defeat people armed with only pistols and rifles, most of them without military experience."

"It does seem strange, doesn't it?" Martín said. "Of course, it is of no interest to neutral Argentina."

"I understand, of course."

The waiter delivered the coffee and placed the bill on a spike on the table. Martín saw that it was the fourth or fifth bill.

"Did I keep you waiting, Milton?" Martín asked, pointing to the spike.

"Truth to tell, I came a little early to escape someone in the embassy I didn't want to talk to."

"I don't suppose you'd give me a name? So that I can avoid him too?"

Leibermann visibly thought that over. "Colonel Almond," he said.

Martín was surprised that Leibermann had given him a name, and that one in particular, but his face did not show it.

Does he know that I had lunch with Almond?

Well, let's see where it goes. I was going to tell him anyhow.

"Apropos of nothing whatever, does the name 'Galahad' mean anything to you, Milton?"

"*Sir* Galahad. If he had a first name, I can't recall it. He's a character in English folklore," Leibermann said. "Sir Galahad: the purest of the Knights of the Round Table—are you familiar with these stories, Bernardo, are they part of Castilian culture?"

"Who alone of Sir Arthur's knights succeeded in finding the Holy Grail," Martín said. "I'll have you know, Milton, I am an Old Boy of St. George's School. I learned much more of English legend than I really cared to know."

"I had no idea," Leibermann said. "So I'll bet you know all the words to 'God Save the King,' right?"

"Indeed I do," Martín said.

"Why do I think you were not testing my knowledge of English legend?" Leibermann asked.

"Your Colonel Almond treated me to a very nice luncheon at the American Club," Martín said. "The name 'Galahad' came up."

Nothing showed on Leibermann's face, although Martín was watching closely.

"Really?"

"He seems to think it is a code name," Martín said.

"A code name for whom?"

"He beat around the bush a good deal; I had to guess most of the time what he was talking about. But I had the feeling that he thinks our friend Don Cletus has someone in the German Embassy who uses 'Galahad' as a code name."

"Past tense, of course. During the brief period during which Don Cletus was mistakenly suspected of being some kind of intelligence officer?"

"Present tense," Martín said.

"But Bernardo, we both know that Cletus Frade has been discharged from the Marine Corps and is now a pillar of neutral Argentine society."

"Of course. I wonder why I keep forgetting that? He's told me himself on more than one occasion. And he certainly wouldn't lie about that, would he?"

"Of course not."

"Nevertheless, this is what your friend Almond believes. The way he put it—between intelligence professionals, that is . . ."

"Is that what you are, Bernardo? I always wondered how you occupy your time in the Edificio Libertador."

"I'm in charge of security," Martín said. "I thought I told you. Making sure the fire extinguishers work, protecting General San Martín's sword, that sort of thing."

"Are you a descendant of General San Martín, Bernardo?"

"As a matter of fact, I am."

"That gives you something in common with Don Cletus, doesn't it? He's a direct descendant of Pueyrredón, or so I'm told."

"I am not going to let you take us off at a tangent, Milton," Martín said. "Who's 'Galahad'?"

They locked eyes for a moment.

"I have no idea what you're talking about," Leibermann said.

Martín nodded after a moment. "Pity," he said. "If you had known, and were willing to tell me, I was prepared to share with you the twenty thousand dollars Almond offered me for the name."

"That's a lot of money, twenty thousand dollars," Leibermann said.

"Your half would come to ten thousand," Martín said.

"Hypothetically speaking, Bernardo: If I knew who this

fellow Galahad is, and I told you, and you told Almond, and he gave you the money, what would you do with your ten thousand?"

"Buy a red Buick convertible."

"No, you wouldn't."

"You tell me."

"You would turn it in."

Martín shrugged but didn't argue.

"And hypothetically speaking, so would I," Leibermann said.

"So he made you the same offer?"

"He's never mentioned that name to me."

"Maybe because he knows you know the name and won't tell him," Martín said.

Leibermann shrugged but didn't argue.

"Galahad now makes me very curious," Martín said. "I think I should tell you that."

"Still speaking hypothetically, Bernardo: If there is such a person, I would be very surprised if he posed any threat to the Argentine republic."

"The problem is, Milton, I'm supposed to be the fellow who makes decisions about who is dangerous and who is not."

"I've found over the years that sometimes you just have to trust your friends, Bernardo."

Their eyes met.

"I could turn that on you, my friend," Martín said. "And tell you that it is now your turn to trust this friend."

"I hope you don't," Leibermann said.

"All right, I won't. But my curiosity is still very active."

"I understand," Leibermann said. "And I hope you will understand that I hope your curiosity will go unsatisfied."

"Why would you hope that? If this man poses no threat to Argentina, why would it matter if I had a name?"

"Let's go hypothetical again, Bernardo. If there were such a person, and Cletus Frade were the intelligence officer you mistakenly believe him to be, why wouldn't his name already be known to Almond?"

"Because Frade doesn't entirely trust the OSS?"

"The what? What's the OSS?"

Martín chuckled and shook his head.

"It could be, if all these hypotheticals were true, that Don Cletus doesn't trust Almond, or the people he works for, to keep a secret. And that divulgence of that secret to the wrong people—intentionally or inadvertently—would probably see not only Galahad, but many other people, innocent people, killed."

Martín looked at Leibermann for a long moment. "Have you heard anything else of interest lately?" he asked, changing the subject.

"Not a thing, I'm afraid. And you?"

Martín shook his head. Then he stood up.

"It's always a pleasure to see you, Milton," he said.

"Likewise, Bernardo. Tell me, have you been to the zoo lately?"

"No, but one of these days I'm going to have to go."

He put his hand out to Leibermann, shook it, and walked back through the Café Tortoni to Avenida de Mayo.

[FIVE]
**The Office of the Foreign Minister
Berlin
1410 25 May 1943**

Parteileiter Martin Bormann was the first to arrive, in reply to a telephone call from Foreign Minister von Ribbentrop. "What's this all about?" he demanded brusquely.

"Something has come up in connection with Operation Phoenix that requires an immediate decision. From everyone," von Ribbentrop said, and then, just a shade sarcastically, "Good afternoon, Martin. You're looking well."

"I left an important meeting to come here," Bormann said. "If I was rude, I apologize. Others are coming?"

"The Reichsprotektor and Admiral Canaris," von Ribbentrop said. "Keitel and Dönitz are at Wolfsshanze."

"What has come up? Or would you rather wait until the others get here?"

Von Ribbentrop handed him several sheets of paper. "Would you like a coffee, Martin, while we're waiting for the others?"

"Coffee? No," Bormann replied, then, "This came in two days ago?"

"It came in ten minutes before I called you. There was some bomb damage to communications, the cryptographic facility. Everything was delayed. You don't want coffee?"

"No, thank you," Bormann said, and resumed reading the message.

Von Ribbentrop summoned his secretary and asked her to bring him a coffee and to make sure there would be coffee for the others when they arrived.

"Jawohl, Excellency," his secretary said, and added: "Excellency, Admiral Canaris called, and said that he cannot make this meeting; he is sending Fregattenkapitän von und zu Waching and Korvettenkapitän Boltitz to represent him."

Bormann looked up from the message. "Canaris is obviously smarter than I am. What is this thing, anyway?

"Once you finish it, Martin, I believe it will all be clear," von Ribbentrop said.

Bormann snorted and resumed reading.

```
CLASSIFICATION: MOST URGENT

CONFIDENTIALITY: MOST SECRET

DATE: 22 MAY 1943 1645 BUENOS AIRES
TIME

FROM: AMBASSADOR, BUENOS AIRES

TO: IMMEDIATE AND PERSONAL ATTENTION
OF THE FOREIGN MINISTER OF THE GER-
MAN REICH
```

HEIL HITLER!

MY DEAR HERR VON RIBBENTROP.

FOLLOWING IS A REPORT OF AN AUDIENCE
WITH THE MINISTER OF LABOR OF THE
REPUBLIC OF ARGENTINA, OBERST JUAN
DOMINGO PERÓN (PERÓN), HELD AT
PERÓN'S INVITATION 22 MAY 1943 IN A
PRIVATE DINING ROOM OF THE OFFICERS'
CLUB ON PLAZA SAN MARTÍN. PRESENT
WERE THE AMBASSADOR OF THE REICH TO
THE ARGENTINE REPUBLIC (LUTZEN) AND
GENERALMAJOR MANFRED RITTER VON
DEITZBERG (DEITZ).

PERÓN ON 20 MAY 1943 PERSONALLY
TELEPHONED LUTZEN AND DEITZ AND SAID
THERE WAS A MATTER OF GREAT PERSONAL
IMPORTANCE TO HIM HE WISHED TO DIS-
CUSS WITH US AT LUNCHEON AT OUR EAR-
LIEST CONVENIENCE, IN THE HOPE THAT
THE GERMAN EMBASSY AND OFFICER CORPS
WOULD BE WILLING TO HELP IN THE RES-
OLUTION OF THE PROBLEM.

BOTH LUTZEN AND DEITZ, WITHOUT PRIOR
CONSULTATION WITH EACH OTHER, IMME-
DIATELY ACCEPTED PERÓN'S INVITATION,
AND INFORMED PERÓN THEY WOULD BE
AVAILABLE AT HIS CONVENIENCE. PERÓN
SUGGESTED 1330 HOURS 22 MAY AT THE
OFFICERS' CLUB.

PERÓN IMMEDIATELY BROUGHT THE PROB-
LEM TO OUR ATTENTION, BY INFORMING
US OF THE PROBLEM, AND WHAT ASSIS-

TANCE HE SOUGHT FROM US IN ITS RESOLUTION.

SPECIFICALLY, MAJOR HANS-PETER VON WACHTSTEIN (HANS) HAS IMPREGNATED SEÑORITA ALICIA CARZINO-CORMANO (ALICIA). HER CONDITION AT THIS TIME IS KNOWN ONLY TO HER PRIEST, THE REV. KURT WELNER, S.J. (JESUIT), AND PERÓN. ALICIA IS ONE OF TWO DAUGHTERS OF SEÑORA CLAUDIA CARZINO-CORMANO (MOTHER).

HANS IS THE SON OF GENERALLEUTNANT KARL FRIEDRICH VON WACHTSTEIN (OLD-WACH) WHO SERVES ON THE STAFF OF THE FUHRER.

PERÓN TOOK PAINS TO POINT OUT THE CONNECTIONS OF THE PRINCIPALS. MOTHER HAD A TWENTY-YEAR-LONG RELATIONSHIP WITH THE LATE OBERST JORGE GUILLERMO FRADE (OLDFRADE), WHOM PERÓN CONSIDERS TO HAVE BEEN HIS BEST FRIEND, AND WHO LOOKED ON THE GIRLS AS HIS DAUGHTERS, AS, PERÓN SAID, HE NOW DOES. MOTHER'S ELDEST DAUGHTER ISABELA WAS AFFIANCED TO THE LATE HAUPTMANN JORGE ALEJANDRO DUARTE, ARGENTINE ARMY (JORGE), WHO FELL ON THE FIELD OF BATTLE AT STALINGRAD WHILE SERVING AS AN OBSERVER WITH VON PAULUS'S ARMY AND WHOM THE FÜHRER IN THE NAME OF GERMAN REICH POSTHUMOUSLY AWARDED THE KNIGHT'S CROSS OF THE IRON CROSS.

JORGE WAS THE SON OF SEÑOR HUMBERTO
DUARTE (BANKER) AND HIS WIFE BEAT-
RICE (BANKER'S WIFE), WHO IS THE
SISTER OF THE LATE OLDFRADE.

HANS MET ALICIA IN CONNECTION WITH
HIS DUTIES IN RETURNING THE REMAINS
OF JORGE TO ARGENTINA. PERÓN WAS IN
BERLIN AT THE TIME HANS WAS BEING
PROPOSED FOR THE MISSION, AND
PERÓN'S APPROVAL OF HANS FOR THE
DUTY WAS SOUGHT, IF MEMORY SERVES,
BY THE HERR FOREIGN MINISTER HIM-
SELF.

WITH THE EXCEPTION OF OLDFRADE'S
SON, CLETUS HOWELL FRADE (YOUNG-
FRADE), WHO IS BELIEVED TO BE AN
AGENT OF THE AMERICAN OFFICE OF
STRATEGIC SERVICES, PERÓN FEELS THE
ENTIRE FAMILY IS VERY SYMPATHETIC TO
THE GERMAN CAUSE, OR AT THE WORST
NEUTRAL. IN PERÓN'S OPINION, ALTHOUGH
HE ASSURED US HE WILL DO HIS BEST TO
CONTROL YOUNGFRADE, YOUNGFRADE, WHO
FEELS AN ANIMOSITY TOWARD HANS, IS
CAPABLE OF TURNING PUBLIC OPINION,
AND MORE IMPORTANT, THAT OF THE
ARGENTINA OFFICER CORPS, AGAINST
HANS, AND THUS THE GERMAN OFFICER
CORPS AND THE GERMAN CAUSE ONCE HE
LEARNS OF ALICIA'S CONDITION, AND
THE IDENTITY OF THE FATHER.

IN VIEW OF THE FOREGOING, LUTZEN AND
DIETZ ARE FORCED TO AGREE WITH PERÓN

THAT THE MATTER IS MORE THAN THE
PRIVATE BUSINESS OF HANS AND ALICIA.
THAT IN FACT IT AFFECTS THE GOOD
RELATIONS PRESENTLY EXTANT BETWEEN
THE GERMAN REICH AND THE REPUBLIC OF
ARGENTINA.

PERÓN IS AWARE THAT HANS IS IN GER-
MANY, AND BELIEVES HANS IS ASSISTING
IN THE INVESTIGATION OF THE DEATHS
OF OBERST GRÜNER AND STANDARTEN-
FÜHRER GOLTZ. IN THIS CONNECTION,
PERÓN TOLD US IN CONFIDENCE THAT HE
BELIEVES THE MURDERS WERE PERPE-
TRATED BY FORMER SUBORDINATES OF
OLDFRADE, ALTHOUGH HE HAS NO PROOF.

PERÓN REQUESTS THAT IF HANS CAN BE
SPARED FROM HIS DUTIES IN CONNECTION
WITH THE GRÜNER/GOLTZ INVESTIGATION
THAT HE IMMEDIATELY BE RETURNED TO
HIS DUTIES IN ARGENTINA, HIS OBLIGA-
TIONS AS AN HONORABLE GERMAN OFFICER
BE MADE CLEAR TO HIM, POSSIBLY BY
OLDWACH, AND THAT HE ENTER INTO A
MARRIAGE WITH ALICIA.

ALTERNATIVELY, PERÓN SUGGESTS THE
POSSIBILITY OF ALICIA GOING TO GER-
MANY, THERE TO ENTER INTO MARRIAGE
WITH HANS.

DEITZ FEELS THAT INASMUCH AS HIS
INVESTIGATION OF HANS HERE HAS SHOWN
NO CONNECTION BETWEEN HANS AND THE
GRÜNER/GOLTZ MURDERS, THE FIRST
REQUEST OF PERÓN SHOULD BE SERIOUSLY

CONSIDERED, FOR THE FOLLOWING REA-
SONS:

(1) PERÓN ALMOST CERTAINLY WILL BE
THE NEXT PRESIDENT OF ARGENTINA.
GRANTING HIS REQUEST WOULD BE PROOF
THAT THE GERMAN OFFICER CORPS DEEPLY
REGRETS THE UNFORTUNATE DEATH OF
OLDFRADE, AND IS WILLING TO MAKE
AMENDS IN ANY WAY IT CAN.

(2) THE MARRIAGE OF HANS TO ALICIA
WOULD BE A MAJOR SOCIAL EVENT IN
ARGENTINA AND REFLECT WELL ON GERMAN
INTERESTS.

(3) THE MARRIAGE OF HANS WOULD VERY
LIKELY BE USEFUL IN CONNECTION WITH
A CERTAIN PROJECT THAT HAS RECENTLY
UNDERGONE CERTAIN REVERSALS. BANKER
MIGHT VERY WELL BE USEFUL IN THIS
CONNECTION AS BANKER AND BANKER'S
WIFE HAVE BECOME INTIMATE FRIENDS OF
HANS.

(4) WHATEVER INFLUENCE YOUNGFRADE
HAS WITH ALL OTHERS WOULD BE GREATLY
DIMINISHED BY A MARRIAGE BETWEEN
HANS AND ALICIA.

(5) JESUIT HAS EXPRESSED CONCERN
THAT TRAVELING TO GERMANY WOULD SUB-
JECT ALICIA TO SOME RISK TO HER PER-
SON AND THE UNBORN CHILD.

LUTZEN CONSIDERS THAT EITHER OF
PERÓN'S REQUESTS BE GIVEN CONSIDERA-

```
TION AT THE HIGHEST LEVELS, AND FUR-
THER SUGGESTS THAT WHICHEVER SOLU-
TION IS DECIDED UPON BE ACTED UPON
AS SOON AS POSSIBLE.

RESPECTFULLY SUBMITTED:

THE UNDERSIGNED PARTCIPATED IN THE
PREPARATION OF THE FOREGOING MESSAGE
AND CONCUR IN EVERY DETAIL.

MANFRED RITTER VON DEITZBERG

GENERALMAJOR, GENERAL STAFF, OKW

MANFRED ALOIS GRAF VON LUTZENBERGER

AMBASSADOR OF THE GERMAN REICH TO
THE REPUBLIC OF ARGENTINA

END MESSAGE
```

When Bormann raised his eyes from the message, he saw that Fregattenkapitän von und zu Waching and Korvettenkapitän Boltitz had come into the office. He sighed, shrugged, and handed the cable to von und zu Waching.

Von und zu Waching had just finished reading the first page when Reichsprotektor Heinrich Himmler and SS-Obersturmbannführer Karl Cranz marched into the room.

"Heil Hitler!" Himmler barked, and he and Cranz gave a stiff-armed Nazi salute. The others returned it. The look on Himmler's face suggested that he didn't think the salutes of von und zu Waching and Boltitz were up to standard.

"Well, Joachim, what's so important?" Himmler asked.

"There has been a cable from Buenos Aires," von Ribbentrop said. "Von und zu Waching's reading it now."

Himmler looked at von und zu Waching, who handed him the page he had read. The look on Himmler's face suggested he thought he should have been handed the entire message, whether or not von und zu Waching was finished. Von und zu Waching passed the second two pages to Himmler one at a time. Himmler read them all before passing them to Cranz.

"You considered this important enough to have me come all the way over here, Joachim?"

"I based its importance, Joachim, on the importance your man von Deitzberg apparently places on it," von Ribbentrop replied.

Cranz finished reading the cable, started to hand it back to von Ribbentrop, then looked at Boltitz. "Have you read this, Karl?"

Boltitz shook his head.

"Give it to him," Himmler ordered.

"The question seems to be simple," Bormann said. "Would sending the fertile Major von Wachtstein back to South America be a major contribution to Germany's good relations with Argentina, or would we be sending the fox back into the chicken coop?"

"I would substitute the phrase 'major contribution to the success of Operation Phoenix' for 'good relations,' " Von Ribbentrop said.

"The question as I see it is whether we can trust young von Wachtstein," Himmler said. "Cranz?"

"Where is he now?" Bormann asked.

"In Augsburg," von und zu Waching said. "And in that connection, I think I should mention that General Galland telephoned to the Führer asking that he be assigned to the ME-262 project. And the Führer approved."

"Damn!" Bormann said.

"Well, Cranz?" Himmler asked impatiently.

"Herr Reichsprotektor," Cranz said, "nothing that Korvettenkapitän Boltitz and I found in our investigation suggests that von Wachtstein is anything but what he appears on the surface. A simple, courageous officer, who, when he can be pried from the arms of some female, executes his orders to the best of his ability. Would you agree, Boltitz?"

"Yes, Sir," Karl Boltitz said.

"What are you going to tell the Führer, Joachim," Bormann asked, "since he approved of Galland getting von Wachtstein?"

"I think I would agree with the Foreign Minister that the Führer has too much on his mind as it is to trouble him with what we all, I'm sure, consider an administrative matter," Himmler said.

"With all respect, Herr Reichsprotektor, I don't believe I have the authority to make a decision in this matter without the personal concurrence of Admiral Canaris."

"Well, then, damn it, the decision will be made without him," Bormann said. "You go back there, Fregattenkapitän, and report to him the contents of this cable, and what we decided to do about it. If he has any objections, he can tell von Ribbentrop or Himmler."

"Jawohl, Herr Partieleiter."

"When do you and the others go to Buenos Aires, Boltitz?" Himmler asked.

"Tomorrow night at half past seven from Templehof, Herr Reichsprotektor."

"Is that enough time to bring von Wachtstein here?"

"I'll have to start making the arrangements immediately, Herr Reichsprotektor."

"Well, then, may I suggest that you and the Fregattenkapitän get about your business?" Himmler said.

Von und zu Waching and Boltitz gave a stiff-armed Nazi salute.

"Jawohl, Herr Reichsprotektor," von und zu Waching said.

The two came to attention, clicked their heels, and marched out of the office.

[SIX]
Guest Room No. 1
Quarters of the General Officer Commanding
Luftwaffe Flughafen No. 103B
Augsburg, Germany
1820 25 May 1943

Major Freiherr Hans-Peter von Wachtstein jerked the sheet
of paper from the Olympia portable typewriter, crumpled it
into a ball, and threw it angrily into a wastepaper basket.

*What the hell! If I ever finish writing this—and it is god-
damned difficult to write it in the first place, not mentioning
having to write it knowing some goddamn Gestapo clerk is
going to read it—it will probably be on the first Condor
some Ami P-51 pilot will luck up on and shoot down over the
Atlantic.*

*Well, shit, I have to write it. I'll give it another shot when
I come back.*

Or will I?

*Will I write Alicia, or will I have a couple of drinks with
Trudi, and then, principleless sex maniac that I am, bring
her up here and fuck her ears off and put off the letter I have
to write Alicia for one more day?*

*Goddamn it, I know what I'll do. I'll go to the hangar office
and write it on one of their typewriters before I come here.*

*I will at least try to do that, as I will try not to fuck Trudi,
and I will probably fail at both.*

He looked at his US Army Air Corps–issue Hamilton
chronograph, exhaled audibly, and stood up.

He was in his underwear. He put on a shirt and a sweater,
then sheepskin high-altitude trousers and boots. He took the
sheepskin jacket from a hanger, picked up the flight helmet,
and left the room.

Oberstleutnant Friedrich Henderver was waiting for him
in the living room. "You look unhappy, Hansel," he said.

"No, Sir."

"I was about to go looking for you," Henderver said. "But I thought you might be entertaining Trudi."

"No, Sir."

"There are two schools of thought about that, you know," Henderver said as he picked up his sheepskin jacket and waved at the door. "One is that a little activity of that sort calms a man down and makes him a better pilot. The other is that one should neither drink *nor* fuck for at least twelve hours before flying, because it slows down the reflexes."

Peter laughed dutifully.

"Well, smile," Henderver said. "Trudi will be here, I'm sure, when we get back."

"Yes, Sir."

"Tonight we are going to combine more stick time for you with an experiment with droppable fuel tanks. Phrased simply, that means, presuming we can get the bitch off the ground with all that weight, we will go to seven thousand meters. If we haven't exhausted the auxiliary fuel getting up there, we will exhaust what's left and then jettison the tanks. If we run out of fuel on the way to seven thousand, we will jettison the tanks at that time. In either case, the tanks will crash through the roof of either an old people's home or a children's hospital."

"What I really like about you, Friedrich, is your cheerful way of looking at things."

Henderver laughed.

Thirty minutes later—just as he thought he was going to run out of runway—Peter finally felt life come into the controls of the two-seater ME-262 and managed to lift it off.

The tanks were jettisoned as they reached 6,500 meters.

"Well, that seemed to work," Henderver said. "And here we are at altitude with nearly full main tanks."

"Which will now crash through the roof of an old people's home, right?"

"And give Herr Goebbels one more opportunity to provide photographic proof of the Amis murdering innocent Germans," Henderver said.

●　●　●

General Galland was in the hangar when the doors closed and the lights went on.

Henderver and Peter climbed down from the cockpit of the ME-262. Both gave the General the military, rather than the Nazi, salute when they walked over to him.

"How did it go?" Galland asked.

"I don't want to know how much over maximum gross weight we were," Peter said. "I had a hell of a time getting it off the ground."

"We need better engines, General," Henderver said seriously, and then added, in a lighter tone, "On the other hand, we got to a little over sixty-five hundred on the auxiliary fuel."

"Tell me, Hansel," Galland said. "If the Reichsprotektor, Herr Himmler, asked you personally to trust him about something, would you?"

"Sir?"

"Watch yourself, Hansel, that's a trick question," Henderver said.

"The bad news, Hansel, is that you're out of the ME-262 program. . . ."

"Sir?"

"And—depending how you feel about Argentina—the good news is that you're going back over there."

"I don't understand, Sir."

"General, we need him," Henderver said.

"According to Herr Himmler, the Reich needs him more in Argentina," Galland said. "He wouldn't tell me why. He asked me to trust him, which translates to mean he would be happier if I didn't register outrage with the Führer."

"I vote for registering outrage, General," Henderver said.

"So do I, Sir."

"Well, you're a nice guy, Hansel, and a good pilot, and this is going to break Trudi's heart, but this is one time I don't think I should get in a fight with our beloved Reichsprotektor."

Their eyes met.

"I'm sorry, Hansel," Galland said. "You know what it is. They call it conservation of ammunition. I don't have that much left."

"I understand, Sir."

"There will be a Heinkel here in about an hour to fly you to Berlin. From the Führer's personal fleet, I'm told. I had your stuff packed. That will give you time for a quickie with Trudi."

"With the General's permission, and aware of the damage I might be causing to the reputation of Luftwaffe fighter pilots, I think I would rather have a drink with you and Friedrich."

"OK, Hansel," Galland said. "We can do that here. I'll send my driver for your stuff and some Champagne."

"Thank you, Sir."

"I'm really sorry about this, Hansel," Galland said.

XIX

[ONE]
San Carlos de Bariloche
Río Negro Province, Argentina
1320 29 May 1943

Don Cletus Frade turned the Lodestar on final, which put him over the incredibly clear and blue waters of Lake Nahuel Huapí, with the village of Bariloche to his right and the Andes Mountains in the background. "Flaps, twenty percent," he ordered.

Lieutenant Colonel Richard J. Almond, U.S. Army Air Corps, reached for the flap control, moved it, and when the indicator showed twenty percent, called back: "Flaps at twenty."

Almond was in the right seat of the Lodestar, in civilian clothing except for his Air Corps A-2 leather flight jacket. Frade was wearing his Marine-issued leather flight jacket, which differed from the Air Corps model in several details, including its fur collar. Almond's jacket had a leather collar. Frade's jacket insignia still included a leather patch with—now faded—gold wings and the legend, "Frade, C. 1/LT USMCR" stamped on it.

"Gear down," Frade ordered.

Colonel Almond reached for the wheel-shaped control and pushed it forward. When the green bulb indicating the gear was down appeared on the instrument panel, Almond reported: "Gear down and locked."

Cletus Frade reached for the throttle quadrant with his right hand.

"One twenty-five," Colonel Almond reported the airspeed, then turned and looked up at First Lieutenant Anthony C. Pelosi, Corps of Engineers, Army of the United States, who was standing between them, supporting himself with one hand on the back of the pilot's chair and the other on the back of the copilot's seat.

"You want to go strap yourself in, Lieutenant?" Almond said, expressing what was actually an order in the form of a suggestion.

"Go fuck yourself," Lieutenant Pelosi responded and didn't move.

It took a moment for Colonel Almond to really comprehend what had just been said to him. But as they were about to land on a gravel strip in remote Argentina with a pilot at the controls who had no more than thirty hours' total time in this type of aircraft, this was not the time to do anything about even such an outrageously obscene refusal of an order from a superior.

"One ten," Almond called to Frade, then, "One hundred."

At ninety miles per hour indicated, Frade gently retarded the throttles and eased back a hair on the Lodestar's wheel, whereupon the airplane stopped flying and the wheels made a gentle contact with the ground. "Dump the flaps," he ordered as the Lodestar rolled down the gravel strip.

Colonel Almond adjusted the flaps. "*Zero* flaps," he reported. It was a gentle chastisement. The proper command Frade should have given his copilot was "Zero Flaps" not "Dump the flaps."

Frade slowed the aircraft to taxi speed long before they had reached the end of the gravel runway.

"Nice landing, Clete," Almond said, giving credit where credit was due.

Frade nodded. He stopped the Lodestar, turned it around on the runway, taxied back to the end of the runway, and then turned the airplane around again.

They were now ready to take off.

But instead of reaching for the throttle quadrant, Frade shut the left engine down, put the right on LOW IDLE, and applied the parking break.

"Get out of the aisle, Tony," Clete said as he unfastened his shoulder and lap harness.

"Yes, sir," Pelosi said.

Pelosi politely and respectfully says "Yes, sir" to Frade, and "Go fuck yourself" to me? That will cost you, Lieutenant, just as soon as we get back to Buenos Aires. Who the hell do you think you are?

Almond had a second thought: *Well, that just may give me the reason to get rid of him. He's entirely too close to Frade. Remove a small problem before it causes large trouble.*

All I have to do is report that obscene insubordination and say that he is obviously unsuitable for service here. And Frade can't protect him; it would be his word against mine.

Almond followed Pelosi and Frade into the cabin and to the rear door. Captain Maxwell Ashton III, Signal Corps, Army of the United States, and Frade's bodyguard, or whatever he was, the Argentine who followed him around like a puppy, carrying a shotgun, started to unfasten their seat belts as they passed.

This was the third time Almond had provided Frade with flight instruction in the Lodestar. The first two sessions, they had been alone (except for Frade's shadow) and the instruction had really been in basic aircraft handling. Loss of an engine immediately after takeoff, that sort of thing. They had used the El Palomar field for that, and had made perhaps thirty touch-and-go landings.

Frade was an apt pilot and had been a quick student. All he had needed was a little instruction.

For their third session, Frade asked for a cross-country flight. Almond had readily agreed. It would give him a chance to see the country from the air, something he didn't know how else he would manage. And when Frade suggested they take Ashton and Pelosi, to give them a chance to see the country from the air, he agreed to that, too, and left notes for them in the boxes at the embassy, telling them to arrange their schedules so they would have two days free starting that Friday evening.

Pelosi had the door open by the time Frade reached it, and one by one everyone in the plane jumped to the ground.

It was piss-call time.

Frade tucked himself into his trousers and turned to smile at Almond. "Tell me, teacher, if that was an official check ride, would you have passed me?"

"Yes, Clete, I think I would," Almond said.

"In other words, you think I'm qualified to fly that bird all by my lonesome?"

"Well, I would recommend, of course, that you have a co-pilot; but sure, you're qualified to be pilot-in-command."

"When you get back to the States, make sure you tell Colonel Graham that," Clete said.

"Excuse me? Who?"

Clete didn't respond.

"Let me have your .45, Enrico," he said.

Enrico Rodríguez reached around, took what looked to Almond like a Colt Model 1911A1 .45 ACP pistol from the small of his back, and handed it butt-first to Clete.

What the hell is he doing?

Clete ejected the clip from the pistol, examined it, and put it back in place.

He was counting cartridges to make sure there wasn't one in the chamber and the pistol was safe. I wonder why he did that?

Colonel Almond erred. Clete had counted the cartridges remaining in the magazine—six—to be sure that the seventh was chambered in the pistol.

He pulled the hammer back, then looked around. He pointed to the side of the runway, where, twenty-five yards away, there was a makeshift runway marker, a large tin can painted yellow.

He raised the pistol and fired.

Even with the muted roar of the left engine, the unexpected sound was shocking. Almond's ears rang.

What the hell was that all about?

"My God, Clete!" Almond exclaimed.

The can came to rest. Clete fired again and the can jumped into the air again. It landed again, and Clete fired a third time, sending the can another ten yards across the field.

"That's all," Clete said. "My uncle Jim was always saying, 'Quit while you're ahead, Clete, quit while you're ahead!' "

Holding the pistol to his side, he looked at Almond and went on: "That's sound advice for you, you sonofabitch," he said. "I hope you're smart enough to take it."

"Excuse me? What the hell is going on here? If this is some sort of joke, I don't like it."

"When you get back to the States, Almond, you will tell Colonel Graham, won't you, that you checked me out in this aircraft?"

"Who the hell is Colonel Graham?"

"This would be a very bad time for you to try to be clever with me, Almond," Clete said.

"Would you please move that pistol away from me?" Almond said.

"I'm not pointing it at you," Clete said. "My uncle Jim taught me never to point a pistol at anyone I didn't intend to shoot. And I haven't really made up my mind whether I'm going to shoot you or not, or let you go to the States and have a little chat with Colonel Graham."

"I have no goddamn idea what you're talking about!" Almond said, aware that his voice sounded a little hysterical. "I never heard of a Colonel Graham!"

"Bullshit!" Lieutenant Pelosi said.

"He may be telling the truth," Clete said. "What the hell, it doesn't matter if he does or not. You, Captain Ashton, in your next communication with Colonel Graham, will report that both you and Lieutenant Pelosi were present when Colonel Almond informed me that I was now qualified to fly the Lodestar."

"Yes, Sir," Ashton said.

"But I think you should tell him that conversation took place at El Palomar, not here. That's not the truth, but we're in the intelligence business, and we can be cut a little slack."

"Yes, Sir," Ashton repeated.

"Who do you work for, Almond?" Clete asked. "And remember that you're an officer and a gentleman, and officers and gentlemen don't lie."

"I'm assigned to the Office of the Assistant Chief of Staff for Intelligence, G-2, in the War Department."

"And they sent you down here to ask questions about Galahad?"

Almond didn't reply.

"Yes or no, Colonel," Clete said. "And I think you should understand that if I think you're lying to me, I probably will decide to shoot you."

"Yes," Almond said faintly, and added: "Yes, that is one of my missions."

"Thank you," Clete said. "I really don't like to kill people unless I have to."

"You were pretty dumb, Colonel, to ask Ashton and me about Galahad, and really stupid to ask Coronel Martín," Tony Pelosi said.

"The thing is, Almond, Galahad is critical to an operation I'm running here," Clete said. "I don't want his identity known to G-2, or the Bureau of Internal Security, or anyone else."

"Those were my orders, Major Frade," Almond said. "You can hardly fault me for trying to carry them out."

"When they interfere with my operation, I can," Clete said. "Nothing personal."

"I'm glad you understand," Almond said. "Frade, we could have talked about this. You didn't have to go through that melodramatic business with the pistol."

Clete raised the pistol slightly and fired again. The bullet struck a rock two feet to Almond's side and went into a screaming ricochet.

"Mother of God!" Almond almost shrieked. "You're crazy!"

"Do I have your attention now, Colonel?" Clete asked.

Almond stared at him, wide-eyed.

"Here's the rules. You stop asking questions about Galahad. If you do, I will find out, and I will either kill you myself or have you killed."

"Do you realize what you're saying, Major?"

"Yes, I do. If you ever appear anywhere near my estancia, or my homes in Buenos Aires, you will be shot on sight. Or, anyway, killed. People here like to use knives."

"Well, then, you better kill me right here and now," Almond said. "Because if you don't, I intend to make a full report of this incident."

"I expect you to," Clete said. "But you'd better consider—and you will have time to think it over in the next couple of days—what you're going to say in your report."

"What I would do, Almond," Ashton said, "if I were in your shoes, would be one of two things. I would report that you compromised your mission here—that you blew it, in other words—and that not only do you feel you can do no more good here, but that you have received death threats—"

"You heard those death threats, Captain, if I have to remind you of that!"

"I didn't hear any death threats," Ashton said. "Did you hear any death threats, Lieutenant Pelosi?"

"No, Sir."

"If I may continue, Colonel," Ashton said. "Or you can stay here, enjoy the good life, and forget you ever heard 'Galahad.' "

"I think you should shoot him, Señor Clete," Enrico Rodríguez said. "Or let me. I don't trust him."

"You can shoot him the first time you see him near Estancia San Pedro y San Pablo, or anywhere near the houses in Buenos Aires," Clete said. "I really don't want to kill him unless I have to."

He turned to Almond. "I really don't want to kill you, but I will if I have to. And for something else to think about in the next couple of days: If I have to, the Argentine government will consider that I've done them a favor."

"What is this 'next couple of days' business? Is that some sort of ultimatum?"

"I think it will take you at least a couple of days to get back to Buenos Aires," Clete said. "Would you give me your wallet, please?"

"What?"

"Your wallet, Almond," Clete said. "It'll be returned to you in Buenos Aires."

"You're not going to leave me here!"

"Yes, I am," Clete said. "Enrico, get his wallet. And make sure he has no other identification on him."

"Sí, Señor."

"When we get home, mail his stuff to him at the embassy," Clete ordered.

"Sir," Ashton said. "I could just leave it on his desk at the embassy."

"Better yet," Clete said.

Enrico professionally searched Almond, and took his money, his diplomatic carnet, his diplomatic passport, and his keys.

"Give them to Captain Ashton, please," Clete said.

"Sí, Senor."

When he had finished, Clete handed him the pistol. "Careful, there's still one in the chamber," he said.

Enrico carefully lowered the hammer, then ejected the magazine and refilled it before replacing it.

"Now march the Colonel over there," Clete said, pointing to the end of the runway threshold. "When I have the other engine running, leave him there and get on the airplane. If he does anything suspicious, you can shoot him in the foot, but you are not to kill him. Understand?"

"Sí, Señor."

"Ashton, you want to ride up front with me and work the controls?"

"Yes, sir."

Clete climbed into the Lodestar, followed by Ashton and Pelosi. It took him less than a minute to strap himself in and restart the left engine. Sixty seconds later, Enrico climbed aboard and closed the door. Thirty seconds after that, the Lodestar reached takeoff velocity and Clete lifted it into the air. "Wheels up," he ordered.

"Wheels up and locked," Ashton reported twenty seconds later.

On the ground, Lieutenant Colonel Richard J. Almond, U.S. Army Air Corps, watched in disbelief as the Lodestar climbed smoothly out over the bright blue waters of Lake Nahuel Huapí.

Christ, I don't even know where that village is!

And then, surprising himself, he was suddenly very nauseous.

[TWO]
El Palomar Airfield
Buenos Aires
1905 29 May 1943

When Cletus Frade turned the Lodestar on final, he saw that the runway lights had not only been turned on but that he was going to need them. "Shit!" he said, then ordered, "Gear down."

There came the sound of laboring hydraulics, then Captain Maxwell Ashton's voice came metallically over the intercom: "Gear down and locked," he said. "Why 'shit'? Have we reason for me to soil my undies?"

"What happened to your blind faith in my flying skill?" Clete asked as he lined up with the runway lights.

"I fear that was a *fleeting* blind faith," Ashton said. "Answer the fucking question, Cletus!"

"I'm not going to be able to fly this thing to Estancia San Pedro y San Pablo tonight," he said.

The wheels chirped as the Lodestar touched down. Clete smoothly slowed the aircraft down.

"God, may I reconsider my rash promise never to sin again if I ever made it safely back to earth?" Ashton asked. "I was under a certain strain when I made the offer."

Clete picked up the microphone. "El Palomar. Lockheed Zebra Eight Four Three on the deck at five past the hour. I will need parking instructions to remain overnight and fuel service, please."

"Eight Four Three, take taxiway Two Right, make a right turn on the tarmac, and park your aircraft in front of the terminal."

"Taxiway Two Right, right on the tarmac to the terminal."

"Correct, Eight Four Three."

"Muchos gracias, amigo," Clete said, and hung up the microphone.

Ground handlers were waiting in front of the terminal to help him park the Lodestar. He shut it down and climbed out of the pilot's seat. "Permit me to say, Captain Ashton, that in all of my vast experience flying Lodestar aircraft, I have never met someone who could handle the flaps and gear controls with such skill and élan as you showed," Clete said.

"I hate to remember that I was a passenger the first time you flew this great big sonofabitch," Ashton said.

"I think it was the second time I flew it, not the first," Clete said, and walked into the cabin. "Enrico, find a phone someplace, call the house on Avenida Coronel Díaz, and have someone drive a car out here. Is Señora Dorotéa's Buick there?"

"Sí, Señor Clete."

"Then have them bring the Buick."

"Clete, I can drive you into town, my car's here," Tony Pelosi said.

"I want to go around town, not into it," Clete said. "But thank you."

"Are we going to do an after-action, boss?" Ashton asked.

"You mean did our theatrics properly impress Almond?"

"Yeah."

"I think so. It went well, I think. I thought he was going to piss his pants when I shot next to him."

"A completely understandable reaction, I would say," Ashton said.

"I hope it went well," Clete said thoughtfully. "I really don't want to have to kill him."

"Are you prepared to?" Ashton asked, very seriously.

Clete met his eyes, then nodded.

"Sometimes, despite the unkind things Colonel Graham said to you, I think you really are suited for this line of work," Ashton said.

"I'm almost sorry Almond doesn't know Graham," Clete said, not responding to the comment. "And I agree with Tony, I don't think he's even heard his name. I thought it would be sort of funny if Almond told him he had checked me out in the Lodestar."

He walked the rest of the way down the aisle, opened the door, and jumped to the ground.

"Welcome to Buenos Aires, my friend," Coronel Bernardo Martín said, stepping out of the shadows. "I was getting a little worried about you."

"I'm touched, but why should you be worried?"

"You left Posadas Airfield at half past eleven this morning, and no one's seen you since."

"Well, it's a long way from Missiones Province, mi Coronel."

Ashton jumped to the ground, then Pelosi.

"You remember these gentlemen, I'm sure," Clete said.

Martín saluted, and Ashton and Tony returned it somewhat awkwardly.

"We don't salute when we're in civilian clothing," Clete said.

"Really? I wonder why not? I don't think that people stop being officers when they put on civilian clothing, do you?"

Enrico jumped to the ground, saw Martín, and saluted.

"You see?" Martín asked, chuckling. "Enrico understands."

"Unless you'd rather stand around here chewing the fat with Coronel Martín, why don't you guys take off?" Clete said. "Call me when you hear something."

"Yes, Sir," Tony said.

"I see Lieutenant Pelosi isn't the only one who can't seem to remember you're no longer an officer," Martín said.

"For which I will order him tarred and feathered," Clete said.

"You're not going into town with them?" Martín asked.

"I have to tie the airplane down, and then see that it's fueled," Clete said. "That'll take thirty minutes. There's no point in them waiting around."

"Then good evening, gentlemen," Martín said. "It's always a pleasure to encounter members of our diplomatic corps, and I'm glad that my fears about your welfare were groundless."

"They were probably intuitive, mi Coronel," Ashton said. "After flying with Señor Frade, I am always tempted to kiss the ground when we finally get back on it."

Martín laughed dutifully, and offered his hand to each of them.

"Go find a phone, Enrico," Clete ordered when they had gone.

"May I ask why?" Martín asked.

"To get us a car to drive to the estancia," Clete said. "My wife's car is at the Coronel Díaz house."

"I'll be happy to drive you to Coronel Díaz. My car is here."

"Thank you, but no thank you," Clete said. "I wouldn't want you to waste your valuable time waiting for me here."

"I insist, my friend," Martín said, smiling.

Clete met his eyes and then shrugged.

"In that case, how would you like to help me tie down the airplane?"

"I would be delighted," Martín said.

"Manuel, this is Señor Frade, and the gentleman sitting beside you is Suboficial Mayor Rodríguez, Retired," Martín said when they were in the blue Dodge.

"I'm happy to meet you, Manuel," Clete said. "Even if I suspect that you're more than el Coronel's driver."

"In a very real sense, Cletus," Martin said. "Manuel is to me what Enrico is to you. Where I go, he goes, and he knows that what he hears or sees goes no further than I tell him it should."

Clete was watching Lascano's face in the rearview mirror. It flushed with pride.

"If he's half as good at that as Enrico," Clete said, "then I would say you are fortunate to have him as a friend, Bernardo."

"I think so," Martín said. "So tell me, Cletus, do you see much of our mutual friend Coronel Almond?"

"No, can't say that I do."

"He's looking for someone called Galahad," Martín said.

"Who?"

"I thought that was perhaps the reason for your tour of Argentina today, Cletus. That you were assisting the Colonel and Major Ashton and Lieutenant Pelosi in trying to find Señor Galahad."

"Bernardo, you couldn't be more wrong," Clete said.

"A man bearing a striking resemblance to Coronel Almond was reported getting on your airplane at El Palomar this morning."

"Is that so? I can't imagine why. Maybe your . . . friend . . . mistook Captain Ashton for Coronel Almond."

Martín smiled. Almond was tall and thin with very fair skin. Ashton was short, dark-skinned, and obviously Latin.

"I suppose that's possible," Martín said.

"You're looking for Coronel Almond, are you, Bernardo? Why?"

"Actually, it's Mr. Galahad who's piqued my curiosity. Do you know him, by any chance, Cletus?"

"Never heard the name."

"I thought you might have been looking for him in Córdoba or Posadas."

"My, you have been keeping track of me, haven't you?"

"I thought perhaps you were headed for Montevideo again, despite what I took to be our understanding that you wouldn't do that without passing through immigration."

"I wouldn't do that," Clete said. "Not only would that be illegal, but it would violate our understanding."

"And what were you doing in Córdoba and Posadas, if you don't mind my asking?"

"I'm thinking of starting an airline. I wanted to take a look at the airfields around the country. Captain Ashton went with me to help me with the controls. And to get a look at the land. He's an assistant military attaché, you know, and they like to learn as much about the host country as they can."

"So I've heard," Martín said. "And I don't think you found Galahad in Bariloche, either?"

"I don't even know who your Señor Galahad is, as I've told you, Bernardo."

"And you weren't in Bariloche, either?"

"San Carlos de Bariloche? I didn't even know they had an airfield."

"Just a simple gravel strip," Martín said. "No terminal. Very few people even know it's there. But you have experience in flying into simple airfields that very few people know about, don't you?"

"A little."

"Well, in my simple way, I've just been trying to put things together," Martín said.

"What things?"

"I had a most interesting report from the Gendarmeria Nacional in Bariloche several hours ago. A man walked into town from the direction of the airstrip, went to the Gendarmeria, identified himself as Colonel Almond, said he had lost his diplomatic carnet and his passport, and requested assistance."

"Was it your friend Colonel Almond?"

"Yes, it was. I spoke with him on the telephone. He was not willing to tell me how he'd gotten to Bariloche, or how he'd lost his identification."

"I wonder what he was doing in Bariloche?" Clete asked.

"I thought maybe he might be looking for Señor Galahad," Martín said. "And I thought maybe you dropped him off in Bariloche while you were flying around the country."

"Why would you think that?"

"A large red airplane was seen flying over Lake Nahuel Huapí," Martín said. "In the belief that it might be landing, the Gendarmeria lieutenant drove to the airstrip. But there was no red airplane when he got there. He said he thought he saw a man who could have been Coronel Almond standing at the end of the runway, but he wasn't sure."

"I wonder who that could have been?" Clete asked.

"What I'm wondering is how Colonel Almond got to Bariloche. There are only two buses a day, and he wasn't on either of them."

"Gee, that is puzzling, isn't it? Did you ask Colonel Almond?"

"He did not wish to discuss the matter. He claimed the privileges of his diplomatic immunity."

"That wasn't very cooperative of him, was it?"

"I thought it was very uncooperative," Martín said. He exhaled audibly and shrugged. "Cletus, my friend, we're getting close to your house. Can we stop fencing?"

"Is that what we've been doing?"

"I have the feeling that you don't want Colonel Almond to find Galahad. True or false?"

"If I start answering questions, do I get to ask questions?"

"Within reason."

"Then I will answer questions within reason. First answer, true. You now owe me one."

"Does Coronel Juan Domingo Perón know the identity of Galahad?"

"I'm sure he doesn't. Now you owe me two."

"Would you like Perón to know his identity?"

"I'll take my first question now," Clete said. "Why did you ask that question?"

"Perón asked the German ambassador for his help in getting someone back here from Germany. I thought it might be Galahad."

"Got a name?"

"The German pilot Major von Wachtstein. That's your two questions."

"Alicia Carzino-Cormano is in the family way. Von Wachtstein is the father."

"That's the truth?"

"Does that count as a question?"

"A small question."

"That's the truth. I got that from my wife, who said Perón is 'taking care of things.' I am not supposed to know either about the baby or Perón."

"OK."

"If I asked how you got von Wachtstein's name, would that be a small question?"

"It would be a very large question, which I can't answer."

"If I were in the intelligence business, I really would like to have someone in the Germany Embassy."

Martín chuckled.

"You know who Almond's looking for, don't you?"

"That would be a big answer, worth a big question from me."

"Agreed."

"Yeah, I know who he is. Will I give it to you? No. So don't ask."

"You don't want me to know, and you don't want Almond to know, and you don't want Perón to know."

"If that's a question, yes."

"It was a statement, but I'll give you a question."

"I'll swap all my questions for one favor," Clete said.

"I'll listen to the proposal."

"If you find out who Galahad is, would you tell me before you tell anyone else?"

"Why would you want me to tell you?"

"I'll throw that question in with the others," Clete said. "Because at that time, I could tell you things I think would color whatever decisions you had to make."

"OK," Martín said. "I make no promises beyond telling you before I do anything with Galahad's identity."

"Deal. We're now even."

"I'll give you an answer without a question. Almond offered me twenty thousand dollars for Galahad's identity."

"I know," Clete said.

"Señor," Sargento Lascano said. "We are at Señor Frade's home. Shall I drive around the block?"

"No, just pull up in front," Martín ordered. He put out his hand to Cletus. "It's always a pleasure to see you, Don Cletus."

"And you, Bernardo."

"One more question," Martín said. "If for some reason—suspicious behavior, for example, like his mysterious appearance in San Carlos de Bariloche—Colonel

Almond was determined to be *persona non grata,* would that please you?"

Clete hesitated a moment before saying, "No."

"Because they would send someone with the same mission?"

Clete nodded, and opened the car's door.

[THREE]
La Case Grande
Estancia San Pedro y San Pablo
Near Pila, Buenos Aires Province
2205 29 May 1943

Señora Dorotéa Mallín de Frade was in the small sitting, knitting blue baby booties—she was convinced she was carrying a boy—when she heard the wheels of an auto crunching the gravel on the driveway.

This was followed by the slam of an automobile door, which made her suspect that it was her husband. He had never learned to *close* a door. He always slammed automobile doors as if he hated the cars they were attached to.

She rose from the chair in anticipation of having a word with her husband.

In a moment, the door to the small sitting opened.

Don Cletus Frade's heart swelled when he saw his wife, the picture of a young mother-to-be, actually knitting whatever they called those things they put on baby's feet. "Hey, precious," he said emotionally.

"You bah-stud," Dorotéa said with precise English pronunciation. "You miserable bah-stud!"

"It was too dark to fly it back here. We had to drive."

"You left here, you bah-stud, at the crack of dawn, telling me you were going to get a few hours' instruction in the Lodestar. You did *not* tell me, you bah-stud, that you were going to fly the plane *alone* to Buenos Aires to get that instruction. You implied that Colonel Whatsisname was here."

"I said nothing of the kind."

"I quote you, Cletus Frade. A few hours from whenever the hell you got out of bed in the middle of the night—"

"It was after six. It was light."

"From after six, if you insist, a few hours translates to ten or eleven o'clock in the morning. I had luncheon prepared. You didn't arrive. I called El Palomar, where a very nice man at the petrol place told me that you had been there about seven, picked up *Colonel Almond* and Tony and Maxwell Ashton, and taken off about seven-thirty."

"Correct."

"You promised me you would not fly the aircraft by yourself until you were qualified to do so."

"That will never happen again, I promise you," Clete said.

"Why do I detect more deception in your tone of voice?"

"You're suspicious by nature?"

"You bah-stud!" she said, but there was a hint of a smile on her lips.

He smiled at her.

"Cletus, I have been sitting here the entire afternoon and the entire evening, knitting these damned booties, with visions of you crashed somewhere. Where the hell have you been?"

"You don't want to know."

"Oh, yes, I do!"

The telephone rang. Clete moved toward it.

"No, you don't! Someone will answer it. Where were you, Cletus?"

"All over the country," he said.

"Specifically."

"Posadas, Córdoba, and Bariloche."

"My God!" Dorotéa said. "I didn't know there was an air-field at Bariloche. Damn it, Cletus, couldn't you have learned how to fly that aircraft without flying all over Argentina? Is that why you lied to me, because you knew I would beg you not to?"

He saw the anger was gone, replaced by sadness.

"Baby . . ." Confirmation came when he saw tears form in her eyes.

"My God, you're about to be a father! Doesn't that mean anything to you at all?"

"I had a reason," he said. "I don't think you want to know what it was."

"Our understanding, Cletus, was that you were to share everything with me."

"I was dealing with Almond," Clete said. "He was sent down here to find out Galahad's identity."

"Sent by whom?

There was a knock at the door, and Antonio entered without knocking. Dorotéa quickly turned away so that he would not see her tears. "I beg pardon, Don Cletus, but el Coronel Perón is on the line, and says it is very important."

"How did you know I was here?"

"I saw you drive up, Señor."

Clete walked to the telephone and picked it up. "Tío Juan, how are you?"

"I have just learned from friends of mine that a friend of ours, as we speak, is on his way back to Argentina," Perón said. "I thought you would like to know as soon as possible."

"Jesus Christ, that's good news!"

"I can only hope that it will alter the opinion you hold of my friends," Perón said.

"Sure," Clete said.

"I thought perhaps Dorotéa might wish to tell Alicia. I have not called Estancia Santo Catalina."

"I'm sure she would. You're very thoughtful, Tío Juan. And I'm grateful."

"We're family, Cletus. I could do no less."

"Well, I'm truly grateful."

"As soon as I have further details, I'll pass them on."

"Thank you."

"Good night, Cletus," Perón said sonorously, and the line went dead.

"You're truly grateful about what?" Dorotéa demanded.

"He came through," Clete said. " 'As we speak,' Peter's on his way to Argentina."

"Thank God!"

"You better get on the phone to Alicia. Or maybe drive over there in the morning."

"We'll drive over there tonight. I want to be there when Claudia finds out."

"I'd rather go in the Buick, if you don't mind."

"It's about out of gas," Clete said, and held open the door of the Horch for her to get in. He was just about to drive out of the garage when Enrico appeared, carrying the Browning shotgun.

Dorotéa didn't seem at all surprised to see him, didn't protest, and then waited until they were on the macadam road through the pampas before picking up their original conversation precisely where it had been cut off: "You were telling me Colonel Almond was sent down here to identify Peter . . . Galahad. By whom?"

Clete exhaled, and decided this was as good a time as any to get it over with. "I originally suspected the OSS, but he says it was the G-2. That's Army intelligence, and I think he was telling the truth."

"He told you this?"

"At the time, I had a pistol in my hand and had just let off a round two feet away from him."

"You threatened to kill him?" Dorotéa asked matter-of-factly.

He nodded.

"Did he believe you?"

"I hope so. Otherwise I will have to kill him."

"You should have told me before," she said. "Then I wouldn't have worried myself sick all afternoon and evening."

"I'm sorry about that, baby."

"Enrico, do you think that man, Colonel Almond, believes Señor Clete will do what he said?"

"Sí, Doña Dorotéa."

"Well, then, it's been a good day all around, hasn't it?" Dorotéa said.

"We still have Claudia to face," Clete said.

"That's right, and for God's sake, darling, let me handle that!"

"Yes, dear."

Doña Claudia Carzino-Cormano received Señor and Señora Frade in her dressing gown, explaining that their very welcome visit was unexpected, and that she had decided to retire early.

Then she looked at them expectantly.

Alicia, also in her dressing gown, came into the room looking very frightened.

"You should have stayed in bed," Claudia said, and turned to Clete and Dorotéa. "She's got some sort of influenza. This morning she was nauseous."

"Mother, for God's sake."

"Alicia," Clete said. "Peter's on his way to Argentina."

"Oh, thank God!" Alicia said, and started to weep.

"Exactly what is going on around here?" Claudia demanded suspiciously. "I'm pleased to hear that Peter's coming back, but couldn't you have telephoned the news? Or wouldn't it have waited until morning?"

"Tía Claudia, there's something Alicia's been trying to find a way to tell you," Dorotéa said.

[FOUR]
El Palomar Airfield
Buenos Aires
1640 30 May 1943

Clete was sitting in the cockpit of the Lodestar. One of the two speakers of his headset was on one ear, allowing him to listen to radio traffic; the other ear was free, so he could converse with the student sitting in the right seat.

He was functioning as an Instructor Pilot, and loving the role, because his student was not only attentive and an obviously quick learner, but absolutely adorable as well.

And then he heard what he was waiting to hear: "El Palomar, Lufthansa Six Two Nine."

"Darling, put your cans on," Clete ordered.

" 'Cans'?" Dorotéa parroted, obviously amused at the term; but she put the earphones quickly over her head. Her husband thought her expression was priceless.

"Lufthansa Six Two Nine, this is El Palomar."

"El Palomar, Lufthansa Six Two Nine is at two thousand meters sixty kilometers south of you, over the River Plate. Request approach and landing instructions."

"Lufthansa Six Two Nine, El Palomar. Permission to approach El Palomar on present course is granted. Descend to one thousand meters. Report when twenty kilometers from the field."

"El Palomar Six Two Nine. Understand and will comply. Beginning descent at this time."

Two minutes later, Lufthansa Six Two Nine called again. "El Palomar, Six Two Nine. At one thousand meters. Due north. Indicating four hundred kilometers. Estimate maybe twenty-five kilometers from your station."

"Six Two Nine, Palomar, continue your approach," the tower said.

"Oh, shit!" Don Cletus Frade said.

Dorotéa looked at him with concern. He pointed out the cockpit window.

El Coronel Bernardo Martín and Manuel Lascano were walking across the tarmac toward them. Both were in uniform. Leica 35-mm cameras hung from their necks.

Enrico put his head in the cockpit. "Señor Clete . . ."

"I saw them."

"What do I do?"

"Open the door and smile," Clete said. "What else can we do?"

"Sí, Señor," Enrico said, and turned and went into the passenger compartment.

A minute later, Martín put his head into the cockpit. "Señora Frade," he said, "how delightful to see you."

"Mi Coronel," Dorotéa said. "Since we're going to be friends, why don't you call me Dorotéa?"

"I would be greatly honored to do so, Dorotéa," Martín said. "My Christian name is Bernardo."

"And what brings you to El Palomar, mi Coronel?"

"I would be honored if you would also use my Christian name, Don Cletus."

"And I would be pleased if you called me Clete, without the Don, Bernardo," Clete said. "You didn't answer my question."

"*Lufthansa Six Two Nine,*" Clete heard over his earphones, "*you are cleared to land on Runway One Eight. There is no other traffic. The winds are from the north gusting to thirty kilometers.*"

"*Understand, One Eight. Winds north gusting to thirty. I have the runway in sight.*"

"I would hazard the guess that I'm here for the same reason you are, *Clete,*" Martín said, and knelt, and then pointed out the side cockpit window. Lufthansa Six Two Nine had its wheels down and was making its final approach to El Palomar.

"Good-looking bird, isn't it?" Clete asked.

"Beautiful," Martín agreed. "For my general fund of aviation knowledge, which is faster, this or the Condor?"

"I think I'm a little faster," Clete said.

"I hope you won't mind," Martín said, "but I asked the authorities to have him park his machine to your right."

"Why should I mind?"

"I thought it would give us a chance to see who's getting off, without appearing too obvious," Martin said.

And make a few snapshots for the family scrapbook, right?

"I'm sure you will be both be delighted to see Major von Wachtstein again," Martín said. "I just wonder which of you is more delighted."

"You think he'll be on that plane?" Clete asked innocently.

"Well, we'll see in a minute, won't we?" Martin asked, and went into the cabin.

"How did he know that?" Dorotéa asked.

"He has someone in the German Embassy."

"Do you think he knows about Peter?"

"I think he suspects."

"And if he finds out for sure?"

Clete held his hands up in a gesture of helplessness.

Ground handlers and customs and immigration officers marched across the tarmac. A moment later, Ambassador von Lutzenberger and Generalmajor von Deitzberg, both in civilian clothing, came out of the terminal and walked quickly after them.

"That's Ambassador von Lutzenberger," Dorotéa said.

"The other one is von Deitzberg, who is an SS officer pretending to be a soldier."

"How do you know that?"

In for a penny, in for a pound, Clete decided. "Martín gave a picture to Leibermann. Leibermann made a copy for me."

"Is Martín on our side?"

"Martín is on Argentina's side. And I suspect that he is just as adept at getting cozy with the Krauts as he is with me."

The Condor taxied onto the tarmac and the pilot skillfully parked it beside the Lodestar. The cockpits were separated by the length of the right wing of the Lodestar and the left of the Condor.

The pilot of the Condor looked down with shameless curiosity at the blonde sitting in the copilot's seat of the Lodestar with earphones over her soft blond hair.

Stairs were wheeled up to the door of the Condor as it opened. The delegation of Argentine officials climbed them and entered the aircraft.

A moment later, a plump man got off.

"Gradny-Sawz," Clete said.

"I know."

"That's von Tresmarck," Clete said as a second man appeared in the door. "He's from Montevideo, where he runs the ransom operation. He's queer."

"Really?" Dorotéa replied, then: "Oh, there's Peter! Thank God!"

Peter, who was in uniform, glanced at the Lodestar.

For Christ's sake, Peter, don't wave!

He was followed by a man in a German naval officer's uniform. He followed Peter down the stairs, where they both gave von Lutzenberger and von Deitzberg stiff-armed Nazi salutes, shook their hands, and then followed them across the tarmac to the terminal building.

"Who was he?" Dorotéa asked.

"I never saw him before," Clete said. From a nearly forgotten portion of his brain, information he thought he would never have to use popped to the top. "He's a Korvettenkapitän."

"A what?"

"It's the same rank as lieutenant commander. The equivalent of major."

"Nice-looking man," she said.

"He's a goddamned Nazi," Clete snapped.

"Cletus, you're jealous!"

A moment later, other passengers began to leave the airplane.

Four or five minutes later, Martín appeared in the cockpit again.

Apparently he's satisfied that everyone who's going to get off is off.

"Thank you for your kind hospitality, *Dorotéa and Clete*," he said.

"It's nothing, Bernardo," Dorotéa said.

"Our pleasure," Clete said. "I don't suppose you know who the naval officer was?"

Martín hesitated before answering. "His name is Boltitz. He's to be an assistant naval attaché."

"I owe you one."

"Are we still keeping score?"

"I'm sure you are," Clete said.

They shook hands, and Martín left.

"Enrico!" Clete called, and when he appeared in the cockpit, "Get the extinguisher, please."

"Sí, Señor."

"What you do, honey," Clete said to his student, "is turn

on the MASTER BUSS. It's already on, because I wanted to use the radios. Then you put the mixture to FULL RICH, the throttle to LOW IDLE, punch the ENGINE PRIME button, then the LEFT ENGINE START."

"OK."

He glanced out the window. Enrico was standing by a large fire extinguisher on wheels."

Clete gave him the "winding it up" sign, and Enrico nodded.

"Do it, baby," Clete said.

"Really?" she asked, and set the controls as he had explained. The left engine ground, coughed, and came to life.

"Let it warm a second, until it smoothes out, then get off FULL RICH, and when you see Enrico is ready with the extinguisher, start the right engine."

A minute later, she looked at him happily.

"El Palomar, Lockheed Zebra Eight Four Three," Clete said, "on the tarmac in front of the terminal. Request taxi and takeoff, visual flight rules to Pila."

Dorotéa looked at him curiously.

He pointed to her microphone.

She smiled and picked it up. "El Palomar, Lockheed Zebra Eight Four Three," Dorotéa said into it, "on the tarmac in front of the terminal. Request taxi and takeoff, visual flight rules to Pila."

A long moment later, the tower replied, disbelief evident in the man's voice.

"Say again, Señor?"

"That's Señora, Señor," Dorotéa said. "I say again, Lockheed Zebra Eight Four Three on the tarmac in front of the terminal. Request taxi and takeoff, visual flight rules to Pila."

There was an even longer wait for El Palomar's reply. "Zebra Eight Four Three, make a left turn from your parking position. Take Taxiway Left Four to Runway Two Eight. Report when you are on threshold of the runway."

"That's enough instruction for one day," Clete said, and took Dorotéa's microphone from her hand to reply to the tower. There was a look of disappointment on her face.

Enrico put his head in the cockpit. "Ready, Señor Clete."

"I'll tell you what, baby, when we're ready to go, put your feet on the pedals and your hands on the wheel, and follow me through."

"Really?"

"Really."

She smiled at him.

What the hell, Amelia Earhart was a pretty good pilot, and women are ferrying everything up to B-17s from the factories. There's no reason she can't be taught to fly.

[ONE]
Estancia Santo Catalina
Near Pila, Buenos Aires Province
1530 12 June 1943

The wedding of Señorita Alicia Carzino-Cormano to Major Freiherr Hans-Peter von Wachtstein posed many of the same problems as the wedding of Señorita Dorotéa Mallín to Señor Cletus Howell Frade . . . and also some additional ones.

For one thing, the thatch roof was in bad shape on La Capilla de Santo Catalina, which (like La Capilla Nuestra Señora de los Milagros on Estancia San Pedro y San Pablo) served as the parish church for its estancia. The roof had been up for twenty-five years, and was leaking. Though Doña Claudia Carzino-Cormano had directed its replacement, until that was completed, a tent was used as a chapel to serve the workers.

When the need for the chapel for the wedding became

known, that process was one-third completed—the old roof
and its rotting supports had been removed. There was no
way the repairs could be completed in less than a month,
which was of course out of the question. As was a marriage
ceremony in Buenos Aires. There was no time for that,
either. A six-weeks-premature baby would be credible,
while a three-months-premature baby would not.

As was to be expected, Señora Dorotéa Mallín de Frade
offered Estancia San Pedro y San Pablo's La Capilla Nuestra
Señora de los Milagros for the wedding, as well as whatever
else Estancia San Pedro y San Pablo had to offer.

Doña Claudia accepted the offer of the chapel but not the
Casa Grande. Her daughter would have her wedding reception in her own home. That was only fitting. Furthermore, a
reception in Dorotéa's Casa Grande would be awkward.
Clete might agree to entertaining the Germans, but he would
not like it; and Clete, like his father, was unpredictable when
forced to do anything he didn't want to do.

It was in fact not at all easy for Claudia herself to be
charming to the Germans, for she agreed with Cletus that
they had been responsible for the murder of Jorge Guillermo
Frade. Cletus was a North American and could get away
with not bothering to conceal his contempt for the Germans,
but Cletus was not the mother of a girl about to bear a half-
German baby. And perhaps, she tried to tell herself, the time
had come to put that awful tragedy behind.

Claudia arranged for six Mercedes buses to be brought
from Buenos Aires to transport the wedding guests and the
Estancia Santo Catalina workers to La Capilla Nuestra
Señora de los Milagros, on Estancia San Pedro y San Pablo,
and back. The trucks of both estancias would be put to the
same use.

Peter, thank God, did not get on his high horse about having a Protestant clergyman participate in the ceremony; and
Father Kurt dealt with the Right Reverend Manuel de Parto,
bishop of the Diocese of Pila, who waived the usual routine
for wedding banns and was pleased to be the celebrant,
assisted by Father Welner.

Another set of problems for Claudia came in the person of Juan Domingo Perón. On one hand, he had arranged to have Peter returned from Germany. The baby would have a father. A good father, from everything Claudia had seen of Peter.

On the other hand, Perón was close to the Nazis who had ordered Jorge's murder.

Not to mention his disgusting behavior. His sick interest in very young girls was at least private. But he had now focused his public interest on that dreadful Radio Belgrano "actress," Eva Duarte, whom he had taken as a mistress.

Worse, the sale of Radio Belgrano had come through. Eva Duarte and her sleeping partners were no longer Cletus's problem, but Claudia's. And the little tramp had already been making noises about being grossly underpaid.

Doña Claudia was a nervous wreck by the time it was over, but the wedding went off without a hitch.

As it turned out, Don Cletus Frade managed to avoid the whole thing, claiming a serious problem at one of his vineyards, San Bosco, in Córdoba Province. He telephoned his profound regret that he would be unable to attend the wedding or the reception.

Claudia saw him, however, peering through the slats of the cloakroom blinds at La Casa Grande, as Major and Señora Hans-Peter von Wachtstein left La Capilla Nuestra Señora de los Milagros between an honor guard of dress-uniformed officers, Army, Navy, and Diplomatic, of the German Embassy.

The only thing that went wrong after that was that the wedding trip didn't go as planned . . . and that wasn't really such a problem. Claudia had arranged for a suite in the Provincial Hotel in Mar del Plata, but the newlyweds never went there.

Instead, they flew in one of the Piper Cubs to God Only Knew Where. Someone, either Peter or Clete, had left it on the pampas for a getaway after they left the reception at Estancia Santo Catalina.

Alicia left her a note: They would be back in seven days.

[TWO]
Avenida Pueyrredón 1706
Piso 10
Buenos Aires
1605 20 June 1943

Having received no response to the ringing of the bell, Major Hans-Peter von Wachtstein let himself into his apartment. "Hey, anybody home?"

"In here, Peter," a familiar voice called.

Peter went into his sitting room, where he found Korvettenkapitän Karl Boltitz, in civilian clothing, behind his desk. His hand was resting on a folded copy of *La Nación*.

"Hello, Karl," Peter said. "What are you doing here? Where's my maid?"

"After she let me in, I gave her the rest of the day off," Boltitz said.

"What's going on?"

"Sit down, Peter," Boltitz ordered coldly, pointing to a leather armchair.

"I'll stand, thank you," Peter said, his temper starting to flare.

Boltitz pushed the newspaper to one side. It had concealed a Luger 9mm Parabellum pistol. "Sit down, Peter," Boltitz repeated.

"What's going on?" Peter replied, but sat down.

"It says here—if we are to believe Reuters, and I do—that Rome was bombed by five hundred American planes last night. Is that what happened, Peter, you decided we will lose the war? And wanted to be on the winning side?"

"I don't know what the hell you're talking about," Peter said.

"While you were flying off on your honeymoon, I took a trip by car," Boltitz said. "To Puerto Magdalena. There I spoke with Lothar Steuben and other members of his family. Now do you know what I'm talking about?"

Peter didn't reply.

"Herr Steuben reported that you left his home, 'to conduct business,' *after* you had convinced Herr Loche that you needed to know where exactly the boat from the *Océano Pacífico* would land on Samborombón Bay. That's how the Americans—or the Argentines, it doesn't really matter—knew where to be, and when. You told them, Major Freiherr von Wachtstein."

Peter didn't reply.

"Do you deny this, Peter?"

"No," Peter said simply.

"Did you know the intention of your friends, vis-à-vis Oberst Grüner and Standartenführer Goltz?"

"No."

"Why, Peter?"

"You know what they are bringing ashore, of course?"

"Radios to assist in the repatriation of the *Graf Spee* officers, you mean?"

"No, I mean cash, and gold taken from the mouths of Jews after they had been murdered in concentration camps, intended to provide sanctuary for the Bavarian corporal and his filthy friends after Germany loses this war."

"You swore a personal oath, on your honor, to the Führer."

"That was a terrible mistake. I spent time in Russia. I know what the Nazis really are."

"The point is, Peter, I took the same oath you did, and I am honor-bound to adhere to it. By your own admission, you are a traitor."

"All right," Peter said, "now what?"

"Your treason, among other things, has kept German submariners on the high seas, starving, in great risk of being discovered and sunk, because the *Océano Pacífico* could not resupply them. Some of them are friends of mine."

"Some of them are friends of mine, too."

Boltitz shrugged. "I suppose that's true," he said. "A generation ago, Peter, if this confrontation occurred between your father and mine, this would have solved the problem."

He tapped the Luger with his fingertips. "My father would have left your father alone with one cartridge in the pistol, and your father would have done the honorable thing, and that would have been the end of it."

"My father would probably have tried to take the pistol away from you," Peter said.

"I wouldn't try that," Boltitz said. "I have a full clip in here, and I could get off three shots before you got out of the chair."

"I think I would rather be shot than shoot myself," Peter said.

Boltitz quickly picked up the pistol and pointed it at him.

Peter felt pain in his stomach.

"I don't really want to shoot you, Peter. Please don't make me."

"If I'm a traitor, why should you hesitate?"

"Because then your treason would have to come out. And that would hurt other people besides yourself. Your father, for one. I am unable to believe that he's aware of your treason. General Galland, for another. He thinks you are an honorable German warrior—"

"So do I," Peter said. "We just see honor differently. My allegiance is to Germany, not Hitler, not National Socialism."

"—and it would be very awkward for General Galland if it came out that an officer he personally asked the Führer to have assigned to him was a traitor."

"Christ!"

"And the child your wife will bear would for all of his life be stigmatized by having a traitor for a father."

"What are you going to do? Turn me loose?"

"My honor forbids that, although, personally, I would like to. I've come to like you, Peter."

"Oh, shit!"

"There is a path you could take," Boltitz said.

"Really?"

"Tomorrow you're going to fly to Montevideo."

"And I should crash into the River Plate?"

"No. That might be suspicious. If you did that, there wouldn't be a body. But if you crashed at El Palomar on landing, it would be considered a tragic accident. Do you follow my reasoning?"

After a moment, Peter nodded.

"Do you agree?"

Peter nodded again.

"May I lay the pistol down again?"

Peter shrugged.

"I suppose this might be considered, under the circumstances, absurd, but will you give me your word of honor?"

"You have it, Herr Korvettenkapitän," Peter said.

Boltitz looked at him for a long moment, then stood up, tucked the pistol into the small of his back, and walked out of the sitting.

When Peter heard the door close, he walked to the nearest toilet and just managed to get to his knees in front of the water closet before he threw up.

[THREE]
The Office of the Ambassador
The Embassy of the German Reich
Avenue Córdoba
Buenos Aires
0950 21 June 1943

"Korvettenkapitän Boltitz is here, Excellency," Fräulein Ingebord Hassell announced.

"Ask him to come in, please," von Lutzenberger said. "And please do not disturb us."

"Jawohl, Excellency," she said, and pulled the door fully open until there was room for Boltitz to pass her.

"Good morning, Karl," von Lutzenberger said. "There's something I want to show you. It's in my personal safe. Why don't you have a seat?"

"Thank you, Excellency."

Von Lutzenberger disappeared from view.

His safe is apparently either under his desk or low on the wall.

Von Lutzenberger reappeared, holding two envelopes in his hand. "You look like you had a bad night, Boltitz, if you don't mind my saying so."

"I didn't get much sleep, Excellency," Boltitz admitted.

"These came on the same plane you did," von Lutzenberger said. "They are addressed to you, but I'm familiar with their contents."

He handed him the two envelopes. One bore his name in handwriting, and Karl opened that one first, because he recognized his father's handwriting. It was a very simple note.

Berlin

22 May 1943

My Dear Karl:

As you embark on your new assignment I must tell you that I take great pride in knowing that you will faithfully execute without question whatever orders you receive from Admiral Canaris.

May God give you strength in this time of great challenges to Germany. I will pray for you.

With much love,

Father.

Boltitz glanced up at von Lutzenberger, who was looking at him. He opened the second envelope.

Oberkommando der Wehrmacht
Office of the Director of Intelligence
Berlin

22 May 1943

Korvettenkapitän Karl Bollitz

Dear Bollitz:

In case there might be some question in your mind concerning your responsibilities in your new assignment:

You are under the direct orders of Ambassador von Lutzenberger and you will comply with his orders as if they had come from me. In this connection, all communications of any kind must be approved by von Lutzenberger before they are forwarded to me or any other of ce.

Heil Hitler!

Canaris

Canaris

Vizeadmiral

Chief, Intelligence, OKW

Karl Boltitz looked at Ambassador von Lutzenberger.

He heard his father's voice in his ears: *"The best advice I can give you, Karl, is to listen to what Canaris is* not *saying."*

Christ, does this mean what I think it does?

"Do you have any questions, Boltitz?"

"No, Excellency."

"May I have the letters back, please?" von Lutzenberger asked.

Boltitz handed them to him.

Von Lutzenberger carefully burned both and their envelopes. "These did not, if I have to say this, come to me via the diplomatic pouch."

"I understand," Boltitz said.

"Major von Wachtstein came to see me this morning before he left for Montevideo. He told me of the chat you two had last night."

"Yes, Sir?"

"In a few minutes, von Wachtstein will land at Montevideo," von Lutzenberger said. "And he should be back here two hours or so after that. I told him I was counting on him to be careful. I missed him when he was in Germany. He's our only pilot, you know."

"Yes, Sir, I know."

"You really should make an effort, Boltitz, to get to know him well. I think you have much more in common than you may have realized previously."

"Herr Ambassador—" Boltitz began.

Von Lutzenberger stopped him with an upheld palm. "That will be all, Boltitz. Thank you for coming to see me."

[FOUR]
The Office of the Director
The Office of Strategic Services
National Institutes of Health Building
Washington, D.C.
1045 22 June 1943

"Got a minute, Alex?" Colonel William Donovan asked, stepping inside the office of the Deputy Director for Western Hemisphere Operations, Colonel Alejandro Graham.

"Truth to tell, Bill, I'm up to my ass in alligators."

"I really need just a minute."

"OK."

"I just had a rather interesting chat with the G-2," Donovan said.

"Really?"

"Someone has apparently told him we have a team in Argentina headed by someone named Frade."

"I wonder who told him that? That's supposed to be Need To Know."

"That's what I told him. He was pretty vague about that. He said he was sorry, but *I* didn't have the Need To Know who told him that. He sort of hinted it came from the White House."

"From the White House? That place leaks like a sieve, doesn't it?"

"I keep telling Roosevelt he should tighten things up," Donovan said. "But you know how he is."

"Yes, I do. Is there more?

"Oh, yes. It seems the G-2 sent a new assistant attaché for air to Buenos Aires. And this man not only got to meet Frade—your friend Leibermann introduced them—but checked him out in that Lockheed we sent down there by mistake."

"Really? I'm not sure I'm glad to hear that."

"And then, the attaché told the G-2, Frade repaid his courtesy by threatening to kill him."

"Maybe the attaché asked Frade the wrong question," Graham suggested.

"I have no way of knowing this, of course—and the G-2 said he had never heard the phrase 'Galahad'—but I think maybe the attaché did ask Frade the wrong question."

"That does seem likely, doesn't it?"

"What do you think I should do, Alex?"

"I think I'd tell the G-2 he should tell his man to be careful."

"I did. I told him that Frade's already killed six people we know about."

"I think the figure is four, but who's counting?" Graham asked. Then, more seriously: "Are you going to have trouble with your friend Franklin about this?"

"I don't see how he can complain to me that Frade threatened this guy without admitting to me he sent him down there to ask a question he promised me he wouldn't ask."

"I don't know which of the two of you is the more devious," Graham said. "I say that as a compliment. Now get out of here and let me go back to work."

Donovan left, and Graham sat at his desk, the events of the last two months whirring through his head.

You dodged the bullet that time, Cletus, he thought. *I hope it doesn't make you cocky. Donovan's not the kind of man to give up easily. Next time, he may not bother to ask the question at all. Next time, maybe you'll be the one on the other end of the pistol. . . .*

And whose hand would be holding it? A German? An American? An Argentine?

He sighed and shook his head.

One more alligator, he thought. *But when you are already up to your ass in alligators, what difference does one more make?*

He turned back to his papers and started to read.